Honour
and
Humility

Honour
and
Humility

A sequel to Jane Austen's 1813 novel
Pride and Prejudice

by GENEVIÈVE ROSE WIMER

SUTTER HOUSE
2002

Honour and Humility is a work of historical fiction. The characters
and locations are based on those created by Jane Austen in her work
Pride and Prejudice, first published in 1813. Other than those well-known
individuals and news events referred to for purposes incidental
to the plot, all names, places, characters, and events are the product of
the author's imagination, and any resemblance to actual events,
locales, or persons, living or dead, is entirely coincidental.
To the extent that real persons and reported events
are mentioned in the novel, the author has included such references
without the knowledge or cooperation of the individuals involved.

LIBRARY OF CONGRESS CONTROL NUMBER: 2002105890
ISBN 0-915010-46-1

Published in the United States by
Sutter House, Lititz, Pennsylvania 17543

Distributed by
Hemlock Hill Book Distributors
P.O. Box 45
Millersville, Pennsylvania 17551-0045

To

My Husband,
Ronald L. Wimer,
And Our Children,
Deborah, William, Jody, Tracey, and Laura,
who have made this book possible

I inscribe my deep love and gratitude to my daughter Jody Weaver. Without her encouragement and constant stimulus, this book would have neither been written nor finished. It is to her that I owe the success of it.

I must record also my steadfast love and gratitude to my dear husband for his support and understanding during the writing of this book. And to our other four children and their families for their forbearance, I remain indebted to you all. Without all such love and understanding, this book would have been far more difficult to write and may never have been completed.

If Honour and Humility *becomes any contribution to society, much of the credit is theirs. To all of them, I am forever grateful.*

IN LOVING MEMORY OF MY SISTER CHARLOTTE

Contents

Introduction

THERE ARE THOSE who are of the firmest belief that when a man takes a wife, she is to be a part of him—not apart from him, and will settle for nothing less than the most violent affections for the woman of his choosing, expecting his bride to share his sentiments on the subject.

Those who are arranged in marriage come to the wedded bed with little or no knowledge of their intended partner, with submission and acceptance of their expected duty in the appropriation of children and in a marriage brought about to unite connections, family and fortune.

Unfortunately, there are those who ignore proper decorum, marrying for fleeting carnal lust or the convenience of total want in propriety or whose momentary decision may cause a most unsuitable wedded state to ensue.

Those fortunate to be amongst the first mentioned find felicity in love, the second are left to mere chance, and the latter frequently proved a union whose partners suffer indifference, insolence and discontent.

Most people desire their children to find felicity in marriage, with the hope of propriety, still others will settle for convenience; however, it is a known fact that some cannot agree on the subject among themselves. In *Honour and Humility*, it was the good fortune of Mr. and Mrs. Bennet, belonging to the modest estate of Longbourn and having birthed five daughters, to recently witness the marriage of their two eldest in a double ceremony to two gentlemen of means, known to be the very best of friends.

Jane Bennet, the eldest and esteemed valued by her mother as the prettiest, was a girl of light chestnut-coloured locks, her smooth skin appearing to have a texture of cream. Her gentle demeanour and reserved style only lured a desire to further witness her beautiful eyes, which rendered fairness to her loveliness. Her general fashion, however simple, added refinement with grace noticeable in her strides. She was a dear, kind, sweet girl, quiet with good sense, always seeking the very finest in everyone. Her countenance revealed a most amiable disposition, and she fortunately, and most advantageously, fell in love with Charles Bingley of Netherfield Park, a man of inheritance and fine character.

Charles Bingley was tall, with light-coloured curly hair, fair complexion and owning gentle characteristics. His fashionable attire, always looking quite debonair, and his energy and bright expression only improved Mr. Bingley's pleasing looks. Falling in love at first sight would indeed describe the consequence of Charles Bingley, who upon meeting Jane desired her company, later intending to spend a lifetime together in felicity.

Her sister Elizabeth dons very different manners; she was more challenging, inquisitive—a higher-spirited young woman whose disposition made presentation of her united frankness, vivacity and good humour. Being fond of the out of doors, she had a quality of freshness in her healthy appearance, which often gave her tanned, silky skin more brilliance. Her dark tresses flattered her face, revealing the splendor of her fine, bright, eager eyes, reflect-ing a delicate complexion of pure loveliness and extreme beauty. Her movements displayed unreserved confidence and more than common gracefulness with charm, giving her form certain elegance. Elizabeth Bennet was of the good fortune, after much anguish and grief, to fall in love with Fitz-william Darcy, a man of vast means whose wealth afforded him the prosperous estate of Pemberley.

The grand estate of Pemberley was thought to be the finest in all of Derbyshire. Its master, Fitzwilliam Darcy, had extremely handsome looks, exhibiting locks of dark curls surrounding his noble mien. His eyes were deep in colour, bright in reflection; his masculine attractiveness captivating, affording a figure advantageous in height and striking in appearance, to which his virile attire so well fitted his form and provided him marked notability. In public he was notoriously sedate but equally known to be well educated and superior. In his air he permeated society with his excellent breeding, making conspicuous his superior qualities which, on first examination, could be mistaken for haughty, arrogant and decided conceit. However, closer inspection exposes the true gentleman, severely honourable, a distinctly unselfish nobleman, flawless in character, tender of heart—the very finest among men. It was equally known amongst his friends that Fitzwilliam Darcy was incapable of willfully behaving dishonourably or ignoring his duty.

As a connoisseur of the fictional world of Jane Austen, I all too soon found myself craving more. Perhaps it is that escape from the realities of everyday life or a mixture of the culture and values that holds the greatest appeal. I believe it is merely a desire to continue a most beloved story that led me to dare such a task as to write in Jane Austen's shadow. I now take you back to the lives of Jane and Elizabeth Bennet on their wedding journey.

The Wedding Journey

A FORTNIGHT WAS SPENT of the wedding journey and the newly wed-ded couples had been seen about London attending plays, assemblies, tak-ing in reviews as well as visiting various shops. The former Misses Bennet, now so advantageously married, were at the threshold of comforts and con-sequences of greatness they had only chanced to imagine. Such connections and family had instantly elevated their rank of society but, more impor-tantly, both found themselves in wedded bliss, having secured gentlemen who shared their mutual love and respect.

Having just breakfasted and escorted his wife above the stairs to their chamber, Mr. Darcy announced to his wife, "Elizabeth, Bingley and I have business to attend in town."

Elizabeth's eyes searched his expression. "Business, will you be gone long?"

"My dear Elizabeth," voiced Mr. Darcy, "Bingley and I shall return before early afternoon to be sure. I believe you and Jane may amuse yourselves until then."

"What is your business?"

He stepped toward her taking both her hands in his and kissed them gently. "I beg you not inquire of my business, you will ruin the surprise."

"Surprise!" Elizabeth declared with a broadened smile.

"I confess, indeed there is. You shall be appraised of it soon enough. I must go now to meet Bingley; I am certain he waits impatiently. You know him well enough; he no doubt will suffer any length of separation from your sister. As for my own situation, well—I shall hasten my return; you may be certain of it."

"Wait I shall, but content, nay it will not do. Only with anticipation shall I wait."

Mr. Darcy bowed, then moved in the direction of the door. He paused, slightly turned to look at her once more. "Until I return," he said, then hastily quit the chamber.

Elizabeth's curiosity piqued. Had they not taken in everything about town? She could not help but venture guesses on her own part, but after giving it further thought, she determined to let it be Mr. Darcy's fashion. She trusted him wholly and completely. She knew whatever it was, it was sure to be pleasing.

She was at liberty now to go to Jane's chamber to pass the time, but first lingered at the window to watch her husband's carriage depart the inn.

Not being at all prone to self-deception, she consoled herself. Although he was now a striking contrast to the man she long ago thought she knew, she was well aware, when out in society, he could be mistaken for haughty, arrogant and decidedly conceited. Having once erroneously judged him ill with her unhesitating prejudice, she would now cry out against the injustice of any implied doubt expressed by anyone who thought him to be anything but honourable. She now suffered the embarrassment of her own recollection.

At his estate, the province where his disposition was sure to possess a freedom of ease, she expected to establish a refreshed understanding of him. Had she not, during the passing weeks, pleasantly discovered his open intimacy, which lacked neither the tendency to conceal his thoughts, concerns or expressions of felicity in his new position as a husband? Although he still retained his quiet reserve, the easiness of his ungoverned demeanour when alone with her led her to anticipate a likeness to be discovered at his home in Derbyshire. He was a man of perfectly good breeding, a gentleman with correct knowledge of etiquette of court. In her newly found prejudice, she viewed him flawless.

The carriage disappeared; there was no reason to linger at the window any longer. I must see Jane. Perhaps Mr. Bingley told Jane where they were directed. She paused, after giving the matter further consideration; she promised herself she would not pry from Jane any information.

Elizabeth knocked on Jane's chamber door lightly.

"Come in," she heard from within.

As Elizabeth entered, Jane quickly rushed toward her. They joined hands, giggled, embraced, then hugged again.

"I'm so happy, Lizzy. I don't know how I shall bear so much felicity. Oh, I'm so afraid I will wake up to learn it has been a dream. I want the dream to go on forever. In time I wish to present Mr. Bingley with a son. Oh, Lizzy, would that not be the most wonderful announcement? Do you believe I am silly for entertaining such thoughts so early in the marriage?" Jane said with hurried discourse, causing the words to roll off her tongue with ease. She blushed, turning crimson red. "After all, we are still on our wedded journey. I'm so afraid; can this be true, are we really here together, or am I dreaming?"

"Nonsense," said Elizabeth, "this is what is meant to be. It is as fate would have it, to be sure. And I'm sure fate will provide you a handsome abundance of children."

"I'm sure you are right, Lizzy. I'm so happy I could burst." Jane's brow crinkled. "But Lizzy——"

"But what, dear sister? What is it that troubles you so?"

"I was thinking, what if something happens to our father?" Jane bit her lip, clenching her hands together. "Mother would be forced to quit Longbourn. She would have no place to go. You know the estate is entailed away from the female line and will go to Mr. Collins."

Elizabeth stared at her sister. "Do not concern yourself of such matters. There is nothing to be done at present. You have such a propensity to worry for naught."

"I shall try, Lizzy," Jane replied, still clenching her hands, letting out a sigh. "I want so much to be a good mistress of Netherfield Park. But Lizzy, Charles' sisters still lodge at Netherfield. You know they were opposed to our marriage," Jane lamented.

Elizabeth gently touched Jane's arm. "Do not fret; Mr. Bingley will tend his sisters."

Incipient tears welled in Jane's eyes. "But—they tried to separate us."

Elizabeth managed a forced smile, with anxiety knotting her stomach. "Jane, do not give way to trouble yourself with that which has not taken place. It would be in their best interest to rekindle those affections they found for you upon your first meeting if they are to continue at Netherfield Park. You know Mr. Bingley is violently in love with you; he will not allow them to injure you, you may be sure of it. Come, let us savour the delights of the day. This is the beginning of happier times. Now Jane, what do you intend to wear at dinner this evening?"

"Lizzy, did not Mr. Darcy tell you of a shopping journey this afternoon?"

"Why—no," replied Elizabeth, noting that Jane had not detected her hesitation.

"Yes, Charles said we are to go to the dress shops to select something of elegance to wear to the ball at the Grand Ballroom near Hyde Park this evening."

Elizabeth's face brightened. Her lips parted with excitement. "A ball!" she exclaimed with glee.

Jane swiftly covered her mouth with her fingers, "Oh gracious Lizzy, perhaps Mr. Darcy was going to surprise you."

"I'll not say anything, Jane, perhaps it is to be a surprise. My husband was very secretive when parting, was Mr. Bingley?"

"Yes, even with his revelation of the dress shops and ball, I daresay it is as you say; he was secretive."

A smile overspread Elizabeth's face. "Well, we shall not ruin their proposal."

"Surely you are aware," cautioned Jane, "this has been extraordinary for us; we are not used to such society as this so steadily. Does it not make you uncomfortable Lizzy?"

"Not at all; I rather think it is easier to adjust to this state of society than to be affluent and find yourself thrust in sudden poverty."

Jane's eyes widened. "Oh, do not say such things, Lizzy, it causes embarrassment."

"You had better get used to it, Jane; we are now to become accustomed to privileges of a society we experienced infrequently, dreamed of often, but never dared to imagine as reality. We must become accustomed; it will be expected of us; it is our duty."

"I suppose it is as you say," replied Jane. "Still, it is like a dream. Lizzy, what do you suppose our husbands are truly about?"

"I cannot venture a guess, nor would I wish to. Perhaps it is their design to end our wedded journey with unrivaled memories," Elizabeth replied, then added, "let us agree to let the men have their do. No doubt they have made excellent plans; we are fortunate to be sure."

Elizabeth moved toward the door. Placing her hand on the latch, she turned. "Well, Jane, I shall return to my chamber to rest until Fitzwilliam returns."

"It sounds like a fair plan, Lizzy, we may require rest for such a fine evening. I am inclined to agree we are indeed fortunate. I cannot help but be happy."

Elizabeth opened the door; but before closing it, she poked her head in. "Jane, I am well pleased our husbands planned this journey together. Next to Mr. Darcy, there is no other I think so highly of whom I would wish to share my wedded journey with. Is it not delightful to think our husbands the best of friends as well?"

"Lizzy, I am sure our husbands are well aware of their excellent plan. I am equally certain they were conscious of the benefits of sharing this time together, for surely it has made it twice the pleasure for all. Indeed I share in your delight."

Elizabeth smiled. "It is indeed a pleasure."

She returned to her chamber. At the dressing table she stared at her reflection in the looking glass. This was to be their last evening in London; tomorrow they expected to journey home to begin their life together. She gave herself up wholly to thoughts of happiness, delighting in the notion of Mr. Darcy and Mr. Bingley taking the pains to escort them to the dress shops. This would be their third visit to the shops. Had he not lavished her with enough finery? To think all we have been through to reach this end, why it is almost inconceivable. But it is not the end, is it? Quite the contrary, it is the beginning, she mused.

Sometime later, Elizabeth was awakened by manly voices outside the chamber door. She detected low, secretive voices before she heard the door latch. Mr. Darcy entered. He immediately directed himself to her side. "I trust you rested well?"

She smiled serenely. "Indeed I did."

"Well then, be off with you, make haste, make yourself ready; your sister and Bingley will be waiting below the stairs."

He neared the window as he waited, looking out at the sky. Its great expanse of blue only seemed to add to the delights of their wedded journey. He thought he could not have wished for a more perfect day than this. After a few moments, he strained to catch a glimpse of a familiar figure of a man in the street. He was sure he recognized the man. Indeed, his suspicions were correct. The man was George Wickham. What is he doing here? he mused. I supposed him to be in the north country. He soon realized, without doubt, the woman with him was not his wife. Upon closer examination, he concluded the woman accompanying him was no stranger to him as well. He cautiously turned to view his wife, then turned his attention back toward the street. He watched as the couple crossed over to the other side. His thoughts of a perfect day quickly dissipated.

It took Elizabeth an instant to make herself ready. She laughed to think, by sheer coincidence—no prodding or prying, but by the mere transfer of general information—she found him out. She dared not put their plan to ruin. That would not be acceptable. She turned to advance toward him; "I am ready to take my leave."

Mr. Darcy swiftly moved away from the window.

"Are you unwell, Fitzwilliam? You look suddenly pale."

"I'm quite well thank you, uh—I was just deep in thought, that is all." Attempting to change the subject, he extended his arm to her. "Dearest, come here." He then guided her to the dressing table. "Study the looking glass. Do you make the same claim as I?"

"And what claim is that, Mr. Darcy?"

"The reflections in the looking glass, they are two so wholly and completely one, are they not?"

"Yes, it is as you say. Should we not direct ourselves below the stairs without further delay? Jane and Mr. Bingley must surely be waiting."

Mr. Darcy neared the window again. Seeing no sign of Mr. Wickham, he turned back to her. "Yes, we must go, make haste."

Jane and Mr. Bingley had not arrived as yet. Mr. Darcy impatiently paced, frequently peering out of the window in search of Mr. Wickham. Much to his relief, he was nowhere in sight. Elizabeth smiled at what she perceived as his seldom seen manner of excitement.

"It is a very fine day; the carriage awaits us," said he.

"Oh," she replied, "do we require a carriage?"

"Yes, we have found a special place we wish to introduce to you and Jane."

"I'll be content to let it be a surprise," uttered Elizabeth sheepishly.

"Indeed you will," replied Mr. Darcy, "for I shall not tell you where it is we are taking you." His voice was pleasantly teasing, causing Elizabeth to burst into a giggle.

Jane and Mr. Bingley finally arrived. Elizabeth noticed Mr. Darcy quietly directed the driver before boarding. They traveled for a time until the carriage halted in front of a row of small shops. "Come," said Mr. Darcy, "we shall start here."

Immediately upon their entry, the shopkeeper advanced toward them. Mr. Darcy directed, "Show the ladies finery, attire fit for a ball, spare no expense." He paused, adding, "Make haste we have other shops to visit."

"Very good sir," the shopkeeper retorted in a spry voice.

Elizabeth immediately found her choice. She was fitted with a dress the colour of sage, garnished with lace edgings, trimmed with a wide sash. How lucky was she to have found a dress so well fitting to her form, thought she.

She owned nothing in comparison. She modeled it for Mr. Darcy, who, much to her delight, was well pleased. He neared her and said, "My dear, you look quite fashionably smart. I daresay I view the shopping a success." His description broached expressions of enthusiastic admiration. His eyes became gentle. "You look uncommonly beautiful, I am certain you will be admired by many this evening."

Jane's choice of a dress in pink with French lace flattered her figure. It added brilliance to her already fine complexion. Mr. Bingley's favour was of no surprise to anyone. His gasping reaction and brightened eyes revealed full approval. He struggled to speak. "I am delighted. Jane, you look absolutely marvelous, indeed splendid."

Mr. Darcy looked at the shopkeeper, then gave a nod. "We shall take them."

After securing the dresses, they were shuttled to several other shops. Before the close of the afternoon, Jane and Elizabeth were in possession of complete attire. Nothing was spared in terms of expense. They were to be newly clothed from head to foot. Nothing was overlooked.

Elizabeth, having been educated of this before parting the inn, had no idea as to the total extent of the shopping journey. She determined she was pleasantly surprised after all. She was glad her husband mentioned the ball; she no longer had to pretend she did not know of it.

"Come, the carriage awaits us," Mr. Darcy announced, once again instructing the driver before boarding. Sitting next to Elizabeth, he exchanged a sheepish grin with his good friend Mr. Bingley, whose expression did little to hide his enthusiasm.

"Why do you smile so; what are you about?" inquired Elizabeth.

"You will know soon enough. Have patience," Mr. Darcy coyly replied.

Mr. Bingley smiled. "You must indulge us."

Elizabeth's inquisitiveness increased. Unable to contain herself any longer, she commented, "I'm sure whatever it is, we shall be delighted to assist you in the adventure."

Their husbands chuckled in a teasing manner. The carriage traveled several blocks, finally coming to full rest in front of a row of shops on a narrow cobblestone street. Having dismounted, the men escorted the ladies into still another shop. They soon realized they had entered a gentlemen's shop.

The shopkeeper afforded them chairs to sit in as they watched their husbands disappear into the rear of the place. About five and twenty minutes following, the gentlemen reappeared. They were fitted with complete evening dress. Spiraling slowly, they neared their wives. The ladies stared in stunned silence.

"Well—" Mr. Bingley smiled broadly, breaking the silence as their wives continued to gape. "Have we your approval?"

Jane and Elizabeth glanced at each other, then simultaneously replied, "Indeed!"

They rose from their seats, giggling at their response.

Elizabeth studied her husband with increasingly greater admiration. His masculine attractiveness captivated her ability to articulate her delighted emotion. His virile attire well fitted his form, providing him unquestionable notability. Although he was generally thought of in this fashion, unto himself he gave his advantageous looks little attention and oft'times failed to see it.

"It becomes you very well," Elizabeth remarked soberly. Staring deep into his eyes, she made herself nearer to him. His striking noble form captivated her. Thinking him a figure of manly beauty, she could not dislodge her eyes from him. He was towering and magnificent, more exquisitely distinguished than ever she imagined. She stood momentarily transfixed. "Oh—my dearest—I can scarce take breath. My heart beats rapidly."

"You approve?" questioned Mr. Darcy with earnest hope.

She felt her face warm. It coloured a deep shade of red as she explained in a low whispering voice, "Approve? How could I not approve? I once thought you to be the most handsome among men; now at this very moment, I confess you have outdone yourself." She swallowed hard, taking in air, adding quietly, "It is just that you continue to astonish me; you take my breath away at the mere sight of you."

Mr. Darcy gazed passionately into her fine eyes while taking her hands in his. He lifted them slightly before affectionately giving them a squeeze, never taking a second to remove his eyes from hers. So taken with each other momentarily, they well nigh forgot where they were. Suddenly, realizing he still held her hands, he inhaled, letting loose as he released his breath. Both lingered speechlessly mesmerized; not another word was spoken.

Jane addressed her husband. "Charming, you look so dashing, very elegant. This suits you well, you look fashionable indeed."

Mr. Darcy regained his poise. He was not disposed to any public display. He viewed such behaviour beneath his dignity, causing him to feel quite undone. "We purchased the attire this morning; shall we continue?"

"I believe we shall," stated Mr. Bingley before the ladies could reply.

The shopkeeper wrapped their previously worn clothing. After settling the costs, they were on their way. They proceeded next to the haberdashery to acquire the accessories the shopkeeper had in his keeping since the morning hours. Their appearance, having delighted the ladies beyond expectation, brought additional pleasure, especially to Mr. Darcy, who now felt a compelling desire to be alone with his wife.

"Now, what do you say we return to the inn, perhaps you ladies might wish to consider preparing yourselves for dinner and the ball this evening?" asked Mr. Bingley.

"Very well," responded Jane.

Elizabeth took the disengaged arm of her husband, snuggling close to him in the carriage. Mr. Bingley brought Jane's hand to his lips and softly kissed it. "I do declare, for all appearances, we are the height of happiness, indeed it is so," stated Mr. Bingley. "I do believe we are the two happiest couples in all of London at present, possibly ever!"

Arriving at the inn, the gentlemen insisted they should like to go for a turn while the ladies dressed for dinner. "After all," Mr. Bingley excused with persistence, "we are completely attired and have time for a turn about the grounds. I do expect we both shall benefit from the freshness of the air. We promise to return directly."

Mr. Darcy nodded in agreement. Having announced their plan, they quickly accompanied the ladies to their chambers, then quitted the inn in haste. Elizabeth again noted their secretive manner. Her propensity to be curious lent disbelief to the vagueness of their claim, more so due to Mr. Bingley's unnatural actions. He was clearly anxious to quit their presence.

Some time thereafter, their husbands returned directing themselves above the stairs. Elizabeth, now formally attired, was sitting at the dressing table when Mr. Darcy made his entrance. As her ladies' maid quitted the chamber, he neared the dressing table. He stood behind her for a moment, admiring her presentation in the looking glass. His face suddenly appeared over her left shoulder. He leaned in toward her, eyeing her through the looking glass, then kissed her softly on the cheek. In a tender whispering voice he proclaimed, "You look absolutely radiant."

Her eyes gleamed as she gazed back at him through the looking glass, captured once again in that hypnotic state as their eyes reciprocally locked, unable to sever. They lingered, momentarily speechless, caught in the rapture of the moment.

"You possess the ability to disarm me with your dark fine eyes," he complained with passionate utterance. He brought his hands from behind his back, circling them around the front of her. He carefully placed an emerald necklace about her throat. Elizabeth's eyes filled with tears of joy as he secured the delicate latch, gently kissing her cheek again with an amorous purr.

"Oh—how—breathtakingly beautiful," she said slowly. "You possess exquisite taste, but I fear you are much too generous. I should never have expected anything this fine," she softly added, her voice trailing in disbelief of the beauty and extravagance of his gift.

Her words startled him to full composure. "Why ever not?"

"I do not know," Elizabeth answered in a small voice, her eyes now looking down at her lap. "I never expected it, never thought of it; it is so beautiful; you are much too generous." She raised her eyes to view the jewels through the looking glass. "The emerald induces me to reflect on the beauty of the countryside."

"It does not do you justice; there are no jewels in comparison to such beauty as yours. Though I thought it rather elegant, I had a severe desire to present it to my handsome wife; I simply decided you should have it."

His praise was gratifying. Her heart was lastingly touched. She remained speechless, embarrassed by his revelation of deep affection. Self-consciousness induced her face to colour, causing her to feel intimately warm. Overpowered by feelings of inspiring affection, Elizabeth stood to embrace him. They stood gazing lovingly into each other's eyes.

"Perhaps we better be on our way," noted her impassioned husband.

"Yes—yes, I quite agree," she replied, realizing their imposing power over each other.

Jane and Mr. Bingley awaited them. "There you are," cried Mr. Bingley. "I thought you would never come. The carriage just arrived," he announced, then added, "Are you unwell, Darcy?"

"Very well, thank you. Why do you ask?"

"Well—when you came below the stairs, you appeared preoccupied, as though your mind were elsewhere. Your face is a bit flushed."

"Allow me to assure you, Bingley, I am well. I look forward to a most complete evening," he replied with certainty. He could not publicly speak of his intimate thoughts of desire, which induced the distraction.

"Oh, Jane, the dress looks lovelier on you now than in the shop," Elizabeth noted.

"What a magnificent necklace," Jane commented as she studied Elizabeth's throat. "It flatters your attire. Mr. Darcy has exceedingly excellent taste, does he not?"

"Indeed he does; and look at you, Jane, your necklace is very beautiful. It complements your dress very well."

"Yes, Lizzy, I agree. Mr. Bingley thought the opal would surely flatter the pink dress. It adds just the right quality to the style, would you not agree?"

"Oh yes, Jane, I believe it does."

They could not control the urge to hug one another. As they exchanged a hug, Jane whispered softly into Elizabeth's ear, "I'm convinced of your earlier declaration, Lizzy; you are absolutely correct—it is fate indeed; it is all meant to be."

Hyde Park Ball

*W*AITING OUTSIDE THE INN was Mr. Darcy's rather large barouche box. Mr. Darcy tapped on the top side to begin their journey. Each inhabitant was quietly reserved in anticipation of the evening. After a brief journey, the carriage came to a full stop in front of the Grand Ballroom. After disembarking, the four stood before the great hall, studying its magnificence with admiring excitement.

"What a grand establishment," observed Mr. Bingley. "Is it not now, Darcy? What say you?"

"It is auspicious in appearance and promises to lack nothing. I am certain the evening will prove to be extremely gregarious."

As the four entered the ballroom, Elizabeth looked about the chamber forming a study of the plenitude of couples. Such fine garments and elegance of presentation marveled her. But foremost, she experienced satisfaction in the knowledge her own formal attire was equivalent or, in a few instances, advantageous to that of the other ladies about the great hall. The population of the chamber was unmistakably distinguished with people of elevated circumstances and couples representing good breeding. Certainly none lacked in social graces, thought she. Ladies curtsied and gentlemen bowed as they passed. She knew no one, but that was of little consequence as Mr. Bingley, her sister and husband comfortably accompanied her. As she crossed the chamber linked in his arm, she became aware of the attention they drew, noticing particularly her distinguished husband, whose superior elegant stature commanded attention from the ladies as he took each courtly stride. It did not take long for Elizabeth to realize her husband was well acquainted in the London society she now permeated. Several gentlemen called him by name as they approached. Until this moment she had given little thought to his connections. Feeling accomplished and refined in her appearance, she detected favour in his eyes as well; but more importantly she experienced her own satisfying fulfillment. Never in the whole of her life had she experienced the concentration of so many eyes upon her person, nor had she worn attire indicative to the height of fashion owning to such an affluent society.

Elizabeth at the moment studied Jane and Mr. Bingley. Jane's elegant style of dress, along with her look of happiness, reinforced Elizabeth's belief that her sister was content in her position as Mr. Bingley's wife. She admired Jane's excellent character, particularly her ability to pursue indisputable goodness in people. For all general determination, she believed Mr. Bingley aspired to the ideal country gentleman. When coupled together, their appearance emanated refined culture saturated with dignity.

Glancing in the direction of her husband, much to her surprise, she caught his amusement in observing her. Her heart beat fast within her breast. Her face coloured. The evening was just beginning and already she was in awe of the activities about her. His appearance stirred romantic notions within her, causing her to turn a deeper shade of red as she now sought to harness her exaggerated emotions.

Mr. Darcy looked at her with an element of alarm. "Are you unwell, my dear?"

"Very well. I find I am experiencing overwhelming pleasure. It is all quite breathtaking to be sure. I confess, I am happily situated at my husband's side."

Suddenly Mr. Darcy turned to his wife, affording her a superior bow. He inquired of her in a teasing manner, "I trust, madam, I may take this opportunity to solicit your hand for the first two dances and all others thereafter for the whole of the evening?"

"Such formality, need you ask?"

"Very well, my dear, shall we dance?" He extended his hand, leading her to the dance floor.

Before she could utter another word, they were dancing, suddenly aware, by sheer coincidence, the melody played was the very same they danced to at the Netherfield ball. This was surely a remembrance of less pleasing times, an earlier dance she would just as soon forget. She did not desire to blemish this delightful evening with such opposing notions from the past.

By slight observation, Mr. Darcy made notice of Elizabeth's frowned expression. With closer recognition of the tune, and having perceived as much, he supposed his wife's thoughts. He resolved not to be silent. No, silence will not do, thought he. It required strategy to rectify it forever. "Perhaps we ought to have some form of conversation while dancing, Mrs. Darcy. Perhaps we should prompt some remark regarding the size of the chamber or the number of couples!" Then he added, "You see, dearest, I do on occasion talk by rule while dancing, is that not so just now?"

Elizabeth could not help but be amused. She knew what he was about.

"You see, I am capable of behaving in a gentlemanly manner. Would you not agree?"

She could tolerate no more of his teasing; it caused her face to colour again. With this, she laughed all the more. "Do not taunt me so," cried Elizabeth, pleading with folly.

"As you wish," he replied. "No further tormenting. I shall cease it immediately by stating: Madam, I am of the firmest conviction, there being no doubt, I am absolutely certain, when I announce I am dancing with the most handsome woman in the whole of the room. I further conclude, the gentlemen occupying the ballroom would be quick to agree with me, if not for the vexed state in which they would find themselves should their partners know they expressed such a notion. I observed the heads you turned upon our entrance. Your loveliness is captivating; surely I noticed you earnestly studied."

"I too noticed the approving attention you received from the ladies upon our entrance. I daresay they were not scrutinizing myself with admiration, but rather desiring perhaps closer examination of my husband?"

"Perhaps they were; perhaps you better remain at my side the whole of the evening; perhaps you should keep a watchful eye on me to be sure," he claimed with playful sarcasm.

"You are very good, Mr. Darcy. I cannot match comments such as these," she laughed. At that particular moment a new tune was heard. Her husband became more reserved, turning less playful, but remained continuously attentive, having succeeded in his desire to divert her attention from sad memories of the past. The delightful ball progressed as numerous agreeable melodies were heard. Many pleasing dances were to be had by the four that evening.

While the four stood to the side talking amongst themselves, a gentleman approached them. He was tall, dominating a slender distinguished appearance. He moved about in a very gracious manner, displaying an immediate sense of duty and honour. His handsome looks revealed dark eyes comple-

menting his dark wavy hair, with fine features expressing a charming mani-
festation of benevolence. Elizabeth noticed his hands were soft looking. She
thought he had unusually long, slender fingers.

He approached them as if he were familiar with them. He was indeed,
with one of the party at least. Mr. Darcy was his acquaintance. The gentleman bowed humbly as he addressed Mr. Darcy in a confident soft voice.
"Fitzwilliam, I believe this is indeed an unexpected pleasure to see you about
in London once again."

"Yes it is indeed," replied Mr. Darcy. "I had not expected it myself since
we last spoke. Allow me to introduce you to my party. This is my dear friend
Charles Bingley, his wife, Jane, and my wife, Elizabeth. This is Mr. Henry
Manley. He is a clergyman here in London." He bowed. "We have known
each other many years," Mr. Darcy added.

"Fitzwilliam, I did not realize you were married!"

"Indeed I am, a fortnight yesterday to be precise."

"Oh, I see, that explains it. You are on your wedding journey. Please
accept my best wishes for your health and happiness; I indeed wish you all
the best," he directed as he bowed to the ladies. "Are you to stay in London
long? Will you have occasion to visit the rectory?"

"I had not intended to do so, although it is a splendid idea," replied Mr.
Darcy. Mr. Darcy turned to Mr. Bingley and the ladies. "Would you be
inclined to consider staying one additional day in London?"

They were all in agreement. "Sounds like a splendid idea. We shall be
delighted and look forward to it," expressed Mr. Bingley.

"Very well, Fitzwilliam, at what time may I expect you tomorrow? Do
you prefer the morning, early afternoon or late afternoon toward evening?
I may say if you choose evening, I would be more than delighted to have the
cook present us with a splendid meal. I would welcome the company," Mr.
Manley expressed graciously.

Mr. Darcy again glanced at the rest of the party. After little discussion,
they all agreed to come late afternoon toward early evening for dinner.

With dinner guests secured, he turned to address Mr. Darcy. "Fitzwilliam, would you allow me the pleasure of dancing with Mrs. Darcy later in
the evening?"

"I am not opposed to it," replied Mr. Darcy, "but you'll have to ask
Elizabeth yourself."

Before he could utter another word, Elizabeth curtsied. "It will be an
honour."

Mr. Manley bowed, excusing himself, then moved on to mingle with others. Elizabeth watched him intently as he departed their company. It was obvious by the recognition he received that he was successfully acquainted and no doubt well admired.

"I like him," voiced Elizabeth. "What a charming creature; he has grace expected in a man of his position. I do believe he is in the right profession. Yes, clergyman suits him well. He has the right manner for it. I do admire his kind demeanour; surely he is a person instantly liked upon introduction."

Jane and Mr. Bingley, now desiring to dance, parted their company.

Now alone, and having no secret with his wife on the subject, Mr. Darcy explained to Elizabeth how Mr. Manley rendered him assistance months back, when he visited London to recover her sister Lydia, who had run off with a regimental man.

The subject pained Elizabeth. Her thoughts reverted to that awful time when her youngest sister, Lydia, only fifteen years of age, had convinced herself in love with a blue coat in a local regiment. Having followed the regiment to Brighton, upon invitation by the Colonel's wife to be her personal companion, Lydia ran off with the man believing a marriage was in the scheme. They remained well hidden in London until Mr. Darcy, through close investigation and with the help of connections such as Mr. Manley, who was instrumental in providing a pathfinder, located them and laid out a large sum to bring a marriage about. Having accomplished all this out of affection for Elizabeth, he saved the Bennet family from embarrassment and ruin. Scrutiny of such discredit, upon public disclosure, would certainly have placed her and her sisters in a disgraceful position. To add to her pain, all this must be kept secret. The whole of the family still believed it was their Uncle Gardiner who brought about the marriage of Lydia. This was a conversation only they could share, as Jane and Mr. Bingley had no knowledge of the events.

She thought, what must he think of my family?

"What is the matter, Elizabeth, you look suddenly pale. Are you unwell?"

With a look of embarrassment, she answered, "Oh, dearest, it just occurred to me, Mr. Manley is apprised of the situation; how humiliating to be sure."

"Do not concern yourself, my dear; there is no need for alarm. Mr. Manley is honourable; his opinion of you is highly esteemed, you may be sure of it. Perhaps we should not speak of it further; let this not interfere with the romances of the evening."

"Yes, I agree, it is best left unsaid. I must say, I find Mr. Manley rather agreeable. I delight in the thought of meeting him again. Perhaps we could invite him to Pemberley."

"That would please me."

As the evening carried on, they danced and laughed. Mr. Manley returned to claim his dance with Elizabeth, who discovered him to be an excellent partner. Upon returning her to her husband, he requested a dance with Jane.

Mr. Bingley was all too happy to oblige; however, he was eager to have Jane to himself again. The three watched as he danced about with Jane.

"His movements are smooth about the floor. As you see, he is light on his feet," claimed Elizabeth. "But," she delightfully added, "although I claim him an excellent dancer, I much rather prefer you, dearest; you are an excellent partner, far superior in fact."

"Why thank you, Elizabeth."

Although she thought it, but dared not voice her opinion publicly, it was his touch alone she felt most wholly and desirously comfortable with.

Mr. Manley escorted Jane back to their party. The gentlemen danced the last two dances of the evening with their new brides.

"As with all such delights, these events do come to a close," Mr. Bingley announced. Just as predicted, so it did; it ended with the fondest memories certain to remain.

Mr. Darcy's eyes brightened. "Although I claimed never to be fond of dancing, I must admit having the good fortune to be joined with an excellent partner certainly changed my whole outlook on the subject. I too confess, I am all too sorry to see the evening end." He turned to his wife. "Elizabeth, you must plan a ball at Pemberley. I do believe I have acquired a better taste for dancing since I may now count on you as my partner. I would welcome such an event."

"You flatter me, Fitzwilliam, but I confess, I enjoy a good dance."

As he secured her wrap, he neared her from behind to say softly in her tresses, for her hearing alone, "It is not flattery, my dear, but earnest truth of your ability. I consider you the best dancing partner of my acquaintance. I daresay it credits my desire to satisfy my romantic inclination to be near you and admire you in public without censure."

A reddening overspread Elizabeth's complexion as she accepted his words of admiration. She felt his passionate gaze sheathe her form as they continued to ready themselves to depart. How passionate was his love for her, thought she. She believed she was beginning to truly understand this husband of hers. He was neither proud nor haughty, just reserved among those he knew least; but, with her, reserve was nonexistent. She believed she was beginning to understand his strengths as well as his weaknesses. That is, if he has any weaknesses, she mused.

As they proceeded to quit the ballroom, Mr. Darcy stood aside allowing a few of the ladies to pass. Elizabeth was quick to notice one of them casting a direct pausing look at her husband. With a faint sly grin accompanied by a slight nod, the woman acknowledged him. Aware of the attention his presence had drawn throughout the evening from several of the ladies, she determined that this encounter held specific significance. And to her further notice was the way in which this woman wished to make her presence known.

Elizabeth had perceived the woman went out of her way to pass in front of Mr. Darcy, so as to be noticed. After passing them, the lady was joined by a rather smartly dressed gentleman, appearing to be of some wealth, although advanced in years. As she linked her arm in his, the woman turned to direct one last glance over her shoulder in the direction of Mr. Darcy. Prior to turning away, she afforded him an amorous smile before departing. Elizabeth surmised the woman knew her husband. She found her interest elevated to a level of absolute diversion. As soon as they were out of sight, Elizabeth inquired, "Are you acquainted with that lady, Mr. Darcy? She appeared to know you!"

"Yes, Elizabeth, I know her; just a business acquaintance, nothing more. You need not concern yourself."

While the woman was somewhat handsome, she did not own to that air of elegance claimed by the female society at the ball. Elizabeth thought she rather appeared overstated and a bit removed from her society. Although her garment held certain appeal, it lacked obvious quality of affluence. The style, being deficient in comparison to the general population of the room, presented her conspicuously. She could not help but wonder how it came to be that she attended such an event, but supposed the gentleman she accompanied had much to do with it.

Elizabeth studied her husband at length. She could not help but notice the change in his countenance such a meeting produced. He seemed absorbed in sober reflection. Her curiosity piqued, but she soon discovered he had no wish to pursue the subject, as he conveniently changed the topic without hesitation. Now convinced her husband was undone by the encounter, she found herself uneasy of the ill effect the woman seemed to have on his disposition.

With her mind dashing from one notion to another, they proceeded to the out of doors. The chance meeting with this lady had a less than calming effect on Elizabeth. She struggled to regain composure. Her breathing became heavy. Her heart beat rapidly with anxiety. Now aware of the attention she drew from her husband and sister, she endeavoured to regain the sense of gaiety of the evening. She managed to snuggle nearer to him as they waited for the carriage, affording Jane an appeasing smile, which seemed at the moment to pacify the situation in her eyes solely.

Elizabeth's altered demeanour did not escape Jane's notice. Jane knew her sister's temperament well. She believed Elizabeth to be perhaps a bit undone by the attentions Mr. Darcy received. She too noticed the encounter, judging it odd as well. She knew her sister was not likely to rest until she knew all there was to know. Finding a bit of amusement in the situation, she concluded her sister perhaps possessed a level of jealous tendencies. She pleasantly smiled back at Elizabeth with a watchful eye.

The carriage was brought around. Before long they were back at the inn.

Alone now in the chamber, Elizabeth willingly did not approach the subject, hoping her husband would offer some explanation. He did not.

Instead, he seemed unusually preoccupied. Finding she could no longer contain her propensity to know all, she asked, "Dearest, is there a reason for your reserve? That lady, does she claim a significant design on you? You are acquainted with her, are you not?"

"Yes, Elizabeth, but our association was purely business."

"What kind of business?"

"Elizabeth, I have no wish to discuss it. It is nothing, my dear; I beg you will put it out of your mind. Your concern is wasted on nothing."

"Nothing! How can you declare it is nothing when you were so displaced by your meeting? Fitzwilliam, the whole of your demeanour took a turn after the encounter. What business exists that could possibly induce you to be so undone? The deliberate manner in which she wished to make her presence known to you did not escape my observation. I daresay she did not appear to possess any air of refinement or level of that society I would expect to discover in any acquaintance of yours. She desired you to make her notice. I witnessed the stare she afforded you," she said searchingly. After a deep sigh, she added, "I could plainly see she is not a woman of your society; indeed she is not!"

It troubled him to witness her now elevated state of anxiety. "You are right, she is not of our society; she was in my employ," he answered with pained voice.

"At Pemberley?"

Mr. Darcy stood with certain calm, but knew he could no longer remain silent. There was a certain irony in all of this, thought he. In his quest to keep their wedding journey so wholly and completely pure from any disappointment or less than wonderful memories, he had to now explain Miss Grey, as well as conceal his earlier view from the window. Anguished feelings overcame him, along with an urgency to clear up the matter at once.

"Elizabeth, come here," he said, taking her hand, leading her to the bed. He sat her down, seizing a place at her side, still holding her hand in his. "Elizabeth, Miss Grey was employed at Pemberley as Georgiana's governess. Once my father passed on, I detected a noticeable difference in Miss Grey. She suddenly directed her attentions toward me. I neither sought nor desired her attentions. I told her so forthright, avoiding any close encounters. She continued to do everything in her power to gain my notice. Although I did notice her, it was not the recognition she intended. I kept a watchful eye on her. One day I returned to the house, having forgotten some papers in my office. I discovered her going through my desk. My presence there startled her. Her explanation was shallow. I erred in judgment when I foolishly chose to extend her further opportunity to prove herself worthy of the position—perhaps it was because Georgiana seemed pleased with her. One night, Mrs. Reynolds abruptly awakened me from a sound sleep. She had been keeping a watchful eye on Miss Grey. She witnessed her quietly attempting to enter my bedchamber. You can imagine my embarrassment and horror. I knew not what Mrs. Reynolds thought at the time. I was forced to dismiss Miss Grey from my employ only to discover Mrs. Reynolds had been watching her for some time suspiciously. Mrs. Reynolds was well aware of her unsolicited attentions. Had it been anyone other than Mrs. Reynolds, I may have been universally gossiped of, but she knows me too well to have any ill thoughts in that direction. She has never spoken of it since. Tonight is the first our paths have crossed since I discharged her from my employ. I must say, I was bewildered to see her there."

"But why did you not wish to tell me?"

"Elizabeth, this is meant to be the happiest of times. I did not wish to cloud our first memories with disappointments of my past. He pulled her close to him in a lengthy embrace, seeking refuge from those thoughts he now felt necessary to conceal. It occurred to him that he had not considered her to be of a sensitive nature. He now viewed her in a new light, detecting she displayed sensitivity of other women viewing him.

"Very well, dearest, perhaps we should prepare to settle down for a restful night," he said, hoping the gaiety of the promised evening was not lost.

"Yes, perhaps we should."

Once in bed he held her close, changing the subject to their intended visit the day next to Mr. Manley's parish. Now all such thoughts of Miss Grey were laid to rest. Having put them in their proper place brought a sense of satisfaction to both parties.

Instead of anticipating a long journey home, which was previously planned for the morning, they now looked forward to an evening with The Honourable Henry Manley.

An Additional Day in London

THE MORNING NEXT, the four, having no particular plan for the early part of the day, remained in their chambers until mid morning. Elizabeth sat at the dressing table brushing her hair. "Are you quite sure we are not upsetting your housekeeper's plans for our return home? Is she expecting us? Should we be sending her communication?"

"Not at all," Mr. Darcy replied with certainty. "I will send a messenger as to when she may expect us. We are not destining for Derbyshire for several days. The plan is to first go to Netherfield Park. I intend to dispatch the message from there. We shall have to spend two nights at best to rest, perhaps three or more if you wish. There is no hurry. I should have thought you might wish to visit Longbourn while in the neighbourhood."

Elizabeth smiled, but before she could comment, he added, "I am pleased you found favour with Mr. Manley. It is my intention, before long, to convince him to take one of the parishes on my property. He has such a propitious nature about him. The clergyman at my largest parish, Richard Green, is contemplating quitting the place. He wishes to retire to reside with relatives in Bath. That is not expected for several months. I have not approached Mr. Manley with an offer, but I certainly wish to entertain thoughts of him. He is quite a gentleman, is he not?"

"Yes, I must agree."

Mr. Darcy walked to the window. He lingered there, staring out at the grounds. He turned his attention to the sun, now high in the sky. The brilliant rays of the sun penetrated its magnificent golden light about the grounds, forcing its resplendent panels of sunlight through the trees. He lingered a while longer, as if he were being held captive. He turned his attention to Elizabeth once again. "I have inordinate regard for the God-given beauty of nature. There are times I find myself in awe of all that surrounds me."

"I have long ago formed an attachment to nature. Indeed I agree, all credit of inspiration regarding such reflections belongs to God. But I confess I have been studying your depth of thought as you stand at the window. I wondered the subject of your reverie."

"My mind was ardently engaged in the desire to secure Mr. Manley to fill the vacancy soon expected at Pemberley. I am convinced it would be advantageous to secure him. It would suit me well to have him situated there, but convincing him may be another matter."

Elizabeth took a step toward him. Her brows slightly united with curiosity. "How so?"

Mr. Darcy peered out of the window once again. He seemed occupied, but then he turned to her. His lips parted as if to speak but hesitated, then said, "It is universally known, some rather prefer the society of town. I am sure you observed Mr. Manley appears well acquainted within London society. It is evident he is suitably respected. I am aware of his many connections. I'm sure it would make the decision difficult."

Walking away from the window, he continued, "Mr. Manley is unwed. For a man of six and twenty, a move to the countryside would limit his selection. He surely will not find a wife at Pemberley Estate, perhaps in all of Derbyshire. I don't know why he has not married. I guessed, or I rather supposed, he had not encountered a suitable mate, or perhaps he shares my sentiments."

"What do you mean?" she inquired with eager interest.

After a silence of several minutes, Mr. Darcy eyed her directly. He played with the ring on his finger for a few fleeting moments. He paused, then took a step closer to avow his heartfelt sentiments. "I was unwilling to settle for anything less than the most extreme affections and deepest love. I once confided in my sister Georgiana that only the deepest love would ever induce me to matrimony. No doubt you can imagine what prompted me to speak to Georgiana in this regard. Nonetheless, I felt it my duty to instruct her of the risky dealings in the matters of the heart, explaining others do not convince you in love. I merely pointed out, a person will experience helplessness in controlling such strong emotions, that naught, including one's own strong willfulness of mind, can deny the heart-wrenching emotions endured when captured in sentiments of such depth of inexplicable feelings. I confided in Georgiana, stating if I were not so fortunate to find that depth of love, nothing would induce me to marry—not even an intended partnership, regardless of wealth and connections. I would suffer to settle for no less."

Elizabeth stepped back to sit on the end of the bed. Soaking up his every word with amused satisfaction, she smiled broadly. His words astonished and flattered her. She could scarce believe her hearing. Had not he expressed that only the deepest love would induce him to matrimony? Hadn't she expressed those very same words to Jane?

Elizabeth cupped her hands over her face. She allowed her torso to fall back upon the bed as she began to laugh. Her laughter steadily increased without restraint.

Mr. Darcy made his carriage straighter, tugged on his coat as he stretched his neck within his collar. Now staring at his wife, his expression emerged soberly stern. Tumultuously pained by her laughter, his looks grew sharp with torment. Struggling awkwardly, his speech in every way turned indignant, causing his face to heighten in colour as he advanced cautiously toward her. Every feature of his face revealed the formed disturbance of his immediate thoughts. At length, with forced calmness and captured composure, he inquired, "I might wonder why—pray—tell me, what is it you find so amusing you suffer difficulty to restrain such laughter?" Then with the appearance of haughtier composure, he went on. "I was serious in my proclamation. All I stated was in earnest. Why then do you find folly in the sincerest confession of the heart?"

Elizabeth immediately apprehended his hurt. With embarrassment impossible to be overcome, she instinctively ceased her laughter. "My dear—dear husband, I laugh at myself alone. I said those very words to Jane before making your acquaintance. Our thoughts are strikingly alike, yet sometimes not. Only the deepest love would have ever induced me to matrimony! You suffered my indifference. I am certain you well remember it. Like others blindly in love, we endured the heart-wrenching denial through our stubborn willfulness, which gave way to our common thoughts of prejudice, a near death to any alliance between us. But our regard was stronger than our denial; esteemed felicity triumphed in the end, the result being mutually victorious I daresay. I could not have settled for less than the deepest endearment myself. I would rather be poor in love than rich in situation, chancing a life of discontent."

"You'll hardly have to worry about that now," he retorted.

He neared himself to her, securing her in his arms. Locked in an embrace, they clung one to the other. "Only the deepest affections," repeated Mr.

Darcy, "only the deepest love," he said again as he rocked her back and forth in his arms.

Moments later, Elizabeth sat on the end of the bed as her husband stood in front of the looking glass regulating his neckpiece. "Mr. Darcy, are you fond of children?"

"So formal is your inquiry, Elizabeth. Why do you ask?"

"Well—it is something we never discussed. It occurred to me, I do not know if you like children. I believe I ought to know your opinion; it is so, is it not?"

There was silence as Mr. Darcy concentrated on his collar.

"What say you?" Elizabeth searched further, impatiently.

"I suppose it is a matter in need of some consideration. Certainly we will indeed have children. But as to whether I like them?" Mr. Darcy continued to work with his neckpiece, making no attempt to continue the exchange.

A dead silence overspread the room. Elizabeth watched him closely. She could only wonder if he had little interest in the subject. She waited, but still no response. Unable to contain herself any longer, she quickly stood up. "Well—what—what is your answer?" she demanded.

"Hum—well—" he replied, with his back still to her, "remember, you inquired. I fear I must be truthful, so the answer is no. I do not like children, Mrs. Darcy."

She viewed his reflection through the looking glass. His answer was explicit; his facial expression remained serious as he continued to alter his neckpiece.

Elizabeth's face paled. With all colours having drained from her face, incipient tears welled in her eyes. She could feel the hot tears make their start down her cheeks. Mortification caused her heart to pound rapidly. It was as if she were being suffocated. Placing her open right hand to her chest, she sat slowly down on the edge of the bed. Gripped with sad thoughts, she tried to regain her regulated breathing. She had discovered him to be a most excellent character, perfectly well suited to her in every manner; but if this be the flaw in his character, it was so extreme she could scarce draw breath at the very thought of it. She fought back tears to no avail; they continued to roll down her cheeks. There was no disguising her disappointment. So taken aback, she could not utter another word.

Mr. Darcy, still fixing his neckpiece, could see her full view through the looking glass. Instantaneously he knelt in front of her, taking her hands in his. With tenderness, he quickly responded, "Forgive me, dearest, I should not have teased on such a delicate subject. What I wish to say is this. No, I should not like to have children; I should love to have children. Dearest, loveliest Elizabeth, children will be the center of our home, and if their likeness is to that of their mother's, they will no doubt be the handsomest children in Derbyshire." Then, taking his handkerchief, he wiped her tears. "I beg you will forgive me. It was abominable of me to tease. I had no idea it would be taken in such a manner to cause pain; indeed you take me too seriously. I presumed you would have been secure in the notion before we married, as was I, to be sure. I never questioned it otherwise. I thought, on the contrary, I predicted more that it would be expected and desired on both our parts. As these things happen by nature, we have no control. I do indeed like children, you may be certain of it. Be happy in your thoughts; indeed it is true, I desire many—the sooner the better."

Mr. Bingley knocked on the chamber door. "Jane and I have long awaited you both, it is but two hours above noon. We entertained thoughts of break-fasting; what say you?"

"I believe our minds engage similar notions; we shall join you below the stairs momentarily. Will that be sufficient?" inquired Mr. Darcy.

"Yes, indeed," answered Mr. Bingley as he closed the door.

Elizabeth inspected her eyes in the looking glass to assure they were void of leftover tears. Mr. Darcy drew himself to her, embraced her, placing his head next to hers as they viewed each other through the looking glass. He smiled tenderly, gently tightening his hold on her.

"Let us start afresh. I see I shall have to be more selective with my teasing. I suppose you had not expected me this playful. No, indeed you did not. I must admit I am quite astonished. I had not expected your reaction nor would I have considered you this sensitive, although it was a delicate sub-ject, was it not?"

"It is all so very strange; perhaps the distance from home is the influence. I confess, I have no understanding of it, none at all." She, being embarrassed by her reaction, faintly smiled at him in the looking glass.

"We shall have to make haste; Mr. Bingley and your sister have long been waiting. No doubt they suffer pangs of hunger. What say you, are you want-ing?"

"I do believe I am; I could eat well just now," she replied as he led her to the door.

"Shall we walk? It is a fine day. I feel rather enterprising and desirous of exercise," explained Mr. Bingley, his eyes bright with excitement.

"That is a capital idea," Jane chimed in as they both looked to Mr. Darcy and Elizabeth for agreement.

"I fancy a walk; so does Mr. Darcy. Is that not so?" added Elizabeth.

"Yes, I do believe I prefer to walk."

Both women secured the disengaged arms of their husbands.

They had breakfasted but were still engaged in conversation. The ladies could not refrain from mentioning the ball. Jane announced, "It was an exceedingly good ball, was it not? There must have been twenty dances at least. We indulged most of them without fatigue."

"Yes, I was impressed by the variety of formal attires. I may say we had our share in elegance of appearance at the ball; did we not, Jane?"

"Yes, Lizzy, I should have never thought we would aspire to such delights."

They exchanged joyful anticipation of their dinner invitation at the parsonage. They were equally anxious to visit the rectory to make a closer acquaintance with Mr. Manley. Mr. Darcy, having already been acquainted with the parsonage, was less eager to see it, but perhaps more anxious to spend valued time with an old friend.

The conversation turned to another subject of interest, especially to Mr. Darcy. Mr. Bingley anxiously reported, "Darcy, there is a very fine book shop directly down the street. Since we have no decisive plans, I am of the conviction we should venture there to see if there is anything tempting to enhance our libraries. While waiting upon you, I conversed with the innkeeper. He mentioned the book shop, noting Mr. Knisely to be an excellent proprietor. Mr. Knisely is known to have distant callers. You will be pleased to know that you may very well find books not only pleasing to your taste, but special bound copies of rare books. And, Darcy, he assured me the shop carried bound copies of current books soon to be catalogued as collectibles, as well as new publications recently put into circulation. I daresay the innkeeper is a well-informed man of good taste and judgment. He told me he is excessively fond of reading and is well acquainted with Mr. Knisely. Judging by the volumes you possess, I thought perhaps you might be enticed to inspect the inventory. Shall we go? What say you, Darcy?" probed Mr. Bingley.

"Sounds as though we are going to visit the book shop," said Elizabeth, before her husband could utter a word. She smiled at him, exchanging an engaging look. "I have had a glimpse of your library. I daresay you possess a vast collection. I am eager to acquaint myself there."

"Then you should know Darcy is not only known for his extensive reading qualities, but for owning one of the finest maintained libraries in Derbyshire. His library is universally known to contain rare books and publications," Mr. Bingley interjected.

"My father had long established a library at Pemberley Hall which consists of much sought after publications. Like his father before him, his love of books never failed him. Any given opportunity to enhance his reading was never ignored. I suppose he well impressed upon me the importance of educating one's mind through extensive reading."

Mr. Darcy's mind wandered. It was Elizabeth's fancy for reading, as well as her fine eyes, which seized his notice. It was no surprise to him that his new bride was equally eager to visit the book shop.

Elizabeth, well aware of his indulgence in books, his hunger for knowledge and further education, was no less eager to witness the excitement such a declaration produced in her husband. Although she had seen his library on one occasion, she had not the knowledge of its contents, having had no specific opportunity to study the rarity of its books. She was eager for him to give in to a special purchase on their wedding journey, something particular that he could lay his hands upon in their advanced years to reminisce back to this time. Nothing would please her more, thought she. It would indeed give her pleasure, especially since he lavished her with so much finery. Surely he should have something more than a suit of clothes—yes, a rare book would do nicely. Her thoughts projected further. She wished she had the means of wealth so that she might purchase a special book for him, but, since that was not possible, she could entertain no such notion. Before she could ponder further, Mr. Bingley sprang to his feet.

"Shall we go?" he inquired, ending her musing.

They walked up the street linked arm in arm. Sure enough, there it was within an easy distance, Archibald Knisely's Book Shop. It was a quaint shop, whose shingle hung, to the excitement of Mr. Darcy, upon its notice.

Archibald Knisely's Book Shop

Upon entering the book shop, they were immediately impressed to view the large inventory. Mr. Darcy's thrill was evident; he immediately began to gape over titles.

"Such a fine shop," expressed Mr. Bingley. Mr. Darcy never looked his way; he was too enthralled in his search to pay him any mind. His complete silence, his display of indulged concentration, made known to everyone present that he was not distracted by any movement or conversation. He was so immersed in his search, he may well have been alone.

Elizabeth looked about the shop, discovering interesting publications which caused her to linger at a certain location. One book of poetry caught her fancy. She studied it for a time, then returned it to the shelf. She found little else to captivate her interest. On most occasions such an opportunity would have been welcomed, thought she—but it seems today I have not the mindset to pursue books; in fact, I find my concentration lacking. She then discovered her attention fixed on her husband, who was obviously captured by a particular book. She studied him at length. His one arm was bent at the elbow with his hand up to his face. The other held a book while he ferociously read.

She strolled about the shop, pausing at the book of poetry once again. She was convinced her choice was induced by the romance of the wedding journey.

It took a little more than an hour for Mr. Darcy to find five books to add to his collection. Elizabeth heard him conversing with Mr. Knisely over a rare book he found on a small side table; not shelf-set as the others. Mr. Darcy appeared to require the book with urgency.

As she neared them, she was fairly certain she understood them to discuss its contents to be that of a family, perhaps a ledger of sorts. Although her husband bargained for the book, Mr. Knisely declined its selling, stating he did not wish to part with it. Her husband emphasized a willingness to pay an impressive sum. Mr. Knisely appeared unmoved. Mr. Darcy persisted, stating he absolutely had to have the book. As she continued her wait, Mr. Darcy slightly turned to view her, then leaned closer to Mr. Knisely, pleading assertively. She noticed him lean still closer as they spoke quietly, keeping the conversation between them. Following a lengthy exchange, Mr. Knisely elevated his head to give a momentary glance in her direction. After returning his eyes to Mr. Darcy, he finally gave way to his wishes, agreeing to part with the book. She watched with renewed interest as they continued a lengthy exchange on other books.

Mr. Darcy, convinced he had what he wanted with the rare book along with four additional books, turned to Elizabeth. "Before I settle my purchases, I notice you have no book. Did not you find anything to your liking?"

"Well—yes, I did find one book of interest."

"I insist you retrieve it at once," he replied without hesitation.

She immediately went to the book of poetry to claim it for herself.

"It pleases me that you have found a book. I value our shared love of books. Surely you know it is a quality I admire." He then took the book from her to settle with the proprietor. Noticing it was a book of poetry, he commented, "A book of poetry—more often than not, poetry is the language of love, is it not, Mrs. Darcy?"

She smiled at him. Her sentiments exactly, thought she.

Although Elizabeth was eager to view his purchases, the distractions of the day, along with the planned visit to Mr. Manley's diverted her attention. All was forgotten for the moment.

Mr. Darcy and the shopkeeper continued to converse. The desire was there to do more of it, but the remainder of the party had been waiting for him to finalize his purchases. He was well aware of their impatience. Mr. Knisely promised to correspond with him if he came in possession of certain rare books.

"Thank you, sir, and good day," Mr. Darcy directed at Mr. Knisely.

"Good day to you," added Mr. Bingley as he neared the door with his purchases in hand.

The Scare

QUITTING THE BOOK SHOP, Jane suggested, "Perhaps it would be wise to return to the inn to rest before dinner at the parsonage."

"Yes, I am quite fatigued, although I cannot imagine why," Elizabeth agreed.

It was a fine day. The air was crisp, making it a pleasant day to walk. But, she suddenly felt weak and rather light-headed. How unusual, Elizabeth thought to herself. Slipping her arm through Mr. Darcy's, she relied on him as a means of support.

Jane and Mr. Bingley walked more advanced of them. Jane, upon turning around to speak, with an alarmed voice asked, "Lizzy, are you unwell?"

Mr. Darcy immediately viewed his wife. Noticing her complexion was ashen, he asked with urgency, "Dearest, are you quite all right?"

"I am well; I just feel a bit light-headed, that is all. There is nothing to concern yourselves with. I am out in the air. You know how I like the out of doors, it refreshes me."

As they neared the inn, Mr. Darcy felt Elizabeth slip from his arm. He was losing contol of her, but managed to catch her just as she reached the ground.

"Good God, she fainted. What shall we do?" cried Mr. Bingley excitedly as he ran back to his friend.

Jane put her fingers over her mouth as if she were trying to keep from screaming. She began to panic, gasping for air. Her body was suddenly overtaken with fear, causing her to become paralyzed with anxiety. She clutched her husband.

"Jane, calm yourself," Mr. Bingley said, giving her a quick pat on the shoulder.

Mr. Darcy, with soundness of mind and calmness of controlled composure directed Mr. Bingley. "Come, Bingley; don't just stand there, assist me. We must get her to the chamber."

Jane inhaled. She collected her thoughts, attempting to calm herself the best she could. The innkeeper came running out of doors with another gentleman.

"I believe we may be of some service to you, sir," said the innkeeper hurriedly.

"Thank you, yes," a composed Mr. Darcy answered.

Wasting no time, they assisted in taking Elizabeth to the chamber. The innkeeper's wife was not far behind with smelling salts.

Jane was in tears. "There must be something seriously wrong; I have never known Lizzy to be anything but strong and healthy." She continued to sob as she followed.

The innkeeper's wife called to the housekeeper, "Dispatch the apothecary at once." She turned to Jane. "There, there now, do not fret; your sister is coming around."

The smelling salts brought Elizabeth to a somewhat alert state. Mr. Darcy looked at Jane. "Rub her hands, Jane," he directed. Within minutes Elizabeth was conscious and feeling rather silly about the fuss her having fainted created.

The apothecary arrived. After examining Elizabeth, he reported, "She merely fainted. I do not expect there is anything of concern, but perhaps rest might prove beneficial. It very well could have been something she ate. Perhaps a bit of undigested food."

Elizabeth soon found herself alone in the chamber with her husband. "Shall I send an express to Mr. Manley with regrets for this evening?" he inquired.

"Certainly not; I will not hear of it. I shall be well, you will see. I believe all I require is a bit of rest. Dearest, why do you not go back to the book shop? I noticed you and Mr. Knisely had much to discuss. I could plainly see our waiting party caused you to draw close your search."

"No—no, I could not go, I shall stay right here with you. I'll watch you rest. I shall be content to read the *Morning Post*. Perhaps when I have finished it, I may enjoy one of my books while keeping a watchful eye on you. Indeed, I could not consider it."

"My dear, I know my sister Jane well. She is no doubt fretting as we speak. I know it will give her comfort to watch over me. You must believe me; it is so, I insist. Now, please go knock on their chamber door. Present this proposition to Jane. You will see how eager she is to come. Then, I would like you and Mr. Bingley, although I do not know that this would be his preference since he did not make many purchases—still, I would like you to return to the book shop. Go now; finish what you started," Elizabeth pleaded.

Mr. Darcy kissed his bride reluctantly, but did as she requested. He soon learned she was absolutely correct, Jane was eager to sit with her.

Mr. Bingley's passion for books was unequal to that of his friend. "If you have no objection, Darcy, I would much rather stay to converse with the innkeeper. I find him a likeable fellow of some education."

"Very well, Bingley, you know where to find me if I am needed. I shall look in on Elizabeth before parting."

Jane, now content to watch over her sister, expressed, "Lizzy, I am surprised Mr. Darcy returned to the book shop; I expected he would have stayed with you"

"Jane, Mr. Darcy did so upon my insistence. I know you all too well. Since it is not a man's province to sit with the sick, I thought he would benefit from a return trip to Mr. Knisely's Book Shop. After all, Jane, I have had little chance to speak with you alone."

"Yes, that is true," she answered, positioning the bolsters to allow Elizabeth more comfort.

"Jane, bring your chair closer."

"Very well, Lizzy. But should not you be resting?"

"Jane, I wish you would not fuss so. Besides, I wish to speak to you. Here is my chance to do so now that we are alone."

"What is so important, Lizzy, that cannot wait?"

"I must tell you. It occurred to me back at the book shop that I had not the means to purchase so much as a book for Mr. Darcy. It would have pleased me to give him a gift. After all, Jane, have we not received so much finery?"

"Yes—but, Lizzy—I do not believe our husbands expect anything. Surely they are aware of our family situation."

"I am certain they are well aware of our lack of means. Even so, Father did mean to grant us a small dowry; he said as much. That was made impossible, thanks to our mother's frequent visits to the warehouses. Poor father, our wedding clothing was all he could afford."

"Come now, Lizzy, I fear you are much too hard on our mother. She does not mean to be unconcerned; it is just her nature to be unreasonable."

Elizabeth abruptly sat forward. "Unreasonable, you call it! Jane, do you not see how she has managed to ignore his pleas for economy? He was greatly distressed. I could plainly see he was mortified in having to provide an explanation of such delicate matters relating to his bookkeeping. He recounted to me that Lydia's extravagant wardrobe, required for her stay at Brighton, and Lydia's wedding clothing and our own, far exceeded his pocket allowance. Sadly, he was not in a position to do us any justice in the matter. I was surprised he made no mention of our mother's propensity to extravagance when relating this; however, you are well aware of her habitual visits to the local warehouses without his knowledge."

"Perhaps, but surely you know our mother does not mean to ignore his wishes."

"Oh, Jane, how is it possible you defend her lack of respect for our father's wishes?"

Jane sighed as she sat back in the chair, folding her arms in front of her. "Perhaps, Lizzy, you are much too severe where our mother is concerned. But, I do confess she does visit the warehouses frequently against Father's wishes. It is distressing to him, I know."

"I suppose we will not be sorry for escaping the delivery of the invoices, surely not the general commotion caused by such. I, for one, will not miss the turmoil. Nor shall I miss our father shutting himself up in his chamber upon their receipt. Little is ever made of his protests on our mother's side. Jane, you must admit, she is amiss to take no responsibility. She refuses to comprehend anything adverse of her expenditures and forbids him further discussion or pleas. It pains me to remember how he hung his head low, claiming he was heartily ashamed of himself for not having put more money aside for this occasion. He just shook his head, deeming himself a failure in the matters of economy."

"Oh Lizzy—do not distress yourself so. We must accept what we cannot change. You would do well to rest now. Put this out of your mind. Mr. Darcy cares nothing if you cannot afford him a book; I am certain of it."

Elizabeth lay back against the bolster. She sighed, affording Jane a meek smile. "Yes, Jane, as always you have that tendency to influence. I shall look to the better of the situation. You are right; I will rest now."

Much to Jane's relief, Elizabeth closed her eyes saying no more.

Mr. Darcy returned in just a little above two hours. He found Elizabeth had rested. She was rejuvenated and in high spirits.

"Jane, I believe she looks well rested."

"I do agree, Mr. Darcy, she looks much better, even appears to be her usual self."

Elizabeth sat up. "I don't know what came over me earlier," she explained. "I do not recall ever fainting in my entire life. No, I'm sure I never have!" She sat back again. This is so unlike me, Elizabeth thought to herself.

"Our mother always threatens to faint oft'times when something of a stressful nature comes forth, but I have no recollection of her actually fainting. I am sure she never did, just threatened she was going to. I know of no one in our family to collapse. I conclude it cannot be a family trait, just a quirk of nature. It just may very well be the altitude. I do believe it was just a peculiarity. I am much improved; I couldn't be any better."

"I am glad to hear it; it is most distressful," Mr. Darcy lamented soberly.

"I suppose we ought to ready ourselves for our visit to the rectory. I must say, I am hungry, such an appetite I have presently. I hope dinner will be served shortly after our arrival. I am excessively famished," Elizabeth reported.

Mr. Darcy studied Elizabeth. "I confess your colour is back. You do look rather radiant. I am relieved."

"I feel refreshed," she pointed out. "I am anxious to get on with the evening. I do believe that nap did me right."

After making themselves ready, they set out to collect the rest of their party. The carriage was ordered and they took their leave.

Visitors at the Rectory

THE CARRIAGE LEFT THE INN, and having arrived at the rectory at the expected time, drew to a halt in front of the ivy-covered parsonage.

Mr. Manley appeared. "How good of you to come; you do me great honour," he said as they eagerly entered the parsonage. Mr. Manley directed them to the sitting room. "Do sit down. May I offer you some tea, perhaps some port?" he inquired.

"Thank you, tea will suffice. Henry, allow me to say again how good it is to see you. Our meeting at the ball was quite unexpected. I made notice your lengthy conversation with the Lady Cassandra."

"Yes, I do believe she was rather lost. The Earl was occupied with Lord Harrington. She was left quite on her own. I suppose she is used to it; it appears she is always quite alone at gatherings."

"It is a great pity, indeed," Mr. Darcy said, as his eyes instantly met Elizabeth's. "I should never think of allowing my wife to wander about alone at a gathering, much less a ball."

All such conversation ceased upon the entrance of the housekeeper, who announced, "Your presence is required in the dining hall."

When the last took his seat, Mr. Manley gave thanks. Mr. Darcy, well impressed with Mr. Manley's eloquence of speech in prayer, intently listened to his ability to turn ordinary words into sacred meaning. He enunciated with the foremost sincerity. A feeling of certainty consumed him. He was now persuaded he must convince this man to come to Pemberley to secure the position he was most anxious to offer, and managed to express his views without further ado.

"Such a wonderful meal," expressed Mr. Bingley. "I do believe the cook made a fine choice. I cannot take credit for such delicacies. I confess the choosing was not my own. I do hope you enjoyed it," Mr. Manley expressed.

"Very much so," stated Mr. Bingley.

Jane smiled. "Lamb is my favourite dish. I could not have wished for better."

"Nor I, Mr. Manley; it was all so very palatable indeed," added Elizabeth.

The conversation about the table centered on London in general, the ball, the plays they attended, as well as Elizabeth's unfortunate faint.

Mr. Manley grew immediately concerned. "Mrs. Darcy, I hope you have fully recovered; this is alarming news. Are you feeling well now?"

"Yes, very well indeed," replied Elizabeth. "It was just a quirk of nature I am sure. Nothing to be concerned of. After resting, I concluded I have never felt better. In fact, I still claim the same. I am well, very well indeed."

To Elizabeth's relief, this seemed to put the matter to rest. She was sorry the subject had been mentioned. To change the discourse, she awkwardly stated, "Mr. Manley, we visited Archibald Knisely's Book Shop today. Are you acquainted there?"

"Oh, yes, I visit there often. I share your husband's love of books. Like him, I possess a collection of rare finds. Perhaps after dinner you may be persuaded to visit my library. I have made many purchases since your last visit, Fitzwilliam. I daresay you will be interested."

"Indeed, Henry, I always have an interest in books. My father once told me I should never be lonely if I have books. I confess they are rather like old friends."

"Yes, Mr. Manley, my husband did purchase several books today, one rare one. Is that not so, Fitzwilliam?"

"Uh—yes—Elizabeth, but I did take the book back to Mr. Knisely's shop when I returned this afternoon," he replied with hesitation. He had indeed taken the book with him; however, he just merely carried it on his person. The evasiveness of his language led all to believe he had returned the book.

Now Jane, who wished to know more of the Lady Cassandra, interrupted him. Much to the immediate relief of Mr. Darcy, Mr. Manley's discussion of the ball changed the discourse. The subject of the rare book was quickly forgotten.

After dinner, Mr. Manley ushered the visitors to his library as he had earlier implied. After the passing of a half-hour of discussing books, predominantly with Mr. Darcy, he all too soon realized his other guests were less enthusiastic. Mr. Manley smiled at Mr. Darcy, then he winked, "Perhaps we should retire to the music chamber."

"I believe that to be a wise decision," Mr. Darcy retorted with a smile.

Upon entering the music chamber, Mr. Darcy noticed the pianoforte.

"Henry, might I request my wife to play your pianoforte? She sings and plays well."

Elizabeth's cheeks overspread with a deep blush. Removing her eyes from her husband, she assured her host, "Although I do play a little, I play very ill indeed. My husband is prejudiced in my favour I fear."

"Oh—Lizzy, you always make that claim. Mr. Manley, my sister does play well."

"I would be happy to have you sit at the pianoforte, Mrs. Darcy."

"Since you insist, I suppose I might play an Italian song, if that is agreeable."

"Very well, an Italian song it is."

Mr. Manley was quite taken with her performance. "Won't you play another for us, Mrs. Darcy? You not only play well, but sing well too. It would be an honour if you did."

"If you wish," replied Elizabeth, this time obliging him by choosing an Irish air.

Elizabeth looked at her husband. He swelled with pride. He enjoyed displaying her talents, although she was less sure of their rapture. When all such entertainment was completed, Elizabeth walked toward Mr. Darcy. She turned to secure a seat next to him, as they applauded her fine presentation.

"Henry plays very well. Won't you do us the honour of hearing you play?" inquired Mr. Darcy.

A hint of modesty overspread Mr. Manley's countenance. He gave not an answer, but instead gave a nod to Mr. Darcy as he hesitantly got up from his chair. To the exposure of recognition, he was somewhat indifferent. Mr. Manley languidly walked to the instrument. He turned to look at Mr. Darcy, then to the remainder of his now gaping guests, as he took his place at the pianoforte. He sat for a moment appearing to be in deep meditation before he delicately began to play a sonata composed by George Frideric Handel.

Jane's eyes widened; her lips parted as she looked at Elizabeth. Mr. Bingley sat wide eyed, unable to remove his attention from the instrument. Elizabeth's face reddened. She looked at her husband as she let out a sigh of embarrassment, which gained his attention. He smiled back at her, then returned his attention to Mr. Manley's performance. Such playing astounded them. Mr. Manley's fingers seemed to glide across the keys with ease. His smooth manner only added to the beauty of the melody.

Elizabeth sat numb, totally mesmerized by his performance. She could not help but think his marvelous effects of tone had a quality difficult to rival. She deemed him a skilled pianist, at least the best of her hearing at a private gathering. His performance gave testimony to the dynamic range of the instrument, from a gentle tinkle to a reverberating roar as he sustained the range of tones. He had the ability to make the percussive bell-like quality admirably well suited to style, as he supplied his listeners with rhythmic accents and rippling embellishments. How subtly and beautifully he managed to deliver the tone, as if falling on ears like raindrops in a pool, thought she. His sudden sharp splash of sound grew fainter and fainter as he concluded the piece. She could only determine it was enough to take her breath away. She fantasized that Handel himself must have been his instructor.

Elizabeth, now embarrassed by her performance, noticed he not only played well, but did so devoid of sheet music. She wondered how this could be. When he finished, they applauded intensely. Mr. Bingley bellowed out, "Bravo!"

"How very astonishing," said Jane in a complimentary, surprised voice.

"Magnificent, simply magnificent. Words are wanting to express such excellence," exclaimed Elizabeth. "At this very moment I wish I had not played first; my playing is certainly inferior to that of our host's."

"Not at all, Mrs. Darcy, you do not allow yourself enough credit; you play very well, and sing well too. I, on the other hand, do not sing. Singing is one of my failings. Although I have a voice for public speaking, it is not to be heard in song. Allow me to assure you, your music was a delight to all ears. It would be an honour to hear you play again." He took a seat in a chair, then added, "We have many visitors here at the rectory, but tonight's company is extraordinary. I find this to be a most delightful evening."

Elizabeth graciously listened with a smile. He was indeed an excellent creature. Her eyes once again became fixed on his long fingers. She thought them to be most advantageous at the pianoforte. She was glad her husband showed an interest in Mr. Manley for the position at Pemberley. Being a valued friend only proved to make him more desirable.

"Under whom did you have the privilege to study music?" inquired Mr. Bingley.

"To tell the truth, I have never studied music, nor am I able to read a note. I simply play by hearing."

"Simply! How very interesting," replied a startled Jane.

"How did you learn to play? How did you discover you could play?" Mr. Bingley inquired, sitting up on the edge of his seat with enthusiasm.

"I was drawn to the music chamber as a young lad. I played on the pianoforte with little notice from the rest of the household, being the music chamber was at the far corner of the house. Occasionally I was discovered, but my parents soon learned I was naturally inclined to play, so they afforded me the privilege of the pianoforte whenever I desired. I entertained myself there often. My mother provided a special pillow to allow me better advantage to the keys. I have always thought God had given me long slender fingers to promote the religious tunes he prefers. I have no pretension of myself as a great entertainer. I am merely a religious man bringing glory to

God's word through music. "

Elizabeth was taken aback by his modesty. "Do play for us again," she requested.

Mr. Manley obliged. Aside from being extremely talented, he proved to be an excellent host. They could only imagine by his speech in prayer that there was sure to be nothing wanting in his sermons.

"I do not play cards. I feel a clergyman ought not to. I hope you will be content to just visit and enjoy general intercourse."

"Although we do play on occasion, we are no great fans of card playing. I much prefer an exchange," Mr. Darcy explained.

Mr. Bingley sat upright. "We are very content to just sit and talk."

"You have a long journey home tomorrow. Are your plans set? Are your trunks made ready? I do hope that you do not meet with any inclement weather."

"Yes, our plans are set; we shall start our journey early. Judging by the night air, I do not expect rain, although one never can tell what the day next will bring," Mr. Darcy answered.

After a few additional hours, Mr. Darcy stood. "Perhaps it is time to bid farewell; we should gain much rest for the journey home. As always, Henry, it has been a delight."

"We have so enjoyed the evening. I do hope to see you again," added Mr. Bingley.

Jane arose from her chair smiling. "Yes, it has been a most delightful evening."

Elizabeth smiled. "It has added pleasantries to the memories of our wedding journey. We do hope to see you at Pemberley."

Mr. Darcy faced his friend, "Henry, thank you for your kind invitation. It proved to be a most agreeable evening, one I shall long remember. You must come to Derbyshire. I shall expect it, in fact; I shall count on it. I am desirous it will not be before long?"

"Yes, it will be an honour," answered Mr. Manley. "I do hope the journey home is a pleasant one. You may be sure I do indeed plan to visit that great estate."

When in the carriage, the two couples chattered all the way back to the inn. The main topic of their discourse was the musical talent of Henry Manley.

The Journey Home

THE LADIES LEFT THE PARTICULARS of their forthcoming journey to the gentlemen. They concentrated on the necessity of having the servants make ready the trunks. To them it seemed but a day or two since their arrival. The chambermaids made ready some of the garments a day earlier, but waited till last to place their finery in the trunks to be sure their new gowns would maintain as fresh a look as possible. Elizabeth was amazed to learn exactly how greatly increased her wardrobe had now proven to be.

At length the barouche arrived. The trunks were fastened to the back; the parcels were placed within as the two couples happily boarded.

Having now quitted the inn, they started their journey home. The air was dry and the roads were a bit dusty, but in spite of it all, it was thought to be a very fine day. They were eager to return home, discovering themselves anxious for the familiarity of their surroundings. Believing now that the pleasures of home promised the assurance of happiness, they grew more eager to venture there. Their journey was long. Having left the London scenery far behind, they afforded a stopover at an appointed inn. Setting out once again, they ultimately found relief when noticing they were within an easy distance of Netherfield Park. The sun was beginning to set. Netherfield Park could be seen off in the distance. Jane, having caught a glimpse of it, suddenly announced, "This is to be my home now!"

"But of course," said Mr. Bingley. He looked at Mr. Darcy. "You two shall have to stay a few nights at best, the team needs a rest. You should stay a few days before you go on to Pemberley. To be sure I would desire you do so. It is much too soon to part."

"Indeed, I had depended upon it," responded Mr. Darcy. He looked at Elizabeth as he lightly caressed her hand. "That will give us time to visit

Longbourn before we set our direction toward Derbyshire. Surely we cannot go on without paying visit there. After all, it is within three miles of Netherfield Park."

Elizabeth certainly had no objection; she was grateful to spend a few additional days with Jane and Mr. Bingley. She would be glad to visit Longbourn; she would see her dear papa again.

"Good gracious!" cried Jane. "Here we are." The carriage halted in front of Netherfield Hall. They disembarked gladly, stretching before entering the house without further delay.

Much to their surprise the housekeeper announced, "Sir, Mr. and Mrs. Hurst and your sister Miss Bingley are from home. They desired me to say they went to visit your sister in Liverpool. They are not expected back any time soon. They quitted Netherfield Hall the day before last. They desired me to tell you it is their plan to be gone at least a fortnight."

"Yes, well—thank you," Mr. Bingley stated with a blank look. The housekeeper left them to themselves. Mr. Bingley, now in close proximity to Mr. Darcy, was afforded the advantage to relate quietly, "How absolutely convenient, Darcy. I daresay I could not have planned it any better."

The ladies busied themselves with the direction of the trunks, following the servants above the stairs.

It was a relief to Jane and a comfort to Elizabeth to learn they were to be alone. It was one less reason Elizabeth would have to concern herself with when leaving Jane behind. How glad Elizabeth was to know that Jane and Mr. Bingley would have their privacy.

The day next, while breakfasting, Mr. Darcy was quick to announce, "Shall we direct ourselves toward Longbourn within the hour?"

Elizabeth afforded him a loving, direct eye. "I should like that; I should like that very much."

Mr. Darcy smiled as he patted her hand. He looked at Jane, detecting she was no less eager to visit her family. Elizabeth's smile broadened; she thought this further proof of his excellence. He continued to strive to equal her fancy of a husband. The very fact that he could give rise to such occasion as visiting Longbourn, without hesitation or reproach, proved him superior as well as sensitive to her situation.

After having breakfasted, Mr. Bingley directed his open carriage to be brought around. It was such a beautiful day, not too hot, nor too cold. It was just what it ought to be, just a very fine day. Yes, an open carriage would do very well on a day such as this.

Longbourn

As THE CARRIAGE PARTED Netherfield destined for Longbourn, Elizabeth examined the familiar countryside. She was happy to be going to the place of her birth to see her dear papa. She was certain he missed her. She chuckled to think of her certainty where he was concerned, knowing full well it was known throughout Hertfordshire that she was her father's favourite. As the carriage made its way around a slight bend, Elizabeth could see Longbourn in the near distance. It is all so very strange, thought she. It has taken on a different look. How less impressive are the grounds. My view of this place is so altered. Have I grown so swiftly used to such finery, I am unable to appreciate the once sufficient modest home of my youth? As the carriage drew to a halt in front of the less than ornate house, Elizabeth suffered pangs of shame for her prejudiced thoughts.

The Bennets were still in the breakfast chamber. Hill ran to announce the arrival of the former Miss Bennets.

Kitty and Mary ran ahead to greet them, with Mr. and Mrs. Bennet not far behind, with all parties equally glad to see one another. Mrs. Bennet fussed over Jane and Mr. Bingley immediately; however, Elizabeth detected a much warmer greeting extended to her husband. Whatever the reason, she did not care; she was just happy to witness it. Mrs. Bennet looked directly at Mr. Darcy, "Come in, come in, we are so happy you are come here."

Mr. Bennet neared Elizabeth and gave her a hug as he quietly related, "I've missed you greatly, my dear Lizzy." In a lower voice, he lamented, "The days seem so much longer without you and Jane. Little else has changed in the way of life at Longbourn, including the lack of sensible conversation along with the continuance of foolery to no end. I suffer greatly in your absence. Take pity on your poor father. I am delighted you are come."

"Ring for tea, Kitty," instructed Mrs. Bennet.

Kitty scrunched her face, letting out a groan, "Why must I always be the one?" she complained as she stomped her foot on the floor. She was gone in an instant but returned in a flash, swiftly regaining her seat. She clenched her hands together. "Tell me," she said anxiously, "you must tell me everything there is to tell about London. What was it like? Did you make notice of the militia? Did you witness a whole regiment?"

"Well—I do believe we did see some redcoats milling about, but very few. I suppose we paid them little mind," Jane reported. Neither she nor Elizabeth could say with certainty the knowledge of witnessing a whole regiment.

"While in London we did see plays, attended a ball and visited shops. Our time was agreeably engaged at every moment," replied Elizabeth.

Mr. Bennet stared at Elizabeth over his spectacles. He raised his brows, then said, "Ah, Hill has brought the tea. Shall we all have some? Well, gentlemen, what say you to some tea?"

Elizabeth, grateful for the interruption, was particularly indebted to Mary, who suddenly inquired, "Did you visit any milliner shops? You mentioned shops; I thought perhaps you purchased a new bonnet? You must tell me of your shopping, I daresay Mamma will be glad to hear of it."

Nothing could divert Mrs. Bennet's attention more than the notion of shopping. Mrs. Bennet, now fully focused on the present conversation, quickly interjected, "Oh yes, my dear, do tell us of your purchases. I have always wanted to visit the established shops in London, but your father insists we have enough with the local warehouses."

Mrs. Bennet narrowed her eyes in her husband's direction. With a voice laced with contempt, she continued. "My long desire to visit the London shops has fallen on deaf ears for some twenty years now. I do think it is quite unfair that my own daughters should visit them before their mother. It is very hard I tell you, indeed it is; it is quite shocking," she added, bringing her handkerchief to her nose. Then suddenly realizing she was in company, her demeanour took a sudden turn. It was to Elizabeth's relief, but Jane cringed with mortification. She sat silent with a reddened face, looking despairingly at her husband.

They had visited less than an hour, before Mrs. Bennet inquired, "Of what dish are Mr. Darcy and Mr. Bingley particularly fond? I wish to know so I may make ready the table for dinner when next you come."

Elizabeth saw her mother's behaviour toward the gentlemen a good sign, especially where Mr. Darcy was concerned. She had approved of Mr. Bingley immediately; however, this was not the case with Mr. Darcy. But on this day she seemed determined to find favour in him.

Before leaving Longbourn, Mr. Bingley addressed Mr. Bennet. "I would be delighted if you will sport with us tomorrow."

"I would be honoured," answered Mr. Bennet. He turned to Mr. Darcy. "Will you be sporting with us tomorrow?"

"I believe I shall, Mr. Bennet."

"Ah, very good then, until tomorrow."

Without further delay, Mrs. Bennet immediately chirped, "Yes, my dear, you should sport with Mr. Bingley; I shall plan on visiting Jane while you are out."

Jane stiffened, closing her eyes. Elizabeth looked at Jane, affording her a sympathetic stare. Poor Jane, her first day at Netherfield Hall and already she had concerns regarding how much time her mother would expect to spend there. Elizabeth looked back at her with a lack of expression as the carriage pulled away.

Upon their arrival at Netherfield Park, Elizabeth announced, "I am extremely fatigued. If there is no objection, I should like to nap."

"Lizzy, are you unwell? I think perhaps you should rest. I do believe you have us all concerned; I don't know what to suppose," Jane expressed nervously.

"Yes, come; I shall see you to the bedchamber, I am concerned. Be assured I shall not be satisfied until I receive a report from Dr. Gordon when in Derbyshire."

"Very well, dearest, I'll not challenge you. I am much too tired to dispute it."

The morning next, the Bennet's carriage arrived early. Since the four had already breakfasted, it was not long before the men departed. The ladies occupied themselves with books and music, but not before a tour of Netherfield Hall, which their mother requested as soon as the men were out of sight.

"Well, Jane, I have seen the breakfast parlour, now I should like to see the rest of Netherfield Hall," she said as she marched ahead. Jane and Elizabeth scurried after her.

"Such fine rooms, so smartly fitted; I don't know when I have ever seen a place so richly furnished. Come now, Jane; I shall see the rest of the house."

Although impressed with Netherfield Hall, she turned to Elizabeth. "What say you now, Lizzy; when might we expect to see Pemberley? From what I hear, it is much grander than Netherfield Hall and promises to be magnificent indeed. I daresay it does make your Mr. Darcy quite the gentleman. Yes, indeed, I have always thought of him as such; no doubt you remember my saying I always favoured Mr. Darcy. I quite admire him. To think my Lizzy is now mistress of Pemberley Hall. We have been very fortunate indeed! Now I must admit Mr. Darcy is the handsomest of men; yes, he is indeed quite handsome."

Elizabeth and Jane exchanged a stare of soured expressions. Remembering their mother's severe dislike of Mr. Darcy, her now altered opinion was no surprise to them. She could be counted on to contradict her own feelings for gain. The only consolation to Elizabeth was the knowledge that Mr. Darcy's reserve most often caused her mother to be apprehensive toward him. Surely she would not wish to insult him now. Since he said very little out in company, her mother could hardly find any common ground on which to approach him.

"Mother, I expect Mr. Darcy would wish to settle in for a time at Pemberley before receiving guests. He has told me so on several occasions. I daresay it would be wise to honour his wishes; he is used to having his own way."

"Yes, yes, you are right, my dear, I do believe we shall be forced to wait upon him."

Such resignation brought Elizabeth a sense of relief. Grateful for the long distance from Longbourn, she felt empathy for Jane, who was less fortunate, being an easy distance from Hertfordshire as to no doubt have to tolerate frequent unwanted visits.

Mrs. Bennet continued to marvel at the size of the rooms, was amazed by the fine furnishings, admired the exquisite draperies and found the wall hangings to be a wonder. She remarked on the plenitude of servants and expressed delight in her daughter's affluence. She moved throughout the chambers inspecting everything in sight, as if she were taking inventory.

Jane and Elizabeth looked at each other in exasperation; their mother's total want for fortune embarrassed them. They were glad the men were out.

Mrs. Bennet clasped her hands together at her chest in excitement. "Oh, my dear Jane, if only the Lucases could see it all. Their lodge is not of this size. You know, they think themselves quite influential since his elevation to the knighthood. I should like Sir William and Lady Lucas to see the whole of Netherfield Park. They will have to admit my Jane has done well, very well indeed."

Jane's stomach knotted; she wrenched her hands, then swallowed hard. "Mother, I have only just come home. Mr. Bingley may one day wish to invite Sir William and Lady Lucas, but I cannot entertain such thoughts presently. Mother, when Mr. Bingley returns, make no mention of this."

"And why not?" she returned in a sharp tone.

"Mother! I do not wish to invite people to Netherfield Park to congratulate myself on having married an affluent gentleman. It would prove insulting to invite to flatter myself. That would be obvious to say the least."

"My dear Jane, you should not stand on such ceremony as to think you need an occasion to invite the Lucases to the park," she argued.

"Mamma, Jane does not wish to crow of her situation, cannot you understand? Mr. Bingley is a man of good taste, situation and rare temper, but perhaps you misread him if you think him a man to display his style ostentatiously in public."

"Now, Lizzy, you quite vex me; there is no need for that sort of language. Jane knows perfectly well I only desire the Lucases to see her now she is married."

Jane stood tall. She protruded her chin with authority, "No, Mamma, I will not invite the Lucas' any time soon; we will end this discussion now."

Mrs. Bennet was speechless. She had not expected such censure from Jane.

Jane, familiar with her mother's strong will, feared she would not always be up to the task of taming her. She was temporarily satisfied to have triumphed. Looking at her mother, she could see that she had disarmed her. Mrs. Bennet was totally undone. Her wish to flatter her own situation was put to ruin. She frowned, plopping herself down in a chair and turning her face from both daughters. She tightened her lips, drawing them inward. In a vain attempt to gain sympathy, she raised her handkerchief to her teary eyes.

Elizabeth and Jane exchanged a look of disgust. Their mother was impossible; she was sure never to change. She was generally uncontrollable, requiring no encouragement.

Mary and Kitty were delighted to look about the house, play the pianoforte, and visit the library. Their behaviour was pleasingly polite, asking only once for a deck of cards to amuse themselves. They were a grateful diversion from the antics of their mother.

Jane and Elizabeth were relieved when the men returned from their shoot. Their mother had less to say.

After supper, the Bennets quitted Netherfield, leaving Jane and Elizabeth exhausted in their anticipated concern of their mother's unwanted opinions, fearing what she may have said next.

"Will you come again tomorrow to sport, Mr. Bennet?" Mr. Bingley asked.

"I believe I shall. You may expect me early. I believe it is not the notion of a good sportsman to lay loose a day's pleasure," Mr. Bennet said, then turned to look at Mr. Darcy. "Will you join us again tomorrow?"

"I'm sorry sir, no. We must be on our way to Pemberley. Perhaps you will delay your sport until the afternoon. Elizabeth and I will visit at Longbourn before we take our leave."

"Indeed you are a good sort, Mr. Darcy; I should like to see my Lizzy again before you take your leave. Very well then, tomorrow it is. Good day to you all."

"Good day to you," smiled Mrs. Bennet.

"Oh, Jane, I am so sorry," Elizabeth turned and said when the carriage departed.

"Well, Lizzy, at least you should not have to worry; you will leave for Pemberley tomorrow. Be assured I shall envy you the distance."

"Oh, Jane, I am indeed sorry," she said again, pondering her own escape.

Elizabeth observed the quiet reserve of her husband. He was very much as he was when he first visited Longbourn with Mr. Bingley. She had not witnessed this state for several weeks. He was as different as night and day. She determined the company he kept altered his manner. She studied him, admiring his handsome presentation, with all the prejudice expected of a wife deeply in love. She thought him advantageously virile, further musing of his irresistibility, contemplating herself anxious to be alone with him.

The morning next, Elizabeth suffered a fainting spell, compelling Mr. Darcy to alter their plans. They would remain another day in Hertfordshire. He sent word requesting Dr. Jones meet them at Longbourn. In vain he struggled to understand the meaning of it all. After about an hour, Elizabeth's condition improved, allowing the four to leave for Longbourn.

Hill announced them. "Good day to you," Sir William Lucas greeted, much to their surprise.

"Good—day—Sir William. Pray excuse my astonishment; it was not ill meant. We simply did not expect to see you today," Elizabeth said, hoping to disguise her dismay.

"I had Kitty fetch Sir William and Lady Lucas to Longbourn to visit with us," Mrs. Bennet smugly said, smiling with obvious satisfaction of her plan.

Jane bit on her lower lip. Elizabeth afforded her sister a stern look. Both Jane and Elizabeth struggled to conceal their exasperating abhorrence at their mother's ill plan. Mrs. Bennet ignored her daughters, granting Sir William Lucas constant conversation. It was not long before she said, "Mr. Bingley, Sir William and Lady Lucas would like to come visit at Netherfield Park, perhaps they may do so in two or three days?"

Jane's eyes widened with shock as she took in air. Her chest ached. She could hardly bear the pain of her mother's humiliating intrusion. She viewed her insensitive meddling as an unreasonable weight of misery.

Before anyone had an opportunity to comment, Mrs. Bennet turned toward Mr. Darcy. "And, Mr. Darcy, we should very soon like to gather a party to visit Pemberley; perhaps Sir William Lucas, his family and my sister Philips with her husband will join us. We desire to see the place; after all, we understand it is grander than Netherfield."

Ignoring her comments with dignified reserve, Mr. Darcy interrupted, "My immediate concern is for my wife; I must see her to her bedchamber. She suffered a fainting spell this morning. I must insist she lie down. I'll accept no argument. I have dispatched Dr. Jones to Longbourn. I expect him directly. Pray, you'll excuse me."

Like lightning, Mrs. Bennet bolted from her seat. She immediately succumbed to a distressed unsettling state. She became nervous, pacing about the chamber and mumbling frantically.

Mary and Kitty ran to fetch Hill to turn down Elizabeth's bed. Those left behind in the sitting room discussed their concern. All thoughts of visiting Netherfield and Pemberley were now diverted.

Jane, caught between her mother's inherent disturbance and Elizabeth's fainting, sat down in exasperation. She buried her face in her hands. Mr. Bingley, not knowing what next to do, attempted to comfort his wife.

Mrs. Bennet was now in an uproar over Elizabeth. She was not to be calmed. Her present state of anxiety could well be heard throughout Longbourn.

"Although I feel better, I must admit I find the frequency of spells quite distresses me. I long to be on the way to Pemberley; it is rather troublesome to have yet another delay. Surely Dr. Jones will think I am well enough to travel," Elizabeth lamented.

"Let us all hope so," Mr. Darcy replied dryly.

As she lay upon the bed, Mr. Darcy sat in close proximity reading a book. She searched the chamber with her eyes; she was bored except for the disturbing notions of her mother. She was grateful her fainting spell provided an escape. Although Mr. Darcy made no mention of it, she had no doubt he was not eager to entertain her mother at Pemberley. Considering her mother wasted no time intruding on Jane's privacy, there was little doubt the distance of Pemberley would hold her back for any length.

Dr. Jones finally arrived to examine Elizabeth. "I find you to be quite healthy. I believe it is safe to journey to Derbyshire tomorrow."

"Oh, thank you; I am anxious to take my leave."

Dr. Jones called Mr. Darcy to the chamber. "She is well. I can find nothing wrong."

"That is of little comfort; I am excessively disturbed. There must be a reason!"

"I'm sorry, sir; no report of illness of any kind. In fact, I see no reason for concern."

"This is not acceptable; I had not expected such a report. I daresay I am less than pleased; I fear there must be a reason for all of this."

"Well sir, I can give you none. I will bid you good day," was all he could say before quitting their presence.

Elizabeth could no longer concentrate on the exchange between Dr. Jones and her husband. Her mother's intrusion chiefly occupied her thoughts. It was more than she could tolerate. She viewed it advantageous to be going a long distance, convincing herself Jane was much more capable of enduring the unpleasantness of their mother's interference. She would surely have words with her mother if she stayed any longer.

Mr. Darcy abruptly halted her thoughts. "Elizabeth, when we arrive at Pemberley, I shall employ Dr. Gordon. Indeed there must be some explanation; I have little tolerance for such lack of understanding. I must see that you are well."

Elizabeth and Mr. Darcy went below the stairs to join the rest of the party.

"Dr. Jones gave us the good news. We are glad you are well," Sir William stated.

"Thank you," was all Elizabeth could say before her mother anxiously interrupted. "Yes, well—now, Jane, you know we talked of Sir William visiting Netherfield?"

Jane tightened her lips, staring long and hard at her mother to no avail. But her mother was not to be persuaded otherwise. Although totally mortified by her mother's forced attempt to put her in a displeasing position, it was rather difficult to dispute the matter in front of Sir William and Lady Lucas. Jane's heart sank. She looked at her husband with despair. His face reddened. The smile left his face as his eyes widened in astonishment. She looked beyond him at her mother, detecting she had not a notion of the embarrassment she induced.

Mr. Bingley looked irritated. "But, of course, you shall come to Netherfield Park day after tomorrow. Will that do?" He remained calm and reserved. Jane knew he was frustrated and angered by the forced intrusion.

Mrs. Bennet's meddling incensed Mr. Bingley. Looking at Jane, he felt the pain she now suffered. His heart sank. He loved Jane so dearly, but feared the nearness to Longbourn a hindrance. At that very moment he envied his friend. His thoughts were interrupted by Sir William Lucas' hardy voice. "Capital, capital idea Mr. Bingley; we should like to visit."

Elizabeth sat in disbelief of her hearing. Poor Mr. Bingley, thought she, her mother had intruded on his good nature already. Poor Jane, how embarrassed and shocked she looked at the moment her mother initiated the subject a second time. She was glad her mother set aside her designs on Pemberley. Perhaps Mr. Darcy's evasive manner inhibited her from bringing up the subject a second time. Nonetheless, Elizabeth couldn't be happier to be quitting Longbourn before her mother had a chance to renew her attempt at initiating a planned visit.

Elizabeth suddenly heard her name. It was Jane's voice she heard calling. Elizabeth's mind snapped back to the conversation. It had been little more above one hour since the tea had been served. Jane was on her feet, bringing the visit to an abrupt end. Comprehending Jane's urgency, she quickly followed her lead. As they neared the door, Mrs. Bennet anxiously followed.

"Girls, are you not going to dine with us today? Had you not planned to do so? I had planned it myself," cried Mrs. Bennet, appearing quite undone by their leaving.

Jane's voice turned cold. "I'm afraid not today, Mamma, perhaps another time."

As they walked out of doors to the carriage, the entire party followed. Mr. Bennet walked within a deliberate distance, far enough away so as not to be heard. "Well, my dear Lizzy, Jane, here you are both leaving me again." He looked around, then expressed, "Well, well now I daresay, I heartily understand and wish you both happy. But think of me. Think of me with consideration, for I shall suffer greatly, amiss as it may be for me to say. I shall miss you both; depend upon it. I suppose I shall have to take to my chamber for a few hours to recover. Good-bye, Mr. Bingley; good-bye, Mr. Darcy; take care of my girls." He stepped back from the carriage, giving a nod of the head.

By now, Mrs. Bennet was all smiles, managing to mark the occasion with her next reply. "God has been good to us, we have three such son-in-laws. It's a pity Lydia could not be here. It would have been such a merry gathering, would it not now, my dear?"

"A great pity indeed!" Elizabeth said in a low voice saturated with disdain.

All such thoughts now tired Elizabeth. They bid their final farewell much to her satisfaction. The carriage pulled away, thrusting her back into the seat.

Netherfield Park

A weary Jane voiced, "It is a quiet evening, is it not?"

Elizabeth yawned as she stretched her arms above her head. "Yes, indeed it is; I suppose I should retire early so I am fresh for my journey in the morning."

"Oh, Lizzy, I shall miss you."

"And I you, but it must be." She turned to her husband. "I believe I must turn in."

"Yes, I will join you," he replied. He bowed to Jane and Mr. Bingley. "Good night to you," he said, nearing Elizabeth.

"Good night, Lizzy; good night, Mr. Darcy," Jane called after them.

"Yes, good night to you both," Mr. Bingley chimed in.

Mr. Darcy, still distressed by his wife's fainting spells, found sleep rather difficult. He lay awake pondering the disturbing and unexplainable situation.

The morning next, when Elizabeth and Mr. Darcy were preparing to take their leave, the Bennet's carriage arrived to see them off.

Elizabeth first embraced Kitty, then Mary, then next her mother. Last but not least, she advanced toward Jane. Jane, finding it difficult to let go, held on to her embrace at length.

"Good-bye, dear Jane."

"Good-bye, Lizzy, I shall miss you sorely," replied Jane softly with a sad expression.

"My dear Jane, you will do well, I'm sure of it. I am no longer needed at your side; you have Mr. Bingley."

"I suppose so," replied Jane. "It is just that—well, you will be a great distance away. Promise you will write often, Lizzy, promise me. And, Lizzy, think of me often, for I shall be mindful of you." Jane began to weep, taking her handkerchief to her tears.

Elizabeth afforded her an encouraging smile. "I promise I shall write often. Remember, Jane, Fitzwilliam claims it is but fifty miles of good road that divides us. Jane, I will think of you often; you know all too well how very dear you are to me, but now you are more dear to Mr. Bingley."

Jane could not help but smile. "I can hardly dispute that, Lizzy."

Lizzy is so consummately right, thought Jane. She felt her heart flutter to be reminded they were man and wife. Never in her life had she thought it would all come to this pleasant end. Here she was, now mistress of Netherfield. How glad she was to take her place as lady of the hall. How shall I bear so much happiness? But I shall be lost without her, she mused.

"Very well then, write I shall," Jane replied with a certain sense of sadness.

"I must go now, Jane." Elizabeth quickly hugged her mother then turned to enter the carriage. She stopped, then said, "Mr. Bingley, might I request you take special care of my sister?"

"Yes, but of course, Elizabeth. I shall indeed; you know I shall."

As Elizabeth entered the carriage, Mr. Bingley faced Mr. Darcy. "You must be sure to give my regards to Miss Darcy." Next he looked at Elizabeth.

"Allow me to assure you Elizabeth, I shall bring your sister to visit you before long."

"Thank you, indeed we shall rejoice when you visit. I trust it will not be long."

Mr. Bingley bowed, "Good-bye, Darcy; good-bye, Elizabeth."

"Good-bye, Lizzy; good-bye, Mr. Darcy. Do return soon. I shall have your favourite dish planned if you write in advance of your coming," Mrs. Bennet called out.

Mr. Bennet discreetly expressed to Mr. Darcy, before he could board the carriage, "I'm quite distressed with the faints; my Lizzy has always been a strong healthy girl. You will surely look after her with extra care, will you not?"

"You may be certain of it, Mr. Bennet; be assured I may be depended upon."

"Yes, Mr. Darcy, I believe you are a man of your word; good-bye then," he said, withdrawing from the carriage. "Good-bye, Lizzy, do not forget your father; I shall surely miss you. Perhaps I shall visit as soon as an opportunity presents itself. To be sure, yes indeed, I believe I shall." Mr. Bennet now stood with his hands behind his back, appearing to have lost his invaluable confidant.

Mr. Bingley closed the carriage door, taking a step back. The Bennets were still offering their last farewells.

"What a relief to be going home at last," Elizabeth turned and said to her husband.

He made no reply.

The Road to Pemberley

"**I**T IS EASILY FIFTY MILES to Pemberley, is it not, Fitzwilliam?"

"Yes, but I imagine it will pass off quite swiftly. The weather is fine; the journey thus far has proven uneventful."

"Yes," she smiled, "I am anxious to start our life together at Pemberley. Perhaps it is a matter of good roads or perhaps it is you at my side that makes the journey so pleasing," she declared as she nestled against him.

He smiled down at her with gladdened eyes as she linked her arm in his. She closed her eyes, appearing to have fallen asleep, but she was merely contemplating her future.

Mistress of Pemberley, thought she. There was a time when she thought all that had escaped her, believing Mr. Darcy was lost to her forever. Mr. Darcy lost to her forever? She pondered such thoughts with distress. Thoughts of his inability to overcome his severe affections for her were comforting.

Even Lady Catherine de Bourgh, his own relation, could not influence him to deny his feelings. His convictions remained unchanged. Well aware her husband remained estranged from his aunt disturbed her. Why could she not forgive him for not honouring a marriage commitment made for him at infancy to her daughter Ann? Was she so totally devoid of feelings she lacked all understanding of his desire to choose for himself? Her violent anger toward his marriage was steadfast. And, now, all communication with her had been severed. This will not do, she brooded. She desired to be everything he had anticipated in seeking a lifelong companion. Thoughts of setting out to win his aunt's approval now enticed her. I know, thought she, I shall be the instrument to unite them. In time I shall extend an invitation to his aunt. But, first, perhaps it would be best to correspond through the post, using language so admirably persuasive that it might even appeal to a woman of Lady Catherine's disposition. Oh, this is not likely to be an easy task, she told herself. But I do desire felicity within his family. I must win Lady Catherine's approval. Perhaps Colonel Fitzwilliam might be an asset in attaining this. Dear Colonel Fitzwilliam, he tried to tell me of Mr. Darcy's affections early on, but I only set out to disprove him. How could I have been so full of error? Such thoughts pained her. She was wrong on so many accounts. She knew it was unlike a man of Mr. Darcy's wealth and situation to settle for a woman of little means as she. Much more was expected of him from family and friends. Surely now he would have to suffer the burden of

securing a wife those of his society would view as beneath him.

The ride tossed her about, depriving her of sleep, but she continued these thoughts with her eyes closed. Feeling secure next to him, she huddled still closer, aware of his impressive character.

Thinking now of the children they may one day birth, amused her. She marveled at his superior qualities, desiring his traits would be re-birthed in them.

Pemberley at Last

MR. DARCY GENTLY NUDGED HER. "We are nearing Pemberley; you are almost arrived. We are atop the hill where the woods cease—look, Elizabeth."

There it was—Pemberley Hall, on the opposite side of the valley, beyond the lake. They went around the turns as they neared the great place. It was just as if it were the very first time she set eyes upon it. She remarked aloud with unrestrained admiration, "I have never seen a place so pleasantly situated."

"And this is to be your home, dearest, loveliest Elizabeth."

They descended the hill, crossing the bridge, as they continued toward the door. Mrs. Reynolds came out of doors at once to greet them, accompanied by many servants.

"Good day. Welcome home, sir; welcome home, Mrs. Darcy," greeted Mrs. Reynolds.

The servants had formed a line on each side of the entrance to greet them. Elizabeth smiled as they bowed and curtsied. She was overtaken by a sense of pride. She thought the sound of "Mrs. Darcy" was pleasing to her taste. Yes, indeed, she liked it quite well.

Georgiana stood anxiously at the portal. "Welcome home, dear brother and sister. I have missed you," said she, hugging each of them, one after the other.

Elizabeth had thought Georgiana to be quiet and reserved, but this day she was quite the reverse. She was caught up in the anticipated happiness of their homecoming.

"When you have settled, I will be most anxious to hear every detail of your journey. I desire to know the sights you visited, your opinion of London society, as well as all that you enjoyed. Elizabeth, you must tell me of my brother. Does he treat you well?"

Elizabeth giggled. "Well, I see we shall have to have a private conversation to discuss him at length," she said, casting him a brief look.

He stared at them before he dared to say, "What might you have to discuss of me that requires privacy? I should think my sister would not be so officious where I am concerned." He rolled his eyes at his wife. He could think of no clever immediate response in his own defense.

Georgiana eyed Elizabeth with mixed pleasure amid astonishment. "Elizabeth, the surprise visit to the shops you wrote of, I have never known Fitzwilliam to own to such romantic tendencies. But then, I suspect that is because I have given no thought to it. It is a side of him I have never witnessed. I daresay, perhaps I have not given him sufficient credit. I am glad he displays a tender heart; it is quite pleasing to think of it. Surely you were surprised by his actions, were you not?"

"Nay, Georgiana, I was touched by his tender heart whilst we visited in Derbyshire many months ago, at which time I was so very fortunate to be the recipient of his sincerest degree of kindness. He has an unguarded affectionate heart. I was saddened by the thought of quitting Derbyshire, but duty awaited me. I had little choice but to leave this beautiful countryside as well as your brother's association." As she spoke, she was well aware her husband listened intently. His expression was rather demure, but the language with which she described him seemed to brighten his eyes. For one brief moment, she detected his behaviour lent an indication of slight embarrassment.

Soon the trunks were taken above the stairs, with Mr. Darcy following close behind. He insisted on unpacking his books, waiting impatiently for the removal of the finery to reach for his belongings with greater ease. He casually stood about while the ladies took their leisure. With the assistance of the maidservant, they continued to undo the trunks. When he sought his chance, he quickly bent at the knees, scouring the bottom of the trunk where he had placed his books. He took immediate possession of them. He stood, then bowed. "That will do; my manservant will know what is to be done. Surely you will tell Silas he may care for the rest of my belongings," he instructed before withdrawing from the chamber, parting their company as though a pack of hounds were at his heels.

Elizabeth eyed Georgiana, shaking her head with a smile. "I suppose unpacking trunks is not liking to a man; his manservant will care for his dress coats to be sure. Having no brothers, I am not accustomed to dealing with a man's attire."

"Nor I, Elizabeth; Silas has always performed such tasks for my father and brother. Surely you will become accustomed to the services rendered here."

"Indeed, my father's attire was generally cared for by Hill. We do afford a few servants, but I venture to guess not near as many as Pemberley Hall. I suppose I should allow the maidservant to finish here. I shall have to get used to the privileges afforded by such a grand estate. Although I am not ignorant of conduct with propriety in the discharge of ordinary matters, I acknowledge to you I am of a rather indelicate sense to aspire to your brother's expectations. In the manner of carrying out governing servants, I suspect I should acquire a greater sense of it. I have had seldom opportunity to enjoy privileges such as those to which you are accustomed. Perhaps you will introduce me to some of the formalities here. Will you consent to it, Georgiana?"

"It would be my pleasure."

One solid comfort in Elizabeth's favour was the knowledge of having already found approval from Mr. Darcy's sister. Although Georgiana was young, she was wise beyond her years. Elizabeth was certain of her affection. Her stature celebrated pure elegance with sophistication. She demonstrated a willingness to introduce Elizabeth into her level of society, matched by an eagerness to form a closer alliance. Georgiana's unlimited kindness induced closeness, causing them to become immediate confidantes. This pleased Mr. Darcy greatly, but such superior character was of no surprise to Elizabeth; she rather expected it.

Georgiana was pleased her brother had the tenderness of heart along with insight to increase Elizabeth's wardrobe, but made no mention of it to her brother or Elizabeth.

"I believe we shall find my brother in the billiard parlour; I heard him tell the servant of his intentions. Shall we go?"

As they ventured below the stairs, Mrs. Reynolds greeted them at the base. "Mrs. Darcy, is there anything particular you would like served at dinner?"

Elizabeth looked at Georgiana, then back again to Mrs. Reynolds. "Oh my," sighed Elizabeth, "I had not given it any thought. Would you be so kind, Mrs. Reynolds, to tell the cook to prepare Mr. Darcy's favourite dish this evening?"

"Very good, madam."

As soon as Mrs. Reynolds was out of sight, Georgiana turned to Elizabeth. "Very good, sister, very well done. I daresay you will need little instruction. I know my brother well enough to predict he will make notice at dinner, you shall see."

Elizabeth just smiled. Georgiana proceeded to show Elizabeth to the billiard parlour. They quietly entered. Mr. Darcy appeared to be attempting a rather difficult shot. Elizabeth noticed his shot to be direct, as was his confidence.

Mr. Darcy bowed upon their notice. "Pray tell me, how are my two favourite ladies getting on?"

"Very well, very well indeed. Georgiana and I are off to the music chamber. My new sister has a great inclination to sit at the pianoforte. I am gain set on reading."

"Gain set on reading?" quipped Mr. Darcy. "Then you do agree? An accomplished woman has much knowledge of music, but also finds substantial improvement of the mind through extensive reading. Never pass up new publications to enrich the mind, is that it?" he shrewdly smiled, then bowed.

Elizabeth sensed Georgiana's solemnity, realizing she had no understanding of the remarks. She tossed her head back with a giggle. "You are teasing."

He smiled. "Yes, enough tormenting, you both possess a great capacity of mind; your application of elegance is equally accomplished to suit me well. I shall join you both later."

They directed themselves to the music chamber. Elizabeth claimed a seat on the corner of the sofa, while Georgiana made her way to the pianoforte.

Georgiana Darcy had a very soft, gliding, smooth style to her playing, which had tremendous appeal. Admiring Georgiana's accomplishments, Elizabeth could not help but wish she herself had practiced more. Oh, to be so at ease, so sure of one's own ability, thought she, as she picked up her book. She concluded her first day at Pemberley could not have provided more pleasure than this.

Mrs. Reynolds and Bessie entered. "I ordered some tea and biscuits, Mrs. Darcy. I thought you might like some." Bessie put the tray down, curtsied, then quit the chamber.

"Thank you, Mrs. Reynolds."

"You're quite welcome, Mrs. Darcy,"

The extraordinary attention Mrs. Reynolds provided was yet additional proof of her goodness; there was no doubt she served Pemberley Hall well.

Elizabeth recalled Mrs. Reynolds' description of her husband when she first visited Pemberley. She was full of pleasing regard. All such praise was comforting; she felt quite contented in her new home, finding a ready welcome as the master's wife.

As her thoughts drew her in, she suffered a lack of concentration of her reading. She loved him so very dearly. At this moment she thought she could hardly contain her romantic tendencies. Even in his absence, she discovered thoughts of him were distracting.

Within the hour, Mr. Darcy joined them in the music chamber to read a book. But before too long, one of the servants announced dinner awaited them.

After taking his seat, Mr. Darcy noticed the dinner consisted of all his favourites. This pleased him. He looked at Elizabeth. "This is your doing, is that not so?"

"Yes, my dear, it is. I wanted this evening to be perfect as was the day," Elizabeth replied with a smile he could not resist.

"Come now," said Mr. Darcy, "we are embarrassing Georgiana. Look, her face has coloured. Pray, we beg your forgiveness for having done so."

Georgiana blushed, forcing a deep redness to her cheeks. She was not accustomed to viewing her brother in love. She believed it to be quite amusing though, far better than his usual sober state. Thinking very highly of Elizabeth, she was pleased with her brother's choice of a wife. As she nibbled at the food, she admired the lively exchange between the two. Although she viewed her brother less rigid, she was completely taken aback by his now teasing manner. Seldom had she witnessed him so open. He seemed more at ease in his own surroundings. She had never quite known him to be other than quietly reserved, surely never open to display teasing tendencies. He allowed Elizabeth startling liberties she never would have imagined of her brother; certainly she would never have attempted to approach him in this manner herself, she mused. All this made the marriage between the two more endearing to Georgiana.

Georgiana Makes Plans

GEORGIANA ASSERTED HER DESIGN to return to London. "I plan to further my education there. Brother, have you connections? My former teacher has quitted London society. He now resides in Paris. Surely you have connections?"

"I gave it no thought. I would have expected you to stay at Pemberley."

"I am grown now—Brother, I should wish to be less governed. You should not have to concern yourself of my welfare. Is it not enough for you to secure me a residence and a good teacher for me to study under? I wish to continue my study of the languages. You know I may do so very easily in London. And, brother, you know how very much I desire London society. Since I am not inclined to have a gentleman caller presently, you should have no worry," Georgiana pleaded.

"Very well, Georgiana, I will look into it."

As Elizabeth sat quietly, it occurred to her that perhaps Georgiana's parting was to allow them opportunity to be alone. The multitude of servants proved that hardly possible, but then perhaps she desired to venture out on her own for a time. She was in the habit of fixing a good education for herself; surely her brother encouraged it. She thought it best to stay apart of this, to let brother and sister decide, until Georgiana looked at her. "What is your thinking, Elizabeth, what say you?"

"Well—" Elizabeth said slowly, giving careful attention to her reply, "I suppose you should do what is in your heart. But you know your brother; you know he is very wise. He knows best; he is always right."

"Yes, to be sure, my brother does know best."

"Do not concern yourself, Georgiana, I will inquire at once; I respect your wishes," added Mr. Darcy, with a somber certainty of duty in his voice.

He did not desire to deprive his sister of her hunger for education. Sense and education were ultimately important in his estimation; surely he believed it should not be taken lightly. He was of the opinion a person should always seek to improve the mind. Although he desired her presence at Pemberley, he longed for her to determine her own future.

After dinner, Mr. Darcy and his new bride took a turn about the massive grounds.

"Beautiful, just beautiful," expressed Elizabeth. "You know how much I enjoy the delights of being out of doors."

"Yes," he replied, "I believe my sister remained behind to allow us privacy. Do you presume that is why she is so persuaded to go to London?"

"I do, I fear it may be so. I shall miss her. She is as dear to me as ever a sister can be, even more so in some instances. She looks to you for guidance, does she not?"

"Indeed, with an admiration I should always wish to be deserving of. She is a delicate creature, yet very strong in character. She'll do well; I must trust her judgment. She has grown, but I cannot help but wonder if some less than deserving fellow might recommend himself to her for gain."

Elizabeth stopped walking; she turned to face him. "If you were my brother, I should admire you, but I confess, I prefer to admire you as my husband."

"And I shall always desire to be deserving of such admiration."

They began to walk again. Elizabeth linked her arm in his, nestling closer to him. She shivered. The air was getting cooler with a stronger breeze coming from the north. Mr. Darcy stopped his walk to remove his coat. He then placed it around his wife. He stood silent for a moment, taking her face in the palm of his hands before he gently kissed her. He viewed her silently.

"I rather like the way you look after me. To have a husband who cares with all his heart, I would have never guessed you were capable of such tenderness. Indeed I like it very much."

"I confess; I rather like looking after you. I daresay Bingley and I have been very fortunate. Perhaps I consider myself more fortunate than Bingley. At least I have not the worry of discontented sisters."

"Quite the contrary, Georgiana and I have become the best of friends. I do wish Jane could claim the same. I fear it is a hopeless matter. Perhaps we should turn back to the house now."

"Yes, I agree. Bingley has other sisters. Did you not know of it?"

"Why, yes, in fact I do; he has five sisters in all, does he not?"

"Yes, one sister to your liking, now that we speak of it."

"Like me? How so?"

"Perhaps not in looks, but she does share similar qualities. She has a quick wit, owns to good humour, has pride, I believe, but not of a false sense." He paused. "Although she is not plain, she does lack your beauty. But I must say, in looks she is quite different."

"Oh," Elizabeth uttered.

"Yes, Emily Bingley is a fine sort."

"I should like to meet her. As for Caroline and Mrs. Hurst, it is of little matter what they feel toward me."

"Yes, but I suppose I am partially to blame."

"How so, Mr. Darcy?"

"Caroline was taken aback by my admiring you. I had long been aware of her designs on me. I have never had any interest there. Her condescending prospect annoys me greatly; she has a false sense of it."

Redness overspread Elizabeth's face. "I cannot believe this."

"Well, my dear, nothing is lost, is it now?" he smiled. "Yes, mastering his sisters will not be an easy task for Bingley. I worry for Bingley. He is so easily taken in by them. There may be other reasons of concern also."

"You are referring to my family?" She frowned. "Do not be alarmed, it is already a concern of my own. I cannot deny the consequence the short distance between the two houses can mean. I know my mother's tendencies as well as the demands she capably puts upon Jane. Jane has always endured her intrusions. Jane is so complying. And, as you are well aware, Mr. Darcy, I am of a rebellious nature. I am surely known for it at Longbourn."

"I was not thinking of your family. Caroline will be forced to quit her rank as mistress of Netherfield Hall. I wonder how readily she will relinquish it? I fear Jane may be challenged whenever Bingley is away from home.

"Oh, I had not thought of it."

At the doors of Pemberley Hall, they stopped to linger at the portal. He drew her close to kiss her again. Then, holding her at length, he looked into her eyes. Prudently, he stated, "There is my aunt to consider; her conviction disturbs me greatly."

"It is just her opinion; I pay little mind to it."

"My aunt is a very rich woman who is used to having her own way. Her ideas are fixed; she leaves little room for the opinions of others—she chooses not to hear them. Your cousin Mr. Collins suits her well. Lady Catherine likes the patronage he lavishes on her. She is probably good for him, as he is for her. It is my cousin Ann I fret for. Poor Ann, all these years she has endured her mother's overprotective shield."

"Yes, Ann does say very little. It is hard to get to know her."

"Surely you must have noticed how Lady Catherine always speaks for her, which is mostly to say that Ann is sickly, unable to do anything. It is outrageous. Poor girl, my mother certainly would not have wished me to marry Ann, had she lived to see the end result."

Elizabeth concluded she had judged he was indifferent to Ann, but such was not the case. It was clear he did care about Ann. She resolved he could not express it for fear Lady Catherine would surely think he was anxious to honour the commitment made so long ago. Perhaps now he would feel in a better position to pay Ann some attention.

The penetrating cold made Elizabeth shiver even more. She was weary, having walked for nearly an hour. The portal did little to shelter them; the darkness was beginning to deepen. The cry of an owl could be heard off in the distance.

They entered the house, hurrying to the sitting room to be near the fire.

Mr. Darcy stood, smiling down at his wife. "Did you know I can see the reflection of the flames dance in your eyes?"

"Surely you quip."

"Not so," he replied, drawing her to him. He closed his eyes as he buried his face in her tresses. They were not in the sitting room long when Mrs. Reynolds brought some tea. The two quickly stood apart from their embrace upon her entry. Mr. Darcy's eyes sparkled like a child who had been caught. His stiff manners surfaced as he addressed Mrs. Reynolds. "Thank you; that will do."

Elizabeth giggled. His formality entertained her. He looked back at her with a curious stare. She could only guess his thoughts. Her first day at Pemberley was drawing to a close.

Once in the bedchamber, Mr. Darcy sat at the secretary to dispatch a note to Mr. Manley in London on his sister's behalf. After placing the seal upon it, he retired to the bed where Elizabeth awaited him. She soon fell fast asleep in the comforting protection of her husband's embrace.

A Message from London

SEVERAL WEEKS PASSED since their arrival at Pemberley. Elizabeth Darcy had engaging, consequential weeks as Mr. Darcy commissioned Mrs. Reynolds to show his wife about the house, introducing her to all that such an imposing property could afford.

"Do introduce Elizabeth to the many chambers. Be certain to point out where the good silver is kept as well as the fine linens. I prefer to show her the library and the great hall of paintings. She must become familiar with the family heritage."

"Very good, sir."

After four weeks following their homecoming, a messenger delivered a letter.

"Georgiana, I have received word from London. Mr. Manley has secured a place for you. You may continue your studies under a Mr. Sheffield of Horizon Manor, a most respected tutor, highly recommended through Eton College. Mr. Manley claims he is quite interesting, and he claims he owns a lively horse. Although educated, he appears to be fixed on racing; it seems he enjoys the challenge of a race. Mr. Manley had taken the pains of researching his background, finding him to be most suitable. You are to stay at Mr. Manley's sister and brother-in-law's manor, a Mr. and Mrs. Cochran. Is this agreeable do you think?"

"It sounds very agreeable; please dispatch a reply accepting the offer. I am eager to once again dwell in London society. I feel confident I will be pleased with the security of Mrs. Cochran, especially since she is Mr. Manley's sister and you speak so well of him."

"Mr. Manley assured me his sister will look after you. He is equally confident you will be comfortable at her home. I will write back at once instructing Mr. Manley to set the plans. Is this your wish to be sure?" Mr. Darcy inquired soberly.

"Yes, I do believe it is indeed."

"Then I shall reply at once."

Later in the evening, Elizabeth advanced to Georgiana's bedchamber. "Might I speak with you?"

"I am always glad to converse with you, Elizabeth."

"I require assurance that your desire to return to London is not to allow your brother and I time alone. Surely you know we desire you to live here with us."

"Elizabeth, I am eager to continue studies. I find the best sources of educators in London. My decision had nothing to do with you or Fitzwilliam."

"I'm glad to hear of it," Elizabeth replied with a sense of relief. "I could not let you go without being absolutely certain your decision was not a result of lack of privacy on our part. Surely you are aware how very much I delight in your company. Be assured I shall miss you. We have become true sisters. I'll not try to persuade you to do otherwise if you are sure your intentions are purely selfish on your part."

"Oh, yes, Elizabeth, my motives are purely selfish. As much as I love Pemberley, you and my brother, I yearn to further my education. Elizabeth, I do miss the excitement of London. I am quite comfortable there."

Mr. Darcy neared the door, requesting permission to enter. Georgiana continued, "Brother, what better place to educate, to experience society but in London? Considering I shall find safekeeping in the sanctuary of Mr. Manley's sister's home, what more satisfaction will you and my sister find than this? Be assured I shall miss you both; I will write often. You will write to me will you not, Brother? You have always done so faithfully in the past. I shall look forward to correspondence from you both often, I daresay."

"Indeed we shall," replied Mr. Darcy. "You may depend upon it. When should you like me to arrange your leave? I shall write to Mr. Manley as to when he may expect you. Would a fortnight meet with your approval?"

"Very well, that will do very well," returned Georgiana. "And, dear Brother, thank you; you are so very good to me."

Mr. Darcy bent forward to kiss his sister on the forehead. He divulged a sober look, but managed a forced smile. "I always miss you, Georgiana, your happiness means much to me. I predict one day you shall be happily contented to live in the country. You are just at that trying age when all things appear unsettled. Well—I bid you good night."

"I'm glad you are so well settled, Brother. There was a time I worried; you seemed exceedingly unhappy, but now you have found felicity. Just think, I'll not be concerned you suffer loneliness. Good night, I trust you will sleep well."

The days following brought Georgiana and Elizabeth closer as confidantes. Georgiana had an intense desire to please her brother, but it was with Elizabeth that she was more inclined to share her intimate thoughts or concerns.

"Elizabeth, might I impose upon you with a delicate question as only you may answer to my satisfaction?"

"Surely, but you look a bit flushed. What causes so much embarrassment?"

"I should dearly wish to discuss the subject of love," Georgiana expressed shyly.

"If you wish."

"Elizabeth, how does one know when one's in love? What signs must I look for? How shall I ever know for sure?"

Elizabeth, not expecting such questions, sat momentarily in deep meditation.

"It is quite obvious you have never been in love. If you had, you would not be inquiring. I fear it is sometimes confused with romantic tendencies of flattery or shallow compliments young girls often contemplate to be love. Of this you must be on your guard. Is there a particular gentleman you are fond of?"

"Not presently, I just wish to know. I thought perhaps you might educate me."

Elizabeth sat down, patting the seat of a nearby chair. With a look of combined innocence and desire to be educated, she sat down, giving Elizabeth her undivided attention.

"Georgiana, you are a young woman of high moral character; you lack no social graces. Your respectable family and esteemed connections I fear place you in a vulnerable position out in the world. Perhaps this is your brother's concern. You are no match for deceitful characters. Guard against supposed gentlemen whose devious schemes may be aimed at robbing you of your birthright. Seek the honourable."

"You mean like Fitzwilliam?"

"Indeed, like Fitzwilliam. It is not to say all men who lack means are deceitful, quite the contrary. There are many both honourable and gentlemanly. My dear sister, love is not only a matter of the heart, but considerably more. It is not to be taken lightly. Both prudence as well as the impulses of the heart must maintain a fair balance, just as social interests and discipline must be harmonious. Flattery, clever attentions with compliments, may make a lady feel virtually helpless. Such men lack scruples; some flatter women into false beliefs with excessive insincere praise, usually given to gratify the recipient's vanity or to win their affection. It is a dangerous practice, hypocrisy of the worst kind."

Georgiana moved restlessly in her seat, perching herself on the edge. With an earnest desire to understand, she cupped her hands in her lap, paying particular attention to Elizabeth's words.

"It leads to lying for gain. Flattery is used to induce a sense of being desired. A truly honourable gentleman has no need to convince; in fact, he usually reserves his affections until he is secure in what he feels. Love happens with honest confession. When it is time for a man to form a serious design on a lady to whom he wishes to direct his honourable intentions, he will know. That is when he will seek her hand in the proper respect, entreating her father. When a man's compliments are excessively strong, perhaps brazenly forward, his intentions may be anything but honourable. A devious, clever character's attentions are carefully planned in a skillful manner. His motives are generally destructive to anyone but himself."

"Yes, I do see a little; that is to say my brother had attempted to educate me on the subject. You know how forthright he can be. I daresay I judged his view was of a manly nature, so I thought it best to seek your view. Elizabeth, I detected my brother's love for you the first time you dined at Pemberley. Mr. Bingley and his sisters were here as well. I confess I was confused by Caroline Bingley's ill manners. Fitzwilliam confessed their design was to injure you. Why do they dislike you so?"

Elizabeth sighed. The very thought of Caroline Bingley pained her. "Caroline Bingley set her designs on your brother. At first I was of little concern to her, until she recognized your brother's interest in me. I believe she viewed my situation so far below his as not to give me a moment's consideration. When she learned otherwise, she did her best to persuade him to dislike me. Being of strong mind, he could not be influenced."

Elizabeth paused. She sighed again, taking a deep breath. Shrugging her shoulders, she afforded Georgiana a direct look, then continued.

"Georgiana, my family is of little means, our birthright is not of noble ancestry, we lack social connections, we are poor in many respects, but not so very poor that we can not afford a cook, housekeeper and a few servants. The Bennet estate is a small one, but fitting. Having no brothers, the estate is written as such that the house, grounds and all the contents are entailed away to my cousin Mr. Collins upon my father's death. Mr. Collins is the vicar residing at Hunsford property at Rosings, to which your aunt, Lady Catherine de Bourgh, is his patroness. His practice of insipid flattery does not offend her. I fear there are those in my family whom Mr. Bingley's sisters view as vulgar, offensive, even scandalous, certainly beneath their society."

Georgiana leaned forward. "But I am sure my brother had never an interest in Caroline Bingley. He would have educated me of it."

"Yes, but a man of your brother's position, to set designs on someone of less importance, offends them. It is not common in today's society, I think. He deplores marriage void of love. I am indeed fortunate to be the recipient of such decided passion."

"And I am fortunate to have you for a sister."

"Thank you, Georgiana, you are very kind."

"No, it is not kindness, but truthfully spoken. Elizabeth, tell me more of your family."

"Very well. I have four sisters. Jane is the eldest, married to Charles Bingley. Kitty and Mary remain at home. Lydia, the youngest, is married, presently residing in the north country."

"So you are the second eldest? I should like very much to meet all of them."

"And so you shall, in due time I would expect. I am anxious for you to meet Jane. She is valued by our mother as the prettiest, although I suspect your brother would give her argument on that account, and I shouldn't be sorry for it. She has light chestnut hair and skin so smooth, like the texture of cream. She is of a gentle demeanour, owning to a reserved style. She has beautiful eyes, which I believe renders fairness to her loveliness. Her general fashion is simple like mine. She is quiet with good sense. I admire Jane most for her ability to seek the very best qualities in everyone. She has a most amiable disposition."

"And your other sisters?"

"Kitty and Lydia were close, silly girls, easily led. But now Lydia is married, so Kitty spends much time with her friend Mariah Lucas. Mariah's sister is married to my cousin Mr. Collins, whom I mentioned earlier. Did you ever meet them while at Rosings?"

"No, I have not. It has been some time since I last visited Rosings. Now my aunt is very angry with Fitzwilliam. I fear we shall never visit Rosings again."

"Are you aware of the circumstances surrounding her anger?"

"I confess I am. She is unable to forgive my brother for marrying you."

"Then surely you are aware your brother and Ann were spoken for?"

Georgiana nodded in acknowledgment and continued to listen intently.

"I am so sorry all this has had an adverse effect on you. I plan to do everything in my power to rectify the matter, but at present I know not how."

"Do not concern yourself on my behalf. Pray, tell me more of your sisters."

"Kitty is a sensitive girl. I daresay she will gain much more intelligence now that Lydia is away. Lydia was a bad influence on Kitty; they continuously sought the attentions of soldiers encamped at Meryton. I must confess, at times they quite neglected the commonest rules of decorum. As for Mary, my mother claims Mary deficient in looks, but I do not agree. Mary likes religious books; she has a great interest in the church. She would do well as a vicar's wife. Mary pays little attention to fashions like other girls. I suppose her youth is at fault, but there is no hurry. She seems unaffected by young men and presently has no desire to seek their company. As for my mother—yes, I will have to tell you of my mother, for I am sure you will one day make her acquaintance. I fear it is best you know in advance what to expect."

"Are you like your mother?"

Elizabeth reached over to pat Georgiana's hand. She laughed, "Heavens no! I favour my father's demeanour, thankfully so. My mother has many opinions and voices them freely with little thought. I suspect any silliness in Kitty or Lydia is directly from her. She excites easily, expects much, is a great talker of little matters and fusses at length. She likes to be disagreeable, I fear at times just for the sake of being so. My mother lives her girlhood fantasies through her younger daughters, puts much stock in a red coat and contradicts her own opinions on most occasions. Jane and I are closer to my father in thoughts and actions."

Georgiana looked concerned. She gasped, "Oh dear, does she disagree with Fitzwilliam?"

Elizabeth let out a faint sarcastic titter, "Indeed! You can well imagine the consequences. Enough talk of my mother. You must allow me to tell you what I truly believe love is."

"Please do, Elizabeth," Georgiana said as she sat up closer to listen.

"It is honour, pure faith, hope amid unrestricted trust. I believe the bond of love I share with your brother is of the purest kind, but it could not have survived without mutual trust and respect. He concealed his feelings until he was certain, then made an honest confession. In fact, one day, realizing he loved me in spite of my inferior family, lack of connections and wealth, he felt he could no longer remain silent. He told me how much he ardently admired and loved me; I rejected him."

Georgiana's lips parted with shock. "Oh gracious, you did? Why?"

"Because I had been imposed upon by George Wickham with falsehoods of Fitzwilliam. I therefore formed an ill opinion of him, later discovering the erroneous nature of my beliefs. Soon I felt quite different toward him, but it was too late learned. Later, I visited Pemberley. We happened upon each other quite by accident, as he was not to return until the day next. Then he introduced you to me. His kindness weighed heavy on my thoughts when I was forced to quit your society to return home. I agonized that I would never see him again. I could not eat nor sleep. I had a heart-wrenching ache so acute, I did not know how I should go on. All I could imagine was that he held ill thoughts of me. Indeed your brother is the best man I know. I hold him in the highest regard. He is secure in his senses. When we marry, the Bible says two become one. When one of us is suffering, the other minds it intently."

"Oh, to find such love would be wonderful indeed," Georgiana expressed.

"When he is from my side, I miss him so very much, almost as though part of me is gone. In marriage there is love and pride. Pride in knowing the man at your side is the very best of men and feeling as if the whole of the world knows it is fact. Pride in knowing that whatever we do, wherever we are or whomever we are with, we are respectfully honoured for being the half of another that is so great that God himself smiles on the union. To love intensely as if your heart depends upon it when your feelings are beyond your control, this is the passion of love in marriage. When you can claim feelings such as these, you are in love. Well, I daresay I hope I did not confuse you."

"Indeed not," replied Georgiana, "I now understand my brother."

Elizabeth stood. She eyed Georgiana with curiosity, "Indeed, how so?"

"When he first educated me of his interest, his eyes gladdened. His speech excelled to a greater pace. His countenance brightened, inducing an excitement I rarely witnessed in him. It was but a short time thereafter, I believe he had just returned from Rosings with our cousin Colonel Fitzwilliam, that I became alarmed. He was greatly pained, suffering an anguish only he knew. When I inquired as to his sadness, he could not speak of it. He spent much time on the end of the sofa pondering his tormented feelings. He paced up and down the gallery at night. I noticed he could not sleep nor eat. He grew pale with darkness about his eyes. I felt hopeless when he quitted Pemberley."

"Oh," said Elizabeth, as she regained her seat, "that must have been after I refused him."

"Yes, I see that now. He announced he needed a diversion to escape his torment. This I did not understand, but when I next returned from London, he announced we were to meet. At the time, although I detected a rather reserved happier brother, I was still aware of his slight melancholy. He was still anguished, almost as if he dared to hope, but hope was out of his reach. Elizabeth, the night you played the pianoforte I watched his face glow with emotion. I knew at once my brother had the deepest affection for you. Oh, I suspected it earlier when he spoke of you, but that night I knew with certainty. When you parted that evening, I heard him wandering in the gallery, then the music chamber. He was very restless. Perhaps some day I'll be fortunate enough to find someone equal to my brother."

"Now," said Elizabeth, "if you keep that in mind, you will have nothing to fear to be sure. Yes indeed, set your sights on a man equal to your brother and in all probability you may make a good match. Indeed such aspirations will not fail you. Speaking of him, we had better find your brother or he'll think we ran off."

"You are probably right."

They ventured below the stairs, finding him in the music chamber, sitting on the corner of the sofa reading. They distracted him upon entering, but he did not seem to mind the interruption. He turned his book over his knee. "Now what have you two been up to?"

"Might I ask who is inquiring?"

"That would be your husband."

"Let me see, we were discussing women's concerns."

"Very well then, I believe I have heard enough," said he, shaking his head as he took up his book, rolling his eyes at them.

Georgiana sat at the pianoforte to play while Mr. Darcy continued to read.

Elizabeth fetched her book of poetry to join him. Altogether the evening passed quietly and uneventfully.

The Fall

THE MORNING NEXT, Elizabeth descended the stairs slowly. Her turbulent stomach seized her customary restrain beyond her command. Inasmuch as the room spun, a light-headed feeling overcame her. She held tight to the railing, carefully taking one step at a time.

Mr. Darcy, now in the library, heard a rather loud commotion. It was Mrs. Reynolds shouting. He then heard Bessie calling for help, hastening him to learn the trouble. He discovered Mrs. Reynolds had found Elizabeth lying at the base of the stairs. She was calling for assistance, while trying to keep Elizabeth's head elevated as Bessie frantically fanned her with her apron. Mr. Darcy took over, directing Mrs. Reynolds to fetch a manservant. Wasting no time, she hastened her return with three.

"Silas, quickly dispatch a rider to Lambton to fetch the doctor. Make haste, tell him to come directly," Mr. Darcy said with authority.

Silas promptly left them with wide, sweeping strides. Mr. Darcy, in control, instructed the servants to take his wife to her chamber.

"Mrs. Reynolds, do we have smelling salts in the house?"

"Yes, indeed, sir, I'll fetch them at once."

"We will be above the stairs in the bedchamber," he called after her.

Mr. Darcy stayed at Elizabeth's side, stroking her face. Georgiana, having heard the commotion, appeared. "Goodness gracious, Fitzwilliam, what has happened?"

"I don't know, but I believe she fainted. Help rub her hands. What takes Mrs. Reynolds so long?" he expressed impatiently.

While Georgiana rubbed Elizabeth's hands, she started to moan. At that moment Mrs. Reynolds hurried into the bedchamber. One of the housekeepers followed behind with a basin of fresh, cool water and a cloth.

"Thank you, Mrs. Reynolds, she seems to be regaining consciousness. I suppose these smelling salts will expedite the matter." Elizabeth moved her head back and forth.

"Elizabeth, can you talk to me?" He checked her eyes as he inquired.

"Whatever happened?" asked Elizabeth.

"I believe you fainted, my dear. Do you remember if you reached the base of the stairs; are you hurt; are you in pain?"

"I did indeed reach the base but I felt light-headed. I suddenly felt uncontrollably nauseated, and the room turned about rapidly; that is the last I remember."

"Thank God you did not fall down the steps. I sent for the doctor. I shall remain here until he arrives; then we will talk about what is to be done. You should not attempt to come below the stairs alone, at least until these fainting spells subside. You do agree?"

"Yes, I believe I should not."

Georgiana viewed his troubled look; Elizabeth could see it too. In spite of his severe expression, he remained in control, giving orders to Mrs. Reynolds as well as the other servants as he busied himself putting the cool cloth on her forehead. "Unless the doctor says otherwise, I do not wish her to be alone."

"Yes, sir, indeed."

Two hours passed before Silas appeared to announce the doctor's arrival. He brought him directly to the bedchamber. Everyone, with the exception of Mrs. Reynolds and Mr. Darcy, quit the chamber. After the doctor questioned Elizabeth, he asked Mr. Darcy to quit the chamber, then closed the door behind him.

Mr. Darcy paced in the hall. Georgiana did her best to keep him occupied, but soon learned he was not to be spoken to. He was too anguished to make conversation. After a half-hour he grew increasingly restless. He sat on a step, putting his elbows on his knees as he buried his face in his hands. Georgiana stayed with him, unsure if she should attempt to speak. She was about to near him when the bedchamber door opened. Dr. Gordon motioned for him to come in.

"Well, Mr. Darcy," started Doctor Gordon, "I have talked at length with your wife. She tells me she has only fainted a few other times in her life, all over the past several weeks. Are you aware your wife has felt ill daily for several weeks now?"

"Why, no." He looked down at Elizabeth, "Why have you not mentioned it?"

"I did not wish to alarm you."

"Shall we have someone with her at all times?"

"That may be wise, although I recommend additional bed rest—no exertion would surely help. Judging by her description of light-headedness, coupled with nausea these past weeks, upon closer examination I would say your wife is perfectly fine. She appears to be a strong woman; yes, I suspect she will do quite well."

Mr. Darcy's face hardened; he became stern. With anguished words, he abruptly stated, "No, I'll not accept that. How can she be well, she continues these fainting spells?"

"Trust me, Mr. Darcy, you have no more concerns than other men."

Exasperation consumed his features. "I must know at once the reason for all of this! Surely you have some explanation!" Growing increasingly frustrated, his tone grew demanding. He immediately sat at her side on the edge of the bed, taking her hand in his.

"Yes, indeed, in fact I do know, but your wife prefers to tell you. We discussed it at great length. She is well aware of her condition. I trust she will take very good care with your assistance; you may dispatch me if needed." Doctor Gordon grinned as he moved toward the door, closing it behind him. Mrs. Reynolds and Georgiana followed his lead.

Mr. Darcy leaned forward to kiss her on the forehead. "Dearest, if anything happened to you, I couldn't bear it. What is it? You must tell me now, put an end to all my misery. I confess, I can hardly endure the struggles of my present thoughts." He sat up again looking at her in anguished apprehension.

Elizabeth sat forward giving him a serious look. "My illness is such that I will no doubt change, dearest; I should never be the same."

His voice was overtaken with anxiety, "Whatever do you mean?"

Elizabeth lay back again. She playfully smiled. Keeping her beaming eyes on her husband as she smiled with pure joy, she calmly replied, "Dearest, I am going to be the mother of your child, that is all."

Mr. Darcy gazed speechlessly. The sober expression on his stunned face just stared back at her. His eyes filled, he kissed her hands, then her face. "Dearest, loveliest Elizabeth, mother of my child, you have made me the happiest of men." Again he sat for a moment gazing at her. "Did Dr. Gordon tell you when we may expect its arrival?"

"Dr. Gordon did only say after much discussion. Given that I fainted in London when only wedded a fortnight, he should expect the happy event to take place about nine months from our wedding. So, within less than six months, you shall be a father."

Mr. Darcy inhaled deeply. He leaned forward, giving her a tender kiss, then kissed her hands again and again. As he stood, she lay watching him for a moment. He was deep in thought. But before another word could be spoken, he moved hastily to the door. He called out for Georgiana, who he presumed was still patiently waiting in the hall. He called to her again, this time his voice filled with urgency.

"Georgiana, come, come here at once."

Georgiana ran down the hall to the bedchamber. She entered with swift strides, now out of breath, with a worried look upon her face.

"Georgiana, Elizabeth is with child; I'm going to be a father. What say you to that?" he chanted. Before she could say anything, he gently pulled her close. As he still held her captive, he looked down at her. "You are going to be Aunt Georgiana, can you believe it?"

Georgiana broke into a relieved smile. "Perhaps my presence is needed at home; perhaps I should alter my plans of joining London society in order to remain at Pemberley as a companion to Elizabeth. Indeed I shall if it is your wish."

Elizabeth quickly replied, "If going to London is truly your desire, then I shall not put your plan to ruin. You should go without reservation, if it is your wish. I am in very good hands, surely you can see that. It is not that I would not wish to have your excellent company; you know that would be a welcome delight for me. I will not have you sacrifice your plans, no indeed. Your brother will see to it that I am well taken care of. Is that not so, Fitzwilliam?"

"Surely you are aware your presence always brings joy, as is your absence a void. Elizabeth will be well looked after. Let this be the end of it. You go, fulfill your desire."

Mr. Darcy quickly went to the hall. He called out, "Mrs. Reynolds, come above the stairs quickly, make haste!"

Mrs. Reynolds hurried above the stair believing there was another emergency. Mr. Darcy seized her hands for a moment. "Mrs. Reynolds, Elizabeth is with child. I suppose you know that already. Is that not so?"

"Yes sir, I do."

"I shall depend on you and Bessie to care for everything. I believe we shall have breakfast here in the chamber. Please see that she has fresh water at her bedside. She will come below the stairs in the latter part of the afternoon. I will escort her below the stairs myself, but request you to be present. Perhaps I may require your assistance; I shall count on you."

"Yes, indeed, sir. You have my best wishes. I can not tell you how relieved I am to finally understand Mrs. Darcy's spells. The thought of an infant in the house once again brings great joy. I believe it has been much too long. Again, sir, my best wishes to you both."

"We thank you, Mrs. Reynolds. Please go below the stairs. Gather the servants together; I wish to make the announcement."

"Very well, sir."

"Georgiana, will you stay here until I return? After I make the announcement, I will go to the library to fetch some books, then return."

"Of course, you know I will."

"Do not be alarmed; surely I may be left alone for a moment," Elizabeth retorted.

He looked at her perplexed. "Indeed not, at least not today," said he, quitting the chamber.

Elizabeth looked at Georgiana, who now occupied her brother's space. "I think it quite considerate of him to make an announcement."

"As with any important event, he'll announce it. They are loyal servants; most have been with us for many years. I notice my brother conducts himself very much as my father did. Surely you must have noticed how dear Mrs. Reynolds looks to him. I know Fitzwilliam planned to take you about the property to introduce you to the families. I believe that shall have to wait now. You will see how twice a year he opens the ballroom to treat the families to a feast. He does this at Christmas as well as harvest time; he looks forward to it. You shall witness how he greets them individually. I was ten when my father died. He has been the best of brothers, but acts like a father to me."

The discussion ended when Mr. Darcy returned. Before long, Georgiana departed their chamber.

"Dearest, you shall not be alone today, not on such an eventful day as this. I desire to be at your side. I wish to watch you sleep, watch you eat; but most of all I believe I shall affably wallow in the felicity of our announcement."

He suddenly looked rather alarmed; his expression turned sober. "My dear, you have not breakfasted yet. I shall summon for it at once. I shall have to go—" Before he could say another word, a servant entered the bedchamber with a breakfast tray for the two.

"Ah, Mrs. Reynolds, she is so very good, I should have known. Mrs.

Reynolds loves children; I should know. She spent much time with me since I was four years old. She is an excellent creature. We are fortunate to have her; surely there is no one better."

"I like Mrs. Reynolds very much indeed," smiled Elizabeth. "When I first met her at Pemberley, I liked her immediately. When she spoke of you, it was with such admiration. With obvious pride she told us you were the best of men. I remember thinking, one would almost have thought she were your mother; there was a definite prejudice in your favour. Her face lit up at the mention of your name. She told us you were a good little boy, saying you never gave her any cause for concern. I know you to be an excellent man. I daresay, according to Mrs. Reynolds, you were an excellent child. I only hope our child will take after you, preferably emulate your temperament."

"Oh, Elizabeth, you know very well I suffer to direct my quick rise to temper. I own to an obstinate nature, sometimes to my abhorrence. I struggle to keep my pride under good regulation, but I have that tendency to speak what is on my mind. Nay, I would wish the child to have your looks as well as your temperament."

"We shall see, dearest; perhaps he shall have a little of both."

"He—shall have both?"

"Oh yes, to be sure; I'm quite confident you shall have a son; I just know it. But we shall have to wait won't we?" She laughed at her own folly.

"We better breakfast, it will soon be too cold to eat."

Mr. Darcy spent the rest of the day with his wife. He quitted her presence only for a few moments, leaving another to sit with her.

It was an eventful day, one sure to be long remembered, thought she. What had begun as a frightful morning, ended with mutual joy. As he fussed over her, she readily gave herself up to the luxury of being taken care of.

Mr. Darcy looked at himself in the looking glass. His smile was broad. He stared at his reflection, concluding the image before him had no misgivings of the future. He thought how intensely that man loved his wife. Not unlike most men, he entertained thoughts of a son, believing that would certainly give him great joy. But then, thought he, a daughter would be welcomed as well. "But I imagined he will have dark beautiful fine eyes like his mother," said he aloud.

"Did you say something, dearest?"

Mr. Darcy turned his eyes upon her. With absolute enthusiasm, his eyes sparkled at the very sight of her. "Just thinking aloud, my dear; my mind is agreeably engaged in the future."

The Invalid

ALTHOUGH CONFINED, Elizabeth maintained her sunny disposition, along with her lively spirit. The significance of her day contrived of affectionate conversations with her husband, whose particular attentions consisted of a mixture of sincere regard, teasing and tender care. There was little time to suffer boredom with a husband who sought to occupy her with demonstrative feelings of adulating regard. He sought to respond to her every emotion.

"Fitzwilliam, I desire to write to Jane. I wish to make announcement."

"Very well, dearest." He immediately saw to it that she was provided with all she required, directing her maidservant to bring her a writing box.

Penning all such thoughts on paper passed off the morning to her delight. After announcing the happy event, she described her days getting acquainted with the great estate. Upon completion of its contents, she secured Mrs. Reynolds to see the letter was sent post. Now she looked forward to the afternoon, which afforded her the opportunity to venture below the stairs.

Mr. Darcy, still uneasy about leaving her alone, stayed continuously at her side. He glanced up turning his book over on his lap. "Dearest, do you think yourself up to going below the stairs for a few hours?"

"Yes, I have looked forward to it."

"Very well then, Mrs. Reynolds will assist us."

Elizabeth descended the stairs as planned. Feeling light-headed, she requested to be brought to the sofa for a rest before dinner. Although he obliged her, Mr. Darcy expressed a concern of her being out of the chamber too soon, turning strict with limitations.

"Fitzwilliam, I am convinced it is smart to be up at the very least for a short time. Anyone may suffer light-headedness if confined at length. You must allow me this much."

"Very well, but you must promise you will not move about without assistance."

"You have nothing to fear where I am concerned. I am a dutiful patient. You may be certain I will honour your wishes."

Elizabeth looked forward to the day next, when she could once again do the same. In the weeks following, she spent most of her time resting or reading. She and Mr. Darcy breakfasted together each morning. He insisted upon keeping her company, for as much as time and circumstances would allow.

"Dearest, this could prove to be a lengthy six months," she warned.

"To be sure," he responded, with his attention still fixed in his book.

"It nears the time Georgiana is to depart from us. Is it not so?"

He turned his book on his lap, providing her with his full attention. "Yes, her trunks will be made ready tomorrow; she will depart from us on the day following."

"I shall sorely miss her, she is good company, we have had fine conversations. I find she is so very much like you."

"Like me? How so?"

"She has poised elegance, with a striking air of superiority in the best sense. She carries herself with dignifying pride; her only desire is to please you."

"You say that with much love. You do not know what it means to me to have a wife so loving to my sister. I am a fortunate man to find such felicity within the whole of my family."

"Well, not all of your relations—you forget Lady Catherine."

"No, I have not forgotten my aunt. I am in a most unfavourable position," he replied coldly, staring off into the chamber with an unyielding expression. His eyes turned glassy. He parted his lips as if to speak, but then said no more on the subject.

"Shall we write to your aunt to tell her of the event?"

He leaned his head back against the chair, closing his eyes for a fleeting moment. Then he looked in her direction. He hesitated. "No, that would not be wise; the news may be viewed as insolent. Had I married Ann, the child would be her grandchild. Surely it would be viewed as designed arrogance; it is best we do nothing at all."

"Perhaps you should write Colonel Fitzwilliam; invite him to visit. We may seek his assistance with Lady Catherine."

"Inviting my cousin is an excellent idea. I am always eager to see him.

Even though he finds favour with her, I'll not have him involved in our affair. I cannot put the Colonel in such a position as to lose her favour; I forbid it. That would hardly be fair. I'll not suffer him. If he is able to break away, I shall be glad to receive him."

"Very well, dearest, we'll not approach him."

"I tell you, Lady Catherine must be dealt with prudently; it is a delicate matter."

He proceeded to write to the Colonel, extending the invitation they spoke of. Then he announced, "I shall write to Bingley as well."

"I have already written to Jane; Mrs. Reynolds sent it post yesterday."

"Well, am I to be deprived of announcing this happy event? Am I not the father in standing?" he said teasingly.

"You know very well I wrote to Jane. How could you not know, you have rarely left the chamber? Am I not the mother?" she came back at him, teasing further.

"Of course I knew you had written; I would have thought you more ill had you not done so."

"Fitzwilliam, I never would have suspected you such a tease. Whatever became of the quiet, reserved, proud man who says little; you quite surprise me."

"I am still that man. I am surrounded with all that brings comforting ease. Here I experience a depth of felicity. Why should I not be content? I follow my father's illustration. At Pemberley he was much the same, but in public, that was another sphere. He was well known for his superiority, distinguished with stylish grace. He was thought to be a great gentleman; never did he act otherwise. But at Pemberley he was all ease, more prone to jest."

Admiring his reminiscence, she noticed when he talked of him he seemed to display an inexplicable longing. "You miss him very much, judging by the mode of your declaration. What is further interesting, is that you give description of your own character."

"That pleases me; I can think of no other footsteps I'd rather follow in. Now, am I to be allowed to continue my book, or do you intend to demand my complete attention all of the day?" He picked up his book, still peering at her from the corner of his eye in a teasing manner.

She gave a laugh. "Very well, I suppose I should rest now." She lay her head back, closing her eyes with pleasant anticipated thoughts of him as a father.

The Departure

THE DAY ARRIVED for Georgiana's journey to London. Having already breakfasted, she made her way to her brother's chamber. She tapped at the door, then entered upon hearing Elizabeth's voice of invitation.

Seeing it was Georgiana, Mr. Darcy stood. "I believe I shall allow you ladies time alone." Before quitting the chamber, he bent forward to kiss his wife, then kissed his sister's forehead as he paused in front of her.

"Who will sit with you when my brother goes to his library, or to sport?"

"I imagine Mrs. Reynolds, although I do not require a guard. I am quite capable of entertaining myself with a book or writing a letter."

"I'm not sure Fitzwilliam would stand for it."

"Do not concern yourself with me; I am a dutiful patient. I am quite certain I may adapt to confinement with a measure of agreeable compliance. Look at you now, all prepared to flee to London. We have rather enjoyed so many pleasant exchanges, have we not now?"

"Yes, I may say so as well. The weather is fine for my journey there."

"So it is, Georgiana, I could not have wished for a better day. I'm glad we have this time alone. Your brother is very discerning where you are concerned." She paused, "You will be sure to write when you arrive—you will write often?"

"You may depend upon it. You must promise to write as well. You must tell me all I am missing. I shall miss our conversations most sorely."

"I too, Georgiana, I too. You know it will not be the same when you are gone. If you find your arrangements not liking to your taste, you will write us, will you not? Promise me, I shall rest uneasy if you are not thoroughly happy. You must promise to do so."

"Do not worry, Elizabeth, read nothing into my reserve. I am always of this nature. Rest assured, I would not hesitate to return directly if I find my situation less than anticipated. I promise you with all my heart. Good-bye, Elizabeth; I will miss our talks to be sure. Be advised, I shall be on my guard of those false flattering, complimenting creatures of the world."

"Very good, Georgiana, you are an excellent student, good-bye."

Georgiana paused to peer at Elizabeth one last time, then quit the chamber in haste.

The carriage arrived. The trunks were fastened to the back. Several servants stood at the threshold to bid her farewell. Mr. Darcy gave his sister one last hug before assisting her into the carriage. He closed the door, then leaned his head in the window slightly. "Georgiana, as always, I shall dearly miss you. You must write to say you arrived in safety."

Georgiana nodded her head. With somber seriousness of expression, he stepped back from the carriage, giving a nod to the driver to take his leave. He stood watching until the carriage was out of sight, then entered the house to return to his wife.

He was in the chamber for several moments before he took up his book. Elizabeth sat up to gaze in his direction after wiping away an involuntary tear. "I see your sadness, I shall miss her too. She has been away many times, has she not?"

"Yes, indeed she has; each time is like the first. I feel helpless in my protection of her; such feelings never cease. I know I must allow her the freedom to become her own. Do not concern yourself with me; I shall recover from the moment. It is my duty to guide her, thus granting her the freedom of her education, although each time I suffer a little more for it."

"To have such a brother, Georgiana is very fortunate in this respect."

"Thank you, my dear, your words are most comforting."

"I shall rest now," said Elizabeth, adding, "I am so very tired, I had little sleep knowing Georgiana was to depart today."

"Before you rest, I believe I must send word to Mr. Manley with regard to Georgiana. I have been meaning to do so on another matter. Have you any objection to an invitation to Pemberley?"

"That would please me, but you will have to receive him. I am certain, under the circumstances, he will not mind. Surely he will understand my confinement, once he is appraised of my limitations. I do believe my absence will be tolerated."

"Very well then."

With this understanding, he went to the secretary to write his letter.

Mr. Henry Manley, Rectory at Wilshire, London
12ᵀᴴ of March

My dear sister Georgiana is presently on journey to London. I trust your sister awaits her expected arrival. The parsonage I spoke of, soon to be vacant, requires closer inquisition on your part so we may come to some understanding on the matter previously discussed. Your presence is most desirous to resolve the matter, and will permit me to engage in the office of pointing out the certain sense and disposition of the status, people, surrounding grounds and parish on this estate. Closer inspection, along with the impartial convictions I afforded you in London, may influence your investigation and decision to my favour. I am certain, once representation is made, we will be of the same opinion; that is to say the parsonage vacancy at Pemberley is most advantageous, affording its taker the promise of security, predominant integrity and a heightened sense of assurance for benevolence in the country. I ask you to pardon the freedom with which I demand your immediate attention; however, I must hasten my search for replacement as the immediate clergy is presently ill and wishes to go to Bath earlier than expected. Remembering everything that passed in conversation between us in London, I am in a position to tempt you with an offer you may find difficult to repudiate once you have come. Allow me to warn you, I shall use my every influence in attempting to hurry your decision to my satisfaction.

Respectfully,
Fitzwilliam Darcy

After addressing the message, he placed the seal upon it. He left his resting wife momentarily to give instruction to Mrs. Reynolds to have it dispatched at once.

He returned to his wife's side with the rare book, along with another he had purchased on the wedding journey. Being secure in the knowledge of her sleeping state, he chanced to examine the book. The contents of the rare book afforded a look into a family ledger, a family of nobility which once resided in Berkshire. The subject drew an urgent desire to know more. On closer examination, he determined its contents might require a visit to that particular area in pursuit of ancillary facts.

Little more than two hours passed, when Mr. Darcy was forced to quickly conceal the book. His wife stirred to a wakened state. With an alternate book in hand, he sat appearing intense in his reading.

"You read much today," she observed.

"Yes, I am content to be at your side. I confess I rather enjoy watching you sleep. Do you believe yourself up to taking a turn about the music chamber? You no doubt are in need of exercise. Dr. Gordon suggests it, but requires accompaniment. I believe you will take it in quite well. Is that agreeable?"

"Oh yes, I believe I'm quite capable. I look forward to the change."

"Very well then, you stay settled. I have something to care for. I will return directly. Promise me you will not get out of bed?"

"You have my word on it."

Mr. Darcy clutched the books in his hand, holding them tight to his breast as he made haste to his office. He now kept the rare purchase locked in a secure place. On his way back to Elizabeth, he encountered Mrs. Reynolds.

"Was my message to Mr. Manley dispatched?"

"Yes sir, at once."

"Very good, Mrs. Reynolds," he said, quitting her presence.

"Well my dear, are you ready for the challenge?"

"Yes, but why could you not wait to take those books to the library? They would have been well enough left in the bedchamber, would they not?"

"Yes, it is quite so, but I thought I heard Mrs. Reynolds; in fact I did. I wished to inquire if my message to Mr. Manley was sent direct. She said it was so."

"Oh yes, I had forgotten it. I do hope he comes; it will be a pleasure to have him visit."

"My sentiments exactly. What do you say we start our walk?"

With all such thoughts of the book diverted, they quitted the chamber. He was not comfortable in his concealment, but suspected she would have little understanding of his search into this particular family ancestry. He wondered, with consideration, how it happened that his wish to do what appeared to be so virtuous had become an unattractive quality of concealment. He was certain it was best to say nothing of his find, at least until he could affirm his suspicions.

After several turns about the chamber, Elizabeth played Mozart's *Menuetto* on the pianoforte, providing him gratifying pleasure as he sat on the sofa with his port, absorbing her beauty. He studied her splendor, continuing his admiring gaze, believing her face to glow radiantly. His thoughts directed to the impending birth. He found solace in his surety that she would be an excellent mother. Her very presence brought him the greatest joy as well as ungoverned satisfaction. What more could any man hope for?

Expected and Unexpected Visitors

A FEW DAYS FOLLOWING Georgiana's departure, Mr. Darcy received word through the post. He hurried to his chamber to share the letter with his wife.

"Dearest, I have a letter from Georgiana; here, you read it."

Fitzwilliam Darcy,
Pemberley Estate,
Derbyshire

My dear brother, fear not. I have arrived safely in London. I am happily situated at the manor of Mr. and Mrs. Cochran. As for my journey, as you may expect, the weather was quite fine, the ride was smooth, uneventful, but tiring. You have my unwavering gratitude for securing me a comfortable situation. My surroundings are more than expected. Mr. Manley's sister, Mrs. Cochran and her husband Sir John are very kind. I have met your Mr. Manley today. I daresay he is just as you described. Although I have yet to start my studies, I did meet with my tutor, Mr. Sheffield of Horizon Manor. I report him to be educated, well informed, as well as handsome for a man of his age. He appears to be an accomplished gentleman of very agreeable character. He does indeed cherish the speed of a horse, for I heard him tell Sir John just yesterday, his horse won at great length after being challenged by a friend. Mr. Manley was sure to invite him in advance of my studies to seek my approval. There is no doubt I am well protected here. I cannot express my satisfaction more than this. I trust you are taking prodigious care of my new sister. Be sure to flatter her with the attention she deserves. I will write when I have more to report. My sincerest regard to you both.

Yours,
Georgiana

That same day a message arrived from Colonel Fitzwilliam stating he was pleased to be invited and would be traveling to Pemberley directly.

After the reading of the letters, Mr. Darcy expressed, "I have a desire to sport today. Elizabeth, would you mind if I did so? Would it be agreeable to you to consider Mrs. Reynolds sitting with you in my absence?"

"I wish you would, dearest; I never tire of Mrs. Reynolds' tales. She may be depended upon to recount tales of your boyhood. Surely you realize, of this I can never get enough."

On this particular occasion, perhaps because his visit was expected, Mrs. Reynolds enlightened Elizabeth how Colonel Fitzwilliam and her master would run throughout the house as boys. "Oh yes, they would chase each other here, there, up and down. They would sometimes hide from one another so they could jump out to scare. They were indeed full of folly, but were always the best of friends. They were such dear, sweet boys."

As Mr. Darcy went out of doors, a carriage was nearing Pemberley Hall. He waited with curiosity to see who the visitor might be. Very much to his surprise, it was Elizabeth's father. Equally surprising was that he traveled alone.

"Mr. Bennet," Mr. Darcy stated with puzzlement, then bowed. "You are alone, sir?"

Mr. Bennet promptly bowed. His eyes twinkled. His smile broadened when he answered cheerfully, "Yes, indeed, my wife set her designs on attending a ball in town, announcing she, Mary and Kitty will spend a week in Meryton with her sister, Mrs. Philips, to which I had absolutely no objection, but perhaps for the frequency to the local warehouses. The nonsense I expected to escape induced a strong urge to see my Lizzy.

Once I was certain Mrs. Bennet's plans were tightly bound, I made the announcement of my intended visit to Pemberley, much to my wife's protest. As you can imagine, of course, it oppressed her, putting her in a nervous state, to which I suffered at length for three days following. As a master in the art of tears, she fretfully wept into the days next with no relief. Can you imagine that, Mr. Darcy? I daresay you can, yes indeed. You know, Mr. Darcy, such artful weeping afflicts a man. I do believe it quite unfair of God to cause a woman to cry with such ease; it is a strategy difficult to repudiate. A weapon of wailing can undo a fellow; I do believe a man is no contender in an arena of tears. A man soon finds himself at a loss to do anything but comfort her, then relent to suffer his own pain in silence. Nonetheless, I did not allow her theatrical performance to alter my plan to come to Pemberley. So you see, here I am," he reported with quick wit and a gleam in his eye.

Mr. Darcy smothered a smile. "Well—Mr. Bennet, I daresay there is some truth in your proclamation. Tears can undo a man quicker than the sword." He could only smile at his father-in-law's lively interpretation.

Mr. Darcy's man was present to care for the carriage. He gave him a nod to do so, then turned back to Mr. Bennet. "Elizabeth will be delighted to see you; I am pleased you are come. When you have settled, you must allow me to introduce you to the grounds; perhaps you would find pleasure in sporting with me?"

Mr. Darcy's expression was sincere and taken as such. Mr. Bennet noticed the alteration of his demeanour; he could only conclude that marriage did him credit.

"Delighted to be sure. Now if you don't mind, I am anxious to see my Lizzy. I don't mind telling you, Mr. Darcy, I miss her severely. I suffer a lack of sensible conversation at the dinner table that I could always count on my Lizzy to provide. Well, well, enough said on the subject; lead the way."

Mr. Darcy could not help but smile at Mr. Bennet's description of his wife and other daughters. He gave a half bow, extended his arm in the direction he was to go, to which Mr. Bennet took heed. He was pleased to have an opportunity to get acquainted with him independently.

Mrs. Reynolds was still telling stories when they heard lively conversation ascending the stairs. Elizabeth sat forward. "I hear someone coming—I believe I hear my father's voice."

The gentlemen knocked before entering the chamber. "Thank you, Mrs. Reynolds," a grateful Mr. Darcy expressed. With a warm gesture, he motioned for her to quit the chamber.

"Father, you have come; I am pleased. Where is my mother?"

Mr. Bennet gave the same report just given to Mr. Darcy, only with language a bit livelier as he winked his eye when through, inducing his daughter's laughter.

"So, you are come alone."

"Yes, yes, it was conveniently planned. I'm not in the least bit sorry for it; quite the scheme I daresay. I'm sure your mother was wise to it, but it was too late, her plans were set and so here I am. I'm certain I have not heard the last of it, you may be sure of that!"

Mr. Darcy brought a chair nearer to Elizabeth for her father. He carefully fixed the bolsters behind her, allowing more comfort in an upright position.

"Well now, it appears I am a most fortunate woman indeed. Before me are the best of men. How shall I ever recover from such an event?"

"You'll get over it, I'm sure," Mr. Bennet replied, viewing her over top of his spectacles.

"I shall leave you both; I will need a word with the cook and Mrs. Reynolds for an addition to the table for dinner," Mr. Darcy declared before quitting the chamber.

"He is quite gallant. I daresay, Lizzy, no uneasiness about him here, quite the contrary. He is positively a gentleman, so attentive to you. He is warm, friendly, but still a bit stiff. I believe you made a good match, my dear; I'm glad for it. I must remember to congratulate him on your report of the upcoming event. You know how happy this makes me, Lizzy. I was delighted when we received the letter announcing it. Your mother, she talks of Lydia's event frequently. But to be frank, Lizzy, I worry of Lydia; she is short on sense. I fear she still owns a foolishness of mind. She lacks intelligent inclinations; whatever is to become of her? I know naught this husband of hers; it is very hard to trust a man who snickers, flatters, pays false compliments all the while scheming to his own advantage, and whose reputation is of little consequence to him."

"Oh, Father," Elizabeth said sympathetically.

He shook his head with despair. "If things had been different, if Lydia had only shown an ounce of good sense, I might have felt differently toward him. It is very hard, and your mother so eagerly welcomes him to Longbourn; such foolery is intolerable."

"Father, do not distress yourself so."

He shrugged his shoulders as he let out a sigh. "I fear your sister will suffer the misery of disappointment through her misguided affections. He seems to possess an independence of spirit. I do believe their marriage is a maneuvering profession where he is concerned. George Wickham is certainly no Mr. Darcy. Well—never you mind that, Lizzy; I couldn't be happier for you. This husband of yours is much more than expected. He invited me to sport. I plan to take him up on it."

"Please do, Father, I know he is sincere in his offer; you may depend upon it. His lake has many fish; I know it has been some time since you had that pleasure. I am sure my husband will provide you with all you require, once he finds it is to your liking. What a happy occasion to have you here."

"Lizzy, I can plainly see you are content with your situation. Allow me to say, while I have you alone, how very happy this makes me. You have made me proud, my dear, very proud indeed." He patted her hand, smiling broadly.

"Oh, Father, he is everything good and kind. I feared you would never understand my choosing. Yes, he is quietly reserved when out in society among strangers; he rarely speaks in public. In such cases as these, he only talks when he has something of value to declare. He is an excellent conversationalist; you will find he is well versed on many subjects. Here at Pemberley he is all ease, as you witnessed. Forgive my freedom in saying so, but I am selfishly glad my mother did not accompany you; I believe this will afford you the freedom to judge my husband for yourself. Was she very angry?"

"She declared she would never speak to me again. We both know that to be impossible. She threw a fit of despair, cried for three days altogether. Her nervous fluttering and headaches ran the chambermaid ragged seeing to her every whim. I daresay, if her dramatic performance were a stage play, she would no doubt receive rave reviews."

Elizabeth laughed at his description. "I can well imagine it."

Mr. Bennet and Elizabeth talked for some time. It was about two hours later when they heard voices nearing the bedchamber. Mr. Darcy entered with Colonel Fitzwilliam.

"Why, Colonel Fitzwilliam, you wasted no time in coming; I am not sorry for it. This is my father, Mr. Bennet."

"How do you do, sir. Well, Elizabeth, I have not had this pleasure since your wedding day. Pray, what is this I am told; you announce a special event?"

"Indeed," Elizabeth responded with swelling pride. She glanced at her glowing husband, then next at her father. Her smile broadened.

"Well now, Colonel Fitzwilliam, my wife says she will give me a son. What say you, is that not the best of news?"

"Well, I should not dispute it, whatever the lady says. I am not a married man, I have no opinion; indeed I cannot say." He looked at one, then the other, then gave a laugh.

"We are so happy to have you here," Elizabeth expressed. "Would you not like to sit down? Was your journey long?"

"My ride went well; I'm quite comfortable at the moment, in need of nothing more than the company before me."

"I shall be coming below the stairs within the hour. My husband here has his guards watching me every moment; he fusses if I make a move alone. He is most attentive, perhaps I should not protest," she said, rolling her eyes.

"Knowing my cousin, I can believe that."

"Well, I'm glad to hear of it; such a delicate state, he is a wise man in-deed," Mr. Bennet added, looking at Mr. Darcy, then to the Colonel, afford-ing them a wink.

"Now, Elizabeth, that is unjust. You failed to tell of the fainting spells. I will not have you alone. In this respect, perhaps, I suppose I am selfish. I shall have my way." He turned to his guests. "She is a good sort of patient. She is not too opposing at times. Let us just say she has not run me ragged, lest not yet."

"Run you ragged? Indeed not! I run the servants ragged," she proclaimed with a giggle.

They all laughed at the tease, then quitted the chamber to allow her maidservant to prepare her to join the party below the stairs. Having taken an immediate liking to one another, the Colonel and Mr. Bennet enjoyed easy conversation as they ventured to the music chamber.

Elizabeth eventually made her way there, too, with her husband's assis-tance.

"I should like to sit at the pianoforte."

Mr. Darcy, seeing no immediate danger, allowed her to do so. Next he poured port for his guests, then excused himself to tell the cook another table setting was necessary. Mr. Darcy returned within minutes and poured himself some port wine before taking a seat. He sat quietly, listening to her music.

Observing the pride in his son-in-law's expression as he sipped his port while watching his wife at the pianoforte, Mr. Bennet determined his daughter's happiness was secure. After completing the tune, he noticed Mr. Darcy wasted little time advancing to her.

Upon his leading her to the sofa, Mrs. Reynolds entered to present Mr. Darcy with a letter, which had just arrived. He opened it without delay. With a look of stunned disbelief, he queried, "Can you believe this? Mr. Manley is to arrive today. I declare, I must speak to the cook; we may require still another place at dinner; this is quite astonishing to be sure."

"There is much excitement here today, is that not so?" Elizabeth noted.

"Indeed," said Mr. Bennet, "perhaps I should have picked a better time to surprise you with a visit, my dear. This seems to be a most inconvenient time."

Mr. Darcy quickly spun around to address his father-in-law's comment. "Nonsense, not at all, I would have it no other way. I daresay we shall be a handsome assembly in the dining hall; there is certain to be no lack of conversation. Pray excuse me," he said, then bowed before withdrawing from the chamber.

Mr. Manley arrived within the hour. He was brought to the music chamber, where the whole of the party was assembled. Once introduced, Mr. Manley fitted himself easily into the conversation. Mr. Darcy couldn't have been more pleased.

The rest of the day passed quickly. The announcement was made to direct themselves to the dining hall, to which no one lingered behind. As they took their places, it was just as Mr. Darcy predicted; there was in fact no lack of conversation. Although Mr. Manley was unknown to Mr. Bennet and the Colonel, it was soon evident he was an excellent man in their view. His manners were viewed impeccable, his style gracious. His well-fitting groomed attire provided him a handsome appearance. As a judiciously educated man with a good sense of reserved humour, he emanated a warm receptive personality of immediate reverence. It was obvious he had chosen the right profession. As a man of the cloth, he represented everything that vocation required in dealing with spiritual understanding of community. Having added much to the conversation, it was noted by Mr. Bennet, "One would not have guessed that we assembled here have just made each other's acquaintance." During the conversation, Mr. Manley expressed, "So eloquent was your letter, Mr. Darcy, I daresay it was finished off handsomely; I view the handwriting to be further affirmation of your excellence."

"Thank you," a humble Mr. Darcy expressed with tranquil reserve. His countenance laid open his modesty. He turned suddenly silent. It proved to be a pleasing evening in every sense.

The morning next, Mr. Darcy left Elizabeth still asleep in their bedchamber whilst he visited his library. Much to his surprise, he encountered Colonel Fitzwilliam.

"Good morning, Cousin, I thought you wouldn't mind my choosing a book to read."

"I bid you good morning. Indeed, I do not mind," replied Mr. Darcy.

"You certainly have a grand variety to choose from. I must say, Darcy, you greatly increased the library since your father's death."

"Yes, I have; I share his love of books; how good of you to have noticed."

"I enjoyed myself last evening, Cousin. I like Elizabeth's father. He is quick of wit, possesses a good sense of humour. Your Mr. Manley is quite a gentleman. I liked him very much as well. I do believe the conversation flowed easily; I daresay it was rather lively."

"Yes, everything you say is so; I have no complaints—the house is lively enough; my wife couldn't be happier; the cook outdid himself; and my cousin is always a welcome sight."

Mr. Darcy took a book from the shelf. As he paged through it, he paused, then turned to the Colonel. "Needless to say, Colonel, I'm so glad you are come; you know your company is always gladly received. Do you care to join Mr. Bennet and myself today for a shoot, if I can get away?"

"No, I think not; being in the Militia has taken the joy out of it, if you know my meaning."

"No, I do not, but I'm sure it is as you say."

"Cousin, I heard Mr. Manley and Mr. Bennet speak of a fondness for fishing last evening; I assumed you might fish today."

"I did not hear of it, perhaps they would prefer to fish. To be sure, I shall have to see that my guests are fitted with fishing tackle. I'm quite glad you brought it to my attention, Colonel. Perhaps you will join in fishing. Well now, I believe I am a bit hungry. Shall we go to the breakfast chamber?"

"Sounds like a capital idea."

"You go, I must go above the stairs to look in on Elizabeth. She will breakfast in the bedchamber. I shall ask Mrs. Reynolds to keep her company. Dear Mrs. Reynolds, she is a comfort to me, so efficient, competent, capable and kind. Elizabeth is fond of her. Mrs. Reynolds relates to her everything I did as a boy; she mentions you on occasion. So you see, Elizabeth looks forward to learning all about past times at Pemberley. Go now, I will join you momentarily."

It was but a short time later when Mr. Darcy came to the breakfast chamber. By this time Mr. Bennet and Mr. Manley had joined the Colonel. What a marvelous choice of people to happen together, so complementary to each other, thought he.

After they had breakfasted, Mr. Darcy asked, "Would either of you care to fish today? The lake is well stocked; are you interested in casting a line?"

Mr. Bennet and Mr. Manley were quick to accept.

"I shall see to it that you are provided equipment; my manservant will lead the way. I beg your pardon to be excused to stay with my wife. She is a bit worn out; I believe she requires a watchful eye."

"I have no doubt we will do very well together. I believe we are both in agreement—you have made a wise choice. We certainly understand your position; be assured there is no objection. We will have much to talk about I'm sure," related Mr. Manley.

Mr. Darcy went to his wife's side, relieving Mrs. Reynolds, whom he had imposed upon in order to entertain his guests.

"Well, my dear, you look a bit tired."

"Yes, I must rest. It is so good to have my father here—what an unexpected pleasure. Mr. Manley is a most welcomed guest and you know how happy I am to see your cousin."

"Yes, I know, Elizabeth, but you will tell me if the excitement is too much?"

"Of course, but how can it be? You do everything for me."

"To be truthful, I take great pleasure in it."

"Oh, you do?"

"Certainly, my invalid affords me more time to absorb her beauty."

"I believe I shall rest now," Elizabeth said with playful sarcasm, as she lay her head back with a smile overspreading her face.

The gentlemen fished the better part of the day. The Colonel entertained himself until the afternoon. Deciding to pay his cousin a visit, he ventured above the stairs.

"I thought I should like to visit with you both."

"Of course, bring a chair here, sit," Elizabeth encouraged him.

"It is so good to be here; I was most anxious to see you both. It has been too long since we last saw one another."

After about a half-hour exchange, Mr. Darcy arose from his seat in order to fix the bed covering along with the slipping bolster behind his wife. After she was well taken care of, he returned to his seat to converse with them both.

"I daresay, Darcy, you are quite the attentive fellow, staying behind to see that your wife is well taken care of, plumping the bolsters behind her and I know not what. Elizabeth is fortunate to have a husband who pays such close attention. I've heard of fellows who, once they are wed, entertain themselves as they please, giving little or no notice to their wives unless the urge moves them."

Mr. Darcy's voice turned cold. His eyes went from his wife to his cousin in a flash as he pressed his lips together in distaste, then quickly avowed indignantly, "These are misfortunes indeed. A man should not take a wife unless he plans a life with her, not about her; or he should think the better of staying single if that is his design." His face grew pale; his eyes became piercingly cold. There was great anger in his raised voice as he wasted little time in expressing his thoughts on the subject.

The Colonel struggled to reply. "Oh—dear, how silly of me. It was just an observation, Darcy; be assured I think the better of you. I was only making comment," defended the Colonel.

"I understand you, Cousin, it is just that the subject angers me. When a man takes a wife for himself, he has understood obligations. You'll forgive my harshness just now; I have no tolerance for the lack of respect some men have for the women they wed. I do suppose these are the results of arranged marriages, where the man and woman have no say; that is the danger in it all for the woman. Parents should think the better of it. They take awful chances with their daughters. You may be sure, if I have a daughter, I will instill in her the merit of settling for nothing less than the deepest affection," he added in a more civil tone. His eyes met Elizabeth's as he regained a sense of calm.

She was taken aback by his less than controlled conversation. Obvious to both her and the Colonel, was his adamant opinion of the subject. The very thought of such a character disturbed him. Colonel Fitzwilliam looked sorry for having mentioned it. Elizabeth, determined to turn the exchange in another direction, quickly asked, "Colonel Fitzwilliam, have you visited Rosings recently?"

"Why, no, I had planned to go but received your invitation; so I decided to come here first." Then looking at his cousin, he inquired, "Have you had any word from Lady Catherine?"

"No, to be sure it may never take place. She has proven herself indifferent to my correspondence. I am determined to let it end," he said, his voice righteously angry. He paused, then with a mode of controlled language he continued, "Come now, surely you know she views my marriage extremely offensive. Her language to me was very frank. She was abusive in her opinion regarding my wife. Besides, she'll never forgive me for not honouring the commitment made for me as a child. She is a foolish woman indeed. If she continues in her convictions, the most she will accomplish is to deprive herself and Ann of the pleasantries of family. In spite of all this, my wife wishes me to overlook these offences, to pursue reconciliation. To be perfectly forthright, I only conceded to honour her wishes. If I were she, I would not entertain such thoughts." He paused for a moment, then stood up, regaining a further sense of control before continuing. "I should tell you my wife is of the belief that you may be of service in lessening her resentment. She believes you have the genius to penetrate the silence of my aunt. I am of the opinion there is no voice to change her. I would not ask that of anyone; certainly I will not put you in a position to have her anger directed at you."

"I am not afraid to approach my aunt; she and I have never quarreled. She has no reason to direct any anger at me. Remember, Cousin, I am the only visitor she has other than the Collinses of Hunsford. I'm sure she would welcome a visit from me. I would be happy to see if I may be of assistance."

"No, no, I cannot expect it of you; I should not feel comfortable you doing it; to contemplate it would be to my abhorrence. If it is to be done, it is my duty alone."

The Colonel quickly jumped to his feet with zeal. "Why should I not, if it is of my own choosing?" His voice was direct but calmly demanding as he exerted his opinion.

Mr. Darcy quickly stood, "You make your visit on your own terms, do not concern yourself with my situation. I possess deep felicity in my marriage, connections and friends. I can certainly survive without the patronage of my aunt's condescension to be sure."

Elizabeth sat forward anxiously. Tears flushed her eyes, streaming down her face. Her breathing became heavy as she tried to speak, but words seemed to fail her.

Mr. Darcy quickly went to her. "Be calm, Elizabeth, there is no reason to become undone. Surely you understand my meaning." He quickly presented his handkerchief to wipe her eyes. "There now; that's much better."

"Pray forgive me, I have no desire to make you anxious."

"I'm quite all right, Colonel; it is just that I wish to bring forth reconciliation. After all, she is your relation. This whole situation intrudes on Georgiana and Ann; you know it is so."

"I agree, Elizabeth, I worry for Ann as well. Darcy, you must see the merit in all of this."

"Colonel, as I said earlier, you make your visit on your own terms."

"Dearest, remember you promised you would try to make amends, if only for my sake; you did promise, indeed you did."

Mr. Darcy sat on the edge of the bed. He calmed his voice patting her hand. "I made the endeavour, Elizabeth, my correspondence was rejected. I'll put forth no more; my tolerance is limited." He stood up. Although his voice was calm, there was no alteration in his disposition.

"Well, Darcy, you know I shall afford you the privilege of my service in spite of your declaration. I do believe I may be of use. I believe you to have made an excellent match. Considering the indignant mistreatment of your wife, I should think my aunt very fortunate that she would even endeavour to consider reconciling. I shall do my best. It would be a pity to carry on this separation, if for no one else than for Ann's sake. Think of Ann, poor girl, she has little in life to look forward to. She has wealth with a dismal future. When our aunt is gone, what is to become of her? Such an insignificant existence, intolerable to think of! Her survival distresses me a great deal. The very thought of her torments me. I must pay visit to Rosings. I intended to do so on her behalf, I had planned it."

It was time to approach the dinner table. Elizabeth was relieved for the interruption. The subject was strenuous, although necessary. She hoped the dinner conversation would prove less severe. The knowledge of other guests in the house convinced her there were more agreeable subjects to be had.

"Your table is well set; I have enjoyed a most excellent meal," said Mr. Manley.

"I enjoy the luxury of employing one of the finest cooks in these parts. I am fortunate in that respect. Tonight's meal was indeed fine, thanks to the fresh fish provided by our guests."

"As you see, there is not a bit of fish to be had on the plate. It was tasty; the empty plate is a good indication, is it not?" asked Mr. Manley.

Later in the music chamber, the colonel inquired, "What of Georgiana, is she in London, Elizabeth?"

"Aye, staying at Mr. Manley's sister's residence with plans of furthering her education. She is being tutored by a Mr. Sheffield of Horizon Manor."

"Did you know Mr. Sheffield is quite a horseman? He likes to race, enjoys the triumph of the challenge," Mr. Manley added.

The evening ended quietly, with the party retiring to their bedchambers in somber dispositions. When alone, Elizabeth consoled her husband, who now expressed grief of his harshness toward the Colonel earlier.

"My dear, be assured the Colonel is aware of the sensitivity of these subjects. I perceived he was sorry for his remarks. You should not take so seriously those comments made only to provide conversation. The Colonel is a reasonable man; he loves his cousin. Surely he did not expect your reaction; most certainly he was taken aback by it. There is no need to reproach yourself for expressing honourable feelings."

"I confess, I was rather harsh with my words. You know me well enough, Elizabeth; there is no pretence in me to disguise my feeling on the matter."

"I, as well as the Colonel, admire your lack of pretence. I must tell you, having taken the whole of the exchange in, I witnessed the integrity of you both. You were less restrained in expressing your inflexible morality. I daresay the alliance between you both affords you the luxury to express your true implacable sentiments without hesitation."

"The Colonel and I have never had words; I confess I feel less than comforted by the thought of it."

Elizabeth struggled to sit up in the bed. The bolsters were slipping; she soon found herself in an awkward position. Mr. Darcy sprang to his feet to assist, then regained a seat on the edge of the bed. Elizabeth, feeling more comfortable, smiled at him. There was a momentary silence as he took her hand and examined it, gently taking his thumb over her smooth skin. She smiled at him once again, studying his demeanour.

"Being privy to the whole of the discussion, I may say, I perceived the Colonel's determination. Although perhaps less forceful, he held tight to his declaration. I determined his opinion could not be altered where your aunt is concerned. I do believe his true worth is in his unwavering allegiance to his family. The tenderness of feeling where they are concerned is pleasingly evident."

"Yes, I agree, Elizabeth. With the Colonel there is unlimited honesty. I'm glad his opinions are not the wavering kind, even if it means he disagrees with my own."

"His concern for Ann is endearing. I could not help but like him all the more for it."

Mr. Darcy faintly smiled, taking her hand in his again. He looked up at her after a thoughtful moment. "Yes, the Colonel is an excellent man." He slightly chuckled. "I did not think he had it in him. I have never witnessed him so bold, but then, we have never had words."

Elizabeth placed her disengaged hand over his. "I am in awe of your regard for one another's opinions. I especially determined your mutual regard in each allowing the other freedom to express sentiments without restriction or condemnation. I have no doubt the Colonel suffers an equal depth of reflection to all of this."

"I'm sure you are right, Elizabeth; I love and admire your ability to have me censure the sensibility of my actions. You are an excellent creature; I highly esteem you for it."

Joining her in bed, they snuggled together. It did not take long before the happy couple was well into a deep sleep.

It was but two days since the Colonel's arrival. He announced his intention to quit Pemberley to go to Rosings within a few days. He assured them both he would do his best to alter the situation. He expressed a determination to draw his aunt to reason, but Mr. Darcy did not lend any encouragement.

As the days faded, Elizabeth grew stronger, experiencing decreased bouts of lightheadedness and nausea. Dr. Gordon, having visited the day last, believed her to be past the trying period.

When the Colonel was ready to take his leave, Mr. Darcy, joined by his wife, went out of doors to bid him farewell, avoiding those expressions of sentiment with regard to the task he was about to take upon himself. Mr. Bennet planned to depart from Pemberley but would tarry for an additional hour. This was the first Elizabeth had been out of doors in weeks. The air was cool, the sky gray with hovering clouds overhead. It appeared the heavens could open at any moment to unleash torrents of rain. Mr. Darcy hoped his cousin would arrive at Rosings before the inclement weather hindered his journey. When the Colonel disappeared from sight they ventured indoors. Finding she was not tired, nor did she wish to sit, Elizabeth decided she preferred to continue her walk.

"Dearest, will you take a turn about the room with me?"

"If you wish." Before starting their walk, Mr. Darcy turned to Mr. Bennet. "Mr. Bennet, may I ask you to remain another day? I wish to take Mr. Manley about the property on business. It would be a great service to me if you stayed to look after Elizabeth."

"How can I refuse? You may depend on me, Mr. Darcy."

"I thought so; you have my gratitude. I had not thought Elizabeth had sufficient time alone with you. I suspected you needed little encouragement to alter your plans."

Elizabeth studied her husband. Grateful thoughts swept through her mind. She was certain his sensitivity was a testimony of her father finding favour in his view.

Mr. Darcy and Mr. Manley were gone virtually most of the day, returning in the late afternoon. The two stood at the portal.

"God has provided you well, Fitzwilliam; would you not agree?"

"Indeed he has; no man could complain of such a situation. I have wealth and felicity in marriage; soon I will have a child. Such riches are more than the value of the note. Yes, I am in a most favourable position. My father's teachings have served me well. I hope to never fall beneath the principle of his wisdom. My father was all that was benevolent; he was an amiable man with excellent judgment. My employs are good people, deserving of the best. I made you an offer today. I beg you consider it at once; you know my wishes. Mine is an urgent need. I require an answer soon. I am used to having my own way, I must admit. But if you accept, you will not be deprived of anything here other than the bustle of town. Make no mistake, I am an anxious man; I seek an answer soon."

They entered the house in time for dinner, managing an hour in the music chamber before retiring for the evening.

The morning next it rained quite hard, but Mr. Bennet, having already stayed an additional day, thought it best he start for home. Being well aware of her discontentment regarding his private visit to Pemberley, he had no desire to anger his wife further.

"Well now, Lizzy, I set my path to Longbourn. It has been a most interesting visit. I daresay, I don't know when I have enjoyed dinner as well as conversation as I have here—most delightful indeed. And to you, Mr. Darcy, you have been a most gracious host. I don't believe I could have gotten to know you better another time. Do take care of my Lizzy. She has always brought me delight; she's in the best of hands now I see, yes indeed she is."

He kissed Elizabeth good-bye. The gentlemen bowed as they watched him enter the coach. They remained at the threshold until the carriage disappeared down the lane.

Mr. Manley was now the only guest at Pemberley.

Rosings Park

THE COLONEL ARRIVED at Rosings Park late in the afternoon. A nervous Mrs. Jenkinson greeted him with news that Lady Catherine was confined to her bedchamber with fever.

"How ill is she?" questioned the Colonel.

"Very," Mrs. Jenkinson replied, her hands fidgeting. With dark circles about her eyes, she seemed lost as she moved restlessly about, nervously fretting. "She took ill a week ago Sunday. She has not been out of her chamber since. She suffered a violent fever. The doctor did not expect she would be with us today. Although she did quit the fever, she looks very ill. She has made strides in health, but oh, Colonel Fitzwilliam, she has not been herself. It has been very hard, very hard indeed."

"And what of my cousin Ann? Where is she?"

"She is in her chamber. I fear she is deeply troubled, poor thing. I hear her weeping at night. The Collinses don't come for fear of the fever. Mrs. Collins is with child, and so they stay away. Several servants have fallen ill as well. I've been on my own; it has been hard. I'm glad you are come. I asked her ladyship if I was to send word to Mr. Darcy, but she would not hear of it. She became angry when I mentioned his name. Very angry indeed."

"Thank you, I shall go directly to Lady Catherine's chamber, then next to Ann's."

Noticing she shook all over, he lightly touched her arm. "All will be well, I'm here now." He could see a bit of relief in her face. He pitied her; she was an amiable woman, a hard laborer with a quick desire to please. He knew from past visits, Mrs. Jenkinson's services were on frequent demand. It took little imagination to realize the tremendous strain of responsibility no doubt imposed on her by his aunt while ill.

He swiftly moved above the stairs to Lady Catherine's chamber. He knocked on her chamber door before entering.

"Why, Colonel Fitzwilliam, whatever are you doing here? Pray tell me, why have you not sent word of your coming? You know how very much I desire to know these things."

"Yes, I know——" was all he could say before Lady Catherine interrupted him.

"Oh, Colonel, it has been exceedingly dreary here. No one calls or comes when my need is greatest. But I must say I am glad you are come, yes, quite glad."

"Well—I am here now, Aunt."

He detected a certain despair of dependency in her countenance, a quality one was not likely to see in a woman who is used to dictating to others with immense condescension, yet he was interested to learn she was well enough to scold him.

"Come here at once," she ordered.

He pulled a chair to her bedside, taking her hand in his. "What may I do for you?"

"Keep watch on Ann. You know, Colonel, how frail my Ann is. I daresay she requires attention; after all, she is quite incapable of looking after her own interests."

"Yes, it is my intention to go next to Ann's chamber."

He was surprised she was receptive to his offer. For such a large woman, she looked tired and frail. Her usual strong, marked features had sunk deeper still. Although she still gave orders, they were less fierce than normal.

"I'm glad you are come. It has been quiet here. The Collinses stay at Hunsford. We see no one but Mrs. Jenkinson," she lamented. "We rely on her heavily, as you can imagine."

"I can believe it; I saw Mrs. Jenkinson in the entrance hall. She looks worn. I'm here now; had I known, I would have come sooner."

"Yes, I believe you would."

He sat back in the chair, letting go of her hand. A tense silence took over. Suddenly she turned to him. "Have you seen your *cousin*?" she emphasized the latter, as she brought her eyes in tight with a squint.

Surprised she would ask; he gave careful thought before answering. He was sure she meant Darcy. He hesitated; if he were wrong, she would surely be incensed, thought he.

"Which cousin is that, Aunt?"

Her voice elevated with anger. "You know whom I'm referring to!"

This was more like the Lady Catherine he knew. Mrs. Jenkinson was right; she was regaining her health. It's a pity Ann did not inherit her strength, he mused.

"Yes, indeed I have; as a matter of fact, I just quitted Pemberley."

"Well, how does he get on?" There was a pause. "Answer me; do not be so impertinent. How does my nephew do?"

The Colonel, taken aback, sat up straight. He stared at her. He started to speak but stumbled over his lost words. He hesitated before managing to utter, "I—had not expected you to inquire after my cousin, but since you have done so, he is well, very well indeed." He paused, then leaned forward. "Would you like to hear of his wife?"

"I DO NOT! Do not mention that odious woman to me! I will not have her name spoken in this house; I forbid it." Her angry tone peaked; her face snarled making her piercing eyes squint as she glared in his direction. Surely she was on the mend. The turn of her countenance revealed a much livelier woman than first encountered.

"Very well then, I guess you are not interested in any news of Pemberley Hall?"

"No, indeed, I have no interest there; allow me to be justly understood; you will talk of another subject, or you will quit my chamber!"

"Well then, what does the doctor report?"

"I am to get well, no need for anyone to think otherwise. I am surely not engaging thoughts of the undertaker, you may be certain of it."

"Is there anything I may get you?"

"No, Mrs. Jenkinson has been attending me."

"Yes, Mrs. Jenkinson, as I said earlier, appears tired. Has she had any relief?"

"Relief? No indeed. I have great need of her; it is her duty."

"I daresay, it will be of no use to you if Mrs. Jenkinson falls ill. Allow me to stay a few days. Allow me to direct the help to take care of you and Ann so Mrs. Jenkinson may rally her strength. You have other servants to assist; she obviously requires some rest."

"Very well, have it your way. I'm too ill to discuss the matter any further. You will stay then, to be certain?"

"Of course I shall stay. And if you don't mind, after I look in on Ann, I should like very much to visit your library to choose a book to occupy a bit of my time."

"Very well then, be off with you; I am tired; I need my rest."

As Colonel Fitzwilliam entered his cousin's chamber, he was discomposed by his cousin's appearance, finding her more frail than he had ever witnessed.

"Ann, are you unwell?"

"I am well enough," she answered timidly. She seemed uncomfortable in his presence. He was greatly pained by the thought of it.

"What do you do in here alone, Ann? Are you occupied with something?"

"No."

"Have you talked with your mother today?"

"No, the doctor said I may not go to her; I only see Mrs. Jenkinson. But she is much too busy with Mother; she has little time to direct to me."

"May I read to you, Ann?"

"Please do, Cousin."

The Colonel, with triumphant approval, accepted a book of her choosing. He began to read. Her behaviour toward him was everything admirable, though guarded. He could not tolerate this with indifference. He was persuaded that attentiveness along with plenitude of nourishment might speedily boast her spirits or at least sanction a strengthened physical nature. He pitied her. She was frail and backward, lacking the comfort of conversation. I would sacrifice all to be privileged to rescue her from her minuscule existence, thought he.

He realized for the present that he could only delight in her desire to be read to. Amidst his reading, he observed a dim but brightened spirit. Still he fretted for his cousin. Her life consisted of nothing more than sleeping and eating. He judged by her appearance that her daily intake of food was insignificant. She is thinner, definitely paler than I remember, thought he.

His anxiety grew as he sought to conceal his concerns. Overcome by desperate feelings of helplessness, he determined something must be done for her. But I know not what, he pondered unto himself.

Conversation proved difficult. Not wishing to intrude on her lack of knowledge of so many subjects, he was forced to remain assertive in the conversation. It was evident she wholly depended upon those around her to provide secondary information.

Ann's mind strayed from his reading. As she sat quietly, her mind centered on the illness about her. She feared her mother would surely die. Tormented by all such thoughts, she was terrified at the notion of being deserted. She studied the Colonel as he read. His presence gave her a sense of security. She had spent days alone in her chamber, oftentimes speaking to no one. She felt anxious but afraid to express such weakness to her cousin, whom she looked up to.

She thought him everything good and kind. He represented all that she knew as virtuously gallant. Although she always felt a close association with him, this visit seemed strange. Never had he visited in her chamber. She felt awkward now that he was there, yet his presence was no less desired. How strange, thought she, most often he visited along with her cousin Darcy, providing little chance for her to ever speak with the Colonel alone. Even then, her mother was always present. She mused over her cousin Darcy, who rarely spoke to her. Even though he was uniformly kind, she thought him stiff in manner, finding she had grown to fear him. She managed to smile at the Colonel as he finished the story. Once again she directed her attention toward him delicately. She felt spiritually attached to him, yet he was almost as far away from her as a few feet could provide. All such pleasure reclaimed from his attentions were now accepted with more ease. The clock in the hall struck six. Since the Colonel had finished his reading, he excused himself, quitting her chamber, but promising to return directly.

He proceeded below the stairs, requesting a servant bring tea and biscuits to Ann's chamber. When he returned, he noticed she was eager to be in his company. Her manners were childish, yet he was well aware of her age being so near his.

The tea and biscuits were brought in. The Colonel watched as Ann took small bites, believing it would take forever for her to finish.

Following the shared treats, Colonel Fitzwilliam left her for the night. He looked in on his aunt before going to the guest chamber. As he lay upon the bed, his tormented thoughts of his findings at Rosings robbed him of a restful night. He anguished over his cousin's state of health. Although she seemed to have escaped the fever, she was nonetheless in want of improving ambience. His mind, taxed beyond reason, experienced a sense of hopelessness in his desperate desire to restore her to good health.

He lay awake, unable to clear his mind of Ann's meager existence. There were no solutions in his notions, nor could he hope to see her gain an opportunity to escape the clutches of Rosings, whose walls only promised to penetrate the certain doom of her existence. When he finally managed sleep, it was to be at the expense of a nightmarish dream of her demise, causing him to awaken in a cold sweat. He sat on the end of the bed with his face buried in his hands. He wept at the thought of her frailty. Since it was too early an hour to rise, he lay quietly awaiting a glimpse of light to appear in the window. He neared the wash basin, cupping his hands to put water to his face. Two hours passing only proved to instill desperate feelings with regards to her rescue. How could he achieve this? He once again lay his head upon the bolster, relenting to a shallow sleep until the bleak light of dawn woke him. Although it was morning, it proved dark and dreary, as torrents of rain soaked the ground. It was just as well to be indoors, thought he.

Mrs. Jenkinson delivered breakfast. The shared breakfast lent opportunity to ensure Ann received nourishment. He noted she ate almost everything on her plate, attributing it to her having someone to share it with. "Ann, do you remember when we were children? Darcy and I would visit. We had fun playing hide and seek, did we not?"

"Surely you remember I was not permitted to play; I was only to watch."

"Yes, that is right. I'm so sorry I mentioned it, Ann."

"That's quite all right, Cousin, I rather enjoyed watching you play. You both took pleasure in amusing me. I remember the times you performed parlour theatricals; you designed the whole of it. It was no doubt silly, but I fancied it just the same. You both did quite well at acting; I thought you very good."

"Why yes, Ann, I had forgotten all about it. I believe Darcy was once a hunter. Indeed, yes, I was the beast acting out the hunt."

"I remember when my Aunt and Uncle Darcy would visit with Fitzwilliam and Georgiana. Georgiana was but an infant. I believe you and Darcy were about ten or eleven. The whole of your family visited then, you as well as your brothers. You were once scolded for calling our cousin 'Fritz.' Lady Darcy was very angry; do you recall it?"

The Colonel chuckled. "Indeed I do; I was punished for doing it a second time. How wonderful of you to remember; I had forgotten. I shall have to ask Darcy of his recollection. Those were such happy times; indeed they were."

"How is my cousin?"

"Oh, Ann—dare—I tell you Darcy is the happiest of men? He has a wife he loves deeply. Dare I tell you she is with child? Does such language distress you?"

"Do not reproach yourself on my account, Cousin. Nay, I am relieved he is well settled. I shall always wish him well. Cousin, will you tell him that when you see him next; will you promise to do so?"

"Yes, indeed I shall, to be sure. I am certain such news will add to his felicity. To learn you bear no ill thoughts can only bring relief. Understanding the arrangement made for you both as infants, I am comforted by your amiable remarks."

"I should not have wanted to marry Darcy; I have grown fearful of him. He very rarely spoke to me when he visited; I have always thought him stiff in manners. His looks are cross, but you have always been of a different disposition; you have a more tender nature, such that I have never reason to fear."

"Ann, you must not judge Darcy ill. Do not form a harsh opinion of your cousin. He has always been concerned of you, but feared to express it for the weight of the commitment your mother held over him. He never sought to injure you. His remote manner is a form of refuge, although I daresay it is in his nature to be reserved. But that is the way with Darcy. I do know he did not desire your mother to continue with the promise his mother made with her. Although Darcy is a very complicated fellow, he is direct with the truth of his feelings. He no doubt feared any expression regarding the promise would injure you. He is good, indeed he is; you must believe me. He is the best of men, in spite of his reserved, starched manner. He often spoke of you when we visited. He wished there was something to be done for you, but never desiring to give false encouragement, he retreated instead. He often expressed sorrow for having felt he slighted you. I know the pain he suffered on many an occasion over his inability to convert your mother's overprotection of you. Each attempt by him was only taken as further proof that he was contemplating his future, forcing him to distance himself from the promise as well as you. Your mother heard nothing she did not wish to hear. Fear him not, he is perfectly amiable, kind and everything that is wholly good. When in the confines of his beloved Pemberley, he is not stiff or rigid, quite the opposite in fact. He does love you, Ann, but he is in love with Elizabeth."

"Cousin, I do love Darcy, but I do not believe I should have ever found felicity wed to him. I am not so devoid of feelings that I would wish to spend the rest of my life married to a man who preferred someone more suitable to his nature. I really have not the feeling for my cousin as I ought to have had to enter a wedded state. I was readily relieved upon hearing of his nuptials. When he married, it ended my uneasiness of the commitment. I regret not having had the courage to tell my mother that I did not desire the planned union. Truthfully, I feared I would have been forced to marry against my own wishes. So you see, Cousin, I am not in the least injured; I do truly wish them happy."

His mind raced to digest her words. Amazed by her revelation, he suddenly realized she must have been tormented by the arrangement. Now believing she suffered a vast deal by the very thought of it, he felt sorrow for the pain she endured in silence. Her description of her being forced to wed without the firmness of will to voice her opinion haunted him. He said no more on the subject.

"I'm glad to hear this, Ann; I shall go to visit your mother now. We shall talk later, if that is to your liking."

"I look forward to it, Cousin."

He quitted the chamber with satisfactory thoughts of her revealed secret, but remained astonished by her honest expression. That is the most conversation he had ever had with her now that she had grown. He felt hard pressed to do something for her before he departed Rosings, but had no inclination what it could be. To this, he would have to give some thought. He made his way to his aunt's chamber. She was sitting up, having just breakfasted. Mrs. Jenkinson was about to depart the bedchamber.

"Good morning, Lady Catherine; good morning, Mrs. Jenkinson; it is not fit weather for anyone to be out of doors."

He reclaimed the chair he used the day last, once again nearing it to her bedside. She was quite annoyed looking, he thought, but, nonetheless, he ventured to speak.

"Well, I trust you slept well."

"Where have you been? I thought you would have visited me before this." Her demanding voice indicated she was insulted.

"I had breakfast with Ann, we talked; I suppose we gave no thought to time."

"And what did you discuss?"

"We discussed our visits as boys when the Darcys and Fitzwilliams all converged upon Rosings at once. Ann reminded me of a funny event, but not so very funny then I imagine." He chuckled trying to make light amidst her negative disposition.

"And what event might that have been?"

"Do you remember when Lady Darcy became rather angry upon my calling Fitzwilliam 'Fritz'? I was scolded the first time I was caught, but when I was found out the second time, I was abruptly punished. Do you remember it?"

Lady Catherine sat forward excitedly. "Why—yes, you were punished; it was so; indeed, I do remember. She did not take your provocation lightly. Your mother and father were embarrassed; they were highly vexed when you did it a second time." Lady Catherine could not help but chuckle remembering the circumstances. "Indeed I do remember," she replied while leaning back into the pile of bolsters she had Mrs. Jenkinson place behind her.

"That was long ago; your little boys are men now. I daresay we loved to visit this house with all its grandeur; it was so lively then. We had so many wonderful hiding places. Those were pleasant days; were they not, Lady Catherine?"

"Yes, they were, now it is lonely. I have not been out of this chamber. Poor Ann is so sickly. We have so few visitors at Rosings," she said with a look of despair.

"Well, Lady Catherine, I am here now."

"Indeed you are, my dear nephew, how good of you. Your cousin's visits I miss. I could always count on his visits; you being with the redcoats, I never know where you are or when I shall see you next. But Darcy—I could always depend on him. What is a poor old aunt to do? What say you about this unhappy situation?"

"Pemberley is lively enough these days."

"Yes, I have no doubt of it. Are the shades fully drawn to hide the shame?"

Her harsh, indignant words caused him anguish. He felt torn, but his loyalty to his cousin remained unwavering. "No, the shades are not drawn, but there is much excitement there. Do you wish to know the most recent news?"

"What is there to tell?"

"Pray aunt, I cannot tell; it has to do with his wife. Since I am ordered not to mention her name, I suppose it is of little matter to you what concerns her." The Colonel deliberately spoke cautiously, watching for a reaction.

"What are you about? Tell me; I want to know."

"I cannot tell lest I mention her name. Do I have your permission?" he daringly teased. Much to his surprise, she did not scold him. She struggled hard to show no reaction, but he could plainly see her curiosity piqued.

"Very well then, if it is your wish, I'll allow you to tell me."

He paused, staring at her for a moment. "Elizabeth is with child; that is the news. I have something further to tell you if you will hear it."

"Humph, with child! He forgot what he owed to his family. I see what you are about. You try to entice me into talking to your cousin. Well I won't hear of it; I certainly will not. Know this, Colonel, I am wise to such trickery. I see through your conniving coyness; you have to get up early in the morning to pull one over on your old aunt. So there, thought you could fool me did you? Humph! Your cousin made his choice; I no longer wish to concern myself with him."

"Very well," said the Colonel, as he arose from the chair.

"You come directly back here; do not try my patience further. I'll not stand for this kind of behaviour."

He sat down. Determined to make her question him, he said not a word. The deafening silence unnerved her. "I demand you tell me what you alluded to earlier."

"I believe my cousin to miss his aunt, but he was determined to allow you to cut him out forever."

"What do you mean, was determined? Am I to believe you have talked to him regarding his absurd choice of a wife? Well—did you show him the error of his ways?"

"Indeed not, not I. I can assure you, Lady Catherine, nothing of the sort was said. I visited Pemberley upon invitation before coming here. I found your nephew in deep felicity. I assure you he is very much settled. I daresay I approve of his choice of a wife."

His frank statements startled her. He was glad he spoke with forced directness.

Her lips parted upon hearing his stern expression. She swiftly sat up, staring directly at him with stunned surprise. Never had she known the Colonel to be direct with her, much less with the force he had just displayed. She gave him a curious look.

Feeling a certain air of triumph in her reaction, he felt satisfied to gain her full attention. He deliberately continued to eye her directly. But it did not take long for Lady Catherine to gain full control of her emotions. Her applied remark was delivered with the same swiftness of her now forgotten surprise at his directness. "Bah, deep felicity indeed, with that odious woman? Your cousin is a fool."

He started to get up, but once again she protested against it. Her affection for his cousin was, as always, obvious, as was her curiosity, which was now getting the better of her.

"I want to know of your visit there. What are you concealing? I must know."

"I shall only tell you if you promise to not interrupt me further."

Lady Catherine lay back, uniting her lips in somber silence. With a controlled voice she carefully answered, "Very well, if you insist."

"As I stated earlier, your unwillingness to accept your nephew's correspondence made him determined to allow you to cut him out forever. His wife, Elizabeth, will not hear of it. It is through her influential persuasion, her perseverance, that he has weakened his steadfast position."

He noticed she raised her brows at the mention of Elizabeth's name, but was equally satisfied she did not interrupt. He drew his chair closer, leaned in to her with a meek smile. "Lady Catherine, I am deeply concerned. This sort of behaviour on both your parts can only bring further injury, resulting in irrefutable damage. However hard this is to hear, you know Darcy would never have encountered such a marriage had he not the deepest affection for her. You know him full well. Do not comment when I tell you she is a very good person, both honourable and kind. She seeks to extend that kindness to you and Ann."

The Colonel noticed Lady Catherine leaned slightly forward. He stopped his discourse. She parted her lips as if to make a comment, but lay back into the pillow.

The Colonel continued, "You insulted her directly, then again through offensive language to my cousin in your written word. Is not this good reason for any woman to settle for estrangement? She cannot, because that is the goodness in her. She cannot help to whom she was born. She did not set out to make my cousin endear himself to her. Quite the contrary, he proposed while she was at Hunsford; she rejected him."

Lady Catherine instantaneously sat forward. Her expression turned puzzled, then cold. Uniting her brows, she looked at him with a cold stare. Her lips seemed to tighten. She found herself momentarily at a loss for words. "Rejected him? My nephew, she rejected my nephew; by what means?" Her voice turned soberly baffled. "So that was the business with your cousin before he quitted Rosings. He was greatly anguished; I thought problems on his estate or perhaps Georgiana troubled him. He would not allow me to pry into his affairs. He became irritable with my inquiry. Humph, she rejected him; how dare she! Humph!"

"Whatever the reason, she refused to stand up with him; it was irrecoverably settled by her. My cousin suffered the severest anguish. Overcome by the rejection, he was distraught by her rebuff; therefore, he quitted Rosings. He could no longer stand to be so near to her. But he soon learned distance only brought him agony of the acutest kind. Later, when you told him of your visit to Longbourn, telling him Elizabeth gave no satisfaction to your confrontation, you afforded him hope. You alone are responsible for his continuing pursuit. You must admit, Lady Catherine, he has a high regard of her to confess his feelings a second time. He dared to ask for her hand once again. He is like his father. I need not tell you how noble a gentleman he was; he was very much the same—proud, very proud indeed."

"Humph," was all he heard.

"You rest now, I should like to look in on Ann," the Colonel said, returning the chair to its proper position. He quitted the bedchamber, leaving Lady Catherine alone with her thoughts. He experienced certain satisfaction in his revelation. He delighted in the knowledge of her curiosity, which forced her to listen. Perhaps he would stay for a few days additionally, at least for Ann's sake, if nothing else.

The few days next were uneventful, except for the talks he had with his cousin.

For Ann, the days represented cherished moments with her welcomed visitor, in spite of the fact her mother lay ill. She looked forward to seeing him each day, anticipating his telling her of her mother's state. She gladly dined with him, delighting in his lively conversations. He was free to tell her of places he had been as well as people he knew. Seldom did she enjoy a conversation so wholly and completely for her alone. She sat at his side as he talked, imagining herself in the places he talked of.

The Colonel took pleasure in his visits with Ann. He thought she looked brightened and improved in colour. He ate his meals with her to assure she was taking in food.

With little thought to it, he had an impulsive plan on this particular morning. Without hesitation or regard, he set out to make it work.

"Ann, if your mother approves, would you like to visit Pemberley with me?"

Ann jumped to her feet with a look of horror overspreading her face. Her lips parted with disbelief, inducing her to draw her hand to cover her mouth, releasing a gasp. "Oh, cousin, my mother should never approve of it; I dare not mention it."

"No need to, I shall. Have you any objection?"

"No indeed, but you should think the better of it; my mother can be mean tempered. I should not want to cross her. Presently, she is very unhappy with our cousin. I daresay I would not mention such a notion."

"Well then, it is settled; I shall approach her."

He stayed with her a while longer, then excusing himself, he quitted the chamber in search of Mrs. Jenkinson.

"Mrs. Jenkinson, come into the library; I must speak with you."

"Very good, sir."

"I must beg your assistance."

She hesitantly agreed to listen to his plan with understanding. She consented to discharge his request with fearful reservation. He waited in the library, impatiently paging through a book until Mrs. Jenkinson came below the stairs, granting him a nervous nod. He waited a half-hour before making his way above the stairs to Lady Catherine's bedchamber, taking a deep breath to collect his thoughts before entering. After placing a chair at her bedside, he studied her intently. "How are you feeling?" he asked with inscrutable meditation amid severe concern.

"Very ill, I am very ill today; I had a much better day yesterday. Mrs. Jenkinson said I look sickly and drawn. She determined I am warm. She fears the fever is returning. Mrs. Jenkinson is concerned for Ann; the doctor warned to keep her a distance from me. I fear she will come down with the fever. You know how frail my poor Ann is. If she were to get the fever, she would surely die. Mrs. Jenkinson is to acquire further help, she says she feels rather poorly. She thinks she may be coming down with the fever. Half of the household staff has fallen ill. Perhaps you should not be here."

Colonel Fitzwilliam stood up. He placed his hand on his aunt's forehead. Furnishing her a troubled look, he regained his seat, taking her hand in his to tenderly pat it. Drawing his chair still nearer, he leaned his body toward her, studying her tenaciously once again. She could not escape his troubled look. "I do believe you are rather warm. Perhaps I should require Mrs. Jenkinson send for the physician."

"I've already asked Mrs. Jenkinson to send for the doctor."

"I am concerned for my cousin Ann; she is much thinner, paler, even weaker looking than usual. I fear it is a risk for her to be down the hall from you. I will go below the stairs now to await the doctor. I would be very interested to converse with him."

He carefully returned the chair to its proper place. Glancing down at her again, he shook his head in somber meditation before quitting the chamber.

Directing himself below the stairs, he sought Mrs. Jenkinson. Approaching her, he smiled with a bit of relief, "Thank you Mrs. Jenkinson, I need to see the doctor immediately when he arrives. I will need to talk with him privately before he views my aunt. Will you see to it?"

"Yes, Colonel Fitzwilliam, but what if her ladyship finds out? She will be angry for certain. You know her temperament, Colonel," a very nervous Mrs. Jenkinson lamented.

"Do not concern yourself, Mrs. Jenkinson. There will be no blame to place in your direction to be sure. Just say you will have me see the doctor when he arrives."

"Yes, Colonel, of course. I shall do as you ask."

When the doctor arrived, Mrs. Jenkinson directed him to the library. Colonel Fitzwilliam closed the door. He proceeded to face his aunt's doctor.

Dr. Pounder was a portly man, long past middle age, with no hair atop of his head. He was extensively well dressed, with an imposing blinding-white collar. He carried a fancy walking stick, well carved with a golden ornate knob. He had a genteel air about him. In a burst of confidence he addressed the Colonel. "I believe you are Lady Catherine's nephew?"

"Yes sir, I am."

"I have been her physician for many years. I am well acquainted with the ills of your aunt and cousin."

"Yes, so I understand," replied the Colonel rather nervously.

"Well, young man, out with it. I have little time to waste. If you wish to speak with me, I suggest you do so now."

Although the Colonel stumbled for words, he managed to express his concerns for Ann in a most convincing manner. Dr. Pounder intently listened with sympathy. He was in full agreement with the Colonel.

"Indeed, I told Lady Catherine years ago Miss de Bourgh is quite capable of carrying on as other girls; however, I did suggest she curtail some strenuous activities. Although she may not be as hardy as most girls, she is capable of enduring much, if given the chance. I too have been concerned of her present condition for some time. This nonsense to confine her has reduced her to a weakened state, making her frail. She is weak; anyone may see that, except perhaps your aunt. I do believe she suffers melancholy, but your aunt is not to be persuaded otherwise. I fear I judge your cousin surely marked for certain doom if she does not escape the confines of this suffocating existence."

This was just what the Colonel needed to hear. He no longer felt nervous. He was quick to impose on the good doctor by requesting he embellish the truth to do service to Ann. He made known his scheme to the doctor, who thought it was a capital idea, if he could manage to get away with it. He quickly agreed to assist him using his influential professional opinion. He wished the Colonel luck, then quitted the library with a grin overspreading his face. Colonel Fitzwilliam watched the doctor disappear above the stairs. He patiently awaited his descent. Some five and twenty minutes later, Dr. Pounder came to the entrance hall. In passing the Colonel, he paused to wink, then tipped his hat before continuing on his way. The Colonel, now realizing the remainder was up to him, immediately went above the stairs to his aunt's bedchamber.

"Lady Catherine, what report did the doctor give?"

"Oh, Colonel, I am not well; indeed it is true, the doctor fears the fever is coming back. He said it would be unwise for Ann to stay at Rosings. Stand back, Dr. Pounder said you should not be here. He says Ann's constitution could not hold up with a fever. He is concerned for her safety. He asked if she could be sent away. The doctor is sending someone to help Mrs. Jenkinson, he fears she has been exposed to me too long and has the fever as well. He requires bed rest for her. You must leave this house at once. Take Ann with you; see that she is well taken care of."

"But, Lady Catherine, surely you know I have no place of my own. My father's house is fully occupied at present. He is entertaining a large party from the north of London. The only place I can conceive to take Ann would be to Pemberley. I know that is out of the question; you will not allow it."

Lady Catherine appeared nervous. All traces of confidence seemed to escape her. She was wholly and completely dependent upon him.

"Yes, yes, I had not counted on such a fever. I have no recourse but to allow you take Ann to Pemberley. Darcy will take care of her; I am certain of it. At this very moment, I have no desire to fret over trivial matters of the discontented situation. How irrelevant it all seems in the face of death; surely you can plainly see that, can you not? You must go, make haste, take Ann; leave this house at once. Do not stand there wasting time, make haste, make haste!"

"Very well, as you wish. We shall leave at once. I will send you word express from Pemberley of our arrival. Lady Catherine, I bid you good-bye."

But before he could entirely quit her chamber, she called to him, "Tell my dear Ann she takes my heart with her. She best not come near my chamber door before she departs. What shall I do without my Ann? Take care of her Colonel. Tell your cousin it is his duty to the family to see that she is well looked after. Lord, if I should be fortunate enough to live to see tomorrow. Go, go, make haste; it is imperative you quit Rosings this very moment. Leave me to this wretched fever, come what will. And tell your cousin, if anything should happen to me, he is to see to it that Ann is well looked after, for I depend upon him. He owes it to the family to grant my wishes. "

"Very well, I shall do as you wish; I will take my leave now."

Satisfaction overtook his countenance, his suspicions were right on the mark; her love for Ann was greater then her distaste for Elizabeth Darcy. He hastened to Ann's chamber with her maidservant, quickly closing the door behind him. She was startled by his swiftness, causing her to become alarmed.

"What is it, Cousin?"

"Dear Cousin, do not be concerned. Promise to ask me no questions at present; there is no time. You must gather some clothing; we depart for Pemberley directly. Tell your maidservant what you wish to take. We must leave here at once, make haste. We have little time, you must hurry." As he spoke, his eyes examined the chamber.

"Very well, Cousin, I should have a trunk brought up."

"No time for that. Have your garments gathered in the middle of the bedclothes. I shall tie them up. Hurry Ann, there is no time to waste. I must run below the stairs to Mrs. Jenkinson; I shall return directly."

Ann was frightened. Although she trusted the Colonel wholly and completely, he did not seem himself. Never had she witnessed him in such haste. By nature, he was a careful planner. She feared his actions were not rational. For a brief moment, it occurred to her that perhaps he had been stricken by the fever as well. She quickly decided to push such thoughts aside, convincing herself she would allow him to be in total control. She proceeded to do as he asked. With the help of her maidservant she managed to gather her garments.

He descended the stairs, taking two steps at one time. Upon locating Mrs. Jenkinson, he hastened her to the library, shutting the door behind them. He related to Mrs. Jenkinson the plan, appealing for her secrecy.

"Do not worry, the good doctor intends to return with a person, unbeknownst to Lady Catherine, to remain here at Rosings. He will be requesting that you do not go in her ladyship's bedchamber until your own fever is cured."

"But—Colonel, I have no fever, I am exhausted that is all."

"Indeed you have a fever, Mrs. Jenkinson. Dr. Pounder told Lady Catherine you must be sent to your bedchamber. I suggest you take this opportunity to get the rest you have been lately deprived of. You see, Mrs. Jenkinson, it is all as I planned. You will have no part in it. You must keep this to yourself; you must not educate the other servants. Stay to your chamber; allow yourself time at leisure. I suggest you find other matters to concern yourself with. I am off to Pemberley with Ann. We have Lady Catherine's blessing. What say you to that?"

"Oh, Colonel, if her ladyship were to ever find out, I should surely suffer her scorn. I do believe you have the best intentions. I will take heed of Doctor Pounder; I will follow his precise instructions. But I have my reservations, to be sure. Her ladyship is a very sharp woman; I rather doubt she will be convinced for any length of time. If you are discovered, she will never forgive you the mockery. Oh, Colonel, the vengeance of her scorn!"

"Dear Mrs. Jenkinson, this is the only hope for Ann. I need you to do exactly as planned. Come now, what say you?"

"Fear not, Colonel Fitzwilliam, I will do as you say. Pray, take care of Miss Ann; she is indeed a dear sweet child. I do worry so for her welfare. I suppose I must do as you say; yes, I will to be certain. I will keep this unto my own self as you have requested;, you need not worry on my account."

She faintly smiled, staring at him. She paused, continuing to fidget with her fingers. "I'm to have a fever, am I. Well, so be it. I shall welcome the bed rest." She fidgeted, then faintly smiled nervously, exhibiting a bit of relief. "You may be assured of my concealment."

"You are very good, Mrs. Jenkinson. Now I suggest you go to your bedchamber. Tend to that fever you have this very instant; wait no longer, be off with you."

"The best to you and Miss Ann, Colonel. I shall think of you often."

"Aye, Mrs. Jenkinson, I am sure you will." Patting her arm, he winked, then quitted her presence, leaving a nervous Mrs. Jenkinson to carry out his instructions.

He had one of the servants bring Lady Catherine's carriage around as well as his own horse. He ran above the stairs taking swift, wide strides. He tied Ann's clothing in the bed coverings, then hurried her below the stairs. Moments after the footman guided her into the carriage, they were moving in the direction of Pemberley.

"Dear Cousin Ann, Darcy is sure to be delighted to see you. A shock it will no doubt be. I had wished to send a message, but had not the time. He will surely be astonished; I confess I can hardly wait to see his reaction. This will be a welcomed relief for you, Ann. I am certain Elizabeth will afford you much kindness. I'm sure it is so; she is very good, yes indeed, you shall see for yourself. This is like an adventure; is it not now? If you get tired, you may wish to consider this side of the carriage to lean your head on my arm. It has all happened so quickly, I can scarce believe we are on our way to Derbyshire. I do hope, Ann, that you see the favour to you in all of this. I do hope you do not reproach me for this in the coming days. Tell me, Ann, are you feeling quite well? Are you at ease?"

He talked with nervous chatter. She just stared at him. She was well aware the Colonel was not his usual self; she still feared he was ill.

She hesitated, continuing her stare of him. "Thank you, Cousin, will you tell me now; does my mother know where I am gone?"

"Oh yes, she knows you are gone. She knows you are on the road to Pemberley. What's more, you have her blessing to do so. Now what do you say of that?"

His speech puzzled Ann. He spoke with the confidence of a conqueror. She had no understanding of what he was about. She found his words hard to believe. She had never known the Colonel to falsify anything, yet this seemed so absurd. She could not comprehend her mother giving her blessing, nor could she imagine her sending her off to Pemberley. Surely there would have to be an explanation for all of this, if it were truth, thought she. She hesitated, then answered him.

"If you say it is so, Cousin, I have no reason not to consider it true. It has been years since I visited the Derbyshire estate. I saw my cousin often, but always when he granted us visits at Rosings. I shall be happy to see it again. Cousin, are you unwell; are you certain my mother has given her blessing?"

"I am perfectly well. I assure you, Ann, your mother has complete knowledge of it."

Although he felt satisfied with his accomplishment, he began to feel guilty where Ann was concerned. Deciding it was only proper that she should be aware of the whole of it, he spent the remainder of the journey telling her how he brought it about, holding nothing to himself. He delicately enlightened her how Doctor Pounder claimed her capable of doing many things, explaining it was his wish to see her expend herself while at Pemberley. He encouraged her to draw strength from this visit. He motivated her to take advantage of this time to do those things she often desired to do but was prohibited doing by the limitations placed upon her. He spoke directly of Doctor Pounder's concerns for her welfare being presently more of a concern than her mother's illness.

"I'm not sure I understand," she said with a perplexed look about her face.

"Ann, let me be frank; Dr. Pounder has been concerned of your health for many years. He found reasoning with your mother a trying task of little success. Dr. Pounder told me he has never successfully been able to make your mother understand that in her determination to shield you from activity, affliction and exercise, she has made you weak and sickly. He exhausted every means he knew to convince her you have the capability to do what other girls your age are doing."

She stared as she listened. Her face gave no expression. He grew concerned. "Ann, I fear I have injured you; I do not wish it so; it is a matter of your mother loving you so very much. It is her desire to protect you from the world, as you are all she had left once your father died. Unknowingly, she has put your well-being at risk, the very deed she tried to avert. Ann, I beg you to try to do a little more each day to make yourself strong while at Pemberley; this is imperative if you are to gain strength. I beg your forgiveness in tricking your mother. I must tell you, your mother is in health. In fact, she suffers no feverish tendencies, but has been made to believe it is so. Do you forgive me, Ann, for the foolery I have placed at Rosings?"

"Oh, Cousin, I fear you have done all of this for me; it is so, is it not?"

"Yes, Ann, my intentions are your well-being alone. Do you forgive me?"

"Yes, Colonel, but I fear if you are discovered, I shall never see you again."

"I have no concern for myself, although to speak the truth, I believe I should shrivel up and die if I could never see you again, Ann. In my heart I know it is a possibility, but it is a risk I had to take. Although it would be to my sorrow, I would gladly give up ever seeing you again if it meant you were well and strong like other girls. Is that not worth the risk? Tell me you agree; I need your consent. Please tell me you see it is for the best."

As she agreed, she moved herself to his side of the carriage to lean against him for rest as he had earlier suggested. She snuggled up against him, linking her arm through his. Titillation raced through his body as his pulse elevated by her unification. He had not expected to feel overwhelmed by her nearness. Perhaps it was the course of events along with the freedom he felt, which now inspired feelings of protectiveness, thought he. Overwhelmed with satisfaction of her understanding, he further believed she possessed a certain confidence in him. He continued to assure himself that she fully trusted his judgment. Ann had not been free to express herself to any other than her mother for years. Such a severe separation from her was rare. He wondered if she had ever been separated from her for more than a few hours. It was his utmost desire this risk would not be in vain. He was determined to see success in his scheme. But feelings of discomfort soon came over him once he had time to consider the fact that he was not as a rule accustomed to taking risks. In fact, never in the whole of his life had he done anything so irrational or hasty, nor was he accustomed to plan anything without thorough consideration of the consequences. On the contrary, his decisions were always based on careful planning.

She remained at his side with overspread feelings of safety. He had always provided her with a sense of his caring; his loyalty to her was constant. She experienced a level of guilt for her desire to be with him, rather than with her mother; yet this was like an adventure she took delight in.

As she slept at his side, he found he had too much time to himself to think. He began apprehensively to wonder where all this would lead. There was certain sadness about the present situation and circumstances, thought he. But still he could not help but feel an unequivocal amount of triumph in such a scheme. His task appeared successful, at least for the moment.

Pemberley's Most Unusual Visitor

WITH ENCOURAGEMENT from Mr. Darcy, Mr. Manley planned to spend the day going about the property on his own, expecting to return in time for dinner. He departed shortly after having breakfasted, leaving Mr. Darcy at Pemberley Hall with his wife.

During the late hours of the morning, Elizabeth was in the music chamber with Mr. Darcy when she thought she heard an approaching carriage. Nearing the window, she peered out, but saw nothing. She stood quietly for a time, listening for the sound of the horse's hooves. Suddenly, there it was, a very large carriage making the clearing. "There is a very large carriage just through the clearing; I wonder who it could be. Are you expecting a visitor?"

Mr. Darcy turned his book over. "None I am aware of."

"Dearest, I am not certain, but I believe it is Lady Catherine's carriage."

As he neared the window, the carriage was approaching the front of Pemberley Hall. His voice turned soberly cold. "Yes, indeed it is Lady Catherine's carriage; we had better see what this is about." Taking wide-sweeping strides, he guided her through the chamber with a stern look about him.

"Now, dearest, you must promise to be civil."

"I will not risk upsetting you, but you can hardly expect me to rejoice; whatever can she be doing here?" he replied with greater annoyance as he walked at a faster pace.

Elizabeth's mind raced with each stride. She hoped Lady Catherine had come to make amends, but knew that wasn't likely. Her ladyship was a hard woman whose harsh opinions could not easily be transformed. She was certain Lady Catherine had not enough time to forget the injury imposed on Ann. She was equally convinced that her ladyship held her at fault for having robbed Ann of the intended marriage. She was well aware Lady Catherine viewed her as a woman who lacked fortune, family or proper connections. Such thoughts caused her head to pound, but she dared not say so. Alarming her husband was not a risk she cared to consider. His disposition was ungracious at present, no doubt because the visit was unannounced, she convinced herself. His rigidity of expression magnified. She could plainly see his mind raced with uneasy anticipation. He was caught off guard, leaving him totally unprepared to deal with Lady Catherine. As he walked with powerful force, his passionate anger increased. Only once had Elizabeth witnessed this look. It was that awful day at Hunsford when she rejected his proposal. She knew how extremely direct he could be in the face of adversity. Knowing Lady Catherine was of the same disposition was of little or no comfort to her. She had experienced her malicious behaviour at Longbourn. She viewed her perseverance to be an equal match to that of her husband's. The vast difference between the two was that he was generous, honourable and used good sense along with an openness of mind, while she, on the other hand, was more selfish, crass, condescending, simple minded and very unlikely to yield. One thing was certain: she considered them an equal match. Both would remain steadfast in their convictions toward her. By now, Mr. Darcy realized he was hurrying Elizabeth. He regained partial composure, slowing his strides on her behalf. They reached the door as the carriage was nearing a full stop. Mr. Darcy threw his shoulders back, then, placing his hand across his chest, he inhaled before he gave a nod to the servant to advance toward the carriage. Together they stepped forward to greet his unsolicited guest.

Mr. Darcy, still in a state of disbelief that his aunt would come all the way to Pemberley, was angered for not knowing her purpose or being forewarned. He did nothing to conceal his angry disposition, as Elizabeth thought he ought to; instead his expression grew austere.

Elizabeth watched her husband, fearing his anticipated reaction to the visitor. His clenched jaw did not escape her observation. She gripped his arm with greater force, but he did not seem to notice. He was determined his aunt would not upset his wife, nor would she be allowed to further offend him with rude opinions. He would not have this on his property. He had the mindset of the upper hand, believing her to be determined to unleash her scorn.

"Unquestionably, it is my aunt's carriage. We shall receive her together. If she means to speak with me, she will see my wife as well. She will conduct herself in a civil manner to my liking, or I shall instruct the driver to turn the carriage about. Indeed, she will be quitting Pemberley as swiftly as she arrived."

His voice soured with icy tones consumed with sarcastic determination. With premature anger, he stood tensely at the threshold waiting for the carriage door to open. The dismal constant rain only added further gloom to the uninvited situation. The carriage door swung open. To their shock, out stepped Colonel Fitzwilliam.

"Good day to you, Cousin. I daresay, a dampened day it is at that. I bring you a visitor, one very anxious to enjoy your company; you may be sure of it. She means to stay at length, a fortnight at the very least. Your man must take care of my horse. We must send the carriage back to Rosings tomorrow after the team has rested. The parcels will have to be brought in as well."

Colonel Fitzwilliam faced them with a widespread grin. His joyful voice sung in the atmosphere, almost like a chant, but full of playful sentiments. He continued his tantalizing smile, realizing they had absolutely no understanding of his folly.

Now perplexed, Mr. Darcy looked at his wife. They stood in a stunned state, unable to speak. They knew not what to expect. This certainly seemed a strange affair.

Colonel Fitzwilliam held out his hand to help his rider exit the carriage. To their astonishment, it was Ann. Rather shyly, she too now stood before them.

Ann suddenly felt strangely disoriented. It had been years since she visited Pemberley. The presence of her cousin Darcy frightened her. She scarcely glanced up. His alarming towering stature caused her to suddenly shrink back nearer the Colonel, disappearing behind him.

"However did you manage to bring Ann here? What have you done with my aunt?"

Mr. Darcy's sober, angry voice scared Ann. She kept a watchful eye on him. Although he faintly smiled in her direction, it did little to comfort her. Elizabeth represented a different demeanour. Ann found her smile welcoming, which afforded her a bit of ease, but not enough to halt her anxiety entirely.

"In due time, in due time, Cousin. Say hello to your cousin Ann. She is most happy to visit here; she looks forward to her stay."

"Of course, welcome Ann, it is good to have you here," Mr. Darcy said, looking down at her. She seemed small as she shrunk away from him. "How are you feeling? It has been quite some time since you visited Pemberley. Be assured we are delighted to see you."

She blushed, saying not a word, as she shrunk back shyly, drawing her arms inward.

"Ann had a message for you, Darcy, but now she may deliver it herself. Now is not the time I think, perhaps later she will apprise you."

Mr. Darcy gave nod to his man to care for the horses, then ordered the carriage to be returned to Rosings the day next. Mr. Darcy, still in a perplexed state, entered the house. He assisted Ann with her damp wrap, handing it over to the servant.

"Well, Cousin," Mr. Darcy said, "pray tell me what this is about. Have you taken leave of your senses? Does Lady Catherine know of Ann's whereabouts? Does she know her carriage is at Pemberley?"

"Darcy, we are famished; we have not eaten. I refuse to answer any questions until my hunger has been satisfied."

"Pray tell me, Cousin, what is this about? You wear my patience thin."

"But did not I say that I will tell all after we have been fed?"

"Very well." Mr. Darcy nodded to the servant. Although it was short notice, the cook managed to delight them with some cold ham, salad and drink.

Mr. Darcy viewed the Colonel impatiently. He looked at Elizabeth, then to his cousins. His looks were stern, his carriage upright, as he sat staring, waiting for the Colonel's laggard explanation. It was obvious to Mr. Darcy the Colonel was well pleased with himself. He thought him to display a sense of egotistical satisfaction. Aggravated and unable to remain silent any longer, he stated, "I demand to know the details that brought all this about. Quit this folly at once! Enlighten me with regard to the nature of your business. My patience grows short; I daresay your tarrying angers me greatly."

Elizabeth noticed Ann could not eat. She determined her husband's angry words frightened her. Ann's eyes widened as she trembled. Her eyes searched from one cousin to the other. Finally, she hung her head. Elizabeth believed she was about to cry. Providing her husband a long stare, she leaned close to him, "Lower your voice, you frighten Ann."

"I beg you, forgive me, Ann. Colonel, please be reasonable; explain this to me," he said in a calmer manner. He turned to look to his wife for approval.

The Colonel revealed all. Mr. Darcy said not a word. Elizabeth chuckled to herself. She never expected anyone to dare fool her ladyship. Any humour induced by such a report did not bring the great depth of gaiety one might have anticipated. Although she thought it was a right smart trick, she could not help but determine the Colonel used poor judgment. Viewing her husband's fixed expression, she perceived she should quietly take it all in, realizing he was less in agreement of the Colonel's doings. Elizabeth extended much kindness to Ann. She tried general conversation, but Ann was a girl of few words. Even so, the few words she did say were more than Elizabeth had ever heard pass her lips. Elizabeth observed that Ann ate a little after she calmed her husband, believing she must have been hungry from the long journey. Although Colonel Fitzwilliam continued his explanation, the atmosphere was sober, with a guarded sense of contentment to know that they had Lady Catherine's blessing to have Ann at Pemberley. Ann's expression revealed nothing. Elizabeth supposed Mrs. Jenkinson to be all nerves, after learning of her agreed involvement. The cooperation rendered to the Colonel by Mrs. Jenkinson as well as the doctor amused her, not to mention the woman brought forth to care for her ladyship with special instructions from one so bold of the medical profession. It was a good prank just the same, thought she. Mr. Darcy was not as confident as was the Colonel, quite the opposite in fact. She knew him well; he had no look of conquering gratification, nor did he show any sign of pleasure in the related scheme.

Attempting to hold back a yawn, Ann appeared weary. Mr. Darcy, with a touch of delicacy regarding his cousin, rang the bell. "Bessie, show Ann to one of the bedchambers. Ann, you settle in; I shall be up to see you before long."

Like a schoolgirl, she followed his instruction, but not before providing him a lengthy stare. Elizabeth wondered what was going through her mind. She watched as Ann allowed herself to be led away by Bessie, who had the keenness of mind to treat her like a delicate flower.

They remained at the table in a sensitive exchange of disagreement, beginning with Mr. Darcy scolding the Colonel as soon as Ann was out of sight.

"This dishonest deed lacks all sense of honour. How foolish of you to risk bringing Ann to Pemberley. I am not of the opinion this was a wise decision; I'm convinced you should not have attempted it. If Lady Catherine discovers your scheme, her wrath will be upon you, not to mention my household. That will be the end of it; you'll think you should have thought the better of it. Lady Catherine is not a woman to be taken lightly. You have never had words with her or borne her scorn. You have never discovered how truly vicious she can be," he said in a warning voice. "She'll not spare you any consequences. Remember, Cousin, you have done this! Ann is the one thing in this world Lady Catherine will not have compromised. It was badly designed, and I'm ashamed for it. From you, I expected better judgment. I am exceedingly displeased."

Elizabeth could not help but sympathize with the Colonel after witnessing the harsh reprimand. He sat there as if his cousin had just crushed every bit of enjoyment of the escapade. The triumph drained from his face with each angry word. She had to agree with her husband's caution. The Colonel risked much. All the fear she felt earlier in believing it was Lady Catherine in the carriage would prove to be nothing if she uncovered the scheme. The result would be tenfold in severity; she had no doubt of this. And I shall be surely blamed for it, thought she.

"Well, Colonel Fitzwilliam, I must say, we have had eventful days here at Pemberley, but none such as this. Indeed, it is a day full of unexpected disorder. You should have seen your cousin's expression when the carriage neared. We thought it to be Lady Catherine herself. You sly thing, I cannot believe this of you. I would have never suspected you capable of such a scheme."

Mr. Darcy quickly turned to his wife, wasting little time addressing her comments. "It is not brilliance of mind to put a blunder such as this into action. This is not like you, Cousin; you have excellent principles. What is this about?" Then Mr. Darcy turned his attention to his wife. "I should think my wife would not encourage him or find humour in such awful plots. Indeed I should desire you to afford him no reassurance." His look was of a forbidding nature as he turned his head from her back to the Colonel, who now spoke.

"Nor should I have expected it of myself. I do not know what came over me. I felt the urgent need to remove Ann from Rosings. The day next I designed the scheme, seeking the help of others. I felt an uncontrollable desperate charge, powerless to discipline my own will. I gave little thought to any danger in it; truly I did not. Now that I have done as much, I'm quite astonished by my actions. But allow me to assure you I'll never reproach myself for having done it—never!"

Elizabeth thought she ought not to say anything further. She felt her husband viewed her prior remarks reproachable. I must learn my place; I must learn to let this to the gentlemen, thought she. Her unwanted opinions always seemed to bring her trouble in the past and she certainly had no desire to revisit old habits. She struggled to repress her natural frankness as she sat in silence, sorry for having injected her unwanted opinion.

"Well, enough of this," stated Mr. Darcy. He once again turned to his wife, reaching for her hand.

"Forgive me, dearest, I am just in ill humour. I was unjust to scold you just then, forgive me. Now if you will excuse me, I am to go to the guest chamber to talk to Ann. Elizabeth, would you mind keeping my cousin engaged in more respectful use of his time?"

Likewise he turned to the Colonel, "Cousin, keep in mind my wife is in a delicate state, not to be left alone, nor to walk without accompaniment. I shall return before long." Soberly, he bowed before quitting their presence.

Mr. Darcy knocked on Ann's chamber door. When he entered, she was seated. Her head hung as she stared into her lap. He took a chair, drawing it near her.

"I'm glad you are come. I do believe it has been years since you spent time in Derbyshire; is that not so?"

"Yes," replied a very shy Ann as she drew her hands in, shrinking back into the chair with her eyes fixed on her hands together in her lap.

At first it seemed a lurid failure in his mind to understand his cousin's fear. His heart sank with disappointment. At first he folded his arms demonstrating his keeping unto himself, but then not wishing to appear commanding, he unfolded them. He clasped his hands together, merging his fingers as he placed them in his lap. He leaned forward slightly, but noticed she once again shrunk back. Pressing his back against the chair, he took in a sigh. The only sounds to be heard at that moment were the sweet chirps of birds hovering in a nearby tree immediately outside the chamber window.

"Ann, I believe you are frightened of me. Can this be possible?"

"Some—sometimes, Cousin. Your look is severe; you were very angry in the dining hall. You are angry I have come."

"Why no, Ann, not at all; you should know that."

She made no reply, but continued to look down at her hands in her lap. She sat awkwardly for a few additional moments. Mr. Darcy took his hand under his cousin's chin to raise it up. "Pray look at me, Ann. How you must have suffered these past years! Forgive me for not having paid closer attention to you; I would not wish you to think I am not concerned of you. Such circumstance never existed. But I do feel I have been unjust where you are concerned. I possibly slighted you, perhaps I may have injured you without intention."

Detecting her uneasiness, he sought to change the subject. "This is such a cheery room is it not? I hope you will be comfortable here. I trust these arrangements are agreeable to you?" He slightly smiled, but was sure she barely noticed.

"Yes, Cousin, I like the chamber." She did not look up, but instead stared at her hands fidgeting in her lap. He noticed her eyes filled and her lower lip quivered.

"What is it, Cousin; is it my wife? Is it unbearable in her presence?"

"Oh no, Cousin, I like your wife," she quietly replied. Her complexion became pale, as if that were possible. All colours now seemed to desert her features. He said not a word, allowing her to compose herself, detecting she wanted to speak further. "I have something to tell you, but I fear——" she weakly said with threatening tears. She could feel the words stick in her throat.

Well aware she was unaccustomed to expressing her innermost feelings so openly, he sat quietly.

Feeling the urgency to address the subject she could put off no longer, which brought so much pain, she struggled to muster the courage to speak. She sobbed in search of words, trying to gain a sense of control. His presence intimidated her. She was glad he was seated, for all she could think of now was how he towered over her at the threshold, frightening her with his stature alone. Her heart pounded with anticipation. Perceiving he had matured to manhood adapting a severe nature did little to ease the tension of his striking presence. Her opposing thoughts only caused her to cry all the more. She struggled to inhale, attempting to cease her uncontrollable weeping.

He allowed her to have her cry. He sat quietly waiting, making an effort to sit back in his chair to gain a less frightening distance, awkwardly searching for less imposing posture.

Her weeping soon turned to sobs. As the sobs turned to sniffles, he patiently waited.

Distressed to know she was frightened of him, he wondered at what point in their lives this had taken place. He thought back to their childhood when they were comfortable together. Now he struggled to understand her feelings. It saddened him to view her in this state of distress.

He removed his handkerchief from his dress coat to present to her. She wiped her eyes. They sat momentarily in silence until he took one of her hands. Placing it between his own, he tilted his head down to her. "Ann, I know I appear quite stern at times, but you must believe me when I tell you I am not an ogre. I have the utmost regard for you. When we were children, I enjoyed making you laugh. It has been some time since I saw you laugh. Do you think I may at least see a bit of a smile now?"

She awkwardly moved her lips slightly, but it could hardly be ranked a half smile. As he attempted to pat her shoulder, he detected her resistance; her body became rigid at his touch. She instantly pulled away from him, turning her shoulder slightly inward.

He noticed she shivered. Suddenly disheartened by her rejection, he wondered what he could do next. He got up from his chair to secure a blanket to put around her, only to have her slightly pull back as he placed the wrap around her shivering shoulders. He returned to his chair to shroud his tallness, deliberately placing his hands together in his lap.

Once again he leaned toward her. "Are you still cold? Shall I have your fire stirred?"

"No—I am not cold, I—I am embarrassed. To be honest—" She sighed, then cleared her throat. "I um—I am just sorry I make you so angry." She frowned. Her eyes filled again, allowing a lone tear to trickle down her left cheek. It now occurred to him—what he mistakenly assumed as her being cold, was in actuality her own crisis of trembling fear. He meditatively struggled to find the proper words to alter her alarm of him. All thoughts of how he may inspire reconciliation failed him. Giving in to his own misery of the undesirable situation, his address was mournfully released. "Oh, Ann, what is it that troubles you so? I would wish that you placed more trust in me." He reached out to touch her shoulder. She pulled herself away from him once more. He immediately withdrew his hand.

Distressed by her fear of him, he sighed, sensing the emphasis of his inward misery. His voice turned low and pained. "Do you think you would wish to tell me now? Shall I come back later? Perhaps you prefer to talk another day? Would you feel more comfortable if I quitted the chamber? I do wish you to be at ease here at Pemberley, but I fear I frighten you. It quite distresses me to think of it."

"Please, do not go. I fear I shall never face you again if I do not unburden myself. I think you will not desire my company, once you learn my true feelings."

"I cannot imagine such a thing. Just say it, Ann; we get on very well. You should have faith in me; I wish you would. Say what it is you wish me to hear."

"I'm happy I am come to Pemberley; it is such a beautiful place. I like your wife very much. She has always shown me much kindness. I am—I am—contented you are happily situated. I am equally glad you find felicity in your marriage. Nothing pleases me more. Do not reproach yourself for the commitment made for us. I——"

Ann stopped. She took a deep breath. Again, she unsteadily gasped for air. Her voice cracked as she began again. "I—would not have been happy in marrying you, nor did I desire it. I love you dearly as my cousin, that is all. I have never been in love with you the way I should have been in the marriage sense. I pray you will forgive me." The tears that had filled her eyes now continuously ran down her cheeks, spilling down onto the front of her dress.

"Forgive you for not being in love with me? Nonsense, oh, Ann, I'm so happy to finally talk openly with you, without the fear of injuring you. You are very dear to me. I have always been deeply concerned for you. We are happy you are come; this is exactly what we wished for. Now, if we can only get your mother to make a turnabout. Well, enough said on that account, this is a happy occasion indeed."

Ann felt a sudden rush of relief. With it came an uncontrollable gush of tears mixed with releasing sobs. She took a couple of deep breaths. She put her hand up to her chest, then inhaled, feeling the still fast pace of her pulse. Her heart beat rapidly within her breast.

"Do I detect a sigh of relief, Ann?"

"Yes, Cousin."

"Let us think no more of it. There is nothing to forgive. Let me see you now; you look well but thin. Perhaps we can change that. It is my earnest desire you make the most of your visit here; what say you, Ann?"

"I should like that very much," she softly replied. Having unleashed all that held her captive in despair, her hopelessness suddenly seemed to dissipate. There was an unexpected naturalness felt in his company. It was almost as if, by sheer magic, the hands of time were forced back to that stage of their lives when they were comfortable in each other's company. An unmistakable serenity shone forth from her eyes as she shyly looked up at him. The many months of heart-wrenching anxiety were over. All that remained was a desire to recapture that sense of ease, which had once united them with joyful contentment.

Now that the words had been spoken, it brought closure to the dreaded circumstances which had long divided them. Realizing he had suffered greatly from his evasive actions at Rosings, she supposed her mother's determination for him to keep his commitment placed a heavy burden upon him. She unexpectedly understood his honour, comprehending how it must have troubled him a great deal to be held to a promise he had not made for himself. She could easily see his tender heart with freedom to feel the caring manner of his countenance, finally at peace for having been so bold to express her own feelings. She could look at him now, without feeling the weight of obligation forced upon them. Understanding he shared the same tortured feelings of guilt for not honouring such a pledge seemed to invalidate the uneasiness of moments ago. She was aware of his caution, viewing him as sincerely concerned of injuring her.

"Are you more at ease now, Ann?"

"Yes, Cousin, I believe I am."

"I cannot tell you how relieved I am to hear you say those words. I am well pleased indeed. We have wasted much time together since we have grown, to be sure. You were always such a pretty little girl. I remember entertaining you. I liked the sound of your laughter. Perhaps we will find much laughter here at Pemberley. I am to go below the stairs now; do you wish to join me?"

"I would like that very much. Cousin, I think your wife is very beautiful."

"Well now, you have my full agreement there; I cannot dispute it."

He noticed a shy smile overspread her face. He put his arm out to escort her below the stairs. After linking her arm in his, he placed his free hand over hers, and lowering his head to her, he expressed, "This is how you and I should be, Ann, cousins as well as very good friends. I can see you are more at ease; indeed I am glad for it."

Ann responded with an affirmative nod as they proceeded to join Elizabeth and Colonel Fitzwilliam in the music chamber.

"I do believe, Elizabeth, you have an admirer here," said Mr. Darcy as they entered. "Ann tells me she thinks you are very beautiful. I daresay I shall not dispute it; I am a prejudiced man; indeed I confess it."

Elizabeth blushed, as did Ann.

"Thank you, Ann, come to me at the pianoforte. Have you ever played?"

"No, I have not."

"Would you like to learn a simple tune?"

"Yes, indeed; do you think I may?"

"I have no reason to suspect you cannot."

Elizabeth spent time teaching Ann a simple tune she learned as a child. Much to her delight, Ann enjoyed it. The gentlemen sat on the sofa drinking a glass of port, watching the ladies at the pianoforte. Having cleared the air of his true feelings, Mr. Darcy now held a general exchange with the Colonel.

"You know, Cousin, your wife is excellent company for Ann. I was quite surprised at Rosings; she was eager to talk when allowed. Poor girl, can you imagine never being allowed to do anything? She would make some man an excellent wife given the chance; she would be receptive to learn anything. I believe her to be rather pretty, if you look beyond the thinness of her face or darkness about the eyes. I do believe sunshine with a bit of attentiveness will do a world of good on her behalf. What say you, Darcy; is it not so?"

Mr. Darcy heard his cousin's words, but his mind was otherwise engaged. His cousin puzzled him. He viewed him a genteel sort of man with tenderness of heart, the sort of creature one finds immediately pleasing—one sure to make friends wherever he went. He was somewhat handsome, rather tall in stature. He determined the kindness of his demeanour showed in his face; there was nothing haughty about him. Mr. Darcy seldom thought of him much before this; however, today he saw his cousin in a different light. Never had he known the Colonel to do anything irrational, dishonest or deceitful, nor to fabricate or exaggerate news or take chances. He always viewed him a straightforward, happy fellow. This was so strange, the invention of such a scheme, then to carry it off in the fashion he did. How extraordinary, thought he. Even he had to admit it was quite a trick to pull on their aunt. He couldn't help but wonder if the Colonel had motives of which he himself was not aware. I must answer him now, thought he.

"You seem to be very sure of yourself, Cousin. Have you reason to believe Ann will be allowed to stay long enough to make a difference?"

"Well—it is my hope something good comes of this visit. I just want Ann to experience life. I could not take her to London; it would not have been proper. What better place is there than Pemberley? I feel we owe it to her, Cousin; would you not agree?"

"Since you put it that way, I fancy I would have to agree. I confess at times I felt at fault for having deprived her of her intended future, yet today she made me blameless, affording me the knowledge she would not have liked to have me. Truthfully, Cousin, I am relieved to hear it. The only disturbing bit of information I learned from her was that she was frightened of me. Certainly I cannot endure her feeling as such; it made me quite uneasy to hear her say those words; it pained me greatly."

"Come, come now, Darcy, don't agonize over it. I set her straight at Ros-ings; I explained your position. Indeed, I flattered you creditably."

"Did you now, Cousin? You are quite a fellow, I must say." He kept a watchful eye on the Colonel as they spoke. He noticed his attentions were in the direction of the pianoforte. Mr. Darcy was certain Elizabeth was not the subject of his intense study.

"Darcy, I should write to Lady Catherine of our safe arrival. Would you furnish me with paper? Better yet, do I have your approval to sit at your desk? Since the carriage is to be sent back tomorrow, I shall have it delivered at the same time."

"Of course, go to it."

The Colonel returned just when the ladies decided to quit the pianoforte. He took his place on the sofa next to his cousin.

"I should like to go for a turn about the room, dearest."

Mr. Darcy immediately arose from the sofa to accommodate his wife.

"What a pleasant way to spend the afternoon," observed the Colonel.

Much to the surprise of all three, Ann quickly turned to the Colonel. "Yes, it is quite pleasant is it not? I too should like a turn about the room."

All three looked in her direction, causing her to turn several shades of red. Her obvious blush gave way to a shy smile.

"You had better be careful now, Ann, in a day or two we may have you laughing."

Elizabeth leaned to her husband instantly. She lowered her voice. "You should not tease; I am not sure Ann is quite ready for it."

In a less than quiet voice, Mr. Darcy replied. "Oh, but Elizabeth, you don't know how we used to make Ann laugh when we were children. We often amused her. She was a right good sport; is that not so, Colonel?"

"Indeed, Elizabeth, she afforded us an excellent audience."

"Yes, Elizabeth, I always took delight in their amusements," Ann added.

The couples ended their turn, then poured some port as they sat in the music chamber in a lengthy exchange.

It was obvious to Mr. Darcy and the Colonel that Ann was now regaining her once lost sense of ease in their presence; but it all too soon ceased when Mr. Manley returned. When he was introduced to Ann, she turned quiet, withdrawing once again from the exchange.

Unaware of the situation, Mr. Manley attempted conversation, asking Ann many questions. She remained shyly reserved, but managed to answer him tolerably well, without so much as looking at him.

Mr. Manley thought it odd that Mr. Darcy's cousin should be so extremely shy, but made no mention of it. He could not make her out. She seemed childish in her manner, yet he could plainly see she was not a child. He was confused by the simplicity of her language. He soon ceased all attempts to converse with her.

Mr. Darcy could clearly see the confusion of his friend, but given no private chance to alter the situation, they passed the next hour with little conversation from Ann. She sat quietly, taking in the exchange around her.

When dinner was announced, the Colonel extended his bent arm to his cousin, escorting her in the direction of the dining hall. Mr. Darcy, with his wife at his arm, walked deliberately slower, to gain a private audience with Mr. Manley.

"Henry, my cousin's shyness, I feel I must explain. Ann has seldom experienced the world beyond Rosings, her home at Kent. I am afraid she is quite frail, having been sheltered most of her life. She has been prevented from doing that which most girls her age do. I fear you will find she is painfully shy among strangers."

"Pray, I do not understand, Fitzwilliam."

"I have an overprotective aunt, who allows Ann to do little. She seldom allows her to speak. This is rare for Ann to be from home."

"Oh, I see. Thank you for telling me; I would not wish to excite her with pressing questions."

When they were all seated, Mr. Manley spoke an eloquent prayer. Ann, now seated across the table from Mr. Manley, was overtaken with shyness when he looked in her direction. She was drawn to his appearance. His well-spoken manner intrigued her, but still she found it difficult to look at him directly without blushing. Her self-consciousness kept her from eating, as she may have, had she been seated elsewhere.

"What an excellent bit of beef," Elizabeth commented.

"You'll find there are very few that cook as fine a meal as we received here; it is always a pleasure to dine at my cousin's table," added the Colonel.

"Thank you, I take great pride in my table; my guests are always well satisfied."

"I can believe it. I think I shall have more; how about you, Ann?" the Colonel asked, but then noticed she had not finished the small portion she had on her plate.

"No, thank you, Cousin, I believe I have had enough."

After dinner, they returned to the music chamber, where Mr. Manley played the pianoforte while the Colonel chatted at length with his cousin. Elizabeth tried to keep a steady conversation with Ann, but it proved difficult. After about an hour, Elizabeth announced, "I do believe it has been a long day of startling events. I fear I am fatigued. I trust you will not think me impolite if I retire for the evening."

"Not at all," Mr. Manley retorted as he stood to bow.

The Colonel bowed, then next looked in Ann's direction. "It is quite all right, Elizabeth. You may be assured we do not mind; do we Ann?"

"Pray excuse my absence. I must look after my wife. Colonel, will you entertain in my absence? I expect to return directly."

"Fitzwilliam, no need to feel you are required to return if you prefer to stay with your wife. I understand your position. Her delicate condition is your first interest. I will not feel the least bit slighted if you do not return. If you have no objection, I should like to visit your library to select a book to take to my chamber; but I do believe I shall visit with the Colonel and Ann a bit before retiring."

"Thank you, Henry, I believe I will do as you say. I should be glad if you visit the library. I have no doubt you will find a book to your liking. I bid you all good-night, then. Good-night, Colonel; good-night, Ann," Mr. Darcy said as he bowed.

"I should like to go to the library first to secure a book to take above the stairs. Do you mind, dearest?"

"No, not at all."

"Good-night, Darcy," expressed the Colonel. "I plan to stay in the music chamber a while longer if you have no objection."

And to their astonishment, Ann interjected, "I should like to keep him company."

"Very well, then, we bid you all good-night."

Mr. Manley remained to keep them company for a time. He had noticed Ann's interest in his playing the pianoforte, so he announced he would play a few tunes in her honour before retiring to his chamber.

Ann smiled at Mr. Manley. She decided she liked him as well as his music. She thought him just the sort of gentleman her cousin would have for a friend. And as for her cousin Mr. Darcy, he grew more to her comfort with closer association. She wondered how it ever came to be that she learned to fear him. She experienced a certain release of freedom at that moment. Unlike her natural inclination to withdraw from conversation, she managed to make a few general comments without prompting. Although she felt strange, she had a sense of control, finding an independence she rarely ever dared to express. There was no one to speak for her, or to halt her expressions. She soon understood that those in her immediate company had an interest in hearing her voiced opinions. Even as Elizabeth and her cousin bid their good-night, she found ease in saying, "I thank you, Cousins, for all I have enjoyed thus far at Pemberley. I look forward to tomorrow."

"Good night, Ann," a surprised Elizabeth commented. Mr. Darcy nodded his acceptance. Having bid good-night to their guests, Elizabeth and Mr. Darcy set off for the library.

"Dearest, I noticed your cousin pays much attention to Ann."

"Yes, I have witnessed it as well."

"How is it that the Colonel never married?"

"I assure you I do not know; I never gave it much thought."

After Mr. Darcy found the books he desired, they proceeded above the stairs. Elizabeth made ready for bed while her husband chose to read a while longer. All was quiet until he turned his book over on his lap. "Elizabeth, you are still awake, are you not?"

"Yes, I am; why?"

"How did Ann like the pianoforte; did she do well?"

"Very well. Having never had the opportunity, I found her to do well enough. These things take time. Why do you ask?"

"I was just thinking of the Colonel; his eyes were fixed for a time in the direction of the pianoforte when you both were there. My cousin was more interested in the business of you and Ann than in our conversation. I found him to be preoccupied, perhaps there is a strong attachment there."

"Aye, I witnessed it myself. Perhaps the Colonel felt the urgency to remove Ann from Rosings for reasons he has not yet discovered. It is not his character to carry out schemes, is it not?"

"No, I'm sure you are right in this. I know him too well. I would never have expected so myself; he is certainly not a person of chance; this is all so very peculiar."

"Well, we shall have to wait until tomorrow to see how he employs himself. I must say, I had not expected a day such as this."

"Nor I."

That seemed to end the conversation. Mr. Darcy returned to his book as Elizabeth lay her head back, fast falling to sleep.

The day next, Elizabeth received a letter from Jane.

My Dearest Lizzy,
Netherfield Park,
Hertfordshire

I can but wonder the excitement you all feel having such a report of a pending event. Our expectations of felicity in marriage are complete in you. We wish to make known our congratulations. Have you heard the news of our sister Lydia? She has a happy event of her own. I daresay her presentation will come before yours. That concludes three, the Collins' happy event is expected soon. Our mother and father are well, Lizzy; we see them often, along with Kitty and Mary. They come often to Netherfield Park and are invited to dine at Netherfield Hall today. Yesterday was spent at Lucas Lodge where we played cards for hours, while Mary entertained with her musical talents. The country is quiet, affording no news at present. I am glad you send such pleasant accounts from Pemberley. Tomorrow we expect Caroline Bingley, the Hursts and Mr. Bingley's sister Emily. You may remember Charles mentioned five sisters in all. Mr. Bingley made mention of a journey to Derbyshire. I know not when, but I will be anxious to see you. I have not time to express all my means, but will do so later.

Yours, Jane

Elizabeth smiled. "Dearest, I have a most pleasing letter from Jane; perhaps you would like to read it?"

"If you wish."

She handed him the letter. After reading it, he turned to her. "I know you are anxious to have your sister visit; but allow me remind you of Bingley's sisters. Since they reside at Netherfield, they would surely expect an invitation. I would discourage it presently. Perhaps you should delay your reply."

"Oh my, yes, I had not given it thought. With Ann and Colonel Fitzwilliam here, perhaps the excitement would be too much. Truthfully, I should not desire the grief of their censure."

Later in the afternoon, another letter arrived; this one for Mr. Darcy penned by Mrs. Jenkinson for the Honourable Lady Catherine de Bourgh of Rosings Park.

Fitzwilliam Darcy,
Rosings, Kent

The conditions of this house are such that the good doctor expects the quarantine at Rosings Park remain yet a fortnight, lest he deems additional time needed. Ann must impose on her cousin until further notice. My compliments to Colonel Fitzwilliam, who had the keenness of mind to bring Ann to Pemberley. Under the circumstances, I consider it your duty to oblige me. Mrs. Jenkinson was well enough to dispatch this letter, but no more. The doctor ordered a special keeper to tend the ill. She is stiff on the rules, allowing me the privilege of this letter alone. I am confined to my bed. My affections to my dearest Ann.

The Honourable Lady Catherine de Bourgh

There seemed to be a quiet sense of felicity. The five dined then retired to the music chamber, where Mr. Darcy shared Lady Catherine's letter. Elizabeth sighed. It mattered little to her that Lady Catherine made no mention of her, but she knew Mr. Darcy was discontented by it.

With the letter still in his hand, he thought to himself, what else can be expected from a mean-spirited, unyielding aunt? The Colonel interrupted his thoughts. "At least she wrote of the goings on at Rosings."

Mr. Darcy detected the Colonel had regained a renewed sense of triumph. Little more was said of the letter, perhaps for Ann's sake. There was no desire to dispute its lack of sensitivity.

Mr. Darcy was impressed by Mr. Manley's delicacy with Ann. He seemed to possess a natural inclination to reach her soul, drawing her from within herself with unaffected ease. He continued to be amazed by her response, noticing she brightened each time he spoke. Mr. Manley delighted in playing her requested tunes on the pianoforte. He seemed to gain a sense of her following. Colonel Fitzwilliam also afforded Ann excessive attention, but that easement had long been established years ago and maintained without interruption.

Ann gained a remarkable expression in conversation with greater ease. There emerged a noticeable physical improvement. Discovery of contentment added serenity to her ambiance. Her eyes brightened with recurring smiles, which gave way to laughter. The circles beneath her eyes grew less and less dark until they ceased to exist, as did the extreme shyness. She was finding physical strength in her short time at Pemberley, along with a greater sense of self-confidence. She was eager to learn, playing simple tunes with one hand on the pianoforte. Elizabeth was teaching her to stitch a pillow slip, to which she took an immediate liking as well.

Elizabeth felt physically stronger each day, as did Ann. Together, they took little turns about the grounds. Elizabeth led Ann to believe it was she who was a source of strength for her.

One particular afternoon they decided to play a silly word game, which induced much laughter. The object of the game was to act out a word given on a piece of paper. Ann's word was chicken. Elizabeth guessed it outright. Ann laughed at her own imitation. When dinner interrupted the game, Ann's disappointment was easily noticeable.

The morning next a message arrived for Mr. Darcy from Jane. Mr. Darcy thought it odd the letter was addressed to him rather than Elizabeth. Surely Bingley would direct a letter to him, but Jane?

Fitzwilliam Darcy
Netherfield Park, Hertfordshire

Pemberley Estate, Derbyshire

Mr. Darcy:

I must trouble you with news to lessen the shock to my sister, as only you can do. Our father is extremely ill. Your presence is required at once. My father is in such a state you may not arrive in time to pay last respects. Presently, this is all the information I can afford. Unfortunately, Elizabeth's happy report presents a risk due to the high fever. Come at once.

Jane Bingley

At the time of the reading the gentlemen were in the breakfast chamber. The ladies were still tucked away in their bedchambers. With grave aspect, Mr. Darcy languidly sat down.

"Fitzwilliam, are you unwell?"

"No, I am tolerably well, Mr. Manley, just the recipient of bad news I fear. Elizabeth's father is gravely ill; we must leave at once for Longbourn. I dread the telling of it. The truth is, we may arrive too late. I must wake Elizabeth at once. I fear she will take it very poorly, of this I am sure. It pains me to disturb her in her condition, but it must be done. Pray excuse me."

"Is there anything I can do for you, Darcy?"

"Yes, Colonel, you must stay here to look after Ann."

"Mr. Manley, pray excuse my necessity to leave, you are welcome to stay with the Colonel. He will have to take charge in my absence. My steward is most dependable. Mrs. Reynolds is an excellent woman as you are well aware, Cousin. They know everything to be done; you may trust them with the particulars."

"Fitzwilliam, I thank you for the kind invitation, but I feel I should return to London, I have stayed too long. Please accept my sincerest sorrow for the situation in which you and your wife now find yourselves. I will indeed keep a prayer open to you for traveling mercies. My sincerest regrets on the illness of your father-in-law."

"Very well, Mr. Manley, as you wish."

"Perhaps this is not the best of times; however, before you go, allow me to tell you I accept your offer. I have talked with Mr. Green. He expresses a wish to leave at once. I shall inform him I depart for London today. Perhaps upon your return, you will find me well settled in the parsonage. I had hoped to tell you today under happier circumstances in the presence of your wife, but I see now that is not possible. This will have to do."

"Thank you, Mr. Manley, it is good news in light of bad. I beg your pardon for not being at liberty to stay to discuss the situation further; it greatly anguishes me not to express the pleasure such an occasion affords, but I'm sure you know how pleased I am. I look forward to seeing you upon our return." Mr. Darcy bowed, then turned to leave, but turned back again. "Colonel, if you please, tell my man to make the carriage ready at once. Make my apologies to Ann; I am certain she will understand. I'll take my leave, good day to you both." He quitted their presence, advancing above the stairs. He paused to gain full composure before entering.

"Dearest, you must get up now to prepare yourself."

"Prepare myself?"

He immediately went to her. Drawing her into his arms, he held her close. "I have had a letter from Jane; do not allow yourself to be undone; remember your health. We must leave at once for Longbourn, your father is gravely ill. I am having the carriage made ready at once. Show me what you will need; I will have Mrs. Reynolds parcel everything while you breakfast. She will be here momentarily with the chambermaid."

"May I see the letter?"

As feared, she became anxious. She sprung to her feet, pacing back and forth, unable to suppress all signs of inward turmoil. She was bewildered. Helpless as a child, she prayed, mumbling aloud between her sobs. Her world was crumbling about her. She quickly sought to sweep away thoughts of her cousin laying instant claim to the family estate. To imagine fully the consequences her father's death would have on the whole of the family seemed only to add to her pain. She reproached herself for such misplaced thoughts. Ashamed of her selfish reflections, she tried not to contemplate the ill effects all this might have on the future. Her lips trembled as she prayed more rapidly to squelch her now pained thoughts, which she could not begin to utter aloud. She tried to conquer her sorrow as she wiped away tears.

Mr. Darcy viewed her state of nervous unrest. In an instant he was close to her. He drew her into his arms, continuing his hold as she cried at length. She tilted her head back to speak. He kept his arms around her as she looked at him with eyes welled up with tears. All attempts to speak seemed to fail her at that moment. Her face was tear stained, with redness overspreading her features.

"Oh, dear Papa, I should be very sad if we do not arrive in time." Tears continued to stream down her cheeks. She tried to prevent them, but uncontrollable sobs claimed her. She quickly composed her thoughts while making herself ready. "At once, we must leave at once; I will make haste. I do not know that I can eat anything."

Mr. Darcy felt helpless in his wish to comfort her. The mixture of tears together with the desire to hurry to Longbourn left little time to console her. I suppose there will be ample time once the carriage makes its start, he thought to himself. Fifty miles of road will surely allow ample time to converse. All thoughts were now of her, his love for her along with his desire to protect her from all the ills of the world. Not being inclined to self-deception, he knew that was impossible. He suffered to think his only authority was to see her swiftly to Longbourn, she hoped before her father expired.

"Very well, I will have something wrapped for along the way; but, Elizabeth, do you think that is wise with your delicate condition?"

"I will be well dear, just lend me your assistance. Where is Mrs. Reynolds?"

Within the hour Elizabeth and Mr. Darcy were on their way to Longbourn.

Mr. Manley, having quitted the place shortly after them, left only the Colonel and Ann at Pemberley.

Fifty Miles of Good Road

℃HEY ARRIVED AT LONGBOURN in ample time. Mr. Bennet was gravely ill, but still taking breaths. Jane and Mr. Bingley greeted them as they disembarked the carriage. It was not long before Kitty appeared, with Mary following closely behind. Mr. Darcy assisted Elizabeth's walk into the house. The atmosphere within was grave. Although Mr. Darcy feared for his wife's now delicate state, he made no mention of it. As they entered, she addressed Jane along the way, "Jane, where is our mother?"

"Mamma is in her chamber with the hysterics; her nerves are in turmoil. She is ill as well, with the fever, Lizzy. She continues to go in to see my father. Oh, Lizzy, she agonizes over him. Lizzy, I am so glad you are come. I do believe she may have a seizure of sorts if she does not make herself calm. I have never seen her this adverse; I do believe she suffers severely. Lizzy, Aunt Philips is here, but she is of little comfort to our mother; she cries ceaselessly. It is hard enough to console Mamma, as you will see, without Aunt Philips trying our nerves. As you can plainly hear, Aunt Philips suffers loudly. Such wailing is unsettling in the face of hopelessness. I can scarcely bear the strain; it is upsetting. Oh, Lizzy, how glad I am to see you," she said, hugging her again.

Mr. Darcy knew Mrs. Philips to be the sister of Mrs. Bennet, who lived nearby in Meryton with her husband. He was equally educated of her time spent visiting the Bennet house with spreadable hearsay. Her lack of restraint he was not familiar with. He could not help but view her presence disconcerting.

Mrs. Philips was a lady of medium height and brown hair, with a robust figure, whose matured face bore little similarity to that of Mrs. Bennet. Both women, though on in their years, gave resemblance to once owning handsome appearances. Whatever the happening in Meryton, it seemed Mrs. Philips was first informed. Once owning to all the details, she quickly saw the news widespread, having many years before learned to cherish the value of spreadable gossip. However unfortunate the circumstances, she could be counted upon to not only repeat, but embellish the facts. It was not uncommon, and in fact occurred quite often by virtue of her meddling, that a slight commotion easily became a scandalous fracas. Her presence annoyed Mr. Bennet frequently. It was well known within the Bennet household that Mr. Bennet, on many occasions, suggested to his wife she should occupy her time more productively. However, Mrs. Philips being her sister, prevented him from having much influence, for when the ladies had their heads together, it was a hopeless affair. Mrs. Philips now fretted loudly of her sister's situation. Her uncontrolled loud state, another quality she was universally known for, was now in full bloom.

"What of Aunt and Uncle Gardiner, Jane? Do they know of the sad state of affairs?"

"Yes, Lizzy, I sent them word express. I am certain they departed London immediately. I expect they are en route to Longbourn as we speak."

"That is perhaps the best news we may expect. Oh, Jane, their goodness may always be counted upon———" Her voice trailed to silence. Elizabeth was lost in thoughts of her own.

"Yes, Lizzy, I am well aware of what we owe to Aunt and Uncle Gardiner. They have been kind to us, have they not now?"

"Yes, Jane, they have indeed."

"Yes, but Lizzy, we must not forget what we owe to them where Lydia is concerned. Why our uncle had to lay out a handsome sum to pay off Mr. Wickham's debts and secure him a new post in a northern regiment. Whatever should we have done if Uncle Gardiner had not rescued Lydia? If it were not for his regard, neither you nor I would be married."

Elizabeth fixed her eyes on her husband's face. There was nothing to be read in his features; he bore a look of perfect indifference. As she plainly spoke, the distraction of her thoughts caused her cheeks to become overspread with the deepest blush. She was certain he heard every word. She felt immovable from her present notions, but shortly recovered herself to once again speak with perfect composure. "Perhaps we should say no more of this, Jane. I am pleased you sent word express; we shall find comfort in their coming."

"Yes indeed, Lizzy, I agree."

Mr. Darcy remained at his wife's side. With all such conversation, his thoughts ventured in the direction of Elizabeth's Uncle Gardiner. Mr. Gardiner, a stout gentleman with good manners, was a businessman in London. His wife was, in all respects, always congenial, kind and caring. They demonstrated the best of sense and good judgment. Mr. Darcy took an immediate liking to them.

Elizabeth turned to Jane. "I must see Father, Jane; take me to him."

Elizabeth neared her father's side. "Papa, can you hear me? It is I, Lizzy."

An extremely feverish Mr. Bennet managed to reply weakly, "Oh, my Lizzy, you are come; I knew you would. I knew my Lizzy would come." As his increasingly feeble voice drifted into an unconscious state, his head fell to one side.

"Papa, Papa, can you hear me?" Elizabeth cried.

He made no response. Elizabeth turned to her husband. Burying her face in his chest, she relinquished all attempts to govern her emotions, yielding to uncontrollable weeping. He held her in his arms, saying nothing, allowing her to have her cry. After having controlled her sobbing, he led her out of the bedchamber. They went next to her mother's bedchamber. There they found her grief stricken, suffering with severe distress. She tried to quiet her mother to no avail; her mother was not to be calmed; she was in a wretched state. Elizabeth quitted her mother's presence, feeling rather helpless. Her younger sisters followed them from chamber to chamber.

"Perhaps we should join the others in the sitting room," Mr. Darcy suggested.

Mr. Darcy, Elizabeth, along with Jane, Mary and Kitty, set out for the sitting room. Suddenly, Elizabeth noticed Mr. Collins. Elizabeth's brows narrowed. She frowned, while quickly halting her steps. Spinning herself around on her heel, she faced Jane. "What is he doing here, Jane?"

"Mr. Collins first came to empathize with us on the unfortunate situation of our father's illness. Now I believe he is taking inventory. I'm sure Mrs. Lucas notified him of our father's condition. Charlotte did accompany him, but returned to Lucas Lodge. Lizzy, she is extremely vexed with her husband; I noticed they had a heated exchange. She appeared embarrassed by his audacious behaviour. She quitted Longbourn in haste," Jane lamented in a whispering voice.

By now, Elizabeth's intolerance for his insufferable behaviour plunged her in a state of unguarded contempt. Before Jane or Mr. Darcy could restrain her, she marched up to him.

She addressed him indignantly. "Mr. Collins, what do you do here?" Demanding and unreceptive, her eyes turned sharp like daggers. While directing her piercing vehement look of abhorrence of his selfish disdain for the feelings of her family, she advanced closer to him. She clenched her teeth until her jaw hurt. The very sight of him repulsed her. Concealment was beyond her will to control.

"I am of the belief my situation in life as clergyman calls upon me to express, to my respectable family, condolences on the enormity of your grief in the near death of your father. Allow me, it being my duty, to offer my sorrow for the severe situation in which you will soon find yourselves." He bowed. His reply held a stagnant air of self-importance. Granting a smug grin, he stood with his shoulders back as he stretched his neck within his holy collar. Confidence flowed out of him with each bold word. His eyes glistened with satisfaction of his intended inheritance. He quite conveniently passed off his actions as the duty of a clergyman to Elizabeth's now appalled state.

"Pray, tell me, Mr. Collins, exactly what situation would that be?"

As Mr. Darcy neared Elizabeth, Mr. Collins humbled himself momentarily, offering a deep bow. He humbly apologized. "It is not my intention to add anxiety to your unfortunate state of affairs; however, certainly you realize the reality of the present circumstances. Why they will no doubt alter the situation of your family drastically."

Mr. Darcy determined it was best not to interfere in his wife's dealings with Mr. Collins, however distasteful he found him to be. She was irritated beyond control. He allowed her the needed relief of correcting the horrid situation, to relinquish her anger rather than reserve it for an ensuing battle. Believing his wife perfectly capable, he resolved to observe without interception, lest it be required.

With scorched words of displeasure, she inquired further, "What situation would that be, Mr. Collins?"

"Why—the near death of your father; surely he is not expected to make it through the night. Surely you are aware of the condition upon which the estate is written? Longbourn will be entailed to a male heir. Sorry as it must seem, Longbourn estate will be my responsibility when he is gone. I simply wish to inspect what will soon be mine. Allow me to remind you, Cousin, my wife, your dearest friend in the world, may present me with a son." He clasped his hands together at his chest, elevating his eyes. "The future heir to Longbourn!" He returned his eyes to Elizabeth. "Certainly you cannot deny me my rightful place. Surely you must realize, I am to inherit all of this upon the death of your father."

"Indeed, but my father lives Mr. Collins, or have you overlooked that fact? Does your station in life provide you with direct knowledge of the surety of his passing?" Her raised voice, coupled with stern promptness, was evidence of her increased anger. His ill manners offended her. As she contemplated his attempts to take liberties at the expense of their sorry situation, she glared at him with intensifying disdain.

He smothered a grin. From the corner of his eye, he viewed Mr. Darcy. With all the insincerity his character could muster, he retorted, "You may be assured you have my earnest desire for you father's recovery, doubtful as it seems. My dear Cousin, as painful as it may be, death is sure to come; they have given him little hope. Surely you do not mean to deny me the opportunity to inspect all that will be entailed to me? If I may be so bold as to suggest, perhaps you too should make some advances to settle the near future of your mother and sisters."

"How so? What is your meaning?" she voiced firmly.

"Why—my dear Elizabeth, surely you know that your mother will be forced to quit this house along with your sisters at once upon the death of your father. I daresay, from what I hear, they may be very well situated at Pemberley."

"Mr. Collins, I daresay you are too hasty! My father still breathes; or is it you fear the contents of this estate may be removed, so as to pillage what you feel you are entitled to? Or perhaps you lack integrity to afford respectability toward those still living? You place a low ethical value on human life, which I find appalling. The very core of your respect for others, for their feelings, sensibilities, their opinions or welfare is severely lacking. Simplicity, coupled with common decency, mold great factors in the conception of good taste. I daresay, I have no notion to you owning to any of it. Thoughtlessness, selfishness, even greed linked to a merciless heart—you obviously boast through your vulgarity. Altogether, you lack an attitude of reverence one expects to witness in a clergyman."

Mr. Collins appeared indignant as she continued with ice-laced tones. "Mr. Collins, I find your actions offensive, arrogant and highly contemptuous. I must ask you to leave this house at once." She glared at him. If he noticed her agitation, it was with insignificant sentiment. He slyly grinned with a confident poise, as he resumed his defiant, almost hostile attitude. "My dear Cousin, consider my rank as clergyman; surely you will require my services." His words were subtle, but he was now caught up in circumstances, emerging as his own worst enemy.

"I think not, Mr. Collins; your presence is not desired here. Perhaps if you require a duty, you may go to the local chapel to pray for the ill; is that not what is expected of you? Should you not be in prayer for my father? Perhaps you should pray for yourself! Yes, Mr. Collins, pray that God does not use his wrath to correct your fallacious ways. Surely your Bishop would not approve of your covetousness or your lack of feeling for the bereaving widow, should my father depart. I find you insufferable. Your decided conceit has long culminated my thoughts of you as being a self-centered, selfish, self-serving individual. I am ashamed to claim you as relation! Your egotistic arrogance and disregard for others, along with your obnoxious presumptions, have long intruded upon my family. These thoughts and words have deliberated upon my lips at length; today I find great relief in expressing them to you. Your actions are unbecoming of a man of the cloth; need I say more?" Elizabeth felt a momentary intense relief at being able to speak her feelings, until a determined Mr. Collins foolishly continued.

"My dear Cousin—" was all she allowed him to say. She stepped closer to him. She raised her voice, emphasizing her words like whiplash. "MR. COLLINS, I shall not ask you again to quit this house! My father still takes in air! Until such time as he does not, your presence here is not desired." Her eyes met his with coldness foreign to her. Never before had she suffered such inward fury; it frightened her. She had thought she could handle him, but his lack of sympathy and want of property was nothing compared to the mockery of his religious calling. Her breathing turned rapid. She seized her stomach in pain. As she felt her heart pound fervently within her breast, the blood seemed to surge through her veins. Her jaw-line tightened; she realized her bluntness escaped his bloated importance. She desperately felt her control declining. Her face turned crimson. First letting out a shriek of disgust, she clenched her fists before thrusting her arms down at her side, still facing him with penetrating eyes.

Mr. Collins stepped closer to her. He appeared determined to challenge her further. Mr. Darcy noticed Elizabeth's trembling state. The consequence to her health now drew him nearer to her. She was breathing heavily, now more distraught with each angry word that passed her lips.

No longer willing to tolerate risking his wife's health, he concluded that Mr. Collins cared little for anyone or anything beyond his own flattering speculation. He quickly stepped between them as Elizabeth rallied herself for another round. He abruptly interrupted. "Enough," he said sternly, "enough." He turned to Jane. "Jane, please convey your sister to the sitting room. I wish to speak with Mr. Collins."

Jane placed her hands on Elizabeth's upper arm. "Very well, come Elizabeth, come to the sitting room."

Elizabeth reluctantly went with Jane, uttering not another word at first. She paused, then turned, allowing Mr. Collins a lengthy, vehement look of disgust. Before she totally quit his presence, she willfully voiced, "Yes, I believe I prefer to seek the purity of less stagnant air to be found elsewhere. Under different circumstances, I might view his self-satisfaction and total lack of true comprehension a constant source of entertainment. Such a ridiculous character is not worth the waste of words." It took several moments for Elizabeth's mind to adjust to the conclusion of the confrontation. Dizziness swept through the whole of her body. Her legs became weak. Kitty and Mary followed close behind, eyeing Mr. Collins as they exited.

Knowing how stubborn she could be, Mr. Darcy was amazed she followed his instruction so readily.

When Jane and Elizabeth quitted the chamber, Elizabeth turned and questioned, "Jane, how long has Mr. Collins been here? Why did you allow him to stay? His presence angers me beyond reason. Could you not stop him?"

"Now, Lizzy, our Cousin means no harm. Although he lacks the sense of good timing, I do believe his intentions were good. I do believe he arrived with the intention of consoling us. He just seems to forget himself, which I believe hinders his ability to see beyond his inheritance; that is all."

"Jane, why must you make excuses for such a man? Cannot you see he takes pride in our suffering and congratulates himself on his position as heir to Longbourn? Cannot you see this, Jane?"

"Come now, Lizzy, surely you know Mr. Collins lay blameless. We cannot hold him accountable for the inheritance being entailed away from the female line. But, I must say, I do agree that it is improper for him to take inventory while father lays dying. It is indeed unsettling."

"Oh, Jane, I wish I could be as generous, but I cannot."

Mr. Collins was a man of no real means, who naturally lacked good sense or intelligence, but somehow was so fortunate to have been assisted by education enough to gain his ordination. Presently, he was fortunate to enjoy the patronage of the Right Honourable Lady Catherine de Bourgh, widow of Sir Louis de Bourgh of Rosings Park, a substantial estate, as well as being the infamous aunt of Elizabeth's husband, Fitzwilliam Darcy. Mr.

Collins and his wife, Charlotte, reside at Hunsford, a comfortable rectory on Lady Catherine's estate. His manners were seemingly formal. He continually humbled himself and apologized frequently for trivial matters which lacked substance, but, most importantly, matters no one else would give notice to. His cunning, insidious ways failed to escape the understanding of those who were well acquainted with him.

He had a stagnant air about him, having grown more pompous through his connection to her ladyship. His obviously felt authority as clergyman made him in sum, a pompous, insufferable, ineffectual gentleman who lacked character. He adapted a combination of overconfidence amid condescension, believing all others beneath his good opinion. He remained unrelenting with self-importance. Humility, he reserved for Lady Catherine; therefore, he managed to contradict himself frequently while trying to impress her ladyship. He proved to be a foolish, self-absorbed individual, whose aim in life was to secure himself a comfortable situation, but yet presented himself as such, that one would believe him to be exceedingly charitable, and, moreover, unconcerned of himself.

Mr. Bennet, being a man of some sense with wit, realized he had no quarrel with him. He could not hold against him the matter to which the estate was written.

Mr. Collins, being a man of seven and twenty, fell short on looks as well as character. It escaped Elizabeth's reason as to why her friend married him, but she alleged Charlotte's acceptance was a matter of duty, supposing him a suitable match. She was well aware Charlotte owned no romantic tendencies, had little desire for more than the comforts of a home and was less inclined to think of passion or love, asserting felicity could be found in situation. Charlotte had comfortably expressed, "It was best to have no longing to be well acquainted with a future husband." Being the ripe age of seven and twenty, she thought it best to accept his proposal.

Securing the hand of Miss Lucas only proved to make Mr. Collins less humble. Upon learning of Lydia's contemptuous public behaviour, he visited the family to celebrate victory of the situation, in the guise of clergy duty. It was apparent that his reason for visiting now was to enjoy the sentiment of inheriting the family estate. It meant little to him that Mr. Bennet was not yet dead. Overcome by his desire to be master of Longbourn, he attempted to capitalize on the Bennets' misfortune by taking inventory. His premature aspirations were viewed unprincipled in Mr. Darcy's estimation. He found he could no longer remain silent.

When the ladies were well out of sight, Mr. Darcy, with a directive gesture of the hand, led Mr. Collins to a vacant chamber. Towering over Mr. Collins, he stepped forward, stopping directly in front of him. He united both hands together behind his back as he confidently edged forward, lifting his heels still higher, leaving only enough room for breathing, as he stared down at him. Looking severe, he cleared his throat. With a voice officially cold, his harsh words were delivered.

Mr. Collins looked fretful. He attempted to step back, only to have Mr. Darcy step closer. Up until this moment, he had not considered the fact that Mr. Darcy was Lady Catherine's nephew. Suddenly, all thoughts of his connection to her ladyship seemed to penetrate his understanding. His brows united with alarm. He rounded his shoulders, attempting to shrink back, affording Mr. Darcy a lowly bow. When he straightened up again, he nodded his head to Mr. Darcy with a faint grin. He was obviously trembling. Mr. Darcy noticed his complexion paled. Mr. Collins pressed his lips together, swallowing hard, before lowering to grant a humble bow once again.

Mr. Darcy talked to him at length, leaving Mr. Collins in an anxious state. After Mr. Darcy excused himself, he checked on Mr. Bennet before joining his wife.

Elizabeth looked beyond him. "What has become of Mr. Collins?"

"I believe the gentleman is on his way to Lucas Lodge."

"Gentleman indeed! What did you say to him?"

"I will talk of it later, but I believe it is safe to say your cousin's revelry of triumph has been lost to him momentarily. Come, we will go to your father again; he is awake."

When they neared her father's bedchamber, they approached quietly. Mrs. Bennet was at his side, crying profusely, preventing her from hearing them near the chamber.

"My dear Mr. Bennet, whatever shall I do; who will care for me?" she wailed, her nervous voice quivering as it echoed the chamber. Mrs. Bennet, with her back to them, still unaware of their presence, went on. "Mr. Bennet, you must get well for my sake, I shall need you by my side; you have always taken care of us," she lamented.

"My dear Fanny, try to control yourself; this cannot be good; you are not well. I am so tired," a very weak Mr. Bennet lethargically stated.

"Oh, Mr. Bennet, what shall I do?" She continued to cry.

"The girls are here, Fanny. They will assist you. There is Hill to help," he told her, as if he were so weary he could hardly get the words out.

"Mr. Bennet, my dear Mr. Bennet, you have been so good to me. Can you hear me. Mr. Bennet?" she cried softly.

"Yes, my dear," he replied, reaching for her hand.

"Mr. Bennet, please forgive me," she managed between sobs.

"Forgive you for what, my dear?" his tired voice responded, gasping for air.

"Forgive me for never having given you a son. I know you desired it. I fear I have cheated you. Can you ever forgive me?" she wept softly.

Still holding her hand, he replied tenderly, "My dear, do not concern yourself with such matters now. God has been good to us; indeed you lay blameless. I should have liked to have a son; it just was not to be. You rest now," his voice trailed off. Mr. Bennet then slipped into an unconscious state.

Elizabeth assisted her mother to her bedchamber. They stayed with her until she finally managed to rest somewhat peacefully, sobbing softly. Elizabeth felt an overwhelming sense of sorrow for her mother's guilt in not giving Mr. Bennet a son. She knew her father did not blame her, but over the years it was often mentioned in a tormenting tease. When her mother was resting, they returned to her father's bedchamber.

Elizabeth took a cloth. After dipping it in the basin of cool water, she placed it upon his forehead. Her father stirred. Choosing to remain at his bedside, Mr. Darcy refused to leave his wife. They witnessed with discouragement, Mr. Bennet's unconscious state. There was little to be done.

Dr. Jones arrived. He remained at the house, expecting the end to be near. The local clergyman, now with his prayer book in hand, was performing last rites.

Several hours passed before Jane re-entered with Mr. Bingley. "Darcy," he said as he bowed, "is anything to be done?" Mr. Bingley whispered as he neared his good friend.

"Unfortunately, no; I see nothing to be done."

"Elizabeth, should you be h——" Mr. Bingley started to say, but noticed Mr. Darcy slightly shaking his head, prompting him to quit the subject. Mr. Bingley quickly reciprocated, saying he expected there would be lamb, salad and fruit to eat in the dining hall, if they were hungry.

"Perhaps I should go to the dining hall. I have no appetite, but suppose for my condition's interest I must take in some nourishment," Elizabeth stated languidly.

A relieved Mr. Darcy accompanied her.

"Jane, I shall stay the night in my bedchamber so I may visit father frequently. I should not wish to be far from him," announced Elizabeth.

"I should like to be in my chamber as well; perhaps we may take turns," Jane replied. "Lizzy, our mother is unwell; she has cried herself into a nervous state. I have come from her bedchamber. She looks rather pale, quite ill. She is excessively warm; I fear she is in need of the doctor's attention. Oh, Lizzy, I fret for both our mother and father. How can this be? It was just a few days ago he became ill. Now the whole house is in uproar."

"I know, Jane, I know. I will go to my mother now."

Mr. Darcy accompanied his wife to her mother's bedchamber. "Mamma," said Elizabeth, gently touching her hand.

Her mother, in a subdued, tired voice, cried, "Oh, Lizzy, your father is so ill; what shall become of us? How shall I get on without your father to direct me? He has always taken care of us. Oh, Lizzy, I am so tired. My head aches; I just want sleep."

"You rest, Mamma. Jane and I are here; we shall look in on Father; you rest," Elizabeth told her with as much tenderness she could afford. Quitting her chamber, Elizabeth turned to her husband. "I should like the doctor to look in on my mother; she is a bit warm. Judging by her tired state and slow manner of speaking, I believe the fever has taken a definite hold."

"I shall see to it."

Kitty and Mary wept outside their mother's bedchamber. Their father was on his deathbed, their mother was of little comfort to them, and they appeared isolated. Elizabeth and Jane had their husbands to console them. It appeared they had no solace of their own. Mr. Darcy, feeling overwhelming compassion for them, directed, "Come girls, stay with your sisters."

They returned to their father's bedchamber, discovering his condition unaltered. There was no response to the medicine the doctor rendered—he had sunken further into a comatose state; his pulse was weaker. The hope of a more auspicious report seemed to be fast slipping away. The smell of burnt vinegar permeated the chamber, leaving its lasting effect throughout the house. Mr. Bennet's existence seemed insignificant, as he lay stretched and still.

The doctor shook his head, anticipating little hope was left.

"I do believe it would be wise to look in on Mrs. Bennet," Mr. Darcy told him, then turned to his wife. "Elizabeth, which was your chamber? I will have the parcels brought up. Perhaps you would like to rest a bit?"

"I believe Jane and Mr. Bingley have already taken care of it."

"Very well then, let us first go to the dining hall; you need nourishment."

He turned his attention to Kitty and Mary, gently directing, "Come Kitty, Mary, you shall sit with us. You have had a trying day, have not you?"

The girls burst into tears. Still sobbing, they responded to his direction, descending the stairs with the rest of the party. Once Elizabeth was seated, Mr. Darcy gently patted Kitty on the shoulder to comfort her. This appeared the only attention she had received. He offered her a chair; then turning to Mary, he offered the same compassionate comfort. Mr. Bingley was quick to follow his example, paying further attention to the girls by helping them reach the platters. The house was busy with people. The servants were hard pressed to keep up with the events of the day. Those despairing had little time to think of anything else but the present sorrowful situation.

Elizabeth finally thought to ask, "What of Lydia? Jane, has she been informed of our father's grave condition?"

"We sent word express, but received no reply. I supposed she would come directly upon receiving it," Jane told her as she burst into tears.

Mr. Bingley, while comforting Jane, passed Mr. Darcy a forlorn look. Uncomfortable in teary situations, he felt helpless.

Mrs. Philips sat close by weeping fervently; she was not to be comforted. She feared for her sister and her brother-in-law. She lamented on stories of spreading fevers in the village years earlier. Her tales of ravaging death did little to ease the situation. They only elevated the occupants of Longbourn to a heightened pitch of tension, but she was determined, as always, to continue to seek out the worst of circumstances. Mr. Philips sat quietly at her side. Almost as though he was used to her exaggerations, he seemed not to take her present state with an ounce of worry. Mr. Darcy thought him rather devoid of feelings, but, after learning Mr. Philips had just arrived, determined the man had little opportunity to understand the depth of the situation.

A servant hurried into the chamber. "Mr. and Mrs. Gardiner," announced the servant. Elizabeth immediately arose from her chair to receive her Aunt Gardiner.

"Oh, Aunt, I'm so glad you are come, my father is not expected to——" Elizabeth could not speak. Torrents of tears streamed down her cheeks. All she had fought to hold back now gushed from within.

"There is no need to explain; I understand," Mrs. Gardiner said, looking despairingly in Mr. Darcy's direction.

The gentlemen bowed. For the moment it appeared they could do nothing else. Waiting was the only activity appropriate.

"I fear," cried Elizabeth, "my mother appears to have the fever as well. I am certain my father's condition is grave."

"Elizabeth, I know you love your father and mother, but should you be here my dear? Should you be exposed in your condition?" questioned her aunt.

Mr. Gardiner added, "I'm sure everything possible is being done. We have great concern for your condition. Do you think it wise to stay in this house?"

"I know what you imply; I have already visited with my father. Perhaps I should have thought the better of it, but I am physically strong; you know how I am. I could not stay away, surely you cannot expect it," she cried as she sat down again, placing her folded arms on the table and lowering her head upon them. Mr. Darcy gently touched her shoulders.

Mrs. Gardner stepped closer. "There, there, yes, we know, we only voice our anxiety of your condition. It would be very hard to stay away, I'm sure of this."

"I know, Aunt." She turned to look up at her husband, took his hand, then continued. "My presence causes my husband much anguish. Although he has not said so, I read it in his face. He knows I need to be here. He has not intruded on the right of a daughter to have a final moment with her father." Then turning back to her husband, she said, "I should like to return to his bedchamber once more; will you accompany me?"

"Of course," he replied, fixing his eyes on her aunt's.

They visited his bedchamber, Kitty with Mary following behind, along with Jane and Mr. Bingley. To their discouragement, Mr. Bennet's state had not altered.

They looked in on their mother. "She appears to be sleeping," Mr. Darcy stated. "Perhaps it is best you ladies return to the sitting room. Charles, would you assist Elizabeth? I should like to converse with Dr. Jones." With a nod of his head, he motioned them all out of the chamber.

Mr. Darcy, now alone with the doctor, suggested, "Dr. Jones, perhaps it would be wise to check Mrs. Bennet; there is reason to be concerned; she is extremely warm."

"Very well, are you in charge, sir?"

"No, I am not. I only seek to keep abreast of the situation. I am but a son-in-law. My wife is a daughter; she is with child. I am concerned of her welfare and that of my unborn child. As for who is in charge, I cannot say. I believe that position remains unclaimed."

"Very well, sir, an infectious fever has taken hold," he replied dryly.

Mr. Darcy accompanied the doctor to Mrs. Bennet's bedchamber. She was in a state of rapid decline. Having taken a turn for the worse, her body now cleaved to a high fever. She gave no response; her pulse was faint, her breathing shallow.

Dr. Jones turned to Mr. Darcy. "Sir, I charge you to send word at once to Dr. Smyth in Meryton. I fear a second opinion from one with more experience with typhus is required."

Having understood his meaning, horror raged within Mr. Darcy. His mind raced; the thought of such a fever haunted him. He was well aware of the danger to all occupants within the confines of the house. Before he could carry out the assignment, Dr. Jones flatly stated, "Sir, I would suggest you not alarm anyone in the house until Dr. Smyth has made known his professional opinion. I believe it unwise to inform the others presently."

"You may be assured of my silence," Mr. Darcy returned. He quit the chamber in haste, now suffering the conviction of the risk to his unborn child. He did not wish to alarm or forbid Elizabeth to be with her father, but he had growing fear that the uncertainty of the infectious illness was not to be taken lightly. In his anguishing position he thought he should go mad with fear. An infectious fever was concern enough, but typhoid? He no longer found comfort in his wife having passed that trying time of feeling sick or light-headed, which had earlier been the only relief he had found in the entire situation. His newfound concerns bred unavoidable torment.

It took slightly more than an hour for Dr. Smyth to arrive. By this time Mr. Darcy was afflicted with a wretched state of dread. He waited outside of Mr. Bennet's chamber with his back to the wall and his eyes shut. The anguishing turmoil of the potential horror of typhoid fever made him ill. With suffocating fear, he perspired profusely. The agony of it all caused his chest to pound without relief. Containing his feelings proved impossible. He had successfully convinced the ladies to gather in the sitting room to allow the doctors to look after Mr. and Mrs. Bennet, devoid of interruption. Mrs. Philips continued her loud, fretful wailing. Kitty and Mary were inconsolable. There was little even he could do. In his despair, he felt desperate to take leave of the house.

Mr. Darcy slowly and gravely approached his friend. "Bingley, would you be so kind to look after the ladies?"

Mr. Bingley eyed his friend closely. Although he was unaware of the degradation of the situation that brought so much pain, he knew his friend was suffering.

"Would you prefer I joined you, Darcy?"

"No, I think not, not this time; please take charge."

"Very well, you may depend on my doing so."

"Thank you, Bingley," he said, hastily quitting their company, unable to bear the trepidation within him. Even he could not conceal the terror in his guise.

Charging his way out of doors, he stumbled in his strides down the graveled path to the copse. A penetrating shiver ran through his body, leaving him with a clammy feeling. He stepped dully; shuffling over a few loose stones along the path as he swiftly plodded along. Mortifying thoughts sent chills down his spine. All such thoughts disheartened him with desolate notions of what might be. In desperation, he fell to his knees beneath a tree, burying his face in his hands. He remained for a time, then began to pray.

"Oh, God, you alone know the nature of my soul; I beg your protection from the painful circumstances of typhus." He found the comfort of prayer was now his only method of release. Humbling himself, he audibly worshiped, "O God of mercy, I beseech your forgiveness for past transgressions. I desire to seek your will alone. Allow me the opportunity to show I am worthy; I am desperate for your divine power."

Choking out words through grief-stricken misery, he asked of God, at once with anguish and humility, that he might grant a miracle. His prayers were unselfish, full of grace and humble adoration. After a hushed stillness, he pleaded with raging energy, by faith, with all his heart's wishes, feeling he could scarcely endure more than his present suffering. Then the Lord's Prayer involuntarily passed from his lips. Unable to contain himself any longer, he wept under the stars, unleashing all he had sheltered inside. A slight wind sprang up suddenly. At that moment, he knew not from whence the voice came, but somehow knew it was the Lord's voice summoning mysteriously. The words seemed to whisper on the wind, voicing, "Peace I give unto you, mighty works shall be known to you this day." He raised his head, attempting to compose himself once more, but remained silent and still. An unnatural stillness seemed to reign. He rose to his feet. Millions of stars lit the sky. He stared up toward heaven as the still night air turned suddenly tumultuous—as if to defy all earthly reason. A strong gusty wind sprung up around him, whipping his clothing with force. He clutched his coat about him as a clap of thunder roared, making the earth tremble beneath him. He stood for several moments unafraid, studying the sky. The fierce wind swirled round and round him, as if to take with it his fear. Never in his entire life had he experienced such an abrupt change in the atmosphere. He reasoned the unnaturalness of the experience came from a powerful source. Overcome by a sense of peace, all that weighed him down seemed to dissipate as if it had been taken over by foreign guidance, leading him to a purer future than he had a right to expect. It was an extraordinary event, contrary to the customary process of nature. In his heart he felt assured it was his faith that now held the substance of all that was prayed for, promising the evidence of that which was not seen. He felt strangely safe from the foe of danger. He fell to his knees to give thanks.

The atmosphere once again became tranquil. With fresh hope and inexplicable knowledge of all, which gave him strength to carry on, he released all hopelessness and sorrows. With an enormous sense of certainty beyond expectation, he was overtaken by peace of mind. In his heart he felt the death-ravishing effects of typhoid had been cheated. A cooler gentle breeze crossed his brow, yet the night was still; but somehow he knew, without reservation, his prayers had been heard. It was an experience he was not familiar with, nor likely to soon forget. It was frightening, yet produced serenity. The thought of the powerful experience caused his entire body to tremble. He looked up to the heavens with a quiet heart, steadily inhaling. He filled his burdened breast with the night air, gaining a sense of composure amid spiritual tranquillity. Like a thunderbolt that strikes, he abruptly felt a forceful urge to return to the house. As he forged his way, his strides gathered speed. At first, he did not join the others, but went directly to Mr. Bennet's bedchamber to find him still in an unconscious state. He sat at his bedside with his head bowed for about half of an hour, pondering on the feelings within his heart. The inexplicable event he felt he could not disclose, for fear its communication would not be met with so much understanding to make a penetrating impression on anyone so wholly connected to him. Without warning, Mr. Bennet began to regain a conscious state. Mr. Darcy raised his head. He looked in the direction of the doctor.

"Sir, I am relieved to report the fever is not of a typhus nature, just an infectious fever. I fear his wife suffers the same."

When Elizabeth entered the chamber, Mr. Darcy moved to allow his wife nearness to her father. She softly talked to him, taking his hand. After a few moments, she looked at the doctor.

"Doctor, I believe he is not quite as warm."

The doctor carefully checked him, then his pulse. He paused. "I do believe you are right; his pulse is stronger, his chances are good."

The doctor looked at Mr. Darcy in amazement. Mr. Darcy nodded in recognition. He was still in awe of his experience, trembling at the thought of the power of prayer. Mr. Bennet was slowly awakening. As he continued at his father-in-law's side, he reached down to put his hand on his. Mr. Bennet stirred, taking a hold of his hand. In a weak voice, he said, "God is so good; indeed he is." He then drifted into a restful state.

The doctor examined him again, then afforded a favourable nod. "I do believe the fever is leaving him; he'll be weak, but his signs are getting stronger. I believe his chances of recovery are greater indeed. I would not have thought it possible. He was much too weak; his pulse was scarcely detectable. I daresay I have never witnessed anything like it."

"You expect him to recover, do you not?" asked Elizabeth.

"I see no reason he should not recover; he will need much rest; improvement may be slow. But, if he continues as he is, he will get stronger with time."

"And Mrs. Bennet, has she come round?" asked Mr. Darcy.

"Dr. Smyth is with her; come, we shall see."

They followed him to her chamber. Dr. Smyth was taking Mrs. Bennet's pulse. She remained in a sedate state. Her pulse was rapid, but the fever still took its hold. She continued to drift off, awakening occasionally to speak, but her words lacked clarity.

Lydia arrived. She was distressed to discover her mother's deteriorating state. Miraculously, Mrs. Bennet regained consciousness, managing a few words to Lydia before drifting back into her previous, unconscious state. She visited with her father, not realizing how very sick he had been. She went below the stairs weeping uncontrollably for her mother. With her handkerchief, she wiped the tears from her paled face. The bloom of her youth seemed to have faded. Although married, her attachment to her mother had not wavered. Elizabeth felt a certain compassion for her young sister, who was swollen with child, looking rather worn from her journey. She felt sorry her sister was alone in her delicate state. The flimsy excuse of her husband's absence was further proof he gave little thought beyond his own concerns.

The week next, Mr. Bennet grew stronger; the fever left him. But that was not so with his wife. She lay still, slipping in and out of consciousness. On the evening of the sixth day since his turnabout, Mr. Bennet was allowed to go to his wife's side. He sat at her bedside as he watched her in her unconscious state. He spoke softly to her. After a bit, she awoke. "You are here, Mr. Bennet?" she asked, her voice faintly trailing.

Taking her hand in his, with tenderness he replied, "Yes, my dear, it is I."

"Forgive me, Mr. Bennet, I so wanted to give you a son."

"You rest, my dear, do not anguish over such thoughts."

"Forgive me, Mr. Bennet," she repeated again weakly.

"My dear, God has been good; he gave us five daughters. You rest now, all will be well." He patted her hand, then stood. Leaning over her, he kissed her forehead as she fell into a sleeping state. He sadly made his way back to his chamber.

Witnessing the exchange put Elizabeth under additional despair; her head pounded. She felt sick to her stomach. Lacking sleep, she was clearly exhausted. Through his insistence, her husband led her to the bedchamber, hoping she would sleep.

"Oh, I wish there were some good news to be had," she uttered.

"Well, my dear, I have had a letter from Pemberley."

"Why did you not tell me? What does Colonel Fitzwilliam have to say?"

"Just that all is well. Ann gets stronger every day. He hoped the situation at Longbourn was not as grave as anticipated."

"Yes, we all hope so."

"Yes, my dear, I am sorry I have not mentioned it sooner. The letter arrived at a most inconvenient time. I had forgotten it. You look very tired, dearest; you should rest."

Elizabeth rested, much to her husband's satisfaction.

The morning next they first visited her mother's chamber. Her Aunt Gardiner had just summoned Dr. Jones upon noticing Mrs. Bennet's state of deterioration. The girls surrounded their mother's bed. The clergy had been summoned as well as Mr. and Mrs. Philips. The whole of the family now gathered in her chamber. She lay unconscious; her pulse had turned extremely weak. There was no response.

After about a half-hour of somber silence, Dr. Jones looked up. He shook his head in sorrow as he sadly told them, "I am very sorry." He slowly pulled the cover over her.

"Are you sure she is gone?" Mr. Darcy questioned soberly.

"Yes sir, I'm afraid so. I have done everything possible; there was nothing more to be done."

"Yes, of course, excuse my insistence," Mr. Darcy added. His sobering voice trailed off, then he further asked, "Did she ever regain consciousness?"

"No sir, I'm afraid not since yesterday."

Elizabeth turned to her husband. She clung to him, crying profusely. He held her to him while she wept. Tired, weak and drained of energy, she began to slip through his arms. He was loosing her to the floor. Mr. Bingley, along with the doctor, helped him deliver her to her bedchamber.

"Pray please, I believe you should examine my wife at once; I fear she is unwell."

"Your wife is with child, is she not, sir?"

"Yes, she is."

"This has been strenuous for her, sir; perhaps she ought not have been here."

"I'm well aware of that," Mr. Darcy replied. "How do you tell a daughter she must stay away under such circumstances? Will she recover without injury?"

"I believe with rest, she will do well. It appears she is strong; is that not so?"

"I certainly hope so."

While the doctor examined Elizabeth, Mr. Darcy entered Mr. Bennet's chamber. "Mr. Bennet, I fear I have bad news. Sorry as I am to tell you of it, it cannot be helped. Mrs. Bennet has perished, sir. I am so very sorry."

Mr. Bennet stared out into the room without responding.

"Is there anything I can do for you, Mr. Bennet?"

"No, Mr. Darcy, you have done much more than we could have anticipated. I am grateful to you, sir."

"Mr. Bennet, it distresses me to leave you, but Elizabeth has fainted. The doctor is with her; I must get back to her."

"Do take care of my Lizzy, Mr. Darcy."

Mr. Darcy nodded his head. He quickly quitted the bedchamber to rejoin Elizabeth.

The smelling salts brought Elizabeth around, but she did not wish to rest. Instead, she insisted she go below the stairs to join the others. She was not up to taking orders and exercised her will of iron to have her way. Failing to convince her otherwise, the doctor helped Mr. Darcy assist her below the stairs.

Mrs. Bennet was dead. It was unforeseen. Those close to her had expected she would make the same turnabout as her husband.

Mr. Darcy stayed at his wife's side. Elizabeth buried her face in her hands and wept. The cry drained her, robbing her of all energy. When she could cry no more, she sobbed, gasping periodically to control her calm, then turned to her husband to bury her face into his chest. Mr. Darcy held her close, the whole of the time wishing she had taken Dr. Jones's advice. Mr. Bingley comforted Jane, while the Gardiners paid their attentions to Kitty, Mary and Lydia. The general mood was somber, as expected. Except for the occasional weeping permeating the room by those grieving, all would have been fairly quiet had it not been for the hysterics of Mrs. Philips. Mr. Philips could do little to comfort her.

Dr. Jones entered the sitting room. "I shall take my leave. Mr. Bennet is resting. He appears to be doing quite nicely. I believe my services today are no longer required."

"Thank you," Mr. Darcy said as he got up to see him to the door.

"Mr. Darcy, I can find my way; perhaps you would do better to stay with your wife."

Hill quickly moved in the doctor's direction to see him to the door, but not before affording Mr. Darcy a reassuring nod.

"I believe you are right. Thank you, I bid you good day," replied Mr. Darcy. He then turned to his wife. "Dearest, I do believe you should rest."

"Very well," she answered, allowing him to lead her away. He sat in a chair near her bed with his book. Finally, Elizabeth gave in to sleep. Finding it difficult to concentrate on his book, he set it aside. Bringing his hands up near his face, he put his fingertips together. He sat silently, reviewing the death of Mrs. Bennet as well as his unusual experience. Securing his book again, he looked over at his wife, then turned the book over on his lap. He had not the opportunity to share his experience with her. He wondered if she would understand. Laying his head back against the chair, he closed his eyes. It took but a few moments for him to fall asleep.

A servant announcing, "Sir, your presence is required at dinner," awakened Mr. Darcy.

"Very well, we shall be there directly."

"Very good, sir."

The brief exchange woke Elizabeth. Together they made their way to the dining hall. There was little conversation; the general mood was gloomy. Without the loud wailing of Mrs. Philips, there was a deafening silence. All that could be heard was the sound of the utensils touching the plates along with an occasional clearing of the throat amidst quiet sobs.

Mr. Darcy was glad when late evening provided an excuse for all to retire. They had looked in on Mr. Bennet several times. Each time he was sleeping.

Since Mr. Bennet was to recover, Jane and Mr. Bingley returned to Netherfield, giving up the bedchamber to the Gardiners. Kitty and Mary shared a room to provide a bed for Lydia.

It was quiet; all inhabitants seemed finally at rest. Mr. Darcy was just about asleep when he heard uncontrollable sobbing. He ventured to the hall. It was Lydia. "The poor girl," thought he aloud, "alone in a family way with no one to comfort her."

He lightly knocked on her chamber door.

"Yes, what is it?"

He hesitated, "It is Mr. Darcy; are you all right? May I have the servant get you anything?"

He could hear her controlling her sobs, "Please go away."

When he returned to the chamber, Elizabeth was awake. "Where did you go?"

"I heard your sister sobbing; I offered to help her, but she would not have it. Elizabeth, tomorrow will be a hard day. It disturbs me to see her alone.

Kitty and Mary look lost as well. It is obvious Lydia's event will come before ours. Surely a woman needs her husband at such a time. The Gardiners, perhaps they will stay near her. Shall I mention it to them?"

"Please do; I'm sure they will be glad you did. You quite astonish me. Such goodness, you have been the strength for us all, even to the wife of someone who tried to do you ill."

"No, Elizabeth, the strength comes from another source. I could never be deliberately unkind. Lydia is your sister; why should I not wish her well? Rest now, you will require much strength. You will need your vigor tomorrow. Tomorrow will prove hard. Poor Lydia, she was deemed favoured by your mother; is that not so?"

"Yes, I know; it will be most difficult for Lydia. I do believe she will feel the sting of our mother's death deeply. Her husband does not afford her the comfort of his company in a situation such as this. Such a sad thought indeed. Have no fear, I shall sleep now; good-night, dearest," she said as she closed her eyes, snuggling closer to him.

He lay still with his arm about her, looking into the darkness, unable to rest. Thoughts of his experience kept him awake. If she cannot understand from where I draw my strength, how will she ever contemplate the holiness of such an experience? Will she ever discover such a profound reasoning power? Will she ever be raised to that level of understanding? All such thoughts now consumed him. He lay still, listening to her steady breathing as he snuggled closer to her, burying his face in her tresses. He closed his eyes as he inhaled her fragrance. This was his favourite time of the day, when he could keep his arms about her. It was a short time before he fell into a shallow sleep.

The Funeral

THE SADNESS OF THE FUNERAL was only slightly brightened through the strength gained by Mr. Bennet. He was too weak to attend, but his heart was deeply rooted there. Hill stayed behind at Longbourn. Mr. Bennet awoke. He sat upright as he looked over at Hill, who had been stationed in a chair at his bedside.

"You are awake, sir, allow me to alter the bolsters."

Mr. Bennet looked at Hill. "Thank you, Hill. The house is quiet; I suppose the family is still at the church. I know you wished to attend, Hill, but I am infinitely obliged that you stayed behind to tend me."

"Yes, sir, quite all right. I imagine it is best to remain among the living."

"It will be a trying day."

"Yes, indeed, Mr. Bennet, it is a very sad day."

"Well, Hill, a man certainly has a lot to reflect upon, does he not? I imagine it will be rather quiet at Longbourn."

"Yes, sir, I imagine it will," he said as Sarah entered.

"You have served Mrs. Bennet well, Sarah."

"Yes, sir, I shall miss her." Sarah wiped the tears from her eyes with her apron after she fluffed up the bolsters behind him.

"Life can certainly be difficult, can it not now, Sarah?"

"Yes, sir, I imagine so, " she replied as she fought to hold back her tears. "Would you like some hot broth, sir? It will do you good."

"Yes, Sarah, I believe that would well suit me just now."

She departed the bedchamber. He closed his eyes as he lay his head back into the bolsters. Before Sarah could return with the broth, he heard a commotion below the stairs, supposing the whole of the family had returned from the churchyard.

Elizabeth and Mr. Darcy immediately went to Mr. Bennet's bedchamber. She scurried above the stairs in haste. "Are you awake, Papa?"

"Yes, Lizzy, I was just lying here thoughtful of your mother." Just then Sarah entered with the broth. As he sat up, Mr. Darcy fixed the bolsters behind him.

"Thank you, Mr. Darcy, you are quite attentive."

Mr. Darcy nodded. He walked behind his wife to rest his hands on her shoulders.

"So, Lizzy, did you stand in for your father today? Was the service to your liking? Was it done properly, according to my wishes?"

"Yes, Father, it was. The people from the village were very kind; many friends and parishioners attended. My sisters have had their moments. It is hard, as you well imagine."

"What of your cousin Mr. Collins, was he there?

"Yes—Mr. Collins was present, but he did not say anything to me. Dear Charlotte did. She expressed her sorrow of our mother's decease. Of course Sir William did so as well. There were many people, Father. It has been hard these past days."

She did not tell him she had ordered Mr. Collins to leave Longbourn. At the funeral, Mr. Collins avoided her, although for a brief moment their eyes did chance to meet. His look was laced with impassioned disregard.

To Lady and Sir William Lucas, Mr. Collins represented everything desirable in a man of the cloth. Such praises were shared frequently. There was no greater pride than that of Sir William Lucas, who took every opportunity to praise his son-in law's character as reverent as well as devoted.

At the funeral, Sir William Lucas approached Elizabeth and Mr. Darcy. "The death of your mother saddens us greatly." He paused, then added, "It has had a great sorrowing effect on Mr. Collins, poor fellow. He feels it most acutely, indeed he does. His attachment to his cousin is commendable. I fear the loss of your mother has thrust him into a melancholy state. Just last evening, out of concern for Mr. Collins, I looked in on him after noticing his melancholy state after informing him of your mother's death, as well as your father's gain in strength. I believe it tormented him; he cried at length. I don't believe I have ever heard a man weep so violently, surely I have not. He knew not that I was in the shadows. I kept to myself, not wishing to embarrass the nobility of his manner. Be assured he was greatly moved by the loss of his cousin's wife, for I heard him talking to God. I distinctly heard him ask, 'Why her, Lord, why did it have to be her?' Dear man, he was so troubled; I dared not interrupt him, not even to console him. I believe I heard him weeping during the night as well."

Mr. Darcy and Elizabeth listened intently. It was obvious that Sir William lacked understanding of his son-in-law's true meaning. Elizabeth could only feel a certain sense of anguish for her friend. She viewed Mr. Collins' rudeness at the funeral as a relief; believing it would have been far more difficult to be pleasant had he approached her. Elizabeth was glad Charlotte had not the opportunity to witness the confrontation at Longbourn, supposing he had not educated her of it. Charlotte was very much with child; upsetting her would prove ill-gained. Reminded now of her father's notorious words of advice—"some things are best left unsaid"—she felt the truth of its meaning. She was abruptly drawn from her thoughts by her father's addresses to her.

"Yes, my dear, your mother is sure to be missed. What of your sisters, are they doing better, or do they fret still?"

"Better yes, they will come to you soon. I believe they have willfully afforded me time alone with you."

"Kitty and Mary seemed melancholy, what of Lydia? Lizzy, she was not doing well. It is not like her to be downhearted; I cannot recount ever witnessing Lydia despondent."

"I know, Father, she seems so severe; she is downcast."

"Well, I'm sure your mother knew Lydia loved her. Tell her come see me alone. I should like to have a talk with her. A sad case my dear, she was always her mother's favourite. I'll assure her of that, perhaps that will elevate her spirits."

"Yes, Father, it just might at that; I'm sure it will."

Mr. Bennet turned to look at his son-in-law. "Mr. Darcy, I dare ask, you were here were you not when I was brought out of the fever? I believe you were; is that not so?"

Mr. Darcy stepped closer. "Yes, Mr. Bennet, I was; why do you ask?"

"I thought it to be so, but I'm confused; I thought someone took my hand."

"Yes, Mr. Bennet, it was I."

"Mr. Darcy, were you present when Mrs. Bennet died?"

"Yes, sir, I was."

"Papa, I talked to mother before she died. She was very tired. I spoke to her ever so gently; I promised to look after you," Elizabeth told him, hoping to ease his painfully anguished thoughts.

"Mr. Bennet," interjected Mr. Darcy, "Dr. Jones was with her in the end, as well as the family. She did not appear to suffer at length."

"Well, I'm glad to hear of it."

"Dr. Jones said she kept repeating something about regretting not having a son; she was sorry for it, that was all," Mr. Darcy said as he altered the slipping bolsters.

"Yes, it must have troubled her; we talked of it as well. My dear Mrs. Bennet, as if she had any authority over it, poor woman. I'm sorry too, she did want a son; it was never to be, that is all."

"Papa, you look so tired; should you not rest just now?" Elizabeth asked, taking the cup from him, handing it over to Hill.

"Yes, Lizzy, I believe I should." He closed his eyes as he lay his head back after Mr. Darcy adjusted the bolsters once again.

Elizabeth and Mr. Darcy went below the stairs to join the others. It was a very sobering afternoon, except for some sobs every so often. Lydia remained withdrawn. She scarce spoke but a few words together. All that could be heard was quiet discourse about the funeral.

Jane and Mr. Bingley stayed the entire day. Lydia had her talk with her father before quitting Longbourn in the afternoon, but not before a brief conversation with Elizabeth.

Elizabeth was glad to see she was in better spirits after talking with their father. Lydia appeared lonely; the bloom she once owned seemed to be fading. Elizabeth thought perhaps the conditions of the journey, as well as being alone when traveling, were partially to blame for her depressed state, along with the loss of her mother. It saddened her to witness it. But when alone, Lydia spun around to face Elizabeth. "It must be quite nice to be so rich. If you could think of me once in a great while, it will be welcomed I assure you. I think we should not have enough money to live without help. Perhaps Mr. Darcy would consider sending three or four hundred a year? Would you ask him, Lizzy?"

Elizabeth stared at length, wrinkling her brow in an effort to understand her lack of shame or pride to seek funds continually. At that moment words failed her.

"Lizzy, would you ask for my sake?"

Elizabeth faintly smiled. "I have sent you twice from my pin money, Lydia. I had rather not appeal to my husband on such a matter, but I shall give it further consideration." She leaned forward to pat Lydia's hand in a comforting manner.

Lydia pulled her hand away swiftly. "Thank you just the same. I can plainly see you have no intention of mentioning it to Mr. Darcy. Very well then, see if I care. Live in your grand hall with all the trimmings. Think of me if you will, but I shall give you no attention at all. I suppose I should be grateful you have the time to talk with me. I'm glad you know how I feel. Even if you do disapprove of my husband, it is of little consequence to me. So there, Miss Lizzy, be happy in your thoughts at your grand estate. Well, I bid you farewell." In a flash she boarded the carriage. She was out of sight before Elizabeth could respond.

Elizabeth watched the carriage take its leave. She had expected Lydia perhaps to look out of the window, but she did not. The view of her hat brim was all Elizabeth could see. Within moments the carriage disappeared.

How very foolish my sister is, thought she. To imagine I would approach Mr. Darcy with such a request. The whole of the conversation pained her. She had no intention of mentioning Lydia's request. Just the same, it was no less disturbing to think Lydia would expect her to ask. The thought of George Wickham pained her. For a brief moment she considered the injustice of it all. How could Lydia suggest such a notion. How dishonourable is this man who sends his wife alone to see her mother buried. Tears welled in Elizabeth's eyes; she wished her sister no ill will. She could not help but think of the recklessness of George Wickham's past. Surely George Wickham was aware of his duty in life. Surely he is aware, if a man does not do what is expected of him, his reputation is doomed; his family surely disgraced. The prospect of George Wickham's lack of integrity was grievously recounted. She could only think him a terrible disgrace. She wished she could tell him how very much she despised him now. She mumbled aloud, but no one was there to hear her. "Mr. Wickham, I am well aware of the dishonour you bestow on my sister as well as my family. I shall never understand how I was ever taken in by you." Elizabeth emitted a dull reprove. She clenched her hands tight, thrust them straight down at her side, then relaxed them again. She then composed herself before entering the house.

The Gardiners left for home shortly after Lydia's departure, promising to visit at Pemberley soon. Mr. Darcy's attachment to the Gardiners for their contribution to his present happiness caused him to extend to them an open invitation to Pemberley.

Elizabeth and Mr. Darcy stayed three additional days. Mr. Bennet was getting stronger. He was out of bed, moving about for short periods and managing to spend time in his room. Elizabeth saw this as an excellent sign of his return to normalcy. However, how normal was that life now? It was certain to be a much quieter place without her mother, thought she.

When it neared time to leave, Elizabeth turned to Mr. Darcy. "I should like a few moments alone with my father. I would like a private conversation with him."

"Very well, go to it."

Elizabeth neared the doorway of her father's chamber. She lightly knocked.

"Come in, Lizzy. I know why you are come. You are taking your leave now, is that it?"

"Yes, Papa, but first I desire a few moments alone with you."

"So your husband parted with you momentarily, did he?" he quipped, then winked.

Elizabeth took a seat at his bedside. She reached over to pat his hand. "Yes, he honoured my request, I knew he would."

"Lizzy, he is an excellent man, the best. I'm so pleased you're happy, my dear."

"Yes, Papa, you have no concern of me; I am well taken care of."

"I suppose it will be quiet now. I suppose I'll have a certain sense of loneliness to speak of; but not to worry, I shall get on with it; I always do."

"Kitty and Mary are here, Father, you will not be so alone."

"Yes, but one day soon they'll run off leaving your poor old father to himself, no doubt."

Even though it was not the proper time, Elizabeth felt it necessary to approach a delicate subject. She moved the chair nearer to him. Taking his hand in hers, she delicately spoke. "You know, Father—many men marry again after a respectable amount of time has passed. Perhaps one day you will." She let loose of his hand. "It is not necessary for you to be alone forever."

Mr. Bennet looked weary. He scrunched his face with disapproval of her suggestion. He looked at her over top of his spectacles, as if to wonder whatever can she be thinking. "No, no, Lizzy, I'm determined to remain alone to the end of my days."

"But why, Father, why should that be?"

"Lizzy, I shall never wish to marry again; life has dealt me my fair share of the marriage state. I do not believe I care to have another round of it. No, I'll not hear of it!"

He spoke with great certainty of opinion. His convictions on the subject appeared to be severe. She felt it best not to press on with the subject any further. She knew her father and mother had not been the best-matched pair. In fact, she viewed their relationship a constant challenge.

"Oh, Papa, I must take my leave. Mr. Darcy wishes to come in to say good-bye. You will write, Father, will you not? Surely you will be up to penning a letter."

"To be sure, Lizzy, now let me see that husband of yours."

Elizabeth withdrew from his chamber. She returned with her husband. Upon his entry, Mr. Darcy bowed respectfully.

"Mr. Darcy, you will be sure to take care of my Lizzy, will you not?"

"You may count on it, sir."

"Thank you, Mr. Darcy, you are a kind man. I'll not soon forget just how very kind. You quite surprise me pleasantly at times, you are indeed an honourable gentleman."

"Thank you, sir."

"Well, well now, come here, Lizzy." Elizabeth moved close to him. She leaned down to kiss her father good-bye. He kissed her on the forehead. "Now get along, the two of you."

"Good-bye, Father," Elizabeth said as she paused at the doorsill affording him a faint smile before departing. The thought of leaving her younger sisters saddened Elizabeth as well. Saying good-bye while they remained downhearted unsettled her. Her sisters would be lost without their mother, she was well aware of it. "Good-bye, Kitty, good-bye, Mary, I expect we will see you at Pemberley for a visit when father is completely well. You must write to me."

"We shall, Lizzy," Kitty replied with a lost look.

Mary looked profoundly at Elizabeth. "I believe we must accept that which we do not understand. And, we must understand that which we are to accept. It is written in the Bible, "whatsoever thy hand findeth to do, do it with thy might; for there is no work, nor device, nor knowledge, nor wisdom, in the grave, whither thou goest." So you see, Lizzy, we must accept; we must go on to do those things we ought to do."

"I'm sure you are right, Mary; life does go on."

They quitted Longbourn to start for home. Elizabeth's mind was filled with the events which hastened their journey to Longbourn, as well as the turn of events which were now instilled in her memory.

As for Mr. Darcy, his thoughts contemplated the experience at the copse.

Return to Derbyshire

Before starting their journey home, the Darcy carriage made a stop at Netherfield Park. Elizabeth touched Jane's arm. "Oh, Jane, these have been hard days, have they not now?"

"Yes, how does our father do today, Lizzy?"

"Very well this morning, Jane. He was in his room; that is good, is it not now?"

"Yes, we shall go there later today. Lizzy, I am so glad you stopped, even if it is for a short visit." Jane's expression soured; her lips parted, unleashing a sigh. "Lizzy, do not be alarmed; Caroline is here with Louisa and Mr. Hurst. They have been very cordial to me, and I expect the same for you. Lizzy, Mr. Bingley's sister Emily has come. She is so very different from Caroline and Louisa. You will like her, to be sure. I expect you will, yes indeed you shall."

They entered the house following Jane to the sitting chamber where the whole of the party was gathered. The greetings began. Elizabeth received a civil welcome from Caroline and Mrs. Hurst. When introduced to Emily, Elizabeth could immediately understand why Mr. Darcy, as well as her sister, thought she might take an instantaneous liking to her.

Emily advanced toward Elizabeth. She curtsied, then greeted her. "I am so delighted to make your acquaintance, Mrs. Darcy. Please accept my condolences on the death of your mother; I am so sorry. My brother Charles has told me much of you."

"I'm delighted to meet you at last. I've heard so much about you too," Elizabeth said as she curtsied.

Elizabeth thought Emily unpretentious with gracious style. She was smaller in stature than expected, and thin, but not too thin. Elizabeth thought it

184

odd she had never married. But then, perhaps she never met anyone to her liking, she mused, as if to find an excuse in her own mind.

Emily's hair was light chestnut in colour. Her features were fine, her skin like milk. She had an appealing face with a pleasing expression, matched to a character emanating certain affability. Impressed with Emily, Elizabeth noticed she walked with all the loveliness expected of a woman in her situation. Although her presentation was superior, she determined Emily did not exhibit herself above her company, a quality both Caroline and Mrs. Hurst lacked. There was nothing haughty, stiff or rigid about her. She was quick to make conversation as an equal, demonstrating a kindness to Jane which Elizabeth found pleasing.

It was little wonder Mr. Bingley appeared proud of Emily, thought she. She glanced over at Mr. Hurst, who lived up to his general reputation of lounging. His manners were lacking as always. He abruptly sat up, letting out a snort before closing his eyes again. Elizabeth viewed his snobbishness to be no match to his general manners or appearance.

Caroline and Mrs. Hurst, although civil, examined Elizabeth. Their eyes combed her entire form as they commented on her new fashions. They restrained from snickering together as they had done in the past. Elizabeth concluded that the watchful eye of her husband must have influenced their manners. Mr. Bingley seemed to be keeping abreast of the situation as well.

Elizabeth was decidedly polite. Quite relaxed in their company, she went out of her way to show marked pleasantry, gracefully accepting their invitation to play a tune on the pianoforte.

Caroline was uncommonly friendly to Mr. Darcy. As suspected, it was of no surprise to watch Louisa Hurst follow Caroline's lead. They spent little more than three hours at Netherfield Hall before parting. Elizabeth was glad to have met Emily at last. Emily, upon learning of the upcoming event, wished them joy.

As always, it was hard to say good-bye to Jane. The same sentiments were expressed and, as always, it was a tearful farewell.

Once the journey began, Mr. Darcy turned to Elizabeth. "I am pleased Caroline and Mrs. Hurst greeted you with civility. I contemplated their allegiance with peculiar regard considering past sentiments. Their display of notable decorum proved this to be a most pleasant interview, would you not agree?"

"Yes, I was quite surprised by it all."

He was not at all surprised to find she liked Emily. As for Mr. Bingley's other sisters, he viewed the reception of Caroline and Mrs. Hurst a representation of future salutations. He supposed their designs on visiting Pemberley in the future induced them to establish agreeable behaviour in his presence.

"Caroline and Louisa Hurst are not likely to utter remarks as in the past. Since they are aware I remember all that has passed, they are sure to remain guarded in my presence, especially with regard to my wife."

"Yes, I suppose that is true."

"I thought your sister looked well. Of course Bingley's felicity one can hardly escape. He intends to invite your father and sisters the Saturday next to spend the day, as long as your father is up to the task."

"I did not know of it," she replied. This pleased Elizabeth; her father would need to be out in society. She feared he would be less likely to visit the Philipses. Although Mr. Bennet liked them, he and Mr. Philips never had much common conversation. Mrs. Philips was always fussing when not gossiping, a trait which annoyed him greatly. Other than a short visit, he was not likely to spend much time in Meryton. She was sure her father would visit at Lucas Lodge, feeling equally certain Sir William Lucas would look in on him occasionally. There were sure to be fewer trips to the local warehouses now that her mother had passed. Kitty and Mary would have to find something else to occupy their minds. That would not be hard for Mary, who always had her nose in a book, but for Kitty it could present a challenge, Elizabeth mused.

Mr. Darcy observed his wife, "You look healthy, my dear, in spite of the hard days you have just experienced."

She smiled at him with a reddened face. Compliments from him were always welcomed, even though his admiring looks induced a blush.

Mr. Darcy turned suddenly serious as he leaned in to her. "My dear, I'm so sorry your mother died. I am sorrier I had not expressed it more strongly to you at Longbourn. Surely you know I understand your pain."

"You have, dearest, perhaps not in words, but surely you and I are clearly beyond speaking when words aren't enough. No words could have made it more plain."

"Your sisters suffer a vast deal, I fear."

"Yes indeed, but you afforded them comfort. Do not think my sufferings prevented my awareness of your kindness. With all that passed, they were lost until you rectified the matter with your gallant rescue of attention paid in their direction."

"I did what any man would do."

"I think not; you exceeded expectations to be sure."

"If you wish to believe that, I'll not try to change your mind on the subject."

"My father thinks you gallant."

"How so?"

"My father may appear to be an ordinary man of simple wit, but make no mistake, he has a way of drawing out the inherent characteristics of people. He has the wisdom as well as the ability to make light of those situations that prove less than pleasing. I believe he simply endures what life bequeaths him. Do you want to know of the conversation we had alone before we parted?"

"If you wish me to know."

"He mentioned how quiet it would be once we were gone. Naturally, he is not alone with Kitty and Mary present. I supposed at first that he meant he would be lonely, but I'm not sure. I believe he existed in the house with my mother, often seeking the privacy of his chamber to escape the fussing. I'm not sure there was much to their relationship on an intimate part. It made me sad to think of it. He could be hard on her at times. To be truthful, he often took enjoyment in his quick wit, which made her nervous or upset to some degree. But he always made it right in the end. He did desire a son. My mother knew that, but never expressed it in a compassionate fashion. I was very much surprised she mentioned it on her deathbed. Oh dear, I ramble on so."

"I do not mind; perhaps it is good to talk of it. He will be lonely, I suppose."

"Yes, I imagine so; he will be lonely indeed. A man needs companionship; would you not agree?"

"Not all men, some are content to be alone."

Elizabeth thought he answered as if he understood. She curiously eyed him, then went on. "Perhaps I should not have approached the subject, but I did tell my father that I believe, after certain passing of respectable time, he should think of remarrying. I should ought not to have done it. I should have thought the better of it."

"Why is that?"

"His answer haunted me."

"Haunted you? How so?"

"All he said was, he'll not entertain such thoughts. He would prefer to remain alone to the end of his days. He thought life had dealt him his fair share of the marriage institution. He was adamant about it. It was obvious he was thinking of my mother."

"And this haunted you?"

"Yes, do you not see? His marriage lacked the felicity one expects. He has had much to deal with. You observed my mother's character. Surely you understand his meaning all too well; is that not fact now?"

Mr. Darcy made no answer; his expression revealed nothing. He looked straight ahead, avoiding any direct look.

"You will not answer me. You refuse to express your opinion, is that not so?"

He placed his hand over hers. He gently squeezed it, keeping it there. "Elizabeth, your father is a good man. Given a respectable amount of time, and if the opportunity presents itself, he may find himself in a position to give such thoughts reasonable consideration."

"You are an excellent creature. You will not speak ill of my mother; no, surely you could not. I loved my mother, but I am well aware of the strained embarrassment she placed on the family reputation. She could be foolish in public—she often said things she ought not to, thinking nothing of it. She lacked a certain quality in her air. You need not say so, but I know you must have felt the sting of having such a woman as your mother-in-law. To be sure, we are all aware of it; but like my father, this is what was dealt to us. We had to abide, endure; it was ours to accept."

"Elizabeth, it does no good to dwell on this."

Elizabeth released her hand from under his. "Yes, but I know it to be truth. I know the less said the better, but should I not be allowed to express my sentiments to you? I could not speak on such a subject to any other."

"Yes, I suppose this to be so, since you put it that way."

"You know how frank I can be. I have said nothing to you that was not truth."

Mr. Darcy remained silent. Believing there was no comfort to be found in undesirable remarks, he simply leaned forward, patted her knee, then put his open hand upon her cheek as he afforded her a comforting smile.

She acknowledged his silence to be exactly as it was meant. Giving it further thought, she concluded his virtues and countenance, coupled with his confidence in his own judgments, directed him perfectly right. She realized that concealed beneath such reserve was his understanding, which she viewed solid as his worth. There was nothing wanting in his character. She knew her esteem toward him was stronger than once believed, if that were possible. She finally felt she totally understood him.

Suddenly Elizabeth remembered Mr. Collins. She quickly turned to Mr. Darcy on the edge of the seat, approaching the subject hastily and with determination. "What exactly did you say to Mr. Collins at Longbourn? Of what did you say to him?" she asked again impatiently, before he could give an answer.

"My presence generally intimidates him, surely you are aware of it. I merely referred to Lady Catherine's opinion regarding ill manners connected to the deathbed, explaining my aunt is very sensitive on the subject, having never gotten over the death of my uncle. I cautioned that she would be angry and may consider releasing him of his position at Rosings, should she learn of his taking inventory, anticipating the death of your father. You should have seen his expression when I reminded him she is not in agreement with such conditions imposed on estates, which deprive female lineage. I suggested he take care that his ill-trodden steps do not trample upon the heels of the future. Then I mentioned my knowing the bishop personally; explaining, I thought I should be meeting with him soon. With such revelations made known, he was mortified and became nervous. He hastily quit Longbourn like his pants were torched; need I say more?"

"Oh—do you know the bishop?"

"Yes, I have long been closely acquainted with him."

"I daresay, you do know the right words, do you not now?" She could not help but chuckle to herself at his descriptive narrative regarding Mr. Collins.

"It was not hard to convince him. And I must say, I do find it puzzling to understand how so much can escape the man."

"I am getting weary."

"Come, come to my side of the carriage. You may lean on me. I rather like having you near me," he said playfully.

When she joined him, he placed his arm about her. With peaceful thoughts of her beloved husband at her side, she fell asleep almost immediately, awakening in time to see the last mile of the beautiful countryside, before noticing Pemberley Hall off in the distance.

Notions at Netherfield

ARTING ELIZABETH'S COMPANY always pained Jane. On this day, the difference was also the loss of her mother. Once Elizabeth parted, Jane sunk in melancholy spirits. Since her desire was to be alone, she retreated to her bedchamber without a word. She sought quiet to contemplate her sober thoughts. Even Elizabeth had not the same sense of loss for their mother, she supposed. "My mother's funeral brings such a definite close to my childhood," mumbled Jane aloud as she viewed herself in the looking glass.

She threw herself across the bed, weeping for her mother. She found such favour in her mother's eyes. Although her mother could be trying at times, it gave her great pain to think she had not lived to see them thrive as a family. She would forever be denied the joy of being a grandmother. Thinking of the many times she had publicly caused them all embarrassment, Jane wondered, forlornly, if her death would bring relief to others. All such thoughts brought further pain along with heaviness upon her chest. Her heart ached at the thought she would never see her again. Curling herself up with her knees drawn to her chin, she continued to cry at length until she exhausted herself into a sleeping state.

An hour passed before Mr. Bingley, who had been searching for Jane, awakened her upon entering the chamber. Startled by his entry, she sat up, gasping as she struggled to compose herself. "Oh, Charles, it is you. I must have fallen asleep."

"Oh, my dear Jane, you must have cried yourself to sleep. Your eyes are puffed; I can plainly see you have been weeping."

"Charles, my mother is gone. I feel an emptiness I cannot explain. I know my mother was not up to your level of society; nonetheless, she was my mother. I do miss her so very dearly," Jane lamented.

"Yes, Jane, I can see that," he said as he neared himself to her, taking her in his arms. His compassion only proved to induce a further cry. He continued to rock her in his arms until she finally cried herself out.

She gave him a generous hug. "Charles, you are so good to me. How shall I ever bear the pain of losing my mother? Elizabeth is gone. How shall I endure the days alone?"

"Jane, you are not alone; I am here with you always," he expressed in delicate terms.

"Pray, forgive me, Charles, I did not intend to slight you. You are my strength, my only consolation. I could not wish for more, except perhaps a child. Oh, Charles, it seems everyone around us makes an announcement. My mother died never having lay witness to being a grandmother. I shall miss telling her news of a happy event when it happens."

"Jane, do not distress yourself. These things have a way of working out. I am equally certain we will make an announcement soon. Do not allow others' announcements to shadow your happiness for their sake. Indeed you are happy for Elizabeth and Darcy?"

"Yes, Charles, I did not mean it in that sense. I am delighted for Lizzy and Mr. Darcy; you know I wish them well. I suppose being the eldest, I would expect to have been the first to make an announcement. But that is not the way of the world, is it now?"

"Jane, would you like me to ring for tea? Would that make you feel better?"

"I suppose so; thank you, Charles."

"My sister Emily wondered where you were. She was concerned; she thought I might find you here. She wishes you to know she is near anytime you have need of her."

"Charles, she is very good indeed. She possesses some of Lizzy's qualities; wouldn't you agree? She has that same discretion of frankness. Perhaps her frankness is in a milder sense than Lizzy's. I like her very much, Charles. If you would be so kind, tell Emily I am well. I thank her for her concern. I do indeed look forward to her company when I am in better spirits."

"Very well, I shall have some tea sent up. I shall allow you time alone with your thoughts."

Mr. Bingley left his wife's presence. Jane's dispirited state concerned him. He supposed it was natural for a girl to pine for her mother, but Jane seemed so very desolated. His inability to reconcile her to the loss of her mother pained him. He had rather expected she would do as she most often did with situations—find a reason for its necessity. But then, what necessity could death possibly hold, thought he.

Jane remained in her room long after having her tea, preferring to pass up dinner. She worked herself into a nervous state. She had no appetite, nor did she wish to be in the company of Mr. Bingley's sisters, to carry on conversation of little or no significance to her. She had not the energy to put up a front to appease those around her.

The morning next, Jane arose feeling refreshed. She decided she would take a walk out of doors. Since Mr. Bingley had already quitted the bed-chamber, she wandered to the breakfast room, finding him there alone.

"Charles, you are alone?"

"It appears I am not, now that you are come. Will you join me?"

"Yes, I believe I will. I believe I have an appetite. I look forward to a much better day than the last. Perhaps you will consider taking a turn about the grounds with me?"

"It would please me, Jane. I am glad to see you are feeling much better today."

"Yes, Charles, I have accepted my mother's death. I delight in the recovery of my father. I am fortunate to have you at my side to comfort me; I find I am quite blessed. I have much to contemplate among the living. I am well, Charles, as you can see."

"Yes, my dear, we shall take good care of you. Perhaps we should plan to visit Pemberley. I daresay you will like it. You have not seen it except through others' eyes. I am certain you will find it extraordinary. We shall invite your father and sisters to come to Netherfield at least once a week; what say you to that, my dear? Would that please you?"

"Very much, Charles. I cannot tell you how delighted I am to have such a concerned husband in whose eyes I am cherished."

"Indeed you are; now eat your breakfast so we may take our turn."

"Very well, Charles," Jane replied, managing a half smile. She lowered her eyes to the plate of food. Her appetite was less than expected, but she managed to eat most of it.

The two walked about the grounds. The remainder of the day seemed to pass rather quickly. Each day seemed to bring the brightness of tomorrow. Jane took one day at a time to recover from the loss of her mother.

Sadness and Gladness

$\mathcal{I}$T IS A DELIGHT TO BE HOME AGAIN in comfortable surroundings, thought Elizabeth, as the carriage neared Pemberley Hall. Colonel Fitzwilliam and Ann anxiously greeted them. Colonel Fitzwilliam approached immediately. "I am so sorry about your mother."

"Elizabeth, please accept my condolences on the death of your mother; we were so sorry to hear of it. Be assured we are pleased to hear your father is doing well. I hope one day to meet him," expressed Ann.

Elizabeth was taken aback by Ann's manner. Although still a bit reserved, she seemed less restrictive. Her colouring was much healthier. Her hair shined in the sunlight. Judging by her appearance, Elizabeth determined she looked to have gained in pounds.

"Why thank you, Ann, that is so very kind of you."

"Not at all," replied Ann, "I was sincere in saying so."

"I believe you were."

"Shall we enter now?" Mr. Darcy suggested. Once they gathered in the sitting room, Mr. Darcy poured himself a glass of port, offering it to the others before taking a seat on the sofa. He was content to be back in the sheltering comforts of his own surroundings.

After taking port together, Ann, who was positioned near Mr. Darcy, reported, "Cousin, Mr. Manley is settled on the estate. I have exercised the freedom of inviting him to dinner. I hope there is no objection."

"Why—no, Ann," he answered in an uncertain gradual voice. Her invitation shocked him. He had not considered she would extend herself so willingly. His dark piercing eyes studied her with curiosity.

"Is anything wrong, Cousin?"

"Why no, Ann, I am astonished, that is all. Look at you, you are at ease.

You have taken liberties to show unexpected kindness. It is to your credit. I am not accustomed to viewing you in this fashion; I must say it pleases me, you may be certain."

"Ann, you have been busy while we were away?" Elizabeth inquired.

"Indeed she has, she has been at the pianoforte playing little tunes, sitting here sewing, reading and I know not what," spouted the Colonel as he patted her on the shoulder.

Mr. Darcy rose to fill his glass; then turned on his heels to face Ann. He bowed as he raised his glass. "To Ann, my cousin, who has astonished me. I am well pleased," then he returned to his former position on the sofa.

Ann blushed. Her natural shyness took over.

"You have embarrassed Ann," added Elizabeth, scolding him slightly.

"It's quite all right, is it not, Ann?" the Colonel asked.

She just managed to blush all the more.

Bessie entered to announce Mr. Manley's arrival. As Mr. Manley entered, he drew everyone's attention. He walked to Elizabeth. "Mrs. Darcy, my empathy for the loss of your mother; I was so very sorry to hear of it. Your father, does he continue in health?"

"Oh, yes, indeed he does, thank you."

"Fitzwilliam, I am well settled at the rectory. I have become closer acquainted with your other clergy on Pemberley Estate."

Mr. Darcy bowed. "I couldn't be more delighted." He walked to the table, poured Mr. Manley some port, then returned to the sofa, saying little. The conversation flowed without him. He was content to sit. He observed Ann, after noticing she brightened in Mr. Manley's presence, but then he noticed the Colonel became suddenly withdrawn. There was something dramatic about his looks as he wriggled in his seat. He was suddenly reminded of childhood days as he watched the Colonel wriggle. It was a habit he displayed when intimidated or uncomfortable. He noticed the Colonel watched Ann steadily. His somber gaze bore a sense of loss. His poignant stirring emotions overspread his face. With clenched jaw, he sat mute, regularly sipping his port. It took little time for him to empty the glass. Mr. Darcy noticed he all too frequently filled it again, as if he were greatly pained.

The Colonel was even more inhibited at dinner. He stared at his plate and said little as he pushed the food about, rarely taking the fork to his mouth. He only spoke when spoken to. Mr. Darcy viewed his sober reflection as discomforting.

"Colonel, are you unwell?" questioned Elizabeth.

"I am just feeling a bit under the weather, that is all."

"Oh, I'm so sorry," she said, accepting his explanation. Mr. Darcy did not. He knew the Colonel too well to accept such a shallow answer. Judging by his countenance, along with his lack of appetite, he detected the Colonel had something on his mind. Mr. Darcy, now in much need of rest, was too tired to wonder speculatively why his cousin was troubled. The whole of the evening passed off as strangely as it had begun. Mr. Darcy was relieved to see the day come to an end. He was eager to escape to his bedchamber to find much needed rest.

Mr. Manley

Mr. Manley, now well settled at Pemberley, discovered his surroundings to be everything favourable. He stood at the window that overlooked his garden for about an hour as the day declined. Pemberley was all Mr. Darcy had professed. It is a strange calm, compared to the lively London society I have grown accustomed to, but I do believe I rather prefer the quiet of the country, thought he, as he watched the splendid sun gradually disappear. He lit another candle in his bedchamber, taking a seat near the fire in a comfortable armchair with his book. After a time, he put his book down to look about the chamber. His immediate thoughts were of his one thriving concern, the extreme reduction of suitable ladies in want of a husband. Having decided long ago to seek only those pure affections most men set out to claim, but few withhold themselves for, he concluded he should prefer to remain alone rather than settle for less then his anticipated notions. No such woman had surfaced to suit him in the whole of London society. Having given London's associations ample opportunity to produce such a partner, he succumbed to dwell among country folk. "I believe I might do just as well in the country," he said aloud, with no one to hear. God will guide my path to the altar if that is his wish, he pondered further. I shall seek an audience with Mr. Darcy to express my delight in my new surroundings. Perhaps it is better to wait; the pair seemed to have enough on their minds. My lodging is more than adequate. Since I have placed my belongings, I find it quite comfortable, he thought with satisfaction. I must remember to thank Mr. Darcy for his orders to the steward to supply me with my needs. He was quite taken with the many fruit trees on the grounds. The plot on which his house was situated was taken up with a vegetable garden at the lower end. He was astonished to find that Mr. Darcy had ordered the under gardeners to look after his garden weekly, paying particular attention to the harvest it expected to surrender. The vegetables were perfectly lined as well as weeded continually. The fruit trees were precisely pruned and appeared to be producing well. The local farmers' wives came to gather the fruit periodically, presenting Mr. Manley with fine jellies from his own grounds. Having no wife of his own, he easily accepted the pleasure of the attentions bestowed upon him, only to learn that Mr. Darcy had left word they were to look after him. He was amazed at the swiftness to which Mr. Darcy's employees carried out his orders.

Since his house afforded him a fine library, he wasted little time in placing his book collection upon the shelves. The church was a delight. Mr. Manley was not surprised to find those who cared for the farms at Pemberley were steady in the church. They actively participated in the continual goings-on there, eagerly volunteering. This reality was unexpected, but then, this was his first country parish. He quickly established a pleasant rapport with the people. Equally amazing was the way in which the people spoke of their master. He immediately learned how respectfully admired was his friend. Through general intercourse, he learned those residing at Pemberley Estate were much envied by those employed in the surrounding countryside. He promptly understood Mr. Darcy paid his people a fairer wage than most and was known to reward his employees when the harvest was exceptional. One farmer expressed, "We here know of no other master who shares his wealth when times are good. Mr. Darcy is an honourable gentleman, as was his father. We are fortunate to be under his estate."

It was no wonder the tenants frequented the church, Mr. Manley thought to himself. Whenever anyone fell ill, they gathered to light candles and to pray together. The church was the center of all the estate.

Mr. Manley determined he did not miss the busyness of London; he only missed the many friends, being well acquainted there. More pleasing were the pleasantries of Pemberley Hall, where he enjoyed fine dinners with excellent company. Presently he was enjoying the company of Ann.

The thought had crossed his mind that perhaps Ann would make an excellent parson's wife. Although ignorant on many subjects, she demonstrated an eagerness to learn. He thought perhaps with some guidance, Ann might respond favourably to such an existence. But it was not long before he determined that perhaps he best consider her elevated society. He had learned Lady Catherine de Bourgh was not a woman with whom one might easily deal, surmising she may wish Ann to marry into a more advantageous society with greater wealth than his. He convinced himself her frailty would not make her a good candidate as a parson's wife after all. And since he had not grown to that passionate state of longing to secure her hand in marriage, he thought the better of it, but did not totally persuade himself to consider her lost to him.

Although Ann afforded him a measure of attention, he witnessed the easy nature of relations which flowed between her and the Colonel. In spite of the fact that she brightened in his presence, he could only conclude that the attachment Ann and the Colonel shared was indeed to remain unrivaled and the strong connection between them created a bond with which an outsider ought not to trifle. He decided to retreat from forming any design, but rather chose to allow any such feelings to develop through Ann.

Although the only disadvantage he could find from his new position was that the country did not afford him much chance in finding a wife, he found he was content in his situation and harboured no regrets.

A Message from Rosings

A FEW DAYS PASSED. Two messages arrived from Rosings: one addressed to Ann, the other to Mr. Darcy. Finding Mr. Darcy in the library, Bessie presented him the letter. He read the letter aloud to himself in a mumbling voice.

Fitzwilliam Darcy, Pemberley Estate, Derbyshire
Rosings, Kent

The confines of Rosings remain unchanged. The doctor wishes to prevent the spread of fever, although I am convinced mine has ceased. His assistant, Mrs. White, carries out his orders well. I remain under her persistent watchful eye. I am still not permitted to leave my bedchamber. It is my understanding, Mrs. Jenkinson continues to improve; however, they allow no contact for fear of a reversion. As you can see, I am forced to write with my own pen. I am indebted to you for your excellent care of Ann. You carry out your duty well. I may say you have not disappointed me. Ann writes she is well and content, I remain obliged to you.

The Honourable Lady Catherine de Bourgh

The Colonel neared the library shortly after Mr. Darcy read the letter. He witnessed his cousin's baffling annoyance as he paced about the chamber with the letter clenched in his hand. He took immediate notice of his cousin's facial expression, detecting a combination of sheer amazement and exasperation mixed with anger. He supposed his chafed temperament was a sign of renewed vexation. He could only guess the letter bore the Rosings seal, concluding his cousin was once again gravely disappointed in the deficiency of the letter. By now, Mr. Darcy was mumbling aloud to himself again.

"Darcy, is anything wrong?"

"I cannot believe it," he answered in an angry tone of incredulity.

"What is it?"

"I just received a letter from Lady Catherine. She writes that she is obliged for the duty I perform. She is glad Ann is content, but makes no mention of my wife. I am grieved! She ignores the very existence of my marriage. Is there no end to her insufferable prejudice?"

"Darcy, come now, it may take time. I do know she has always loved you. In fact, I've always viewed you favoured by her."

"Yes, and we both know the reason for that!" he answered fiercely, stretching his arm in the air with the letter clenched in his fist.

The Colonel hurriedly raised his hand to quiet his cousin. "Shhh—quiet Darcy; calm yourself. You would not desire to upset Elizabeth. Surely you know how hard it is for Lady Catherine to set aside her resentment; that should be of no surprise to you."

"I suppose not," he replied with less agitation. His momentary resentment began to fade. The Colonel's calming persistence induced him to civility.

"Give it time, the situation will improve; I'm sure of it."

"Well, I'm glad you are certain of it," Mr. Darcy replied sarcastically.

The Colonel neared his cousin, gripping his forearm gently, "Come, Darcy, the ladies await us in the music chamber."

Mr. Darcy put the letter in his dress pocket. Placing his hand flat against his chest, he deeply inhaled before squaring his shoulders. His resentment dwindled with regained composure. As the gentlemen entered the music chamber, Elizabeth was instructing Ann at the pianoforte. The lessons were not as melodious to the ear as an air, but the gentlemen endured their reverberation, occasionally glancing at each other with raised brows. Although they admired Ann's perseverance, there was certain gladness when she quitted the lesson. The repercussion of sound made it difficult to concentrate on a book or conversation.

The ladies joined them. After sitting for a time quietly, Ann stated, "I have had a letter from my mother. She writes she is still confined to her chamber until Mrs. Jenkinson is fully recovered." She sheepishly giggled, realizing her mother was completely taken in. She continued, "I sent my mother several letters; none made mention of my activities here. I fear she would be angered, Cousin," Ann related, looking in Mr. Darcy's direction. "She instructed that I not exert myself. When I return to Rosings, I shall continue to play the pianoforte, read, embroider and perhaps I shall try to write plays. I shall show my mother I am strong and capable. Indeed I am not to be persuaded otherwise."

Among the three there arose an unspoken astonishment at the assertiveness never imagined in Ann. The three sat eyeing her with amazement. Their reaction startled Ann to embarrassment. Rather shyly she announced, "I shall tell my mother I should like to be out."

"Out?" Mr. Darcy questioned.

"Out, as in society," she said shyly, with a touch of innocence.

Elizabeth delicately replied, "That is all very well, Ann, but should you not do it in a gradual state, so as not to shock your mother all at once?"

"I suspect she will be pleased with me; do you not imagine it so, Elizabeth?"

"She loves you; I'm sure your happiness will bring satisfaction."

"I'm sure of it," the Colonel added.

"Your mother's propensity to protect you may be a bit difficult to repudiate, but you no doubt will persevere; I am certain of it," Mr. Darcy added soberly.

Mr. Darcy was not only contemplative of Ann; his mind was unpleasantly engaged with regard to the communication earlier received. Still agitated with his aunt's language, he desired the diversion of sport. He looked at his wife. "Elizabeth, do you feel quite well?"

"Why, yes. Why do you inquire of my health?"

"I should like to sport today."

"You may shoot if you like. Do not concern yourself on my account, Ann is here."

"Cousin, will you join me?"

The Colonel did join him, leaving the ladies to enjoy a quiet afternoon. Both ladies decided to nap to refresh themselves for dinner, which in the end consisted of the pheasant provided by the shoot. It was an enjoyable dinner with easy conversation, followed by a quiet evening—the four sat comfortably, each at rest with a book of their choosing.

A few days following, the ladies were alone in the music chamber. Ann sat on the sofa doing needlework, while Elizabeth indulged herself in a book. Ann put down her needlework. "My heart beats with felicity, my head with notions; I shall never be the same, nor should I desire to be. Perhaps I shall never be strong as you, but I have taken strides, I depend on doing more."

"Well—well now, Ann, that is what I was hoping to hear."

"Yes, is it not strange how a person can change?" she replied mystifyingly.

"Ann, you astonish me. You arrived here extremely shy; now see how much you have altered. It is good to see you smile, even better to hear you laugh. I am glad to see it. I would venture a guess that you will convince your mother of your abilities."

"You have been good to me."

"And why should I not be?"

Ann turned quiet for a moment. With a voice scarcely above a whisper, she replied, "My mother has been very heartless to you; she resents your marriage. I know it causes you great pain and I——"

Elizabeth stretched forward, patting Ann on the knee to halt her speech. "Mr. Darcy and I have no secrets, Ann. He told me of your conversation. You must know by now that I delight in your companionship. I am proud of having been partly accountable for your accomplishments. Your mother will be taken aback by the very sight of you. Constant pursuit of reconciliation will heal the wounds, fear not. I should believe one day your mother will visit Pemberley; I'm sure of it," she said with notable assurance. Elizabeth smiled warmly as she ended the discussion.

"Ann, I beg you excuse me; Mr. Darcy extended a dinner invitation to Mr. Manley this morning. I believe I must inform the cook we require another plate."

"I'm glad he comes."

Elizabeth quitted the chamber. When she returned, Ann was playing at the pianoforte. As she sat on the end of the sofa, she once again picked up her book. Lacking the required concentration to read, she lay her head back to close her eyes, engaging her mind on thoughts of her own happy situation.

The gentlemen returned two hours before dinner in the company of Mr. Manley. Again Mr. Darcy watched Ann brighten in his presence. The Colonel seemed to be attentive at first, but soon became increasingly out of sorts. His actions were of a competitive nature, quite foreign to his demeanour. Mr. Darcy hoped his guest did not notice his cousin's unnatural expressions.

The rest of the evening passed without any exaggeration of temper. Mr. Manley appeared not to make notice of the Colonel's challenging manners. Mr. Darcy was rather glad to have it end; his cousin's actions concerned him.

When he retired, Mr. Darcy could not so easily fall asleep. He was too busy pondering the evening's folly.

The morning next, as Elizabeth and Mr. Darcy entered the breakfast chamber, they noticed the Colonel sitting with his head down, staring into his cup.

"Good morning," they said.

There was no comment in return. The Colonel remained in a trance.

Elizabeth stopped her walk. She turned to her husband, raised her shoulders, and looked back at the Colonel before inquiring, "I trust you rested well?"

"No, not at all."

"What do you mean, 'not at all'?" retorted Elizabeth.

"Just that—I have not slept," replied the Colonel in a most unusual meditative state. He continued to stare into his cup with heavy-laden eyes.

"Why ever not?" Elizabeth persisted.

"Are you unwell?" inquired Mr. Darcy.

"No, I am not ill."

"Then what is it, Cousin?"

"I'm just fatigued, that is all."

While breakfasting, the three sat quietly with very little exchange. Mr. Darcy and Elizabeth kept a watchful eye on the Colonel. He sat with rounded shoulders, slumped in the chair, looking rather unkempt. Visible was the darkness encompassing his weary eyes.

"Cousin, you look excessively troubled. What is wrong?"

"Darcy, are you being disagreeable with me?"

"No, Cousin, you flatter yourself; I merely want to be sure you are not unwell."

"I slept not a bit."

"Might I ask why?"

Elizabeth intently listened. Her husband was a clever man; she knew he had something on his mind.

"Well, if you must know, I had not a wink of sleep all night. I paced at length; I slept very little the night before; I have the same to report for the night previous. What say you to that, Darcy?" he asked challengingly.

Mr. Darcy and his wife looked at each other, then back at the Colonel. He seemed unreasonably annoyed, so the three sat quietly for a few additional moments.

"Is there a concern I should know of, Cousin? Have we offended you?"

The Colonel blurted out in a nervous rapid voice, "My intentions are honourable to be sure. I have nevermore had such twilight of revelation. I did not sleep. It became clear to me once alone———" He halted his words, thrusting his elbows on the table. With his head now cradled in his hands, he once again stared into his cup, letting out a deep sigh. After a few moments he sat back in the chair again with his eyes closed. His hands gripped the edge of the table. When he did continue, his dialogue slowed. He mumbled, "For years I visited Rosings with you. I never allowed myself to reflect upon my own affections; instead, I ignored them. I often imagined taking Ann away. I don't know what came over me, Darcy. I had this urgent, desperate need to take her away at any cost. Even your scolding did not alter my conscience. I have no regrets, nothing to reproach myself with. Last evening Mr. Manley's presence tormented me. She reaches to the depth of my soul until I can scarcely breathe. I am not ashamed to tell you—I love Ann, I believe I have for years."

"You walk on dangerous ground, Cousin; I'll give you that!" Mr. Darcy stated.

"Lady Catherine's love of Ann was greater than her abhorrence of your wife; my love proved greater than the risk I took. I had no knowledge of it until last evening. I anguished over the thought of her and Mr. Manley together. Oh, Darcy———"

The Colonel buried his face in his hands again as his voice quivered. "Help me see this through. I love her; I always have. You could never see for playing to whom I entertained. All I ever desired was to see her smile, to hear the sound of her laughter. As the years passed her laughter lessened until it fell silent. These past weeks she blossomed like a delicate flower in the spring. My feelings I cannot repress—it's too late—I am violently in love with her. I watch her here in this house, such a sight to be seen. She is pure sweetness; she is all my heart desires." With his face now buried in his hands again, he wept. He was overcome with his revelation, distraught as well as exhausted.

"Come, Cousin, allow me to get you to your chamber; you do not wish to have Ann see you undone. You must rest to enjoy Ann refreshed," Mr. Darcy said convincingly.

Relinquishing himself to his cousin, he faintly agreed. "Very well, Darcy."

"Elizabeth, ring the bell; ask Bessie to bring some warm milk to the Colonel's chamber."

"Very good, dear, I will."

When Mr. Darcy returned to Elizabeth, he smiled as he took his seat. "My cousin is indeed in love; his sincerity is not lacking. He is anguished over the thought of asking Lady Catherine for her hand in marriage. Yes—

I more than suspected this. I have no opinion on my aunt's expected reaction. I am at a deprivation to venture a notion. Perhaps when her mother sees her full of life, refreshed with colour, doing things she was never taught to do, she'll think the better of it. Truly I wish it to be so. My aunt can be mean-spirited, but not toward Ann. One happy thought—my aunt loves the Colonel. I believe she now feels indebted to him for getting her out of the quarantined house."

Elizabeth slightly laughed at the thought of his aunt being taken in. Mr. Darcy chuckled as he brought his cup to his lips. After taking a sip, he put the cup to the saucer, adding, "He may consider it fortunate his scheme was successful." His smile broadened; they looked at each other as they burst into laughter.

"I do believe the Colonel is very much in love," reported Elizabeth.

"It is so—in love with Ann all these years. There can be no other explanation to reason why he risked such a silly scheme. He is not a man of folly; his actions were totally out of character." Mr. Darcy stated, touching her hand in a playful manner. "I am in recognition of his torment; it was not so long ago I suffered the same plight."

"What will he do?"

"I will be in no position to assist him; that is certain."

"I would imagine it will take time."

"Yes, Elizabeth, I'm afraid so. He will suffer much indeed."

"Dearest, I understand his feelings; I have felt his suffering."

"Well, I'm glad to hear of it!"

"You are glad to hear of it?" she squealed.

"Yes, I suffered greatly. It is inconceivable I should have suffered alone. Have you no concept of the wretched turmoil I endured, the sleepless nights, the lack of appetite, the haunted thoughts of life without you, with no mercy in sight? I did everything in my power to forget you. It only proved to worsen my torment. Surely such suffering was not in vain. I daresay, I'm glad we had something in common at that wretched time, even if it was insufferable torment of the acutest kind."

"Well, I suffered a great deal as well," she returned willfully.

"How so, dearest?"

"I could not sleep, nor eat. I had this horrid fear I should never see you again. I could not bear it. The very notion that you would be out there somewhere thinking ill thoughts of me caused me severe anguish. Thank goodness I had Jane to comfort me."

"Indeed, it appears we both suffered. Now you must endure the consequences of marrying a man who adores you, a man scandalously in love. What should you say to that?"

"Well, I should have to give it some thought."

"Humph," he grunted.

They laughed, her hand in his, caught up in each other, until Ann entered the breakfast room. Ann's face coloured. She acted as though she did not know what to do.

"Come in, Ann, join us," motioned Mr. Darcy, as he released Elizabeth's hand.

She neared the table with her plate of food, taking a seat across from her cousin, appearing rather intrusive and embarrassed for having caught them at such a moment.

"Ann, you look refreshed. I daresay you look rather well."

"Thank you, Cousin, I am well."

"We have already breakfasted, but will keep you company."

"Thank you. Where is my cousin?"

Mr. Darcy and Elizabeth shared a look of secretiveness. "He went up to rest; he could not sleep all night," Mr. Darcy reported.

"Oh, I do hope he is well. He seemed irritable last evening. Did you notice it, Cousin? I cannot imagine what ailed him."

"Why, yes I did; I'm surprised you noticed."

"Oh, I always notice everything regarding my cousin. It quite distressed me all evening. I should not like him to be unhappy—he had that look about him, so I thought."

"Indeed," uttered Mr. Darcy.

"Yes, I always view him to be rather cheerful, he most assuredly was not himself."

"You are very observant."

"Oh yes, of my cousin to be sure. I habitually observed him for years. He is the most amiable, agreeable man, such kindness, I know no other to be his equal. Surely he is a most wonderful creature."

"Is that so?" Mr. Darcy answered.

He and Elizabeth had their suspicions of the Colonel, but this was a fresh revelation. Mr. Darcy turned to Ann. "Ann, I have influence in a more prestigious regiment and was thinking of securing a post for the Colonel, but I was not sure of it, because it may mean he would be away from these parts for perhaps two years or more. What are your thoughts?"

Ann quickly burst from her seat with zeal. Like lightning, the thought of his absence sent her into a state of despair. Her eyes filled, her breathing accelerated, causing her face to pale. Her anguished thoughts of losing him were immediately known by the look of horror upon her face. Appearing nervously distressed, she leaned toward Mr. Darcy, "Oh, Cousin, I beg you will not; please, Cousin, I could not bear it; please, no. I could not have him sent away—" Her voice quivered with apprehension.

Mr. Darcy quickly voiced, "I know Ann, we could not do without the Colonel, so I must think the better of it. I believe I must leave him as he is." He could see the relief in her face as her anxiety receded. Mr. Darcy reproached himself for testing her. It was not his wish to excite or upset her. His only design was to assure himself of her true feelings.

"Oh, thank you, Cousin, we are of the same thoughts."

"You better eat your breakfast; it's getting cold."

Elizabeth looked at him in disbelief. She gave her husband a scolding stare as she poked him in the leg beneath the table.

A few hours later the Colonel reappeared, asking Ann to take a turn about the grounds. She quickly obliged. Mr. Darcy watched as they quitted their presence, wondering what he would say to her, if anything.

That evening, dinner conversation was quietly forced with polite conversation. The Colonel in particular was less than civil. He remained out of sorts when gathered quietly in the music chamber. The air seemed stale with certain tense sentiment. The Colonel met any attempt at conversation on Mr. Darcy's part with sarcasm. Elizabeth was relieved to retire. The strain of the evening had taken its toll.

Once in the bedchamber, Mr. Darcy announced, "I must go to the Colonel. He is troubled; I believe he is angry with me. I must know why. I shall return directly."

Mr. Darcy knocked on the Colonel's chamber door, then entered. "I believe we must talk."

"Whatever for?" the Colonel said in an angry, annoyed, less than civil tongue.

"Are you angry with me, Cousin?"

"Indeed I am; I have every right to be."

"If I injured you in any way, I wish to know of it."

"I warn you, do not use your influence to get me out of the way!"

"Is that all?" he chuckled, but then noticed the Colonel did not see any humour in it.

"What do you mean is that all? I pour my heart out to you. In the midst of my suffering, you seek to get me out of the way. What are you thinking? You and I have never had words; this is a first!" he raised his voice in anger again.

"No, no, you misunderstand, I beg your forgiveness. Ann's regard toward you is that of an endearing woman. I just wanted to see her reaction to add certainty to the reality of her feelings. The reaction from Ann was just further proof that she is in love with you, that is all. I realize now I should not have attempted it."

"To be sure?" said the Colonel in a calmer inquisitive manner. A grin of satisfaction overspread his face with astonishment.

"Yes, that is all. I should not have done it; her reaction told me that."

"What do you mean?"

"She became anxious at the thought. I had to quickly say something to calm her; I upset her beyond my intention; I have reproached myself for doing it."

"Indeed?"

"I think, Cousin, you'll sleep tonight," Mr. Darcy said nudging the Colonel's arm.

"Indeed I shall."

"Oh, Colonel, am I to believe you have not approached her with your feelings?"

"No, I did not. I am doubtful of our aunt. I do not believe she will find it pleasing. I shall have to give it time."

"Yes, it is a wise choice."

"Well—good-night, Cousin."

Ann lay awake in her chamber contemplating the course of events which had now changed the whole of her life. I am happily free at Pemberley, she mused. Here I may do whatever I wish without restriction or the scrutiny of a watchful eye. How shall I ever relinquish such freedom? She looked about the darkening room, feeling vaguely comforted, but her mind was dull with painful thoughts of home. For a moment she thought of the little things she cherished from her stay at Pemberley—the pillow slip she stitched, the turns about the beautiful grounds and the general exchange of which she was encouraged to be a part. She sat up, bringing her knees to her chin, wrapping her arms around her legs as she lay her head upon her bent knees. She thought of the pianoforte she wanted so desperately to master. She swelled with the spirit of a young woman blossoming into a cultured lady of society, vowing not to know defeat. Even if her mother forbid her freedom, she would conquer all that stood in her way. *I am determined to stand up to her,* thought she. Thoughts of enduring her mother's constraining nature caused her head to ache. Torn by the knowledge of her mother's estrangement from Mr. Darcy, she started to weep. Tears flowed freely as she sobbed at the thought of parting from all that which represented the new Ann. She loved Elizabeth as a sister. The closeness she now claimed with her cousin Darcy, she could not bear to relinquish. Surely she could not turn back. Her experiences only caused a desire for greater liberation. Although she swore to start afresh, she had no disillusionment of her mother's inevitable displeasure upon learning all that was not revealed in her letters. But she cared little of anything else, other than the independence of the last weeks. *If only she could delight in my alterations; I shall never be the girl I no longer recognize. I must make her mend the disagreement with Darcy,* thought she. But then she remembered her mother's will of iron, her straightforward controlling temperament, which could be vehemently unyielding. She never dared to contradict her in the past. She feared she lacked the strength to confront her with her opinions. Just the same, she told herself, *I have no choice but to do so, or I shall surely die in the hopelessness of my past life.* She hoped the Colonel's presence would ease the judgment her mother might place upon her cousin and Elizabeth for allowing her the freedom of her own will.

She stretched herself out upon the bed. The moonlit night provided a source of light within the chamber, enough for her to stare at the ceiling. She knew the time drew near for her return home. She knew the good doctor and Mrs. Jenkinson could only stretch the falsehood of the fever for so long. She twisted her body around, pressing her face into the pillow, crying uncontrollably until it was saturated with tears. Her head pounded at the very thought of being parted from all that she loved. Her face felt hot from weeping at length, her eyelids felt weighted. Unable to endure any further thoughts of the painful truth, she cried herself to sleep.

Rosings Renewed

ANN HAD BEEN AT PEMBERLEY for a little less than six weeks, when two messages arrived from Rosings, one for Mr. Darcy as well as one for Ann.

Fitzwilliam Darcy
Pemberley, Derbyshire   Rosings, Kent

The quarantine has been lifted; all occupants of the house have fully recovered. The doctor reports Ann may return home. I will send the carriage, Tuesday, May 15. We shall expect Ann to return directly. I remain obliged to you, nephew; my compliments on your kindness.

The Honourable Lady Catherine de Bourgh

Mr. Darcy read the letter. Once again he fumed at the trenchancy of his aunt. Her sentiments regarding his marriage obviously remained unchanged. Although the letter was a bit soft hearted toward him, it still did not satisfy his longing. He remained angry.

Since Ann received a letter as well, Mr. Darcy supposed she knew of the intended carriage. After about an hour he looked for Ann. He found Elizabeth in the music chamber reading a book. "Excuse me, Elizabeth, have you seen Ann?"

"Yes, she was rather upset; I know not of what; she would not confide in me. I believe her to be in her bedchamber; I thought I would look in on her in due time."

"She received a letter from Rosings. My aunt is to send the carriage for her tomorrow."

"Poor girl, that would be unsettling," Elizabeth replied, struggling to raise her now swollen figure from the sofa. Mr. Darcy put up his hand. "No need for you to go; I shall go to her."

"Very well. I hardly know what to say; I suppose it must be."

"Yes, it must be," replied Mr. Darcy before quitting the chamber. He knocked on her chamber door, then entered upon request.

"Ann, I received a letter as well. You know of the carriage?" It was plain to see she had been weeping. His heart ached with overwhelming compassion as he pulled up a chair near her. "I am sorry you must go. We have had many delightful days, is that not so?"

"Yes," she replied sadly. He thought she might cry again at any moment.

"We have become the best of friends, have we not now, Ann?" As he completed his sentence, she burst into tears falling against him. Mr. Darcy just patted her in comfort, allowing her to have her cry, giving up his handkerchief to her. Attempting to make light of the situation, he noted, "Why does not a lady have handkerchiefs when needed?" But Ann did not respond to his remark; she was too busy sniffling.

"I know Elizabeth has discovered you a pleasant companion."

As she continued to sniffle, he continued to converse. "It will be hard to return; that is so, I know; but surely you knew the day would come?"

She continued to sniffle, unable to control her tears.

"I have no standing with your mother to be advantageous to you, Ann. I am sorry for it; you do understand?"

"Yes, Cousin, I know," she managed to say.

"You will write to us, will you not?" he asked. She gave no response. "The Colonel will accompany you to Rosings, but he must leave directly. You know he is required to return to his regiment. I am aware you enjoyed your stay with us; you will visit again, I am certain of it. Perhaps my aunt will even consider it; her letters to me are kinder now."

"I hope so, Cousin."

"The Colonel took his horse for exercise. I expect him back at any moment. I shall invite Mr. Manley to join us for dinner. I will tell the cook to prepare something special. Now, what would you like?"

"Anything, Cousin, whatever the cook makes is always a delight."

"Perhaps the next time you come, it will be under far different circumstances."

"What do you mean, Cousin?"

"Uh—just that it may be with your mother, that is all."

"Oh, yes, that would be delightful indeed," she answered. Although she had been weeping, she was much calmer now.

"I am going to leave you now; you come join us; enjoy your last day here."

"Yes, Cousin, I shall," she said as she got up to follow him. When he realized she meant to come down immediately, he extended his arm to her. They walked below the stairs together.

"Do you remember, Ann, weeks ago when we had our little conversation? We became friends again. I assisted you below the stairs in this very fashion."

"Yes, Cousin, I was in complete relief that day; such a burden was lifted."

"All this has been good for you, you would agree?"

"Yes, I do indeed."

"Elizabeth, look who I found above the stairs."

Elizabeth looked at Ann affording her a broadened smile. "Ah—Ann, your cousin accompanies you like a gentleman."

"Indeed, he is a fine gentleman."

"I wholeheartedly agree; I have no wish to dispute it."

"Tomorrow I shall leave Pemberley, but I shall never be the same as I was; I am determined to do it."

"To do what?" inquired Elizabeth.

"Why, I am just going to tell my mother—no, I'll show her. I'll make her glad to witness my change," she voiced with determination.

"I'm glad to hear of it."

"Pray, excuse me, ladies, I am going to charge the cook to prepare a special farewell dinner. Then I shall go to the parsonage to invite Mr. Manley to join us."

"Thank you, Cousin, I should like that very much."

Dinner conversation capitalized on Ann's pilgrimage home. Although she was sorry to be leave-taking, there was a specific happiness in her countenance. Mr. Darcy supposed his cousin anxious to demonstrate her new character, or perhaps to get on with the business with her mother. Such a pity was the present state of affairs, thought he.

Later in the evening, Mr. Manley played the pianoforte after they played a few word games. The pleasant activities provided a needed diversion for Ann.

"Mr. Manley plays a lively tune; I suppose under different circumstances I would be dancing," Elizabeth exclaimed.

"I have never danced in the whole course of my life," announced Ann.

The Colonel's lips parted with astonishment; he immediately jumped to his feet. A smile overspread his features and his eyes became merry. "I cannot tolerate the thought of it. Mr. Manley, would you be so kind?"

"Indeed, Colonel, it will be my pleasure."

"Excellent," chirped the Colonel as he walked up to Ann. He bowed, "May I have the pleasure of this dance?" As Ann arose from her seat grasping his extended hand, he continued, "Please accept my apology for not having thought of a dance before this. I shall show you a few simple steps." He looked to Mr. Darcy. "Elizabeth, Darcy, won't you join us? It is not difficult, Ann; we shall demonstrate."

"Very well, but I'll only allow Elizabeth one dance—her delicate condition, you know."

"You are much too protective, but I will be the first to admit, I like it," Elizabeth added.

As the four danced, Elizabeth engaged her attention on Ann. "Ann, I am impressed; you catch on swiftly."

"Perhaps it is the result of watching others dance all these years. You forget, although I was never allowed, I had the pleasure of studying the demonstrators."

"Well, that is very hard to imagine. You are indeed quite capable," said the Colonel.

It seemed Ann's last evening at Pemberley was everything gay, as Mr. Darcy desired it would be. Elizabeth played a tune, allowing Mr. Manley a dance with Ann. The lively chatter, united with laughter, had nearly made Ann forget the impending journey.

Mr. Manley quitted Pemberley Hall around seven o'clock, at which time, Mr. Darcy insisted Elizabeth retire early.

"We bid you good night. Colonel, I should wish you not to keep Ann up too late, she must be refreshed when she arrives home. We would not want Lady Catherine to think Ann has overextended herself."

"Yes, of course, Darcy, good-night."

The morning next, Mr. Darcy had one of the servants help Ann parcel her belongings. Ann's heightened spirits puzzled Mr. Darcy. The notice of the waiting carriage did not seem to alter her temperament. Having just breakfasted, Mr. Darcy gave the order to have the parcels placed in the carriage. Colonel Fitzwilliam made himself ready for the journey. It was a bittersweet farewell for all. Although Ann shed a few tears, which was to be expected, she then bid them good-bye, boarding the carriage with a pleasing smile as she waved. Mr. Darcy closed the carriage door. He stepped back, giving a nod to the driver.

It seemed extremely quiet at Pemberley, but they soon agreed it was pleasant to be alone at last. The quietude and solitude, together with the scarcity of amusement, proved to be a pleasing variation, opposed to considering a day of gratifying visitors.

A few days following, when in the music chamber, Mr. Darcy intently read while Elizabeth played Italian songs on the pianoforte. Mr. Darcy glanced up and turned his book over on his lap as he observed her. For some time she remained unaware of his audience, until he said, "Dearest, I wish you to sing; would you do me the honour?"

"Very well, what is it you wish to hear?"

"A song of your choosing, my dear." After obliging him one song, she then joined him on the sofa, snuggling next to him. He reached over to place his arm around her, drawing her nearer to him.

"Hum, such felicity," he purred.

"Is it now?"

"I adore your music. When first I heard you perform, I was impressed by the magnitude of your abilities."

"Well, you shall have it on demand. How can I refuse such a flatterer?"

"Flatterer? No indeed, I speak only the truth."

"I beg your pardon; excuse me, sir, a letter from the post has come," Bessie interrupted, handing him the letter.

"Thank you, Bessie," he said, taking the letter in his hand. As Bessie quitted the chamber, he glanced down at the seal. He immediately looked at Elizabeth. "It is from Rosings. Why, it is from Ann."

"I am pleased she writes. I was concerned we had not heard from her. What does it say?" she questioned as he read. Then he read the letter aloud.

Fitzwilliam Darcy
Estate of Pemberley, Derbyshire

My dear cousin, I must ask you to forgive the tardiness of my correspondence. To tell the truth, I find little time to write. I have been occupied, shocking my mother with all I have learned. She is well aware my alterations I owe to my visit at Pemberley. Although she speaks of it often, she still remains unyielding in admitting she was in error where your wife is concerned. However, I do believe she bends. She herself repeats her name, which is more than was afforded prior. Yesterday my courage rose. I expressed my true feelings regarding the commitment made for me at birth, much to my mother's surprise. It is done; she forgives me for it. I daresay I am the happiest creature in the universe. I am kept busy answering letters from our cousin, Colonel Fitzwilliam. Through his letters to me, he sends his utmost regard to you and Elizabeth. Mrs. Jenkinson is astonished by my alteration. My mother means to present me at court as soon as our cousin can take his leave in about five months; I requested as much. My sincerest regard to Elizabeth; I miss her companionship. Do be sure to tell her so.

Yours,
Cousin Ann

"What a rewarding letter, my dear. Do you not think so?" Elizabeth asked, noticing his mind seemed to be elsewhere.

"Oh, yes, quite so. I was thoughtful of Lady Catherine. How very hard for a woman who spent years forming her pious opinions and her self-righteous principles to be humbled through her own daughter as well as you, to whom she condescends. Her lessons are hard, her opinions obviously erroneous; acknowledgment will be tardy, I am sure of it. I know my aunt; her relinquishment will come in due time, however reluctant, if it is to be. I do hope she yields to what she must know in her heart is right and just."

"We have it to look forward to; that is more than we had before. I'm glad for Ann. I am surprised she remained so assertive, are not you?"

"I worried she would retreat; but let us not forget Ann is in love, and we know the power of such things, is that not so?" he said, looking at her expecting a smile of agreement.

"Indeed it is; I do believe she derived her strength from it."

"Well, my dear, that brings a sense of satisfaction."

"Yes, indeed it does."

In the evening when they retired to their bedchamber, Mr. Darcy, as he did frequently, penned a letter to Georgiana. Elizabeth wrote a letter to her father as well as Jane. As they prepared for sleep, Mr. Darcy stretched his arm around his wife. He suddenly realized how very swollen she had become. Without hesitation, he inquired, "Elizabeth, did you visit the nursery?"

"The nursery?"

"Yes, when Mrs. Reynolds took you about the house, did she take you to my mother's bedchamber? Did she not show you the nursery?"

"I don't recall it; there were so many chambers; I was tired."

"Tomorrow morning I shall show you myself." Both being so completely weary, sleep did not take long.

The morning next, Mr. Darcy directed his wife to his mother's bedchamber. He opened an adjoining chamber door; there it was before them, the nursery. He took her by the hand, guiding her entry. "Oh, dearest, look!" Elizabeth cried. "It is a beautifully decorated chamber; the crib is handsome." Stroking her fingers across the fine finish of the richly carved wood, she carefully examined the style.

"I slept in that crib, so did Georgiana," he said softly.

Elizabeth noticed his voice held certain tenderness. He stood behind her with his hands upon her shoulders as they looked down into the little bed. There was a distinct seriousness about him. His voice was reserved but a gentle tone; his expression was sober. It was obvious his mind was established in memories of another time in his life. His eyes glazed with approaching sentiment, but he did not stir.

"The chamber is wonderful, so cheery; it has a rocking chair; look—a silver rattle, some books over there. It is perfect, just perfect," she described, breaking his thoughtful trance.

"I'll have the servants make it ready with the necessities."

"But, it is so far away from our bedchamber."

"We shall move you in here, you shall take my mother's chamber, it is larger. It is handsome and richly furnished, is it not?"

"Yes, but it's, it's——" she could go no further with her decree. Her voice quivered with anxiety, her heart pounded within her chest as she swelled with concern. The enthusiasm of moments ago quickly dwindled, leaving her suddenly weak. The colour drained from her features, exposing her immediate agony.

"What, Elizabeth, it's what?"

"Well, it's your mother's chamber?"

"Yes, what of it?" he pried further.

"Did your father, did—did he have a bedchamber to himself?"

"Yes, he did, it is down the hall. Why do you ask?"

"Well, I don't——" again she could not continue to speak her mind. Her thoughts consumed her, her concern grew, fearing the changes he desired.

"Elizabeth, what is it? Are you unwell?" he said impatiently.

"I have no wish to be away from you; I should have thought you would want us to be together always."

He started to laugh as he dropped himself in a nearby armchair. He gestured for her to draw near him. Reluctantly honouring his request, her eyes searched for answers while she approached him. He reached out, drawing her onto his lap. Shaking his head slowly, he smiled. "My dear Mrs. Darcy, or shall I call you 'mamma', whatever am I to do with you?"

"What is your meaning?"

"Do you imagine I desire you separated from me?"

"Well, to what purpose then would you be down the hall?"

"That invariably has been my chamber since boyhood. I at no time gave notion to take another. I surmise, with my father's death more than five years ago, I thought it sacrilegious for a son who admired his father such as I, to take his chamber."

"Does this mean you will receive your mother's bedchamber with me?"

"Certainly, none other will do; it is reasonable, is it not?"

"I suppose so."

"You suppose so; this is incomparable to my chamber. Alter it in any fashion you favour. Order the servants to move furniture in, remove furniture, direct new draperies fabricated of your choosing; do what you wish with it, please do, indeed. We can transfer your things here following the improvements. You may convert this to our bedchamber; the nursemaid will reside on the other side of the nursery."

"Very well, but it may take time."

"Well, judging by your figure, it's a matter of a few months."

Elizabeth blushed; she was sensitive, quite mindful of her appearance. His open opinion of her person embarrassed her. He had little reserve in his language to her. His replies were always honest, however disconcerting she viewed his truths. "Elizabeth, I've one request; it's about the——"

"I do not desire to change the nursery; it is perfect as it is," she replied before he could finish his thought.

"Do you mean it? My mother died when Georgiana was two. I visited the nursery frequently, oftentimes in the morning. I have always felt a closeness to her here. Does it disturb you dearest, does it cause unpleasantness?"

"No, not at all. It is comforting to have a husband who loved his mother; you never talk of her, only your father."

"I was almost twelve when she died, Georgiana two. She sang to us in this chamber. She had the softest skin, with dark tresses and fine eyes like yours. She cherished us, always caressing or rocking us when the thunder was frightening. Invariably she had time for us."

"I am sorry I did not get to know her."

"I was lonely when she died; I often visited the nursery for comfort. When I matured to manhood, I ceased to visit the little chamber, but a man becomes a child once again upon entry. I felt that a moment ago. It is so strange; I had forgotten this chamber until last evening. I was anxious to reveal it to you; the morning could not come soon enough. Now I am being sentimental, am I not?"

"Mr. Darcy, you continue to amaze me."

"You better give some thought to this chamber; your time is limited," he said, studying her swelled form with pleasure. "Come, Elizabeth, it's time we breakfasted."

His affections for his mother were of a sensitive nature. There was an inescapable openness in his manner toward her memory, with no deficiency to conceal his innermost thoughts or feelings, which he expressed with pleasing naturalness. He was a man of little levity, a principled gentleman, yet so sentimentally endearing to all he loved. The vast difference in him when alone with her continued to intrigue her. On a few occasions she witnessed his character totally unguarded. In spite of his periodic surprises, she was confident she knew the depth of the man she married. He was complex to be sure, but still, each new experience only enhanced her notions of the surety of her profound knowledge of his identity.

Pemberley's Pride

SEVERAL WEEKS PASSED with little excitement at Pemberley Hall other than the visits by Mr. Manley.

On one particular afternoon, as Mr. Darcy returned to the house, a horseman delivered a message. Since he recognized the writing to be that of Jane, he hurried to present the letter to Elizabeth. She quickly opened the letter, sitting down to read it.

Pemberley Estate

My Dearest Lizzy,
Netherfield Park, Hertfordshire

Be assured we are all well at Netherfield Park. Caroline, Emily Bingley and the Hursts continue to stay on here. Our family at Longbourn is well. Our father, Mary and Kitty are invited often to dine at Netherfield Hall. Lizzy, I must tell you of my distress. Kitty writes to Lieutenant Denny regularly. Fearing she lacks good judgment, I could not rest until telling her of the embarrassing circumstances she may suffer in doing so. The word, originating from Lucas Lodge, is that she is engaged. She tells me she is not. I am hard pressed to make her understand the implications attached to penning letters to the other sex. That is all I have to report on the subject at present. With much happier thoughts in mind, I must relate to you our latest adventure. It has come to the attention of Mr. Bingley, the availability of an estate within six miles of Lambton desirous of a new owner. My husband expresses a keen interest in viewing it. We plan to travel in that direction at once. I am no less eager to oblige him. To think, it would bring me neighbouring to you, my dear Lizzy. If acceptable, we may take possession by Michaelmas. My only regret will be parting from the nearness of Longbourn. Our dear father will be lonely should we quit the place. We plan to visit Pemberley soon. Pray write at once if you will receive us. I imagine Mr. Darcy will be anxious to see his friend Charles as I, you.

My dear Lizzy, I have more to tell. Our own dear Lydia has a little girl named Hannah. We received word yesterday. Lydia is well, but does not expect to visit too soon. There was a sadness in her letter; I believe she pines for our mother. Lizzy, have you heard Mr. Collins and Charlotte have a son? His name is Richard, now to be about four weeks, and it is said that Mr. Collins celebrates in the knowledge that young Richard will one day be master of Longbourn. We understand Charlotte to be well, although Sir William Lucas mentioned she wrote of an infectious fever at Rosings, a cause for concern. By all accounts they avoided the great house. Fortunately nothing came of it and all at Hunsford remained safe. It was reported Lady Catherine was extremely afflicted, in fact, we learned of her confinement to her bed-chamber. I believe this to be the same time you wrote of Ann coming to Pemberley. Perhaps the circumstance of your visit here prevented you from speaking of it. Sir William Lucas swells with pride and has gone to Hunsford with Mariah and Lady Lucas to see the boy. I must bid you farewell now, Emily requires my company. I believe I have told you all there is to tell; I must conclude.

Yours, etc.

Elated to read the news, Elizabeth immediately informed her husband of its contents. The notion of seeing his good friend was more than pleasing. He requested Elizabeth write at once an answer conveying their delight to receive them at Pemberley. He was pleased to hear her father was doing well, saying he hoped he would visit soon. Her husband had little to say concerning the birth of Hannah, only commenting his wish for her family's health and happiness. Elizabeth pressed no further for discussion, although she felt sad to learn her sister did not expect to see her family for a length of time. Remembering her conversation with Lydia after the funeral, she bore the burden of her concerns alone. Although it was in her power to once again send Lydia something out of her private pin money, she chose to ignore her last request. If they neglected to concern themselves with the future, so be it, thought she. She was certain any relief granted to them would lead to further foolish spending. No, she decided, I will not recount this to my husband, nor will I honour such a request; that is my final resolve.

Upon reading that part of the correspondence pertaining to her cousin Mr. Collins, Mr. Darcy smiled. They were pleased Charlotte was in good health as well as the child, but he suspected their absence from Rosings added needed relief to Charlotte, who often bore the direction or correction of his aunt.

Pleasant thoughts lingered as Elizabeth celebrated her sister's impending visit. Much time had passed; she was sure Jane would be surprised to see the alteration of her form.

An invitation to dine at Pemberley Hall was extended to Mr. Manley. On this glad occasion, Elizabeth took delight in informing him of the expected visitors. He expressed his desire to entertain them all at the rectory one evening of their visit.

Dinner was not long completed when Elizabeth sat back in her chair. It was all she could do to stay awake, having had a long tiring day planning the restoration of the prior Mrs. Darcy's chamber. She had spent much of the day with the servants, giving instruction regarding placement of certain pieces of furniture. She directed them while they hung the new tapestry she had commissioned for the window coverings.

"I confess I am fatigued. I fear I am physically unfit to remain in your company. I beg you'll excuse my early departure."

Mr. Darcy helped his wife from the chair. Her developed figure was more visible. Easily noticeable was her struggle to rally her energy. Mr. Manley rose from his chair, then bowed. His face became drawn, the creases between his eyes grew deep with concern. "Mrs. Darcy, I do indeed excuse you. I do hope you feel refreshed in the morning; now, I bid you good-night."

"Thank you, Mr. Manley, do stay, visit with Fitzwilliam."

"I shall, thank you."

"Pray, you'll excuse me momentarily. I wish to accompany my wife above the stairs; I shall return immediately." It was not long before Mr. Darcy returned to the sitting room.

"I trust you have Mrs. Darcy well settled?"

"Indeed."

"Fitzwilliam," began Mr. Manley as he sat his cup of tea aside, "I should like to express my contentment. I am exceedingly happily situated here in the country; indeed I have no regrets accepting this position. I find a ready welcome amongst your people. They demonstrate eagerness to involve themselves in the workings of the church. I must say I was quite impressed with the housing provided when I visited each home individually. Such amenable provisions I had not expected. Your generosity goes beyond that of most men."

"Thank you, Henry," a modest Mr. Darcy answered as he got up from his chair to pour two glasses of port.

"They express the warmest gratitude for my sermons. I daresay the rewards of my position come not from what you afford me, but from the satisfaction afforded through their generosity. The parish exceeds expectation; it provides me with all the necessary tools required by any clergy to achieve success in sacred work. I wish to express my deepest gratitude to you, Fitzwilliam, for the freedom you extend me in charging the parish. You honour your promises well; I am privileged to be the vicar here. I am well aware of the advantages it affords me. Allow me to say, your tenants are good people; the very mention of your name engenders respect. I do believe life is good here for them. Indeed, this must be very satisfying to you, is it not?"

Mr. Darcy kept his quiet reserve momentarily. Mr. Manley's complimentary words pleased him; it was further proof he was following in his father's footsteps. "Thank you, Henry, for your compliments. They are indeed good people; they deserve to be rewarded for the merits of the labour they perform. I am aware of their regard; I respect them. Such lessons I learned at my father's teaching; he was an excellent man."

Mr. Darcy sat forward in his chair before going on. "Although my father sought superiority, he never did so at the expense of those who served him. He was fortunate to possess good business sense; I am fortunate he was my mentor. He once told me, man is not measured by wealth in God's eyes, but by how he treats other men. Our servants receive fair wages; the houses provided are well kept. I make it my business to pay particular attention to their needs. The church remains an important center for all, including my family. I too derive joy from your sermons; I believe every master should be an important presence worshiping among his people. Yes, God has been good to us; I am well aware I am fortunate to have such good people."

He paused to take a sip of his port. "In part, Henry, that is why I sought you for the position; I witnessed none better. I sought the best for my people. I was determined to have you here. You being a valued friend made the selection all the more specific," he declared in unequivocal terms.

Mr. Manley set his glass aside. "Fitzwilliam, you allow me many advantages, but I must tell you I consider your friendship the most rewarding privilege afforded me. You are indeed a man of honour. I declare I am better for having you to claim as friend. You speak little of it, but I do believe you to be a religious man in the best sense. Perhaps your reserved nature prevents you from discussing it?"

"Henry, I do believe God has been very good to me. I should not wish to dishonour Him; it is difficult at times, but a man must strive to always do that which he knows in his heart to be just and pleasing in His eyes. I have felt God's presence; I have been touched by His mercy; I know what wondrous things He is capable of. I—I have been witness of his claim on my life."

As Mr. Darcy once again arose to fill their glasses, Mr. Manley detected that the depth of the conversation threw Mr. Darcy into deep meditation. He could not help but feel he had touched on so tender a subject as to slightly embarrass his employer. He watched as Mr. Darcy took a sip of his port, staring into space. His eyes turned glassy; he appeared to be distracted, almost lost in recollection.

"Fitzwilliam, your seriousness of language, your innate sincerity with such sober declaration, leads me to believe you have had an experience of some magnitude."

"Yes, I confess I have."

"I thought as much. You suddenly became distracted, indeed your mind was elsewhere. I daresay you have, Fitzwilliam, you humble yourself. I have always judged you to be an excellent man. Your honesty overwhelms me at times; but tonight your modesty does not surprise me. I have witnessed it on previous occasions."

"Have you, Henry? I appreciate your notice. I believe a man's real worth is the value of his character; if he cannot face himself in the looking glass with pride, with some measure of self-respect, he is a failure indeed. I do my best to hold myself accountable to these beliefs. He has rewarded me greatly for it."

"My profession requires me to be an inspiration, but at this moment I find myself the recipient. I would be attentive to discover the nature of your encounter, should you wish to bestow upon me such an honour."

Mr. Darcy quietly meditated. He stared mutely, sipping his port. Soberly, he began. "No doubt you recall Elizabeth and I hastily quitted Pemberley to go to Longbourn when her father lay severely ill. I was in a most deplorable state. Nothing I owned, family or connections ever prepared me to face the degradation of horror I was to experience. The doctor more than suspected typhoid. The house was fully occupied, among them my wife and unborn child. I dared not breathe a word until another physician confirmed it. I sank amid my fears, unable to conceal the torment in my guise. I vacated the house at once, fleeing to the copse. I remember taking wide strides, in desperation, with no real design, as I sought refuge from the boundaries of my despair. I dwelt in the thickest darkness. I fell to my knees, less courageous as I humbly shed stormy, heart-wrenching tears, begging a prayer in desperation. May I never again have a necessity to beg to heaven so hopeless and so agonized a prayer as I did in that hour when so much despair passed over my lips." Mr. Darcy turned silent for several moments, taking a sip of his port. He pondered his experience before continuing. "I prayed fervently, laying my soul at His feet, begging not to be forsaken. My grief was beyond degree; I felt helpless." His voice trailed off as he stared into his port. He arose to fill their glasses again, then reclaimed his seat. After taking a sip of his port, he lay his head back and closed his eyes with his glass still in hand. With pressing expression, it was clear his mind was deeply submerged in the subject.

"Fitzwilliam, do go on."

Mr. Darcy did not look up, but gently brought his shoulders up as if to shrug away his reserve. Then he carefully swirled the port in his glass, studying its flow. He nodded his head as he collected himself, clearing his throat before continuing. "Henry—I exhausted all earthly reason. Any attempt to rationalize or resolve such a dilemma was beyond me. I turned to Him as my father taught me to do. I cast my burdened heart at His feet. I plunged deep into distress as I felt death's close embrace, with faint hope expiring. I dared to ask He permit me not to be a stranger. I begged, 'God of mercy, do not forsake me in my hour of need.' I poured on Him the weight of my fear, setting free my burdened breast of its fatiguing oppression, pouring out my soul. My cries sought His charity. As His grace employed my humbled tongue, I clung to His mercy. I remained there still, my hope hovering round every word. The violent passion of my pleading cries trembled throughout my entire being until I felt completely emptied."

He paused for a brief moment as if he were going over every trace of the experience in his mind. Mr. Manley sat quietly, waiting for him to continue.

Mr. Darcy arose from his seat to near the fireplace. After studying the flame for a few moments, he turned once again to Mr. Manley. He looked at him with moistened eyes as he took in a breath of air before continuing.

"Not knowing what else I could say or do, I recited the Lord's Prayer. I remained frozen for I cannot tell you how long—it seemed forever. I felt His mighty hand upon me. Although my body trembled in fear, I remained on my knees. The comfortable night air turned suddenly tumultuous as I looked to the heavens. I was frightened at first. Then a strange peace filled my entire body as the atmosphere once again turned tranquil. I arose with humbled confidence. The night was still, yet a breeze crossed my brow, taking with it my fears. I knew I experienced His holiness. When I filled my breast with the night air, I felt death had been cheated. I knew my prayers had been answered. He answers our prayers in mysterious ways, does not He?"

"Yes, Fitzwilliam, He does indeed."

"Henry, I had not told a soul of this until present." Mr. Darcy's expression remained sedate. His eyes stayed fixed on his glass.

Mr. Manley's admiring eyes were fixed steadily on his friend. He studied him. He became fascinated with the gravity of his countenance, discovering, as never before, the depth of simple honesty in his expression, which emanated a nobleness that flowed out of him humbly.

"Fitzwilliam, you no doubt felt quite alone at that particular time."

"Indeed, the fear of typhoid was not to be shared. I was convinced the fever was more than infectious; I just know it was, Henry. My wife was warm when she lay down; I thought she too would fall ill. You can imagine the anguish I suffered."

"Yes, I believe I can. The Lord commands the day; His ways are just, His counsels wise. You threw yourself in His mighty path. I do believe your prayers were answered. Some men live a lifetime never realizing the power of prayer. Yes, Fitzwilliam, I am certain you were touched by His hand."

"Henry, I was indeed in His favour, but it is not something one can share with easy understanding. I did not tell Elizabeth; I feared her mother's death would not allow her such understanding. Henry, earlier you spoke of my goodness to the servants; you upheld my integrity. I am ashamed to confess it was not so long ago, I confused my superior sense of pride with ill judgment of others. Oh, I have always appeared upright to my workers. Although superior in status, I treated them the same as I do presently. But, Henry, be not impressed by me; I am not worthy of such admiration. My superiority, my false sense of pride, coupled with my selfish disdain for those I viewed beneath me, well nigh cost me the affections of my precious wife."

"Would you consider me impertinent if I inquired of your meaning regarding your wife?"

"Certainly not. But you think you know me, you do not. My father taught me good values, but I fear I interpreted them to think meanly of the world beyond my society. I foolishly proposed marriage to her, insulting her in the same breath with my ill opinion of her lack of wealth, family and connections, having the mordancy to tell her, that in spite of my better judgment and her lack of worthiness of me, I ardently admired and loved her. Her reproof I shall never wish to forget; she thought me devoid of all proper feelings. It was painful when applied; it tormented me at length. She left a strong impression upon me; it was a bitter lesson I fear, requiring me to see the truth of the man I had become. The challenge of her words forced me to cast off my prejudice. Do not lay the burden of greatness upon me; I cannot own it. I am not worthy."

"Very well, Fitzwilliam, your modesty prevents it, I see. Nevertheless, I am strong in my convictions of you. After speaking with you this evening, I am convinced my decision to accept this position has afforded me the very best a clergyman could hope for. What do you say we call it an evening? It is getting quite late; I should not have expected this much time has passed."

"Yes, it is late; we have talked much. Henry, I find solace in your friendship; I'm grateful to have it."

Mr. Darcy walked out of doors with his friend to bid him good-night. As Mr. Manley parted his company, he could not help but think of the exchange of confidences that united them with such openness when recollecting the holy experience at the copse.

Mr. Darcy stood at the threshold looking up at the sky, feeling a great sense of satisfaction. He was overcome with inexplicable feelings of comforting contentment as he continued his thoughts aloud. "Yes, God is very good indeed."

A Joyful Occasion

MRS. REYNOLDS APPROACHED Mr. Darcy just as he entered the drawing room. "Sir, a carriage is approaching."

"It must be Bingley," Mr. Darcy surmised.

"Oh, such a happy occasion to see them once again," cried Elizabeth, as they made their way to the front of the house.

"Jane, I'm so glad you are come. How did you leave our father, Kitty and Mary?"

"Our father is very well, Lizzy, he sends his regard; he expects to come soon with our sisters; I was to tell you so."

"I'm glad you have finally come. How was your journey; did you enjoy the countryside?"

"Lizzy, the park is beautiful; I can see why you like it here. At first I thought we would never see the house, then we came round a bend, continued through the clearing and there it was. It is such a pleasant setting; the grounds are lovely; we passed the lake, ponds, and I know not what. I knew at once why you like it, Lizzy, since you are so very fond of the out of doors, although I don't suppose you are out of doors running so much these days," she exclaimed, looking over Elizabeth's form.

"Jane, how did you manage to come without Caroline Bingley?"

"Charles made no implication to invite them. Indeed I was surprised; he talked of our visit in their presence, but he went no further on the subject. I do believe Caroline was a little put out. I shall talk more of this later, Lizzy. You did read in my letter of Lydia's little Hannah, did you not? Oh, Lizzy, I imagine she is such a sweet little girl. I do hope Lydia is well; they move from place to place you know. I have so much of which I wish to speak to you; perhaps we should go into the house now."

The gentlemen were engrossed in conversation, making plans to sport.

"Darcy, I brought my new shooting jacket."

Mr. Darcy turned. "Elizabeth, Bingley and I plan to go directly to the parsonage before we sport. First we must follow the trunks and retrieve Bingley's jacket. If there is no objection on your part, I should like very much to invite Mr. Manley to dinner."

"Why no, certainly, no objection at all."

"Very well then," he said. The gentlemen hastily made their way into the house to obtain their sporting attire, so absorbed in conversation they barely noticed the ladies followed close behind as they entered Pemberley Hall. Once indoors, Mr. Darcy turned to Jane and Elizabeth.

"I beg your pardon, forgive my inadvertent slight; I suppose the excitement of seeing my good friend is the defect."

"I believe we did not deem it such a severe failing; be off with you, enjoy your sport," Jane answered.

"Yes, Charles, it is pleasant to see you together again. Be assured we have much of which to talk. I have no doubt we will have our equal share of delights," added Elizabeth.

Within moments the gentlemen were out of sight. Together they fetched the dogs, then proceeded on their way with rapid strides.

"I do believe Fitzwilliam longed for his friend after leaving Netherfield. I detected as much; he was very attentive to me, but our conversations lack discussion of sport, perhaps business concerns, too."

"Yes, I believe it is so with Charles as well. When you quitted Netherfield, he was left behind with just ladies, well—Mr. Hurst too. I fear Mr. Hurst is not the best company. Oh, Lizzy, since we speak of it, oh dear, you don't think Mr. Bingley finds he is not content, do you?" Jane asked, fretting nervously.

"No, Jane, you worry so; I'm sure Mr. Bingley is content, but the situation of his sisters—I have no thoughts on the matter nor do I wish to risk supposing. You do know Mr. Darcy invites Mr. Manley for dinner frequently. The two provide a bit of fresh fish for dinner on occasion. Jane, he is such a pleasure. We shall request that he play the pianoforte after dinner. Oh, Jane, I was so embarrassed in London after my performance at the rectory. I could scarce believe it when he sat down to play. Such playing I have never heard. To think he does not read a note of music. I should like to play so fine as he with sheet music," Elizabeth exclaimed as they both laughed.

"Yes, I know your meaning; I too was astonished; I should have never expected it. Now, Lizzy, I must tell you of father and our sisters. They are invited to Netherfield often by Charles. I do believe Charles enjoys father's company. I do know he likes sporting with him, he has told me so. He says father is a good shot. When Kitty and Mary visit, Mary usually has her books, but Kitty—" she paused with frustration, then let out a sigh. "Honestly, Lizzy, I am at a loss as to know what to do with her; there are rumors of her interest in the regiment, still. We did one day play quoits in the back; then we took a walk. I talked in general to her about guarding her reputation. But, Lizzy, when we entered the house, Caroline and Mrs. Hurst just sat surveying us. Often Caroline will just leave the room. As you can well expect, thither also goes Mrs. Hurst; I do believe they are quite put out when the girls visit. Emily is so very different. She will stay to converse with them. It is the only relief I get when they visit. She does pay them attention, Lizzy; I like her very much. She has been a delight; I don't know how I should endure the presence of Caroline and Mrs. Hurst otherwise."

"Jane, you fret so; you forget Caroline and Mrs. Hurst will mind their manners to be sure, if they desire to stay at Netherfield. And I must say, for a man who has such an elevated opinion of himself, I do believe Mr. Hurst to be rather dull, actually rude at times, even to his wife. Why he falls asleep most anywhere."

"Lizzy, that is unkind, although I must admit, what you say does own itself to an element of truth. Well, look at you now, Lizzy, you have changed, your time is near, very near, I think."

"No, I do not believe so, not for another month or better. Mr. Darcy and I have only been wed for one week and eight months. Jane, I am so glad you are come; I should like to show you the nursery. I am exceedingly excited. Jane, now that you are come here, we have much to talk about. You are to stay some weeks; how good it will be to have company. Should you move close, we shall see each other often. Now come, follow me. This is the library as you can see."

"Charles has told me much of it. Mrs. Hurst mentioned it on several occasions as well. Both she and Caroline are quite taken with Pemberley."

"They have spent some time here in the past. Oh, Jane, I am very eager to have you within an easy distance of Pemberley."

"Yes, Lizzy, but I am grieved to be leaving father. It has been some months now; he seems content enough, but it must be odd, surely a bit lonely at the very least, do you not think?"

"Yes, I would imagine so. Even though our father and mother were of different opinions, she always provided certain anxiety, lively spirit or emotional conversation within the household. I'm sure our younger sisters are not up to her level of excitement. I always believed our father rather enjoyed helping her into a nervous state, as I am equally certain he derived satisfaction in being the source of consolation in providing the remedy. It must be quite different, as you say."

The two continued to talk as they walked through the chambers, stopping occasionally to commiserate. They stopped in the music chamber. "Jane, this is one of my favourite chambers. Fitzwilliam and I enjoy many hours together here."

"Oh, Lizzy, it is such a beautiful room. When I read your letters regarding Pemberley, I had not the slightest notion it was this grand. It is richly furnished with exceeding good taste. Lizzy, Mamma surely would have had much to talk of had she the chance to visit."

"Perhaps, but I am heartily ashamed of my own thoughts on the subject at times, Jane. Let us talk of other things. Come, let us venture above the stairs."

"Perhaps you are right. Now I must speak of Kitty. Lizzy, I'm concerned of Kitty; she continues to correspond with Lieutenant Denny. He is still encamped at Brighton. She does not seem to realize the implications of her actions. I tried to explain that ladies do not correspond with frequency unless engaged. I fear she has acquired a bit of Lydia's foolery. You know how Kitty overlooked Lydia's bad judgment. She never seemed to understand the consequences such undesirable behaviour can bring about. Will you speak to her, Lizzy, when she comes? I believe she will listen to you; I should not want another bad situation to arise."

"Nor should I. This way, Jane, follow me. I must first talk to Mrs. Reynolds; she is preparing the guest chamber. It will not take long." Elizabeth made a brief stop to talk with Mrs. Reynolds before directing Jane down the hall.

"Very well, Jane, this way." As they walked, Elizabeth took hold of Jane's arm, guiding her toward the nursery.

"Now, we were talking of Kitty. If I am to speak with her I shall have to give it much consideration; I don't know if she will regard my sentiments, but I shall try. I recollect Lieutenant Denny. He seemed a nice enough fellow, certainly in possession of good manners; I believe he has a good sense of decorum. I should think we do not have to concern ourselves with recklessness on his part. He disapproved of card playing, showed no tendency to any public display, nor did he promote himself boldly."

"Yes, but, Lizzy, allow me to remind you how you were quite taken in by George Wickham. You saw all the goodness in his looks; you believed all his tales. Even our father thought it queer for a man to gain sympathy with stories of woe."

"True, but, Jane, Lieutenant Denny was pleasant; he was not at all of a forward nature. He displayed excellent character, always appeared gentlemanly. I do not believe we should judge his character by that of George Wickham's, horrid man that he is. Lieutenant Denny is worthy of our respect until he proves otherwise. Now, is that not fair? Surely you must agree?"

"You are right, Lizzy, he was a nice young gentleman, but a young woman cannot be too guarded. I am concerned Kitty has set her designs on him. If father discovers it, he will be angry. He will suffer no further nonsense as in the past, especially since our mother is no longer here to prevent him from acting upon it. He will have the last word, you may be certain."

Elizabeth stopped her walk. She turned, then reached out to touch Jane's arm. "You may be right, Jane; our father now has the freedom to express himself devoid of a challenge, but you know he bends. He finds it difficult to carry out his threats. But I shall speak with Kitty about it if that is your wish. What of Mary, how does she do?"

"Mary most often can be found reading. Kitty runs about with Mariah Lucas. I believe Mary to be tardy in the female sense; she lacks the desire to present herself stylish or to make an impression like others of our sex. Do you not see that, Lizzy; do you understand my meaning?"

"Yes, Jane, I believe it is so; perhaps Mary never received those directions from our mother. She was too busy attempting to marry you off. Surely you remember our social instructions. I do believe we remained too sensible in our direction sometimes to our mother's dismay. Now, regarding our mother's dealings with Lydia—Lydia was too young to be out; I see that now. I do suppose the advancement of her natural appearance was of little aid. She was always so much more robust than the rest of us. No one ever seemed to pay much attention to Mary's concerns; she has always been left to seek her own style, which appears to be lacking. Perhaps upon their visit I should make it a point to seek Mary out. Perhaps it is time I pay her closer attention. Without a mother to guide her, I suppose the responsibility should fall upon an older sister."

Elizabeth stopped at the threshold of the nursery. She turned. "Now, Jane, prepare yourself." She opened the door, taking Jane by the hand, leading her inside.

"Oh, Lizzy, such a wonderful little chamber it is. What a beautiful crib, so splendid; it is delightful, so full of cheer," she exclaimed with glee.

"Yes, it is, Jane. Would you believe I have not done anything to it? It is just as it was. My husband slept in this crib as well as Georgiana."

"His sister is from home, is she not? I should very much like to meet her."

"Yes, she is. I am anxious for you to meet her. Now look, Jane, see this rattle? This rocking chair is where Mrs. Darcy rocked Fitzwilliam; he told me so. Jane, he is remarkable; I have grown to admire him greatly. Such a man, he has the tenderest heart. I believe I understand him wholly and completely at last. He is more wonderful than I ever imagined. Although he is reserved apart from here, or perhaps in company, his character is altered in the comforts of Pemberley; you will see he is more at ease."

"Oh, Lizzy, I did notice a different man in London. I like him, I like him very much. He is a man of few words in public but he is more at ease around me just now, though I suppose that is due to him and Charles being such great friends."

"True, but, Jane, although you will see a noticeable difference here at Pemberley, you are certain never to view him in absolute informality. It seems my husband is quite a tease when we are alone in our chamber. I should have never suspected it of him. He may slightly tease amongst family or close connections; nevertheless, when we are alone, he is quite unrestricted. At times he is somewhat guarded around the servants, though."

"I should have never imagined him to be so, Lizzy."

"Nor I," Elizabeth replied, her complexion having turned a deep shade of red.

"Are you quite all right, Lizzy?"

"Yes," answered Elizabeth, still caught up in her own thoughts. She moved as close to Jane as she could possibly get. Lowering her voice to almost a whisper, she related, "Jane, perhaps I should not speak of it, but Mr. Darcy is very unguarded when we are alone. He lacks no reserve whatsoever. He quite often teases—why he even jumped out to grab me one afternoon when I entered the bedchamber. I did not know he was there. He quickly shut the door and swirled me about the room. I would have never guessed him to own such romantic tendencies. I was quite taken by surprise."

"In the afternoon? Whatever did you do, Lizzy?"

"What do you mean, what did I do? I endure his flattery with great enjoyment. I do not care if it is early or late afternoon to be sure. I delight in his open intimacy. I'm just surprised by it, that is all. You shall say nothing of it."

"Surely I will not. But, Lizzy, I confess I am quite surprised; here I thought Mr. Darcy was commonly reserved."

"There is something genuinely artless about his romantic notions. I believe I am excessively fortunate to have such an attentive husband. He exhibits exceedingly good sense with regard to fanciful sentiments of his unguarded affections."

"We are both fortunate indeed, Lizzy. Charles is such a fine husband. He is as you see him, always easy; seldom does he alter his composure; perhaps just every so often," Jane replied as though she had something on her mind.

"Whatever do you mean, Jane?"

"Lizzy, I did not write of it, but I received a letter from Lydia; she requested we send money, claiming they have not enough to live comfortably. Charles saw the letter quite by mistake. He was very displeased. For my sake, he said he would send a note, but he thought we should think the better of it, pointing out no amount of money would satisfy their appetites for what they cannot afford. They continue to spend, mount debts, then move on to avoid settling them. Charles did not believe we should do it. Lizzy, I am concerned for the child; I do hope she is well taken care of. Lizzy—I understand Lydia makes another announcement. This alarms me; can you imagine Lydia with two children? How shall they ever afford it? Moving from place to place with a child; it distresses me to think of it."

Jane's voice cracked with concern; she let out a deep sigh. Believing she might cry at any moment, Elizabeth moved closer to her, taking hold of her arm. With a look of guarded curiosity, she inquired, "Did you send them money, Jane?"

"No, I thought I should not. Once started, how would we put an end to it? Do you suppose Lydia sends requests to our father? You know he does not have much, but with mother gone there is less foolish spending. Do you think she imposes upon him?"

"I do not know. I dare not guess; I should not wish to ask him either. Twice I sent relief from my pin money. I do know, Jane, she never wrote again once I denied her last request. As for the amount, it mattered not. I feared what was to follow. The expense would not be the impediment, but the knowledge of its spending may surely be. I will no longer send her a farthing of my pin money. I, like you, believe it best not to start it. Jane, I did not inform Mr. Darcy of it; I seriously doubt that I ever will. It saddens me greatly to think of it. One cannot help but be concerned."

"I saddens me, Lizzy, such a poor choice of a husband."

"I do believe Lydia makes foolish decisions in any event. Although foolish, I am of the opinion she would not have compromised herself had she not been in love with him. No matter now, that is all in the past. Let us think of better things. How much time do you intend to spend here?"

"I do not know; some time I expect, three weeks at the very least. Charles is anxious to spend time with Mr. Darcy. He means to look at the estate of Foxshire. I am glad we are come. My husband lacks suitable male companionship. Mr. Hurst is not much company, as you may well imagine. He lies around all day, does nothing more than excessively eat. The only time he goes out of doors is to sport. Even when we gather in the sitting room, he is usually slumped over the sofa, snoring aloud, no less. It is quite unsociable, somewhat embarrassing, I believe. Other than sporting or cards, he and Charles have little in common. They do not share the same notions, not that Mr. Hurst expresses any."

"Caroline and Mrs. Hurst, tell me, Jane, do they treat you well?"

"Yes, they do, Lizzy. I do believe they look upon past actions with regret, or at least they appear so. I have not yet let my guard down. I cannot overlook how they tried to separate me from Charles. His sister Emily is quite the opposite, she accepts me indubitably. I like her very much; we have become good friends. I detect Caroline and Mrs. Hurst a bit envious of the naturalness of our relationship."

"Oh, Jane, do be careful. I fear I cannot be as generous as you, but, I confess, I was greatly impressed with Emily Bingley."

"I should like you to get to know her better," Jane said, reaching out to touch Elizabeth's arm. "She is very kind to our father and sisters when they visit Netherfield. She showed Father about the grounds. I do believe he enjoyed it; they appeared to find much to talk of. She taught Kitty a new stitch. Would you believe she has introduced Mary to books of poetry? I was surprised to find Mary so receptive."

"How very interesting. Well, I thought all was dull at Netherfield, but from what you tell me, it appears to be quite the opposite. I'm glad to hear of it."

After seeing Jane was well situated in the guest chamber, Elizabeth asked, "Shall we go below the stairs now, Jane? I must tell the cook to prepare for three additional settings, although, knowing Mrs. Reynolds, she has already done so. Oh, Jane, Mrs. Reynolds is excellent. She takes prodigious care of our household. I cannot conceive what I should do without her; her efficiency is not wanting."

The ladies made their way below the stairs. Just as Elizabeth suspected, Mrs. Reynolds had taken care of her concerns.

"You see, Jane, it is exactly as I thought; she has taken care of everything."

Later in the afternoon, the ladies noticed the gentlemen returning across the field with the dogs. It was obvious they enjoyed a successful hunt.

A few hours later Mr. Manley arrived. He bowed humbly. "Mr. Bingley, Mrs. Bingley, it gives me great pleasure to see you again. Mr. Darcy tells me you are looking at Foxshire Estate, just outside of Lambton. How very nice it would be to have you within such an easy distance. I trust your journey was not harsh; it appears you had fine traveling weather."

"Yes, we did, very fine weather; the good roads made the journey quite comfortable. We are delighted to be here and quite pleased to see you once again," Mr. Bingley returned.

"Yes, we were elated to hear you were to come to dinner; we looked forward to seeing you again. I hear congratulations are in order on your new position at Pemberley," Jane added.

"Come now, this way, we shall have a little entertainment before dinner," Mr. Darcy added, as he stretched his arm to the direction they were to go. Elizabeth took her husband's arm as she looked up at him with a pleasing smile. She was delighted to have Jane and Mr. Bingley visit. Having Mr. Manley there made it all the more delightful. Her husband looked down at her, placing his right hand over hers. Pausing, he turned to her. "Elizabeth, will you entertain us with a song at the pianoforte? I would so much like to hear you."

"If you wish," she said, as he escorted her to the pianoforte. Just as Mr. Darcy was about to refill their glasses, dinner was announced, directing the whole of the party to the dining hall.

There was never a reason to suspect there would be a lack of conversation at the dinner table. This evening proved no different. Mr. Manley's invitation to visit the rectory was quickly accepted, as anticipated. Mr. Darcy announced they should expect to have pheasant for dinner tomorrow evening, which, as he pointed out, was the day's shoot. The ladies discussed fabrics, bonnets, as well as the beef served, while the gentlemen were caught up in their own subjects. After much food, drink and laughter, the dinner table was cleared, prompting a move from the dining hall. The gentlemen ventured to the billiard room, while the ladies directed themselves to the music chamber, where Elizabeth played the pianoforte. Jane sat on the sofa enjoying the comforts of her unfamiliar surroundings. When Elizabeth completed her tune, she joined Jane.

"I may say, Lizzy, you are more proficient in your playing; perhaps Mr. Manley's residence here induces you to practice more?" Jane stated with a sly teasing grin.

"I confess I do practice more. Georgiana has helped me as well."

"I wish I could perform half as well as you, Lizzy. I just cannot seem to develop a constancy of practice. I have never desired to play well enough, I suppose." After a long pause, she said, "Lizzy, Pemberley is much larger than imagined; I don't know if I have ever been in such a place—why a person could get lost."

"It is rather majestic; I am still unsure that I have discovered everything there is to see. Fitzwilliam has taken me turns about the house explaining family history. You must have witnessed the many paintings in the gallery, did you not?"

Before she could finish, Jane interjected, "Why, yes, I am most impressed with the painting of Mr. Darcy. Why, Lizzy, he does make a rather noble subject, but I don't suppose I need inform you of it."

Elizabeth blushed, then went on, "When in the gallery he introduced me to those in the paintings. I fear I shall never remember them all; there is quite a history here. Dear Georgiana showed me about the place as well; she is such a dear, sweet girl. I have missed her greatly since she went to London. We became quite closely connected. We have come a long way, Jane; have we not now?"

"Yes, indeed we have. When you think of all that has taken place. Now here we are together once more."

The gentlemen finally joined them. At Jane's request, Mr. Manley delighted them with a tune on the pianoforte. An evening of good company, great conversation, music, love and admiration—what more can anyone ask for? Elizabeth thought to herself. She was wholly content in her situation. How delighted she was to be privy to a party such as this.

A Change of Plans

TWO WEEKS NEXT, on a particular day, Elizabeth and Mr. Darcy were the first to arrive in the breakfast chamber. Jane and Mr. Bingley followed a short time thereafter.

"Darcy, after we have breakfasted, I believe we should go directly to the rectory to fetch Mr. Manley. He plans to go to town with us."

"Very well, Bingley. I believe the ladies intend to join us as well."

"Yes, Charles, Elizabeth and I plan to visit the village shops."

Not being in any haste, they breakfasted, sitting for some time in constant conversation. Elizabeth drew a breath as she stretched, then turned to her husband. "I am excessively full of energy; I cannot imagine what has come over me. I am eager for the trip to town."

They conversed as they sipped on coffee for another half-hour. Elizabeth again turned to Mr. Darcy. "I awoke this morning with an awful pain in my back; surely I must have twisted in my sleep. Perhaps I should not go to town. The pain comes then goes. I declare it gets increasingly worse."

Mrs. Reynolds had entered the chamber to assist one of the housekeepers in clearing the dishes away. She advanced in the direction of Mr. Darcy. "Mr. Darcy, I beg your pardon, I have a situation in the kitchen I should need you to address at once."

"Please care for it, Mrs. Reynolds; I believe I trust your judgment."

"No, Mr. Darcy, not this occasion; I believe it is a matter only you may decide."

"Mrs. Reynolds, I know of no situation you are incapable of dealing with."

"Mr. Darcy, I insist, this is a matter of urgent need, your presence is required."

"Well, what is it? Surely you can tell me, Mrs. Reynolds."

Mrs. Reynolds stared at him before taking a troublesome breath. She soberly composed herself, pulling her shoulders back without removing her eyes from his, "Very good sir, but I do believe your assistance is required. Pray excuse me, I shall return in a moment."

Elizabeth observed the manner in which Mrs. Reynolds fastidiously stared at her husband. Convinced of her excellence, she felt it must be a matter of great importance for her to persist in gaining his full attention. She waited until Mrs. Reynolds was out of her sight to address him quietly. "Fitzwilliam, while I understand your desire to discuss your plans of business in town, I cannot believe you spoke so coarsely to Mrs. Reynolds, it is not like you."

"Coarse? I did not think I was coarse."

"Yes, indeed, her intrusion seemed to annoy you. I daresay it is uncommon for Mrs. Reynolds to be persistent. Your swiftness to irritation, I am certain, was taken with a grain of embarrassment. And—oh, oh—" Elizabeth arched her shoulders back, thrusting her torso forward with a groan as she gripped the edge of the table, making her knuckles white. "My back aches, it is excessively painful."

"Are you quite all right, dear?"

"Oh, yes, it is going away. Now, getting back to the matter of Mrs. Reynolds. Fitzwilliam, your annoyance was not well hidden in your guise."

"You are perfectly right. I suppose the tenaciousness of her attitude did seem to annoy me. I shall apologize to Mrs. Reynolds when she returns. What is it, dearest, is it the pain again?" Mrs. Reynolds had entered the room, positioning herself directly at Mr. Darcy's side. Her face grew more severe as she looked him straight in the eye, "Sir, I insist you come to the kitchen with me at once!"

Mr. Darcy's expression was perplexed but turned adamant upon hearing her stern tone. He stood up from his chair. He towered over her. "Mrs. Reynolds, I am hard pressed to understand your persistence."

Before she could answer, Mr. Bingley broke in, "Go, tend to your business; I will wait."

"Very well." He obliged by following Mrs. Reynolds out of the chamber.

Once Mrs. Reynolds had him an easy distance not to be overheard, she quickly turned, spinning around on her heel. She startled him, stopping his strides as he almost ran into her. "Mr. Darcy, I do not wish to alarm you, but you cannot leave the house today."

Before she could go any further, he sternly interrupted. "Mrs. Reynolds, of what are you speaking? Surely I may take leave of the house today if I wish," he replied with saturating authority. She could plainly see he was insulted by her direction.

"Mr. Darcy, you will be required to remain here; I do believe your wife's time has come. I believe you must be prepared to send for the physician."

Excitedly, he demanded, "Are you sure of it?"

"Mrs. Darcy speaks of back pain. I heard her say the pain comes, then goes, getting stronger with each episode. Foremost, you must remain calm; do not alarm Mrs. Darcy. Calmly continue as before. Inquire if her pain lies in the small of her back, right here." She demonstrated taking her hand to his lower back. "Do not excite her; these things take time; she is strong and healthy, she will need to reserve that energy. There should be no need for concern. You must be yourself, Mr. Darcy. I have always known you to be collected of your senses in extreme situations. This is no different; you will keep your calm."

"I should send for the doctor now?"

"I will have a rider dispatched at once. You follow my instruction; all will be well, I'm sure of it. Now, you must return to the breakfast chamber, learn where the back pain is. I daresay you and Mr. Bingley will be changing your plans."

Mr. Darcy nodded his head. He returned to the breakfast chamber taking his seat aside of Elizabeth. He nonchalantly looked at his wife. She is vibrant, her face glows, thought he.

Her eyes brightened as she smiled at him. "Is everything all right in the kitchen?" But before he could answer, she stiffened her body forward in the seat as though she were experiencing pain again.

He tried to remain calm as he answered her. "I uh—I believe we need to purchase a new cooking vessel, that is all, just a slight mishap. Dearest, you appear uncomfortable. Did you say you suffered from back pain? Where does it settle?"

"Here," she demonstrated, putting both her hands behind her back, directly below her waist. "The pain comes fitfully. I experienced it when you quitted the chamber; it's rather uncomfortable, I do believe it is more severe."

Mrs. Reynolds remained nearby, pretending to fix the serving dishes on the sideboard. Upon hearing the description of Elizabeth's back pain, she gave a long stare to Mr. Darcy, then commented, "Mr. Darcy, the matter in the kitchen; perhaps you should see that it is taken care of immediately. I have no way of knowing the extent of the damage; I do not expect it should be taken lightly." Mr. Darcy immediately arose from the table. He bowed as he proceeded to follow Mrs. Reynolds out of the chamber.

"Mr. Darcy, collect your calm; you will need to be tranquil for her sake. All will be well."

"How do you know all will be well, Mrs. Reynolds, when she is in pain?"

"Mr. Darcy, there is no reason for concern; many women give birth, many men have gone through what you are now going through. I see you are getting excited; take a deep breath, calm yourself, think of your father, this experience he suffered twice."

"But not I, Mrs. Reynolds, not I. What of Elizabeth, should not we tell her?"

"She has time; she will realize soon enough. There is no reason to excite her. I'll be above the stairs preparing the bedchamber for the event; I expect she will not last out the morning before the awareness sets in to be sure. I shall require Bessie and Sara to assist me. You continue to present yourself as always. Mark my words, your wife will let you know when it is time. No doubt it will not be much longer. When the realization sets in, bring her above the stairs; we shall be waiting. You must remain calm; now go, now take a deep breath before you return to your wife. Just do as I say; trust me, all will be well."

Mrs. Reynolds parted his presence. A less confident Mr. Darcy returned to the breakfast chamber. After sitting for a time sipping his coffee, he looked at Mr. Bingley. "You know, Bingley, I do not believe I shall leave the house today. I would much rather stay here to look after things. Perhaps later we may play backgammon or cards."

"What, not go to town? Darcy, I thought you were gain set on town, you said so yourself. Why put it off? I wanted you to view the lease with me. I looked forward to it, counted on your coming!" he lamented, his voice in exasperation. "I fail to see the reason for the alteration." He persisted to unsuccessfully influence Mr. Darcy, much to his obvious displeasure.

"Come now, Bingley, I have the matter in the kitchen. I've just realized I need to be here today; besides, tomorrow will be time enough, or the day next perhaps."

"Tomorrow or the day next? Come, Darcy, I am not of the understanding as to why you would suddenly change plans. Are you unwell? Why in heaven's name would you alter our set plans?" Mr. Bingley continued to plead.

"Bingley, please do not challenge me, humour me this once; it soon will be of your understanding. I will go with you tomorrow," he said sternly, knowing Mr. Bingley to be easily convinced.

"I daresay we all seem rather unsettled today," Jane interjected. Mr. Bingley looked at his wife, then pressed his lips together in frustration as he let out a slight gasp.

"Very well, if we must."

Mr. Bingley looked at his friend. Mr. Darcy stared at him with sober expression. Not wishing to challenge him further, he decided the subject was better dropped at present.

Mr. Darcy conveniently changed the subject, continuing to speak in more general terms, the whole time keeping an inconspicuous watch over his wife.

Jane and Elizabeth, in an exchange of ideas regarding dress material, paid little attention to the gentlemen. After about five and twenty minutes, Elizabeth placed her hands in the small of her back. She leaned back. Mr. Darcy noticed she held herself in that position for quite some time. He watched as she released her hands, then continued to converse with Jane. After another twenty minutes, Elizabeth repeated her past actions, moaning with pain.

"Whoa! I must take a deep breath; I'm so sorry but it is really all that bad." Her mouth opened again to gasp, as if she could no longer tolerate the suffering. She arched her back, holding it in the same position for a few moments. Upon releasing herself, she turned to Mr. Darcy, "Dearest, I do not believe this is ordinary; I believe it is something more. Pray, do not be alarmed. Perhaps you should send for the physician. I believe the time has come."

"I already have—the physician is on his way."

"You have!" she retorted in a startled voice.

Jane and Mr. Bingley sat in stunned disbelief. Jane's eyes widened as her mouth dropped open with shock. Mr. Bingley sat frozen in his seat. His eyes grew wide as he looked at his wife, shrugging his shoulders. Their heads turned from one to the other as Mr. Darcy and Elizabeth conversed. Neither said a word but sat in total silence taking in the events about them, periodically exchanging perplexing looks as they listened.

"Yes I have, Mrs. Reynolds' problem was not in the kitchen; she instructed me to send for the physician after recognizing your earlier signs. She is presently above the stairs preparing the bedchamber. She did not wish to alarm you. She claimed you would know soon enough," he said with his speech growing faster as he arose from his chair to summon the servants to help take her above the stairs.

"Mrs. Reynolds is very perceptive, quite remarkable; I daresay I am fortunate to be in such good hands."

"Yes, now perhaps we should go above the stairs. Mrs. Reynolds has plenty of assistance. She awaits you."

Mr. Darcy turned to Mr. Bingley, "Bingley, go to the rectory; request Mr. Manley come. Tell him I require his presence; tell him it is Elizabeth's time."

An astonished Jane and Mr. Bingley were left behind in the breakfast chamber. They watched as the servants helped Mr. Darcy take Elizabeth gently away. Bewildered, Jane exclaimed, "Charles, Elizabeth was not expecting this today, I'm sure of it; she said nothing to me of it."

"Well, Jane, surely it must be time. It is no wonder Darcy did not wish to leave the house suddenly. I thought he was not quite himself getting angry with me for pursuing the subject, when little more than two hours ago he was talking of sporting and all sorts of business in town. I best fetch Mr. Manley, do you wish to join me, Jane, or shall you stay?"

"I believe I shall join you. If I stay I'll have no one to talk to; I'll be alone, worrying. You know how my imagination runs away with me whilst I worry."

Several hours passed; the physician had long arrived. Preparations were set, anticipating the event to take place rather soon. Mr. Darcy was at his wife's side wiping her forehead, holding her hand, conversing with her to keep her calm.

"Mr. Darcy, I believe it is time for you to leave the chamber; we have work to do. If you exercise some patience, I speculate you will be visiting with your wife and child within the next several hours. I suggest you find something to occupy yourself," instructed the physician.

Mr. Darcy nodded his head. "Very well." He stood up from the chair, taking one last look at his wife. He bent down to kiss Elizabeth's forehead, then kissed her hand before releasing his long hold on it.

"I shall be waiting, dearest," he stated, then withdrew from the chamber in haste. He went below the stairs for a drink. He noticed Jane, Mr. Bingley and Mr. Manley in the sitting room upon his entry.

Mr. Manley bowed, "Well, Fitzwilliam, the day has arrived for the blessed event. I am glad you sought me out, I have already prayed for you both. Be assured I shall continue to do so; I am sure all will be well. You need not look so worried, my friend; many women have given birth, many men are fathers; it is common enough."

"Why do people find it necessary to bring this to a man's attention, believing it to be of comfort?" he inquired with frustration.

"Just conversation, it is hard to know what to say to a man about to become a father, especially one who is so obviously nervous. What can one expect to say to bring about calm?" Mr. Manley replied, smiling broadly.

"Forgive me, you are precisely correct; I'm not quite myself. I have little experience in such matters; I suppose I lack patience. I believe it is the hardest thing in the world to witness the suffering of one so dearly loved," was all Mr. Darcy could manage to say as he paced about with a serious look on his face. "I hardly know what to do to occupy my time."

Jane and Mr. Bingley remained seated, not knowing what to say, unsure if they should say anything. Mr. Darcy looked concerned as he paced the floor. Moments later he sat down, played with the ring on his hand, arose from his seat, then paced about the floor again. He finally sat down, but then stood shortly thereafter, venturing to the window. It was but a few moments until he returned to the sofa again. He got up and filled his glass before reclaiming his seat. Within seconds he was up from his seat moving in the direction of the window again. It was all so unsettling, so Jane thought. "Is there anything we can do for you?" asked Mr. Bingley.

"Yes, Fitzwilliam, may we occupy you in some way?" Mr. Manley inquired.

"No, no, I believe I should go above the stairs and wait it out; I cannot bear not to be near. There is nothing to do but wait," he said, as he filled his glass to take with him. He quitted the chamber in haste, leaving his company to themselves, not stopping to excuse himself or bow, as was his normal behaviour. He just simply walked out.

"I've never witnessed Darcy in such a state," Mr. Bingley observed.

"Nor I," said Jane; "did you not see his serious-mindedness?"

"I've seen this many times; it's quite natural, no reason for alarm," Mr. Manley said.

Jane looked at her husband, then at Mr. Manley. "Mr. Darcy is fortunate to have a perceptive woman in his employ. How did Mrs. Reynolds know?"

"I'm sure Mrs. Reynolds is well acquainted with these situations; they are in good hands. There is no reason to be concerned; I do believe your sister will do well."

"I suppose you are right, Mr. Manley," Jane voiced.

"Yes, I expect she will, but Mr. Darcy, well—he may require a bit more patience than he is known to possess. He is quite the fellow, but short on patience; the wait might do him in. I do believe it is not so often Mr. Darcy finds circumstances to which he lacks the power to control. Indeed, waiting is most likely to be intense. This could prove to be his ultimate challenge," Mr. Manley reported.

"Yes, I know Darcy; his tolerance for pain upon those he loves is short; he would much rather endure it himself. I suspect he will suffer a long, hard wait," Mr. Bingley added.

Mr. Manley let out a chuckle. "Mr. Darcy will no doubt survive, I'm sure."

Mr. Darcy paced the floor. More than three hours passed listening to the moans and groans of his wife's struggles. He heard the muffled voices of the physician and Mrs. Reynolds. Mrs. Reynolds appeared periodically to give him a report. He paced the hall in an unsettled state, thinking his presence of mind might desert him. Finally he sat down on the step only to be jolted from his seat by the louder painful cries of his wife. He continued to pace once again, playing with the ring on his hand. The waiting was taking its toll; he felt helpless, shut out and alienated. He thought for sure he could not endure her cries of suffering at any length.

His mind began to race with a multitude of thoughts. "Is it all going badly? Why must she suffer so? I had the notion of distinguishing myself rather well prepared, but I suppose I was quite mistaken. I had expected to bear it with perfect firmness. Have I fallen short of my expectations?" he mused aloud. As thoughts of complications consumed him, he stood with his back to the wall.

He continued to pace when he heard his wife's screams of pain. After a few moments he sat on the steps in anguish, burying his face in his hands with each outcry. It seemed to go on forever. Just when he thought he could tolerate it no more, there came an unnatural, quiet lull. Moments later he heard a baby's cry. Slowly removing his face from his hands, he stood waiting impatiently, wondering why Mrs. Reynolds had not come to him. He straightened himself, then took out his handkerchief to wipe his brow. Finally Mrs. Reynolds appeared, holding the baby wrapped in a blanket. "Mr. Darcy, you have a fine son," she said as she turned the baby into his arms. He looked down at him with relief. "Elizabeth, how is Elizabeth?" he asked instantly.

"I'll not withhold anything from you, Mr. Darcy. It is uncertain; the doctor is still with her," she said in a tearful voice, taking her handkerchief to her eyes now welling with tears. In a shaky voice, she continued, "Dr.

Gordon is not pleased with her present condition; such suffering should have ceased, but it has not yet left her. She is in excessive pain, Mr. Darcy, but rest assured he is doing everything there is to be done."

Mrs. Reynolds looked directly at him, understanding his frightful guise. She took hold of his upper arm. She squeezed it tight. "Be calm, be strong, Mr. Darcy, for your wife's sake. Perhaps a prayer might help."

"Will she be all right, Mrs. Reynolds? Tell me at once!" he demanded to know.

"I cannot lie to you sir, as yet he cannot say. Sir—she is still in much pain. I fear she suffers a vast deal; I wish I could tell you otherwise. The doctor said something is not quite the way it ought to be. To be truthful, she has lost a lot of blood. Mr. Darcy, I believe she is in good hands, but perhaps you should say a prayer, indeed you should, you must." Before she could go any further they heard Elizabeth cry out in extreme pain, more severe than her earlier cries. Mr. Darcy grew more alarmed. He looked at Mrs. Reynolds. "You must go back; be with her."

Mrs. Reynolds disappeared into the chamber. Within moments, the chamber door opened. Bessie emerged to take the baby from him. She too disappeared into the chamber.

Mr. Darcy sat on the steps with his face buried in his hands. Unable to endure her screams, he suffered the torment of her distress. As each scream pierced his chest he grew more overwhelmed, making it difficult to concentrate on a prayer. He attempted to pray with earnest desire, but still the severity of her cries continued, causing a total lack of application. On two occasions, those waiting in the sitting room heard the intensity of her harrowing screams. His breast ached with anguish, his mind raced with the thought she may be lost to him forever. Then came the most violent of screams, followed by total silence. He slowly lifted his head in a rage of fear. He no longer heard Elizabeth, just the cry of the child. He stood upright, waiting for Mrs. Reynolds to appear, but she did not. His hair was wet from perspiration. He wiped his brow. His face was drawn with anguish as the fear of not knowing the circumstances behind the closed door was tearing him apart. The deafening silence disturbed him, leaving him at wits' end. Alone with his tortured thoughts, he began to reason the worst. Why was it so quiet; why could he not hear her? The stillness tormented him beyond forbearance. Then he realized he no longer heard the physician or Mrs. Reynolds. Surely he thought he would hear them. He sat on the steps burying his face in his hands, infinitely distraught beyond his will. It seemed like eternity.

At last the door opened. A weary Mrs. Reynolds appeared again, holding the baby. She stood in front of him, placing the baby in his arms. "Mr. Darcy, you have a daughter; do not be concerned, your wife is well. The doctor will summon in; be patient, Elizabeth is doing well. He requires a bit more time. You will find her very tired; she has had a hard day."

Mr. Darcy's stunned face stared at her. She smiled back at him, repeating herself, "Mr. Darcy, you did hear me say you have a daughter, did you not?"

"Mrs. Reynolds, we have a son—and a daughter?" he said, slowly comprehending her words in disbelief. As the distress drained from his face, he felt his anxiety release, allowing him to breathe with less difficulty. He looked down at the baby in his arms, then turned to look at Mrs. Reynolds with a questioning look upon his face.

"Yes sir, two, Mr. Darcy, your wife gave you a son first, then a daughter."

"I am most anxious to see her," he said, looking down at the child he held to his breast "They are so small, would you not agree?"

"Yes, Mr. Darcy, most babies are; perhaps yours are smaller than most. Allow me to take the child back to your wife. You will see her soon enough."

Mr. Darcy brushed his hand over his face when Mrs. Reynolds disappeared into the chamber. He stood solitarily motionless in wonderment of all that had taken place. His thoughts were of all those horrid assumptions that rose in his mind just moments ago. Now freed from his apprehensions, he contemplated his new situation with greater ease. He stared at the closed chamber door for several minutes, running his fingers through his hair, then down the back of his neck. He clasped the base of his neck, holding his hand there for a time, pondering his last exchange with Mrs. Reynolds. His first instinct was to run below the stairs to tell those waiting, but his desire to be right there when summoned was greater. Oh, to see my Elizabeth, thought he. He impatiently paced until the physician urged him to enter.

He immediately went to his wife's side. Touching her hand gently, he leaned over to kiss her. At her side, well tucked in her arm, lay his son, wrapped neatly in a blanket. As he sat down next to her, Mrs. Reynolds brought the little girl to him. After she placed her in his arms, he gently raised her to his face, delicately kissing her soft new skin. Still speechless, he intently studied his new daughter. He barely noticed the physician taking his leave. Mrs. Reynolds and Bessie followed close behind, quitting the chamber, leaving them alone.

"What are we to do?" he quickly asked of Mrs. Reynolds as she attempted to depart.

She smiled. "I'll return directly, sir. I wish to give you a moment with your wife and children; ten minutes, Mr. Darcy, I shall return in ten minutes with Bessie and the nursemaids. They shall be well taken care of," she instructed, closing the door behind her.

With eyes glazed with tears, he kissed his wife's hand. "Dearest, loveliest, Elizabeth, you have made me the happiest among men." She smiled at the sound of his tender voice. She thought she could easily see the increased value of his affections, if that were possible.

"Dearest, did I not tell you I would give you a son?" a very weary Elizabeth spoke, managing a faint tease.

"So you did, but a daughter, too? I am a fortunate man indeed. I see you are in much need of rest; you are barely able speak, my dear."

"Yes," was all she said before closing her eyes, "my energy is depleted."

He watched her with admiration. He could feel the devotion swell within his breast. He looked down at the baby in his arms. Drawing her up to him, he kissed her soft skin once again, then studied her little face as he held her to him. Never in his life had he such an experience of overpowering torment, immediately followed by overwhelming love. He once believed he achieved incomparable emotions when finally securing the love of Elizabeth, but at this moment he knew what it was to love so wholly and exclusively beyond his imagination or description. He felt complete as a man. His visit with his wife was cut short by Mrs. Reynolds' and Bessie's return.

"Mr. Darcy, you shall have to purchase another little bed. I will place them together presently, but that will only do for a short time. Mrs. Darcy requires rest now; you'll have to go below the stairs. I will sit with your wife; remember you have guests."

"Thank you, Mrs. Reynolds," he said as he started to leave, but then turned back to her. "Mrs. Reynolds, what would we do without you here? Indeed you take prodigious care of us. Now there are two more to look after."

"Mr. Darcy, you leave that to me; I suggest you remember that you have anxious guests awaiting you," she reminded him once again, in a motherly fashion.

He bent down once again to kiss Elizabeth on the forehead. "Mr. Manley is with your sister and Bingley, I shall go to them with the news. Thank you, Mrs. Reynolds, thank you," he uttered before hastily quitting the chamber.

He descended the stairs in haste but stopped short before entering the sitting room. He straightened his carriage, threw his shoulders back, then ran his fingers through his hair. He pulled his shoulders back again, then tugged on the front of his dress coat before making his entrance with reserved natural strides. Once he entered the chamber, he immediately poured himself a glass of port.

"Well," said Jane, "what is it? I can see by your face it is over; tell us what it is. How does my sister do?"

Mr. Darcy emptied his glass before answering. "I have a son," he announced. But before he could go any further, Mr. Bingley's bellowing voice erupted, "A son, our compliments, Darcy, a son. That is marvelous news, splendid indeed."

Mr. Darcy nodded, then he casually added, "I have a daughter."

Jane viewed him inquisitively, her brows united in confusion. She stood up to face him directly. "Did you not say it was a boy; that is so, is it not?"

"Yes, it is a boy, but there is a daughter too!" he proudly announced, taking great delight in shocking them. Consumed with pleasure arising from their stunned expressions, a broadened smile overspread his features.

He reveled in his pride, adding, "My wife did say I shall have a son; she presented him first, followed by a daughter. Indeed she is a woman of her word. How fortunate can one man be?"

"You are a fortunate man, Fitzwilliam," Mr. Manley offered.

Amid the chattering gleeful voices, Jane called out, "Is Elizabeth doing well; how does my sister do?"

"Indeed she is; she is very tired. Mrs. Reynolds practically threw me out of the chamber, telling me we shall have to purchase a little bed."

He moved across the room to pour himself a cup of tea, looking a bit tired as he sat down with his cup. His mind was pleasantly occupied with thoughts deeply concentrated on the most recent event.

Mr. Manley studied his friend. "Fitzwilliam, a son and daughter, you are a twice blessed man. What man wouldn't feel himself proud to make such a claim?"

Mr. Darcy directed himself to the secretary. Before sitting down, he turned to Jane. "I shall send a message to your father at once, then to the Gardiners and Georgiana."

"Oh yes, Mr. Darcy, he should like that very much, so would Lizzy."

Mr. Bennet, Estate of Longbourn, Hertfordshire, England

Be not apprehensive in receiving this letter. With pleasure I bring this proclamation to your attention. You daughter Elizabeth has presented me with a son. That would be enough to please any man; nonetheless, I would like to further inform you, she has also presented a daughter. We are twice blessed! I believe sir, your presence at Pemberley is desirous at once, an undertaking of utmost urgency. I believe a visit most agreeable just now. Be not alarmed, Elizabeth is quite well.

Fitzwilliam Darcy

To the Gardiners he made the announcement suggesting they might visit within a month, but to his sister he advised she should come as soon as convenient. He gathered his servants to announce the happy news, telling them a celebration would be forthcoming, that they shall share in his happiness.

Mr. Darcy took his letters to one of the servants, requesting they be sent at once by messenger. He poured himself another cup of tea, then sat down, fully contented. Feeling quite gratified in his new position—first husband, now father—he was entirely caught up in his thoughts. He did not hear the conversations around him nor did he hear Mr. Manley say, "Fitzwilliam, the servants have called us to dinner."

He sat unmoved by Mr. Manley's announcement.

"Fitzwilliam!" repeated Mr. Manley, as he gripped his shoulder.

"Yes, what is it?" he finally answered.

"Dinner awaits us; our presence is requested in the dining hall. You are in need of nourishment; you should come now."

"Yes, of course, my mind was pleasantly engaged on my wife and children. Henry, I am a father, can you believe it? Two at once! I can hardly believe it; can you imagine it?"

Mr. Manley smiled as he gestured for him to follow to the dining hall. Upon entering, he turned to him. "Fitzwilliam, you are exhausted; you certainly have had a long day, much to contemplate, I daresay. This day did not go as planned; I do believe your intended designs were altered by your wife's presentations. I know you did not expect such a diversion. I believe my work here is done, so it is my intention to leave directly after we dine. I am of the opinion you need to retire to your chamber."

Being a man of his word, Mr. Manley took his leave directly after dinner, but not before once again congratulating Mr. Darcy.

Mr. Bingley and Jane amused themselves for the remainder of the evening as Mr. Darcy went directly above the stairs to look in on his wife. She was peacefully asleep.

He entered the nursery. They lay two in one crib, sleeping peacefully as was their mother. He marveled at the sight of them. Both had black hair, little pink plump cheeks and lay with their little arms up revealing their little fingers. He stood over the crib studying them. His frame filled with a sense of overwhelming joy. He observed them for another ten minutes. Feeling overwhelmingly blessed beyond his deserving, he closed his eyes to give thanks to God. After his prayer, he lingered a few moments longer to watch them sleep.

He returned to his wife's chamber. He sank into the armchair, watching her sleep peacefully. He lay his head back, surrendering to sleep. Some time later he was awakened by the sound of the infants' cries. Within minutes, Mrs. Reynolds appeared with the nursemaids. His wife was awake amid the organized confusion, which now seemed to permeate the chamber.

"You may go to your former chamber to acquire needed sleep. Mrs. Darcy is in good hands. She will be well taken care of," Mrs. Reynolds announced.

It was now he realized their life was never to be the same. He felt a certain sense of loneliness in being parted from her, but did what was required of him. After making himself ready for bed, he lay his head upon the bolster. Although exhausted, thoughts of the wonderful event persuaded him that the excitement surely would not allow him rest, but he was heavy with sleep within seconds.

The morning next, feeling more refreshed and fully in charge, he declared to Mrs. Reynolds, "I should like to have my breakfast brought up with my wife's; I shall breakfast with her."

"Very good, sir."

Hearing the infants awake, he immediately went to the crib, picking up his daughter. He scooped her up in his arms, studying her at length. The newness had not worn; he was still in wonderment of the joy such a little creature could command. He carried her to her mother, then sat on the bed next to her with the infant still in his arms. "She is beautiful like her mother, dark hair, fine eyes, but her eyes are blue?"

"I believe all new babies have blue eyes at first, my dear."

"Well now, she is absolutely the most beautiful baby in Derbyshire, and has a brother the most handsome. I am absolutely certain of it."

"Such judgment only a father can make," Elizabeth said with a broadened smile.

"Indeed I am prejudiced, I admit it wholly and completely; yesterday morning I had the most beautiful wife, today the most beautiful son and daughter as well."

Elizabeth beamed; such deep felicity, thought she. She was more alert now, having had a good measure of sleep. She expressed a desire to hold one of the children.

"This is very fortunate, Fitzwilliam. This event obviates our first disagreement," she said, her eyes twinkling with merriment.

"How so, Elizabeth?"

"Why, my dearest husband, we each have a child to hold. Although I may not deny we just might disagree as to which one of us should have him or her!"

"Well, my dear wife, I see you have taken on a little bit of my teasing tendencies."

"Perhaps I have," she smiled tenderly.

"I believe your sister Jane would wish to visit with you today."

"I should like it very much," Elizabeth expressed with eagerness.

"I sent a message to your father yesterday afternoon, Elizabeth. I told him his presence was required immediately at Pemberley."

"You did? You sent for my father, why?"

"I should think you want him here. Surely he should see the children; is it not so?"

She laughed. "Yes, dearest, I had not expected you to have him come so soon. You are very good. I should like to see my father again. I am certain he would like to be introduced to the children. What of names? We have only discussed it briefly; how is that so?"

"I gave it thought yesterday; I suppose we had not expected them so soon. I would imagine you have some notion. What names would you give?"

"I prefer to hear what names you would give?"

"My father's name was Joseph; I should like to name the boy Joseph if it meets with your approval?"

"Joseph is a strong name; I like it very much. Joseph it shall be."

"What name would you give?"

"I should think Deborah would be a fine name."

"I should have expected you to say Fanny, was not your mother's name Fanny?"

"Yes, but I rather prefer Deborah."

"But Deborah was my mother's name, surely you are not choosing it on my account," he said with noticeable astonishment.

"I am; I like it. I prefer Deborah to Fanny, so Deborah it is."

"My dearest Elizabeth, you continue to astonish me with so much added joy." To have such an endearing wife is certainly comforting, thought he. He delighted in her honour to his family.

After they had breakfasted, Elizabeth announced, "I am in need of rest. Would you be so kind to tell my sister that I will receive her in the afternoon?"

"As you wish, I will leave you now to rest." He kissed her, then quitted the chamber reluctantly.

He found his guests breakfasting. Having already had his, he joined them with a cup of coffee. He immediately talked of the infants—how delicate they are; their hair is black, skin like silk; he went on and on. Mr. Bingley and Jane listened intently. After a half-hour passed, Mr. Darcy looked across the table at the two. "Well, have you two nothing to say?"

"What can we say? You gave us not a chance to speak; you are totally engrossed in your prolific family. Darcy, it is absolutely wonderful to see you so wrought up. We have been friends for a long time; I daresay I don't believe I have ever witnessed you this excitable," Mr. Bingley proclaimed.

"I believe I am guilty of being happy beyond reason. Jane, Elizabeth wishes to see you above the stairs, but not until this afternoon."

"Very well, the afternoon it is."

In the afternoon, Mrs. Reynolds sought Jane. "Your sister will receive you now."

Without hesitation, Jane ventured above the stairs.

"Oh, Lizzy, I'm so very happy for you and Mr. Darcy. Lizzy, you should have been in the breakfast chamber. Mr. Darcy sat for five and forty minutes talking of nothing else but you and the infants. Charles and I could not get a word in, then what do you think?"

"Do tell me, Jane."

Jane laughed, "He wished to know why we had nothing to say." She laughed again, asking, "Have you names yet?"

"Did not my husband tell you with all his chatter?"

"No, he did not, at least I do not believe he did."

"Their names are Joseph and Deborah."

"They are wonderful names. Lizzy, may I peek in the nursery?"

"Yes, you may; just go in but try not to wake them."

She was gone for a time, studying the babies.

"Oh, Lizzy, they are beautiful; such dark hair, beautiful skin, they are precious. I can see why Mr. Darcy excessively talks of them. They are wonderful; it is just as he said."

"Jane, I must tell you, I am so happy. Did you know my husband sent for Father? He told him to come at once, can you believe it?"

"Yes, I know, he told us he sent the message. He sent a message to our Aunt and Uncle Gardiner; he requested they come in about a month."

"In all his excitement, he has forgotten to tell me of the letter to our aunt and uncle; how very thoughtful he is."

"Lizzy, I do believe your husband is very fond of Father now that he has gotten to know him better."

"Yes, I believe that is so. Well, Jane, I believe I should need some rest now."

Jane hugged Elizabeth, then directed herself below the stairs. Although she was happy for her sister, it was with a bit of infinite sorrow she craved to some day soon provide news of an event of her own.

Mr. Bennet Visits

SEVERAL DAYS AFTER RECEIVING the message to come to Pemberley, Mr. Bennet's carriage arrived at the great estate. Kitty and Mary were overwhelmed by the beautiful countryside. Kitty thought it might be a bit far from town but was impressed by its grandeur. Mary was eager to walk about the grounds after finding pleasure in Pemberley Hall's library.

Mr. Darcy had just returned from sporting with Mr. Bingley. Upon entering the music chamber he encountered the three. He bowed. "Well, this is a pleasure to be sure."

"Mr. Darcy, thank you for your letter; I made arrangements to leave at once. We have just arrived; I have not seen my Lizzy as yet. Perhaps you may arrange for me to do so?"

"Yes, to be sure, Mr. Bennet, at once. I trust you are well?"

"Indeed I am, sir; I believe the ride did not seem so long this journey."

"If you will excuse me, I will see if Elizabeth will receive guests just now. Make yourself at ease; I shall have Mrs. Reynolds order tea to be brought in, or perhaps you prefer some port after such a ride, Mr. Bennet?"

"Port will do very well for me, Mr. Darcy, but I believe your housekeeper has already ordered the tea. The girls will have tea, is that not so?" he said, winking, looking to them slyly for approval.

Mr. Darcy poured him a glass of port, then begged to be excused. He rang the bell, instructing there would be six plates required in the dining hall at dinner before proceeding to go above the stairs to announce Mr. Bennet's arrival.

"I shall require about an hour to prepare myself. Would you be so kind to tell them?" Elizabeth expressed.

"Of course, will one hour be sufficient?"

"I believe so."

Mr. Darcy returned to his newly arrived guests to find Mr. Bingley and Jane had joined them. "I see you returned."

"Yes, we inspected Foxshire Estate near Lambton, interesting place indeed. We shall sit down with the owner tomorrow to make further study of the papers. Perhaps you would wish to join us. We have some little time until Michaelmas, so the matter does not require an immediate decision," Mr. Bingley reported.

Jane looked at her father. Feeling guilty, she felt an explanation was due him. "Father, Mr. Bingley is looking at an estate a short distance from Lambton, which is but five miles from Pemberley. We have a party interested in viewing Netherfield Park."

"That's quite all right, my dear; do not alarm yourself on my account. I can see that you are concerned; Jane, that is not necessary."

"Oh, Father, I have no desire to abandon you, but Mr. Bingley longs for the company of his good friend. To confess the truth, I should like to be near Lizzy."

"Jane, my dear, do not fret so; you must not suffer yourself. That is what young ladies do when they marry; it is expected of them." Without hesitation, he turned to Mr. Bingley. "Mr. Bingley, I should like very much to know my girls are within an easy distance looking after one another. It would give me great comfort; I approve of the move."

"Thank you, Mr. Bennet."

"Very well then, I trust your family is in health, all those at Netherfield Park?" Mr. Bennet inquired.

"They were all very well when we came away," replied Mr. Bingley.

"Mr. Darcy, have we names for these two fine children to whom we are hoping to be introduced?" inquired Mr. Bennet.

"Yes sir, Joseph and Deborah."

"Good strong names, Mr. Darcy."

"They were my father's and mother's names, Elizabeth insisted."

"Just the same, I like them."

Mary and Kitty's eyes examined the unfamiliar surroundings. Having thought Netherfield large, they realized, in comparison, Netherfield was definitely outdone. Within the hour they were able to visit with Elizabeth as well as the infants. Kitty found more excitement in them than Mary, who remained her usual reserved self. Mr. Bennet took delight in the sight of them.

"Well, Lizzy, a son and a daughter, you are sure not to be outdone. Such fine children, I daresay beautiful little creatures they are indeed. It's been a long time since we had little children about. Your Mr. Darcy wasted no time in commissioning me here. I suppose you know Lydia has a daughter; don't know if we'll ever get to see her, sorry case I do say." There was a definite sadness in his voice when he spoke of Lydia, thought Elizabeth.

"Oh, Father, they are rather dear, are they not?"

"Yes, quite so," he added, "I believe you should rest now, Lizzy, you look as though you could use it."

"Yes, I am weary."

"Very well, come girls," Mr. Bennet said, directing them both out of the chamber.

Mary and Kitty discovered the shared guest chamber large as well as pleasing. Pemberley was quite busy over the few weeks next. Mary and Kitty became well acquainted with the grounds; Mr. Bennet, Mr. Darcy and Mr. Bingley sported while Jane and Elizabeth spent much time together. The nursemaids were busy tending the infants, who proved to have been blessed with strong lungs.

With the passing of three weeks, Elizabeth was finally gaining her strength, feeling more her natural state for longer periods of time. She was pleased with the nursemaids; they were excellent people, efficient as well as very nurturing, thought she.

Today would be the first day she would venture below the stairs for a brief period. She was glad to quit the bedchamber; she was anxious for a change of scenery. Mary and Kitty were planning a picnic in the afternoon with their father down by the lake. Mr. Bennet planned to fish, while Mr. Bingley and Mr. Darcy were to go to town on business.

"Dearest, are you agreeable to having dinner below the stairs this evening; do you feel quite up to it?" Mr. Darcy inquired.

"Perhaps if I go above the stairs to rest a bit after I have breakfasted, I believe I should wish to join you all late in the afternoon. Why?"

"I thought I should like to invite Mr. Manley for dinner; I have not done so these past weeks while you were in confinement."

"Do invite Mr. Manley. I shall indeed rest so I am present in the dining hall when it is required of me. I am certain I will feel up to the company; besides, Mr. Manley will not mind if I excuse myself early in the evening to be sure."

"You are certain of it?"

"Yes, dearest, I should like very much to see Mr. Manley."

"Very well, then. Bingley, we shall stop on our way to town. Dearest, did you know your father and I visited the rectory the day before last? The girls accompanied us as well. Henry inquired after you; I thought it would be pleasing to have him here."

"Yes, I would be delighted to receive him."

In the afternoon as she rested, Elizabeth heard the girls in their chamber. They seemed to be talking with Bessie at length. Thinking little of it, Elizabeth proceeded to nap.

Late in the afternoon, nearing the time for dinner, Mr. Darcy went above the stairs to his wife, "Do you feel strong enough to join the party at dinner?"

"Yes, I have made myself ready." After quitting the chamber, they directed themselves to the sitting room, where the party was gathered awaiting announcement of dinner. Upon entering, Elizabeth looked about the chamber. The gentlemen stood to bow. Mr. Manley expressed his gratefulness to being invited to dinner once again. Elizabeth noticed Mary sitting on the end of the sofa; her looks were altered to a definite degree. Her dark hair was fixed in a fashionable style with curls flattering her face. In her hair she sported a ribbon which matched her dress. Elizabeth recognized the dress as one belonging to Kitty, noting it well flattered her slender form, making a pleasing presentation.

"Why, Mary, you altered your look; I must say it meets my approval."

Mary's complexion reddened. The formality she displayed impressed Elizabeth. She supposed the absence of her mother's continued stirring antics promoted a more natural transition to womanhood. Elizabeth observed with interest, Mary with Mr. Manley. Having never known Mary to be responsive to any male, she was amazed by her sister's sophisticated reception of the attention. Aware religious reading had long been Mary's interest, and upon hearing fragments of the conversation, she concluded her sister had little difficulty owning a conversation with clergy. Her knowledge surprised Elizabeth, but more surprising was her lack of reserve when the subject was raised, speaking diversely to Mr. Manley with ease. She was pleased to discover Mary listened very well, noticing she responded with fact without making herself an authority, as she was prone to do in the past.

At dinner, Mary managed to acquire a seat next to Mr. Manley. Conversation moved about the table freely with three different subjects stirring at once.

Elizabeth eyed her father after noticing he studied Mary with curiosity. It was a truth commonly acknowledged that seldom did anything pass Mr. Bennet's notice. His eyes shifted about the table from conversation to conversation, although he himself had little to say. While Mr. Bingley, Jane and Mr. Darcy discussed the estate near Lambton, Kitty was busy asking Elizabeth questions about the infants. Altogether there was no lack of subjects about the table. Following dinner, the whole of the party retired to the music chamber, but Elizabeth felt fatigued, having had ample exercise for one day. With the aid of her husband, she excused herself to retire to her bedchamber. Mr. Darcy remained with her to ensure that she was settled comfortably.

"My sister Mary looks quite altered this evening. Not only has she borrowed Kitty's dress, she has fashioned her hair. Had you noticed?"

"I did, but not at first, until dinner when I noticed her next to Henry."

"With her hair curled about her face, she looked rather delightful. She acts more delicate, I believe."

"Yes, that must be the difference; if you say it is so, I'm sure it is."

"My sister conducted herself with a bit more sophistication."

"How so?"

"She seems to delight in the attention Mr. Manley affords her. I heard their conversation regarding the church; I must say she is well educated on the subject."

"You may be right, or it may be that you never realized how well informed she is."

"We shall see. You had better not keep our guests waiting any longer; we will speak of this later."

When Mr. Darcy returned to the music chamber, Mr. Manley was playing the pianoforte. Mr. Bingley and Mr. Bennet were playing backgammon while Kitty and Mary watched eagerly. Within the hour, Mr. Manley announced he should be directing himself to the rectory. While Mr. Darcy studied Mary to determine if his wife's calculations were accurate, Jane addressed her, "Why, Mary, you curled your hair; it is very flattering, you look quite pleasing."

Mr. Bennet, now looking over the top of his spectacles, added, "Yes, my dear, quite a difference to be sure, an improvement I daresay." Mary blushed to a deep shade of crimson. Mr. Bennet, still looking over his spectacles, shifted his eyes in Kitty's direction. "Kitty, my dear, you look quite nice as well."

Kitty conducted herself in a more reserved, less girlish fashion. She looked at him. "Thank you, Father, might I be called Kathryn? Kitty no longer becomes me, I believe it is rather childish; do you not think so?"

Mr. Bennet raised his brows, scrutinizing her over top of his spectacles once again. "Very well, Kathryn, yes, that is a more fitting name for you."

"Thank you, Father."

"Yes, I think Kathryn sounds so much more sophisticated," Jane agreed.

Since the game of backgammon was over, Mr. Bennet announced, "I believe I should like to retire, pray you'll all excuse me. Good night, Mary; good night, Jane; good night, Kathryn." He bowed before quitting the chamber. It was not long before the rest of the party followed his lead, except for Mr. Darcy.

Mr. Darcy remained alone. The whole of his life seemed perfectly proper. His immediate thoughts directed his attention to the source of its success. He lay his head back, closing his eyes. The natural result of his sober reflections caused him to recount his own joyful situation. As he opened his eyes, he glanced in the direction of the pianoforte. A burning desire swept through him like a tempest. Feeling isolated by the dull ache of his cravings, he yearned to have his wife at his side. On this particular night he missed her sorely. The very thought of her in his arms only proved to heighten his masculine desires. The concept of brushing his face against her soft skin, with the notion of burying his face in her dark tresses, now seemed but a faded memory. He supposed his induced desires were the consequence of seeing her in the music chamber, it being the first time since she birthed the children. How beautiful she appeared at the pianoforte. Altogether, it was a scene he could not help but dwell upon with pleasure. She brings to me the promise of her heart and treasure of her love; what more could a man desire? he mused.

After pouring a glass of port, he returned to his seat. Hearing a crinkle in his dress pocket, he reached in to remove a letter he received earlier from Georgiana. He had forgotten to tell Elizabeth of the letter; he read it again.

Fitzwilliam Darcy, Pemberley Estate, Derbyshire

My dearest brother: With a joyful heart I write this letter. How much more wonderful is the news to learn that I am Aunt, but to learn it is twice over. I look back once more to the day you brought Elizabeth to live at Pemberley. I delight in the pleasant thought of it. I look forward to the day when you shall introduce me to my new niece and nephew. How proud our mother and father would be to know you named your children after them. It is such an honour indeed. You may expect me at Pemberley before a fortnight. I shall journey home as soon as may be with all the excitement expected of an Aunt in want of viewing her precious relations. I look forward to telling you of all I have learned. Mr. and Mrs. Cochran send their regards and best wishes on the birth of Joseph and Deborah. My finest regards to Elizabeth.

Yours, Georgiana

He was always proud of her musical accomplishments, but more so delighted that she sought to further educate herself. Protecting her across the miles was difficult. Her inherited wealth was reason enough for any unprincipled rogue to attempt to flatter her to the altar. He thankfully found peace in the knowledge she possessed good sense, equally glad she had learned from past experience to be cautious. He must remember to bring the letter to Elizabeth's attention, thought he. He knew it would please his wife; she missed Georgiana as well. He sat alone sipping his wine, then decided to venture to the picture gallery.

With his lamp in hand, he walked the length of the gallery, only stopping once in front of his own portrait. He studied his likeness, resolving Elizabeth deserved the credit of taming his temperament. He could not own unto himself all that had passed to alter him improved. Only in a private audience with Elizabeth did he allow himself the luxury of openness. He secretly desired that uncomplicated level of relaxed comfort when alone with his wife. The totality of their consummated uniqueness afforded him a place of unimpeded indulgence, freeing him of all inscrutable behaviour. He was equally delighted in her ability to draw from him that freedom of spirit he never dared allow himself. Oh how he desired her at that very moment. All such thoughts amused him as he stood for a time reflecting on the family portraits. The hall requires a likeness of Elizabeth, perhaps the children as well, thought he. Lost in the tranquillity of reflections, he marveled of her taste for nature, her vivacity to strive to be unaffected by opposition, along with her desire to yield to his instincts—both trusting and wholly dependent on his wisdom. His present harmonious situation within the walls, which had always provided sanctuary, no longer seemed lacking, but wholly fulfilled. Yes, that is exactly what the gallery requires, a portrait of my family, he continued to muse.

Letters from the Post

THE MORNING NEXT, Mr. Darcy shared Georgiana's letter. "I must apologize for not having told you of the letter, I suppose when distracted, I put it in my dress pocket. I remembered it last evening, but you were already asleep."

"That's quite all right, my dear."

"I answered the letter immediately."

"I shall be happy to see her; it's been too long."

Before another week passed, Jane and Mr. Bingley declared they should make their start to Netherfield the day next.

Elizabeth, gaining in strength, reacquainted herself with her former style. Mr. Darcy was no less eager to have her at his side. Since Mr. Darcy and Mr. Bingley planned to visit the rectory, Mr. Bennet and his younger daughters planned a journey into town. Inasmuch as the young Miss Bennets had not been away from Pemberley Hall since their arrival, the notion of visiting shops induced great excitement. The unfamiliarity of the shops provided the promise of new fashions. Within minutes, all had quitted the place with the exception of Jane and Elizabeth.

"Elizabeth, parting your company is always difficult. I have so enjoyed our stay, but I shall be happy to return to Netherfield. Caroline, Emily and the Hursts expect our return. I do believe Mr. Bingley's sisters were discontented not to come here. They said not a word regarding it; there was no need to, their looks made their disappointment plain. Charles never suggested they accompany us. Still, Emily is sheer delight. She is a bit like you, Lizzy, but advantaged in years."

"What is her age, do you think?"

"Oh, I know her age; she told me she is five and thirty."

"Five and thirty?" Elizabeth gasped.

"Yes, her appearance is deceiving; she hides her age rather well; would you not agree, Lizzy?"

"Indeed," Elizabeth replied, "I wonder why she never married."

"She told me that too."

"Well, are you going to apprise me of it or not?"

"Oh yes, she was once engaged to a businessman; he was in trade in London, I believe on Fleet Street. They were very much in love, but her family objected to the marriage because he was not wealthy, nor did he have connections. Her father demanded he break the engagement. He refused as a matter of honour. Shortly thereafter, his business was put to ruin, leaving him little or nothing left to recommend himself. She is certain her father was responsible. She heard her betrothed was shipped to Botany Bay due to debts incurred from his failed business. She never saw him again, but did mention that her father asked her forgiveness on his deathbed, claiming to have learned too late in life the value of a man's honour. Is that not the saddest of tales, Lizzy?"

"Indeed, such scruples, how does one come up against such adversity? It's tragic, I must say, Jane; it is a sad case indeed."

"Yes, Lizzy, it makes me sad; she is so very kind. She liked you instantly. When you and Mr. Darcy left Netherfield, she praised your performance at the pianoforte, saying she thought you beautiful. And, Lizzy, she announced what a handsome presentation she thought you and Mr. Darcy portrayed. Oh, how I wish you could have seen the expressions on Caroline's and Mrs. Hurst's faces. Charles not only agreed with her, he went on to say how violently Mr. Darcy's affections were for you and how he tried to repress them to his own torment. Caroline and Mrs. Hurst dared not exchange a glance while Charles studied them continually. Lizzy, I have never taken delight in the misfortunes of others, but in this, I confess, I did enjoy it. Father oftentimes talks of being a connoisseur of human folly; well, that was a test of it, I'm sure. I'm ashamed to say, I did enjoy it very much."

Elizabeth laughed. "Oh, Jane, I should have never imagined I should hear you say such things; my how you have become less innocent—you shock me, indeed you do."

Mrs. Reynolds appeared, presenting two letters. "Thank you, Mrs. Reynolds."

"You're welcome, madam," she replied, before departing.

"Two letters! One is from Rosings for Fitzwilliam, the other is for me from London," Elizabeth squealed with delight. "Oh, Jane, how delightful, I do believe it is from Georgiana." Elizabeth's expression turned severe. Her voice turned cold, announcing, "No, I recognize the writing; it is from Lydia. Why, Lydia must be in London!"

"Oh, Lizzy, I do hope she is not making inquiries regarding money."

"Well, Jane, we shall soon see," Elizabeth said, opening the letter, then reading it aloud.

My Dear Lizzy,

I bring you glad tidings from London. My dear Wickham and I have a daughter Hannah. I suppose you have long known that. I understand you will soon have an announcement of your own; I wish you great delight when it happens. I do hope you think of us often; we have moved again. The rent is more than we can be expected to pay. I do hope, dear sister, since you are so very rich, you might see your way to ask Mr. Darcy to intervene so that my Wickham might get a place at court; we should require more money to live on. I wrote to Jane of my further announcement, more joy to be added. I shall close now, asking if you would be so kind to speak to Mr. Darcy; he is so rich as not to miss the money.

Yours, etc.

Elizabeth's mouth flew open, she gasped for air. "Oh, can you believe it, Jane? I am glad Mr. Darcy is from home; how should I have hidden my reaction to such a letter? How foolish of her to apply to me for assistance again."

"Oh, Lizzy, if they have not the rent, I worry the child may be hungry. Should we mention this to our father when he returns?"

Absolutely not, Jane, say nothing of this to Father; he may know of it already. Of course, I doubt it, or why would she write? I'll not send her a farthing of my pin money, Jane; I'm sorry for it, but it cannot be helped. No indeed, I shall not do it, nor will I say anything to Fitzwilliam."

"It is uninviting to be sure, but she insists on inquiring. Surely Mr. Wickham would not let his child go hungry, would he now. It worries me; what say you, Lizzy?"

"Who knows what Wickham would do? I wonder what he does with his money, except run up bills with every proprietor in the neighbouring town. How is such a man to be dealt with? It would not surprise me to learn he directed her to send the letter, much less use the child to gain sympathy.

Lydia is so silly. Foolish, foolish girl, I can hardly reflect on it; it is exceedingly troublesome. At least she has the good sense not to think she can come to Pemberley."

"Calm yourself, Lizzy, there is no reason to get yourself undone; there is nothing to do about it. I believe we choose wisely in not granting her request; if we send money, the solicitation will surely continue."

In her moment of anger, Elizabeth had crumbled the letter in her fist. Looking down at the letter in the palm of her hand, she then tried to smooth it out. She pressed her lips together in anger with each swipe she took to smooth it. "Yes, this is true; now I shall hide the letter. Do you know what really makes me angry?"

"What, Lizzy?"

"The very fact that I hide this from my husband. Mr. Darcy and I have no secrets, except for this," she said, shaking the letter in her fist. "It makes me furious, how dare she; Wickham is the most worthless of men. I have no desire to tell my husband; I fear he will assist for my sake. That I could not tolerate; it would be to my abhorrence considering Wickham sought to do my husband ill. It is not fair, Jane, you know it is not," Elizabeth's voice quivered.

"I see you are vexed; calm yourself, the men are to return soon. Put the letter away, Lizzy, you must not allow it to undo you so."

"Yes, yes, I am so sorry, Jane, to dwell on such a letter when you are soon to take your leave. It was an impulse of anger; instantly regretted. Well, tell me, Jane, do you think Mr. Bingley's sisters will move with you to the new estate?"

"Indeed, the house is equal to Netherfield Hall; I do believe it is large enough. It has a handsome ballroom. You never did have your ball."

"No, I could hardly have a ball in my condition; perhaps in a month or two I shall do just that. After all, did not my husband tell me I should?"

"Yes, he did, I remember he did. Lizzy, you seem to be stronger; do you believe you will be up to a ball in a month or so?"

"Why, yes, Jane, to be sure. I have only danced one dance since the Hyde Park ball. You know I am excessively fond of dancing. Perhaps I shall wait until you move near Lambton to give the ball, then you will not have so far to come."

"That would prove splendid indeed, but you know, Lizzy, Caroline, Emily and the Hursts will expect to be invited if that be the condition; that would be alarming."

Elizabeth laughed. "Jane, do not alarm yourself. I would expect to invite them. Caroline Bingley and Mrs. Hurst will be too busy with other connections to pay any mind to me. No doubt they will be on their best behaviour if they expect Mr. Darcy ever to invite them to Pemberley again. Make no mistake, although my husband is compassionate, I learned from experience he can harshly demonstrate his convictions if he feels justified. He can be counted upon to be forthright when directing his opinion. One should not trifle with his temper; his disdain can be severe. Yes, Jane, I have no doubt he will not hesitate to express it."

"You are referring to your rejection of his first proposal of marriage?"

"Indeed I am, he was extremely vexed; we both said horrible things to one another. I know his emphatic anger; his directness can be very intimidating. I should not wish to revisit that day. I imagine Caroline Bingley and Mrs. Hurst have never gained sight of him in such a state."

"There is hardly a chance for that, Lizzy."

"I should say not," Elizabeth said; then upon hearing footsteps, she added, "Jane, I do believe the gentlemen have returned."

Elizabeth handed Mr. Darcy the letter from Rosings. As he read the letter to himself, he stood with a half of a smile upon his face. He looked at Elizabeth, "Here, you read it." After handing the letter to her, he watched her reaction as she read.

Fitzwilliam Darcy,

I continue to amaze my mother, but fear she still finds it difficult to release me, always wanting to protect me. I talk of Pemberley often. I fancy she will write soon to praise you, Cousin. She now mentions your wife's name; a good sign, I believe. She is well aware what I owe to you and your wife. She has asked many questions, another good notion. Although she talks of writing you a letter, I believe she finds the quill a bit weighted.

Our cousin writes faithfully, always sending his regards to you and Elizabeth. My mother looks upon him with favour. Although Mr. Collins is quite taken aback by my alteration, he speaks little of it, or of Elizabeth. Little Richard Collins is a dear, sweet child. I take him for turns about Rosings Park. I hope to visit Pemberley one day soon. I send my earnest affections to your dear wife Elizabeth.

Yours, Cousin Ann

Jane remained seated while they conversed.

"It is from Ann; how sweet of her to write. Surely I thought it from Lady Catherine herself," Elizabeth told him.

"I can believe she finds it difficult to write. In view of the circumstances, she would find it very difficult; my aunt is not used to admitting her opinions at naught."

"I for one will be relieved when it is settled."

"I have invited Mr. Manley to dine with us. I trust that meets with your approval?"

"Yes, he is always excellent company."

"Good, then it is settled," he said as he attempted to quit the chamber.

"I should like to see Mr. Manley before we take our leave," Jane said, then added, "Before you depart, Mr. Darcy, where is Charles?"

"He was behind me, but stopped to play with the dogs. I expect he will be in directly." He turned to Elizabeth, "I requested the cook make a leg of lamb; I do hope this is to your liking. I thought since it is a favourite of Jane's that might be desirable."

"How thoughtful, dear, quite to my liking, thank you."

He then quitted the chamber, leaving the ladies alone once again. Since the letter was read in Jane's presence, Elizabeth felt it necessary to explain the situation regarding Ann. She told her of Ann's stay, but made no mention of the Colonel's scheme. Elizabeth was aware Mr. Collins wrote of the horrid fever at Rosings to Charlotte's home at Lucas Lodge, which would surely be made known to those at Longbourn, and thus follow to Netherfield. She allowed the story to stand as was.

Mr. Bennet returned from town. The girls were full of excitement, thanking their father for the unexpected funds he granted them, which allowed for a few purchases. Mr. Bennet waited until Mr. Darcy returned to the sitting room with Elizabeth. He stood in front of them presenting two very small silver drinking cups inscribed with the children's initials.

"Oh, Father—these are wonderful," Elizabeth declared with reservation. She neared her father, whispering, "This is more than expected; should you have done this? Perhaps they are too extravagant?"

He quietly whispered back, "Do not concern yourself, my dear, I had some little money set aside for special occasions; I saw this as being one."

"Mr. Bennet, how very kind of you; our deepest appreciation, sir. You have excellent taste, thank you," Mr. Darcy stated.

"Yes, thank you, Father."

"Lizzy, are they not fine? Father was selective in his search; he would not allow Mary or me to assist. And, Lizzy, what do you think, Father allowed us a purchase at the warehouse. We have had a very fine day," Kathryn reported.

Elizabeth smiled. It was amusing to think of her father at the shops.

Mr. Darcy stood aside of his wife. "Mr. Bennet, Elizabeth appears to be surprised at a gentleman such as yourself visiting a silversmith, picking and choosing; I wonder if these ladies will ever understand us gentlemen."

"You are quite right, Mr. Darcy; I believe I have surprised her. They will indeed never understand us. I daresay, we will never understand them, either," he added with quick wit, then laughed.

Mary entered the chamber with a book of poetry from Mr. Darcy's library. As she sat down to read, Mr. Darcy, standing nearby, thought the book looked familiar. He neared her, studying the open book. "Ah, Mary, poetry, I believe you will find that book captivating."

She blushed, turning rather shy, but managed to say, "Yes, I have diversified my reading, I find I rather like poetry once I gave it a chance."

"Very good, variety in reading; I'm sure you'll think it rewarding," Elizabeth added.

"Yes, I already have," she returned earnestly.

Elizabeth was impressed with Mary. It gave her satisfaction to see her making social gains. She looked forward to observing her once again in Mr. Manley's presence.

On past occasions Mr. Darcy called upon his clergy to give the dinner prayer; this evening he announced his preference to do so himself. Mr. Darcy asked his guests to remain seated as he stood. After bowing his head, he prayed a prayer proving to be so eloquent in speech, indulgent in gratitude, giving exultation of adoration to God, then closing it with a hallowed Amen, that his guests were left mute with magnified astonishment by his humble declaration of praise. Mr. Manley consciously digested the reverence of his friend's words. At length, the entire table remained silent as if no one wanted to be the first to speak after such acclamation.

Mr. Darcy, broke the silence. "Shall we eat?"

Mr. Manley leaned toward him to say quietly, "Fitzwilliam, so eloquent a prayer—my regard for you has long been of the highest magnitude; up until present I had not thought my judgment possible to improve upon; you prove me wrong, my friend."

"Thank you; coming from vicarage, I should consider it a most welcome compliment."

Mr. Darcy, now wishing to detract notice from himself, changed the conversation to the dinner, which guaranteed to be a feast. After Mr. Darcy carved the lamb, the servant took the platter, holding it before him. He helped himself to a bit of lamb along with mint preserves. The meal was followed by the presentation of a cake, specially made to mark the occasion. He had opened a bottle of French wine, giving a toast, first to his wife, then the infants and the company before them, closing with thanks be to God, maker of all things.

Mary once again managed a seat next to Mr. Manley. The continuance of her new presentation did not go unnoticed. Mr. Bennet, as well as Elizabeth, kept a watchful eye on the manners of his other daughters. Mary varied her conversation to adapt herself into the social arena. With dark curls about her face, she appeared delicate, her skin was fair but tanned, her small nose gave authority to her commanding eyes, bright with wit. She sat up straight with an air of superiority. Elizabeth studied Mary's attire, noticing she dared to lower her neckline, which made clearance to reveal her figure. A chain holding a cross hung from her long, sleek neck. She could only reflect on how very plain she was upon arrival; it was hard to imagine it was the same girl— she was decidedly altered.

She turned her attention to Kathryn, who had also taken on a new style. Her hair was made into curls about her temples. Her remaining hair was pulled back with ribbons to complement her dress. Kathryn had already reached the point of desiring attention through the influence of Lydia, but she presented herself with more sophistication. Kathryn was medium in build; her face had such petite features, her nose small, her rounded eyes wide with eagerness, revealing expressions of innocence, bursting with a pleasing personality. Elizabeth observed her father. He paid close attention to his younger daughters. She wondered of his thoughts as she watched him inspect them over top of his spectacles.

Distracted by a question directed at her, Elizabeth's attention was now on her husband, who asked, "My dear, after dinner would you consent to play the pianoforte? I believe the girls would like a dance."

"I would be delighted."

Much to Elizabeth's amazement, the girls displayed a reserved excitement in the plan, not the silly foolish reaction she had expected. This was turning into quite a surprising evening, thought Elizabeth, it continued to be full of surprises. Elizabeth sat at the pianoforte to play a few Irish airs. After Mr. Bingley turned to the floor with Jane, Mr. Manley bowed, requesting the pleasure of a dance from Mary. To Elizabeth's shock, her father directed himself to Kathryn. He then put out his hand for her to dance with him. It was a delight to see her father enjoying himself with ease. As Elizabeth continued to delight in the recreation, she rapidly grew conscious of the change in her father; it was as if he had come alive. He seemed to be a much younger man. Mr. Darcy stood near the pianoforte observing the dance while sipping his wine, enjoying the delightful events with satisfaction.

"Elizabeth, I do believe your father a rather good dancer," he said as his eyes followed her father's movements.

"I cannot tell you when I saw my father dance last; it has been some years," she retorted with astonishment.

"Kathryn and Mary certainly are enjoying the evening," he added.

"Yes, I see they are—Kathryn?"

"Yes—Kathryn. Of course, you retired early; you do not know of Kathryn's request. Kitty asked your father if she might be called Kathryn. I believe she has outgrown Kitty."

"I see," Elizabeth noted.

"I shall have to ask Mr. Manley to play a tune so I may dance with my wife. Do you feel up to a dance with an admiring partner?"

"I shouldn't want to end the dance for Mary; perhaps we can wait, another time."

"Certainly not, I am of a selfish nature just now; I desire a dance with my wife; I do not wish to be denied the pleasure. I'll settle for one dance," he said, teasing quietly.

"Very well, but tarry, allow them a few more reels," she whispered.

"You reason hard; you force me to stand here, sip my wine, adore my beautiful wife from a distance with a lack of patience, a sacrifice to be endured. It is quite insufferable," he lamented, teasing in a low voice.

"Mr. Darcy, I may prove worth the wait."

"Indeed you shall be, I demand it," he teased edging closer to her.

"Mr. Darcy, careful you do not draw the attention of our guests."

"Mrs. Darcy, you lure me with those fine eyes, then expect me to stand near with no reaction; I'll not stand for it."

"You are already standing." She laughed at her own poor wit.

"Mrs. Darcy, you seem to have the upper hand presently, careful of the turnabout," he continued to tease, edging his way closer still.

"My father is looking this way," she said with alarm, trying to muffle her voice.

"What of it, Mrs. Darcy? It was he who gave me your hand."

Since her tune was at an end, she quickly stood. "Mr. Manley, my husband tells me he desires you to play a tune; he wishes to dance with me."

"Fitzwilliam, why did you not say so?"

"Uh—my wife was impatient to dance; I should have asked sooner," was all he could reply after being caught off his guard. He took Elizabeth's hand. As they started to dance, he smiled, rolling his eyes at her for putting him on the mark.

After the dance, Elizabeth reclaimed her position at the pianoforte. To her surprise, Mr. Darcy reclaimed his position near her.

"Do you stand here, Mr. Darcy, to further tease me?"

"Well, are you satisfied?"

"I? It was not I who pressed to dance."

"Yes, I did; I admit I enjoyed it, too" he replied, smiling admiringly.

Before the night was over, there were many dances to be had. Excluding Elizabeth, Mr. Bennet managed to dance with all of his daughters.

A Most Trying Day

$\mathcal{I}$T WAS EARLY. Jane and Mr. Bingley's trunks were brought below the stairs. The carriage was waiting. Leave-taking always brought a sense of sadness. "I'm so sorry you cannot stay a few additional days, Jane. Georgiana is due home any day. I so wanted you to know her. I suppose it will have to wait."

"Yes, Lizzy, I'm sorry too."

Mr. Bennet turned to Jane. "My dear, do be careful, you have a long ride back to Netherfield. I suppose you will be making several stops along the way?"

"Yes, Father, I imagine we shall." While bidding their last farewell, the sudden rapid sound of horses' hooves caught their attention. Local farmers approached at a steady fast pace, stopping short where they gathered. A young farmer jumped from his horse excitedly. "Sir, there has been a terrible accident, a chaise and four has met with disaster, it has overturned below the clearing, beyond the trees about a half-mile. It appears the horses took fright; the driver's reins are broken. I believe the driver to be dead, sir. There is a young woman in the chaise; we left two other farmers there."

Frightened, Mr. Darcy cried out, "Tell me at once man, the woman, does she live?"

"I fear not, sir, she lies beneath the carriage. She did not move, nor did she answer us when we called out to her."

All colours drained from Mr. Darcy's face. Instant horror consumed him. With natural inclination, he jumped on the man's horse, following the other to the mishap. Mr. Bingley ran to the stables to secure a horse. Mr. Bennet told the footman to advance in the same direction, as he boarded the carriage. The ladies clung to one another. Elizabeth surrendered to

271

hysterics. Jane tried to guide her into the house, but she would not have it. Wiping tears from her eyes, she turned to Jane, "I cannot bear the thought of it."

"Yes, I know, Lizzy. Poor Mr. Darcy, what must he be feeling?" Jane embraced her. "Go ahead, cry, Lizzy, there is nothing to be done at the moment; perhaps the man was wrong, perhaps it isn't Georgiana after all."

Elizabeth just cried all the more. She trembled, believing the worst. For the ladies, it seemed forever. They stayed out of doors, hoping to see a horse or carriage. They heard what they thought was a gunshot from off in a distance. Finally they could see the carriage Mr. Bennet had taken coming toward the house with natural speed. Mr. Darcy and Mr. Bingley followed. The ladies rushed to the carriage. Mr. Bennet could easily see the torment his daughter was suffering. "Well now, Lizzy, catch hold of yourself, no need to cry. Miss Darcy is not badly hurt."

Elizabeth placed her hands on her chest to calm her pounding heart. Rubbing her fingers under her eyes, she wiped away tears, then clung to Georgiana after she exited the carriage. Georgiana's dress was dirty and torn; other than a few scrapes and bruises, she had the good fortune to survive the mishap.

Elizabeth clutched her stomach before placing her right hand over her mouth. The strain of emotions surged through her body. She instantly ran a few yards away. Now ill, she released all at a nearby tree. Mr. Darcy ran to his wife, seizing her by the waist. He continued his hold until there was nothing left to lose. When she stood, he drew her to his breast, keeping a grasping hold on her. "How are you now, my dear?"

"I am so relieved Georgiana is safe. I suppose I worked myself up to this terrible end."

"Oh, Elizabeth," he said, kissing her forehead, "you don't know what it means to a man to have a wife who loves his sister as you do."

"I am so thankful she is well; I prayed that she would be unharmed."

"She was rendered unconscious for a bit, but has came around, although I am certain she will suffer the pains of her scrapes, no doubt. Otherwise, I expect she has nothing of which to worry," Mr. Darcy said, as he led her back to those waiting at the portal.

The driver was dead; the reins were broken, causing the chaise to overturn. The most they could account for was that something frightened the horses. One of the horses had to be put out of its misery. It appeared Georgiana Darcy fell, landing on her left side, which took the brunt of the blow;

however, she escaped any serious injury. They took her into the house to refresh her as well as calm her nerves.

Mr. Darcy ordered one of his men to come into the house, another he had sent to retrieve Mr. Manley. He ordered the carriage be put away, announcing no one was leaving Pemberley.

Elizabeth and Mr. Darcy entered the sitting room where the whole of the party gathered. "You are pale," Mr. Darcy said, grasping Georgiana by the shoulders and assessing her face. The left side of Georgiana's face revealed scrapes. Taking his hand to her chin, he turned her head, examining her. "Thank God you are safe, such a scare. I see Mrs. Reynolds has already cleaned your wounds." Releasing his hold on her, he went on, "Allow me to introduce you to Elizabeth's father, Mr. Bennet, her sisters, Kathryn and Mary. This is Jane, who is married to Mr. Bingley, whom, of course, you already know."

"Good day."

"Miss Darcy, I am equally grateful you escaped severe injury," Mr. Bennet said.

Kathryn and Mary curtsied rather shyly.

After the brief introductions, Mrs. Reynolds whisked Georgiana away to her chamber for immediate rest after her ordeal.

"Bingley, I have terminated your journey; I ordered the carriage away for the day. I thought it best; you may depart tomorrow." It was to Jane's relief. The carriage mishap was enough excitement for one day. After several hours had passed, Mr. Manley arrived at Pemberley Hall to see Mr. Darcy on the matter of the dead driver.

Mr. Darcy approached his wife. "My dear, Mr. Manley may very well join us for dinner."

"Mr. Manley, it is always a pleasure to have you at our table."

In the interim, after seclusion in her chamber, Georgiana had come below the stairs in time to ready herself for the evening meal. After thanking Elizabeth for the invitation to dine, Mr. Manley turned to Georgiana. He bowed. "Miss Darcy, I cannot tell you how relieved I am you were not severely injured. It is so good to see you again; I do believe you gave your brother quite a scare."

"Yes, Mr. Manley, I'm afraid I did."

Elizabeth studied Mr. Darcy's manner. She may have well predicted his insistence that Jane and Mr. Bingley stay the night.

Mr. Darcy excused himself after realizing the cook had not been notified of the four additional settings required at the dinner table. He encountered Mrs. Reynolds. "I have already informed the cook. I took the liberty, Mr. Darcy; under the circumstances, I knew you were distracted. Mr. Darcy, I need not tell you how relieved I am Miss Georgiana escaped injury. Such a dreadful loss."

"Yes, it was ghastly. Poor fellow, I understand, after talking with Mr. Manley, he was a young man of one and twenty, engaged to be married."

"Sad to be sure, sir."

"Mrs. Reynolds, I thank you for your thoughtfulness," he stated, then excused himself.

"There he is," announced Mr. Bingley as Mr. Darcy entered the chamber.

"Georgiana, perhaps you would like to see the children?"

"Yes, I wish it very much; we were waiting for your return." Elizabeth, Mr. Darcy and Georgiana made their way above the stairs. To their delight the children were awake and being attended to by their nursemaids. Mr. Darcy placed his son in Georgiana's arms; next he placed his daughter in his wife's arms. He stepped back for a moment. "Now, that is quite a sight."

"They are so small," Georgiana observed.

"Babies are small; you should have seen them a few weeks earlier," returned Mr. Darcy with authority. "You two visit; I must return to our guests."

"Elizabeth, they are precious; I believe I shall like being their aunt."

"I'm sure you will. I have missed you, Georgiana. Your letters were well received. I know your brother looks forward to them as well."

They returned the babies to the nursemaids, deciding they should return to the guests.

"I'm so sorry my mishap upset you to a point of illness."

"Say nothing of it, Georgiana. I am just happy you did not suffer severe injury."

"Your sisters are very agreeable; Mrs. Bingley is the eldest, is she not?"

"Why, yes, she is; I come after her."

"It must be nice to have sisters; I'm glad you are my sister now.

"Yes, it was nice growing up with sisters, especially one as close as Jane is to me; we were always together, the very best of friends." By now they had joined the others. Tea had been served; the gentlemen had wine and the girls were nibbling on shortbread.

"I beg your pardon, sir, but there is a very large carriage bearing a crest, nearing Pemberley Hall," Bessie announced, then curtsied before quitting their presence.

brows and wrinkled her nose, looking rather stiff as she stared at him, waiting for his answer.

Inasmuch as her questions irritated him, his voice turned stern again. "Yes, since you inquire, yes, I was painfully angered, the refusal tortured me; she did not think me a gentleman."

"What? Not a gentleman? What does she mean my nephew not a gentleman? Whatever can be wrong with that girl?"

"Lady Catherine, I was not a gentleman to her; she was justified in refusing me. I was angry, demanding, my actions were deplorable," he told her in a voice less civil.

She changed the subject, employing a less hardened voice. "I want to talk about Ann."

"Very well."

"I see changes, need I say more?"

"Lady Catherine, Ann has changed; she is not physically strong like other girls, but she is equally capable; she requires temperance, that is all," he said straightforwardly.

"I am aware it is to you I owe this change," she returned in a mellowing tone.

"No, Lady Catherine, that is where you err; it is much my wife's doing." Knowing she was aware of this, he looked her straight in the eye.

"I am well aware your wife taught her needlework, as well as a few simple tunes on the pianoforte. I must say her playing leaves a lot to be desired. I find it quite annoying at times. I hired an instructor; nevertheless, I never expected your wife to show kindness to my Ann."

"Why should she not show kindness toward Ann?" he boldly stated, pulling his shoulder back. She made no attempt whatever to dispute his comment.

"Colonel Fitzwilliam tells me it is your wife, not you, who wishes to make amends. I know this cannot be true; I am determined to correct this falsehood once and for all," she stated with certainty, her voice extremely irritated once again.

"Indeed it is true; why should you doubt the Colonel?"

"*What!*" she screeched. Her lips parted with shock. She sat momentarily gazing at him with disbelief. "Fitzwilliam Darcy, do you mean to inform me, you were content to never speak to me again?" she demanded, sitting forward in her chair acutely shaken.

"Indeed, it is true."

"I'm glad your mother is not here to witness such language as this."

"Lady Catherine, your opinion of my marriage is extremely indignant; I find your language to me on the subject to be very frank, abusive, most offensive, I daresay. You told me you would never forgive me for not honouring the commitment. These are your convictions; your own diffidence prevented your reason. In spite of all this, my wife wishes me to overlook these offences, to pursue reconciliation. To be perfectly forthright, I flatly refused," he said in a strong voice as he arose from his seat. He placed the palms of his hands on his desk as he leaned forward glaring boldly at her. He could not have been more honest or strict in his attitude. He desired her to understand his position wholly and completely.

"I demand to know why would you not marry Ann," she uttered indignantly.

Given the delicacy of the subject, Mr. Darcy softened his voice. "I love Ann, but not as a man should love the woman he marries. I knew she could not make me happy and I believe I could not make her so," he replied, regaining his seat with more reserve.

She stared at him as she took in his words. "These are Ann's sentiments exactly. She used the same language with me," she informed him smugly, turning her face from him, elevating her chin.

"Lady Catherine, what are your intentions?" he said, altering his voice with more civility.

She abruptly came back at him as if she were confused. "Whatever do you mean?"

"Why are you here?" he asked, lightly drumming his fingers on his desk impatiently.

"I wish to make all this perfectly clear," she said, turning sideways in the chair. She turned her head away from him. He felt her discomfort, but found no reason to pity her.

"Aunt, surely you have not come here to quibble; what is it you hope to achieve?"

"I come because of Ann. I know what I owe to you," she hesitated, "and your wife," she finished, her voice trailing off as if it pained her to say the words. Such admission stuck in her throat, but the delivery was not lost as Mr. Darcy caught each faint word.

"Lady Catherine, I wrote you a letter seeking reconciliation; you ignored it. I wrote another; you ignored it as well. At my wife's insistence, I wrote another. My own willful reasoning prompted me otherwise, but I conceded to honour her wishes. I was prepared to end our relationship, but Elizabeth would not allow it. Now, may I ask, to what does this visit tend?"

Her lips parted, "Why, Fitzwilliam, such language, this cannot be endured; surely you do not mean to tell me this is truth?" she replied with shock.

"Indeed it is; I'll not deny it."

"This is not to be endured; you would never speak to me again?"

He could see she was clearly mortified, but that mattered little. Discovering it increasingly difficult to keep his anger under control, he raised his voice, delivering his opinion swiftly without regret. "Why should that shock you? Your language regarding my wife was abusive; you not only refuse my letters, when Ann was at Pemberley you chose to insult me further through your written word."

"Whatever do you mean?" she demanded again.

"Your letters were wanting and insulting."

"What do you mean wanting and insulting; I demand to know? I must be satisfied."

"You ignored the existence of my wife, then further insulted me, telling me it was my duty to care for Ann. I did what any man would do; it was not a matter of doing one's duty. I was pleased we had time together, but your letters while she was at Pemberley angered me greatly; they were insufferable," he finished resolutely.

"I was still angry when I dispatched those letters." Once again she turned from him stubbornly, with her nose in the air. She then attempted to change her countenance, realizing her excuses were lacking. A noticeable attempt was made to soften her voice, but it was obviously difficult for her; she was not accustomed to yielding.

"Pray tell me, why is it you are come?" he said, putting her in an awkward position, attempting to force her into a commitment.

"I am here because of Ann, she talks of nothing else. Ann is all I have left in the world. Our dispute makes her unhappy; she tells me so daily. Both she and Colonel Fitzwilliam tell me I am wrong with regard to your wife, that is to say, about her character. I believe they have swayed my opinion; perhaps I have erred in judgment; perhaps she has risen above her lack of wealth, family and connections." She paused, taking a deep breath, then went on, "I have not come to berate your wife; I have come to make amends. It appears I have made a grave error."

His voice softened, "Well, Aunt, I hardly expected you to say thus."

"Do you expect her to receive me now?" she asked sternly.

"Lady Catherine, we have but five minutes until my wife walks through that door." He rose from his seat again. He leaned toward her with the weight of his body dependent on his hands, which now rested upon the desk. "This is my home, let me be properly understood; if you mean to make amends, I am receptive, but I warn you, I'll not compromise where my wife is concerned." His words were delivered with all the authority of a man in charge of his destiny, all the while looking her straight in the eye without a flinch. She sat quietly astonished, saying not a word, but fidgeted with her hands for a brief moment, granting him the certainty of her uneasiness.

His continued stare was deliberate. "Well, Aunt, I believe I hear her coming," he stated as he once again sat down with his hands clasped in front of him.

Elizabeth walked into the office chamber. She walked around Lady Catherine's chair to take her place next to her husband. As she curtsied, she bore a serious look upon her face, not knowing what awaited her.

Lady Catherine slowly nodded her head in acknowledgment.

"Lady Catherine sent a message of her coming; we had not received it as yet."

"Oh!" was all Elizabeth could manage to say. Although the two gave no indication to the outcome she was to expect, it was evident her husband portrayed an air of confidence.

"Miss Bennet, uh—may I call you Elizabeth?" she asked in a civil tone, but direct.

"Why, yes, of course," Elizabeth answered with an element of surprise in her tone.

"I am come to give your marriage my blessing. I know it is late, but a change in circumstances has caused me to reconsider my position."

"Thank you," Elizabeth reluctantly replied.

"The kindness you showed my Ann while here at Pemberley has been greatly taken into consideration. She returned a changed girl. I do believe you to be sincere to my Ann, as she has told me on many occasions. She also told me she had no desire to marry Fitzwilliam; I understand the feelings were mutual. I know now that when I visited Longbourn you were telling me the truth, you were not engaged to my nephew. I further understand that it was your wish to reconcile us against his wishes, is that not so?"

Elizabeth's eyes widened, "Why—yes, it is," She answered with surprise.

Lady Catherine's eyes quickly shifted from Elizabeth to her nephew. Her lips parted, as she looked at him with disbelief. "Why, Fitzwilliam, I thought this could not possibly be true; I refused to believe it, but now I see it is so. Why—I am quite vexed, to say the very least!"

"Lady Catherine, I explained earlier, your assault on my wife's character was not acceptable; your conduct was unsatisfactory. I bore the insults to myself, but not the hurt inflicted on the woman I love; it is that simple. You love Ann very much do you not?"

"Why—yes, of course," she answered him as if he had asked the stupidest of questions.

"Lady Catherine, would you consider your love for Ann greater than the distaste you thought you had for my wife? Was it not your love of Ann that prompted you to send her to Pemberley when you were ill?"

"I suppose if you put it in those terms, yes that is true."

"Well then, you certainly understand; love for another outweighs the love we have for ourselves, would you not agree?"

"Perhaps so. It was Ann who insisted we come; she has been talking of nothing else; she desperately desired to see you again, Elizabeth. I must thank you for your kindness to my Ann; I should never have expected her so changed; no, I daresay, I was quite surprised."

"No need to thank me, Lady Catherine."

"I have been here too long. We have guests waiting, what are your intentions, Lady Catherine?" he asked, now standing, placing his hands flat upon the desk again, leaning forward at her boldly. He stared into her face, well aware he had the upper hand.

"What do you mean?"

"I wish it to be perfectly clear. Are we reconciled or do we remain indifferent?" he asked boldly, as if he were her superior.

"I thought the matter settled," she came back at him. She looked away; the pressures of his demands were making her uncomfortable.

"Lady Catherine, I want a frank declaration one way or the other. I must have it; it must be declared."

"Very well then, you have my word; we are reconciled," she stated cautiously.

"Your declaration made no mention of my wife."

"I gave your marriage my blessing; I thought that proof it included your wife."

"I just wish to be clear on the subject. I demand clarity."

"I consider the matter closed; you may consider it settled," she added, her attitude was such that she sounded as though she were doing him a favour.

"Very well, then," he replied, allowing the subject to be closed as he came out from behind the desk. Standing over her, he stated, "Since you have come this far, I believe it is too late to journey home. You will have to stay the night. You are aware we presently entertain many guests, are you not?"

"Yes, what of it?"

Still towering over her with his advantageous height, he continued. "Our guests consist of Mr. Manley, my vicar; Mr. Bingley accompanied by his wife, who is Elizabeth's sister; Elizabeth's father and her two younger sisters, and Georgiana as well." After delivering his announcement with challenging temperament, he leaned forward slightly, awaiting her answer.

"Well, I guess I'll have to be introduced," she replied, much to his surprise.

"You will make them acceptable to you, will you not?" he asked straightforward.

"Yes, yes, I am very anxious to see how my Ann does out in company."

Elizabeth stepped closer to Lady Catherine. Compassionately, she spoke, "Lady Catherine, I cannot tell you the happiness you bring to Fitzwilliam and me in accepting the invitation to stay. I consider it an honour to have you here. Ann is a lovely girl; I have come to love her dearly. Do accept my profound sincerity in saying these words to you." She curtsied, granting Lady Catherine a faint smile.

"Well, you certainly are a surprise, I'll give you that. I must admit, I am relieved we have come to this end," Lady Catherine said nodding.

"Lady Catherine, we will join the others now. If you judge my guests offensive, I suggest you appeal to me discreetly and you will be shown to your chamber. Remember, you are not at Rosings." He bent his arm, offering it to his aunt. Elizabeth was glad to follow behind; she was relieved, but still the evening was fresh, thought she. She could not help but view the anticipation trying, nor could she deny it could prove to be a lengthy, strenuous affair.

Once having entered the sitting room, Mr. Darcy introduced Lady Catherine. Although she was well received by them with warm welcomes and lively conversation, she mainly sat observing everything. She appeared to be quite comfortable in her present situation. Ann gained a seat near her mother. It was obvious she was doing her best to secure her mother's comfort.

One of the servants entered. "Sir, I believe dinner is about to be served."

Mr. Darcy immediately thought to himself, two more for dinner, no one had warned the cook. But after a few moments, he judged Mrs. Reynolds no doubt informed them of the two additions required at the table. Upon entering the dining hall, he noticed they were short two place settings. At once he realized no one accounted for Lady Catherine or Ann. Upon seeing the table required two additional settings, the servants scurried to make it right.

"Pray be seated," voiced Mr. Darcy.

It had been such a trying day, he thought to himself. He leaned toward his wife to whisper his resolve. "What else may we expect from a day such as this?"

Meeting One's Match

ELIZABETH WAS STILL SLEEPING when Mr. Darcy directed himself below the stairs to the breakfast chamber. Mr. Bennet and Lady Catherine, having already breakfasted, were indulged in favourable conversation, much to his bewilderment.

"Uh—good morning, I expected I would be the first. It is early, you two quite surprised me," he said. It was quite evident that he was caught off guard.

"Why should you be surprised? I always rise early," Lady Catherine replied.

"Did you sleep well, Aunt?"

"Very well, I found last evening most interesting."

"How so?" Mr. Bennet asked with his lively wit and a twinkle in his eye.

"You quite surprise me, Mr. Bennet; I find you well informed. I indeed enjoyed our conversation. I realized I have not been in company for some time; yes, I quite enjoyed myself," she responded with a bit of amusement in her voice.

"I'm glad to hear it," he replied, then added, "it was a fine evening, Mr. Darcy."

"Mr. Bennet, are you aware my nephew has not introduced me to his children? As of yet, I have no proof they exist."

Mr. Darcy, pouring himself a cup of coffee at the sideboard, turned to regard his aunt suspiciously. "When Elizabeth rises, I will take you to them," he mystifyingly responded. He had not expected his aunt to be doing as well as she was in the presence of his guests, especially Elizabeth's family. The fact that she teased quite stunned him along with the ease of their amicable repartee.

"Two at once, Fitzwilliam, that is quite an achievement," she called out.

"Indeed it is, a boy first, then a girl at that," Mr. Bennet chimed in.

"I understand they were named after your mother and father."

"Yes, my wife insisted upon it," he stated proudly.

Within moments, Mr. Bingley, Jane and Georgiana appeared in the breakfast chamber. Ten additional minutes following, Elizabeth entered with Ann, shortly succeeded by Kathryn and Mary.

"Quite a crowd my nephew has here," Lady Catherine called out to anyone who would listen.

"Indeed," responded Mr. Bennet. He then glanced in her direction. With a warm smile, he asked, "Lady Catherine, are you still going to allow me that game of backgammon later this morning?"

Mr. Darcy, now at his wife's side, shifted his questioning eyes in her direction. Ann immediately swung around on her heels to view her mother skeptically. Georgiana afforded Mr. Darcy a dubious look, while Mary eyed Kathryn, forming a similar exchange. Mr. Bingley eyed his friend with inquisition, raising his brows with widened eyes. Elizabeth turned to capture Jane's expression. Jane's mouth, partially open, projected undeniable amazement, providing an open display of the collective thoughts among those witnessing the two seated at the table. With the entire party in disbelief of their hearing, no one dared utter a word. They simply continued sheepishly to await the response.

"I suppose if you insist, Mr. Bennet, but I warn you, I am very good."

"We shall see, Lady Catherine, we shall see. I believe we'll play after the young people take their leave."

A nervous Elizabeth turned to her guest, "Lady Catherine, did you sleep well?"

"Yes, I did," she answered with no complaints whatsoever.

Mr. Darcy remained at the sideboard intrigued, wondering; could this possibly be the start of another peculiar day? He could not believe the difference a good night's sleep could make. He had not heard a word of condescension pass her lips since she was introduced to his guests. She conversed with Mr. Bennet with ease. This was too much to comprehend so early in the morning. He thought he should go out to sport, perhaps get some fresh air, anything to clear his head.

Jane and Mr. Bingley, anxious for home, planned to depart after breakfast. Mr. Darcy had directed his man to bring the carriage around. Soon after breakfasting they arose to bid farewell.

Standing in the threshold, Mr. Bingley stated, "Surely we will get our start this morning; I trust it will be an improvement over yesterday."

"Yes, it is not likely we'll have another day like yesterday," replied Mr. Darcy.

Mr. Bennet, Mary, Kathryn and Elizabeth bid farewell to Jane, while Lady Catherine, Georgiana and Ann stayed in the house, having already wished them a safe journey. Parting was always a difficult task for Elizabeth and Jane; today proved no different.

"Good-bye, Elizabeth, I shall write; I am anxious to settle closer to you; it will not be long, I imagine."

"No, it will not be long; I should look forward to it."

After the painful adieus, the remaining party watched the carriage until it was out of sight. Elizabeth, along with her younger sisters, quickly went into the house leaving Mr. Bennet and Mr. Darcy alone for a few moments out of doors.

"Well, I suppose I should go in for my backgammon game just now."

"Mr. Bennet," Mr. Darcy said as he neared him, stopping short, directly face to face with him. Donning a puzzled expression, he inquired, "How did you ever get into the good graces of my aunt?"

"Whatever do you mean, Mr. Darcy?"

"Sir, I know my aunt; she is not commonly receptive."

"Whatever do you mean, Mr. Darcy? I quite simply made conversation with her last evening; she seemed to enjoy it; I was a dutiful listener."

"How did you get her to agree to play backgammon?"

"I simply mentioned it; she claimed to know it well, so I challenged her, simple as that, Mr. Darcy, simple as that," he commented, giving a wink of his eye.

"Very well, Mr. Bennet, I am in your debt."

"In my debt, how so?"

"Well, Mr. Bennet, you have eased a burden, that is all. Shall we go in now?" Mr. Darcy said as they both made their way into the house.

Kathryn was showing a very interested Ann her needlework. Mary sat in a chair reading, while Lady Catherine listened to Elizabeth play the pianoforte. As soon as they entered the room, Lady Catherine at once declared, "Fitzwilliam, am I ever to see the children?"

"Yes, Lady Catherine, come with me. Perhaps you would like to come too Ann?"

"Oh, yes, I should like that very much."

Mr. Darcy turned toward his wife, giving her a nod, along with a look expressing he desired her to join them.

Some time later they returned to the music chamber. Lady Catherine, quite taken with the children, could not imagine so much black hair, and was decidedly taken with their plump cheeks. She not only viewed them, but requested to hold one of them. Mr. Darcy, utterly amazed, felt a sense of satisfaction at her more then anticipated reaction.

Later in the day, Mr. Darcy discovered a welcomed opportunity to talk alone with Ann. He invited her to take a turn about the grounds. Once outside, he inquired, "Ann, enlighten me, I'm at a loss to understand your mother; how is it she is so suddenly altered?"

"It is not so sudden, Cousin. Upon my return to Rosings, I noticed a difference. She truly wished to come sooner, although it was hard for her, I am certain. I truly believe she thought she should die with the fever. I did not expect her so readily to receive the changes in me. I am convinced death's door forced her to recognize she will not always be here to protect me. I suppose she understands I need to be more independent. You'll be interested to know she encourages it now."

"She loves you very much, Ann."

"Yes, I never doubted it, though I do believe it has taken on new meaning."

"Well, for that I am heartily glad."

"When I told her I should not have married you she was disappointed in me, but not angry. I do believe her knowing my not wanting to marry you allowed her to think clearly."

"I know I was a disappointment; no nephew could have been more loved."

"No more than my revelation. I do believe mine holds a deeper meaning. Your rejection of me made her very angry; it was more accepting to think I would not have you."

"I suppose that would be so," he uttered.

"I have talked at great length of my stay here; I have showed her everything I learned. I deliberately talked endlessly of Elizabeth, knowing I am the one person she would never refuse anything."

"You did this, Ann, for us, did you not?"

"No, Cousin, it was selfishly done. I should always wish to come to Pemberley. I still look forward to your visits to Rosings. Do not you see— all would have been lost."

"You quite surprise me, Ann."

"Colonel Fitzwilliam talked to her at length. While I do not know the whole of the conversation, I am convinced he forced her to believe she misjudged your wife."

"I owe the Colonel a great deal."

"No, I believe the Colonel did it for all of us, including himself."

"Well, I shall have to thank him just the same."

"I noticed other changes you have not yet witnessed, such as her temperament with the servants—she is much more obliging. She goes out of doors more; I do believe being confined to the house, her bedchamber especially, helped bring about the change. I knew her harsh opinions were shrinking once she asked questions, mentioning your wife's name. Earlier, no one was allowed to say her name in the house, myself included. I do believe she is still of the opinion you should have married a woman of wealth, family and connections, but she is resigned you are happy in your choice. The knowledge I should have refused to marry you seemed to make a vast difference."

"Yes, perhaps it softened her position. Ann, you are remarkable."

"I must say I was surprised she and Mr. Bennet got on so well," she said.

"Yes, as was I."

"I believe, not having been out in company for many years, she enjoyed herself, giving little thought to status or connections. Think of it, Cousin, she believes me to be altered for the better; I view her precisely the same."

"I am well pleased for you both. Now, shall we return to the house?"

They returned to the house in time to witness the last move of the backgammon game, a victory for Lady Catherine to a great degree of satisfaction. Lady Catherine was now wishing to take her leave, much to Ann's dismay.

"Before I take my leave, I would wish a private audience with you, Fitzwilliam."

"Very well, shall we go to my office?"

"Yes, that will do."

Once in the office, she comfortably seated herself. She spoke with the utmost sincerity. "Fitzwilliam, I should very much like to visit again. I have not enjoyed myself this much since Sir Louis de Bourgh was alive. I admit, when I arrived yesterday, I was still very much displeased with your choice in marriage, but I felt I could overlook these conditions for Ann's sake. This morning I feel quite differently; I could not be displeased with you forever, you know. I confess your wife quite surprised me; I felt she was sincere in her declaration of my being here. I believe I see now it is your happiness, not her own, which concerns her most."

"And I confess I'm quite shocked by your declaration."

"Why should you be? You know me well enough to know if I have something to confess, I deliver it with frankness."

"You are pleased with the changes in Ann, are you not?"

"Very much so."

"I'm glad to hear of it."

"I owe it all to you and your wife; I'm convinced of that now."

"Thank you, it means a great deal to hear you say it."

He noticed she swallowed hard, slightly turning her head from him. "Well now, where is that girl? We must be on our way," she said, as if she needed to change the subject. Mr. Darcy detected a bit of embarrassment in Lady Catherine's demeanour, a sight seldom witnessed.

As they stood on the threshold after bidding farewell, they watched the large carriage make its way from Pemberley, disappearing beyond the clearing as it entered the woods. Those left behind felt contented relief for having a turn of events so unexpectedly pleasing.

Homeward Bound

At breakfast, Mr. Bennet declared he would depart the day next after dawn, much to the discouragement of his younger daughters. Mr. Darcy desired to take in a few hours of sport while Mary, Kathryn and Georgiana remained in the music chamber. Georgiana granted Mary an audience on the pianoforte, affording Elizabeth time with her father alone.

"Father, I am obliged for your kindness to Lady Catherine."

"Of what are you talking, Lizzy?" he asked innocently.

She smiled slyly. "Father, I watched you allow her a win at backgammon; I know you too well, you are too good at the game."

"Oh, you profess to know me that well, eh?" he returned with quick wit.

"Yes, indeed, I viewed the moves you made; I know you too well."

Mr. Bennet eyed his daughter over top of his spectacles. He grinned, "Well, well, my dear, keep that to yourself. I felt a lady of her stature deserves a win every now and again. It was awfully hard for her to come here, Lizzy."

"True, but I must confess, Father, you quite amaze me," she smiled with satisfaction.

Still peering at her over top of his spectacles, he smiled. "I surprise myself at times. I daresay, I do indeed," he reported in a half whisper.

"Father, I noticed a welcome change in my sisters. Kathryn, as she prefers to call herself just now," Elizabeth rolled her eyes, then continued, "is more poised, more ladylike, lacks that foolish wildness. Mary is a curiosity; what happened to bring about such change? Have you done something with them? They are quite altered."

"I talked to each alone, Lizzy. Uh, Kathryn, as we refer to her just now, is a bit more difficult; she is strong willed. I did, however, lay the law down; I fear she still owns to some of the same foolery Lydia possessed. I am pleased

290

she is on good behaviour here; that is a comfort, but I confess I am concerned."

"What of Mary, Father, what have you done to alter her so?"

"Not much to tell; I simply spoke with her instructing her to listen more, voice her opinions less. I was forthright regarding her singing. She sings off key; I told her so. Although it suffered me to do it, I felt it necessary. I praised her abilities to play, but discouraged the voice. I delicately explained that if hosts desired her to entertain, they would appeal to her to do so. I asked that she not take it upon herself to assume people desired her amusement. As for her new appearance, I had nothing to do with it; it is as much a surprise to me, indeed it is."

"That explains it. Mary was not so anxious to sit at the pianoforte; she only played twice. I wondered why she did not sing. Well, Father, you have been quite busy."

"Yes, well, Lizzy, they need guidance; I'm not up to further nonsense. That sort of thing ceased to amuse me. Just the same, I must tell you, I am concerned. Kathryn writes to this Lieutenant Denny often; she does not listen to me in that respect; it concerns me a great deal. What's a father to do?"

"Yes, Jane is concerned too. I'm sure it will all work out well."

"Perhaps it will, my dear," he said with sadness in his voice.

"Father, what of yourself; what do you do now?"

"What is there left to be done? I enjoy what I have left."

"Are you lonely, Father?"

"Lizzy, it is possible for a man to be lonely in a house fully occupied. You need not concern yourself on my behalf, I do well enough."

"Very well, Father, I shall not press further."

"Well, Lizzy, I believe I can use a bit of port about now."

In the afternoon another carriage arrived. Much to Elizabeth's delight, her Uncle Gardiner managed a few days away from the trade business.

"I'm glad you are come; it is wonderful to see you here," Elizabeth exclaimed.

"It was so thoughtful of Mr. Darcy to invite us. I thought we should never arrive. Even so, you know we are fond of Derbyshire. I find the mountains such a delight, so breathtakingly beautiful," her Aunt Gardiner described.

"Mr. Darcy should not be long; he is from home just now."

"Well, Elizabeth, let me look at you; I see you are well, very well indeed," Mr. Gardiner commented.

"My father is here with Mary and Kitty. I should warn you, it is no longer Kitty; she wishes to be called Kathryn just now."

"Kathryn it is," her Aunt Gardiner repeated.

"Georgiana is here, Aunt, she will be happy to see you again."

"Such a lovely girl."

"Come in now," Elizabeth urged as they neared the door.

"Father, look who has come," Elizabeth said, entering the sitting room.

"Ah, Mr. Bennet," Mr. Gardiner commented.

"Delighted," Mr. Bennet called to them.

Georgiana greeted the Gardiners with sincere regard. Kathryn and Mary were glad to see them as always. Mr. Bennet and Mr. Gardiner discussed plans to fish, stating they hoped Mr. Darcy would return in time or it would have to wait until the afternoon next. Elizabeth suggested they fish to provide the main course for the evening meal. They gladly agreed they should do so if the opportunity presented itself in their favour.

The Darcy babies were thought to be a definite delight. Elizabeth, unable to wait upon her husband's return, proceeded to acquaint them at once.

Mrs. Reynolds ordered preparations of a guest chamber after directing the Gardiners' trunks be taken above the stairs.

When Mr. Darcy arrived, Mr. Manley accompanied him.

"Thank you for the kind invitation; it is our plan to only spend a few days, Mr. Darcy, if that meets with your approval." Mr. Gardiner stated.

"Delighted, it is always a pleasure."

"Thank you again for the invitation, Mr. Darcy; it was most welcome. Of course, we wanted to see the children," Mrs. Gardiner expressed.

"Not at all, think nothing of it."

"We could not wait your return; we viewed the children. They are wonderful, delightful little creatures; enjoy them now, they grow up so very fast," Mrs. Gardiner informed them.

"Would it be an imposition if I were to ride back to London with you? Inasmuch as I have business to settle, riding in your company will make the journey that much more pleasant," Mr. Darcy said, addressing the Gardiners.

Elizabeth was not only shocked but also embarrassed for not having known of his plan. It took everything in her to hide her disturbance. She stared at him in wonderment.

"That would be delightful," Mr. Gardiner answered.

"Mr. Darcy, would you mind if Mr. Gardiner and I borrowed some fishing tackle?" Mr. Bennet requested. "We would enjoy fishing about now."

"Not at all, I'll have my man fetch the tackle. Mr. Manley, would you like to fish?"

"Yes, I believe I would."

"We shall all go, if that is satisfactory." Mr. Darcy exclaimed.

"Sounds delightful," Mr. Gardiner expressed.

"We should have plenty of fish for dinner. Shall I have Mrs. Reynolds tell the cook we are to have your catch for dinner?" Elizabeth inquired.

"With four fishing we shall have ample supply; yes, that would do very well." Within minutes the men parted their company leaving the women to themselves.

"Aunt Gardiner, your family, are they in health?"

"Very well, Elizabeth, thank you. Robert is learning to read; Kate and Alice are taking lessons on the pianoforte, while William is learning to ride his horse. I venture to guess, it won't be long before your children are doing all sorts of learning."

"Aunt Gardiner, do you see the militia near London?" asked Kathryn.

"No, a soldier once in a while, perhaps, not a whole company. Why do you ask?"

"Just wondered."

"Mrs. Gardiner, I am so happy to see you again," added Georgiana.

"And I you. Are not the babies wonderful?"

"I am delighted to be an aunt."

"If you girls have no objection, I should like to take a turn with my Aunt Gardiner."

"Not at all," Georgiana replied. Mary and Kathryn nodded their approval.

Elizabeth and Mrs. Gardiner disappeared above the stairs to the nursery. Elizabeth thought they could find a quiet place for conversation apart from the girls.

"Well, Aunt, I have not seen you since my mother's funeral. I was grateful to have you at Longbourn, so much time has passed."

"You appear well situated, Elizabeth."

With a sense of urgency, she replied, "Indeed I am, but I fear I have another pressing matter to speak to you of."

"Elizabeth, you seem anxious; what is it child?"

"Do you see Lydia in London?"

"Yes, I had several visits from her; she comes alone, her husband never accompanies her; it is always Lydia with the child."

"I am sorry to be so bold, but has she applied to you for funds?"

"Yes, Elizabeth, she has."

"Just as I suspected, so frustrating, she matched herself to the most worthless of men. Oh, Aunt, I don't know what to think," Elizabeth said with distress.

"What is it, my dear?"

"I must be bold again; have you given her anything?"

"No, Elizabeth, your uncle and I should not want to start it."

"Thank goodness, she has applied to both Jane and myself."

"Oh dear, what was your reply?"

"I sent her relief on occasion. We both thought it best not to accommodate her."

"Elizabeth, I must be frank; Lydia looks drawn, her eyes boast darkened circles beneath them. She is pale, tired, quite ill looking, I believe. I daresay I am concerned for her health."

"Oh, Aunt, what is to be done?" Elizabeth cried.

"Lydia is not your concern; the match was her own making; she foolishly chose this life."

"I know, but what of the child? I worry she may be wanting."

"To tell you the truth, when I visited her last I brought fruit, bread, a bit of beef, but I would not give her funds. It appears what they have is spent extravagantly. The flat they live in is more than their income affords, yet it is not commodious. I know not what they spend on."

"This is distressing indeed."

"You know, Elizabeth, she has another announcement; are you aware?"

"Yes I am, so soon, oh Aunt, what is to become of her?"

"Does Mr. Darcy know she applied to you for assistance?"

"No, no I have not told him. No one in my family is aware of the honourable deeds my husband has done. Can you imagine, if he had not gone to London and found them out, no one, not even Mr. Darcy would have dared to marry into such a family; I cannot ask more of him." Elizabeth dropped into a nearby chair. Putting her hands to her face, she wept.

Mrs. Gardiner patted her shoulder. "There, there now, Elizabeth, all will be well, you must not cry; it is not your doing."

"Aunt, if I were to ask him to help her, he would for my sake as well as for the child's. It is not fair; I refuse to do it." Elizabeth cried.

"Elizabeth, you have made the right decision; do not allow yourself to feel guilty; it is not your concern. I beg you, do not reproach yourself."

"I know you are right in this, but it is hard, very hard," Elizabeth lamented.

"Elizabeth, if Mr. Darcy were to give him a letter of credit or funds, it simply would not be enough. Mr. Wickham would squander it away, probably not pay the debts."

"I know you are right. Poor Jane, she would like to be with child; it has not happened as yet. Here I am with two at once, Lydia with one, announcing another event to come. It doesn't seem fair; Jane's desire is so severe; it is not fair."

"Elizabeth, there is surely ample time. Jane is youthful; it is only a matter of time until she will write of an event, I'm sure of it."

"Yes, I am being witless now, am I not?"

"Tell me, Elizabeth, how do you and Mr. Darcy do? Do you get on well?"

"Oh, Aunt, you know him to be a good man. I do believe I understand him perfectly now, that is to say, I am now of the understanding what makes him so honourable. He strives to maintain the highest level of integrity, always putting duty first. He has but few flaws, always toiling for perfection; in my eyes he is matchless."

"Well, Elizabeth, I am glad to hear of it; you should have no concerns; be happy in your situation. You must no longer concern yourself with that which you cannot command."

"You are right, I know, always owning an understanding of my weaknesses. Now, shall we go below the stairs to join the others?"

"Yes, I believe we should, but you had better go to the basin first to apply water to your face, my dear, your eyes look like you have been weeping a bit."

"Very well," Elizabeth said, moving toward the basin.

The women directed themselves below the stairs to join the girls. Georgiana was playing Mozart's *Rondò alla Turca* on the pianoforte. They slipped into the room, quietly taking a seat.

"She plays well," Mrs. Gardiner expressed in a half whisper.

"Yes, indeed, she does play well," Elizabeth whispered, then added, "pray excuse me, I believe I will ring the bell for tea."

When she returned, Elizabeth held a book in her hand. "Aunt, look at this book; it was purchased on our wedding journey. Is it not wholly marvelous?"

"Indeed it is; I enjoy Shakespeare as well," her aunt told her after paging through the book, noticing Elizabeth's marked pages.

"I find his work has meditative energy and lyric melody, very profound."

"Yes, indeed, Elizabeth, I enjoy poetry myself, so I must agree."

"My husband would tell you it is the language of love," Elizabeth whispered.

"He would be right."

Bessie arrived with a tray of tea and shortcakes. The girls joined the ladies, taking tea together along with a delightful exchange of notions.

Within a few hours, the gentlemen returned. They brought with them a very successful catch, proclaiming there was to be no lack of fish at the dinner table. Mr. Manley, having caught the greater number, was certain to join them, as if that made the distinction.

Mary excused herself to go above the stairs upon hearing Mr. Manley was to stay. Elizabeth whispered, "Observe Mary when she comes to dinner; she will be dressed well; be sure to take notice of her seating."

Her aunt nodded with a smile.

As predicted, Mary was formally dressed, managing a seat next to Mr. Manley. Mrs. Gardiner glanced at Elizabeth, catching her look. It proved to be quite entertaining. The gentlemen divided themselves between two different conversations, while the ladies competed for conversations of their own.

That evening, Elizabeth remained silent of her husband's intended trip to London. He offered no information. She wished he would explain; he did not.

The morning next seemed to creep upon them. Elizabeth's father gathered the girls to bid their adieus as they reluctantly lingered.

"Lizzy, I fear we must part, my dear; you take care of Joseph and Deborah until I return. No doubt they shall be running about before long. Well, my dear, say good-bye I must." He kissed Elizabeth on the forehead, then turned to enter the coach.

Kathryn and Mary bid farewell. It was evident they were sorry to be taking their leave.

"Mr. Bennet, it has been a pleasure," Mr. Darcy said, then bowed.

"Indeed, Mr. Darcy, you take care of my Lizzy; I will send you word express." In an instant the carriage had gone. Mr. Darcy announced he would like to sport, inviting Mr. Gardiner to join him. The two men were off, leaving the three ladies alone.

Georgiana stood by a window. She suddenly turned to the ladies. "It is a very fine day; perhaps we should plan a picnic one day soon. I believe I should like a picnic; we do little of that in London."

"You are right, my dear, in London we seem to forget such things," Mrs. Gardiner continued in her thought.

"That sounds like a splendid plan, perhaps tomorrow; we shall invite Mr. Manley as well; that will make our party three couples," Elizabeth delightfully noted.

"I should like that very much," Georgiana expressed.

"Very well then, tomorrow it is. I will go tell Mrs. Reynolds; it is certain to be a success. As always, she will plan the finest details to be sure."

"Since it is a fine day, I suggest we ride to the rectory to ask Mr. Manley at once. Georgiana, do you wish to accompany us? Mr. Manley should be approached with the invitation today," Elizabeth announced.

"That is an excellent thought, my dear," Mrs. Gardiner proclaimed.

Within a half-hour they were on their way to the rectory to pay their respects. They found Mr. Manley at the church. "What a lovely church, Elizabeth," Mrs. Gardiner observed.

"Yes, it is. I enjoy attending services here; Mr. Manley speaks very profound. He is definitely situated in the proper profession."

Mr. Manley graciously accepted their invitation to picnic. After tea at the rectory, they returned to Pemberley Hall to await the gentlemen.

Elizabeth informed them of the plan for the picnic the day next. Mr. Darcy, wholly agreeable to such a plan, suggested it might be pleasant to be down by the lake.

The day next proved to be just as Mr. Darcy predicted, a fine day for a picnic. The six relaxed after the picnic lunch with a shade device to guard them from the sun.

Mr. and Mrs. Gardiner announced their plan to quit Pemberley in the morning. Consequent to learning this, it occurred to Elizabeth that her husband failed to discuss his London business. He had not referred to the trip to her directly, all her knowledge was acquired through overheard conversation. His leaving the day next unsettled her. She felt incensed that he had not spoken of it, but, more so, curious as to why he remained silent of his intentions. Surely she expected an explanation; surely she thought he would understand her need to be informed. She understood even less his wish to ride in the Gardiners' carriage. How in heaven's name is he to return home, she wondered. The thought gnawed at her, but she was determined not to force the question, least not until they were alone.

As the day faded into night, Elizabeth found herself alone in the bedchamber with her husband as he gathered a few books to take with him. She heard him earlier with his gentlemen's gentleman giving, instruction regarding his trunk.

"Fitzwilliam, tomorrow you depart. Are you aware you have not discussed this with me? I first learned of it when you spoke to the Gardiners requesting to share their coach. May I inquire why you chose not mention this before?"

"Dearest, I decided to go when they announced they were only staying a few days. I must be away; I have business to attend in London. I thought perhaps I might as well do it while I have companionship for the journey."

"You will not stay away long? What is your business, dear? And I might wonder how is it you expect to journey home?"

"I had thought of purchasing a larger barouche box. I viewed this an opportunity to do so without too much trouble. I sent word ahead as to my expectations. Besides, I will be in the best of company; surely you would agree with me on that account? I am to be but a few days, no more. As for my other business, there is nothing you need to be concerned with, just business in general."

At first she attempted to pry no further, general knowledge was all she sought. As she continued to feel slighted by his nonchalant evasiveness, she grew more curious. She could not help but ask, "Does this have to do with the estate Mr. Bingley desires?"

"Not at all, Elizabeth, it is just business. I assure you I will return directly. I will miss you, long for you, surely you know that." Though his answer was reserved, it was delivered in earnest, but did not emulate his normal ease.

"Very well, dear, at least tonight I have you to myself."

"Indeed you do. I shall be gone but a few days, two or three perhaps, hopefully no more."

"Two or three, perhaps more?" she cried, alarmed at the thought.

"Dearest, I have business in London; surely you understand men have business to attend."

"Very well," she said as she pulled the covers up to her throat. She stared at him moving about the room. She felt sad; this was the first time he would be away for any length. It troubled her that he made light of it; surely he would have known she would be anxious, so she thought. She closed her eyes, pretending to sleep to conceal her disappointment.

The morning came too soon for Elizabeth. Anguished thoughts made it difficult to hide her melancholy. Before his leaving, she noticed he spent much time in his office with her Uncle Gardiner.

While in the office, Mr. Darcy turned to her uncle. "Mr. Gardiner, I have an imposition; I must ask for your assistance. I shall need someone to make inquiries for me. It is just novice activity, a side interest of mine, which may prove gratifying in the end. Are you willing to assist me?"

"Mr. Darcy, it is always a privilege to assist you; whatever it is I'm sure we can come to some understanding."

"Mr. Gardiner, I plea for secrecy. I prefer your wife not know the nature of the deed; I must insist you conveniently overlook my seeking your assistance."

"Very well, Mr. Darcy, I prefer my wife not to know; Elizabeth cannot pry from her that of which she has no knowledge. I shall forget all when the deed is done."

"Thank you, Mr. Gardiner," Mr. Darcy said as he unlocked his desk drawer, removing the little rare book he purchased on their wedded journey. He shared his findings with her uncle, explaining his desire to research the family book. Since it was a family ledger, particular entries, which bore familiar names, had his attention. He slipped it into his pocket before they exited the office. Then turning to Mr. Gardiner, he expressed, "Thank you, Mr. Gardiner, as you know my wife is of a curious nature; I fear she surely would not understand. I am inclined to favour history; thus, this has become a minor obsession. You must agree it is exciting. To search, much less discover, can be quite an adventure."

"Mr. Darcy, I know my niece to possess the curious nature you expressed, in that I have complete understanding, but perhaps you underestimate her ability to accept. Nonetheless, I shall not try to convince you otherwise. You may be assured of my secrecy."

"Thank you, Mr. Gardiner, I knew I could count on you."

When the time came to part, Elizabeth's heart sank. The very thought of his being away brought displeasure. She found it awkward to say good-bye to him; it seemed strange to part with unanswered questions in her heart along with loneliness of mind. The thought of separation distressed her, but she suffered the torment as she fought to hide the felt disappointment as she lovingly bid him farewell with all the sentiments expected of a dutiful wife.

He tenderly bid her good-bye. His eyes remained glued on her as the carriage pulled away. Her heart sank as she stood with Georgiana, feeling abandoned.

London on Business

THERE WAS CERTAINLY NO LACK of conversation between the Gardiners and Mr. Darcy, whose journey to London provided ample time for a varied exchange of subjects. Mr. Darcy inquired, "By chance do you see anything of Lydia?"

"Yes, I am afraid so—a real pity, a sad case indeed. They live in a flat in London they can ill afford, spending money on I know not what. Lydia does not look well; I worry of her, Mr. Darcy." Mrs. Gardiner reported.

Mr. Darcy appeared discouraged. "There is little I can do to alter the situation, the man will not reverse his pernicious ways nor will he make sufficient his present means. I fear Lydia will suffer the consequences. I had not expected it to turn out as bad as this. George Wickham surely continues to sink beneath his learning. He no doubt insists on running up debts wherever he goes. Have you seen the child?"

"Yes, she is a sweet little girl, but, sad as it may be, Lydia has made another announcement. They live rather poorly. I do believe he mounts gambling debts, then finds the rent a difficulty, moving often."

"Are you acquainted with their whereabouts?"

"Yes, I'm afraid so, Mr. Darcy," Mr. Gardiner interrupted, then elaborated further. "I visited there not wishing my wife to go the neighbourhood alone."

"What of Lydia, is she well fed; what of the child?" Mr. Darcy continued to inquire.

"She does not look well; she has sunk in spirits, her bloom is gone. She is thin, pale, her bright eyes have long faded; I daresay she looks old before her time."

"Mrs. Gardiner, did my wife inquire of Lydia?"

"I cannot lie to you sir, indeed she did."

"So she knows of Lydia's fate," Mr. Darcy said with hopelessness.

"Elizabeth questioned me most precisely; you know your wife well, Mr. Darcy, she is inquisitive; her concern is quite natural."

"Yes, certainly, I would have expected no less from her."

"Mr. Darcy, consider a stay with us while in London," stated Mr. Gardiner.

"No, no, I shall not impose upon you."

"It is no imposition; please allow us to return your kindness."

"No, it is best that I do not; another time perhaps, not this voyage."

Mr. Darcy needed to be free from company. He needed time to research the book, to take notes, a task he was unable to perform at home for fear of discovery. He had determined a room at an appointed inn would surely provide him that opportunity.

"Very well," said Mr. Gardiner, "perhaps next, when Elizabeth accompanies you; we so much desire to have our turn to entertain you both."

"You may count upon it. I shall be at your place of business early in the morning, Mr. Gardiner, if that meets your approval?"

"Yes indeed, I shall expect you."

The trip was lengthy, dry and dusty. They were delighted to reach London, having then parted with expectations of seeing one another in the morning. Mr. Darcy secured a room at a local inn, spending the remainder of the day in his chamber studying the rare book he had purchased at Mr. Knisely's book shop. As he read, he jotted notes of preparation for his instructions to Mr. Gardiner. Mr. Gardiner, being a man of resource, had parliamentary connections, which afforded him the advantage of investigation to which Mr. Darcy could not make public himself without exposure. The Gardiners had become intimate friends. All thoughts of them always brought him pleasure.

Placing the book down, he lay upon the bed staring at the wall, thinking of Elizabeth with passion as he suffered pangs of loneliness parted from her. He sensed her apprehension upon departure. With ample time to recall their last moments together, he accredited his evasiveness as having pierced her, causing her to endure unintended torment. Wishing now that he had managed to announce the journey with greater artifice, he suffered the painful thought that through his secretiveness she perhaps suffered in his absence. He desired to be near her to comfort her. Now he could only hope to complete his business within a few days and to return home directly. He closed his eyes to envision her face, settling for what little comfort his thoughts of her provided him, longing for them to sustain him through the night.

Desiring to know the whole of the family connection, he felt driven by the book. This history, which invariably intrigued him, provided opportunity to research a rare find. It was exciting to discover a family ledger of this nature.

His mind turned to Mr. Bennet, whom he had grown to respect. His own dear father being deceased, he felt a closeness to him through Elizabeth. He admired her love for him. His only desire was for her happiness. With Mr. Gardiner handling the investigation, no one need know of his research. As these thoughts flowed through his mind, he finally fell fast asleep, awaking very early the morning next.

Preparing himself to go to Mr. Gardiner's place of business, he decided it was entirely too early. The streets appeared desolate. Although dawn was just beginning to reveal itself, he decided to walk before breakfast. He quitted the inn to walk despite the dreary weather.

There was a slight mist of rain, just enough to have covered the streets, making everything exposed, moist. The air was still with the start of fog rolling in. The streets were devoid of the hustle and bustle expected within the few hours next when the promise of another business day would bring industrious people about the town as usual. His eyes wandered over the dim and moistened paths. Light struggled with constancy to shine hazily through the rain. He determined a walk would do him good as well as occupy his time. He could hear an occasional clopping of a horse and carriage from the street next, then the quiet again, allowing him to hear his own soft footsteps with each stride as he walked down what appeared to be so lonely a street.

As he walked several blocks at a leisurely pace, he felt the cold chill of dampness as it began to rain a bit harder, but he continued on, pulling his collar up around his neck. Then suddenly, up ahead, he noticed the posterior of what appeared to be a familiar figure of a man. Advancing several additional hesitant steps, he purposely stopped, leaning back into a doorway to briefly watch from a distance. His observation proved his suspicions correct. The man turned slightly, it was George Wickham. Mr. Darcy hung back in the shadows contemplating his escape, having no desire to be noticed.

Mr. Wickham, leaning in a doorway with his arm elevated against the doorsill, was in the company of a woman. His piercing, cold observations made public that she most assuredly was not Lydia. The woman appeared wanting of innocence—a low, insidious, ominous woman of heavy charge, scantily dressed in a diaphanous garment, her aspect divulging the hardened expression of experience. His heart sank as he realized the familiarity of the woman. It was Miss Grey. Now thoughts recanting his wedding journey filled his head. He dwelled on his past notice of her with Mr. Wickham from the chamber window at the inn, then later his shocked encounter with her at the Hyde Park ball, when she deliberately made their association known, inducing Elizabeth's inquisitiveness. Now he was witness to all that offended him. They appeared to be exchanging parting passions, with Mr. Wickham's physical exhibition flaunting an open public display of indecency, yielding further proof that he truly was as unprincipled as his reputation.

Mr. Darcy desired to go no further, preferring not to be noticed, feeling the desperate need to escape. He could see Mr. Wickham's manners were still self-engaging as always; his actions came as no surprise, as he was known to be clever in his pursuits. He was caught off his guard; this was not a situation he expected to witness personally; such reprehensible behaviour distressed him. He had not imagined encountering George Wickham, especially indulging in the delights of the flesh in the wakening of dawn. He viewed him as shameful, disgusting, an immoral man whose arrogant wickedness was with ease displayed publicly, devoid of remorse, and who was unfortunately married to his wife's sister.

However foolishly silly his wife's sister Lydia was known to be, even she did not deserve such a fate. George Wickham proved to be an evil scoundrel; her sister had been easily guided into his entrapment. Although Lydia had made a bad match, he could not deny his role in bringing them together.

He quickly turned, walked a block before making a left turn onto another street, avoiding recognition. He lost his appetite, his contempt grew, the thought of their near encounter revolted him.

Intrigue

Mr. Wickham's insufficient character, his obvious void of feelings or concern for his wife, matched with his total absence of self-respect, was too much to be endured. Mr. Darcy's tolerance for such behaviour was lacking. He walked at a faster pace; his steps pounded the walkway. With each stride he grew more troubled, angrier at the thought of his observance.

He returned to the inn, requiring solitude with his less than propitious thoughts. He tried reasoning that the manner in which George Wickham conducted his life was really not his affair. He had done everything he could on several occasions to provide him a fresh start, but each time only proved to make the man more indulgent to his own extravagant desires.

His thoughts were now of Wickham's father, his own father's steward. Aware that Wickham's father was a principled man whose ethics were unchallenged, known to be well respected as a decent man of impeccable character, whose only fault lay in the over-indulgence of his son George. He could scarce understand how such goodness escaped the son. Had his father lived, he would have been discouraged of his son's character, Mr. Darcy pondered with conviction.

He moved toward the window, noticing the sun behind the clouds desperately attempting to make its presence known. He observed that the air appeared dry, the atmosphere calm, while the streets remained moist from the morning rain, revealing fresh footprints as the town came alive. Believing he should take his leave, he once again quitted the inn, directing himself to Mr. Gardiner's place of business on Sloane Street with his research tucked safely away in his waist pocket along with the rare book.

"Well, good morning, Mr. Darcy; how do you do?" Mr. Gardiner greeted him.

"Very well, Mr. Gardiner, am I too early to take a bit of your time?"

"Certainly not; draw nigh my office, secure a seat."

Mr. Darcy once again presented the book to Mr. Gardiner, unveiling his suspicions. "I quite accidentally discovered the rare book while on the wedding journey here in London, finding it to be most intriguing. I thought I should never convince the shopkeeper to part with it. In truth, it was not for sale. I happened upon it quite by mistake. The shopkeeper had not the opportunity to catalogue it, nor had he time to inspect it. You can imagine the difficulty I had in convincing him to part with it."

"Indeed," replied Mr. Gardiner, "and does my niece know of the book?"

"She did, but I am ashamed to confess I led her to believe I returned it. I did not lie to her, but it was an indirect fabrication of which I am indeed embarrassed. She had no notion as to what the book tends."

"I would venture to guess, Mr. Darcy, you did it with good reason."

"Yes, Mr. Gardiner, I fear there is good reason. I'm sure you will agree once I explain."

Mr. Gardiner, now more delighted to assist him, detected the findings fascinating as well. He too was captured by the intrigue of its possible revelation; the prospect of the genuineness of circumstances could prove rewarding to Mr. Bennet. Mr. Darcy explained it was not his wish, if his suspicions turn truth, to lay claim to having any part in rectifying a wronged past. Once again he stipulated concealment necessary, should a favourable conclusion be the end result. Although he was unsure at the moment how to proceed, he made clear to Mr. Gardiner he desired to settle the matter legally. If the truth were revealed through Mr. Darcy, it might be construed as his desire to have his father-in-law made a nobleman for his own gratification. His only desire was to expose an injustice to Mr. Bennet's grandfather. It would require further research to prove valid, a task he could not risk himself. Mr. Gardiner's contacts at Parliament would be of the greatest advantage, which he found very agreeable.

The gentlemen came to an understanding on the actions to be taken. Mr. Darcy provided the monetary means, covering all incurred expenses. Both satisfied in their current adventure, the men parted as always, accomplices of honour, confessing mutual respect.

Mr. Darcy, having now quitted Sloane Street, decided he must satisfy his agonizing hunger pangs. The direction in which he seemed drawn to walk was the neighbourhood of none other than George Wickham, of which he was well aware. As he neared the address Mrs. Gardiner provided, he wondered if Lydia would take notice. Approaching, he noticed the shades were drawn. The whole of the place appeared dark and vacant. As he neared the building, he observed a notice upon the door in plain view; it was that of an eviction. As he stood interpreting the printed matter, he heard the muffled coughs of a little child, then the familiar weeping. He realized it was Lydia. He hesitated at the threshold, contemplating his next move. He paused as his disposition sank to intense haunting anguish for his sister-in-law's suffering. Immediate concern overwhelmed him. Without further hesitation he ripped the notice from the door, setting out to settle with the landlord. From directions provided by the local smithy, he found the owner, Mr. Briggs.

Mr. Briggs was a forceful man whose conduct was extreme, resolving to enforce the eviction. He determined Mr. Briggs' lack of compassion for Lydia or the child disturbing. It was further evidence Wickham's conduct was so unacceptable the man desired to rid himself of such occupants.

The men debated the situation at length while Mr. Darcy pleaded for forbearance for the child's sake. It was only after Mr. Darcy promised to provide him with six months' payment in advance, along with gratuity for his inconvenience, that Mr. Briggs did surrender. It was a hard transaction, particularly with Mr. Darcy not wishing to reveal his identity. He provided one month's rent along with the back rent, with the understood assurance the balance would be delivered before the close of the morning. Mr. Briggs reluctantly agreed, granting him a requested receipt for the month's rent as well as the back rent.

Mr. Darcy left Mr. Briggs, returning to Mr. Gardiner immediately. It was not his wish to provide Mr. Briggs any evidence to his identity, thus requiring legal tender. With the aid of Mr. Gardiner, a messenger was dispatched to Mr. Briggs with the bank draft promised. Having done so, they waited for the messenger to return with a receipt.

Morning was fading into the early noon hour. Mr. Darcy discovered himself extremely famished, having not yet had any nourishment. Upon invitation, he accompanied Mr. Gardiner to his home. Over a dish of mutton they discussed the unhappy situation. Once again, Mr. Darcy requested his intervention be shrouded. He did not wish his wife to worry of her sister's welfare, concluding there was no need to make her anxious.

He was grateful for the kindness he always found in the Gardiners. Their presence was always a source of joy, although sometimes the circumstances which united them was not. After thanking them for their hospitality, he then walked Mr. Gardiner back to Sloane Street, where they parted ways.

Without hesitation, Mr. Darcy made his way back to Wickham's neighbourhood to purchase meat from the local butcher. In doing the same at the grocer, he requested their anonymous delivery to Wickham's home, a deed he had not shared with the Gardiners. His inherited goodness was inbred through the inspired teachings of his father. His father held honour far above worldly possessions, teaching him to adhere to principled actions worthy of God's desiring, and that without such, man is void of soul, therefore naught. He simply could not reason the thought of a child in want.

He had attained the realization there was nothing to be done for George Wickham to change his evil ways; he was lost. The knowledge that Lydia and the child were secure for six months brought comfort. His was a sense of duty. He thought of his own children, how their situation differed; they were not likely to ever suffer wanting of either food or the necessities of life. To be poor was one thing, but to squander what little one had on drink, women and gambling, aware one's child is in want, was inexcusable. Wickham was a man devoid of every proper feeling; there was nay doubt the man possessed little regard for anything beyond his own selfish desires, greed and lust, not even for a small child of his own flesh or the flesh of the child his wife carried within her womb. All such thoughts distracted Mr. Darcy.

In the latter part of the afternoon Mr. Darcy visited Archibald Knisely's bookshop. Mr. Knisely remembered him well as having bought the rare book with which he was reluctant to part. Once rekindling their mutual regard, Mr. Darcy passed much of the afternoon looking about the shop, examining a few books of interest to him. He was equally pleased to have found some works by William Shakespeare for his wife.

Mr. Knisely mentioned his wife Margaret was from home visiting a sick relative, inquiring if Mr. Darcy would be interested in a bite of supper with him, stating he would enjoy the company. Having no set plans, he accepted the invitation with the knowledge their passion for books gave them much to talk about. He welcomed a diversion from the unpleasantness of the day.

Mr. Knisely was well educated, owning to good business sense. He and Mr. Darcy shared a passion for collectible books as well as a hunger for knowledge. He was advantageous to Mr. Darcy in age but not stature. The two well-dressed gentlemen were equally matched in taste with respect to their attire. Archibald Knisely was tall and lanky with light hair, sporting a tidy presentation. His manner was agreeable.

For Mr. Darcy, the evening proved satisfying. He enjoyed a pleasant dinner with Mr. Knisely. The variety of conversation was everything pledged.

After parting company, he returned to his room, considering himself fortunate to have had the evening occupied as well as his thoughts distracted. His dinner engagement diverted his thoughts to more enjoyable subjects. More importantly, it calmed his longing for his Elizabeth for the better part of the evening, at least until Mr. Knisely's flattering words spoken of his wife brought the freshness of his desires to the surface once again, reviving renewed pain of her absence, making her prominent in his thoughts. He admired the way in which Mr. Knisely spoke of his beloved Margaret as well as their children. The evening ended altogether with fond words of appreciation for books and wives.

Twilight proved the loneliest of times. Although united to his Elizabeth in thought, he discovered the acutest pain in their separation. His heart ached with desire, causing inexpressible agony he could scarcely conceive. He was wholly possessed by thoughts of her. Such intolerable endurance of misery he had not expected. Try as he could to comfort himself, his pining for her was excessive. Without her, he discovered himself incomplete. To his own amazement, he had not felt such pain of separation since he first was from home as a child. He had not expected to revisit such obtrusive pangs of yearning as an adult. The flood of his passion turned tormenting.

As he lay upon the bed, reflective in thought of their shared intimate divine love, he could only conclude it defied description. He himself could not find the proper words to characterize it well enough to do it justice, making the separation no less severe to endure. He wished he were more tired; more than anything else at that moment, he desired sleep as a refuge from his pensiveness. He tried reading the books he purchased. Nothing eased the restlessness of his wanting. Alone, with little but his thoughts to comfort him, he suffered the distressing strain of the tedious night. After many lost attempts to recover his influenced will, he finally, after several unsettling hours, surrendered to shallow sleep.

A Lonely Journey Home

Two additional days passed before Mr. Gardiner found he was unable to secure the facts or documents needed to prove their suspicions correct. They concluded this was going to take additional time, much more than allotted, perhaps months. Mr. Darcy had spent the last evening at the Gardiners' home, having been invited for dinner.

The Gardiners' children provided temporary diversion from the happenings of the past days, but induced a longing for his own. Mr. and Mrs. Gardiner were delighted to witness his tenderness with children, noticing their own took to him without hesitation.

He appreciated the consumption of surplus time a visit such as this provided. The intimate terms of their relationship eased his anxiety of being from home. Somehow being with Elizabeth's relations consoled him, bringing her a little closer to him. Their knowledge of her as a child provided him with stories not yet heard.

He announced his plans to quit London the morning next, estimating he had been from home too long, as this was his third night in London. "Surely Elizabeth eagerly awaits my return," he confessed. After bidding them farewell, he went to his room at the inn, deciding he would retire early. The morning next he went to that part of town where Wickham resided. He impatiently waited for the butcher to open. He once again purchased a bit of meat to be delivered, along with a delivery from the general store. Feeling satisfied he had done as much as possible, he set out on his journey home, taking advantage of a few additional planned stops along the way.

First he was required to pick up the barouche box and horses he had requisitioned. As promised, a driver was waiting to be of service to him. Upon close examination, he found himself quite pleased with his purchase.

He was well satisfied with the family crest he had ordered placed on each door.

Next Mr. Darcy made his way to the West Side of London to pay a brief visit to Mr. and Mrs. Cochran. He arrived at their home about the time they were breakfasting. He joined them upon invitation, giving him opportunity to express his heartfelt gratitude for their kindness to his sister. The visit provided realization of the fortunate conditions to which his sister was entrusted.

After a two-hour visit he bid them good-bye, continuing his journey home. Their acquaintance made him comfortable. To him, Mr. Manley was the best of men; he expected no less of his sister and her husband. His assumptions proved correct; they were fine people. He knew his sister found them to be so through her letters to him. Determining it his duty to stop while still in London to pay his respects, he departed their company with contentment.

With happier thoughts he was now on his way home. He had one additional stop to make before deporting himself happily from London. He desired to visit a special shop to make a purchase, which delayed him another hour.

The sky was dark with a driving rain, making the journey more cumbersome, delaying the time of his arrival at Pemberley. The continuous rain descended, soaking the ground, making the air cold and damp; it was hardly a day to be out. He viewed the dismal misty landscape. Feeling a sense of desolation, he turned his thoughts to home, his wife, children and sister.

By the time he reached Pemberley, the rain had ceased, but the air was still damp. The clouds were clearing, giving way to an imposing rainbow of brilliant colours which seemed to expand across the sky, commanding observation. How beautiful Pemberley looked from a distance. The fresh rain enhanced the greenery. How inviting, thought he, anticipating being greeted. Finally, the coach pulled to the front of the house. He hastily threw open the carriage door and gave instruction to the footman as he departed from him in haste. He flew through the door, anxious to see his wife.

Mrs. Reynolds neared the door, "Welcome home, sir, I believe your wife is in the nursery."

Without restraint, he ran swiftly above the stairs, taking two at one time, wasting not a moment more. He hurried his way to the nursery. There she was, standing over the cribs looking down at the children. They were awake, serenading her with their gibberish. He paused for a moment to admire her, then neared himself to her. She quickly turned upon hearing his steps.

"Dearest, it is you; you are home at last."

He immediately pulled her to his breast, holding her close in a prompt manner. "Dearest, forgive me, I've been too long away," his voice peacefully whispered in her ear. He stroked her back as he buried his face in her tresses, taking in her fragrance.

She pulled herself back to look into his face, unable to repress her sheltered feelings. "I've missed you so, surely you have no notion how lonely the nights have been."

"Indeed I have felt it too; it is the worst of times; I know it well."

"I looked for you to return home each day."

"I thought the journey would never end; my sole comfort was my thoughts of you and the children." He looked down at them. Joseph was playing with his feet. He picked him up and held him close. He kissed him, lay him in the crib, then took Deborah in his arms. After having done the same, he returned her to the crib.

"Dearest, you look weary."

"Yes, I have not had a complete night's rest since I quitted Pemberley."

"Perhaps you would like to rest?"

"No, no, I should like a bit of port, perhaps then some tea. Will you join me?"

"Yes, to be at your side is all I wish for just now."

"Where is my sister?"

"Last I observed, she was at the harp in the music chamber."

When they entered the music chamber, Georgiana was at the pianoforte singing. Upon noticing them, she stopped. "Brother, it pleases me to see you home."

"Georgiana, you have a delightful voice, you should sing more," Elizabeth said.

Georgiana's face coloured. "Not very well, but thank you for the compliment."

"No, I will not accept that, you do sing well, very well indeed; you just are not aware of it nor do you allow yourself the merit deserved, that is all."

Georgiana smiled shyly. "Elizabeth, you are prejudiced in my favour."

"Not at all, I speak the truth as I witness, that is all."

"Continue to play, Georgiana; it is most enjoyable," Mr. Darcy added.

Mr. Darcy poured two glasses of port, then took a place aside of his wife on the sofa after having rung for tea. As Georgiana played, he turned to Elizabeth. In a low, quiet voice only meant for her hearing, he whispered, "I confess the solitary nights only heightened my love for you. In my desire to have you near, I realized how incomplete I am without you."

Having no mind to respond to such a statement, Elizabeth smiled, knowing he missed her excessively; his revelation only endeared him to her. At last, content that her husband was home, she felt whole once again. He was home where he belonged, at Pemberley, at her side.

The Present

As the day next was the Lord's Day, that drew them to church. Mr. Darcy, his wife and Georgiana took their proper place. The great estate of Pemberley afforded a more than modest parsonage, a rather large church and Mr. Manley, who, according to Mr. Darcy's testimony, possessed the most superior qualities of any clergyman.

Mr. Darcy, having adhered to the enthusiasm of the house of worship, realized the importance of good sermons matched with clear delivery. Above all, he understood the importance of the estate owner setting a fitting example. His presence was made known faithfully, expecting those of his estate to follow the same participation. He saw it not only as duty, but also as a time the whole of his estate came together as one, having learned this from his father before him as honourable and fitting of a master.

Early in his relationship at Pemberley as vicar, Mr. Manley became familiar with the respect Mr. Darcy drew from his people. But none so much as this day, when he chanced to witness for himself the regard of his master, when he announced, "So concludes the sermon for today; but before you depart, Mr. Darcy wishes me to announce a celebration at Pemberley Hall to honour the birth of his children. You are all invited to attend tomorrow evening at 6:00 at Pemberley Hall."

The evening next Mr. Darcy held the estate gathering in the ballroom. Mr. Darcy enjoyed sharing happy news; in the past, his father always did much the same, recognizing the residents as an extension of the family at Pemberley.

Elizabeth stood at his side to greet each one of his tenants and servants individually into the great hall. Proudly, Mr. Darcy welcomed them. Georgiana joined them, taking a place aside of her brother.

Mr. Darcy arranged to have Joseph and Deborah below the stairs for the celebration.

Mr. Manley, impressed by the reception, had not expected such extravagance in presentation. The tables were lined with assorted varieties of meat, fish and poultry; platters of vegetable dishes, fruits, nuts, desserts garnished with delightful preserves, dried fruits, wine, tea, and biscuits—surely a feast fit for royalty, thought he. Musicians were placed at the far end of the room. He watched as Mr. Darcy mingled, conversing with his people with ease.

Mr. Darcy turned to Elizabeth. "It gives me great pleasure to do this, I hope they derive equal pleasure from it."

"No doubt, yes, I am sure they do."

Mr. Manley, taken in by the whole of the celebration, was most impressed by Mr. Darcy's request to offer the blessing over the feast to be made final by the clergy's blessing.

A few days following, Mr. Manley received a message from Pemberley Hall.

Henry Manley,

I desire the presence of my good friend this morning at Pemberley Hall if it is convenient. Having now been home several days, I am inclined to fish. I believe fishing provides as good an excuse as any to spend leisure time with a valued friend. If it is not convenient, please send word at once.

Fitzwilliam Darcy

Although they had fished much of the day, their adventure provided little more than amusement. There simply were no fish to be had at the dinner table. In the end, they concluded it was the company that mattered most to them.

After dinner, the party gathered in the music chamber. It appeared Georgiana enjoyed Mr. Manley's company as they talked and played leisurely the pianoforte. "Mr. Manley, you play difficult concertos. I am in awe; I have studied for years; I should never play with such ease."

"Miss Darcy, your playing is exquisite; you are too modest; your style is so much more refined, I assure you."

"Thank you, but I fear you are being kind."

Mr. Darcy viewed the two with interest. It was hard to discern if his friend was just being polite. He knew Mr. Manley was not the sort of man to be frivolous by nature. He could not help but wonder if his sister and Mr. Manley were forming an attachment.

The week next Georgiana was to return to London. The house would become quiet again except for the periodic exercise of Joseph's and Deborah's lungs. The children were spending more time alert, demanding more notice as they discovered their voices along with their ability to command attention. The nursemaids were kept busy with the daily routine.

Frequently Mr. Darcy played with the children. There were times when Elizabeth remained in the nursery to rock one or both of them. He took pleasure in watching her, remembering his mother in that very room. He enjoyed observing her with the children, especially when she sang to them, cuddling them close. So much love has always filled this room, thought he. Now it is my wife who cradles my own flesh. It was satisfying to feel secure in one's situation.

The time had come for Georgiana to take her leave. Remembering the carriage mishap, Mr. Darcy grew a bit anxious. Although she promised to write often, he was once again reminded of the past, when her departure always left a void; this time was no different. Mr. Manley made it a point to be present to bid farewell.

Once the carriage was out of sight, Mr. Darcy turned to face his friend. "Well, Henry, perhaps you should plan to dine with us today."

"I wouldn't think of it," he announced to a shocked Elizabeth.

Mr. Darcy looked at him soberly. "Whatever do you mean?"

"This will be your first day alone, I'll not interfere."

Elizabeth smiled. "It is quite all right."

"Nay, I insist; I shall have it my way."

Mr. Darcy continued his stare. "Very well then, I shall not dispute it."

Dinner was indeed a pleasure as they conversed alone with no interruptions or outside conversations, allowing them to share an intimate exchange.

Mr. Darcy lovingly looked at his wife. "Mr. Manley is a wise man."

"Indeed, I quite agree."

After a few silent moments, Mr. Darcy patted Elizabeth's hand. "I should very much like to retire early."

"Very well, if that is your wish."

"Yes, I believe it is; I would like that very much."

Elizabeth smiled at him. She could not help but think it had been some time since they had any time alone other than in the bedchamber. As she continued her stare at him, her smile broadened.

Mr. Darcy suddenly beamed. "I have a surprise."

"A surprise? What is it?"

"You shall have to be patient."

"And from where did you acquire this surprise?"

"I purchased it while in London."

"You purchased a surprise in London? Dearest, it nears the close of a fortnight. You are just now telling me of it?" she squealed with amazement.

"Yes."

"Fitzwilliam, why ever would you wait?"

"For the appropriate moment."

"And when might that be?"

"When we are above the stairs I shall present it to you, not before."

"Very well then, as you wish," she replied with a slight glance.

"Indeed I will have it my way; am I not the master of this house?" he teased.

"Yes indeed, quite," she said, bowing her head at him to return the tease.

"Perhaps I shall change my mind; perhaps I shall stay below the stairs at length."

"Fitzwilliam Darcy, you are a tease to be sure."

"Yes, Elizabeth, I suppose I am."

"I shall bear the torment and declare you a terrible tormentor."

His look turned serious as he reached over to caress her hand. With sober countenance, he then searchingly asked, "Have you any notion how ardently I admire and love you?"

"I believe I do," she replied, staring into his dark, alluring eyes.

He raised her hand to his lips, kissing it gently. In unpretentious silence, with eyes fixed upon each other, they were captured in oneness, happy to be alone, willfully entrapped in passionate desire.

"As I previously said, Mr. Manley is indeed a wise man," his voice whispered, his eyes still entranced by the sight of her.

"Indeed," she replied in a low, soft voice.

It was not very long before they quitted the dining hall to direct themselves above the stairs. Once in the bedchamber, Mr. Darcy produced a small package. Seated on the edge of the bed, she accepted it with swelled affection.

"Oh, Fitzwilliam, William Shakespeare, wherever did you find this?"

"In Mr. Knisely's Book Shop."

"Oh, you visited Mr. Knisely's Book Shop; did he remember you?"

"Yes, we dined together; his wife was from home. Since I had no immediate plans, I gladly joined him. He is quite interesting."

"That was conveniently to your favour I am sure."

"Yes it was; it was a welcomed diversion."

"Diversion, from what were you diverted?"

"If you must know, the nights were tediously lengthy. The conversation of books helped ease the torment of the emptiness experienced in want of you," said he, as he once again experienced the fixing of his look into her dark, fine eyes. Growing increasingly tender, in a mystic abstraction he continued, "Elizabeth, your nearness enhances the sensations of my affections; I could hardly abide the separation, I suffered tormenting pain."

"Dearest, I must confess, apart from you was not to my liking either, especially in the bedchamber; I missed you most severely," she murmured quietly.

"And I you," he whispered benevolently in return, with deepened amorous sincerity as he made himself closer to her.

"How is it you are able to repress secrets at length?"

"I am a man."

"A man indeed, you are a tease to be sure."

"Oh, but I derive such pleasure in furnishing you with gifts. I wanted to present the book but did not wish to share the moment with any other. I believe tomorrow you may enjoy it without interruption."

Elizabeth's look searched his eyes. "Fitzwilliam, how good you are to me."

He took the publication gently from her hand, placing it on the floor aside of the bed. His eyes remained fixed on hers as he drew himself nearer to her.

A State of Uncertainty

THE POST HAD COME, delivering two letters, one for Mr. Darcy from Lady Catherine as well as one for Elizabeth from Jane. Since Mr. Darcy was not presently in the house, Elizabeth put his letter aside on the mantel and eagerly opened the letter from Jane.

My Dearest Lizzy,

I trust you are all in health. We remain well at Netherfield. Our father, Kathryn and Mary forward their best wishes to you, Mr. Darcy and the children. I am gladly pleased with your account of the children, I imagine they are growing faster than desired. Lizzy, I have the most excellent news; Mr. Bingley and I wish to make announcement of an event of our own. I confess I have long waited to write such a letter. My dear Charles has an excellent heart; his kindness in making me comfortable is overwhelming. In his treatment of such, one might think I should surely break. The news brings rejoicing to our father's house. I shall close now, Lizzy; I am to write to our Aunt and Uncle Gardiner with news of the event. Forgive my hurried letter, my less than tidy writing.

Yours, Jane

Elizabeth was wholly pleased. This was just the news she hoped for. She was sorry Mr. Darcy was from home, she so wanted to share the news with him. He was certain to be delighted for his friend Bingley. This was a long-awaited pleasure indeed.

For a brief moment she thought her life was filled with happy thoughts. But all thoughts were not of a pleasant nature. She gave regard to her mother's death, her poor father alone with her sisters, matched by the undesirable situation with Lydia and Mr. Wickham. Such sadness she had not expected.

Returning her thoughts to the letter from Netherfield, she once again smiled at the gaiety of the event. She could not imagine a happier life. She could only give thought to what wonderful plans he had for the future of their little family. "Oh, where is my husband?" thought she, impatient to share the news; but it was some hours before his return. Elizabeth anxiously awaited him with enthusiastic spirit. Finally he arrived.

"Fitzwilliam, I have most excellent news," she stated as he entered the room in a most unlikely fashion. His expression seemed confused, his manner lacking the normal disposition. His essential appearance was very unlike him. He was all undone.

"What is it?" he managed to say with effort, making her well aware something was not quite rational.

"A letter arrived today from my sister Jane," she started. Elizabeth's voice slowed almost to a halt. She observed his conduct as she quickly forgot her intended conversation. She eyed him with apprehension. "Fitzwilliam, are you unwell. You look pale, you perspire profusely; what is it, my dear?"

Her immediate concern caused her to forget the letter. He now stood in front of the fireplace leaning his head into his bent arm against the mantel. He looked fatigued. His normal articulate speech slurred. His eyelids were visibly heavy as he leaned for support. The whites of his eyes appeared gray; his speech took effort, while his strides seemed unstable. He clung to furniture, slowly feeling his way to a chair. He staggered, as if groping in the dark. The very thought of his actions caused terror to govern the whole of her body; she swiftly moved in his direction to assist him, clutching his arm. He walked with leaden legs, trembling with fatigue as he strained with each hard stride until at last he reached the armchair. She studied his feeble, unsteady movement, unsure if he heard her. She touched his face with the palm of her hand. It was hot; he swayed his head from side to side mumbling.

"Dearest, you have not answered me; are you unwell?" she inquired raising her voice as though he were hard of hearing. "Dearest," she cried louder.

He sat in the armchair with his head back, swallowing hard as he closed his eyes. She noticed his chest shallowly swelled with each difficult breath. He was not responding as promptly as she would have liked. When he did, his voice was a forced whisper, short in breath. It was apparent he was having difficulty focusing. His response was lethargically faint. Fearing he had dropped off into an unconscious state, she shook him by his shoulders. "Dearest, are you able to hear me?" she demanded with an alarmed voice.

"Yes," he struggled to answer without opening his eyes.

"Do you think you are well enough to make it above the stairs?"

Elizabeth panicked when he made no answer. She shouted, "Dearest, answer me—please, you must answer me!" When he did manage to finally speak it was with delirium. She touched his forehead, realizing he was shiving with cold from the clammy sweat which soaked his body, yet he burned with fever. Her heart raced with alarm.

"I shall return directly," her fearful concerned voice cried as she quitted his presence. She ran through the house calling loudly for Mrs. Reynolds first, then Bessie. Bessie happened upon her cries, responding immediately.

"Bessie, I need help. Mr. Darcy is unwell, very ill indeed; he requires the apothecary. Send an express at once. I shall need help getting Mr. Darcy to his bedchamber, but send for the apothecary foremost; make haste! I believe we have no time to lose, he requires attention immediately."

By the time the servants delivered Mr. Darcy to his bedchamber, he had plunged into a feverish stupor. She was eager to learn if Bessie had followed her instruction immediately. A very anxious Mrs. Reynolds appeared before Mrs. Darcy. "Excuse me, ma'am, shall I send for Mr. Manley for the master?" Holding her handkerchief to her face, her voice quivered and her eyes filled with tears.

"Oh yes, Mrs. Reynolds, by all means, please do," cried Elizabeth as she watched Mrs. Reynolds hastily depart her presence.

She wiped his brow. He no longer responded to her cries; he just lay restless, moving his head from side to side mumbling her name. His manservant provided compresses, but she insisted on tending to him, unable to stand idly by. Thoughts of the apothecary taking too long caused her anxiety. As fear consumed her, she allowed his manservant to take over. His lips appeared parched. She dipped a cloth in the basin, then put it to his lips while she continued to talk to him, hoping he would hear her as she watched for a response.

He continued to murmur, moving his head about while she grew impatient, finding the wait torturous. With feelings of helplessness, she observed his unsettling irregularity as she tried to revive him. She noticed he moved, slowly raising his hand to his throat, believing perhaps he was responding, but it was not to be. His hand collapsed in its place, his head fell to the side. As he lay motionless, she placed her head upon his chest to listen to his shallow breathing. Weeping, she continued conversing at him; he still did not react. She wept softly at his side.

Mrs. Reynolds reentered the bedchamber stating, "I received word Mr. Manley will be here directly. Mrs. Darcy, may I help?" Although her speech was meant to be comforting, she grew more anxious for her master. Her affection for him was evident; she was clearly worried.

Elizabeth continued to sob. Mrs. Reynolds gently placed her hand upon her shoulder. "There, there, madam, Mr. Darcy will come around; I'm sure of it. His affections for you will give him the strength that he needs to go on."

Elizabeth did not respond; she continued to sob uncontrollably; she had no better relief for her concerns.

Bessie led the apothecary to the bedchamber. Elizabeth remained, observing his examination of her husband. Upon lifting Mr. Darcy's eyelids, she noticed his eyes rolled back in his head. Although he had ceased to perspire, he burned with fever. His pulse was weak and his breathing remained shallow. The apothecary turned to Elizabeth, "Mrs. Darcy, allow me to strongly recommend an express be sent to fetch Dr. Gordon in Lambton. He is an eminent physician; I'm afraid there is little hope. He requires more than I can offer. I shall remain here until his arrival."

"Very well," Elizabeth replied as she hastily fled the bedchamber to seek Bessie or Mrs. Reynolds. Her search was not long; Mrs. Reynolds, now in tears, was anxiously awaiting word on Mr. Darcy's condition immediately outside of the bedchamber.

"Mrs. Reynolds, will you please send express for Dr. Gordon in Lambton at once?"

"At once," Mrs. Reynolds responded, instantaneously in motion.

"Mrs. Reynolds, you and Bessie remain near at hand; I may require your assistance," she called after her.

Upon returning to the bedchamber, the apothecary imposed her to have the servants fill the bathing vat with cold water, suggesting the nearby lake water to be very cold presently. Before she was able to carry out his orders, he hastily called out, "He is convulsing, there is little time; it may be advantageous to take him to the lake. Get help, make haste, my carriage is waiting; I shall require assistance at once."

Again Elizabeth appealed to Mrs. Reynolds to carry out the apothecary's request. The carriage hurriedly made its way to the lake. The servants shivered as they submerged him according to instruction. Elizabeth waited in the carriage watching the whole of the event. In little less than two hours the fever finally subsided to a safe level.

Elizabeth held him in the carriage, stroking his face as they made their way back to the house. Throughout the whole of the brief journey she continued to talk to him between sobs.

It did not take long to return him to the bedchamber. Shortly thereafter, Dr. Gordon's carriage was making its arrival at Pemberley Hall.

The apothecary looked at Elizabeth. "Mrs. Darcy, although he is not yet responding, his temperature has been reduced greatly. Listen, I do believe I hear Dr. Gordon making his way above the stairs."

"Yes, I believe it is so," she replied, feeling comforted by his revelation. She swiftly moved to the chamber door to greet the doctor. Dr. Gordon entered. "What are your findings?" he addressed the apothecary.

"Mr. Darcy's fever was extremely high."

Dr. Gordon immediately examined Mr. Darcy. "What has been done? Why is his hair wet? His skin is moist as well; what have you done?"

The apothecary wasted no time with his answer. "We submerged him in the lake; the water is very cold."

"What! Good God, man, are you mad? You mean to tell me you submerged him in the lake?" Dr. Gordon came back at him with fury, with eyes piercing with rage.

With a defensive voice, he was quick to make his answer. "Yes sir, he suffered a feverish attack; he sank into a stupor. He began to convulse, so I did what I thought best to reduce the extremely high temperature. I believed he would have died in his own heat had I not done so. Although I know it is not the custom, it occurred to me that the lake water was very cold; therefore, such constancy would surely drive down the fever. There was no time to waste."

"He was that extremely hot?" Dr. Gordon shot back at him.

"Yes sir, indeed he was."

"Well, I would imagine it had to have helped; he is no longer feverish."

"Yes sir, I thought it the only proper treatment; I did the only thing I knew to bring the fever down," the apothecary replied defensively. He pressed his lips together, extending his chin, pulling his shoulders back with a stern look on his face, studying Dr. Gordon.

Once again Dr. Gordon looked up at him. "No neglect was implied by this, sir; perhaps you saved this man's life. I apologize for my severity; I was alarmed by your revelation; such irregular practice is not done. He appears to have a putrid sore throat, not good."

"Doctor, will my husband recover?"

"Mrs. Darcy, I cannot tell you just now."

"Doctor, what of his pulse; is it stronger? Does his breathing remain shallow?"

"Please wait out of the bedchamber, Mrs. Darcy." His words were straightforward. He appeared agitated as he motioned for her to leave the chamber without answering her questions.

Elizabeth complied hesitantly. She heard the doctor inquire what Mr. Darcy's signs were upon the apothecary's arrival, wanting all the details. The only satisfactory element of overheard conversation was hearing the doctor say the apothecary's quick actions to the lake no doubt saved his life. She heard him claim Mr. Darcy to be gravely ill, requiring constant observation. To her dismay, she also learned she was to be kept away from him as the putrid sore throat condition was highly contagious. The doctor related how he witnessed its destruction at a school where several students died.

Dr. Gordon exited the chamber. Now face to face with Elizabeth, he acknowledged, "Mrs. Darcy, I tell you what you do not wish to hear; he is gravely ill. He suffers from the putrid sore throat; he had an infectious fever. I did not purge him for fear his body had endured enough shock today. He may not recover, Mrs. Darcy; he may never respond. You must brace yourself; he requires constant observation. It will be days before we have anything to report. I make no promises; you must prepare yourself for the worst. These things must take their course. I fear you will have to occupy yourself elsewhere. Mrs. Darcy, it is not my wish to cause alarm, but to educate you truthfully. Now, this great estate has clergy does it not?"

"Yes sir," she faintly replied between sobs.

"I suggest you seek guidance from your clergy. He can do what I cannot do. Do you understand, Mrs. Darcy? You may, under no circumstances, enter this bedchamber. The apothecary has agreed to stay until the nursemaid arrives. You shall not go in there!"

"Yes, I understand," she answered, still sobbing.

"Mrs. Darcy, are you aware I was summoned to Pemberley estate at daybreak to administer services for the very same illness on one of your husband's farms?"

"No, I was not aware of it," she said between sobs, trying to gain control. Dr. Gordon was so severe, thought she. He seemed almost angered by her earlier questions; now she felt he lacked understanding toward a wife who loved her husband so dearly as she. Surely he must be a compassionate man, she thought further. How is it he can be so cold?

Arriving in time to hear the doctor's orders, Mrs. Reynolds observed Elizabeth weeping. Distraught herself, she tried to be of comfort to her master's wife. The two women descended the stairs.

Having arrived earlier, Mr. Manley waited with anticipation in the sitting room. Almost as soon as they entered, he bolted from his seat like a stroke of lightning. "Mrs. Darcy, how does he do?" His asking caused Elizabeth to burst into uncontrollable weeping. Between sobs she shook her head, powerless to respond.

Mrs. Reynolds informed Mr. Manley of everything she knew, then quitted their presence, weeping uncontrollably with her apron to her face.

Mr. Manley accompanied Elizabeth to the sofa. "My dear Mrs. Darcy, he is in God's care now. I have prayed for my dear friend; I have no doubt my prayers were heard. You must conduct yourself as the doctor requested; you cannot allow the strain of his illness to impose on your own health, surely that would not prove beneficial."

"Yes, I am afraid that is so," she sobbed, gasping for air, unable to restrain the pace of her weeping. "Mr. Manley it is, it—is—just," she wept, unable to continue.

"Mrs. Darcy, you must collect yourself; this will not do."

"Yes, I know," she sobbed. "it is just that I love him so very much."

"Yes, I know, he is a lucky man."

The following twelve days proved to be very hard. Mr. Darcy's condition remained questionable. Dr. Gordon gave no encouraging news.

Mr. Manley presented himself daily, arriving early. Duties prevented his stay invariably; one of those duties involved the burial of the farmer's son. Dr. Gordon, unable to do anything for the child, declared he was a frail little fellow before being taken ill. The child died of the putrid sore throat, the very illness Mr. Darcy now suffered.

Mr. Manley learned Mr. Darcy had visited the farm the very morning of the day he fell ill. The boy's death did little to calm the concerns of Elizabeth or the servants. There was little she could do to solace her wretchedness of fear for her husband's life.

Elizabeth had sent word to Georgiana regarding her brother's illness, summoning her home directly. The message avoided the whole truth in respect to the death of the child, not wishing to alarm her further. She communicated through a messenger, telling Lady Catherine of her nephew's illness.

The atmosphere encircling Pemberley remained somber. Mrs. Reynolds was beside herself, often entrusting Bessie to deal with Elizabeth. She determined her own present state of apprehension would prove to be of little use in consoling her master's wife.

Georgiana arrived home within two days. As a consequence of her learning of the seriousness of the circumstances, she fell into a low-spirited state. Mr. Manley's visits did little to relieve the gloom which was overspreading Pemberley Hall, but the low spirits did little to discourage him. He persisted in providing encouraging words, saying daily prayers with Georgiana and Elizabeth in spite of their despair, and encouraging them to consider their blessings.

Elizabeth attempted to occupy her time by overseeing domestic duties. She intruded on the servants the whole of the period, suspecting they found her intrusions tiresome. They remained gracious, kind and understanding as they continued to endure her questions and opinions with dispatch. They received her well. In turn, they gained her high opinion of their merits. They were sensitive of her required release from her thoughts, consequently providing situations which sought her guidance, even conjuring up questions of which they already knew the answers.

Georgiana spent much time in her chamber in solitude. Her only source of relief from her pensiveness seemed to be Elizabeth's belief that he would conquer this illness. "Georgiana, we must have faith; Fitzwilliam would desire it. I remain steadfast in my conviction that he will find the willful strength to defeat this wretched illness."

When alone, Elizabeth thrived on hope—prayer matched with the strength of her deep abiding love for him. She wrote her father, the Gardiners, and Jane and Mr. Bingley, telling them the sad state of affairs at Pemberley. She continued to correspond of his progress. She penned letters to Rosings, providing complete reports.

Elizabeth's comforting, reassuring words uplifted Georgiana's spirits. She saw the many days of survival as a sign of his strength to hang on to life.

On the eighteenth day, Dr. Gordon made his usual stop at Pemberley. Elizabeth waited in the hall as she did each day of his visit. On this day, when quitting the bedchamber, he stopped. "Mr. Darcy is responding; I trust he will survive."

Before he could utter another word, Elizabeth inquired, "May I see my husband?"

"I'm sorry, Mrs. Darcy, allow another day or two. I do believe we have the apothecary to thank, ingenious of him to do what he did. I shall use that strategy myself. Unfortunate for the little farm fellow though; I believe he lacked a strong enough constitution from the start; such a pity we arrived too late to immerse him in cold water."

"Doctor, you do expect recovery?"

"Yes, Mrs. Darcy, but do not expect much at first; he is weak to be sure. He will require constant rest; he has had a hard fight."

"Oh, thank you, Dr. Gordon, will you return tomorrow?"

"You may depend upon it."

She felt a sense of release; breathing became easier. For three weeks, the fate of her husband's illness had been pressing on her chest. The news was gratifying; she desired to see him, to touch his hand, to look into his face. "Tomorrow is forever, the day next an eternity," thought she aloud. "How shall I ever sleep the night through?"

She hurried to Georgiana's chamber to give her the good news. They embraced at the happier thoughts they now enjoyed.

Three days expired before Dr. Gordon allowed Elizabeth in her husband's presence. Two restless nights she anxiously lay awake in anticipation. Now free from restraint, she entered the bedchamber, observing him just as Dr. Gordon warned. He was weak, his mind cloudy as he mumbled her name. She touched his face with the palm of her hand; it was cool. His eyes opened for a lingering moment, but then he appeared to sleep.

Georgiana entered to view her brother. "Elizabeth, he appears very weak. I do not believe he suffers; I rather doubt he knows the day of the week. I have always had the good fortune to see my brother in health. I must say this is distressing; would you not agree?"

Elizabeth took hold of Georgiana's hand. "Yes, but we must give thanks that we see him at all. I fear he was very near being lost to us forever, Georgiana; I cannot imagine life without him. I am so glad you are here with me; until your arrival I felt so alone in my grief."

"Yes, but, Elizabeth, I fear I was not much comfort; it was you who had to comfort me. Just the same, I would not have wanted to be elsewhere."

"Georgiana, comforting you granted me daily diversions; indeed I needed that."

Georgiana left the chamber to pursue a tune on the pianoforte, hoping her brother would hear the music.

Elizabeth stayed at his side. It was difficult to see him so weak, but the days following proved to be more consoling when Mr. Darcy slowly regained consciousness, appearing increasingly alert. The fourth week ending, he was in full recognition of her, Georgiana and his surroundings. Although he continued to lie in a weakened state of fatigue, he was acquiring strength.

Mr. Manley was constant in his visits to Pemberley Hall. On occasion, his good friend Mr. Darcy, still not well enough for conversation, just listened with closed eyes as the discourse remained one sided. Although Mr. Manley's visits were indicative of his calling, those residing at Pemberley Hall, who had now become so wholly connected to him, knew his visits were by no means carried out as a sense of duty.

Elizabeth wrote to Lady Catherine, her father and Jane faithfully, proclaiming the triumph of his recovery. Mrs. Reynolds and the house staff rejoiced. Once again Pemberley was full of promise.

The Recovery

SIX WEEKS HAD PASSED. Mr. Darcy, now fully alert, found it hard to imagine himself ill and incapable of leaving his bed. Able to sit up to participate in conversations, it was frustrating to tire so easily without warning.

Elizabeth sat near his bedside reading a favoured book. His eyes were closed. Putting the book upon her lap, she studied him at length. "Dearest, you are looking much better."

"I feel greatly fatigued."

"Dr. Gordon claimed it may take an additional month until you are decidedly better."

"How long have I been like this?"

"More than six weeks."

"I have no recollection of it."

"Do you remember entering the sitting room, ill?"

"No, I do not believe so."

"You were very ill; perhaps it is best you not remember."

"Were you here with me the whole of the time?"

"No, I was not permitted; I was forced to occupy myself. I thought I would take leave of my senses had Mr. Manley not come daily."

He opened his eyes. "I would expect as much."

"Dearest, I confess, I placed much strain on the servants in an attempt to keep myself employed. I fear I intruded on their domain, asking questions, giving orders."

"And how did they do?"

She smiled. "Very well, they endured my intrusion with understanding. But poor Mrs. Reynolds was beside herself; I noticed she avoided upsetting me with her uncontrollable weeping."

"Mrs. Reynolds has been like a mother to me since my own died; I was fortunate then and still now. I am so weary, Elizabeth."

"Yes, you appear so. Perhaps you should not try to put forth effort just now."

"I am entirely fatigued," he said, closing his eyes again.

Elizabeth remained at his side. When she felt secure he was resting peacefully, she visited the nursery. She wondered if the children missed Mr. Darcy's frequent visits. Feeling a chill flush through her body, she clutched her shawl about her, quitting the chamber immediately with alarming thoughts. She instantly sought Mrs. Reynolds' opinion. Since Dr. Gordon visited every third day, she would have him examine her for the putrid sore throat, she thought to herself.

"Mrs. Darcy, you are quite well; it was a mere chill, no more," he said to her satisfaction. "Your husband's progress is gradual, slower than expected; but I am certain he will attain full recovery. Has he requested to read?"

"Not of late, he has not."

"Excellent, see that he does not, no strain on the eyes. I am not convinced, Mrs. Darcy, that you quite realized the depth of his illness; I had not expected him to survive. I am delighted he proved my prediction erroneous; he certainly has a driving force within him. It is a pleasure to come to this great hall under brightened circumstances. You see to it that he is kept quiet; I shall take my leave."

"Thank you, Dr. Gordon," she replied as she watched him descend the stairs.

Within two weeks Mr. Darcy grew stronger, but more restless. Her insistence on routine frustrated him, though he occasionally convinced her to allow him to sit by the window. He had little appreciation for taking orders. "I should like to read."

"I'm sorry, Fitzwilliam, I cannot allow it. If you like, I shall read to you."

"I resent being read to. You know I am quite capable of reading on my own. Am I not the master of this house?"

"Indeed you are; however, it is of little matter. You may not do as you please."

"I see my demands fall on deaf ears; you ignore my requests with such ease. I cannot conceive of it; I protest. You allow very little sympathy for my wishes."

"I am sorry, that is Dr. Gordon's orders. I demand you not press further; I have a book here I shall read to you."

Elizabeth read to him in spite of his contention. Georgiana took a turn at reading to him but discovered him too commanding to handle. "Elizabeth, I prefer you not leave him in my care. I have never been in a position of giving orders to an older brother; he pays me little mind."

"Very well then, we shall see who has the upper hand; I will be sure not to leave you alone with him. I daresay, Georgiana, he must be getting better if he gives us this much trouble." They could not help but laugh at their design. Although he was a hard patient to deal with, they had no intention of letting him have his way.

"Elizabeth, have compassion," he begged after several weeks passed.

"Yes, dear, but you require rest. Surely you remember when I was confined; I remained at the mercy of your orders."

"Ah, I see, the situation is reversed, is that it?" he asked coyly.

"No, dearest, rest is necessary."

He tried flattering her into submission without success. "Dearest, I do feel I am much better. I should like to visit the music chamber; I long to hear you play. It would give me great pleasure. Surely it would not be strenuous; what say you?"

"Dearest, Dr. Gordon is expected to return in two days. Although I am sympathetic, I fear you shall be required to wait patiently for his approval."

"I shall remember this when I am well."

"I'm sure you will, but I'll not allow you to challenge me further," she said as she rolled her eyes at him, adding, "I am sure you will remember, no doubt more then the day you fell ill; it happened so quickly. As I look back on it, I wanted to tell you about Jane's letter—oh, Jane's letter, I completely forgot," she cried.

"What letter?"

"Oh, dearest, there were two letters. You received a letter from Lady Catherine and me, a letter from Netherfield; the Bingleys made announcement."

Mr. Darcy sat forward. "Well, well now, an announcement. I'm glad to hear of it; well now, Bingley, I daresay it has been long awaited indeed."

"It's been such a time; I shall fetch the letter from Lady Catherine."

"Have you read it?"

"Certainly not, it was addressed to you. Your illness distracted me; I completely forgot the letters; I will fetch them at once." She left the room, returning in several minutes with the letters only to find him standing at the window.

"Fitzwilliam Darcy, am I to believe I cannot trust you for one and twenty minutes? You know you must remain in bed."

"Dearest, my legs are stiff, I yearn to stand; surely you would not deprive me a moment at a window."

With posture commanding authority, she stood at the threshold pointing toward the bed. "If you desire the letter you must return to bed."

"Such suffering at the hand of my wife," he mumbled.

"Well, now, I daresay you must feel better; you are being a tease."

"Most certainly not, not I, never," he replied with a grin.

"I have it on good authority, Dr. Gordon may release you this next visit."

"Oh, liberation at last."

"Not so, it is in my care he releases you."

"Well now, I am a grown man, am I not?"

"I am capable of requesting Dr. Gordon not release you," she told him, swaying back and forth holding his letter to her chest with both hands, keeping it from him. He reluctantly returned to the bed; his vanity wounded as he gazed at her with a look of discontentment. Noticing the pitiful frown he bore, Elizabeth burst into laughter.

"You dare laugh at me?"

"Indeed, you are a difficult patient, surely one who requires pity."

"Do you admit I near complete recovery?"

"Perhaps."

"Say it is so; you know it is."

She stretched out her arm. "Fitzwilliam, do read your letter." He was doing his best to manipulate her. She knew she was no real match for him; in the end he would triumph, of this she was certain. To her relief he read the letter without further ado.

"It is an invitation to the 'presentation at court' for Ann, to be held in little more than a fortnight. By proper decorum we should have responded by now."

"Dearest, I am sorry the announcement remained unopened. Although I had forgotten it, I wrote to Lady Catherine advising of your grave illness. I wrote again when you began recovery, as I did with my father, the Gardiners and Jane."

"Well, I mean to answer it at once; I should like to attend."

She read the invitation, giving no response.

"Uh hum," he cleared his throat; "I should like to go; that is if the head-master will allow it," he scoffed.

She flippantly addressed his desire to attend. "If you comply with my wishes."

"If I comply?" he replied, summoning her to him with a gesture.

"Oh no, I have not the slightest intention of weakening; I cannot be taken in by your charm; indeed you are mistaken if you suppose it."

With a voice containing that seriousness of business he was comfortable with, he exclaimed, "Dearest, be reasonable, I must reply at once to Lady Catherine."

"Very well, yes I do believe we may attend."

"Very well then, I shall take my rest now."

"So now you dismiss me?"

"Indeed, I am a sick man; I need rest," he smiled impishly, with marked sarcasm. He knew he was gaining the upper hand; it pleased him.

"Very well, you rest; I shall send word of the circumstances of our tardiness, accepting the invitation at once."

Mrs. Reynolds entered to announce Mr. Manley's arrival. Presently he was visiting with Georgiana but wished to see the patient. Since Mr. Darcy thought he could endure a visitor, Elizabeth gave permission to have him sent above the stairs.

Mr. Manley entered. "Well now, how is the invalid?"

"Very well, rapidly improving, I daresay."

"I understand you presently lack the cooperation you gave some weeks ago when your will was less copious," Mr. Manley stated.

"Perhaps I have been falsely represented."

"Oh, I think not."

"Oh I see, she has you taken in," he said, glancing at his wife.

Mr. Manley smiled back at him. "Not at all, Fitzwilliam, I simply acknowledge how we men are; mine is the voice of experience."

"Indeed," Elizabeth chimed in.

"I am anxious to move about, go sporting, anything."

"All in due time, Fitzwilliam."

"You see, Mr. Manley, he is impossible," she lamented.

Having noticed she embarrassed her husband, who now glanced her a look of disbelief, she decided to take leave. "I shall allow you both time alone," she uttered, then quitted the bedchamber.

"Now that you are recovering, I feel it is time to discuss a certain matter. I understand from Dr. Gordon that the day you fell ill you sent for him to look in on one of the farmers' sons, ill with fever; do you remember it?"

"Why, yes I do; I did indeed send word express to fetch him. The poor little fellow was burning with fever. Do you know how he is, Henry?"

"Mr. Darcy, I am so sorry."

Mr. Darcy closed his eyes with painful thoughts. He swallowed hard, then opened his eyes again. "It grieves me to think the boy died; I did not know. Until this moment I had no notion of it."

"The boy's fever consumed him; you suffered the very same illness. We thought it best to wait until you were well enough to receive the news."

"I touched the boy; I felt his fever; his little frail body was on fire as he lay helplessly limp. I have given him thought these past weeks, Henry; I suppose I feared to ask of him, hoping the reason no one mentioned him was because all was well."

"That explains it; you later became violently ill."

"What of the boy's family; have they the fever?"

"No, they were fortunate."

"My wife told me of the apothecary's doing; I have no recollection of any of it; I am a lucky man indeed. Still, the boy, this is despairing to be sure. Do the farmer and the other tenants know why I have not been to visit these past weeks?"

"Yes, they are aware; they requested a special service to pray for you. Even in his grief the farmer felt responsible for you."

"No fault of theirs to be sure; it could not be helped. I was fortunate to have been under such good care."

"I believe the grace of God saw you through it all."

"Yes, of course, I believe that as well."

Mr. Manley stayed for a short visit, not wanting to fatigue his friend.

The week next passed at a moderate pace. Mr. Darcy, now regaining his strength rapidly, was spending more time out of bed. Elizabeth, forced to relinquish her control over him, watched him take charge. To his own satisfaction he was reading. In the end, the ravaging fever left no ill effects. He returned to his routine of visiting the nursery frequently. He visited the farmer who had lost his son to express his sorrow for his loss. He showed appreciation to his entire house staff, who assisted his wife with affability.

As for Mrs. Reynolds, he requested a private audience with her in his office. To her, he expressed his appreciation for her dedicated caring service. His thanks were not only for himself but also for his wife as well as his entire household. As always, he remembered the happiness of so many depended upon him. He used his power as landlord to bestow his gratitude. With pride, he made known the respect he acquired for their merits. Not wishing to overlook their value, he ordered special baskets filled with fresh meat, fruit and nuts for each household.

One morning Mr. Darcy stood at a window overlooking his vast estate. This day it attracted his keenest attention. He viewed it with earnest contemplation, noticing its woods, valleys, the stream with trees scattered on its banks and the beautiful walks. He viewed it as never before, not as he was familiarly acquainted, but rather as if he were a stranger to the place. He gained new recognition for its beauty, concluding his near-to-death illness had given him a new appreciation of its grandeur as well as its beauty; or perhaps, just perhaps, it was his present state of felicity. Feeling as though he had cheated death, he viewed it as finding favour in the heavens. He could not help but look up to the sky with a smile. "What a glorious day to be alive," he found himself saying aloud, then concluded with, "Amen to that."

On the Road to Rosings

THE TIME HAD FINALLY COME for the carriage to depart Pemberley to attend the presentation assembly at Rosings. Elizabeth experienced a certain excitement to be going to Rosings Park.

Taking their leave the morning prior to the event, Elizabeth hoped Lady Catherine had perpetuated the alteration of character she exhibited at Pemberley. In light of the fact they were invited to spend the night, it seemed a pleasing indication that indeed she had maintained her new disposition. Feeling tired, Georgiana fell asleep almost immediately.

Mr. Darcy was less concerned, explaining, "Dearest, had you known Lady Catherine as I did as a young lad, you would surely realize the person you believe she has become is little more than the person she once was."

"How so?"

"Lady Catherine's relationship with Sir Louis de Bourgh was that of deep affection. She held him in the highest regard."

Elizabeth could not help but reply with enormity of surprise. "Really!"

"Yes, you may believe it; Lady Catherine held him in high esteem."

"This is so very interesting; do tell me more."

"It was only when he died did she isolate herself in that house, losing almost all connections with friends. From birth she supposed Ann to be delicate, but upon his death, her protection of Ann took a suffocating turn, treating her as incapable of doing anything Lady Catherine postulated as strenuous."

Elizabeth's face glowed with surprise. "I had no idea; I'm quite ashamed of myself; I once thought mean of Ann."

Mr. Darcy looked perplexed, his brows slightly united in a questioning manner. "Why should you hold ill feelings toward Ann?"

Elizabeth's face coloured with embarrassment. "I confess I thought her sickly and cross looking; I thought her a good match for you."

"Why, Elizabeth, I am shocked; I am indeed surprised."

"I'm quite ashamed of it now that I know Ann."

"And what of me?"

"I am indeed sorry, Fitzwilliam," her face coloured again.

"I should wish so."

"Tell me more of Lady Catherine."

"Very well. After Sir Louis died, the family continued to visit, but her strong opinions devoid of feelings distorted her eccentricity, making it extremely difficult to be in her company. She often made it rather tiresome to visit, in truth, quite intolerable at times."

"How is it you and the Colonel returned often then?"

"The Colonel visited, as did I, for Ann's sake. I dare admit I often visited out of a sense of duty. I deliberately visited knowing you were at Hunsford. My uncontrollable desires beckoned me. And now that we speak of it, you totally confused the poor Colonel, a most unpleasant curious situation, such an error."

"Whatever do you imply? In what way?"

"I had confided in him my deepest affections, expressed my desire to create for myself a nearer interest, anxious no less for him to make your acquaintance. I poured on him my ideals of an agreeable pursuit. As every attempt to converse with you became a provocation in his presence, he became bewildered indeed. I believe you went so far as to challengingly embarrass me at the pianoforte; you did indeed indulge in taunting me exceedingly."

"Let's not recollect those awful moments."

"Yes, we have better memories, have we not now?" he said as he looked down at her. He noticed that her face was coloured still. He could not hide a smile, observing that his declaration caused the blush; nor could he see any reason to be sorry for it. It was almost as if he had salvaged a particle of triumph from those awful memories. He enjoyed the liberty of the tease, realizing soon they would arrive at Rosings, where he would adhere conscientiously to elevating himself to his usual reserve, giving a striking appearance of composure.

Georgiana, now awake, noticed they were nearing Rosings. She expressed a desire to stretch her legs.

"Whom do you suppose Lady Catherine invited?" Elizabeth was curious to know, then continued, "Surely Ann had been out of touch with local society, perhaps we shall only see a few from town. I suppose we may count on the Collinses' presence."

"I would guess you will meet the Earl of Matlock as well as his five sons, one of whom you are already acquainted."

"Yes, Colonel Fitzwilliam, I shall be happy to see him again."

"I should expect people from the village, young ladies and gentlemen of high social design no doubt."

"Brother, did you know our aunt has re-entered the society she once frequented? I had a letter from the Colonel; he told me so."

"Well, I had not heard of it; but then I have been kept in solitude by a strict headmaster who relinquished nothing in the way of privileges."

Elizabeth made no answer. Her mind was engaged in wonderment of the Earl of Matlock. She tried to imagine the character of the other sons. Attempting to recapture her attention, he asked, "Mr. and Mrs. Collins will be there I imagine; should you be glad to see them?"

"I will be happy to see Charlotte again."

"And what of your cousin Mr. Collins?" She just rolled her eyes.

"Dearest, are you uncomfortably anxious to be nearing Rosings?"

"Yes, a little I suppose, I should hope not to feel awkward."

"Do not be. Let us not underestimate Lady Catherine; allow her a fair chance."

"You are right, my dear," she said as the carriage ride became rougher. He looked at her surprised expression as they were being tossed about. "Some ill country lanes; I do believe we are nearing Rosings; it won't be long now."

"Elizabeth, you will be happy to know Lady Catherine looks upon you with favour; the Colonel has related to me my aunt's appreciation of your letters, which kept her informed of Fitzwilliam's progress. It must be so."

"Thank you, Georgiana; that is good news, is it not?"

They were anxious to exit the carriage, which was now coming to rest in front of the small gate which led to a short gravel walk to the house. Greeted by one of the servants, they entered the grand entrance hall where they immediately happened upon Mrs. Jenkinson.

"Mr. Darcy, how nice to see you at last," she stated, smiling with ease, absent the impressionable nervous manner he was accustomed to. They followed her through the antechamber to the chamber where Lady Catherine and Ann were anxiously awaiting. Lady Catherine and Ann rose to greet them.

"There is my nephew. Come in all of you; I thought you should never arrive."

"Oh, Cousins, I am so glad you are come at last," Ann expressed with angelic sweetness.

"I hope you will take tea with us. Have you dined? Are you tired?" Lady Catherine queried.

"We should like some tea, if it is not too much trouble," Mr. Darcy replied, approaching to afford his aunt a hug, much to her surprise.

"Fitzwilliam, you astonish me, you have not done so in years."

Elizabeth approached her with a full curtsey. She smiled. "Lady Catherine, we were honoured to receive your invitation; once again, we apologize for the delay in answering."

Lady Catherine immediately looked at her nephew. "Why yes, Fitzwilliam, you look well; you must have suffered the same fever that attached itself to Rosings some months back to be sure. It was very vexing to sit here in thought of such a dreadful fever upon that great estate. Why, Ann and I were concerned for you all; what of your dear children, they are well I trust?"

"The children are well, but sad to say one farmer's boy on the estate fell ill, poor little thing was too frail to make it through," Elizabeth explained.

"Such a hard thing," Ann sadly interjected.

"Indeed," Lady Catherine added. "Georgiana, Elizabeth, will you not sit down? Make yourself contented," said Lady Catherine. "Mrs. Jenkinson, call for tea, perhaps a bite of something to go with it."

Elizabeth thought it strange. She was in this house again but under very different circumstances. Lady Catherine's manner of greeting them was pleasant; there was no hesitation in her speech. She noticed her face lit up when they entered; surely this was a good sign. Ann was no less eager to see them. Elizabeth glanced over at Lady Catherine. She could not help but admire the change, which at one time she would have judged impossible. His aunt, obviously less condescending, spoke with a more diminished authoritative tone as had marked her self-importance on her first visit to Rosings. Her composition of speech rallied around the accomplishments of Ann as opposed to faults and ridicule of others.

Ann was nearing completion of a purse she was netting. Not far from her chair was a screen she had been covering. Elizabeth noted with pleasure the advancement of her skills seeing the precision of her stitches. The neatness of her work displayed a flattering selection of colours, all proof Ann indulged her work with enthusiasm.

"Why, Ann, this is excellent work," Georgiana expressed.

"Ann, you are netting a purse, how clever," Elizabeth stated with surprise.

"Yes, Mrs. Jenkinson showed me how to do it, but, Elizabeth, did you not notice my screen covering? My mother instructed me of it."

Elizabeth quickly turned her attention to Lady Catherine. "Lady Catherine, this is fine work indeed. Ann takes to the needle well; would you not agree?"

"Why, yes, Elizabeth, indeed. I surprised myself; why I had not touched a needle since I was a young girl. I do believe that to be so; I believe I rather enjoyed it and so did Ann."

Lady Catherine was very direct, but with a sense of pride in assisting Ann. Elizabeth thought it a task his aunt should never have attempted; surely she would eye it as beneath her. Now, thought she, Lady Catherine is indeed full of surprises. Amazing how the love of a daughter can influence, making it all very astonishing, quite amusing.

Lady Catherine still maintained a certain air of superiority in her rank, but willfully sought to be careful to treat her visitors with equality. This was a bit of a struggle for her. It was obvious that many years had been spent condescendingly dictating to others. Even so, Elizabeth thought her to have made exceptional strides in alteration. She thought it pleasing to feel a part of it. So happy in her findings, she determined she would not miss a chance to show his aunt the respect she now felt was deserved. There was a time she would not have given her the charity of doubt, but now she enjoyed her ladyship's company, viewing her in a new light, actually deriving pleasure from an exchange of conversation, which now flowed with comfort.

"Elizabeth, I do hope your family is in health; tell me, how does your father do?"

"Oh, very well, Lady Catherine, very well indeed."

"And your sister Jane and Mr. Bingley?"

"They are well; my sister made an announcement of an event."

"Yes, I know of the announcement, I had the information from Mrs. Collins. My congratulations to her and Mr. Bingley if you please; perhaps when you write next you will make mention of it."

Elizabeth was taken aback by this inquisition—Lady Catherine inquiring of her family? She noticed she did it void of hesitation, displaying sincere interest. Inheriting some of her father's wit, she thought, perchance that game of backgammon was one of her father's best moves, perhaps she was the winner.

"Delighted to do so, Lady Catherine," Elizabeth told her after a bit of delay.

"Mother, may I educate my cousins of our plans for tomorrow?"

"Why, yes, do."

Ann expressed with elevated excitement, "My mother has acquired wondrous musicians. She has ordered specific music to be played. We will display fine table settings, as well as dancing. I am expected to open the first dance."

Elizabeth looked at Ann. "That will be delightful."

She noted the pleasure her ladyship reclaimed from watching Ann speak, almost as if she were revisiting something lost. She sat in her chair studying Ann as she continued to go on with respect to the attendees expected. Mr. Darcy sat quietly at the end of the sofa sipping his wine. Elizabeth noted his reserve, believing him to be as he was upon her first seeing him at Rosings. His quiet reserve identified his manners in public as not having changed.

After taking a sip of his port, Mr. Darcy looked at his aunt. "When does my cousin Colonel Fitzwilliam arrive?"

"Oh, the dear Colonel shall arrive late tonight or early on the morrow; we are not sure at this moment. He was unable to inform us of his exact arrival, so we know not when to expect him."

Mr. Darcy put down his port. "I have not seen him for six months or better."

"He has requested the first two dances," Ann proudly expressed.

Lady Catherine sat up straight. She looked at Ann with expectations of earnest consent. "You shall have many dances, Ann; there will be so many acceptable gentlemen. Just remember, you did promise if you feel tired you will sit one out."

"Yes, Mother, I will be sure to do so."

Lady Catherine momentarily slipped in conversation, representing her former superior rank in authority. Upon catching herself, she changed her tone, further proceeding cautiously. She was then talking of the servants' duties; however, Elizabeth was impressed by her quick turn of countenance. This proved to be the first of many times she would witness her self-governing.

Mr. Darcy said little; he merely observed as he sat quietly with guarded reserve.

Georgiana said little more the remainder of the evening; she was exhausted from the journey, expressing her eagerness to retire.

Elizabeth thought that although he was very much like he was the last time they were together at Rosings, the circumstances were totally different, believing he should be at more ease. This evening there was no reason for Lady Catherine to demand her share of the conversation, claiming such for herself or Ann, as the general exchange was equal for all participants.

The Colonel Arrives

COLONEL FITZWILLIAM JOINED into the conversation directly as he entered the room, having just arrived in time to surprise them all. He was in high spirits as he enthralled himself in the sight of Ann, obviously delighted in what he saw. "Good evening," he promptly said with a bow. "I am pleased to arrive this evening; now I shall visit with you all gladly. When do you expect my father and brothers?"

"Sometime late tomorrow morning."

The Colonel turned to Elizabeth. "Will you play the pianoforte for us?"

"Oh, yes, please do," Ann added.

Elizabeth went to the pianoforte with the Colonel and her husband. From the start Ann remained on the sofa near her mother. As Elizabeth sat down to play, her husband stood over her with his cousin at his side. "Do you mean to come all this way, Mr. Darcy, to hear me play?" she said teasingly. She noticed he did not smile. Mr. Darcy, not comfortable with the tease, remained reserved in his aunt's quarters. He delivered his reply with sober reflection.

"Yes, madam, I have come to hear my wife play, such as a wife may expect."

Elizabeth taking his cue quietly answered, "Very well, is there a specific tune you desire?" She suffered to conceal her embarrassment as she avoided looking at him directly.

He looked down at her, "You shall choose."

Unable to look up to view him directly, Elizabeth wondered if he were cross with her. She reproached herself for her stupidity.

"Ann, do come to the pianoforte to hear Elizabeth play," the Colonel urged.

Ann quickly responded, while Lady Catherine continued to sit in her chair, contented to observe from a distance.

Mrs. Jenkinson had re-entered the room, taking a seat near Lady Catherine.

"Pray, Aunt, would you mind so terribly if I went to my chamber, I can hardly stay awake; I am so exhausted."

"Why, not at all, Georgiana, one of the servants will show you to your chamber. Good night, my dear, you rest well."

"Thank you." She bid them all good night, allowing herself to be directed above the stairs.

Lady Catherine turned to Mrs. Jenkinson. "Elizabeth plays and sings well, I am forced to admit, it is so much more enjoyable than the little tunes Ann tries to play. Mrs. Jenkinson, she requires further instruction, there are days when her practice grates my nerves. I should not like to discourage her, but, you know, she leaves much to be desired in her presentation of music."

Mrs. Jenkinson, hardly knowing how to respond, could only manage the words, "Yes, ma'am." She had never heard Lady Catherine use complimentary language regarding Elizabeth. Although she was witness to the many changes at Rosings, she had not quite expected such a change in her character toward her nephew's wife. Although she had no understanding of the whole of the situation, she did believe it a welcomed change. It pleased her to see the young people making it a joyous occasion, especially for Ann's sake.

Mrs. Jenkinson had been taken aback with Lady Catherine so frequently in the six months past that she hardly knew what to imagine at times. She continued to smile at her in disbelief. She noticed she too had changed; she now lacked that nervous wandering about the house awaiting orders, contradictions or unreasonable demands. Now her ladyship even talked to her as if she were a friend or confidant.

"Well, Mrs. Jenkinson, you needn't agree so readily," Lady Catherine scolded her. Then she smiled at her before bursting into a chuckle. "Yes, I daresay she does require further training; perhaps one day she will play well, but we cannot lay claim to that presently."

Mrs. Jenkinson continued to smile.

Elizabeth, believing herself to be tired, quit the pianoforte, returning to the sofa with the gentlemen and Ann not far behind.

"This is the most merriment this room has witnessed in too long a time; just look at my Ann, I can scarce believe she is the same girl. Oh, Ann, come take a seat by your mother; I so wish to have you near me this evening for the morrow brings you out like the spring. We expect so many agreeable young men and young ladies."

Elizabeth, long distracted by Lady Catherine's enthusiasm of Ann's alteration and accomplishments, estimated her ladyship ignorant of the Colonel's affections for Ann or Ann's attachment to him. Perhaps Ann remained unaware of her love for the Colonel, thought she. Clearly Lady Catherine was gain set on securing one of the gentlemen of the neighbouring society, one promising in character as well as propriety.

Although she lately afforded much where her nephew Mr. Darcy was concerned, she obviously maintained her opinion regarding marriage within one's rank as duty. Surely the proof of her steadfast beliefs regarding rank surfaced with her next statement.

"Tomorrow will be most interesting, Ann; the most eligible of gentlemen residing thereabout in Kent are expected. Surely you may find one agreeable to you. I assure you, those invited are equal in rank. So you see, my dear, you must not be afraid to consider one of them; I have already taken the pains of checking into their backgrounds. I understand they are all very highly regarded; indeed there is to be no lack of variety tomorrow evening."

Elizabeth listened with interest. The Colonel had little to offer but his pleasing disposition and less than average looks. Although Lady Catherine loved him a great deal, she did not afford him any consideration as a match for Ann that she could detect, quite the opposite in fact.

Elizabeth and Mr. Darcy begged to be excused to direct themselves above the stairs for the evening. After affectionate good nights to the rest of the party they withdrew their presence, once again eager to be alone.

Once behind closed doors, the subject turned to the pending event.

"Dearest, Lady Catherine thinks nothing of the Colonel requesting the first two dances; do you believe her aware of the attachment between those two?"

"I'm sure she is not."

"To be sure, I fear you are right."

"Yes, she is quite captured by Ann's accomplishments. She is also swallowed up in her own alteration; she sees little else at the moment, I'm afraid."

"I see, the party should prove to be interesting; would not you agree?"

"Yes, indeed. Dearest, are you quite comfortable here?"

"Yes, I am; why do you ask?"

"I wished you to be so; I thought Lady Catherine managed herself well."

"Yes, I have no reproach; she is very altered toward me."

"I am pleased to see it."

"Yes, one could not help but see it. It does indeed bring much relief."

"Lady Catherine seemed well informed of my feverish situation; perhaps those letters of yours, keeping her appraised of the situation of one of her favourites, drew heightened appreciation as well as increased affection."

"She deserved no less from me; after all, you are her nephew. I thought it a delicate business; I did it out of duty as well."

"Even so, your kind generosity I'll wager did not go unnoticed. I know my aunt; the words may come hard; just the same she interpreted the sincerity in your writings. I am sure of it," he said as he made himself ready for bed. They lay silently beneath the covers for a few moments, until Mr. Darcy spoke. "I must say, although my wife enjoys a tease as I do, I wish she would not do it out in company. I should wish you would think the better of it hereafter. I am not accustomed to such compromise with an audience so near. Is it too much to ask that you refrain from doing so in the future?"

"Fitzwilliam, the only audience was your cousins. I confess, to that I saw no great harm. I do admit that once having done so, I soon realized your mortification; I did try to rectify the matter before long."

"Indeed you did. I must say I was exceedingly relieved at your quick perception; I was grateful to you for it. Perhaps you will use better judgment hereafter. You know I love a tease, but not in company; I thought you aware I have no taste for it publicly. True we were among family; however, that does not alter the fact that my propensity toward a reserved temperament should secure the understanding of one so endeared and wholly connected to me. Surely you realize I fail to possess that familiar vitality in public that most men display with a sense of common easiness. I find I am ill at ease amidst such exhibition. I—fear being viewed as precarious."

"Forgive me, Fitzwilliam, I should have thought the better of it; you may count on my future knowledge of it."

Elizabeth let out a lengthy sigh, feeling stupid for not having known better. She scolded herself for having committed such a foolish offence, after having lately boasted with pride of comprehending him so intimately well.

Mr. Darcy looked at his wife; the sober reflection on her face troubled him. He did not wish to scold her, but rather to make her understand his uneasiness. He reached out, drawing her to him. "Elizabeth, I assure you I am not angry, nor do I wish to make you uneasy; my only desire is to share my true feelings, to grant you further understanding of my character. It is important you learn my intimate conduct. He held her close, stroking her hair as they snuggled together.

Elizabeth closed her eyes. She mused over her lack of foresight, which brought her husband pain. She did not consider her error of judgment to have caused him to agonize, but rather his necessity to set her on the right path. She could only imagine what degree of suffering those words to her cost him. She reproached herself for the effect her faulty views placed on his countenance. Each time she prided herself with understanding him, she was only to discover she had much to improve upon. She could only question if she were doomed to never fully behold his honour or constant loyalty to duty, which made him noble. She felt so full of error and lacking in judgment.

All Elizabeth wanted now was rest. The anticipation of arriving at Rosings, the long journey, as well as her foolishness, had worn her to a point of exhaustion. She was glad to lay her head upon his chest. She closed her eyes as he held her close. It did not take long for her to slumber, giving way to more pleasant thoughts of what was to be expected the coming evening.

The Earl of Matlock

BREAKFAST HAD SCARCELY CONCLUDED before Mrs. Jenkinson entered, announcing, "The Earl of Matlock, your ladyship."

The Earl entered gallantly with his sons and daughter-in-law. After Lady Catherine greeted them, he turned to Ann, next his son, followed by Georgiana and Mr. Darcy, who then took it upon himself to introduce his wife. "Uncle, this is my wife Elizabeth."

"So glad to make your acquaintance."

Lady Catherine turned to Elizabeth. "Elizabeth, the Earl is my brother. Lady Anne Darcy, your husband's mother, was our sister, but I do expect my nephew has explained it to you by now; did he not?" "Yes, to be sure, Lady Catherine, he has indeed."

To Elizabeth's surprise, the Earl was not quite as tall as she had anticipated. He was a man of medium height and possessed a small frame. He was not a handsome man, his nose being a bit too large for his face—a face which bore deep character lines, giving him a rough look. His hair was gray, prompting unruly locks about his face. He walked upright with his shoulders back, almost as if he thought that posture would make him appear to be taller. Having entered into conversation, it was evident to her that his pleasant address, along with his gentle manner, unveiled a true gentleman of very fine character. He was graciously friendly; she proposed to like him instantly.

Next she was introduced to the eldest son, Lord Fitzwilliam. He was a man of six and forty, medium height, fair complexion, with a stocky build, making it obvious he was not wanting at the table. His brown locks were as unruly as his father's; he possessed rough features as well. Although he could not be considered handsome, he made a pleasant appearance, displaying excellent manners with a touch of superiority. His wife Fanny accompanied him, projecting immediate peculiarity in her manner.

Fanny was advantaged in height to her husband. In spite of the fact that she could not be labeled pretty, she was acceptable to look at. Her light hair was neatly pulled back, presenting curls to flatter her fair pigmentation, with all the features of her face being equally fine; however, she was not to be considered anything out of the ordinary. Her poise bore an air of un-friendly elevation, which Elizabeth immediately thought utterly odd given the present company. She remained at her husband's side, staring at those not making her direct notice. Her clothes were made of the finest material and on her neck hung a lavish necklace almost too much for her propor-tions. Elizabeth noticed the cold manner of her greeting coupled with her total lack of regard for Lady Catherine, who graciously welcomed her. Lady Catherine's fortune, being so advantageous to that of Lord Fitzwilliam and Fanny, made it difficult to understand Fanny's lack of warmth for the society she now permeated.

The second to the eldest introduced to her was James, he being five and forty. Elizabeth favoured him immediately. He was not unpleasant to look at, thought she; perhaps it was his pleasing manners which made him more handsome than his presentation. He had a commanding forehead; his eyes were small and round; his nose was average giving way to a small rounded chin. He was not unattractive; on the contrary, his smile laid open his pleasing personality, full of grace together with good manners. His attire was neatly suited to his form. His well-mixed humour, coupled with lively wit, gave the impression he rather liked to enjoy himself in company. Al-though he was more outgoing than his older brother, Elizabeth supposed having no wife to confine him allowed him freedom to act accordingly. Obviously delighted to be at Rosings, he wasted little time joining in in-stant conversation.

After James came Charles, a man of four and forty with a rather reserved disposition. Charles was the tallest of the brothers, but very thin and frail, requiring a walking stick to assist his limp. Elizabeth noticed he dragged his left foot. She could not help but wonder if his serious nature revealed the pain felt when walking. She decided she must be right when she noticed he was quick to be seated after introduction. She thought him somewhat hand-some but plain; his locks of brown hair were well groomed. His face was long, exposing a high forehead. When he spoke it was with the softest voice. In spite of his reserve, he had an agreeable manner. At first Elizabeth thought he seemed rather lost amongst the rest of his party. She watched Lady Catherine afford him heightened attention, more so than the others in the party.

After Charles followed Francis, three years his junior. He immediately requested to be referred to as Frank. Frank was advantageous in height to his eldest brother. He could not be called thin, but just what a man ought to be, thought Elizabeth. His attire was impressive, very well fitting to his form. His elevated conduct seemed to bring about a certain air. Elizabeth was not secure with her thoughts. His present manners confused her; she could not make him out. She considered him somewhat handsome, noticing he walked intentionally straight with his shoulders back as did his father. His hair was brown but uncurled, hanging loose around his oblong face. His eyes were piercingly dark, his features fine, sporting a dimple in his chin. After being introduced, he directed himself to Charles. Elizabeth noticed the attention he paid his brother, which led her to believe she had perhaps misjudged him upon introduction. He humbled himself to his brother, assisting him with a pillow to support his back. She noticed his attentiveness as he took his brother's cane to an out-of-the-way corner. She instantly retracted her original thoughts of Frank; he was not haughty as first believed, quite the opposite in fact. She decided she admired him, intending to hold him in high regard.

Each of the new arrivals made mention of Ann's alteration, flattering her with encouraging compliments. Lady Catherine stood amidst them, very much involved in the exchange. She was clearly proud, seeming to enjoy the attention almost as much as Ann. After several moments of continued observations of Ann's development, Lady Catherine turned to Elizabeth, then her nephews. She held out her hand for them to draw near. Elizabeth moved toward her. "I owe it all to my nephew Fitzwilliam, his wife, and your brother for giving me back my Ann."

Elizabeth was speechless until Mr. Darcy rescued her. "That is not quite true; the praise belongs to my cousin the Colonel, without him nothing would be possible."

"Yes, indeed it is all owed to the Colonel," Elizabeth added without hesitation. Aware the Colonel risked everything for Ann's sake, she was not comfortable taking credit.

"They all had a hand in it to be sure," Lady Catherine said with delight.

The afternoon passed all too quickly. There was hardly enough time to speak to all her husband's cousins. Elizabeth managed conversation with Frank and Charles. She learned both Frank and Charles were clergymen on their father's estate. James was a lieutenant in a regiment up north. Elizabeth, wishing to make conversation, explored. "How is it four handsome brothers still remain unattached? Are none of you in want of a wife?"

This induced smiles to all their faces. "I do have a fancy for a young lady, but she presently has no knowledge of my interest," Charles announced.

As Georgiana played the pianoforte, Elizabeth noticed Fanny sitting on the sofa alone. Visibly bored, she sipped her tea. She thought she should attempt to converse with her. She ventured to the sofa, taking a seat near her. "How often do you come to Rosings?"

"As little as possible," Fanny replied sarcastically.

"I see, and how was your journey here?"

"Those horrid country lanes tossed me about; I was quite vexed."

"Yes, they were rather rough," Elizabeth replied. "Ann's presentation tonight shall be quite an affair. I understand Lady Catherine has spared no expense in bringing it about. Are you fond of dancing?"

"I suppose dancing is acceptable."

"My husband tells me all his cousins are fond of dancing."

Fanny quickly turned her blaring eyes on Elizabeth. She wasted little time answering with a sharp tongue. "You could hardly expect Charles to dance!"

"Oh, forgive me, I was not thinking when I spoke just then."

"Obviously not," Fanny replied with disgust.

Elizabeth, finding conversation increasingly difficult, began to feel Fanny's annoyance of the uninvited exchange.

"Perhaps I shall take my leave now. How pleasant it was to speak with you," was all Elizabeth could say before quitting her company in haste.

Elizabeth was glad to depart her company; she was sure she had done nothing to offend her, yet her disposition was rudely indifferent. It was difficult to sketch her character; she was unfriendly, offering no attempt to recommend herself in general intercourse. She wondered if Fanny was always inclined to be disagreeable. There was a natural callousness about her she found difficult to tolerate. She decided it was of little matter; there were more pleasant conversations to be had, so she resolved to pay her as little attention as possible.

As Elizabeth walked across the room to rejoin Frank and Charles, Colonel Fitzwilliam seized her. "Elizabeth, there is sure to be no scarcity of gentlemen this evening, certainly not with all the Fitzwilliam brothers present, not to mention those invited."

"I should think not, Colonel; I understand you requested the first two dances. I imagine you are eager; is that not so?"

"Yes, indeed, does not Ann look well? What say you of my aunt, Elizabeth? I believe her quite remarkable. I noticed she pays you much attention. You were modest when she tried to give you credit; you deserved much of the praise indeed; you are well aware Ann responded to you at Pemberley. Can you believe it, Elizabeth? The wretched fever did all this."

Elizabeth quickly hushed him. Just above a whisper, she intimated, "You had better keep your voice low. You are a fortunate man Colonel; my husband had not expected success in your adventure; he was quite taken by surprise. It was a bit dishonest you know, but I daresay one must admit it proved beneficial for more than one person, including Lady Catherine."

"Do you believe I reproached myself for having done it?"

"Certainly not," she replied, then added, "It is such an honour to meet your father and brothers as well as Fanny. Does Lord Fitzwilliam visit Lady Catherine often?"

"No, Edward is too busy with Fanny and the children; they place heavy demands on him, I'm quite surprised he is here, and more shocked that Fanny accompanies him."

"Why is that, Colonel?"

"Since Edward is the eldest, he is heir to the family estate. Fanny enjoys her own wealth; she inherited a flat sum of £5,000. She is all society; the flow of invitations keeps them busy. They presently live in a house on her father's estate, which affords them a life advantageous to many, most assuredly to be admired or perhaps envied. She is pleasant enough in other company I suppose, but Rosings has never had anything to attract her. I confess, Elizabeth, I'm shocked my brother Edward convinced her to attend; I had not expected it. Edward has a kind heart, although, since his marriage, he has been unable to warm it to anyone without Fanny's approval. She is kind to Father but has little time for any other in the family. I suppose the less said of the matter the better."

"Well, I am delighted I had the opportunity to meet them, even if what you say is true; I agree, some things are better left unsaid. I have so enjoyed meeting your other brothers as well. They are charming; I had a most pleasant conversation with Frank and Charles. I noted the care your brother Frank grants Charles; it is quite admirable."

"When both were boys, Frank and Charles played in the grassy field with their horse. A terrible accident deprived Charles of his former abilities, leaving its impression on Frank; I don't believe he has ever recovered from that awful day."

"Does he feel responsible for the mishap?"

"Indeed Frank has suffered distress of the bitterest kind."

"I'm sorry for him; I very much admire the attention he pays Charles."

"Ah yes, Frank does pay much attention to Charles; they were always close. Charles accepts his limitations without reproach."

"Well, I enjoyed my conversation with them; I intend to continue it later."

"It was quite gratifying to see my aunt proud to introduce you into the family. I'm astonished, I had not expected such change; indeed this is a happy occasion. My cousin is coming out, my other cousin is here upon special invitation with his wife and I have managed to secure the first two dances. What could be more delightful or wanting?"

"There is nothing more to hope for. Now, if you will excuse me, I should like to speak with my husband." Giving a curtsey, she departed from him.

Elizabeth's mind drifted to Fanny. It was hard to imagine the influence she had on Lord Fitzwilliam. Perhaps Lord Fitzwilliam insisted they attend for Ann's sake or his aunt's. It is best not to dwell on this longer, she told herself.

"Elizabeth, come," Lady Catherine said, with outstretched arm.

"Elizabeth, Lady Catherine has suggested we prepare ourselves; time is limited; within a few hours guests will arrive."

"Yes, my thought precisely; I shall tell Georgiana to come as well."

"Elizabeth, might I impose upon you to look in on Ann? She is presently above the stairs making herself ready. Although she has Sara's assistance, she may desire more youthful advice; you are more equipped than I to give it."

Elizabeth's lips parted with pleasure. "I would be delighted to do so." Elizabeth curtsied before quitting Lady Catherine's company along with her husband.

"Well, dearest, how did you get on with my cousins?"

"Very well."

"What of Fanny; did she make conversation with you?"

"Fanny's mind seems to be fixed elsewhere. I am inclined to think Fanny would prefer not to converse with anyone."

"Yes, I'm sure she does not reflect on the visit with satisfaction. I expected as much; our society has never been suitable to her taste. Fanny prefers the aristocratic society of London. Elizabeth, give no credit to her actions, she deserves none; she is as insufferable as always."

Georgiana joined them. The three ventured above the stairs to prepare for the evening. As they neared the door of the bedchamber, Elizabeth turned.

"I shall check on Ann; I promised Lady Catherine."

"Very well, you will come directly then?"

"Yes," she said, smiling. Elizabeth left her husband at the chamber door, sensing his eagerness to have her to himself. She was aware he was anxious for her to make visible her new apparel. She continued to Ann's bedchamber, knocked, then entered.

"Ann, I come to see how you are getting on."

"Oh, Elizabeth, I am filled with excitement; I am so very glad you sought me out."

"You must remain calm. This is a most desirable event for you; is it not?"

"Oh yes, I should have never thought my mother to consent to it."

"I believe her love for you increases by the minute. Ann, she is so unquestionably proud of you; she speaks of little else."

"I have you to thank for much of the change."

"That is not so, Ann; your own desire to change brought this about."

"I can think of no one else I would rather share these moments with, indeed no one else. I shall never depart from my gratitude to you. I am aware it had to be my desire to change, but you gave me the strength to do so. Elizabeth, come here, look at my gown. Is that not the most wonderful gown you have ever witnessed?"

"It is very beautiful. I admire the affluence of the fabric; I especially like the little tuck on the sleeves. The colour reminds me of the sky on a beautiful clear day in summer; indeed this blue is the proper colour for one so fair. This lace is very fine, such elegance; surely it must be French lace, is it not?"

"Yes, it is, Elizabeth; my mother's acquaintance at the local dress shop imported several dresses from France. This is the one of my choosing; I believe it is beautiful."

"It is very beautiful, but no more beautiful than the one who shall be wearing it."

"You are so very kind to me."

"You deserve it; I am so proud of you."

"Elizabeth, my mother is changed too; can you not see it?"

"Oh, how can one not help but see it? Quite a contrast, I daresay."

"Yes, indeed; but, Elizabeth, she is a very proud woman."

"Yes, I know. She is very proud of you."

"No, that is not my meaning. What I meant to say is, my mother's pride makes it difficult for her to fully express her affections for you, but I know them to be genuine. She told me one evening that she misjudged you; she now holds you in the highest esteem. She is of the opinion that my cousin made his match according to his own will, using sound judgment. I wish you could have seen how anxiously she awaited your arrival. She is so much kinder now, gentle-hearted. She speaks to me now like a friend as well as her daughter. It is strange, is it not? Indeed it is so very much like living a new life."

"Although she has not said so directly to me, I feel her sincerity; I am grateful it has come to this; I should not have wished it any other way. Perhaps we have all grown a bit more tolerant. Now, Ann, the time—should not you be making yourself ready?"

"Oh, yes, Elizabeth, would you send Sara or Mrs. Jenkinson in to assist me with my attire? Mrs. Jenkinson is so delighted for me; she is very kind, very kind indeed."

"Yes, I shall. I believe she is not far, she will find Sara. Do not worry; I'll send her in. Is there anything I may do for you, Ann?"

"I should like you to see me before any other. May I send Mrs. Jenkinson for you?"

"Of course," Elizabeth said, giving her a hug. "I shall be honoured to be the first."

Elizabeth quitted Ann's room to rejoin her husband. He was completely attired when she entered, just fussing with his collar. Elizabeth came up behind him. Putting her arms around his middle, she rested the side of her face against his back.

"Well, my dear, I see you have returned; how did you find my cousin?"

"Excited—she wishes me to be the first to see her in her dress, so I better make haste. Mrs. Jenkinson will be here shortly to fetch me."

While Elizabeth proceeded to make herself ready, Mr. Darcy excused himself briefly to allow the chambermaid to assist Elizabeth with her gown. Within a half-hour she was attired except for a few finishing touches. Once he entered the room, he sat in a chair observing her quite slyly as she stood in front of the looking glass, swaying from side to side, seeking her own approval.

"Mrs. Darcy, I daresay you are exceedingly lovely," he said as he stood. Nearing her, they viewed each other through the looking glass. Bringing his hands around the front of her he placed a beautiful jeweled necklace about her throat. Once he secured the latch, he placed his arms around her. "There, this will do for my beautiful wife."

"Oh, dearest, it is extraordinarily beautiful; I'm at a loss for words," she told him in a soft voice verging on tears. "You are so full of surprises, so good to me."

He whispered, "Say nothing of it, dearest; I am pleased you approve of it; I stopped prior to leaving London to make the purchase. I have long anticipated a special occasion to present it; there is nothing else to be said. You are exquisite."

He continued his hold on her, swaying slowly. Glowing with satisfaction, he spun her around. "Have I failed to mention my severe affections for you, dearest? Have I faltered in expressing my devotion? If I am guilty of such unpardonable behaviour, I fervently beg your forgiveness; it was unconsciously done, I assure you."

"No, not at all; perhaps not in words, but it is every day implied. I feel it when you smile or when I catch your watchful eye upon me. Yours is a face of expression, you require no words; indeed I am aware of your true feelings."

"Elizabeth, I confess to be the happiest among men."

"That would make me the happiest among women," said she, as Mrs. Jenkinson came knocking at the chamber door.

"I will come directly, but I do require just another moment," Elizabeth promised.

"Very well, Mrs. Darcy."

Elizabeth smiled at him lovingly as she embraced him. "Mr. Darcy, I believe I shall expect the first two dances as well as all those thereafter." To this they both burst into laughter.

Grand Entrance

*V*ERY WELL, ELIZABETH, you had better go to Ann; I shall wait here. We shall descend the stairs together. I do believe that would be advantageous to Ann."

"Yes, dearest, I believe you are right." Elizabeth quitted the bedchamber. She first went to Georgiana's chamber, only to find that she had already joined the party below the stairs. She hurried next to Ann's chamber, finding her anxiously waiting. Elizabeth remarked with glee, "Look at you, Ann, you look like a princess; you are absolutely beautiful. We must not tarry; I believe your mother is most anxious to view you."

"Do you believe she will approve?"

"Approve? Of course she will; who could not approve?"

"You are so very kind."

"Ann, I do believe many guests have arrived; Mr. Darcy and I will descend soon; perhaps you should descend following us, what say you?"

"Yes, I believe I shall. Elizabeth, your gown is outstanding; wherever did you get that exquisite jeweled neckpiece? It is breathtakingly beautiful."

"Your cousin just presented it to me."

"He has exquisite taste, does he not?"

"Yes, he does; I must go to him," she said, granting her a quick hug. "You'll do well; take every opportunity to enjoy each moment. When we reach the base of the stairs, you begin your descent." Then she quickly exited her chamber to join her husband. He was sitting in a chair awaiting her return.

"Ann is pure loveliness; we must descend now so she may make her entrance."

Elizabeth took her husband's arm as they gracefully descended the stairs. When they reached the landing, Lady Catherine neared them. "Elizabeth, you look quite beautiful." Glancing at her nephew, she added, "Fitzwilliam, do you not agree your wife is enchanting?"

Elizabeth just smiled; she could not keep from blushing as he answered, "Yes, she is quite lovely." Elizabeth's face reddened deeper still.

"Fitzwilliam, such a beautiful necklace, you have your father's exquisite taste. I do believe the jewels to have found their proper owner; she does them justice."

"Thank you, Lady Catherine, now observe above the stairs; I do believe you have a surprise about to descend. Watch as this creature of loveliness makes her appearance."

Ann was poised as she gracefully descended. There were several people standing near the base of the stairs, among them Colonel Fitzwilliam. Elizabeth, having already viewed Ann, now focused her attention on Lady Catherine and the Colonel. Lady Catherine stood in awe; her mouth opened slightly. She watched Ann make her graceful descent. The Colonel's eyes filled with excitement. His face beamed with affection; it was easy to see he was struck by her loveliness.

"Oh, Ann, I am so proud. Come dear, come this way, you shall make your entrance in the ballroom now. Allow us to enter first; give us a moment then you shall enter. Colonel Fitzwilliam, will you lend your cousin an arm? Will you escort her into the chamber? I'm sure it will afford you both much distinction," Lady Catherine stated.

"It will be an honour," he replied, marveling at Ann.

Lady Catherine, Elizabeth and Mr. Darcy entered the ballroom. They each immediately turned to await Ann's entry. The Colonel, presenting a natural formality, made entrance to the party with Ann engaged on his arm, pausing at the arch, allowing the gentlemen to bow and the ladies to curtsey as they captured the attention of the entire population of the chamber. The music had begun to play. The Colonel bowed and gallantly extending his hand to Ann, leading her to the floor to start the first dance of the evening.

Elizabeth observed how gallant the Colonel looked, extremely honoured to be Ann's partner. Ann had maintained a sense of poise, making her entrance with all the charm and sophistication expected of a young lady of her rank in society. It was the first Elizabeth witnessed the Colonel dance formally. She was quite surprised by his easy precision, which made a flattering demonstration of his abilities. She thought Ann very lucky to enjoy such an excellent partner, especially for the first two dances.

Lady Catherine sought Mr. Darcy's assistance, leaving Elizabeth to herself for a few unguarded moments. Having been left standing alone momentarily, Elizabeth became aware of two figures coming toward her. It was her cousin Mr. Collins, accompanied by his wife Charlotte. She delighted in seeing her friend again, but was less enthusiastic to meet with her cousin. They had not spoken since that awful day at Longbourn when she happened upon him taking inventory. Until the present, he had managed to avoid her, but now, perhaps, he thought enough time had lapsed. *His ill manners I can never forget,* she mused at the sight of him approaching. She took in air to collect her calm as they drew closer.

Mr. Collins bowed humbly. "I bid you good evening, Cousin Elizabeth. Such a wonderful party; would you not agree?"

"Yes, it is a very nice party."

"So many delightful people, I flatter myself at having been invited to such an important event; however, there was no doubt of our invitation, no doubt indeed. You are aware Lady Catherine regularly requires our presence at all assemblies here at Rosings? We are essential to all gatherings; her ladyship depends on our companionship. How fortunate she extended an invitation to you; I daresay no doubt it is a result of your husband; yes, indeed it must be so."

"Indeed, Mr. Collins," Elizabeth replied apathetically.

Mr. Collins studied her. He frowned, uniting his brows, then studied her attire with greater scrutiny. While his eyes canvassed Elizabeth from head to toe, his lips parted as if he discovered her appearance appalling. "Elizabeth!" he gasped. "I do believe your attire is overstated. After all, my dear cousin, any attempt to elevate above Lady Catherine's rank will not be met with favour. Surely you realize her level of society must be preserved. You should have considered your choice of so elegant a frock. Why, it may offend a woman of Lady Catherine's rank. I daresay, Cousin, you should have thought the better of it. The very fact that you are Mr. Darcy's partner in life should secure wisdom of such delicate matters. You must learn to draw the line of distinction. There is Mr. Darcy's sister to consider as well. You must keenly remember your station, so as not to promote yourself to Miss Darcy's peak of society. Nonetheless, you are expected to dress beneath the level you have so obviously chosen to aspire to; after all, you must remember the association from which you were born. I do believe you erred in judgment in your dress. Such pretences will be viewed scandalous no doubt, no doubt indeed. Perhaps Lady Catherine will forgive this offence once she considers your descent. Yes, indeed, perhaps she may take pity on your lack of good judgment for Mr. Darcy's sake."

"Charlotte, I am pleased to see you," Elizabeth spoke, aiming at ending his foolish conversation of seemingly ridiculous insults.

"Eliza, have you had any word from Hertfordshire? I understand the regiment has returned to Meryton; has your father written of it?"

"No, he has not. I trust your family is in health. What of Mariah; how does she do?"

"Yes, they are all well. Lucas Lodge has been rather quiet, although with the regiment returning, perhaps my father will see his way clear to giving a ball."

"Sounds interesting."

Before Charlotte could say another word, her husband commented, "We enjoy the advantage to mention Mariah is such an agreeable girl of good sense. We congratulate ourselves that there is nothing imprudent in her nature. Her conduct is devoid of any reckless or ill-advised schemes. She demonstrates a high level of decorum, more so than most families can revel. I have taken the liberty to educate her on the importance of her associations; young ladies can never be too guarded. After all, once a reputation is ill marked, there are few that will connect themselves with any regard. The Lucas family's reputable circumstances are valued in Hertfordshire, to which we may boast; indeed it is most highly in our favour. I have heard your sister Kitty has been writing faithfully to a soldier; perhaps we missed the announcement of her engagement?"

Elizabeth's face grew crimson with anger. Determined to hold her tongue, she hesitated, in an attempt to change the subject.

Determined not to be silenced, he hastily continued, "As clergyman, I feel it is my duty to promote and establish harmony. I flatter myself in allowing you, my dear cousin, this opportunity to heal the unfortunate understandings of past offences, especially now that you have found what appears to be felicity in a marriage exceedingly advantageous to a level far from which you were accustomed. I trust you have adjusted to your present level in spite of all you must have had to overcome. It must be very hard indeed, considering your younger sisters. Lady Catherine does not look upon such behaviour with a friendly eye. No, quite the contrary, she condescends to such forbidden actions. We must consider to whom you are now married; it is of the highest importance that your sisters do nothing to cast a veil of contempt on your marriage partner. Nor should you aspire to change in an attempt to elevate your society beyond your known reputation. My dear Charlotte and I are of the same opinion, are we not now?" he asked, turning to his wife seeking agreement. Charlotte, obviously embarrassed by her husband's remarks, remained momentarily at a loss for words; her eyes were wide with shock as she faintly gave a grin, appearing to give no credit to his statement of shared opinion.

"You discharge your opinions with little restraint; perhaps you claim too much, Mr. Collins. I must say I do not hold such pretences. One of the elements of perfect character is the practice of good sense as well as good manners; surely they are prevalent to every good society. Proper decorum does at times come into question indeed, but I feel one who pretends to a virtue he obviously lacks is as dangerous to society as one who prevails upon others that his virtue holds aesthetic value, when in actuality it is for decided conceit, selfish gain or false pride. I assure you I have not changed, neither have I found you so, Mr. Collins; you are just as rude and self-serving as always. Charlotte, I look forward to conversing with you later. Now, I beg your pardon, I'm afraid I have been long desiring my absence from such fatuous intercourse as this," Elizabeth said, hastily parting their company.

Mr. Darcy, now free from Lady Catherine, advanced to rejoin his wife, only to find her immediate presence when he turned about, almost trampling over her.

"Why, Elizabeth, are you unwell? You are pale; has something happened?"

"Insufferable conceit!" she cried in an angry voice.

"What is it, dear, has someone offended you?"

"I'll allow you one guess."

Mr. Darcy looked beyond his wife, immediately catching a glimpse of Mr. Collins. "Oh, Mr. Collins no doubt."

"Yes, Mr. Collins, who takes every opportunity of reviving painful circumstances, making known he is aware of all the particulars of present dealings in the Bennet household; I am beyond displeasure."

"Calm yourself; perhaps we should go to the bedchamber to discuss this."

"Perhaps we should. I am presently of the opinion it is imperative I unburden myself. I do believe it will prove beneficial." The two quickly ventured above the stairs.

Elizabeth conveyed the whole of the exchange to her husband, which angered him as well. He held Elizabeth in a secure embrace.

"The night is young; Mr. Collins has yet to contend with me. I should have thought by now your cousin learned not to encroach on my domain.

He forgets Lady Catherine is my aunt; perhaps he lacks awareness of our favourable circumstances here; nevertheless he is about to be edified."

"What are you going to do?"

"Just let it to me."

"No, dearest, I must know what it is you plan to do."

"It's best you have no prior knowledge of it."

"Oh dear, what of Charlotte and little Richard? I would rather you not do anything. I have no doubt I made myself clear; I should not allow him to agitate me further. Perhaps you should say nothing more on the subject."

"Very well, Elizabeth, I shall try. Such a fatuous excuse of clergy; he lacks all things expected of a man in his position. It is indeed difficult to regulate my propensity to confront such an odious simpleton. I shall try, but I cannot promise you anything. Now, are you prepared to rejoin the others? Are you feeling better?"

"Yes, I suppose I am."

They descended the stairs to rejoin the party. They were instantly approached by Mr. Collins. "Mr. Darcy, such a lovely affair. Your wife is elaborately dressed for the occasion; will you not agree?"

"Mr. Collins, I daresay I am well pleased with my wife's appearance." Before continuing further, Mr. Darcy stepped directly in front of him, leaving enough room to perhaps pass a narrow ribbon between them. Now placing his hands together behind his back he stood tall, swelling his breast as he looked down upon him. His dark eyes drew piercingly narrow, uniting his brows before discharging his next comment. "She is most suitably dressed for such an occasion; will you not agree?"

Mr. Collins viewed him with all the mortification he could muster. He parted his lips as if to speak, but words failed him. He shrunk back only to have Mr. Darcy step to him again. Mr. Darcy turned to Charlotte and Elizabeth. "Elizabeth, Charlotte, might I impose upon you to excuse us. I do believe I should like a few private words."

Not waiting for a reaction from his wife or Mrs. Collins, Mr. Darcy escorted Mr. Collins away by seizing him by the elbow, guiding him out of the chamber.

Charlotte's face turned red. She became apologetic, "Lizzy, I am greatly distressed by Mr. Collins' approach to you regarding your family."

Both ladies now walked to the chamber door. There in the entrance hall, they could see the two plainly, although to Elizabeth it seemed her husband had the upper hand.

"Charlotte, I am sorry for it as well; it pains me; we have always been the best of friends. I confess I have not the understanding of his necessity to bring these past situations to my attention; whatever can his motive be?"

"Eliza, I am sorry for it; I am certain he does not wish to inflict pain. Surely you do not believe I agree with the whole of it?"

"You make it sound as though you do agree in part."

"Why yes, I must admit, much of what he says is true; however, I do not feel it is necessary to bring it to your attention whenever we meet."

"I should say not; just the same it pains me that you agree somewhat."

"Eliza, I wish to put this behind us; we have no quarrel."

"Very well, Charlotte, but allow me to caution you, I have no secrets from my husband; at this very moment he is extremely displeased."

Looking in the direction of her husband, Elizabeth noticed Mr. Collins appeared rather uncomfortable. His face bore a look of disturbance. Mr. Darcy moved from his presence, leaving Mr. Collins to himself, rejoining his wife about the time Charlotte was nearing her husband.

"It looked serious; what did you say?"

"I merely stated it was a lovely party. I told him how wonderful life is when you find deep felicity in a marriage where there are no secrets between husband and wife. I believe he needs time to contemplate. I do not expect him to catch on too easily."

"Apparently not today at the very least."

Elizabeth, hurt by Charlotte's confession, felt devoid of her friendship. Her thoughts were discomforting. Her husband turned to her, extended his hand, then slightly bowed. "Dearest, indulge me, I desire this dance." Interrupting her thoughts, she allowed herself to be led away. The dance provided desired relief. She hoped this would finalize Mr. Collins' need to approach her, at least for the evening.

The first two dances were long past. Elizabeth noticed Ann turning a reel with a gentleman unknown to her. He was tall. Although his face gave a youthful appearance, his manners suggested he was a man of some significance. After the dance, Ann walked him in the direction of Elizabeth and Mr. Darcy, introducing him as John Gibson. Upon closer examination, Elizabeth determined his expression older than his looks. She viewed his character to be superior. Ann appeared delighted with his attentions. It was not long before he requested another dance and the two disappeared.

Elizabeth eagerly observed the crowd; contented to sit out a few dances to view the amusement provided by unsuspecting guests. Capturing Georgiana in her view, she noticed she was involved in conversation with a gentleman from town. Next, she intently viewed Lady Catherine's interaction with several guests. Looking about the chamber, she made notice of Lord Fitzwilliam's success in attempting to get Fanny on the dance floor. The Colonel was himself dancing with a young lady from town. Elizabeth wondered where Lady Catherine encountered so many guests. She noticed Charles and Frank sat side by side, while James danced and the Earl stood along the side, watchful of the evening events. Elizabeth and Mr. Darcy directed themselves to Charles and Frank.

"Why are you not dancing?" Mr. Darcy inquired.

"I have no wish to dance," Frank replied.

"Nonsense," said Charles, "he refuses to dance because I am not able to; he feels he must sit it out to entertain me."

"Elizabeth and I welcome the opportunity to make conversation with you Charles. Frank, please consider dancing," Mr. Darcy urged.

Frank reluctantly ventured across the room to Lady Catherine, who introduced him to a dancing partner almost immediately.

"My brother denies himself pleasure for my sake; you have provided him opportunity to leave my side. He has such a serious temperament, he requires society but rarely allows himself the pleasure of a lady's company."

"Perhaps tonight the circumstances may change. Tell me, how do you do, Charles? I have not had the pleasure or opportunity to speak with you for more than a few moments."

"Very well, Darcy, I am very well indeed; I enjoy my work; Frank takes me wherever he goes. So you see, I want for nothing."

"That is good news indeed."

"Elizabeth, I was admiring your jewels, an outstanding piece."

"Thank you, Charles, your cousin presented them to me this very evening; I am fortunate he has such exquisite taste; is that not so?"

"Indeed. Well, Darcy, I am impressed, you have a beautiful wife whom you unquestionably revere; I understand you have a son and a daughter. It is said you have clearly found unmatched depth of felicity in marriage."

"I confess it is so," Mr. Darcy answered with obvious satisfaction.

Elizabeth blushed; such flattery was too much for one evening, thought she. The present dance had ended. They watched as several couples returned from the dance floor. Frank did not. He managed to secure another dance with the same partner. Lord Fitzwilliam and Fanny left the dance floor, directing themselves toward Elizabeth, Mr. Darcy and Charles.

"Where is my brother Frank?" Lord Fitzwilliam inquired.

Mr. Darcy nodded in the direction of the dance floor.

"Well, well now, however did you accomplish such a feat?"

"We simply suggested he dance, requesting time alone with Charles for private conversation. He really had no choice in the matter, although I do believe he has decided to take advantage of the opportunity; he is on his second reel. Lady Catherine introduced him to the young lady; he has held her captive, I believe."

"I am glad to hear it. Isn't that wonderful, Fanny; do you not agree?" Lord Fitzwilliam asked.

"Yes, how nice of him," she replied in an icy tone. Elizabeth wondered if her remark was capable of an ounce of sincerity.

"Fanny, your gown is lovely," Elizabeth decided to say to be kind.

"Perhaps so, thank you."

"This is such a lovely party, is it not?" Elizabeth asked.

"I suppose one might consider it so, but it is entirely too warm in here, I should need some air; Edward, some air please." She stretched her arm to link with Edward's. Lord Fitzwilliam bowed, obeying as he offered his arm. Within seconds the two disappeared from sight.

Charles looked at Elizabeth. "Do not be alarmed; my sister-in-law is resentful to be here; my brother had to move mountains to convince her to attend. Though she granted him the party, she is determined he shall not delight in it. Do not concern yourself nor look for her to improve on closer acquaintance; save the effort—she is living proof that wealth cannot keep sorrow out of rich people's houses. I believe I am happier in my situation as a cripple, living on a meager income, than she as a woman of wealth who cannot enjoy her comforts. If she finds her life miserable, it is of her own choosing. She does little to expend herself in an amiable fashion. She is most often determined to be uncivil, looking down her nose at most everyone she meets."

"How very sad, I feel sorry for her."

"Oh, do not be sorry for her; why should you? She chooses to offend; I am resolved to think of her no more. Look at my brother James, Darcy; does he not take to the ladies? He has had dances with every girl in the room; I daresay they find him attractive. Darcy what is my brother's concern? Look at him, he looks rather vexed."

"Of whom are you speaking, Charles?" Mr. Darcy asked, leaning into him.

"Why, the Colonel; observe, he is not dancing, only watching the dance floor. Look at his countenance; he looks cross, downright miserable. Whatever can the problem be?"

"Perhaps I shall go see. Dearest, do you mind waiting?"

"Not at all," she answered, as he walked across the room to the Colonel. Although she felt sorry for him, there was little she or her husband could do, especially not on this night. She continued to keep an eye on her husband from across the room.

"Cousin, compose yourself; your frown reveals you. I know what pain you endure; I am exceedingly sorry for it, but you would not wish to injure or put to spoils the happiest day in the life of the one you love; it is so, is it not?"

"You are entirely right, Cousin; I should not wish that. My heart sinks, Darcy; it pains me to watch her in the arms of a stranger. Do I really disclose my discontent?"

"Yes, you look vexed. This is Ann's evening; surely you would not desire her or Lady Catherine to witness you in such a state. Perhaps you should dance with another to divert your thoughts from the present situation. There are some pretty girls in want of a partner," he suggested. He then added, "You'll have to be introduced."

Much to his surprise, the Colonel did just as Mr. Darcy suggested, seeking introduction through Lady Catherine. Mr. Darcy was free to return to Elizabeth.

"Dearest, I was just telling Charles of our plans for a ball at Pemberley following the feast of Michaelmas; we expect all your cousins to attend; is that not so?"

"Yes, to be sure, Charles, you must attend."

"I should like that very much; I'm sure Frank will be delighted."

"Charles, it's been years since you last visited Pemberley; come before the ball and accompany me fishing. I do recall you were always fond of the sport; is that still the case?"

"Yes, indeed it is; I should very much enjoy it, to be sure, Darcy."

"Very well then, I shall depend upon it."

"Indeed, Charles, we should be glad for your visit," Elizabeth added.

Lady Catherine and the Earl joined them.

"I see Ann is still dancing; she did promise to sit out a reel if she were to tire. I'll not approach her on the subject; she will have to make that decision."

"I am certain Ann will keep her promise. There are a great number of couples here this evening, Lady Catherine. I daresay the lavish food displays are splendid; I cannot remember when we had such a delightful evening. It does a father good to see all of his sons under one roof. I do wonder though how you managed to get Frank to dance. He seems quite captured with the young lady. It appears James is making his rounds to each and every unattached lady in the chamber." They all chuckled, having made notice of it earlier.

Mr. Darcy turned to the Earl and Lady Catherine. "If you two would be so kind to keep Charles in conversation until our return, I should very much enjoy a dance with my wife."

"Of course, Darcy, I should like to watch you dance," Lady Catherine gleefully retorted.

"Very well, then," he said, once again extending his hand to Elizabeth. As they danced, Elizabeth noticed Ann. She was radiant, a vision of loveliness as she danced about the chamber with yet another gentleman from town. Her face was bright, glowing, full of colour. Within her view was the Colonel, who had managed to secure a dance with Georgiana. Elizabeth suddenly noticed Mr. Gibson dancing with Fanny, who miraculously seemed to be savoring the delights of the evening. James had still another partner, while Frank continued to dance with his first choice. The delights of the evening only made her anxious for the time she would plan her own ball at Pemberley.

When the dance ended, Elizabeth glanced around the room, apprehending Lord Fitzwilliam and Fanny standing side by side watching the whole of the party. Elizabeth made specific notice of Fanny's fixed study of John Gibson, as he now danced with Ann. Wondering how Fanny managed to be so disagreeable, she knew not why she was drawn to scrutinize her manners, but found it impossible to control the urge to do so. It was with extreme misfortune that her intrigue led her to study Fanny at length. In doing so, she witnessed what she believed to be a licentious exchange of expression between Fanny and Mr. Gibson. Not quite certain, but fairly sure was Elizabeth of her interpretation, having caught the amorous exchange of eye interplay with Ann's dancing partner; she desired to believe it could not possibly be so. She quickly judged such thoughts were best forgotten and quickly looked in another direction. The bold impression reminded her of the Hyde Park ball when Miss Gray passed her own husband an amorous look to gain notice. All such thoughts troubled her.

When the immediate dance ceased, they returned to Charles, allowing Lady Catherine the opportunity to move amid other guests. The Earl remained behind with them.

The remains of the evening passed more quickly than Ann desired. She danced many dances with John Gibson. Lady Catherine seemed quite impressed with him, stating she thought him to be a prospective match for Ann. Ann appeared to desire a further acquaintance. His excellent manners lent him much distinction. Although they seemed equal in propriety and wealth, they were unequal by nature. He was comfortably gracious in company while Ann was more timid, reserved and content to be less daring. She seemed lost when coupled with him, as he advantaged her in every essence of their personalities. He found conversation easily comfortable; Ann was uneasily backward in strange company. Having traveled extensively, he had witnessed and experienced worldly adventures; Ann had seldom escaped the confines of Rosings. She was little acquainted with the world beyond Kent. Nonetheless, the young man seemed quite captivated with Ann. He expressed a desire to call on her in the near future, to which Lady Catherine quickly consented after receiving a look of eagerness to pursue his company from Ann. Such a delightful end to a wonderful party, but not so for the Colonel, who thought his heart would surely break.

Confessions

THE MORNING NEXT, Lady Catherine arose early. Mr. Darcy, being the second to enter the breakfast hall, joined her, allowing a measure of private conversation.

"Good morning, Aunt," he said nearing her, granting a slight hug.

"Why, Fitzwilliam Darcy, I confess I have so enjoyed your attention; that is twice now you have hugged me since your arrival. This has been a fine visit indeed. Was not last evening the very best we have enjoyed in a long time at Rosings?"

"Quite so, to be sure it was."

"I suppose Ann never tired; she only sat out two dances."

"Was she not a sight to behold?" he commented, waiting for a reaction.

"Indeed, Rosings has come to life at last. What think you of this John Gibson?"

"He seems gentleman enough; what say you?"

"He is the eldest son of a wealthy baron; he stands to inherit a vast estate."

"Is it your desire for Ann to marry into wealth?"

"Be not alarmed, my desire is her happiness. I enjoyed felicity in marriage. However, I am sure you realize the importance in a marriage of equality. You'll forgive my saying so, but I maintain the belief that when one marries within one's own rank, bringing to the union equal society as well as position, it is celebrated as a more perfect union. You know my frankness well enough to know I do believe the parties should have some level of affection as well," she stated with certainty.

"Well, I can hardly dispute your notion, but one best have strong affections toward one's intended; surely you desire a match as equal partners in love? Surely you must agree that one must be loyal to his heart?"

"Yes, I must agree; I enjoyed such felicity."

"I'm convinced it is so; yours was a desirable match. I'm inclined to believe your aspirations the same for Ann; are they not?"

"To be sure, it's astounding how unattached one becomes with age."

"Are you speaking of yourself?"

"Most surely I am indeed."

"Reality can be alarming, denial destructive, but change can be gratifying."

"Indeed, I confess it is so," she mentioned with sincerity.

"What of this John Gibson; does he express interest, Aunt?"

"He requests to call; Ann encourages it. I shall not interfere; I believe I have learned from past offences. If she believes herself in love, she must learn to rely on her own decisions."

"Careful, perhaps she still looks for your guidance or regulation."

"Yes, I suppose you are right in some instances."

"Yes, I am sure of it, we all seek guidance; age is insignificant."

"I admit I hold my tongue these days. If he be the man of her choosing, I shall not be the source of division; he is a fine catch, you must agree."

"Perhaps it is wise to use caution when speaking, but voice your opinions just the same. If he is all that Ann desires, you must guide her to some degree."

"How did you gain such wisdom at so young an age?"

He chuckled. "I have not the slightest idea of your meaning."

"Indeed, Darcy, you are wise beyond your years, enough to teach an old aunt."

"Before the others venture below the stairs, I should like to express my happiness regarding your approach of my wife."

"I'm an old woman, Darcy; toward your wife I was unkind, toward you I was dreadfully vexed, to myself I beset embarrassed circumstances. Perhaps I learn lessons hard, but I am not above reproaching myself when I find error in my convictions. Truly I should have preferred you married Ann or someone of your own rank. As far as connections are concerned, you could have done better, but, as for wealth, I am now of the opinion your wealth lies in another form, a fortune acquired perhaps more valuable than money."

"That is very generous of you."

"Not at all, difficult to confess, but once having done so, I found I could not rest until I disclosed the truth of it to you. Can you ever forgive my misgivings, the turn of my countenance toward you?"

"Say no more of it, Aunt, it is forgotten."

"Well now, that is very generous of you."

"Well, thank you just the same; you know we did enjoy the party immensely."

"Yes, I made notice of you with Mr. Collins; you seemed to distress him."

"He astounds me, provokes me too."

"How so?"

"On more than one occasion I have been exceedingly unhappy with his behaviour. I cannot understand the mordancy of the man. He is such a foolish imbecile. Forgive my language, Lady Catherine, it cannot be helped. Last evening was not the first I confronted him. Surely I did not wish to intrude on the evening with such nonsense, but he is consistently cruel to Elizabeth."

"It has made my notice on past occasions, but I am not understanding of it. Why would that be; why is he so intent on injuring her?"

"You really do not know? You have no knowledge of the whole of it, do you?"

"Are you going to tell me or not?"

"After he was long settled on this estate, upon your suggestion that he find himself a wife, Mr. Collins visited Longbourn intending to recommend himself to one of the Bennet girls. He applied for Elizabeth's hand in marriage, but she rejected him. He has never forgiven her for it. He took great delight in communicating the ill manners of her sister. Think it out; from whom did you learn of her sister's running off with George Wickham?"

Lady Catherine sat contemplating his words. After a few thoughtful moments, she returned her cup to the saucer. "I see your meaning."

"Indeed his punishment is to never allow her to forget from where she comes."

"Sometimes it is wisest to leave the past in the past, pity he has not learned it."

"I agree, Aunt, he possesses a perfidious nature. He is determined in his pursuits and indeed never seems to learn."

"Mr. Collins means well but lacks sense, perhaps that is why I enjoy having him about, for surely in his company I am most decidedly superior." She laughed at her statement, believing it to be truth. She smiled before taking another sip of her coffee, then added, "His treatment of Elizabeth is most disturbing."

"Why—you do really like her, do you not? Now surely you can tell me."

"Yes I confess I do like her. I conclude we are a little similar; we are both strong willed and steadfast in our convictions. Yes, I acknowledge I was wrong. It is not so very easy for me to admit it; I daresay such words are difficult. But in confessing it, I must tell you she can stand up on her own to be sure. Come now, Darcy, see how you weakened me."

"Oh, Aunt, that is what I admire in you; I am glad to have you back."

"Whatever do you mean, have me back?"

"You are once again yourself. When my uncle died you became hard in your opinions, quite insufferable to endure. There, that is my confession."

"Oh, such confession at my expense. I hear movement in the hall; I'm glad we seized the opportunity to speak frankly, Darcy; now behave yourself."

They smiled at each other owning to a conversation solely for their own ears, exchanging words of honesty, compassion, confession and truth amid new-found admiration, discovering faded respect rekindled.

Parting of Company

BOTH MR. DARCY AND LADY CATHERINE remained seated at the breakfast table, secure in their individual thoughts. As the room became increasingly busy with hungry houseguests, Mr. Darcy stood to bow before regaining his seat next to Elizabeth. Georgiana gained a seat on Elizabeth's other side.

The table was finished with fine food, laughter and simultaneous conversations, most of which regarded the evening past. Elizabeth communicated the planned ball at Pemberley to inform those present to anticipate invitations, which created excitement in the thought of sharing time together again. Most agreed the separation had been too long, with the brothers discussing the length of time between their last meeting together as an entire family.

Fanny, who chose to be unapproachable, took a seat aside her husband. He was occupied in conversation, while she remained her usual disagreeable self. Most ignored Fanny's disagreeable countenance except Lord Fitzwilliam, whose bondage through marriage doomed him to dote upon her with charmed attention. He endured her ill manners, but after a brief time his attentions were focused on the conversations about the table. She managed to sit out the breakfast with a disgruntled expression, appearing to be quite content to be alone amid a crowd.

Elizabeth was seated within easy distance of Lady Catherine and Fanny. She did her best to make conversation. "Do the splendors of a ball at Pemberley pique your interest, Fanny?"

"Perhaps we shall consider attending."

"I do wish you to come."

"Thank you, Lord Fitzwilliam and I shall discuss it."

"My cousins have not visited Pemberley at length; I have no doubt the ball will be a splendid affair; I do wish you to consider," Georgiana injected shyly.

"And I—of course I expect you and Ann, Lady Catherine to be sure."

"Indeed I should not wish to miss such an affair."

"I so look forward to planning it."

"Is there a reason you wait until after Michaelmas?" Lady Catherine inquired.

"Yes, Mr. Bingley will settle on Michaelmas for the Foxshire Estate, an easy distance of Pemberley. I cannot tell you how happy I shall be to have Jane imminent to me."

"Are you speaking of Charles Bingley and his sisters Caroline and Louisa?" Fanny inquired with interest.

"Indeed I am," Elizabeth answered.

"Quite interesting," Fanny retorted.

"Indeed!"

"I am acquainted with Mr. Bingley and his sisters," Fanny abruptly revealed.

"Why, Fanny, I was not aware of it."

"Yes, I know Charles quite well."

"Oh, then you must attend the ball; surely he will be happy to see you."

Elizabeth thought her proclamation the source which influenced Fanny's sudden interest. It caught Elizabeth by surprise; she had not expected such attention or civility. She was glad to finally come to a common ground of conversation, but once again the cold chill of Fanny's demeanour surfaced as she managed to dampen the moment with her sarcastic reply.

"Perhaps, we shall see if it agrees with our plans," then she arose from her chair, directing herself toward the sideboard with her nose in the air. It was difficult to determine if Fanny was genuine. Nonetheless, Elizabeth was determined to feel warmer toward her; she hoped for Lord Fitzwilliam's sake she would consider attending the ball.

Ann eventually made her entrance after most had already breakfasted. Even so, they remained about the table, providing her with attention of comments on the evening past, contributing generous statements of her captured loveliness.

"Good morning, Ann, I trust you slept well?" Mr. Darcy asked.

"Indeed I did," she said, taking a seat next to the Colonel, who eagerly awaited her.

"Good morning, Ann; dare I say you delighted us all last evening. I am quite sure you were not aware of your elegance," the Colonel told her.

"Why, thank you, Cousin, we made a handsome pair on the dance floor, did we not now? I had no idea you could move about with such grace."

"Oh, be assured, I am quite fond of dancing. He then turned his attention to Georgiana. "Georgiana, I had wished to capture you for an additional dance, but I daresay you were certainly not in want of partners."

Georgiana shyly felt her face warm. "No, I was not, but I did notice your pleasure in dancing with Ann; you two do very well together."

"That was obvious; how fortunate for me the Colonel requested the first two dances. It was a splendid start to a most agreeable evening."

"Yes, but that was all I managed; I had rather wished for more," he said with a complaining voice that drew unrelenting jeers from his brothers.

Ann laughed as his brothers continued to jeer while Elizabeth and Mr. Darcy afforded him a consoling look. Elizabeth pitied him, realizing no one present knew or understood his pain as well as she and Mr. Darcy, not even Ann.

"Ann, what of this John Gibson?" asked the Earl with piqued interest.

"He is very agreeable indeed; I liked him very much."

The Earl leaned forward. "Is he not of extensive wealth?" the Earl continued his inquiry.

"I believe he is; yes, Uncle, indeed he is."

"Very good then, Ann, you have my blessing."

Again Elizabeth pondered the hurt the Colonel now suffered. Such words of encouragement from his father's lips were certainly piercing. Fanny provided her wish for a change of conversation.

"Mr. Gibson is quite handsome; he is surely a most desirable catch, with great wealth about to be his. If I were not attached, I would surely do my best to secure him, indeed I would."

With all faces drawn silently in Fanny's direction, the stillness was interrupted by Lord Fitzwilliam. "Well, my dear, that is not the case now is it?"

"Indeed it is not," Fanny coldly answered.

The unsettling words dampened the perspective until Elizabeth changed the discourse. "The food was extravagant, Lady Catherine, I thought the music delightful as well. You must have worked very hard to bring the whole of the evening about."

"I believe I enjoyed the planning of the event; I do indeed view it a success. You know I had not done such an assembly in years. Rosings was once a frequent social stop; we enjoyed parties and balls quite often. Where does time go?"

"I believe last evening was a night of remembrance," Charles added.

"Indeed I enjoyed myself far beyond expectation," Frank retorted with satisfaction.

"Thanks to Darcy here, who practically forced you to dance. The fact that you continued to dance did not go unnoticed," Charles said with obvious glee.

"Now I am embarrassed," Frank said as his face coloured to a deep crimson.

"Come now, Frank, we so enjoyed watching you," Elizabeth reported.

"To be sure, you were much admired indeed," the Earl chimed in.

"Perhaps we should employ another subject; how about James?" Frank added.

"Speaking of James, how was it you convinced so many ladies to agree to dance with you? Why you must have danced with half the ladies in the chamber!" Lord Fitzwilliam teased.

"I simply smile at them."

"You sly thing, you flatter yourself, or should I say them," Frank injected.

"But of course, I confess they must find me irresistible."

"I see we are modest too!" Frank teasingly returned.

Elizabeth looked at Mr. Darcy. "We enjoyed a few dances, did we not now, dear?"

"I confess I did. Indeed, having the proper dancing partner makes an immense difference; surely I may lay claim to superiority in that respect."

Ann looked at Lord Fitzwilliam. "What of you, Edward; did you not enjoy dancing?"

"To be sure, I always enjoy a good dance."

"And, Fanny, did you as well?"

"Yes, Ann, it was agreeable," she replied flatly with little expression.

Elizabeth was surprised she found it agreeable. She was happy Ann did not appear affected by Fanny's demeanour.

Now mid-morning, the parties gathered about the table discussed departing Rosings. It was obvious it was not Lady Catherine's desire to have the whole of the party quit the place at once, as she no longer desired quiet habitation.

"Darcy, perhaps you might agree to spend an additional night?" Lady Catherine directed with anticipated hope.

Mr. Darcy turned to his wife, who afforded him an agreeable nod, then next to Georgiana, who was equally eager to concur. "I believe we shall; it is settled then; I will send a message to Pemberley at once," he said, rising from his chair to care for the matter.

Lady Catherine was clearly pleased with the decision. Ann spoke with excitement. "Perhaps we may journey into the village this very afternoon?"

"Yes, I don't see why not. We shall all go, if that is agreeable?"

Elizabeth nodded her pleasing approval. She considered her ladyship's appeal a most welcome declaration of her earnest desire to be in her company.

Lady Catherine extended the invitation to the remaining company; however, most were required to return home except for the Colonel, who believed he could stay an additional night as well, which was congenial to Ann.

It pleased Georgiana to stay an addition day. Ann's altered state was comforting, but no more than the consolation of seeing her brother once again in the good graces of Lady Catherine.

The Earl, along with his sons and Fanny made their departure shortly before noon. Although Elizabeth was sorry to see them go, the absence of Fanny was not viewed as a great loss. Fanny's presence seemed to place an exhausting burden on the gathering. She possessed little or no interest in her husband's family unless the subject revolved around wealth or superior circles. Elizabeth could not overlook Fanny's brightened demeanour with the mention of Mr. Gibson. The very mention of his name appeared to pique Fanny's interest, therefore prompting her to inquire further of his family situation. Elizabeth wondered if anyone else made notice how, upon learning of his certain inherited wealth, Fanny took an immediate liking to his character. Try as she did to suffer Fanny, the whole of her company was particularly straining. Fanny's only driving force seemed to revolve around her self-serving desires. Elizabeth was none too sorry to part from her company. It took quite extensive time to bid farewell, and no one, perhaps with the exception of Fanny, was too eager to take their leave. The gentlemen promised her ladyship a return visit before long, to which Lady Catherine expressed her enthusiasm that hopefully she would be receiving them again soon.

The Gentleman Caller

As the carriage departed Rosings, Ann could not conceal her delight in the prospect of going into the village. The Colonel and Mr. Darcy rode their horses alongside the carriage.

It is all so beautiful, thought Elizabeth. Well aware it was her temperament to admire nature's beauty, she was ceaselessly pleased with the picturesque countryside.

Ann was in the highest of spirits as she looked out of the carriage window with widened eyes. "Oh, the delights of last evening's party, at times I think I should have to pinch myself to make certain it was real. And to think, all plans have been arranged to everyone's mutual satisfaction. Now here we all are, such a triumph."

Lady Catherine leaned forward to look at Ann. "Yes, but, Ann, you must be careful not to over extend yourself."

"Yes, Mother, but you must agree, I am quite vigorous for having had such an exciting evening. I do believe it has had no ill effect on my health; would you not agree?"

Elizabeth looked at Lady Catherine, awaiting her answer. "Yes, I confess your colour is good; I suppose it has had no ill effect on you. I still require time to accustom myself to it all."

"Up ahead is the vicar's house. Mother, look, look—there is a man frantically waving off in the distance. Look how he runs after the carriage. Why—why, it is Mr. Collins!" Ann voiced excitedly. "It is plain to see he wishes us to make his notice."

The carriage started to slow its pace. Lady Catherine leaned forward, placing her face near the open carriage window. With a determined air of superiority, she elevated her voice, "Colonel, tell the driver to continue on."

The Colonel did as she requested, but noticed Mr. Collins continued his pursuit of the moving carriage as he crossed the lawn to greet it. With the carriage regaining its steady pace, Lady Catherine merely nodded as the carriage passed him by.

Mr. Collins, by some imperceptible measure displayed a consciousness of all that shattered his hopes of recognition. With impertinent freedom, he shouted, "Lady Catherine, you must stop!" He was out of breath, slowing his chase with unrestrained wonder overspreading his looks. His brows united in mortification as he halted his pursuit of the carriage, which had now left him to stand in its dust. Elizabeth thought it odd that Lady Catherine did not acknowledge him beyond a nod. It was of little matter, thought she, quickly drawing her attentions back to the picturesque countryside.

Shortly after the carriage entered into that part of the village where the shopping district was so alluringly situated, the driver stopped. The footman assisted the ladies to the cobblestone walk, where a variety of shops displayed their finest in the windows. Lady Catherine was eager to promote the necessity of a purchase. Elizabeth noticed Georgiana's selective taste and careful inspection. They managed a few purchases before wandering across the cobblestoned street to view a smart bonnet in a milliner's shop window. Ann viewed the bonnet. "I have a severe desire to own it."

"Well," said Lady Catherine, "there is no question; you shall have it."

As the three turned to enter, a gentleman afoot crossed the street, moving in their direction. Having caught their attention, he now crossed over to them.

"Why, Mr. Gibson, we had not expected to see you; good day to you, sir."

"Good day to you, Lady Catherine, Miss de Bourgh, Mr. and Mrs. Darcy and the rest of your party," he nodded, then bowed confidently.

"It is a fine day, is it not?" Ann quickly stated.

"Yes, quite so! What brings you to the village?"

Lady Catherine perked up. "Ann decided we should visit some shops."

"What a happy chance we meet," said Ann with unrestrained excitement.

Mr. Gibson quickly made himself the principal spokesperson and Ann the object of his attentions. He scarce took his eyes from her. "I would so very much like to stop by Rosings this evening. I confess I must beg to be excused presently, I have pressing business which requires my immediate attention."

"Very well, Mr. Gibson, we shall expect you this evening; perhaps you would consider joining us for dinner?" Lady Catherine said before his parting. He was quick to accept the invitation. Without further hesitation he parted their company.

The Colonel, appearing rather agitated, neared Elizabeth to whisper, "He is very smooth; he is exceedingly anxious to become acquainted at Rosings."

Elizabeth made no answer; she merely gave him a slight stare. The Colonel stood quietly, having nothing more to say; his mind was unpleasantly engaged in the thought of losing Ann's affections. Elizabeth could see his instant depressed state clouded his previous happy temper. Lady Catherine seemed distracted with the anticipated visit, giving no sign of noticing the sudden turn of countenance in the Colonel.

Ann's excitement was no less visible than her delight to shop. Elizabeth and Mr. Darcy managed to smile pleasantly, avoiding meeting the Colonel eye to eye.

As they entered the millinery shop, Ann's eyes fixed on a bonnet. "Mother, I do believe you would look well in this; I dare you the purchase."

Lady Catherine tried it on. "I believe you are right; I shall take it."

Mr. Darcy eyed his wife and sister intently as they milled over the many choices available. "I insist you both make a purchase."

Elizabeth wasted little time in executing his wish. In the beginning, Georgiana searched but found nothing to please her taste, but at last she came across a bonnet she could not resist.

"Since you ladies dawdle at length, the Colonel and I will cross over to the haberdashery. We shall return directly to settle with the shopkeeper."

"Very well, if you insist," Lady Catherine was quick to answer. It took little time for the gentlemen to exit the millinery.

Mr. Darcy purchased gloves as well as a new top hat, but the poor Colonel's thoughts were still fixed on the possibility of Ann being lost to him forever, so he lacked the concentration of a purchase, quitting the shop empty-handed. The gentlemen crossed the street again to the millinery shop. When the ladies made their exit, each had a new bonnet, professing it a successful afternoon. The gentlemen were glad to terminate the shopping journey. They were eager to return to the confines of Rosings.

At Rosings they sought a quick bite of nourishment before directing themselves into the drawing room. The Colonel appealed to Elizabeth to play the pianoforte. Elizabeth neared the instrument to play two tunes before joining her husband on the sofa. Upon Elizabeth's insistence, Georgiana now took a turn. The whole of the party listened intently while she played. Ann expressed her desire to some day play well, while Lady Catherine rolled her eyes at the thought of her lessons.

Mrs. Jenkinson entered the chamber. "Lady Catherine, Mr. Collins has come to inquire if her ladyship would like him and his wife to join your party this evening?"

"I had not given thought to it—no, tell him no; I have ample companionship this evening; tell him I would prefer to invite them another time."

"Very good, ma'am," she replied, then quit the chamber.

Lady Catherine looked at Mr. Darcy; the irritation of the uninvited request perturbed her. She first pressed her lips tight, but then parted them to speak. She leaned toward Mr. Darcy. "The absurdity of that man; I believe I see your meaning where he is concerned. It must unsettle him to know your wife is welcomed here. Have you any notion of the frequency of letters through the post scrutinizing the events at Longbourn?"

"One can only imagine."

"Yes, I believe I see more clearly now."

Lady Catherine was now distracted by the return of Mrs. Jenkinson. "I beg your pardon, ma'am, but Mr. Collins wishes me to say, he and Mrs. Collins have no fixed engagements this evening. He wondered if you might wish to reconsider since his cousin is one of your guests; he believes I misunderstood your meaning, suggesting perhaps that I misdirected your answer."

"Tell Mr. Collins I have no desire to see him. Be sure to tell him not to press the matter any further. I do believe we can do without his company," she stated with displeasure. Then she mumbled aloud, "Foolish man."

Lady Catherine leaned toward Mr. Darcy again. She said in a low voice, "I think it curious he should stoop to such a request, having never done so before. I find it equally odd he comes himself to inquire; why did he not send a servant?" She sat silent for a few moments, then stated, "I do believe your presence concerns him; yes, it must be so; it is quite ill mannered of him, to say the very least. I am displeased with his intrusion, especially in light of our most recent conversation. I am greatly vexed."

Mr. Darcy retorted, "I am resigned now to reflect upon the merit of his sincerity."

Another half-hour passed before a servant entered to announce the arrival of John Gibson. He bowed graciously. He was quick to join in conversation, paying particular attention to Ann. Ann applied to Elizabeth for entertainment in the form of a song at the pianoforte to entertain her guest.

Colonel Fitzwilliam slumped into a rather reserved state, while Lady Catherine grew excessively talkative. Mr. Darcy picked up his glass of port. He conveniently placed himself at his wife's side at the pianoforte. Mr. Gibson and Ann claimed a place near the instrument as well. Although he enjoyed listening to his wife play, on this particular occasion Mr. Darcy engaged his attentions upon Mr. Gibson. Mr. Gibson seemed eagerly pleased with everything Ann said. He was all politeness, attentive and seemingly proficient with compliments. Ann was without doubt eager to receive those attentions so obviously unfamiliar to her. Mr. Darcy would have expected more reserve from a gentleman of wealth. His eagerness for acceptance was equally puzzling. He said not a word but continued to view the situation curiously, lifting his glass to his lips periodically.

When Elizabeth completed the two tunes, they returned to the sitting area. Mr. Darcy kept a watchful eye on the situation, hoping Mr. Gibson would do or say something to contradict his affected behaviour, but Mr. Gibson represented himself well.

Elizabeth solicited Georgiana to play a few tunes. To Elizabeth's comfort, the Colonel joined her at the pianoforte. Elizabeth worried of the pain the Colonel was sure to be suffering.

After dinner, the card tables were assembled. Although Elizabeth and Mr. Darcy did not frequent card playing, they made exception on this particular night, affording Mr. Darcy closer opportunity to consult his own feelings regarding Mr. Gibson. The Colonel did not play; he instead moved a chair near Ann, realizing she was not well acquainted with the game. Lady Catherine, so engrossed in the game, paid little attention to anything else. After looking at his pocket watch, Mr. Gibson stood. "Pray you'll excuse me, I am expected home early. I fear I am required to take my leave at once."

Ann's lips parted as if she wished to speak, but the opportunity soon passed when Lady Catherine asked in a surprised voice, "Must you leave so soon, Mr. Gibson?"

"I fear I must. Thank you for your kind hospitality; it was indeed a pleasure. Rosings is such a beautiful estate, but no more beautiful than the young lady who resides here," he said as he bowed. He kissed Ann's hand, looking into her eyes with an irresistible, unduly favourable pause, then bid his final farewell, directing the whole of his charmed attention at Ann before quitting their presence with expedient decorum.

"Is not he exceedingly fine?" Ann inquired, clutching her hands together to her chest, releasing a pacifying gasp.

Lady Catherine wasted not a moment. "He is quite a fine gentleman."

"What say you, Cousin?" Ann inquired, turning to the Colonel.

"Uh, he is quite the fellow; I'll give him that!"

Ann turned to Elizabeth, "Elizabeth, what say you of him?"

"Well now, he seems quite the gentleman, very handsome indeed."

"He appears to be a rather fine gentleman," Georgiana added.

The whole of the party turned their attention in the direction of Mr. Darcy, who sipped his port. He looked in their direction with his lips slightly parted, realizing all eyes were on him. He remained silently reserved, saying not a word until Lady Catherine interrupted his solitude. "Well, Darcy, you seem to be the only party with no opinion on the matter; speak up, what say you?"

"I know nothing of the gentleman to pass judgment one way or the other. He seems well enough; what do we really know of him?"

"Darcy, I'm shocked; are you so reluctant to give a favourable opinion?" Lady Catherine asked, her brows knitted together.

"Until such time I sketch his character, I am of the notion I should make no commitment on the matter. You wish me to delight in the fine prospect, which you profess to describe; I am inclined to reserve my opinion until such time as one is formed of my own doing. As I stated, he seems gentleman enough, represents himself well I believe."

"Cousin, I am surprised; do you not like him?" Ann inquired.

"Ann, it is not a matter of like or dislike; I have no knowledge of the man."

"Very well then, I'm disappointed in your answer."

"I am earnestly sorry, Ann; I cannot tell you what you wish to hear merely to please you, that would be less than honourable. Surely you realize I hardly know the man; what do we know of him?"

"He comes from a celebrated family. Darcy, I am not understanding you," Lady Catherine retorted.

"I cannot give opinion where none exists. I have not said anything against the man; I merely stated I do not know him. Allow that I am more reserved, read nothing into it," he explained, attempting to direct attention from himself.

Lady Catherine looked vexed. Shaking her head, she pressed her lips together. "Very well, I see it is a hopeless matter to expect an opinion."

Elizabeth eyed him. She knew it was his nature to reserve his good opinion in any case. However, believing she knew her husband well, Elizabeth surmised he preferred not to make known his concern. She proceeded to assist him in a change of subject.

"Well, Colonel, was Ann able to learn any card tricks from you?"

"No, I daresay there were none to be had."

"I must say I am extremely fatigued; it's been a long day has it not?" Elizabeth mentioned, hoping for collaboration to end the evening on a positive note.

The Colonel looked at Elizabeth. "I confess I am weary as well; since I must take my leave very early tomorrow, I believe I will turn in."

A very tired Georgiana agreed. "I believe I would wish to rest as well."

"Well, I suppose if everyone is turning in, I might do so myself. It has been busy here, you know," Lady Catherine announced to Elizabeth and Mr. Darcy's satisfaction.

Less tired was Ann, who lingered in the steady excitement only a gentleman caller could provide; but soon she also announced, "I suppose I will go to my chamber to read."

"Well, Ann, I shall be gone when you awake tomorrow. I must return to my regiment; I shall leave very nearly 5:00 a.m., so I will bid you farewell tonight," retorted the Colonel. After a long, hesitant view of her, he bowed, then quickly disappeared above the stairs.

Elizabeth and Mr. Darcy were no less eager for the escape. They departed to their bedchamber directly after the Colonel. Elizabeth, now enthusiastic for further discussion of Mr. Gibson, turned swiftly to her husband as soon as they entered the bedchamber. "Dearest, do you have a serious regard for Mr. Gibson; whatever were you contemplating?"

"It was exactly as I stated; I have no opinion on the subject."

"I know you too well, something troubles you."

"No, Elizabeth, I prefer not to discuss it since there is nothing to discuss."

"Very well then, have it your way if you will," she told him, feeling slighted by his refusal to discuss what she obviously felt was a concern.

The morning arrived all too soon; the Colonel rose early taking his leave at 5:00 as planned. Mr. Darcy and Elizabeth breakfasted with Ann and Lady Catherine before bidding their good-bye.

Lady Catherine faced Elizabeth. "Thank you, my dear."

Elizabeth smiled. Putting her hand on Lady Catherine's upper arm, she replied, "We expect to see you both at the Pemberley ball."

"Yes, indeed, we most certainly expect to be there; we surely should not wish to miss it," Ann called to them as the carriage pulled away.

Reservations

As the carriage passed over the rough country lane, Elizabeth eyed her husband. "Do you have ill feelings with regard to Mr. Gibson?"

"No, not at all, quite the contrary; in fact, I'm exceedingly disturbed for having no feelings of him; I simply afford no opinion."

Georgiana just sat, taking in the whole of the conversation, paying particular attention to her brother.

"I'm not understanding you, dearest, of what are you speaking?"

"I cannot reproach a man I find no fault with; I see no blemish in his countenance; his character seems good enough, I suppose. I am unable to form an opinion when I feel nothing either incontestable or opposing, yet I find I am indifferent to him." He hesitated, then stated, "I have reservations I cannot illustrate."

"Am I to understand he concerns you, but you find no reason for it?"

"In that respect, yes."

"So, although you do not feel unfavourable toward him, you are uncomfortable to think favourably of him; is that not so?"

"Perhaps your understanding is much greater than anticipated."

"Yes, I believe I do see. You have inherent perception you are unable to determine as yet because you feel something unexplainable."

"To be sure, Elizabeth, I own to a most uncomfortable feeling."

"What do you intend to do?"

"What can I do? He only visits at Rosings; I have no right or wish to cause alarm."

"You believe he has set his designs on your cousin?"

"Yes, I believe that is so. I am not of the understanding as to why a man of vast means, family and connections advances in haste. His perfection

384

disturbs me; he is too eager to please. He conducts himself in a manner to be agreeable in every instance. Much is required of a man whose fortune is entailed to him."

"Are you judging him by your own actions?"

"Perhaps, but I think not."

Elizabeth turned to Georgiana. "What say you, Georgiana, of this John Gibson; what is your opinion?"

"I cannot say; I suppose I found him very agreeable. He solicited me for a dance. Although he conducted himself as a gentleman, I did believe he asked me far too many questions concerning Pemberley as well as my situation. I had not anticipated him to be so interested in my connections or wealth; I thought it rather odd of him to inquire to such a degree."

Elizabeth turned to her husband. "What of your cousin Ann; what are your feelings where she is concerned?"

"While Ann's recent accomplishments may be intrusive to the situation, it would be presumptuous of me to bring this to the attention of my aunt; would you not agree? Ann had not had the direction young girls normally receive."

"Whatever do you mean?"

"Consider the swiftness to which her life altered; she knows little of men."

"Well, dearest, one has to start somewhere," Elizabeth resolved compassionately.

"Perhaps you are right, my dear."

"I have no suggestions. I do empathize with the Colonel, although I am of the opinion he appears to be accepting his position well," she added sadly.

Georgiana looked puzzled. "Does our cousin have designs on Ann?"

"The Colonel has nothing to recommend but himself; he is in no position to make any claims. His affections are known only to us, and now you, Georgiana. You must keep this to yourself. It is true, our cousin loves her; always has, I believe. You must forget what you have heard. Our aunt may not see him as a suitable match. What has he to offer?"

"Oh, Brother, it is very sad; you know the Colonel is an excellent man. What a pity he is not the eldest; certainly our aunt would be quick to agree to such a match. But, Brother, what of Ann; does she know the Colonel is in love with her?"

"We believe so, but we are not certain. Now I fear it may be lost on Mr. Gibson."

"Yes, I see your meaning," she uttered as she sat back in the seat.

"Georgiana, we must hope for the best," Elizabeth stated.

"Brother, I should like to quit Pemberley early in the morning to direct myself toward London."

"Why so abruptly, Georgiana?"

"I wish to continue my studies. Since I am to return for the ball, I should wish to leave right away. You will not think ill of me for desiring London society, Brother?"

"If that is your wish, Georgiana, so be it."

"Oh, Georgiana, it is always hard to say good-bye to you."

"And I you, Elizabeth."

The rest of the journey was uneventful; beyond speaking of the Colonel and Mr. Gibson, they now discussed how anxious they were to see Deborah and Joseph.

A Matter of Concern

ELIZABETH'S SITUATION AT PEMBERLEY provided ample opportunity to enjoy grounds advantageously distinct, uniting beauty with enterprise. The estate of Pemberley was known to shelter the finest land in all of Derbyshire. Since her marriage, she had enjoyed frequent turns about the grounds, reasoning one could easily boast of its rich woods of fine timber. The lush valleys, which snugly spilled into rich meadows with several neat farms scattered about, equally captured her admiration. The three occupants of the barouche box were quick to agree how happy they were to be home at last.

Mr. Darcy and Elizabeth immediately went above the stairs to view the children. "Dearest, they are awake. Look, they are playing," Elizabeth said, as Mr. Darcy picked up Deborah while Elizabeth took Joseph. Happy for all maternal feelings, she now experienced extreme satisfaction in her position as wife and mother. They spent several hours in the nursery before the children's nap. When they ventured below the stairs, Mrs. Reynolds approached them. "Several letters were delivered post; the letters are in your office upon your desk."

They quickly went to the office. One letter was from Jane, another from Archibald Knisely and yet another for Elizabeth, unmarked by its sender.

Mr. Darcy sat down to read his letter from Mr. Knisely. Elizabeth quickly opened the letter from Jane, which had just arrived that very day.

My Dearest Lizzy,

Something unexpected has occurred which could prove to be serious. Mr. Bingley and I have been called to London immediately; we take our leave today, Monday. Our dear sister Lydia is gravely ill. We are called upon to take

Hannah, as she has not the ability to care for her. I am not aware of the nature of Lydia's illness, although I must assume it cannot be taken lightly considering she is with child.

Mr. Bingley and I plan to stop at Pemberley after leaving London. It seems an age since we were last together. You may expect us on Wednesday or Thursday at the very least. We trust all is well at Pemberley; our regards to Mr. Darcy.

Yours, Jane

After reading Jane's letter, Elizabeth sank back into the chair, her eyes staring into space. Her looks bore a mixture of concern and distress. Upon noticing his wife's demeanour, Mr. Darcy inquired, "What is it, dearest?"

"Jane and Mr. Bingley are on their way to London to pick up Lydia's child. Lydia is gravely ill; she is unable to care for her."

"What is being done for her?"

"I do not know; they will come to Pemberley from London."

"When are they to be expected?"

"I believe today or tomorrow, according to her letter."

"Very well, who is your other letter from?"

"I have not yet opened it," said Elizabeth, deep in thought, thinking of her sister. She felt guilty for having done nothing to help Lydia; perhaps if she had— "What has Mr. Knisely to say?" she asked, attempting to keep her mind off Lydia.

"He has come into the custody of a rare collection of books by Couper he believes I may desire. I shall request he send them to me. He wishes us to stop on our next trip to London. He desires to welcome us at his home. He wishes to introduce us to his wife Margaret, the remainder is general information."

"I should like that, I believe," Elizabeth smiled, expressing a desire to go to London as well. Elizabeth decided to open the second of the letters. As soon as the seal was broken, Elizabeth realized the letter was penned by Lydia's hand. She sat up straight in the chair as she frantically read.

My Dear Lizzy,

I suppose you have known long already Mr. Darcy paid our rent as well as laid out money for the six months following. I hope you don't think ill of me for not writing sooner to thank you for responding to my letter asking you to speak to Mr. Darcy on our behalf. It did not escape my thoughts. I now express those thanks to you. Do be so kind as to thank him for the beef as well as the other goods he had delivered to our household. Mr. Darcy did not leave his name with the landlord or grocer, but the description fit him, so I knew you sent him. Little Hannah walks now. I can scarce believe how lively she is. I must close now, Lizzy; I am so very tired I must rest; I have not been well. My sincere regards to your husband.

Yours, Lydia

"Dearest!" she said with some alarm.

Mr. Darcy raised his head from his reading. "Yes?"

"Did you pay Lydia's rent while in London?"

"For what reason do you ask?"

"This letter is from Lydia; she writes, here—" Elizabeth sighed, "here, you read it." She handed him the letter. He leaned forward in his seat as he read with his arms on the desk. She continued to watch him. He let out an extensive sigh as he frowned before raising his eyes to meet hers. He swallowed hard, then drew his lower lip in before addressing her, "I confess it is so; I did pay the rent while I was in London."

"But you never mentioned you saw Lydia."

"I did not see Lydia while in London."

"I am not understanding your meaning?"

"Your Aunt Gardiner informed me as to where she lived. I visited the neighbourhood, discovering the door bore an eviction notice. I looked up the landlord and paid back rent along with six months in advance. Yes, it was I who sent the goods. I desired to hold no secrets from you, but surely you understand my not wishing to concern you; there was nothing pleasant to tell. My only reason for secrecy was that I feared it would cause you suffering; my intent was to spare you the pain of her situation. Dearest, do tell me, this letter indicates she wrote to you requesting assistance; is that not so?"

"Yes," she sighed, "she needed assistance; I refused to tell you of it. I am neither fond nor comfortable keeping anything from you, but I was embarrassed. I had not the notion she truly was in want. I did, on a few occasions, send her a bit of my pin money. I desired to spare you the pain of Wickham's bad manners, believing him the source of her writing."

"And I chose not to concern you of my deed so as not to worry you. We certainly are a match, are we not, my dear?"

"Did you see George Wickham while in London?"

"I saw him; he did not see me."

"Why would you do this for a man so undeserving of your assistance?"

"Surely it was not for him it was done. The place appeared vacant, but I heard the child's cry. I could not allow a child in want. Your aunt informed me of the sad situation. They had been providing assistance as well. It was within my power to abet. I had not expected her to inquire as to who laid out money for it, nothing more."

"Nothing more. I can scarce believe this!" she said in a shocked voice.

"Elizabeth, surely you are not angry with me?"

"Not at all, quite the contrary."

"Very well then, both these letters are a matter of grave concern. Lydia may be alone as well as ill. I shall send a messenger to catch Bingley to bring her here if need be."

"Why do you believe she may be alone? You have not told me the whole of it; is that not so? Yes, that is it, I see it in your manner; you must tell me this instant."

"The landlord informed me George Wickham is about town, never home."

"Dearest, she has made a foolish match, I fear she suffers for it now, but is it our concern? Why should it be your concern after the way Wickham treated you?"

"The child is our concern, Elizabeth. I shall dispatch a messenger immediately; perhaps we can catch Bingley through your uncle. If she is very ill they should bring her here; truly your aunt claims Lydia is looking very ill. I did not like the sound of it whilst I was in London. I can hardly turn my back on your sister; surely you would not have me do so. I would do as much for a servant or the people on my land."

"Are you sure you wish to do this?"

"Yes, there is nothing else to be done; pay no mind to Wickham's treatment of me; she cannot depend on him. I learned as much in London. He is a blackguard of the worst kind to be sure. When I first went to London to pay his debts as well as to see that he did the honourable thing by your sister, I realized then how very much she loved him. In spite of all her foolishness, it was obvious she had an innocent, misguided notion of him as a man. I am sure she had not expected him to turn this bad; surely I myself would have never imagined it."

"Very well, if you are sure—very well—" she replied, searching his expression.

She had thought she held him in the highest esteem, but never so much as this very moment. She watched him rapidly write the note. Looking stern, he dispatched it immediately. His desire was to care for another man's wife who, although her sister, was also the wife of an unprincipled scoundrel who sought to do him ill—yet still he could not tolerate her sister's suffering, nor the want of a child.

The rest of the day passed quietly. The expected Bingley carriage had not arrived. It proved to be a long night, especially for Elizabeth; the anticipation of the arrival of Jane and Mr. Bingley weighed heavily on her mind. They knew not if the message reached its destination in time, leaving little to do but wait.

The Sickbed

M R. DARCY AND ELIZABETH were early to rise, anticipating the parting of Georgiana. By sunrise her trunk was secured, all that remained was the painful parting. Although it was desired she continue her education, it did little to lessen the ill effects of saying farewell. It was but a short time before they watched the chaise disappear down the lane beyond the clearing.

One of the servants announced Mr. Manley's arrival. Mr. Darcy arose from his seat. "Mr. Manley, do come in." He turned to Elizabeth. "Dearest, I failed to mention I invited Mr. Manley to breakfast with us. With the parting of Georgiana, as well as the anticipation of Bingley's arrival, I suppose it escaped my thoughts."

"Mr. Manley, I know my husband was to see you yesterday; do come in."

"Thank you, Mrs. Darcy. Fitzwilliam, I carried out your request."

Elizabeth quickly looked at her husband questioningly. "What request?"

"Your husband asked me to say a special prayer for your sister; he also requested I light a few candles in the church, which I did last evening as well as this morning."

"Well, I hardly know what to say," she said, exasperated, viewing Mr. Darcy intently. His eyes turned glassy. His countenance took an embarrassing turn, then he grew somber. Reflecting upon the deed, his face revealed a look of sheer compassion. He had the ability to speak volumes without saying a word. She had never in her life known anyone who could pour out such depth of feeling through expression alone. He continued to amaze her. She thought of the awful fever that could have robbed her of him; what if he had expired? Whatever would I do?

After they breakfasted, they took a turn about the grounds, carefully staying near the house in hopes of seeing the carriage approach. Morning blended into afternoon. Mr. Manley returned to the parsonage but planned to rejoin them in the early evening for dinner. It was now late afternoon; still there was no sign of a carriage. Mr. Manley returned, joining them as they waited restlessly. Mr. Darcy had the cook plan the dinner later than usual, hoping the carriage would soon arrive. Elizabeth sat at the pianoforte to pass the time. Both were grateful for Mr. Manley's presence, which provided them with a welcomed diversion.

While they waited, they told him of the party at Rosings as well as Elizabeth's meeting Mr. Darcy's cousins. Then Elizabeth explained Mr. Collins to Mr. Manley.

"He sounds like an oddity, especially to find such satisfaction in distinction. I should very much like to meet him. I daresay I have never known a fellow clergyman such as you describe."

"Heaven forbid you should meet him. He seeks every opportunity to gloat at the misfortunes of my family; I fear he does not do his profession credit."

"He sounds like a challenge."

"Challenge? He is thoughtless as well as indiscreet in passing his condescending opinions, I would certainly be embarrassed, especially since he is my cousin."

"Henry, you must understand, he confronts Elizabeth with regard to her family at every convenient opportunity."

"Truly, I should so like to meet him just the same."

"Well I'm afraid you'll have to go to Rosings for that," Mr. Darcy replied flatly.

"Then you do not expect to invite him to the Pemberley ball?"

"Certainly not," Elizabeth said without hesitation. "I believe it is safe to say, Mr. Collins and his wife will never have reason to cross over the threshold of Pemberley, not on the night of the ball most assuredly." Elizabeth sat quite for a moment, then added, "His wife Charlotte was my good friend, although since her marriage she has grown more to his thinking than I am comfortable with. No, Mr. Manley, I see no reason to send an invitation to the Pemberley ball."

"Perhaps we could——"

Just then Mrs. Reynolds hurried into the chamber. "Sir, I believe a carriage is nearing the front of the house."

They hastily ran to the threshold, arriving in time to see the coach come to a full stop. Mr. Bingley exited the carriage. With grave expression he turned to reach inside to retrieve the little girl. In doing so, he turned to Mr. Darcy, "We need assistance; fetch help, Darcy, I fear Lydia is extremely ill, much too ill to make it on her own account."

Mrs. Reynolds immediately ran into the house. Several male servants hurried out to help carry Lydia. It was evident she was very much with child but totally unaware of her surroundings. Elizabeth quickly turned to Mrs. Reynolds. "You know where you are to take her?"

"Yes, ma'am, to be sure."

"Good God, Bingley, she is very ill indeed; how did she ever survive the journey?" Mr. Darcy asked with anguished voice. "I assume you received my message?"

"Yes, we were with the Gardiners when your message arrived. Darcy, we were forced to make several stops; I thought we should never get her here alive. I had the footman stop in Lambton, I was able to secure a Dr. Gordon, whom we expect to arrive directly."

"Good thinking, Bingley, you do yourself credit."

Then realizing Mr. Manley stood nearby, Mr. Bingley anxiously related, "How do you do, Mr. Manley, it was not my intention to slight you."

"That is quite all right, Mr. Bingley, I in no way feel slighted."

"Come, Jane, let us enter the house," he directed his wife. He was still holding the child, who had fallen asleep in Jane's arms, unwilling to give her up to a servant.

"Elizabeth, we require a bed as well as a nursemaid for the child," Mr. Bingley directed.

"Yes, Mrs. Reynolds is prepared for you; take her above the stairs. Bessie or Mrs. Reynolds will meet you; they have waited all afternoon for the child."

"Lizzy, I thought we should never make it; I'm so scared! It was truly awful; Lydia was alone. The child was tending herself. There was no sign of Wickham anywhere."

"What did you do, just take them?" Mr. Darcy asked.

"We left a note, although I did not say we were directing ourselves here, just that Lydia and the child were with Charles and me. I am sure he'll assume we went to Netherfield. I do not expect him to follow. Lizzy, I'm so scared; I fear Lydia is gravely ill," Jane cried.

"Jane, you look pale and tired; are you ill?" Elizabeth asked.

"Lizzy, I could not write of it; I have not been well. Lizzy, there is no announcement, I— I—" was all she said as she started to weep uncontrollably. Mr. Bingley had returned to Jane. In eyeing Elizabeth, he sadly nodded his head to affirm, having arrived in time to hear that part of the painful conversation that caused his wife so much sorrow.

"Oh, Jane, I am so sorry; I did not know," she said as she hugged her, allowing her to have her cry. "Come, Jane, come with me," said Elizabeth as she led her to the office for privacy.

"Lizzy, I could not bring myself to pen it. Charles wanted to write, but I just couldn't tell you. Oh, Lizzy, it was a little boy," Jane said, crying all the harder.

"Oh, Jane, this is all too much; I am so deeply sorry. Perhaps all this is too much for you? Jane, will you be strong enough to care for Hannah?"

"Yes, Lizzy, I will be fine; it is hard not to dwell on the matter. It distracts me; I think of him often, wondering what might have been. I have suffered severe melancholy this last month. Poor Charles hardly knows what to do. I sometimes weep for hours. I confess, until I received Lydia's letter I had rarely left my chamber. It is too hard to be in company. Emily Bingley is so very kind, making every attempt to cheer me; she was as dear to me as you would be, had you been there. She brought me fresh flowers nearly every day and read to me. Lizzy, sometimes I would close my eyes, imagining her you. You are both so very much alike in manners. Even so, I still had no Elizabeth to comfort me; I missed you sorely."

"I am so sorry. My poor Jane, indeed you are pale and tired; it must be very hard for you just now. How does Charles do with the loss?"

"Charles has taken it very poorly; he does not like to speak of it. Emily has been a comfort to him as well. Caroline and Mrs. Hurst do their best, but you know, Lizzy, I believe they lack understanding. I cannot help but believe their feeling to be shallow. Charles has been quiet these past weeks. He is disheartened; I fear he has lost the gleam of excitement he naturally expresses. He often times looks so sad, Lizzy, I can scarcely bear it."

Elizabeth hugged her again. Just then, Mrs. Reynolds approached the office in haste to find Elizabeth. "I beg your pardon, ma'am, Dr. Gordon has arrived; I directed him above the stairs to your sister's bedchamber."

"Thank you, Mrs. Reynolds, we shall follow directly."

"Lizzy, about Lydia's condition, I'm afraid she is much worse off than we realize."

"Jane, I cannot believe her declining condition; she appears very ill indeed; to be sure she has been neglected. How did you find her upon your arrival?"

"Lizzy, we were forced to seek the landlord to gain entry. We found Lydia on the floor with Hannah near her, sobbing. Oh, Lizzy, it was awful to say the very least."

"Well, Jane, you are here now. Dr. Gordon is above the stairs; there is little we can do but pray for Lydia. We had no way of knowing if you received our dispatch; it was a hard wait. I'm so glad you did bring her here. Jane, are you all right? Shall Dr. Gordon have a look at you? Can we get you anything?"

"I will be fine, Lizzy, thank you just the same. I believe little Hannah has captured our hearts, somehow presently filling a void. She is so very precious, is she not? Poor thing, who knows what thoughts occupy her little mind. To be quite honest, Lizzy, if Mr. Darcy had not sent the message, we would have brought Lydia here just the same. I could not leave her in such deplorable condition."

"Jane, we better make our presence above the stairs just now—come."

The two ladies promptly disappeared above the stairs. After Dr. Gordon examined Lydia, he had several questions, most of which remained unanswered. All Jane could offer was that Lydia remained in the same state in which she found her. Dr. Gordon determined Lydia to be far advanced in her term. He observed movement, expecting that was the most positive report he could provide at that moment. He gave instruction to the servant, saying he would return tomorrow to reexamine his patient. He asked she be kept quiet and warm, suggesting she should be carefully watched as well.

Jane and Elizabeth stared at Lydia as she lay unconscious.

"Jane, she looks frail; her looks are indeed altered; she is big with child— not at all like the Lydia we know. She's dark around the eyes. Her face lacks colour; she certainly does appear most harshly unwell."

"Lizzy, it is so unsettling."

"Jane, when Fitzwilliam was in London several weeks ago he visited Lydia's landlord. He settled the back rent. He purchased groceries along with meat from the local butcher to be delivered to her flat. Lydia assumed I informed Mr. Darcy of her letter to me requesting funds. I just learned of this in a letter I received from her yesterday. At first I was uneasy he had done so, now I'm glad he did not deny her needs. Did you advance her a draft, having had time to give it thought?"

"No, I did not."

"Fitzwilliam came across an eviction notice on the door. Surely Lydia must have been taking care of herself with what little others provided. Where do you suppose Wickham was? Surely he was not concerned with their economy so much to engage himself about town. Whatever could he be thinking; what of his children? Blackguard!" With each word Elizabeth became more distressed. She once again glanced down at Lydia. Seeing her sister motionless, she grew angrier.

"Lizzy, Mr. Darcy is indeed a good man. To think of how vilely Wickham treated him. Jane continued with amazement, "Just think of the oddity, Lizzy! Wickham's wife is here at Pemberley, where he grew up. The man Wickham sought to destroy now administers to his wife; there is something so repulsive in it, is there not now. Is there no justice?"

"Jane, my husband continues to astonish me. He demonstrates continuous honourable distinction, the likes of which I have never known in any other—constancy, unwavering constancy— We must descend; the gentlemen no doubt wonder what has become of us."

The two ventured to the sitting room to join the others, leaving Bessie to sit with Lydia. It was a quiet, gloomy evening, not much talk until little Hannah was brought below the stairs after her nap. Charles Bingley seemed to come to life. With unguarded attentiveness he read to her, affording her the privilege to sit upon his lap, hugging his arm. Jane sat with them, holding the book. Elizabeth watched his gentle nature as well as Hannah's eagerness to capture both with her innocent charm.

Shortly after dinner, while they were congregating in the drawing room, Bessie entered hurriedly. "Mr. Darcy, your sister-in-law is awake. She seems very unsettled, sir. I believe she is scared; perhaps she does not know where she is."

Before she could finish, Mr. Darcy hastily arose from his chair, urgently making his way above the stairs, with Elizabeth and Jane not far behind him until he reached the steps, which he took two at one time. By the time they reached the bedchamber, Mr. Darcy was at her bedside. They heard him gently say, "Lydia, it is Fitzwilliam Darcy; you are safe, you are at Pemberley. Jane and Elizabeth are here, as well as your daughter Hannah."

Lydia was awake, but appeared alarmed; he was sure she was scared. Mr. Darcy was doing his best to calm her, to no avail.

When he heard the ladies, he turned to them. "Quickly, bring Hannah; make haste, I believe the child's sight will ease her alarm."

Lydia was restless. Her eyes widened in a cold stare; her hands were making signs as she continued to mumble what sounded like 'Hannah,' although it was not quite clear. She was incoherent; her speech slurred as her eyes grew wild with fright. He pitied her; she was like a lost soul; it was his desire to console her and perhaps give her a sense of peace.

Elizabeth descended the stairs to fetch the child while Jane remained with Lydia and Mr. Darcy. Jane stood near, listening to him talk to Lydia. It did not take long before Mr. Bingley entered carrying the child. After placing her by her mother, Lydia's face drained of the anxiety within her. As her alarm subsided, Mr. Darcy placed an additional cover over her.

"I suspected as much," Mr. Darcy said, facing Lydia now as he gently put the palm of his hand on her cheek, then wiped her brow with a wet cloth. The whole of the time he spoke to her. "You are safe, Lydia; there are many people to tend you here; we shall see to it that you are well looked after. You have had a long, rough journey, indeed you have."

"Lydia," Elizabeth spoke softly. "Lydia, can you hear me?" She moved in closer to her. "It's Elizabeth. Jane and Hannah are here, too."

Although she did not speak, her eyes gave a look of understanding. Hannah snuggled next to her mother, outstretching her little arm to fit around her as best she could.

"Lydia, would you like hot broth? Here, take my hand; squeeze it if you wish," Elizabeth directed.

"Very well, she does; please see to it."

"Yes, ma'am, at once!" replied Bessie.

"I'll go," said Mr. Bingley, adding, "We exited the room so quickly we left Mr. Manley to entertain himself; I will tell Mrs. Reynolds, then join Mr. Manley."

"Bingley, he's quite understanding; I'm sure he has taken the situation into consideration."

"Just the same, Darcy, I shall keep him company." Mr. Bingley turned to quit the chamber, but instantly turned back around. "Shall I take Hannah with me?"

"Lydia, may Hannah go with Mr. Bingley?" Mr. Darcy asked delicately. She moved in agreement, allowing the little girl to be taken below the stairs.

Jane and Elizabeth stayed. Mr. Darcy continued to talk to Lydia. He sedately inquired if she were in pain, hungry, or had any need. He offered to read to her and asked if she were warm enough. Her response was evident with the mention of pain; she squeezed his hand slightly while trying to utter words they could not understand. When he mentioned he would go now since the broth had been brought up, Lydia became alarmed. Mr. Darcy inquired if she preferred he stayed, only to have her touch his hand again.

He delicately replied, "It would please me to stay, Lydia; I shall stay as long as you like; you may depend upon it."

Elizabeth noticed Jane's puzzled look. Her lips parted in disbelief. She continued to watch Mr. Darcy, then urgently motioned to Elizabeth to step outside the bedchamber.

"Lizzy, I do believe your husband affords her security. I confess the manner of his speaking was ever so gentle; he has gained her trust. I declare earnestly I'm quite taken aback by it! Your husband provides her comfort. And to think it was not so long ago that she could not stand the very sight of him; now she became alarmed at the thought of his leaving her side."

"He is concerned, Jane."

"Oh, I'm so sorry, Lizzy, I only meant, it is odd, is it not? We are her sisters; I should have thought that she would desire our presence; after all, we are family."

"Yes, Jane, lest we forget, she is of the understanding it was he who paid the rent as well as provided nourishment. She no doubt heard his fast,

alarmed pace to the room, all this heightened by his recognition of her desire to see Hannah. Do you not see, Jane? It is indeed obviously unmistakable; he represents understanding of her situation, affording the comfort of ease. Having been touched by his kindness, she is simply responding to his sympathy."

"Lizzy, he speaks with such tranquility; his voice is gentle. I do believe our sister does indeed feel safe. Is Mr. Darcy invariably as such? Is he like this most often? He seems always so quiet, reserved, but I do see he has another side."

Elizabeth could not help but smile at her description. "Yes, Jane, as I mentioned earlier, he continues to astound me with his virtuous attributes; he is invariably as such. I daresay he is most definitely my superior; I am no match to his kind, gentle nature. He feels so deeply for others; if you only knew his generosity there would be no question. Quite honestly, Jane, I know not how I am ever to deserve him."

"Well, Lydia, without doubt, is touched by his generous nature."

"It may be so, Jane; I believe it is important she remains at ease. If Fitzwilliam is the instrument, so much the better."

Elizabeth walked back into the bedchamber. "Dearest, I shall descend now with Jane; I'll order hot tea brought up, perhaps a few biscuits."

"That will do well," he replied, looking back at Lydia, raising his brows while nodding his head. "Yes, I can clearly see she is receptive to hot tea."

Elizabeth entered the sitting room. "Pray excuse me, I must order tea above the stairs; please forgive my absence, it cannot be helped."

Mr. Manley stood upon her entrance to bow. "May I be of service?"

"No, that is quite all right, Mr. Manley, we are occupied with Lydia just now, but I fear I am neglecting my duties regarding entertainment of my guests; I do hope you understand."

"To be sure, we are quite fine, no neglect at all, no apologies necessary."

Elizabeth returned above the stairs. Mr. Darcy looked up as she entered. "She sank into a dozing state; we were fortunate she received the broth. Perhaps she should rest now. Bessie will look after her." He turned to Bessie. "You will call me at once if I am needed?"

"At once, sir."

"Very well, dear," Elizabeth answered in a low voice, "perhaps rest is what she needs." They descended the stairs to rejoin the rest of the party. By now Hannah had been put to bed and the room was quiet with soft conversation.

"What do we do now?" Elizabeth inquired.

"We wait; Dr. Gordon will return tomorrow," Mr. Darcy instructed.

"We shall have to stay a few days at least, Lizzy. I believe it is important Lydia has Hannah present," Jane explained.

"Indeed, if it is convenient with you, Darcy," Mr. Bingley added.

"Of course, indeed, she must be here; it is imperative."

"Is there anything I may do before I take my leave?" Mr. Manley asked.

"A prayer would be most appreciated," Mr. Darcy replied.

After fulfilling Mr. Darcy's request, Mr. Manley started to take his leave, but not before Jane despairingly unleashed her thoughts aloud. "I had not thought George Wickham as bad as this!"

Jane received a disapproving look from her husband.

"What is wrong, Charles?"

"I just thought Darcy perhaps did not want family matters aired publicly."

"It's quite all right, Bingley; Mr. Manley knows the whole of it."

"I cannot believe this; he is a true blackguard!" Elizabeth voiced angrily.

"Elizabeth, beyond neglect, we know of nothing else he has done."

"Oh, Fitzwilliam, how is it you can defend him?" Elizabeth demanded.

"Dearest, we know him to be selfish, neglectful, nothing more. Truly I say he is a blackguard. Yes, I admit he has inferior character. Wickham is a scoundrel indeed, but he would not strike her; he is not of an extreme brutal nature in that respect."

"Neglect is sufficient enough, is it not?"

"Lizzy, this does no good; our concern is Lydia's well-being."

"Perhaps you are right, Jane. I confess, I'm beyond belief to understand the whole of it. What sort of man could look at his own image in a looking glass without reproaching himself for the neglect of his family?" Elizabeth said in heightened exasperation.

"We should think of retiring," Mr. Darcy announced.

"Splendid idea. Jane, you should have rest; you have not been well," said her husband. He wearily desired sleep himself. The four went above the stairs, but before taking to their bedchambers they made one final stop at Lydia's chamber. She appeared to be sleeping contentedly, so they retired, leaving her under the watchful eye of a servant for the night. Mr. Darcy gave strict instruction to fetch him instantly if need be.

As the dismal four parted to their own chambers, the ladies hugged each other in consolation. They bid their good-nights, not knowing what sort of night Lydia would experience, wondering what tomorrow might bring.

Dawn until Dusk

THE SUN HAD HARDLY RISEN when a servant came to Mr. Darcy's bedchamber, urgently requesting he come at once to his sister-in-law's chamber. Mr. Darcy quitted his own in haste.

Lydia was conscious. She appeared to be responsive; her eyes were open and she had been asking for him. He immediately went to her bedside.

"Lydia, you've awakened. You realize you are at Pemberley, is it not so?"

She responded, affirming with a slow nod of the head, then in a low, whispering voice she managed to say, "Mr. Darcy, Hannah is here, is she not? I thought I remembered her being here as well as you." She lay back quietly, taking in short breaths of air.

"Yes, Hannah is here; I am happy to see you alert. Do you remember the hot broth?"

She slowly nodded to afirm. With tear-filled eyes, she spoke, "Thank you, Mr. Darcy."

"There is no need to thank me, Lydia; it is my wish you make yourself well again. Little Hannah—she is the prettiest little girl. I do believe she even favours her mother."

"Mr. Darcy, your kindness is very much appreciated. I am much obliged for your goodness. Indeed my sister is fortunate. I trust you know I acknowledge all you have done. You have made me feel safe; there are no words to express my gratitude."

"No, no, Lydia, not at all, do not speak of it. Think nothing of it. It will afford me great pleasure to see you well again."

"Mr. Darcy, I feel strange," she said, raising her palms to her temples. "I can hardly abide the suffering of so much pain. I am so tired; would you mind if I rest now?"

"Not at all, Lydia. You must reserve strength; you must get well again."
Again she moved her head to afirm his message.

"I shall return to my chamber now; rest assured you are safe at Pemberley
with people to look after you. Dr. Gordon is expected to return today; do
you recollect his being here?"

"No, Mr. Darcy."

"He is the finest doctor in these parts, he'll attend you; I've commissioned
him. You rest; it is best you oblige me," he said, patting her hand.

Although her appearance left him disturbed, he parted the chamber comforted that she was alert. Her general colouring was pale, her speech lethar-
gic. She was clearly weak and drawn. Her constitution lacked all the past
luster of her youth. He noticed her once-bright eyes were dismally gray with
agony. It was hard to imagine her the same girl he first met in Hertfordshire.
Remembering he viewed her so full of energy, although thinking her to be
extremely foolish, it was difficult to conceive she was the same girl. He once
lacked tolerance for her public silliness, believing her marked conduct assured public ridicule. Her life appeared to consist of nonsense and folly,
easily influenced by the flattery from the regiment of infantry camped at
Meryton. She sought to follow after a regiment of soldiers until she finally
settled on the worst of the lot. She was in the best of health back then, full
of life, robust in form, with a most excellent complexion. Now, in comparison, she lay just the opposite. He had no wish to deny himself justification
of his past view, only to feel a sense of sorrow for her present suffering. He
could not take responsibility for George Wickham's actions; he had assisted
him in every way possible; now he was faced with the realization there were
sure to be no alterations there. He reached his own bedchamber to find his
wife awake. She was anxious to hear of her sister's condition.

"Lydia is awake, alert and understands where she is. I believe she feels
safe, realizing she will be well looked after," he expressed with a sigh. With
a tired, unsettled voice, he continued, "I will do everything in my power,
Elizabeth."

"Dearest, you take too much upon yourself. Your kindness means much,
but surely you do not believe Lydia our responsibility?"

"Certainly not, but, just the same, she is your sister. How can I possibly
justify not doing everything in my power? If anything happened to her, how
should I forgive myself for ignoring a situation I may have turned about? I
have no regrets. I should like to see her well again. We must do all we can to
make her well; it is fitting and proper."

"And what of Wickham; is he not expected to do what is fitting and proper?"

"Elizabeth, is it not obvious George Wickham will never do what is honourable or befitting unless, of course, it benefits him. I fear Lydia will have to reside at Longbourn when all is well; surely she cannot return to London. What else is there to be done unless you prefer that we have her taken care of quietly in the country? If that be your wish I shall grant it. Dearest, I have no answers."

"A decision such as this is distressing. Will Lydia agree even for her own general welfare; nothing so easy, I fear," she lamented.

"I believe I shall prepare myself to descend the stairs; I am restless. Elizabeth, do you intend to inform your father of the situation?"

"I thought the better of it; I thought it best not to alarm him. I'm sure once Dr. Gordon turns her about she will be well enough to carry on. The problem is, will Lydia do what is best for her and the children?"

"Yes, there is much to be concerned about. I suggest you reconsider and inform your father. Are you coming directly? I should like us to breakfast together."

"Yes, dear, I suppose I should write to Father. I will come directly, but first I must see Lydia."

"Very well, then," he said, parting her company. Mr. Darcy was well out of sight when a very excited servant rapidly sought Elizabeth to come quickly to her sister's bedchamber. Elizabeth ran after her hurriedly, arriving to find Lydia in excruciating pain.

"Good God, run, tell Mr. Darcy that Dr. Gordon is required at once!"

"At once, ma'am," said she, quitting the chamber in haste.

Mr. Darcy, responding from the intense pressure of the circumstances, fled above the stairs with such thunder, accelerating each step hastily as he tread the matting that his heavy steps awoke Charles Bingley and Jane, who were now alarmed and on course to understand the frightful commotion. Lydia's screams absorbed the atmosphere; the children were awake and crying; there was no one left at rest.

Mr. Darcy entered the bedchamber to find his wife madly attempting to hold her as she thrashed about in agonizing pain. Mr. Darcy neared his wife.

"How long, how long until Dr. Gordon arrives?" Elizabeth called out. She nervously held Lydia to her as she rocked her. Her words were spoken with such urgency, as she herself breathed heavily. In her face he could read the horror of her fear.

"The servant has long gone to fetch him; I'm sure her screams instilled the necessity for urgency along with my instructions. He will arrive as soon as may be; I have no doubt."

Lydia, still screaming with suffering, was attempting to lean forward. Her form would not allow much bending. Elizabeth was alarmed, her eyes widened as she looked to Jane, who was weeping. Mr. Bingley removed his wife from the bedchamber. Mr. Darcy endeavoured to get Lydia to lie back, only to find she was bleeding profusely. The bed was stained with an abundance of blood. Mr. Darcy touched Elizabeth's shoulder. "Elizabeth, place the bolster under her legs; I shall leave you with Bessie for a few moments."

Once in the hall, he secured Mrs. Reynolds. "Please fetch linen, water and several blankets." He then ran back to the chamber.

"Lydia, you must lie back; the doctor is en route," he told her, watching her reaction as he viewed his wife, who was now anxiously pale. He exited the room again, only to hear Lydia screaming violently in pain once more. He ran his fingers through his hair. There was nothing to be done but to wait. Mr. Bingley and Jane hurried to him. Jane trembled as she sobbed. Mr. Bingley attempted to calm her. Mrs. Reynolds, along with two servants, hurried down the hall toward them, arms filled with the particulars Mr. Darcy requested.

"Mr. Darcy, Mary here has experience in assisting in cases such as these; she wishes to be of service, sir."

"Excellent, of course, go right in." He turned to his friend. "Bingley, you and Jane get dressed; check on Hannah. The poor child may realize it is her mother screaming."

It was in Mr. Darcy's mind to give them a useful occupation to engage Jane in a diversion.

"Yes, very good, excellent notion; come, Jane." They were gone in an instant.

Realizing it was best for him to remain outside the bedchamber, Mr. Darcy waited at the door for Dr. Gordon. Another five and twenty minutes passed, bearing witness to Lydia's agonizing screams. What seemed like hours was in reality minutes when finally the doctor arrived, hastily making his way above the stairs with his bag in hand.

Dr. Gordon sent Elizabeth out of the chamber. They waited in the hall impatiently. The wretched screaming was both troubling and piercing. As Mr. Darcy held his wife in comfort, she buried her face in his chest, weeping. It was five and forty minutes before the screaming subsided and they heard the sound of a baby's cry. Elizabeth ceased her sobbing. Mr. Darcy looked at his wife with a smile, then drew her close to his breast reliving the day she had put him through the same torment.

Dr. Gordon appeared in the hall, motioning for Elizabeth to enter the chamber. "She is your sister, I understand?"

"Yes, she is."

"I urge you to keep her calm; sit at her side until I return." He quit the room, closing the door, leaving Mary and Elizabeth to watch over Lydia.

"Mr. Darcy, allow me to talk with you in your office."

The gentlemen hastened to the office, closing the door behind them. "Please grant me some paper, post haste. I must send word to the Apothecary to answer any concerns that arise in my absence. I shall remain here as long as necessary. Mr. Darcy, I must be frank; I fear this young lady will not make it through. The child is a boy, appears healthy, a nice size—he will do well. You shall have to secure a wet nurse for him; his mother is unable to perform her duty. Preparations should be made, Mr. Darcy; you must prepare your wife. I see no good coming of this. I fear she has lost too much blood. The young lady is weak; she has neither the strength nor endurance to rally through this. Mr. Darcy, I fear she demonstrates absolutely no longing to put up a good fight. I understand she is your wife's sister. May I inquire, where is her husband?"

"He is in London at the moment, sir."

"That will not do; I fear there is not sufficient time left. He cannot possibly arrive in time; we shall be forced to do without him."

"Dr. Gordon, do you believe her husband's presence will afford her a chance?"

"No, I'm afraid not, Mr. Darcy; the truth is your messenger would not make it half way to London before her expiration; we are only speaking of perhaps one or two hours. It is a most serious situation. She is much too weak; she is hemorrhaging. I fear life is fast draining from her. I advise you to summon your clergy. Now I must return; I have wasted no words. Think not that anything will alter the final resolve, there is nothing else to be done," he stated. He then handed Mr. Darcy his message to the apothecary, requesting, "Please see this message is dispatched without delay."

"Very well, then I shall tend to the clergy; please send my wife from the chamber so I may inform her. I will be there directly after securing her sister Jane."

"As you wish."

They parted company. The doctor went above the stairs while Mr. Darcy sent a servant to fetch Mr. Manley. He sent another to ride to Lambton to deliver the message. He bounded swiftly above the stairs to make known the situation to his wife and Jane.

He first found Jane and Mr. Bingley. Bringing them together with Elizabeth, he appraised them of Dr. Gordon's revelation. Overcome and terror-stricken, they began to weep uncontrollably. Jane put her hands up to her face, unable to stop the flood of tears, which now consumed her. Elizabeth sobbed in disbelief, but managed to say, "I cannot believe this— I do not understand it at all; something must have gone wrong. We had better send a messenger to our father at once; he must be informed."

She continued her cry. Bewildering, fearful thoughts scourged through her entire being as tears of fright splashed down over the front of her dress. She felt weak and helpless. Although Mr. Darcy held her close, the supporting arms she would normally find pleasing gave little comfort in the thought of sure death. Mr. Darcy gently secured her by the arms to hold her away from him. Turning stern with forced calm, he looked at her emphatically. "I will send a message to your father at once, advising him of the circumstances. Lydia has little more than two hours at best; employ your last moments suitably; refrain from this weeping. I understand she owns sufficient alertness to speak. You must collect your thoughts. Gain control; there will be ample time for weeping. Now, both of you compose yourselves at once to make your presence and affections known while there is still time; now go, make haste."

It was inexpressibly painful to be so austere. Had he not felt it imperative they understood the time limitation, surely he should not have spoken with such severe language. Comprehending precious moments were not to be squandered, he gave up his handkerchief whilst they readied themselves with fresh composure to enter the grave bedchamber.

The ladies disappeared into the chamber, leaving Mr. Bingley and Mr. Darcy alone. Mr. Bingley stared at his friend. "Darcy, is this true; are you certain?" an alarmed Mr. Bingley asked. His face grew severe, making his eyes wide from the shock.

"Yes, I fear it is so."

"Darcy, does the child live? I heard it cry."

"Yes, he is healthy; Dr. Gordon claims him a nice size."

"What of the children. What is to become of them; who will care for them? Surely Wickham will claim them, or will they be orphaned?"

"I'm sure Wickham will find them an intrusion; I am fairly certain of it."

"You believe he will abandon them?"

"He will not petition them. While in London, I learned much of his time is spent with courtesans. My wife is unaware of it; the time was never proper for revelation. For the moment, I do not wish her to know of it; it would cause unquestionable pain. Bingley, say nothing of this."

"Why, Darcy, whatever can it matter now? We cannot protect them from all unpleasantness; surely they are grown women capable of some understanding."

"Well, allow me to give it more thought, perhaps you are right— But frankly, Bingley, I am not in a disposition to discuss the wicked ways of such a man at present."

"Very well, you know, Darcy, I should be glad to receive the children."

"You would?"

"Yes, Darcy, I should like that very much. In these last hours I have become quite attached to little Hannah; she is such a dear, sweet little thing, so dainty. I should like it very much; I'm sure Jane would."

"Well, you and Jane must decide. Bingley, I must say I think it rather admirable."

Mr. Manley, having just arrived, was fast approaching them. Mr. Darcy informed him of the situation, suggesting he go straight to the chamber. As Mr. Manley entered, he noticed the ladies at Lydia's bedside. Dr. Gordon stood off to one side as they attempted to speak with her. Mr. Manley took a position near the doctor. He immediately bowed his head to pray.

Lydia appeared alert. She lay with her head slightly elevated. Although she looked ashen, she was well aware of her surroundings. She spoke with equanimity, as she sought to make conversation amidst her pain. Although she spoke slowly, her words were deliberate, as though each word was so important as to be her last. She was no longer disoriented or frightened; instead, there appeared certain tranquility in her countenance. Her manner of speaking caused Elizabeth to believe that perhaps she was aware her time of expiration was nearing, almost as though she could feel the last of her life slipping away. Although the baby had been placed at her side, it was evident she was too weak to hold the child.

"Jane, will you promise to look after my children?"

"Of course, Lydia, until you are well enough."

"No, Jane, I am too weak to go on."

"Lydia, you must not say such things."

"Jane, name him Charles if it meets with Mr. Bingley's approval; for if he had not rescued me, perhaps the little fellow would not have made it. I regret I have nothing for him except my love. The cross I bore around my neck is all I have for Hannah."

"Lydia, please, do not say such things; I cannot endure it." A single tear ran down Jane's cheek; her voice quivered with each painful word. Her heart wrenched with anguish at the thought of her sister's impending demise.

"I reproach myself of my foolish past; I was stupid. Had I been more like the two of you, perhaps my fate would have taken another turn. I beg you forgive my unguarded behaviour. Lizzy, Mr. Wickham is not what he appears to be, but you knew that, did you not?

"Lydia, we must think of better things. May we get you anything?"

"No, Lizzy, he should have made a very fine stage actor. It pains me to think of the false, reckless blame he made against your husband. I refused to see the truth at the start, but I am well aware now where his values lie. I allowed him to flatter me and cloud my judgment with false promises. I was blind to the danger of my pleasure seeking. I know now he only sought to take advantage of our family situation. Lizzy, one awful night in his drunkenness, his anger encouraged his exposure of all that he had long felt with regard to me. He cruelly revealed his only desire in marrying me was to have his expenses settled and the purchase of yet another commission. He was angered to learn our father lacked the economy to settle for me."

Elizabeth gently wiped Lydia's forehead with a damp cloth. "You must not speak of it; it does little good to torment yourself with such thoughts."

Lydia tried to sit forward to no avail. She easily slumped back into the bolster, giving up all the desire to force her body against its will. She became unsettled. "Lizzy, I fear I must tell you of it."

"Very well, Lydia, if it brings you comfort."

"Yes, Lizzy, you must hear what I feel I must say. Wickham further claimed in the end it was Mr. Darcy who purchased the commission and paid the debts, including settling on a sum of £3,000. He claimed Mr. Darcy owed it to him. He said it was Mr. Darcy's fault for foiling his marriage to Georgiana. He claimed he could have lived rather nicely on her inheritance. He confessed he cared nothing for me and only desired the wealth such a marriage would afford him. He said it was you he loved, Lizzy, claiming Mr. Darcy stole your heart away from him. You can imagine how I felt hearing those words."

"Oh, Lydia, I am so sorry."

"Do not be, Lizzy; I hold no ill thoughts where you are concerned. I am wholly ashamed for seeking such a man whose whole character is a mockery. For all my engaging folly, I was led to an uncertain life because I was impulsively blind and taken in by his flattery. My only feelings now are indifference and contempt. If nothing else be said of me, say I was a good mother. Jane, please, I should like our father aware I was a good mother. And, Lizzy, do tell Mr. Darcy I know him to be truly kind."

She gasped then took in air, then slowly continued, "Be not afraid for me. I am not afraid to die; I have no fear of dying, perhaps just the fear of living." She paused at length before uttering with a weakened voice, "I am so weary."

With eyes filled with tears, Jane looked at Elizabeth. She reached to place her hand over Lydia's. "Lydia, shall I lift the little fellow to your face so you may kiss him?"

"Please do, Jane, I should like it."

As Jane neared with the child, Lydia mumbled, "It's getting very bright now is it not? I am so very tired." She sighed as she struggled to kiss the child.

Elizabeth viewed the pained looked on Lydia's face. She understood the slight attempt to raise herself up caused her excruciating pain.

"Jane, he is yours now. Do promise you will always say I loved them."

"Oh, Lydia, please say no more of this," Jane quietly said, as the tears streamed down both her and Elizabeth's cheeks. The sorrow was too much to avoid; they could hold back the tears no longer as their chests became heavily burdened with anguish. They stared at her now. Their expressions of despair were unavoidably exposed.

Mr. Manley granted Lydia her last rites. He prayed over her, granting unto her all the ceremonious attention expected of a clergyman. Lydia was now in a seemingly unconscious state. Dr. Gordon moved in to check her pulse. He sadly shook his head. There was little hope.

Lydia stirred, she murmured, then gasped for air as she weakly moved. She briefly opened her eyes. "Lizzy, Jane," she struggled to utter, "do not cry; tell Papa I regret the disgrace I brought upon him. Give him my love, and I—I—" was all she managed. Her voice trailed off. She gurgled and moaned, letting out a last gasp before her head fell to the side, her face now in the direction of her newborn. She lay stretched and motionless; her body went limp, with all signs of life departing from her.

Elizabeth frantically shook her. "Lydia, wake, wake! Lydia!" Elizabeth was overcome with hysteria. "You cannot leave us, Lydia," she cried out uncontrollably. In her disbelieving grief she was unable to accept the reality of death in one so young. Jane, in a more sedate state, just stared as Dr. Gordon closed Lydia's eyes.

Hearing his wife's loud shouts, Mr. Darcy, without delay, entered as Dr. Gordon was attempting to remove the ladies from Lydia. Jane was a much easier task. He merely placed the infant in her arms. He attempted physically to separate Elizabeth from Lydia. She clutched Lydia's body, pulling it to her own, sobbing with words visibly trembling upon her lips as she continued discourse, expecting and demanding a response, obviously reluctant to acknowledge the deprivation of the life gone from the body to which she now clung.

"Dearest, do come away," Mr. Darcy softly said, placing his hands on her shoulders while she continued to rock Lydia in her arms. He tried to help Dr. Gordon separate her from her sister's body to no avail. She resisted them, still clutching Lydia with unyielding strength. In the end it took Mr. Manley's assistance to forcefully remove her from Lydia. As they walked her to the doorsill, she suddenly collapsed to the floor.

Jane was now in the hall cradling the child, with Mr. Bingley as her comforter. She fared well compared to Elizabeth. Her thoughts were engaged with the children who now required her full attention. Her mind was clearly on the living.

Elizabeth was revived and taken to her own bedchamber, sobbing ceaselessly until the tears dried up and she fell asleep. She finally gained composure in late afternoon. When she united with the rest of the party, she appeared pale. Her chest still ached from her lengthy cry. Her tormented, gloomy eyes were still red with swelling. Every so often she gasped for breath while trying to control a sob.

"Dearest, draw near me; do sit down," Mr. Darcy said as he hastily quitted his seat to render assistance. He nodded to Mr. Manley to fetch her a goblet of wine as he gently led her in the direction of the sofa.

"Pray receive some port; sip it slowly," he instructed her. His voice turned tranquil. "I sent a messenger to your father; I believe Lydia would wish to be next to your mother. We'll depart at dawn; Lydia is en route to Hertfordshire. Jane made the decision; I hope this is agreeable to you. Do you approve?"

She sat stable, nodding in agreement. She continued to sip the wine, staring into space, next fixing her eyes on the fire. Hannah distracted her with brisk movements in her attempt to climb upon Mr. Bingley's knee. She watched with curiosity as he lifted her to his lap. Elizabeth observed how she responded to him with ease. He allowed her to prattle with freedom, which channeled all thoughts in her direction. Elizabeth now concentrated on Hannah, remembering how timid she first was upon her arrival, talking to no one. Turning now to Jane, she said, "Jane, is she not the very image of Lydia as a child?"

"Yes, Lizzy, had not you noticed before this?"

"No, I confess I had not," she answered her in a quiet, somber voice.

"Lizzy, Lydia lives; surely she lives through her children."

"To be sure she does indeed," Elizabeth agreed with resignation.

"Are you feeling better, Lizzy?"

"Yes, I have accepted what must be."

Her statement was a relief to Mr. Darcy. He supposed earlier resistance to his assisting Lydia was now imposing upon her with feelings of guilt. He could only now wish her not to be haunted by the ghost of regret. He knew Elizabeth wished Lydia no ill will and wholly understood to whom her anger was directed. Now he grieved for his own wife's state. He felt her pain along with her guilt of her learning of her sister's suffering. Surely these were the trials of life that advantages could not improve upon, thought he. His entire day was consumed with guiding the feelings of others, hardly allowing time for his own concerns. He suddenly found the revelation of her acceptance a great comfort. Seeking to distract his wife further, he said, "I spent time with Joseph and Deborah; they were so playful this afternoon."

"I visited with them before I joined you; they are busy little ones, are they not?"

"Yes, they are at that, very busy indeed," he agreed.

"Mr. Manley, forgive my company; I am not quite myself."

"Mrs. Darcy, allow me to comfort you in saying your sister is at peace."

"I know, Mr. Manley; I pray you'll excuse my inferior behaviour earlier."

"Dearest, think of it no more; it is a natural reaction. Do not reproach yourself. Surely it is an honour to be loved so dearly. Henry understands your sorrow."

The evening finally brought closure when Mr. Manley bid them good night to return to the parsonage. Those grieving retired early, hoping to find needed rest.

Elizabeth made herself ready for bed but stood by the window above an hour, staring into the evening sky. She watched the light withdraw from the heavens until the last ray vanished, leaving her in total darkness.

Sad Moments

THE TWO CARRIAGES DEPARTED Pemberley Estate for Hertfordshire at daybreak. It was a dreary day; the sky was dark with clouds seemingly low, discharging a gentle, steady drizzle. The clopping sound of the horses' hooves along the road was made more evident by the somber silence within the carriage. They made several stops along the way, enabling the wet nurse to tend the newborn.

Halfway to their destination, Elizabeth requested Hannah to ride in their carriage for the continuation of the journey. Mr. Darcy thought this advantageous, as the child's presence was soothing to Elizabeth, forcing her to focus her attention on the living.

He sat back, watching her with the child. Once Hannah recovered her initial shyness, she clung to Elizabeth. He put his head back and closed his eyes, giving thought to his own dear children, which seemed to be immediately desired. He was fatigued, having had a sleepless night, aware of every twist and turn his wife had taken until the awakening of the dawn provided him a reason to rise. Hannah was full of energy. Her prattle seemed endless as Elizabeth encouraged her to view the passing scenery. As the carriage moved along, Mr. Darcy, with his head still back and eyes closed, suddenly became aware of Hannah attempting to climb upon his lap. He drew her up in his arms, holding her there. As he hugged her, a sense of satisfaction comforted him. She placed her little arms about his neck. Elizabeth smiled, deriving joy from Hannah's playfulness. That was the first he saw her smile since Lydia's death. He believed her to have gained resignation of the regretful occurrence, at least, all the while hoping she was on the mend.

Finally the carriages reached Longbourn, where an anxious Mr. Bennet waited. The greetings were sober. Mary and Kathryn each reached out for

Hannah. The baby began to cry, prompting Jane to lead the wet nurse to a private place for feeding. She entered the sitting room, where all were gathered. Longbourn was once again a gloomy, busy place except for the delight little Hannah cast on the sober atmosphere. It was strange, quite ironic, that Lydia's own child would divert the gloomy attitudes into bright little moments. Comments could be heard regarding the likeness of Hannah to her mother.

"What's to become of the children?" Mr. Bennet inquired with a worried look.

"Father, Lydia asked Mr. Bingley and me to look after them."

"What of Mr. Wickham, has he been notified?" Mr. Bennet inquired further.

"Yes, sir, I dispatched a notice at once; I directed him here. Elizabeth and I will stay at Netherfield Park; we thought Mr. Wickham would be comfortable here with you, if that is to your satisfaction?" Mr. Darcy replied.

"Yes, indeed you have thought of everything, Mr. Darcy."

"If you will excuse me, Mr. Bennet, I should like to walk to the church. You will accompany me, will you not, Bingley?" Mr. Darcy asked his surprised friend, who had no prior knowledge of his plan.

"But of course," Mr. Bingley responded without hesitation.

When they departed the house, Mr. Darcy stopped. He turned to his friend. "Thank you, Bingley, for not questioning me in there. You have no objection to Elizabeth and me staying at Netherfield, do you now?"

"But of course not."

"I thought it would be agreeable to you. It would be unadvisable to stay the night under the same roof with Mr. Wickham; it would prove discomforting for all."

"I certainly understand your position; we shall be delighted to have you. Why are we going to the church, Darcy?"

"Oh, I thought I would settle on the arrangements; it will save Mr. Bennet the trouble. I'm sure the circumstances are difficult enough, Bingley; the man should not have to suffer further hardship. It is no great trouble for me."

"Indeed, Darcy, you do think of everything. I shall be glad when we move near Pemberley, I hold much value in our friendship. I confess I dearly miss your company."

"Yes, Bingley, and I you." Changing his voice endearingly to his friend, he went on to express in the tenderest of terms, "Charles, Elizabeth apprised me of your loss, I cannot tell you how deeply sorry I am for you; you take it hard I see."

"Darcy, I have struggled to be strong for Jane. It is very difficult indeed."

"It pains me to see my friend suffer; I comprehend it to be true. It is not like you, Bingley, to avoid a subject with me, indeed it must be painful. I always have an ear for my friend. I too am anxious for Michaelmas; we shall delight in your nearness. We shall be very pleased when you make your move. There will no doubt be happier times to be had, and I am sure it is only a matter of time before you make another announcement."

With sad, agonizing eyes, Mr. Bingley looked at Mr. Darcy but made no answer.

Realizing his friend's pain and discomfort, he changed the subject. "And what of your sisters, Bingley, are they still at Netherfield?"

"Indeed, but no mind of that, Darcy, they will greet Elizabeth with charm and grace. I am certain they have abandoned all resentment in view of the loss. I'm convinced they will converse and flatter as insincerely as ever. Even though they are my sisters—perhaps I should not mention them with such unflattering description—I am aware of their imperfections. At least Emily is genuine; she has an unblemished affection for Elizabeth as well as Jane."

"That is generous of you, Bingley; it certainly is appreciated."

"Not at all; it is settled then, you will both stay at Netherfield Hall."

When they reached the local parsonage, Mr. Darcy settled upon all the necessary arrangements for the burial ceremony that had been set. It was to take place the day next. As they walked back to Longbourn, Mr. Darcy stopped along the way, turning once again to his friend. "Bingley, you will seek me out if ever you need me to listen? I know it must be hard to endure a loss in silence. The torment suffered alone to avoid inflicting further pain on the one you love can indeed leave a man feeling desolate. Do not hesitate to confide in me, Bingley. I should suffer greatly if I knew you needed me and did not seek me out."

"Oh, Darcy, I cannot bear the loss." Mr. Bingley hung his head. His eyes filled as he choked on his words. He reached deep into his pocket to fetch his handkerchief. "Thank you, dear friend. I confess it would have been most advantageous if we were at Foxshire Estate. I longed for your company. If it were not for Emily, I don't know what I should have done." He blew his nose before gaining his upright stature. "I'm quite all right, Darcy, surely I am."

Mr. Darcy clutched Mr. Bingley's shoulder with strength. "I wish I would have been there." Seeing the subject was too painful to discuss, he said, "Very well, Bingley. We had better be getting back."

When they returned to the house, the Gardiners had arrived. Mrs. Philips was obviously present as well. She cried louder and longer than any other, upsetting the children with her wailing, which one might have believed could be heard in the village. Kathryn tried to comfort her to no avail; it was as though she needed to be heard.

"Thank you, Mr. Darcy, for the prompt message; we arrived as soon as we could. Poor Lydia, thank you for the kindness you granted my niece; you certainly have taken much upon yourself. We tried to locate Mr. Wickham before leaving London but were unsuccessful," Mrs. Gardiner stated soberly, looking at him with tearfully sentimental eyes.

"I sent word to him at once. I'm sure he will be here, Mrs. Gardiner," replied Mr. Darcy in a sorrowful voice.

In a voice equally sad, Mr. Gardner spoke. "It is all quite hard to believe, Lydia—dead. I should have never expected it."

"None of us did, Mr. Gardiner; it's quite shocking. Had you witnessed her unhealthy state upon her arrival at Pemberley, you would have better understanding."

"Quite so, Mr. Darcy. The child is well, I understand; they have taken him above the stairs, I did not get a glimpse of him as yet," explained Mrs. Gardiner.

Elizabeth approached Mrs. Gardiner. "Aunt, I'm certain you would be welcomed above the stairs if you choose; Jane is there."

Hill came running into the house. She stopped short in front of Mr. Darcy. In a voice wanting of air, she gasped as she struggled to breathe before announcing, "Mr. Wickham has just arrived. He is presently nearing the house."

Mr. Darcy composed himself with intentions to exhibit kindness in spite of his contempt. Although he dreaded to be in Mr. Wickham's presence, he could not deny him his rightful place, nor could he express feelings of displeasure against him, however sharpened they were by his disappointment in his character. His own honourable character would not afford him to corrupt Lydia's memory by reproaching her husband at such a mournful time.

Mr. Darcy stood tall as Mr. Wickham entered the room. He slightly bowed, standing next to Elizabeth, who stood frozen, unable to move. Elizabeth would not allow herself to look in his direction; her countenance was a mixture of sorrow and contempt. Mr. Bennet afforded him more comfort offering him a seat and tea; however, Mr. Wickham requested something much stronger, no doubt to numb his present uncomfortable situation.

Mr. Wickham appeared tired from the journey. With anxious discourse, he expressed his regret for not having been with Lydia when she died.

Nearing Mr. Bennet, he said, "I cannot believe Lydia is dead. I had not a notion of her being so ill. I am sorry, Mr. Bennet." With an appearance of being distressed, he hung his head low. He precariously lifted his head, looking beyond Mr. Bennet at a painting on the wall, not really absorbing its beauty but rather blankly focused on something, anything, to take away the uneasiness he obviously felt.

Since he demonstrated a sense of sadness, Mr. Darcy believed he was indeed feeling the loss or, perhaps, guilt. Mr. Wickham, now unmistakably uncomfortable, gulped his port without difficulty, asking for another as soon as his glass was emptied.

Mr. Bennet, wishing to add to Mr. Wickham's comfort, went out of his way to rectify the situation by offering him a bedchamber for the night, which he quickly accepted.

Elizabeth studied him intently. He consumed several drinks, perhaps to soothe his mind or ease his conscience, thought she.

Mr. Darcy observed the way in which he hastily drank one drink after another, asking nothing of the children. He thought it rather odd. Then much to Elizabeth's dismay, Kathryn asked, "Mr. Wickham, did you know you have a son?"

"Yes, I am obliged to Mr. Darcy. I was notified of my responsibilities. Is he here? Is Hannah here?"

Elizabeth thought it quite convenient of him to inquire once the children were mentioned, seeking to recommend himself as the wounded under these distressing circumstances. She blurted out, "Yes, they are above the stairs. Lydia asked Jane to care for her children; do you have any objections to it?"

Noticing Elizabeth's expression was said in a less tranquil voice, Mr. Darcy dared her a look, attempting to halt her incivility. When she ignored him, he touched her arm gently to quiet her. He did not wish her to reproach Mr. Wickham in front of Mr. Bennet, who was struggling with the loss of his youngest daughter.

Elizabeth's mind was overtaken with angry thoughts of Mr. Wickham's false public hints regarding her husband's letter, suggesting Mr. Darcy advised him of his responsibilities. She, having witnessed the dispatch, knew it hinted nothing of it. Any attention, forbearance or patience she would have to afford George Wickham seemed injurious to Lydia's memory. Once again she felt Mr. Darcy slightly caress her arm, causing her to realize she should not dwell upon contempt. Attempting to lift her spirits amid her grief, she tried to alter her demeanour for her own dear father's sake.

Mr. Wickham hung his head low, staring into his drink. After an unsteady intake of air, he quietly answered, "Why, no, I have no objections if that be her wish," much to Mr. Darcy's relief. He continued to drink, avoiding eye contact with Mr. Darcy or Elizabeth.

Mr. Darcy surveyed him, amazed he had not asked to see his own children as yet. Perhaps his lack of curiosity would prove advantageous to his friend, he mused. Surely Mr. Wickham possessed no real means to provide for them, while Mr. Bingley's comforts could render them advantageous amenities.

Mr. Bingley thought they should start for Netherfield, announcing they would return in the early morning. Jane made her way below the stairs with the infant in her arms, with Mr. Bingley following close behind, holding Hannah, the wet nurse behind him. Mr. Wickham got up from his seat to approach them. He unfolded the blanket to look at his son. He vaguely smiled. "He is a fine boy, is he not?"

"Yes, he is, Mr. Wickham," Jane replied compassionately.

With forced restraint, Elizabeth observed Jane's kindness to him, which now was so offensive to her, that it caused an inability to completely control the harsh feelings within. Her looks became fixed with a noticeable expression of contempt. Even though she often admiringly longed to share her sister's invariable search of worth in others, Elizabeth had no desire to extend any benefits to such a man as George Wickham. The very sight of him repulsed her.

"Should you like to hold him?"

"Please," he responded, as Jane passed the baby to his arms. He held him for a few moments. In returning him, he turned to Hannah. "Hannah dear, come," said he with outstretched arms. He gave her a clutching hug before returning her to Mr. Bingley. He looked at Mr. Bingley. "I'm comforted knowing they shall be well taken care of. I am indebted to you, sir; you are indeed an honourable gentleman."

Of what would he know of honour? Elizabeth pondered.

"But of course we shall be happy to fulfill Lydia's dying wish," Mr. Bingley answered.

"Very well then, good night," Mr. Wickham said, as if to excuse them.

Again Elizabeth, exceedingly vexed, found her resentment unappeasable. She now discovered it was almost impossible to expel the gravitation toward hate, which she was never formed to possess.

Jane, relieved to quit Longbourn, discovered generosity a strain. In parting, Elizabeth still could not bring herself to look in Mr. Wickham's direction. Upon Mr. Darcy's notice of her reaction, he was relieved he had not mentioned the prostitute.

The subject of Mr. Wickham's insinuation promptly arose as the carriage quitted Longbourn. Little Hannah had fallen asleep almost immediately, adding relief to the unpleasantness of the day. Elizabeth, clearly agitated by Mr. Wickham, was unable to afford him any doubt or kindness.

As the carriage made its way to Netherfield, Jane curiously eyed Mr. Darcy. She made several attempts to part her lips to speak, only to yield to restraint. He looked at her inquisitively. After much pondering, she finally voiced, "Mr. Darcy, when Lydia fled to London with George Wickham, it was you, not my uncle, who settled his debts, bought his commission and gave him £3,000. I know it must be so; is it not now?"

Mr. Darcy said not a word; he merely stared out the window. He swallowed hard; his lips remained united in silence. He slightly turned to respond, inhaling as if to begin his reply, but instead united his lips again before lowering his eyes.

Curiously, she continued, "Lydia confessed it on her deathbed; it was you the whole of the time. Indeed it must be so."

Mr. Darcy remained momentarily silent. His astonishment was unavoidably obvious. He looked at Jane with an expression of being caught in an unguarded moment of truth he honourably could not deny, further inducing fresh pain. After recovering from a deep blush, he restrained himself regaining perfect composure, instinctively addressing Jane.

"I must confess I am at a loss of words to express my sorrow of your having ever been informed of the deed. At that time I was of the conviction that had I not allowed my erroneous pride to interfere, had I not felt it beneath me to lay open to the world my private actions, Wickham's worthlessness would have been understood. His evil character would have been exposed and never a young woman of character would have sought to love or confide in him. I felt it my duty to step forward to remedy the situation at once, to bring about a marriage to salvage your sister's reputation. Having done so, I should have never thought George Wickham as evil as this, to treat shamefully cruel a woman who innocently professed love and would have devoted her life to him. It torments me to think of it."

Elizabeth eyed her husband. His voice was soberly pained. The subject lay open old wounds publicly. Her heart now ached for him.

Mr. Darcy leaned forward, burying his face in his hands. Overcome with irrefutable anguish, he felt depleted. Feeling the weight of vulnerability seldom exposed, he was caught in a position of deficiency. Agonizing thoughts consumed him. He sought to do the honourable, but now suffered the realization his deed was to no avail.

Before he could utter another word, Jane voiced with great anxiety, "Mr. Darcy, please, surely we do not hold you accountable for Lydia or Wickham's actions. Everything you have done is honourable, nothing less indeed. I forbid you, never speak of it again. The only other persons in the bedchamber at the time of her revelation were the doctor and Mr. Manley. Mr. Manley knows the whole of it; you said so yourself did you not? No, I'll not hear of it, Mr. Darcy; I charge you to bury this secret with Lydia. Certainly Mr. Wickham will not repeat it to others, that would be admission of his guilt, not to mention it would expose him as was."

"Dearest, I fear your virtue places a heavy burden on you. You are the best man I know. I'll not have you reproach yourself. Enough said on this subject. Jane, Mr. Bingley, let us never speak of this matter again."

"Yes, Lizzy, I agree. I'm so sorry I spoke of it, Mr. Darcy, quite sorry indeed!" Jane said with suffering for having mentioned it.

"Darcy, I assure you, your actions were indeed honourable and are of no astonishment to me. I would expect you to do what is just. Perhaps if I had given it further thought, I should have realized it as such," Mr. Bingley added with unsettled feeling for his esteemed friend.

"You are all much too kind."

"Not at all, very grateful, Mr. Darcy, it is indeed an honour to be acquainted. Although you are my brother now, I prefer to think of you as friend," Jane assured him.

"Let us agree to say no more of this; let us not further hone a point exceedingly sharp as this," Elizabeth said as the carriage neared Netherfield.

Upon entering Netherfield Hall, the servants informed them that the rest of the party had already retired for the evening, much to Elizabeth's relief. The day had been hard; the anguish they suffered was enough without giving concern to thoughts of Caroline Bingley's or Mr. and Mrs. Hurst's unpredictable reception.

Restless Night and Morning Plight

HAVING HAD A RESTLESS NIGHT, Mr. Darcy stood robed at the bed-chamber window. He stood in the darkness, awaiting a glimpse of light over the horizon. His reason focused on his wife's resentment toward George Wickham, whose deceitful character once imposed on her understanding with flattering words succeeded by fabrications regarding his past actions, prior to his depravity of her sister. His internal instincts reflected the instilled decorum so rigidly taught to him as a child, which was surely to be tested this very day. He was now freshly tormented by the impending false magnanimity he should have to afford a man so offensive to him. For the sake of circumstances, he would forbid his pride to reach beyond the comfort of his understanding in the sight of death. He felt compelled to forget the injustice, to repress his deep-rooted disdain toward such an unscrupulous character, yet since he abhorred disguise of every sort, it would make the task a degradation; it would do little to lessen his ill opinion of him.

The sun arose slightly, providing a dim pattern of light within the chamber. He turned to eye his wife, who now tossed about restlessly, her anguish having prevented a peaceful night's rest. Again he turned his attention to the horizon, giving thought to his father, who once was his source of guidance. He was in want of his presence at this very moment, owning a strong desire for the comfort of his wisdom. Feeling misery of the acutest kind for the pretence he should have to display for his wife's sake would certainly prove a struggle to his endurance. He had no regrets of the advantages he afforded Lydia in her last days, only sorrow for her suffering, coupled with sadness for the loss of one so very young.

He stood a while longer until the sun gave greater light, then he approached the bed to make his wife awake.

"Dearest, it is time you made yourself ready; we have a long day before us. We shall have to breakfast before we return to your father's house."

"Very well, were you able to rest?" she inquired.

"Yes, a little, I was aware of your restlessness; how do you feel?"

"Somewhat rested, I suppose. Do not concern yourself on my account, dearest, I shall be quite well; surely you should have no worry with regard to me."

"Surely I shall concern myself with you always."

After hearing his words, she neared to embrace him. She required the strength of his affections, finding him always a comfort; but now she realized his pain was equal to hers.

When they entered the breakfast room, Jane and Mr. Bingley were present along with Caroline and Emily, who were about to sit side by side across from their seating. As Emily and Caroline were not yet seated, they curtsied. Emily was eager to address them. As she placed her napkin in her lap, she said, "Elizabeth, Mr. Darcy, I was hoping to see you before you departed for Longbourn. Elizabeth, my sincerest sorrow for the loss of your sister; indeed it must be very hard. We shall expect to arrive at the church at ten o'clock. How do your father and your sisters do; are they well under the circumstances?"

"They are as well as may be expected; I fear my father has taken it rather hard; my sisters are no less affected. Yes, I imagine today will test our endurance. I thank you for your kind inquiry. I am convinced my father will appreciate the attendance."

Emily's introduction to the conversation with kind discourse reflected her to be truly well bred. She smiled as she continued to further gain intercourse with friendly ease, affording Elizabeth the understanding of her earnest desire of the regard and welfare of her father and sisters.

Much to Elizabeth's surprise, Caroline Bingley proved to be receptive and polite, treating her with much more civility than anticipated, although Elizabeth dared to imagine her husband's presence influenced her temperament. Elizabeth remained guarded as Caroline submitted herself in a warm, friendly manner. In a notion to give her the benefit of doubt, Elizabeth surmised that perhaps the absence of Louisa Hurst, coupled with the presence of Emily, put Caroline in a more receptive spirit. But today it was of little matter; Caroline's behaviour was of no concern when she had the funeral to endure.

"Elizabeth and I shall be withdrawing soon after we breakfast. We shall see you at the church," Mr. Darcy told them.

"Lizzy, we plan to depart for Longbourn soon after we have breakfasted; perhaps we might travel together?" Jane inquired.

"Darcy, we shall take Hannah, we intend to have the infant remain here at Netherfield; or do you suppose we should not?" Mr. Bingley inquired.

"Bingley, I am convinced the child should go. Since you will require the wet nurse, it would be smart to take two carriages. I believe his presence should be made known. Perhaps Wickham would take pleasure from another glimpse of the boy."

"Yes, of course Darcy, I gave it no thought; of course he shall go."

"Very well, perhaps we should breakfast now," Mr. Darcy said soberly, eager for less conversation. Lydia's funeral occupied his thoughts as well as his wife's demeanour along with the prognosticated actions of George Wickham. He expected an exhausting day, anticipating much time spent keeping his wife disassociated from George Wickham to avoid flaring temperaments. He possessed no appetite, therefore he ate little. His quiet, sober appearance gained the notice of Caroline Bingley's curiosity.

She viewed him intently, even hesitating before saying, "Mr. Darcy, you scarce eat or speak. Are you ill; does something distress you?"

Mr. Darcy's dark eyes piercingly stared at Caroline with unrelenting disbelief. Her careless lack of decorum angered him. His voice became low with strength, answering abruptly. "Not at all, there is nothing so miraculous of the consequence of a funeral; I should think it easy to understand the somberness of such an occasion. I'm at a loss to understand why you should seek an answer of such?"

Caroline fixed her eyes on her plate. Her face coloured by his stern reply.

Mr. Bingley's countenance was that of affliction, disbelieving his sister would attempt to be so foolish as to challenge his friend under such circumstances. He understood all too well his sister's insinuations; she expected him to lack feelings for George Wickham's wife. He looked across at Caroline with dissatisfaction, rolling his eyes, now slightly shaking his head to acknowledge his disbelief. His embarrassment for his sister's unfeeling innuendos was distinctly conveyed.

Jane said not a word; she understood her husband's annoyance was for herself as well as Elizabeth. Jane, whose character sought the goodness of others, failed to comprehend her cruelty, further astonished that a supposedly refined individual would display such bad manners under mournful circumstances. She anxiously desired to part her company, privately wishing Caroline would not attempt to attend the funeral, viewing her intended presence a discomfort to her and her sister. She eyed Elizabeth, who sat expressionless. She noticed she had hardly touched the food on her plate, just nibbled daintily on a biscuit. As she started to fix her eyes in another direction, she noticed Mr. Darcy reach under the table to Elizabeth, touching her leg in a moment of compassion. Thinking it consoling, she reached down doing likewise, causing her husband to furnish her with a comforting smile.

Emily Bingley's expression was that of confused shock. She appeared embarrassed by the conversation, but said not a word; instead she continued to breakfast, searching the faces of those on the opposite side of the table. Mr. Bingley gazed across at her as he raised his brows in wonderment.

Mr. Darcy, aware his wife had no appetite, said, "Shall we, dearest?"

Elizabeth, understanding his full intention, promptly replied, "Yes, I am ready to depart. Are you, Jane, or do you require to extend the hour?"

"Yes, I am ready indeed."

"We shall leave you now," Mr. Bingley announced.

The gentlemen bowed, the ladies curtsied as they departed, satisfied to suffer the pain of Caroline's company no longer.

Farewell to a Sister

THEY RODE TO LONGBOURN in two carriages, with Elizabeth and Mr. Darcy taking little Hannah with them for comfort and distraction.

Elizabeth, glad to be parted from Caroline Bingley, now faced the insufferable company of George Wickham. She determined Caroline's society perhaps the less of the evils. Although Caroline sought to wound her occasionally, her only design was to injure with words implicative of her family connections, whereas George Wickham, she believed, had deprived her sister of a will to live, therefore inducing an early grave. In the carriage she sought her husband's hand to gain strength to face the sadness of the obsequies. First they would have to endure Wickham's presence at Longbourn, yet another feat to conquer, thought she.

Jane appeared to be managing rather well. The children, who occupied her concern at every moment, now diverted her attention. Her husband gladly accepted the children as his own, proudly consenting to call the infant Charles, finding honour in Lydia's request. Jane found her husband's fondness of children rewarding. She cherished the notion of Lydia at peace, knowing they would be afforded advantages and love.

When the carriages arrived at Longbourn, Kathryn, Mary and Hill approached to assist them to the house. The party was still gathered in the breakfast room. Mr. Wickham bowed when they entered, acknowledging them with a nod of his head. Before reclaiming his seat, he viewed the boy and softly spoke to Hannah, making no attempt to hold either of them.

Mr. Darcy and Mr. Bingley bowed. Mr. Bingley occupied a seat after agreeing to a cup of coffee offered by a servant. Mr. Darcy accepted a cup, but preferred to remain standing. He settled upon an advantageous position, should he find it necessary to provide urgent attention in a hopefully improbable situation. He felt on this day, at least, that he dared not leave anything to chance, noticing his wife's avoidance of Mr. Wickham.

Elizabeth managed to secure a seat advantaging her no direct view of Mr. Wickham. Her thoughts were of her last words with Lydia. As Mrs. Gardiner neared her, Elizabeth expressed concern for her younger sisters, seeking her aunt and uncle to remain near them for comfort, resolving they had no mother to render such duty. As always, the Gardiners happily obliged, having had already sought to assist prior to the asking. Elizabeth desired to stay at her husband's side but also wished to be near Mr. Bennet. Her father looked tired and drawn. The anguish, which was clearly visible upon his face, presented him despairingly.

Suddenly they heard loud wailing. The entire party knew at once that Mr. and Mrs. Philips had arrived. As always, she managed to cry louder than anyone. She entered the breakfast room in an uncontrollable state, not surprising to anyone, except perhaps Mr. Wickham, who really was not as closely acquainted. Mary tried to console her, only managing to make matters more severe. She refused to be calmed, turning more excitable at every attempt of comfort. No one wished to ignore her; however, her loud wailing served no purpose except to arouse the children to an unsettled state. Jane was incensed by her lack of control. She had the children taken above the stairs to remove them from the displeasure of the impression.

The dreaded time had arrived for the burial. The whole of the party left Longbourn for the church, including servants who witnessed Lydia's growth from the time of her infancy.

As they walked, Elizabeth stayed at her husband's side, encouraging her father to stay near. Along the way, Mr. Bennet neared Elizabeth. "Lizzy, what is there good to be expected when a man buries his youngest child? This is affliction of the bitterest kind. Her mother would be deeply unsettled; she was her favourite. Surely it is a blessing she is not here to gain witness of this event."

Elizabeth looked at her father. She took in a breath to steady herself. He looked back at her with saddened hollow eyes, which sunk into his disappointed face.

Mr. Bennet's words quivered past his lips as he sought to compose himself. He then continued, "What's a father to think? Perhaps it was neglect on my part; it is a most unfavourable affair. Oh, Lizzy, I should not have said it, it does no good; I suppose the less said the better," he continued to meander as he walked alongside of her.

"Papa, do not distress yourself so. I regret not having had the opportunity to speak with you in private. I must tell you, Lydia's last words were to tell you of her love. She asked that we tell you she was a good mother. Father, Lydia desired forgiveness for the reckless behaviour of her youth; she fully understood the ill merits of her past. She preferred you have knowledge of it. Lydia died in childbirth; she was too weak to see it through. Clearly there was nothing else to be done. Mr. Darcy acquired the most celebrated doctor in Derbyshire. You are not to blame; surely no one is to blame. I am certain Lydia would not wish you to reproach yourself."

"Very well, Lizzy, I suppose I shall have to accept it," he said sadly.

Mr. Darcy reached over to place his hand over hers, which was linked in his arm. She reached out to console her father, forgetting her own imbedded sorrow, deriving strength in consoling one she loved so dearly. He took pride in her action. It eased his mind to know she was distracted from Lydia's revelation or at least to know she did not wish to burden her father. It was clear—he was eased having heard the comforting words Elizabeth afforded him as she honoured Lydia in death, endearing her memory to her father as well as herself. Mr. Darcy felt he no longer needed to be concerned of her guilt. He believed she had finally reduced herself to resignation and acceptance. He could not expect greater joy than this on such a sorrowful day.

Although the infant was left at Longbourn, Hannah attended the funeral. Jane generously offered Hannah to Mr. Wickham. He accepted, holding her throughout the entire service. It did appear to provide consolation.

Elizabeth offered him no comfort of any kind; she rationalized Jane's reasoning and accepted it. But for herself, she remained less generous; it was not in her nature to search for goodness in a character whose honour was so inferior. She wished for her husband's sake she were more yielding, but she could only trust in his understanding.

It was a beautiful day; the air was crisp with a gentle sweeping breeze. The sky was clear, appearing powdery blue, not a cloud in sight. The ladies required shade devices to guard against the brightness of the sun. They stood at the grave, somber in spirit, sad at the parting. Elizabeth looked about, noticing Caroline and Emily Bingley with the Hursts. Turning her head slightly, she caught a glimpse of Mr. Collins with Charlotte standing near Sir William and Lady Lucas. Up until this moment, she had not given thought of their attending. The clergy announced the reading of "That Time of Year," written by William Shakespeare, which was chosen by her younger sisters at the suggestion of Mary.

That time of year thou may'st in me behold
When yellow leaves, or none, or few, do hang
Upon those boughs which shake against the cold,
Bare ruin'd choirs, where late the sweet birds sang:

In me thou see'st the twilight of such day
As after sunset fadeth in the west,
Which by and by black night doth take away,
Death's second self, that seals up all in rest:

In me thou see'st the glowing of such fire
That on the ashes of his youth doth lie,
As the death-bed whereon it must expire,
Consum'd with that which it was nourish'd by:

This thou perceiv'st, which makes thy love more strong,
To love that well which thou must leave ere long."

The clergy's closing words brought torrents of tears. It was no wonder to anyone present that Mrs. Philips' wailing could be heard over the weeping and sobs of the others. Surely had their mother been alive, she would have given her sister tumultuous competition, thought Elizabeth.

Mr. Bingley held Jane as she sobbed, while the Gardiners comforted Kathryn and Mary. Even Mr. Wickham was seen clutching Hannah with glazed, teary eyes. Elizabeth buried her face in her husband's chest, embracing him with all her strength. Managing to free an arm, Mr. Darcy gripped Mr. Bennet's shoulder, giving up his handkerchief to him. To his wife he gave another. He looked down at her, softly speaking, "Lydia is at peace now, dearest, surely you acknowledge it. You and Jane were fortunate to have had the occasion to speak with her, while the others must rely on your words alone. Your remembrance must be devoid of reproach; she would not desire it. Where her untamed past is concerned, a good memory is unpardonable; let this be the last you recollect her imperfections. Place your love in the proper perspective—love her forever, love her children, be not sad; she would not covet your despair; she proved sensible and strong in the end, facing death bravely. Remember her parting words of love, it is essential to the preservation of your regard for her existence."

Elizabeth eyed him with ardent admiration. His reverence created a sense of calm. She placed her sole dependence upon him. There was so much to be thought and felt. Quieting her sobs, she looked up at him with serenity, still embracing him. This embrace was one of affection, respect with endearment directed at him. He was quick to respond with sensitivity. Letting out a sigh of relief, he faintly smiled. He could not help but think the moment acquired greater value of love amidst the adversity of sorrowful pain. The heartfelt affection shared by the two provided mutual gratification of exchanged regard.

"Yes, I know it to be so, you must not be anxious for me," she told him, adding, "Lydia will live through her children; it is just all so very sad. But I am resigned; you bring me desired peace. I find I am more fortunate than ever I realized. Your tenderness pierces the center of my emotions so much that I can scarce contain my admiration of your excellence; truly I am dependent upon your devotion."

"Dearest, you may depend on my ardent love; you shall always have it. We have been involved in our own concerns; look there, your father has a comforter."

Elizabeth turned to view her father. He was speaking with Emily, Caroline and Mr. and Mrs. Hurst within an easy distance. She watched Caroline and the Hursts express condolences. He seemed distracted from his pain. Much to her astonishment, he invited them to the house for refreshments. Even more surprising was their eager acceptance. The thought of Caroline and the Hursts at Longbourn had no adverse effect on Elizabeth. Somehow she found their distraction to be advantageous when she considered Mr. Wickham's presence. Although offensive on occasion, they now appeared to be of such a different nature and by no means equal in magnitude. Before she could continue her thoughts, Caroline approached. "Elizabeth, allow me to express my sincere sorrow; I realize the pain you must be suffering from the loss of one so very young." All this was mentioned with such civility that Elizabeth felt confused. Perhaps the sober impression of the funeral caught Caroline in an unguarded moment of reality, stimulating a bit of sincerity. Elizabeth decided that, if this be the case, so much the better.

As expected, Mr. Collins and Charlotte approached them with Mariah. Elizabeth sarcastically wondered what words of wisdom she should expect to pass his lips. She was sure he would not ignore an opportunity to mention her sister's lamentable past. That would be too much to hope for.

"My dear cousin, allow me to offer my sincere condolences in the passing of your sister. Although she will be missed, surely her death will quiet all past indulgence; the family must now find solace in the passing of such a member. Although I share your sorrow, you must agree she reaped the fruits of her own ominous offences—a poor, misguided girl whose guilty, shameful behaviour was conceived at an early age. I am quite certain, given time, all will be forgotten."

Elizabeth grew more resentful of his continued impervious inclination to pompously pursue his unrestricted arrogance. Nothing, she could say or do would ever alter his insipid mirth of condescension. Nonetheless she could not walk away from yet another paltry attack on her family's reputation. After staring at him for a moment, she discovered she was too angry to unleash her true feelings under such tender circumstances. Her voice turned sarcastically cold. Not wishing to lay open publicly her exuberant disgust, she breathed deeply before stating, "Thank you, Mr. Collins, your generosity overwhelms me; as always you manage to flatter your own shallow character with statements of your misguided sentiments. You will excuse me now, I must speak with my father."

Charlotte stepped closer. "Elizabeth, allow me to express my sincere sorrow of Lydia's passing; I know the pain you must suffer." Mariah wept softly with a handkerchief to her face, but her eyes grew wide upon hearing her brother-in-law. He furnished Mariah a look of annoyance as if to deny her the opportunity to grieve for a lost friend. In her own mother's loss and now her sister's, he still injured through unguarded insult.

"Mr. Collins, I daresay I believe I shall be visiting the bishop very soon. Is there anything you wish me to say, for I have much to tell him?" Mr. Darcy asked, intending to cause discomfort or alarm of the undisclosed comments.

"No, Mr. Darcy," he replied. But, giving it further thought, he went on, "Perhaps you will mention my warmest felicitations to his Eminence. I flatter myself upon recognizing him occasionally with note of commendation, which I am convinced provides praise so deserving of a man of his stature. I view it my humble duty as a clergyman."

"Come dear, my father awaits us," Charlotte said, tugging on his arm. Her face turned a deep shade of red as she backed away from Elizabeth, obviously anxious to have him part their company.

Mr. Collins' failure to understand Mr. Darcy's meaning came as no surprise. It was not the first time his diplomacy lay waste on Mr. Collins, who lacked the aptitude to understand his own display of impervious foolery.

Elizabeth could no longer feel sorry for her friend. Although she felt Charlotte did not share his sentiments, on occasion her expressions seemed bent in his direction. If she sought little more than comforts of home when she set her designs on him, any suffering was now her own doing. She could no longer afford her friend sympathy in regard to her marital affairs.

A Day of Mourning

SCARCELY ANYTHING WAS TALKED OF the whole of the day but the funeral. There was great sadness connected in the loss of one so youthful. Mr. Bennet, along with his daughters, managed to occupy the respectful mourners, attempting to greet each with an exchange of dialogue which most often proved painful, but, dreary as must be, it was nonetheless a task they could not avoid. The task of receiving empathy provided busyness, which in a very small way afforded shallow diversion. Mrs. Philips continued to weep loudly, drawing attention in her direction, rekindling fresh sorrow and constant pain of the occasion.

Recurrently, Jane and Mr. Bingley disappeared to look in on little Charles, while Hannah remained with Mr. Wickham, who had by this time enjoyed several strong drinks. Elizabeth was slightly puzzled by the attention he afforded the child, but reasoned he perhaps felt more comfortable with her on his lap. She wondered why he lingered at Longbourn, knowing he was not looked upon with favour. Perhaps he stayed knowing nothing would be said of him in his presence, she mused. She wished him to quit the place to provide her much needed comfort. His presence agitated her, causing an uneasiness she certainly would not be wanting. She noticed he was quick to seek the attention of her sister Jane and Mr. Bingley, having once followed them above the stairs. His sudden attentive actions enhanced her curiosity. Her father granted him kindness, but then he was not aware of the deplorable conditions of Lydia's demise. She decided to make her way about the chamber to speak with those who mourned the loss of her sister, as she ought to do.

Sir William and Lady Lucas declared their sorrow with sincerity, quite unlike the expressions received from Mr. Collins. Sir William, not knowing the deficiency of his son-in-law's integrity, managed to praise him, drawing attention to his connections to her husband's aunt, Lady Catherine de Bourgh. It was all Elizabeth could bear to hold her tongue. Mr. Collins' good opinion of himself and selfish disdain for the feelings of others, escaped Sir William Lucas. Thinking perhaps if they were not so ignorant of his manners, they would not so freely praise him publicly. She thanked them for their attendance, then quickly parted their company.

She looked about for her husband. She inquired of Mary if she knew his whereabouts, but Mary had no knowledge of the situation. Her sister Kathryn was busy with Hannah and could tell her nothing. She then suspiciously looked for Mr. Wickham. She approached her father, who was occupied with Caroline, Emily and the Hursts. She noticed Caroline looking about the chamber with inquisitive smugness, examining all its belongings; it was obviously less richly furnished than Netherfield Hall. Elizabeth believed Caroline in all probability found Longbourn rather insignificant in comparison to the grandeur she was accustomed to. She became momentarily distracted by their conversation upon hearing of dinner arrangements for Kathryn, Mary and her father at Netherfield the day next. Fearing her inquiry might be misconstrued, she preferred not to ask of Mr. Wickham's whereabouts. She continued her search but saw no sign of him. Perhaps he decided to take his leave, thought she, with a sense of satisfaction.

She joined her Aunt and Uncle Gardiner in the sitting room where they conversed with her younger sisters, while little Hannah played off to the side. Her Aunt Philips joined the conversation, making the whole of it morbid with her dramatic sentiments. Elizabeth thought she should have to quit the room if she began to wail loudly. They talked for five and twenty minutes until Elizabeth heard Mrs. Philips mention Mr. Philips being above the stairs. Her curiosity piqued, she anxiously inquired, "Whatever would he be doing above the stairs?"

"How should I know, child? Hill was sent to fetch him!" Aunt Philips blurted out in a startled loud tone. At that very moment Elizabeth saw the likeness of her mother.

"Excuse me, I shall return directly," Elizabeth stated as she hastily parted their company, directing herself toward the stairs. Upon her passage to the entrance hall she noticed her husband descending. He approached her in haste, expressing his desire for a drink. Elizabeth's suspicions arose when he guided her to the sitting room with strides faster paced then normally supposed.

"Well, Elizabeth, I see you found your husband," Aunt Gardiner commented.

"Yes, I was above the stairs to see little Charles; he has gone to sleep now. Jane and Mr. Bingley will descend directly; they are with him."

Elizabeth was dissatisfied with his behaviour. His facial expressions made it difficult for him to conceal anything. The tête-à-tête with her husband seemed unnatural. He appeared to be making conversation for its own sake, eventually talking of Mr. Knisely's book shop to her Uncle Gardiner.

Mr. Philips entered the sitting room, claiming a seat nearest his wife. Although he said nothing, Elizabeth attempted to read his expressions with no results, but still wondered why Mr. Philips would be commissioned above the stairs. She noticed her husband's expression as he conversed more naturally, seeming to have regained composure. She was puzzled. She once again looked about, but seeing nothing unusual she was forced to abandon all suspicions.

Mr. Bennet entered the sitting room. He directed himself to Elizabeth. "Lizzy, Caroline Bingley and the Hursts are returning to Netherfield Park. Do you know the whereabouts of Jane and Mr. Bingley, are they above the stairs?"

"I believe they are, Father."

"Very well then, Emily has agreed to stay. May she ride back to Netherfield with you and Mr. Darcy?"

Elizabeth viewed him with curiosity. "Why—yes, Father, we shall be delighted to have Emily accompany us."

Although her father seemed rather happy to have her stay, Caroline Bingley and Mrs. Hurst seemed less delighted. They appeared surprised at the design. Their faces revealed unguarded, displeasing looks fixed on each other at the mention of the plan.

"Very well then, Emily and I shall escort the ladies and Mr. Hurst out of doors," he said as Mr. Darcy arose to join him, bowing. Elizabeth, taken by surprise, quickly decided to do the same. She turned to those remaining. "Pray excuse me," she said as she curtsied, parting their company.

When they re-entered the house, Jane and Mr. Bingley were descending the stairs. They both had a placid look about them; almost smugness, thought Elizabeth. Again her curiosity piqued, forcing her to approach Jane. "Why were you so long above the stairs?"

"Charles and I were just enjoying little Charles, that is all, Lizzy; he was awake."

"Very well then, Jane, I do believe Mr. Wickham has taken his leave; Caroline and the Hursts have gone as well. I must say I am relieved, indeed."

"Yes, Lizzy, I understand your meaning. I believe I just saw Emily with Father. Did she not return to Netherfield with the rest of the party?"

"No, apparently she is to keep our father company. I can easily see he is refreshed with her presence; she is definitely a value at such a time."

"Yes, indeed," Jane answered, but her mind seemed to have misplaced the conversation as her thoughts appeared elsewhere.

Elizabeth viewed her with concern. "Jane, are you quite all right?"

"Oh, yes, Lizzy, very well, I'm sorry; I was just thinking of the children. Look at Hannah; she appears tired, does she not?"

"Yes, she rubs her eyes. Our sisters have afforded her much attention. I do believe they have completely fatigued her."

"Lizzy, would you mind if Charles and I took the children back to Netherfield Park? I am weary as well; I believe I should like to return immediately. Do you mind staying? Emily, may she return with you?"

"Oh, Jane, it was already settled. Emily is going to return with us. I suppose Fitzwilliam and I shall have to stay a while longer to allow Father some time with his guests. Very well then, it is settled; you go, we will join you later."

"Thank you, Lizzy, I shall find Charles now. I believe he is in the entrance hall with your husband," she said as they parted company.

He was not. Mr. Bingley had gone above the stairs. Mr. Darcy remained in the entrance hall with Mr. Gardiner. Mr. Gardiner now quietly appraised him of the investigation of the Bennet family mystery they so eagerly sought to resolve. They, having once believed it to be Mr. Bennet's great-grandfather, learned in actuality it was his great-great-grandfather. Mr. Gardiner learned that a noble title once belonging in the Bennet family had been sold. The investigation quitted at Mr. Bennet's great-great-grandfather, revealing Longbourn not to be the original estate; its location was in the high country, proposing to be considerably grand. Unfortunately, Mr. Gardiner had nothing beyond this news to tell. As Mr. Bingley descended the stairs, his re-entering the entrance hall forced the confidential discourse of the two gentlemen to end.

It was but a short time until Jane returned to secure Hannah, who had fallen asleep on Kathryn's lap. They bid farewell to those remaining, then quitted Longbourn. Since most of the guests had parted, Mr. and Mrs. Philips announced they should take their leave as well.

Hill had several servants set out a fresh display of food for those left behind. They gathered in the dining hall, those remaining now consisting of Mr. and Mrs. Gardiner, Emily, Elizabeth, Mr. Darcy, the two girls and Mr. Bennet. "Well now, our party has decreased in size, has it not?" Mr. Bennet asked.

"Yes, Father, to be sure," Elizabeth expressed; then she asked, "Father, when did Mr. Wickham leave?"

"Well now, that is strange, Lizzy, I gave no thought of him until your inquiry at this very moment; I suppose he left without saying a word. Strange fellow, I cannot imagine him lingering as long as he did. Lizzy, he had very little to say, I did think it odd he never mentioned Lydia once. I should have thought he would show more compassion, very strange fellow indeed!" he said, his brow wrinkled with puzzlement.

"Did you see him leave, Aunt, did you Mary, Kathryn?" Elizabeth inquired.

"No, not at all, he was here, then gone just like that; perhaps he decided he delighted us long enough with his presence," Kathryn stated sarcastically.

"We did not see him leave, Elizabeth; we cannot tell you when we last noticed him. Can you dear?" Mr. Gardiner said, looking at his wife.

"Why, no, Elizabeth, it escaped my notice."

"I must confess I was relieved when I thought him gone; it is strange though, I should have expected he would have taken a moment to thank you for your hospitality, Father."

"Never mind that, Lizzy. Mr. Darcy, I received a very kind message from your aunt, Lady Catherine de Bourgh, regarding our loss, very kind indeed. Would you care to read it?" he asked as he started to take leave of his seat.

"That's quite all right, Mr. Bennet, you remain seated. I thank you for the information; it pleases me to know she sent you a message."

Elizabeth, so taken aback, managed to say, "One finds unexpected kindness in the oddest places. I had not anticipated your aunt to respond; after all, her connections here are vague; how very kind of her."

"Indeed, she speculated when we should meet again at Pemberley for a game of backgammon, Mr. Darcy," Mr. Bennet added.

Mary injected, "Father, you will have an opportunity to play backgammon with Lady Catherine, but not for several months I suppose. Indeed you do plan a ball at Pemberley; is that not so, Mr. Darcy?"

Mr. Darcy sat silent for a few moments before answering. Uncomfortable of talking of a ball under such sad circumstances, he cautiously addressed Mary. "Uh—we do have a ball planned at Pemberley as soon as Jane and Mr. Bingley settle in our vicinity, I believe sometime after Michaelmas. I expect you, my aunt, your father and sister will attend. Emily, I believe we shall have the pleasure of your company as well."

"A ball! Mary, did you hear of it, a ball at Pemberley," Kathryn cried out with joy. Her voice went from sheer excitement to trailing sadness before she burst into tears. It was not hard to understand what caused her weeping. Lydia always longed for a ball. It was simply another reminder she was lost to them forever. Since Kathryn had done so well the whole of the day, Elizabeth supposed the subject caused her repressed feelings to finally surface, and the sting of death now caused her suffering.

"There, there, Kitty," Mr. Bennet said, "you have your cry out; it will do you credit to be sure; your day has been hard. Forgive me, Kathryn, I forget you are not to be called Kitty; here, take my handkerchief," he said, handing it to her.

"Is there anything I can do for you?" Emily inquired.

"No, thank you just the same," Kathryn said, suppressing her sobs.

Mary remained seated, her eyes filled with tears. The pain of the day's events became fresh again, casting somberness upon the whole of the conversation.

Kathryn composed herself. She studied the handkerchief at length. Viewing the initials on the handkerchief, she said with curiosity, "This is not yours, Father, it says 'FD' " still forcing back a sob or two.

"You are in the right, my dear, that indeed does not belong to me; it is Mr. Darcy's. I forgot he gave it to me at the cemetery."

"That's quite all right, Mr. Bennet. Kathryn, are you feeling better now?" Mr. Darcy inquired.

"Yes," she answered, letting out a sigh as she reached over to hand him the handkerchief.

"Perhaps you better keep it; you may need it again."

"No, Mr. Darcy, I am quite fine now."

"You are staying the night?" Elizabeth directed at her Aunt and Uncle Gardiner.

"Yes, we will take our leave in the morning."

"We must entertain thoughts of taking our leave now," Elizabeth said, looking at her husband for approval, then at Emily.

"To be sure, it is getting rather late; we should not wish to disturb all those at Netherfield Park upon our arrival," Mr. Darcy pointed out.

"It was an honour to meet you, Mr. and Mrs. Gardiner; I do look forward to meeting you again some day, perhaps," Emily stated.

Mrs. Gardiner smiled. "Likewise, to be sure."

"I trust you shall all come together at the Pemberley ball," Elizabeth stated hesitantly for Kathryn's sake.

Emily turned to Mr. Bennet. "Mr. Bennet, a pleasure indeed, I have so enjoyed the company at Longbourn. Upon our meeting next, it will be under more desirable circumstances to be sure."

"It is my pleasure indeed; I believe I shall walk you out."

"Kathryn, Mary, it was a pleasure, pray please send a message if there be anything to be done where I may assist," Emily told the girls.

Elizabeth marveled at the reaction of Kathryn and Mary. Both advanced to her, granting an embrace; it was obvious she had captured their friendship.

Last Stay at Netherfield

WHEN THEY REACHED NETHERFIELD, Caroline and Mrs. Hurst were awaiting Emily's return while Mr. Hurst lay sprawled, covering most of the sofa. Jane and Charles had retired early, Louisa announced. Caroline immediately approached Emily. "So how did you enjoy your little visit at Longbourn?"

"Quite well; why do you ask?"

"Louisa and I discussed the visit; we thought it odd you desired to stay. We rather expected you to return to Netherfield in our carriage," Caroline told her slyly.

"I rather enjoyed the evening—good food, fine conversation with excellent company—although I daresay I prefer better circumstances. It's too bad you chose not to stay; we were served the tastiest pudding, wouldn't you agree, Mr. Darcy?"

"Most definitely."

Elizabeth stated with sincere civility, "In the end there were eight of us gathered round the table; it was soothing to be sure, quite pleasing."

"Quite, I suppose," Caroline retorted.

Mr. Darcy touched Elizabeth's arm. "Dearest, shall we retire now?"

"Yes, I believe we shall."

As they quitted the room, they fixed their eyes on each other. They were sorry to leave Emily to deal with her sister's impertinent remarks.

They made their way above the stairs, so happy to close the door to the bedchamber. When they lay in bed, Mr. Darcy soberly began, "Dearest, I must make known to you of a situation today. Forgive my late revelation, but I thought it wisest to withhold the truth until present. I feared your knowing would provoke inappropriate uneasiness, perhaps unleashed anger. I could not conceive your direct response amidst the Longbourn population, surely disguise would have been laborious."

"What is it dearest, you sound so severe?"

"When I descended the stairs, I did so as having been a witness of legal documents."

"What legal documents would you have witnessed?"

"I was commissioned above the stairs by Bingley, he dispatched Hill to fetch me. When I joined them, George Wickham was present. Wickham approached Bingley regarding the children; claiming poverty, he asked Bingley to consider affording him £5,000."

"Heaven forbid! What?" Elizabeth squealed.

"Shhhhhhh, Elizabeth, you must keep your voice low. Although he did not claim payment for the children, he hinted he might be forced to take them with him. Bingley convinced a settlement of £2,000, but insisted it be legal, making it necessary to secure the services of Mr. Philips, who penned the papers. I witnessed them. Truthfully, Wickham sold his children. Can you believe his arrogance?"

"Good God, I can scarce believe this, how unfortunate to find a man so disagreeable to be a father—the poor children. Is there no limit to his evil ways?" Elizabeth cried with horror, putting her hand up to her mouth.

"Elizabeth, calm yourself; this is the very reason I concealed this from you at Longbourn. Jane was witness as well. Think of it, dearest, it is best; he cannot return to claim them."

"Oh, gracious, does my father know this?" she wanted to know at once.

"No, he has not been informed as yet, but I do believe it would be best we enlighten him lest Wickham tries to contact your father in the future for favours."

"Yes, truly, I can scarce take breath; it is a melancholy thought, quite shocking!"

"The whole of it, Elizabeth, is this: once he received the bank note he fled with not a whisper of the children. I am of the opinion your sister asked Jane to look after them, realizing his dishonourable nature; she no doubt feared for their welfare. Even I should have not thought George Wickham as unfeeling as this."

"I am grateful that he allowed Jane and Mr. Bingley to initiate the claim then."

"Indeed—Elizabeth, I fear there is more to tell."

"What more horrid thing can be said of him?"

"Dearest, forgive me my lack of disclosure; I saw no good in it before this. To be truthful, I was pleased I had not told you the whole of the truth; such a revelation would have made today more unbearable."

"Whatever can possibly revolt me more ill than a man who sells his children?"

"Dearest, when in London I learned Wickham spent much time in the company of prostitutes. Lydia was left to care for herself as well as the child."

"Uh—I can hardly believe what I am hearing. Can this be true? By whom can you have heard it mentioned?" she gasped.

"Had I not settled with the landlord, she would have been abandoned, I believe, having no food as well. At first your aunt and uncle believed they made frivolous purchases, but that was not so. She was wanting; her shame caused her to withhold the truth from your aunt, until Mrs. Gardiner visited, witnessing her poverty. Your Aunt and Uncle Gardiner provided for her the nourishment needed for some time. They were not aware of the rent. I happened upon that myself quite by accident."

"What did he do with his wages? With whom were you so intimate to learn of his dealing with prostitutes? Did the landlord enlighten you of his acts?"

"No, he did not. I do know he quit the commission purchased for him; to what end he managed I know not. I only confirm the prostitute with certainty."

"How is it you can claim with certainty?"

"Unable to sleep, I ventured to walk very early one morning. I saw him in the prostitute's portal, her occupation there being obvious. Luckily, he did not make my notice. I ducked into a postern, then quickly quitted the area after witnessing his ill behaviour. I cannot begin to tell you of my immediate feelings. I was appallingly discouraged by all I witnessed. Truly I tell you, to parley with the tempter is always a danger. George Wickham lives life extremely ill. If the wages of sin is death, I believe George Wickham has died many times."

"I can scarce take this all in."

"I fear there is more to tell."

"More? I tell you faithfully, I can scarce believe this. You must tell me; do go on."

"Bear in mind our wedded journey, the day of the ball at Hyde Park. We were about to join your sister and Bingley below the stairs. I had walked to the window as I habitually do. I made notice of Mr. Wickham with a lady other than Lydia. They were obviously on very familiar terms. To divert your attention from the view at the window as well as delay going below the stairs, I captured you at the looking glass, keeping you there for a time in deliberate conversation. I did not wish you to be a witness to such ghastly impropriety. It was my sincerest desire to keep our wedding journey pure. I wanted nothing more than to secure untarnished memories of those days. I worried of your sister and Mr. Bingley's discovery of them. I feared such happiness would be hindered. Fortunately, they did not come below the stairs prior to our arrival, and for a brief time all was safe."

"Why do you say a brief time?"

"You will well recall the Hyde Park ball. A Miss Grey made deliberate strides to gain my notice of her. You witnessed the sultry look she afforded me. You will no doubt recall later that evening, due to my failed attempt to hide my shock of seeing her there, your curiosity caused you to seek an explanation."

Before he could go further, she asked, "What does this have to do with George Wickham?"

"I had not thought it possible that the ill effects of George Wickham would interrupt my wedded bliss, but indeed it was so. Miss Grey was the woman I witnesseded with George Wickham outside the inn. When I saw her at the Hyde Park ball, I thought surely she was there with Wickham, but we then noticed her leaving with another gentleman. The shock you witnessed had little to do with Miss Grey's presence, but more so with the presumption of George Wickham being in close proximity. The prostitute in the portal I witnessed with George Wickham on my business journey was none other than Miss Grey. I confess I have further thoughts on the subject."

"What more can there be?"

"That day in London, on our wedding journey when I made their notice from the window, it troubled me to think of past circumstances. My explanation to you of Miss Grey was not entirely whole. I was pained by the imposition. I did not wish to disturb your thoughts of happiness, so I concealed the whole of the incident."

Elizabeth listened intently. He paused, his voice taken with sober reflection. She could only anticipate his next words.

"You will remember my telling you Miss Grey was Georgiana's governess. Mrs. Reynolds, being well aware of Miss Grey's unsolicited attentions toward me, scrutinized her every move. She uncovered Miss Grey's close relationship with George Wickham. By chance, she heard them discuss a plan to discredit me by way of tarnishing my reputation. Their plan was to conveniently have another servant witness Miss Grey departing my bedchamber. Had it been anyone other than Mrs. Reynolds, I may have been doubted, perhaps the recipient of universal gossip, but she knows me too well to have any ill thoughts in that direction and lay to ruin their plan. Miss Grey planned to enter my bedchamber out of design, a scheme undoubtedly thought up by George Wickham. Mrs. Reynolds' observation unquestionably prevented their charging a public slander in my direction. Miss Grey was dismissed from her post at once."

"Oh, dearest, to think that night I begged an explanation. Oh, Fitzwilliam, what must you think of me? You chose to suffer in silence to protect my memories of our wedding journey. The whole of the time you endured the ill effects of their tarnishing your own." Elizabeth threw her hands to her face. Her eyes welled with tears, soon spilling down her cheeks in despair.

"Come now, dearest, let us put this behind us. Our esteem for one another can surely endure the test of time, even George Wickham. There now, wipe your eyes," he gently said handing her his handkerchief. He was drained of all such feelings that he had constrained for so long, now experiencing a certain sense of relief from the revelation.

"My dearest Fitzwilliam, such impediments you endured to protect me. How you must have suffered—surely you must have."

"Elizabeth, when I arose this morning I dreaded the day before us. George Wickham's conduct is exceedingly vile, such lack of character I would have never guessed. I fail to understand a man who uses his children ill without feelings of remorse. The only good that has come of it is that Jane and Bingley have legal validation for the children; surely his performance affords him no credit of character. It appears his coming here is a most insolent act indeed; I can't imagine he presumed to do so. Even his presence at your sister's funeral was a mockery; his only design in coming was to sell his children or salvage his image. Let us delight in his absence."

"Dearest, I'm so sorry; surely you agonized keeping this from me. There is one bright spot in all of this. I confess it is equally fortunate for us never to have any dealings with Mr. Wickham ever again."

"Yes, that is so. Nonetheless, I shall never understand. His father was an honourable man. His upbringing at Pemberley advantaged him every privilege. As children we called at the parsonage, often learning a depth of integrity from such visits. When a man loses or compromises his principles, his integrity is lost to him forever. If he does so and manages to conceal his lost principles from the sphere of his society, he still must view his reflection in the looking glass. It is that reflection he cannot escape, because it is that image that is fully known to him alone. The man looking in the glass knows what harbours in his heart; he cannot conceal it from himself, lest he deny it—then the looking glass becomes his worst enemy. It is required that a man lead a life that is pleasing to God; the truest test of a man's character is when alone with Him."

"Fitzwilliam, your words are so profound."

"Why should they not be? A man may easily measure his success or failures by his thoughts. I should think it not so very hard to understand at all. But I confess, when I think of Wickham, I cannot understand his thinking. He grew up at Pemberley and was educated at Cambridge with privileges few could boast. He was guided by a father who loved him, then by my own father. He had a most advantageous future before him, but in the end he chose to cast it aside for fleeting lust and greed."

"Fitzwilliam dearest, you feel so deeply. Let us speak no more of Wickham; it is as you say, we are done with him. We no doubt will never have reason to be acquainted with him ever again. Words of him are so indecorously unworthy of the breath wasted in mentioning his name. It pains me to think my sister had not the affections or esteem we enjoy, but then George Wickham has not the depth of your character. Your principles prove you incapable of compromise, lending understood distinction of your character being no less than you present it to be. Truly I tell you, I honour your loyalty."

"Say no more, dearest; come close, allow me to hold you," an exhausted Mr. Darcy said with his eyes closed. His voice was now fading fast as he struggled to stay awake.

Elizabeth lay silent, attempting to eliminate all thoughts of George Wickham from her mind. She could not. She thought of the tragic death of her sister. She was reminded of her judgment upon Lydia's arrival at Pemberley. It was she who continued to question her husband's constant generosity. She saw it as an encumbrance on her husband, but he only saw Lydia in desperate need of assistance. He easily used his power to relieve her situation with undistracted ease. The fact that Lydia was married to George Wickham did not alter his generosity. He extended to her every comfort without indecision, while she struggled awkwardly regarding his obligation with spoken, marked reservations. His constant generosity to Lydia frustrated her at the time. She was haunted now by her opposition to her husband's actions. Oh, if I were only more like him, thought she. He lay next to her, breathing heavily as he slept. She was drawn to his powerful presence. She slowly moved her open palm across his chest, taking in his influential significance, wondering how she deserved such a man. His honour was constant, but the force which guided his goodness seemed to elude her. He was uniform in his loyalty to duty. She was disposed to be inquisitive in nature; he, on the other hand, was quietly reserved, often edified of all around him. She always questioned his duty, while he invariably did his duty without question. She could only wonder how she could have been so full of error. She desperately desired sleep. His heavy breathing seemed to beckon her to join him. She snuggled closer. Her thoughts gathered more resolution of the worst being over. Together they lay silent until, at last, sleep overcame her.

Unpleasantness Made Known

ELIZABETH AND MR. DARCY AWOKE at sunrise, surprised at having had a restful sleep. As they lay close they discussed when they should make known to Mr. Bennet the whole of the truth regarding George Wickham. They agreed to leave Netherfield after having breakfasted to allow Mr. Bennet the better part of the day to recover from the wicked tale, considering he was expected to dine that evening at Netherfield Park.

Upon entering the breakfast chamber, they discovered that they had been the last to rise.

"Elizabeth, pray tell me, of what dish your father is fondest? Is there anything particular?" Emily inquired.

"Why, yes, he is fond of lamb, a leg of lamb with mint preserves. But he eats anything; he is not so very particular."

"Father likes potatoes," Jane added.

"Very well then, we shall have the cook prepare his fondest dishes. And your sisters, are they fond of lamb? Oh, Jane, is it agreeable to you that I may direct the meal? I thought you would be busy with the children."

"Why yes, of course, Emily, I thank you. As for my sisters, they will delight in whatever is prepared; you may depend upon it."

"Elizabeth, may we get you anything? I see you have no appetite for the serving this morning," Caroline made note, looking across at her plate.

"Thank you, but I fear I have no appetite; no, nothing else thank you," she said. She was puzzled again by Caroline's attempt to be kind.

Elizabeth leaned forward. "After we have breakfasted, Mr. Darcy and I will be going directly to Longbourn; we shall return in the afternoon."

Jane looked at Elizabeth with marked speculation. "Shall we go with you, Lizzy?"

"No, no, that is not necessary. We are just going to visit with Father, that is all."

"Very well, if you are sure, Lizzy."

"Quite sure, Jane, do not concern yourself with us; I'm sure you would prefer to stay with the children."

"Very good then, I should wish to stay with the children."

Mr. Bingley stood from his chair. He parted his lips with all the enthusiasm expected from one so wholly and completely happy. "Caroline, Louisa, Emily, perhaps it is best to inform you the children are our children now; Jane and I have legal papers stating so."

Caroline gasped. "Upon my soul, Charles, can this be true?"

"To be sure," he smiled, stating further, "The boy's name is Charles; he is my son, yes indeed. I have great plans for him."

Louisa Hurst's face turned sour. Her eyes squinted in confusion. She swallowed hard, parting her lips as if to speak but merely took in air. She directed a look of disbelief to Caroline. Caroline's expression bore no less snobbery. To avoid further displeasing glances, Louisa allowed her eyes to look down upon the table. She managed to deliberately step upon Caroline's foot. Together they stared at their brother opposite them, who swelled with undeniable pride.

"Charles, Jane, I'm so very happy for you," Emily told them pleasingly.

Louisa questioned, "Charles, you will raise the sister's children?"

"Yes, indeed, is there an objection I should be aware of?" he asked challengingly. His manner was less civil than before.

"Of course not, Charles, it was a mere inquiry," Louise said, her voice softening with sweetness as she deliberately pressed the sole of her shoe upon Caroline's foot once again.

He was aware she and Caroline avoided eye contact. He fixed his eyes on them, daring them to question further. "From this day forward they are our children. No one is to call them anything else; am I understood?"

"Oh, yes, indeed, Charles, to be sure," Caroline added, her eyes wide with surprise, fearing to make expression or utter another word.

Elizabeth, Jane and Mr. Darcy remained silent as they witnessed the taming. They had not expected Charles to be this stern or forceful. To their own surprise they found it quite impressive as well as entertaining.

Mr. Darcy looked at Elizabeth. "Dearest, shall we start for Longbourn?"

"Very well, I bid you good day; we shall return in the afternoon," Elizabeth said, then curtsied before quitting the chamber with relief.

When they reached Longbourn, Mr. Bennet was in his library. They knocked, then entered upon invitation.

"Well, now, this is a pleasant surprise. I had not expected to see you before this evening at Netherfield Park."

"Father, we have news, unpleasant news of an alarming nature I fear; you must be made aware of it," Elizabeth stated without hesitation.

"I fear what these revelations tend. Very well, then, if you must. I daresay by your melancholy expressions, perhaps I should have some port to hear it. Mr. Darcy, Lizzy, will you join me?" he asked as he arose from his desk.

"Yes, I believe I would, Mr. Bennet; would you, dearest?"

"Yes, in such cases as these I believe I should, it may provide relief."

After pouring a glass of port for Mr. Darcy and his daughter, Mr. Bennet received the information they so painfully related. They watched the colour drain from his face upon learning what a true blackguard Mr. Wickham was,—aghast to learn he sold his children, but even more horrified to learn of the painful circumstances Lydia suffered; however, was not surprised to hear of the prostitute. His eyes became saddened by the revelation. Upon conclusion, he looked at Mr. Darcy with sober reflection. "Mr. Darcy, I confess, when you requested my Lizzy's hand, I had thought she should think the better of it. I only wish my Lydia had made half such a match, she was youthfully silly, perhaps more than most, but she was my daughter just the same. There were times I had not afforded her the sense with which she was born, just referred to her as silly and ignorant, more so than other girls—always chasing after the officers, always seeking balls and flirtations of any sort. But even so, no young lady deserves such treatment as you describe—shameful, truly shameful. She was innocent, guilelessly unsuspecting, certainly no match for such a wily adversary." He thought for a moment, then gasped. "Good Lord, I suppose her dying spared the family further disgrace; what an awful thought—I comprehend your purpose in telling me, no need to concern yourself now. George Wickham shall never set foot in this house again. If he is a man with any sense at all, he'll never seek to approach me. He shall be prohibited from having any contact with any of the girls. We should have known there was no good to be expected, but what makes the present situation more pitiful is his selling his own children. I am exceedingly astonished. He deserves no attention. Such a man is he who lacks honour, duty, gratitude; a black-hearted villain indeed, owning to the contempt of the world." Mr. Bennet unleashed his feelings, growing violently vexed at the thought of Wickham. His voice grew sternly loud, with anger clearly visible in his expression. Elizabeth feared the toll such anger might have on his health.

"Oh, Father, calm yourself, this is not helpful; there is nothing to be done. Father, before Lydia died she was sensible but aged well before her time. I do believe he robbed her of her will to live. Had circumstances been a bit different, perhaps she would still be with us. It pains me to enlighten you of her sorry state upon her arrival at Pemberley. Oh, Father, we quite despaired," she said, burying her face in her hands, allowing the tears to flow freely.

Mr. Darcy comforted her until she regained composure to speak.

"Mr. Bennet, although grievous news to be sure, we have determined that full disclosure is necessary. Do not underestimate Mr. Wickham's boldness. He may very well contact you for gain. The £2,000 note Mr. Bingley afforded him will be squandered in haste; I have no doubt of it. He lacks principle, and he will falsify to acquire his desires. It was not our intention to cause distress, but rather to put you wise to his cunning nature. We fear he may try to secretly correspond with Kathryn or Mary," Mr. Darcy explained.

"Lizzy, do not despair on my behalf; I'll get over it soon enough perhaps."

"Father, I believe it wise to inform Kathryn and Mary of a portion of this revelation. I'm not quite trusting of his arrogance; he may write to them. Considering their youth, he may very well appeal to their innocence; he is entirely corrupt, truly he is."

"Yes, Lizzy, I quite agree; allow me to inform them in private. Oh dear, this is most burdensome, such a horrid man to have penetrated our family, such sad business."

"Well, Father, I hope he will think the better of it. Let us say no more of this; indeed he is repulsive."

"Yes, let us say no more," he answered, just as Hill knocked on the door to announce the cook had prepared a noon meal for the company, expecting their presence directly in the dining hall. Elizabeth was wanting for not having been able to eat breakfast. Mr. Bennet appeared glad for the interruption; the strain of the conversation wore heavy on his expression. It was easy to see the pain he endured. Kathryn and Mary joined them, appearing to have returned to their normal dispositions. Elizabeth perceived that Mary had persisted to don her fresh look. Decidedly, she flattered her, causing her face to redden. Kathryn continued her poise of a more ladylike manner, almost as if the very change in name had spun her about. The conversation passed off affably, with less somber ambience as not to eliminate the pleasantries of family discourse. After much talk, Elizabeth said, "Father, we intend to quit Netherfield in the morning."

"I would expect as much, Lizzy, your children await you."

"Mr. Bennet, might I challenge you to a game of backgammon? I assure you there is no obligation to play favourite, allowing my win," Mr. Darcy said, catching him quite by surprise.

"What is this you speak of, Mr. Darcy? I'll not allow you to win if possible to be sure; you may depend upon it," Mr. Bennet came back at him in a spirited manner.

"I am aware the allowances you afforded my aunt," he told him, much to Elizabeth's astonishment.

"Lizzy, you said you would not speak of it?"

"Father, I said nothing. Dearest, tell him; indeed I did not!"

"Nay, Mr. Bennet, I have eyes; that was very generous of you. I've watched you play; your strategy is quite keen—you play well. The game did not escape my notice."

"Well, I've been found out. I didn't realize I had an audience; I shall be more cautious in the future. I daresay, Mr. Darcy, your aunt needed a win that evening."

"Yes, indeed, Mr. Bennet, I believe she did. Now shall we play?"

Elizabeth watched the men for a time. Then, tempted by the fine weather, she decided a turn about the grounds would give her pleasure. Pursuing a walk down the familiar path, her mind wandered from the past to the present, from the first she set eyes on Mr. Darcy to Lydia's fresh grave. And having done so, she realized she had walked in the direction of the churchyard and was now near the cemetery. She walked to Lydia's fresh grave. Looking down, she spoke as if her sister might apprehend her words. "My dear sister, we shall ever be denied your earthly presence. Fear not, your children are in the best of hands; that should give you comfort. Oh, Lydia, forgive my stubbornness; had I truly known, I should have sent you something more out of my pin money; this will always remain my regret."

She stood over her grave for a time. The air was calm with a gentle breeze that whispered through the trees as if to say "all is well, Elizabeth, I am at peace." Her grave was peacefully situated on a slight, sunny hill. She looked at her mother's grave nearby. Stepping to it, she reached down to touch the earth where she lay. She stood for a few moments before turning to make her way back to Longbourn, feeling a sense of serenity.

She learned the first backgammon game had been won by her husband, the second by her father—and both gentlemen, having claimed victory, ended their challenge.

Mr. Darcy and Elizabeth returned to Netherfield Park. In the afternoon the two managed a turn about the grounds. Mr. Darcy stopped his walk. "One day whilst you visited Netherfield Park, I thought you a fine prospect from that very window," he said, pointing his walking stick. "I watched you intently. The feelings you inflamed in me, I effortlessly rejected. In vain, I tried to escape my fascination by concentrating on a book, but such denial drew you nearer. My dearest Elizabeth, how you made me admire you with those captivating eyes." Looking down at her, he continued, "My heart would not allow my will to prevail."

"I had not known I made such an impression."

"Indeed, you did."

She laughed at him, then took his hand as she started to step lively. Short of breath, they entered Netherfield Hall, having trotted back at an exuberant pace.

"You are short of breath; pray where were you?" Caroline inquired.

"Running about the grounds," Mr. Darcy playfully answered. He turned to Elizabeth. "Dearest, shall we venture above the stairs to rest a little before dinner?"

"Very well," Elizabeth replied.

Caroline and Mrs. Hurst, with faces overspread with astonishment, watched them disappear above the stairs in haste. Smiles erupted to laughter as Elizabeth and Mr. Darcy closed the door to the bedchamber.

"Did you see the expression on Caroline's face?" she asked giggling.

"Indeed I did," he smiled, drawing her close, holding her to him with a feeling of love and admiration. If it were possible, thought he, I would wish to hold her in my arms forever.

Dinner at Netherfield

Elizabeth and Mr. Darcy, having descended the stairs, directed themselves to the sitting room, where Louisa was playing the pianoforte. Appearing lively and refreshed, Elizabeth and Mr. Darcy made their entrance. Upon Louisa's notice, she raised her brows in Caroline's direction. Nonetheless of the notice, they made themselves receptive to all the principal people in the chamber, including Caroline and the Hursts. It was not long until Mr. Bennet and his daughters were announced, and after an hour exchange they were seated for dinner.

"Well now, I have reason to suspect someone has ordered a dinner in my favour!" Mr. Bennet said, noticing his most desired dishes seemed to have been singled out before him.

"Indeed, Father, Emily inquired this morning of your favourite dish. Oh—pray, I beg your pardon, Emily, I see I induced a blush. Forgive me, perhaps I should not have spoken," Jane said, witnessing the blushed cheeks of her sister-in-law.

"Well now, allow me to express my gratitude, Emily. It is exceedingly delightful to be treated with such favour; I daresay I am not used to such pleasantries."

During dinner, Caroline and Mrs. Hurst scarcely spoke a word, while the rest of the party found ample conversation, beginning with the praise of a highly admired dinner well done through the excellence of cookery, followed by Mr. Bingley's admiration of his new family. Caroline and Mrs. Hurst listened intently to Mr. Bennet and Mr. Darcy in an exchange over the backgammon games shared that afternoon.

"Mr. Bennet, may I have the privilege to recommend myself an opponent in backgammon? I enjoy a challenge," Emily expressed.

"I would be delighted with such an opportunity," Mr. Bennet accepted.

"Very well. Might I say you are very forbearing to accept such a dare from a lady."

"Not at all! I'm delighted. Considering the inducement of a dare, I find I am more eager; I find my anticipations quite elevated."

"Mr. Bennet, my sister is excellent at backgammon; I daresay the circumstances of her abilities slant highly in her favour," Mr. Bingley added.

"I shall not reflect the outcome. Mr. Bennet is quite skilled. I believe he might be considered quite an accomplished player, the praise not being exaggerated. I heed you fair warning, Emily," Mr. Darcy told her with a smile.

"Would you care to wager that, Darcy?" Mr. Bingley added, winking at his friend.

"Perhaps, Bingley, a wager will indeed make it more interesting." Mr. Darcy said challengingly.

"Very well then, you may depend upon it. You approve five shillings, Darcy? No great wager I grant you, a mere trifle, not enough to make anyone uneasy, but a wager just the same." Mr. Bingley added.

"Very well, Bingley, five shillings it is."

The rest of the party laughed at the thought; it added such intensity to the game. Elizabeth found the subject interesting as she watched her husband and Mr. Bingley smugly relaxed in their seats with anticipated victory, although she was not convinced the subject matter between them was the five shillings. Kathryn and Mary sat with questioning looks, while the Hursts and Caroline shared a look of disbelief.

"Well, well, this should provide interesting entertainment for the evening," Mr. Bennet reflected with delighted wit.

"Indeed, I'm excessively fond of a challenge," Emily retorted.

The communication excited many subjects of joy. At length the urge to resolve the wager neared. They all gathered in the sitting room, where the backgammon board was strategically placed, advantageous to the spectators. As the competitors intensified their attention to the game, the remaining party gathered round them, taking their stations between and behind. A hush fell over the chamber. It proved annoying to Mr. Bennet, who commissioned Elizabeth to play the pianoforte to distract from the silence. With seriousness of mind Emily and Mr. Bennet were now highly concentrating on the board, deep in thought; each seeking to claim victory. The two appeared to play with mutual satisfaction, each confident in their strategy, each cautiously regarding every competitive move with all eyes fixed upon them. Elizabeth, having quit the pianoforte, was once again amidst the watchful crowd as the anxiety grew with each move. As the game neared its end, they all remained seated for some time without speaking a word, with no resolve to break it, until suddenly the game was won.

"Well, Bingley, I do believe you owe me five shillings," Mr. Darcy stated. "You shall have it."

"I confess quite a challenge; indeed a partner of such equanimity is rare, if you'll pardon my saying so, Mr. Darcy. I indeed found you a challenge, you may be sure of it." Mr. Bennet told him with quick wit.

"No offense taken, Mr. Bennet," Mr. Darcy replied, grinning with satisfaction.

"It was indeed a refreshing game, Mr. Bennet, one I hope you grant me the privilege to challenge at a later date so I may prove myself worthy of a win."

"You may depend upon it, Emily, to be sure."

"Father was quite worried. I could sense it; were you not, Father?" Mary asked.

"Perhaps a little, although a gentleman may not wish to reveal such notions," Mr. Bennet said with a wink of the eye.

"Indeed, Father most always wins," Kathryn managed to say.

Elizabeth kept a close eye on Caroline's rather nettled expression; she showed particular interest when her sister asked for a challenge at a later date. Caroline and Mrs. Hurst exerted themselves in a shared, detectable, suspicious exchange of looks. They were obviously annoyed in spite of their smiles, which now overspread their faces. Caroline announced, "Emily, dear, we had not expected your long stay at Netherfield; do you not believe it is time to return home? I should think you would be pining for the north."

"No, she shall not leave, no not at all; I wish her to stay, in fact I demand it," Mr. Bingley interjected before Emily could respond.

"Why, thank you, Brother, I would so very much wish to stay at Netherfield for a time. I find I am quite comfortable here. I wish further opportunity to enjoy the children; I so dearly love them, indeed I do."

"Very well then, it is settled; you shall not only stay at Netherfield Park, you shall join us when we settle within an easy distance of Pemberley. Yes, I insist upon it; I'll hear of nothing else." he stated with certainty.

"Perhaps you would care to join us at Longbourn for dinner tomorrow evening. It is nothing to Netherfield I know; nonetheless, we believe it quite comfortable. You will discover we do employ an excellent cook; what say you?" Mr. Bennet asked.

"We shall be glad to come. Emily, to be sure you would; what say you Caroline, Louisa?" Mr. Bingley asked.

Caroline arose from her seat. In an air more than usually gracious, she said, "Louisa, Mr. Hurst and I have other plans. Charles, perhaps Emily would do better to join us?"

Mr. Hurst, still lounging across the sofa as usual, sat up upon hearing his name. "What! What is it you request of me, Louisa?" Before he could receive an answer, he lay down again and resumed his snoring. Although considered the son of a country gentleman, it was not unusual for him to lounge frequently, occasionally managing alertness for sporting, cards, dinner or port. He was not known to be a great conversationalist or lover of music, further discovering he found little entertainment in a gathering, preferring sleep, as was now the case.

"I think not; I should be delighted to accept your invitation, Mr. Bennet," Emily told him, causing redness to rise in her cheeks. Her eyes brightened when he returned her smile, placing Mr. Bennet in the highest of spirits. Although Elizabeth was sorry they should miss the party, she was anxious to return home.

"Well, Mr. Bennet, it appears you shall have guests tomorrow evening after all!" Mr. Bingley announced, well pleased with himself.

Caroline avoided her sister. With the rest of the party present, she could pay no particular attention to the subject of her immediate desire. Her face was tight with contempt. Although Caroline claimed she and the Hursts had plans, they did in fact have none. Caroline's invention to prevent Emily from going to Longbourn was to be the cause of her own demise. Any pain inflicted was only to be felt by her. There was little question by her guise that she was not delighted to view Emily at Longbourn.

Elizabeth turned her eyes to Mr. Darcy, catching a glimpse of his general affability. He, now aware of her eyes on him, grinned with satisfaction at the lack of success Caroline drew from her scheme. Elizabeth saw it was of little importance to Mr. Bingley if his sisters viewed her father's dinner arrangements with ridicule or censure. The exchange of looks between her husband and Mr. Bingley led her to believe the men found gratification in the foiled plot to separate Emily from the Bennet household. Quite contrary to Caroline's disposition, the two gentlemen appeared to be entertained by the whole of the conversation, which now appeared the source of amusement.

Mr. Bennet and his two youngest daughters stayed above another half-hour. When they arose to depart, Mr. Bingley called upon Emily to join in expressing their anxious await of the evening next. Caroline and Mrs. Hurst, attempting to avoid further embarrassment, expressed pleasure in having them at Netherfield for the evening, granted an elegant curtsey, then parted their company in haste.

As for Mr. Darcy, his thoughts were on the morning journey. He longed to return to Pemberley to see his children. He again expressed regret in not being available to accept the invitation so graciously extended, declaring his eagerness to return to the concerns at his estate. Elizabeth was in agreement, further construing the pleasure to be gained by a lesser party number. On this account she found herself content with the intimacy of those attending, surely the evening would prove pleasant. Elizabeth and Mr. Darcy bid them farewell, expecting to see the three at Pemberley soon.

Kathryn and Mary were drawn to Emily. They showed a keen interest in her intended visit. The friendly, natural willingness to accept her valuable qualities was motive enough for them to seek her out to teach them to embroider their cushions with finer stitches. It was settled between the whole of the intended party that the carriage should arrive at Longbourn around four o'clock in the afternoon.

The Great Estate

$\mathcal{I}$T WAS WITH GREAT RELIEF that Mr. Darcy and his wife returned to the estate of Pemberley. The diversity of the grounds was as beautiful as that of a pastoral dream. The carriage continued until they reached the lowest point, where they traveled for a time through the rich wooded area, immense over an extended portion of the property. She knew they neared the great place when they ascended but a half mile, finding themselves at the top of considerable elevation where the woods ended, entering into the valley to the winding road which revealed Pemberley House, situated across the valley, stately, perfectly proportioned in celebrated majesty. The house appeared more imposing to Elizabeth as she admired the magnificence surrounding it with an absolute lack of awkward taste. The ridge of high woody hills complemented a stream in front, which swelled into a greater lake, enhancing the beauty of the property. Its banks were neither formal nor falsely adorned. The natural beauty of the park remained well preserved by the grounds-keepers. Elizabeth was exceedingly delighted to be home. The thought of basking in Pemberley's bucolic splendors provided great appeal. The very thought of taking the children for a walk through the gardens, to be at home again, at peace with their beautiful surroundings, was comforting.

Further delight was added upon their view of Joseph and Deborah, who seemed to have advantaged in size over little more than a week. "Elizabeth, I believe I shall commission to have a likeness taken of you. Would you prefer a solitary sitting or one with the children? I do believe they are perhaps old enough to be captured with a brush."

"Dearest, the very subject has entered my thoughts. I am at a loss to decide the very same. I do believe perhaps an entire family likeness would be my wish; what say you?"

"If that is your wish."

"I believe it is."

"Very well, then, I shall inquire at once."

After a quiet, uneventful evening, the two decided to retire early.

"Elizabeth, pray you'll excuse me. I would like to look in on my sporting dogs. I will join you directly."

"Very well, I shall await you above the stairs."

Mr. Darcy ventured above the stairs not more than a half hour later. Upon nearing the landing, he heard weeping. Recognizing it to be his wife, he followed her cries, finding her in the bedchamber where Lydia died. He slowly pushed open the door. He drew her to him. He held her, allowing her to have her cry as she clung firmly to him.

After a time, he looked into her tear-stained face. "Dearest, do come away; do not allow the temptations of this chamber to make you downcast, Lydia would not desire it; surely you believe that," he said, discovering his words caused further torment. He held her to his breast, stroking her.

Finally she raised her tormented eyes to his face. Securing comfort from his expression, she allowed him to lead her away.

"I'm quite all right now, dearest. I've had my cry; really, I should not have dwelt upon it. Lydia would not wish it. I was drawn to the bedchamber, contemplating my own felicity. It reduced me to tears to think her short life ended in such misery. I promise I shall dwell on it no more. Perhaps our felicity is the very thing that saddens me; she certainly was not touched by such devotion."

As she lay at his side, Elizabeth felt her husband's powerful, impassioned love. Such happiness, felt before in their exchange, was once again expressed by his sentiments, providing a deeper inducement of heartfelt emotion. Hers was luxury felt of assurance regarding her importance to him. His constancy of dedication provided her certainty of the goodness governing their union. His actions generated a feeling of security, conviction and magnanimity. She felt altogether comforted by him. Experiencing the safety of his arms about her as she lay next to him, she believed it was improbable there could exist a greater love than theirs. A feeling of contentment diffused over her as she found herself entangled in the serenity of shared emotions.

As they lay close for a time, Mr. Darcy, now gradually dozing into a shallow sleep, was stirred by Elizabeth's voice. "Dearest, I'm curious, that backgammon wager, was that something more? I detected it was, but had no understanding of its meaning."

Aroused to alertness by her novelty of attention, he replied, "You are perceptive, are you not? Bingley and I had talked of the noticeable attentions Emily affords your father. As we discussed a frivolous wager regarding his sister's attentions, we were interrupted. The wager was forgotten until the game reinstated the thought, and thus was used to disguise the challenge."

Elizabeth sat up at once in astonishment. "Her attentions?"

"Elizabeth, I'm shocked indeed; surely I thought you perceived the whole of it. Emily Bingley draws the attention of your father. She affords him attention in return. How is it possible it escaped your notice?"

"I had not given it thought. I thought she was being kind or neighbourly."

"Being kind! Come now, dearest, surely you witnessed Caroline's envy as well as Mrs. Hurst's disagreeable sneer; how could you not?"

"I was unsure of the intended meaning."

"Well, now, I'm truly astonished; could you not tell the enjoyment Bingley and I derived from the situation? I thought it quite obvious to you."

The expressed pleasure of her husband's reply now piqued her interest as he went on to say, "If you were aware of the very delight to us, you would have noted the inducement to alarm Caroline and Mrs. Hurst. I suppose one should not delight in the shortcomings of others; however, those two deserve the pain they inflict upon themselves with their pious opinions. They would deny Emily happiness; further, they are jealous of her, as they are of you. They try very hard to convince Bingley and myself of their sincerity toward you and Jane, their only desire being to continue to reside at Bingley's table and keep an open invitation to Pemberley. Although he shows no sign publicly, in my confidence he expressed his knowledge of their designs. Bingley is no fool. They are senseless to underestimate him. What of the ball, should you be uncomfortable inviting them?"

"Not at all, quite the contrary. Each occasion Caroline Bingley witnesses our felicity, especially at Pemberley, she will ever be reminded you belong to me and I to you. Caroline will never forgive me that, to be sure. I confess I have enjoyed the folly at times; I suppose it is a weakness in my character to take delight in such thoughts."

"Perhaps we share a weakness that exposes us to ridicule the ridiculous. Unfortunately, Caroline and Mrs. Hurst suffer the erroneous notion they are superior. As for Caroline, I should beg the difference. She mistakes her haughty manners as elegance, striving to endeavour to educate Bingley and I of her disapproval of our choice of partners. She overlooks her solitary status. More importantly, she overrates the charm of her society." Mr. Darcy chuckled. "No one dares inform her the reason she continues in want of a partner. Should I have desired a partner so gratified with her own character, perhaps I would have set my designs on her. The thought of her as a match never appealed to me. Beyond the rank of her society, even without my Elizabeth, I should have never entertained thoughts of Caroline intimately. I should perish at the revolting thought of it."

"I believe I am very grateful I appealed to you."

"You believe, you believe! Well, indeed you ought to admit it. Come closer to me. Allow me to hold you close. Appeal indeed, yes, very much indeed," he mumbled.

With all such thoughts put to rest, they soundly slept the night away.

Pleasantries at Pemberley

THREE WEEKS PASSED before Mr. Darcy's commissioned artisan arrived at Pemberley for the sketching of the portrait.

"Mr. Armstrong, is this the sum of your business?" Elizabeth inquired while maintaining a resolute composure of countenance in his presence to ease her discomfort. Elizabeth was fidgety, since this was her first likeness. Except for an occasional glance at her husband, she required no assistance in her pleasure making conversation.

"Why, yes, ma'am, I have great passion for my work. I have done countless subjects throughout England, even having been commissioned for a portrait within the royal family."

"Indeed," she replied with interest, "I have long admired the skill of your hand at Georgiana's portrait; it hangs most handsomely in the gallery."

"It is a pleasure to be sought by Mr. Darcy," he said, preparing his instruments. After placing his sketching material conveniently, he turned, instructing, "I require you to place yourself here on this seat, ma'am." In doing so, he continued, "turn slightly this way, placing your hands thus. Mr. Darcy, I shall necessitate you slightly behind, but to this border of your wife, if you will. Very good now, it has been my study children will only sit for short lengths; they have a propensity to move about frequently. They bore easily. This affords me opportunity to start, allowing the children very little required time at the sitting. Pray do not concentrate on the length of time with the children; I have no doubt of my success in capturing their image."

"Very well," she uttered. Mr. Darcy said little, just did what was required of him, while Elizabeth found her steadiness wanting, prompting her belief that the success of the children in a portrait was impossible. As she remained fixed, she noted the ease with which Mr. Armstrong worked. She was impressed by the speed of his labour. He appeared intensely pleased with his accomplishments thus far. He continued his progress, then requested the children be brought to the sitting. After having fixed the children to his satisfaction, Elizabeth perceived the swiftness of his instrument. His hand moved across the surface of his board effortlessly. After a few moments, the children engaged in an exchange of prattle. He continued to approach the children employing his mesmerizing soft voice, which seemed to capture their full attention, allowing Elizabeth to believe his countenance an art in itself. It was above five and twenty minutes additional until he announced his conclusion. The children were tranquil, causing Elizabeth to view the sitting a success.

Once the children were taken away by the nursemaids, Elizabeth and Mr. Darcy ventured round to see the initial drawing. Elizabeth unleashed an expression of pleasure to find the detail so involved. The facial expressions captured their character. Mr. Darcy stated he believed there to be no wanting of likeness in the drawing, that it had been sketched to his satisfaction. Elizabeth thought her own likeness exceeded her expectations, which caused a blush to her cheeks upon viewing it. Both were anxious to have Mr. Armstrong return in a few months with the final image.

Days passed into weeks without any dilemmas on the great estate. One day, Elizabeth, having little to occupy herself, descended the stairs. Happening upon Bessie, she inquired, "Bessie, pray do you know where I might find Mr. Darcy?"

"I believe you'll find Mr. Darcy in the billiard parlour, ma'am."

"Thank you, Bessie," she said, continuing on her way. She startled him as she entered, disrupting his shot.

"Dearest, I believe I should like to learn to play billiards."

"Have you never done so?"

"No, the opportunity never presented itself. Will you teach me?"

"To be sure, but I warn you, I'll not allow a win as your father would afford you," he said teasingly. Perhaps you had better use the mace instead of the stick."

"Why must I use the mace? Are there only three balls required?"

"We wouldn't want you to tear the cloth, and, yes, Elizabeth, there are only three balls."

As the weeks passed, Elizabeth learned to master the game to her satisfaction. She was still unable to defeat him. Try as she did, when the games were won, she invariably had made not one successful shot. Taking pride in her mild accomplishments, she planned to challenge her father when he visited next. She had heard years before that he possessed excellent skill of the game.

Mr. Manley frequently visited Pemberley Hall at the request of Mr. Darcy for dinner, sporting, and even, occasionally, a billiard game. Although Elizabeth was making strides in her billiard skills, any attempt to gain a win from either gentleman failed, convincing her she'd never encounter an equal competitor. While the gentlemen afforded her no advantages, she decided the fun of the sport provided ample reason to persist, causing her to continue to endure their teasing.

Little more than two months passed before Mr. Darcy received communication from Mr. Armstrong regarding delivery of the portrait. Elizabeth anxiously awaited his arrival the two days following. At last he came. He brought the portrait to the sitting room, where he strategically placed it to be viewed advantageously.

When the portrait was unveiled, Elizabeth gasped with pleasure. Then she remained expressionless, caught in awe as she fixed her eyes on the images in sheer amazement. Mr. Darcy, well pleased with the end result, received the strong likeness of the children with joy. He admired how the strokes of the brush captured their skins' softness, revealing fresh life and vigor, every detail so correct, so exact. Elizabeth viewed it with unexpected delight, believing her appearance elegant. She thought it reflected a sense of charm, providing her much credit. Having no criticism of her likeness, she expressed extreme pleasure with the whole of it. Mr. Darcy appeared as a fine, tall, handsome man of nobility with an expression of confidence, very much like that of the true man. Elizabeth thought it a perfect resemblance of his facial features. Together they asserted their gratefulness to Mr. Armstrong on the excellence of his abilities. Upon compensation, he was informed he would be called upon in the future for additional work as Mr. Darcy still desired a portrait of his wife alone.

It pleased them to have the portrait placed in the gallery just in time for the visitors to see, for the Pemberley ball was but a month away. Elizabeth, having sent out the invitations the day prior, was excited to think it would be viewed by her family.

Within the week, next during Michaelmas, Mr. Bingley was scheduled to settle on the lease. Anxious for them to be settled within an easy distance to Pemberley, Elizabeth prepared to invite the whole of the party to Pemberley for dinner the day next, after settlement. Two days before Michaelmas, Elizabeth was surprised to see a carriage arrive at Pemberley.

"Father, what do you do here? I had not expected you for another two weeks at least, closer to the ball," Elizabeth said with surprise.

"Well now, Lizzy, I had a notion to see my daughter and grandchildren as well as my son-in-law. I thought we might sport together. Mr. Darcy expects me, perhaps not this soon; when we played backgammon we discussed it."

"My husband is from home, but we expect he will return this afternoon. Mr. Manley should be returning with him. Perhaps I better warn the cook of additional guests. Father, has Jane left Netherfield yet?"

"No, Lizzy, they have not; I anticipate their start two days following. I understand Mr. Bingley will come ahead to secure the place. I do believe Mr. Darcy invited him to stay at Pemberley until he settles the lease."

"Yes, it is so; I do believe we expect him tomorrow. Well, Kathryn, Mary, you must be tired from the journey; come into the house."

"Lizzy, just you wait until you see the embroidering I carry, Emily has taught us new stitching. Lizzy, she plans to accompany us to the local warehouse to purchase fresh attire for the ball here at Pemberley," Kathryn anxiously told her.

"I shall be very glad to examine it, Kathryn."

"Oh, Lizzy, I had so wished Mariah to come to the ball at Pemberley, but Charlotte and the Lucases insisted she not attend; she must go to Hunsford instead. It was all so very strange, indeed it was. I felt sorry for her; she cried at length. I am not of the understanding why they were so angry with her for the asking. It was extremely strange; what do you suppose was the concern?" Kathryn expressed, then added, "Lizzy, perhaps you should like to see my embroidery after dinner; Emily says I'm much improved."

"Yes, Lizzy, Emily intends to assist me in finding the proper colour suitable to my complexion," Mary added.

Elizabeth smiled. "We intend to invite Mr. Bingley and the whole of the party to dinner when they arrive at Foxshire Estate."

Mr. Bennet's face brightened with joy. "Delighted to hear of it."

Upon entering the house, the three requested to see the children. They were brought to the sitting room, where Mary and Kathryn immediately took a child to play, inquiring if they should be allowed to take them for a turn about the grounds. Elizabeth, being very cautious, suggested they wait until the children were more acclimated to them, since Deborah seemed to sniffle when Mary picked her up. They were very good about company; however if one were to become strange it was sure to be Deborah; Joseph was more outgoing and, unlike his father, quick to take to strangers.

Above an hour passed before Mr. Darcy arrived in the company of Mr. Manley. They had been visiting the tenants on the estate. Mr. Darcy was surprised to see Mr. Bennet, but very glad he had come just the same.

"Mr. Bennet, a pleasant surprise," Mr. Darcy said, greeting him with a bow.

"Mr. Bennet, so good to see you again," expressed Mr. Manley.

"Indeed, always a pleasure," Mr. Bennet returned.

Mary and Kathryn said nothing, just curtsied, then continued their attentions to the children. Elizabeth, seeing the children contented, gave permission to take them out of doors.

"Father, I have learned to play billiards."

"Is that so?"

"Well, I do play; not very well I grant you; just the same, I play. I do remember hearing you to be excellent at billiards; is that true?"

"Well now, Lizzy, it has been some time since I last played; my skills are no doubt deficient."

"Well, Father, perhaps after dinner we may challenge Mr. Manley and my husband."

"Perhaps, Lizzy, we shall see."

Mr. Manley and Mr. Darcy excused themselves for a moment to take care of business in the office, promising to return within the hour.

"Father, do you see Jane often?"

"Oh yes, very often indeed. We dine at Netherfield at least twice each week, and they with us once weekly."

"So often, is that necessary?"

"Why, yes, Lizzy, one should not expect to be away from family for so very long. And considering their intended move, I thought I should take advantage of the situation. And speaking of family, Lizzy, what say you; your cousin Mr. Collins paid visit to Longbourn."

"Whatever for, Father?" she asked with a look of mixed surprise and displeasure.

"Well, I shall speak frankly. He learned through Lady Lucas, who no doubt acquired her information from Mariah, that Kathryn was still writing to Lieutenant Denny. His purpose in coming was to spare the family further disgrace. His connection to the Right Honourable Lady Catherine de Bourgh, as he spoke so eloquently of her praise, would surely be displeased with any further disdain on the family name now that her nephew has been wholly connected to us through marriage."

"Well, Father, is Kathryn still writing to him?"

"Yes, but the letters are seldom now. After your revelation at Longbourn of Mr. Wickham's unfavourable character, I talked with the girls. Kathryn revealed to me the letters sent by him, offering me the privilege to read them. Kathryn was writing out of concern for Lydia. You see, Lieutenant Denny would seek information whenever possible. Unfortunately, Kathryn had some indication as to the sad state of affairs in which your sister lived. She attempted to enlighten me on several occasions, but did not, for fear I would get angry and fight Wickham. I felt no need to censor the letters; there is no real attraction or connection there; she assured me of that."

"Mr. Collins takes much upon himself with delight, I'm afraid," thought she aloud.

"Yes, I agree. Mr. Collins states his wife's alarm of further unsettlement at Rosings should Lady Catherine hear of additional grievous circumstances involving the Bennet family."

"Such an insufferable, odious, despicable man! Father, do you believe Charlotte is agreeable to such language; what say you; what is your opinion?"

"Sorry for you to hear of it; yes, I confess, Lizzy, I do. Sir William Lucas had a letter penned by her hand. I am of the opinion she is all that you have heard. Her letter expressed concern; they apprehend our relations will induce their demise at Hunsford should Lady Catherine find displeasure in the Bennets, since they are cousins, of course." Having related this information, he sighed, then sat back in his chair with a hint of despair upon his features.

"While I agree it is wise to exhibit appropriateness of family position and surely concern of respectability is sensible indeed, I cannot condone the constant reverberation of discourse regarding an apprehension of wickedness that has yet to occur. I find it rather troublesome. I am of the opinion the Collinses' place far too much importance on the beleaguered possibilities than on fact. What's more, I fear they will never lessen their ill opinion of our family. Knowing, as I do, that Charlotte's marriage to our cousin, Mr. Collins, was for comfortable means alone, I suppose I should not be surprised of her failing friendship. Indeed, their own happy situation is of more importance than any pain or suffering they may inflict. Still, Father, I find I am highly disappointed in her. Surely the letters between Hunsford and Meryton pass frequently upon learning any bit of news which may gain insight into the Bennet situation. It is all quite disheartening indeed."

"I see you take my view of the subject, Lizzy."

"Well, Father, I confess I am relieved Kathryn has no interest in Lieutenant Denny."

"Lizzy, the alteration in your sisters is refreshing; their conduct is admirable. I do believe Emily's attention increases their complaisant actions. Our home is quietly reserved and orderly, no reason for concern. They so look forward to our dinners at Netherfield. They enjoy Emily's visits to Longbourn as well. Why, Emily has enchanting wit, exceedingly fine manners as well as superior character; her company is most desirous. I believe they are the happier for it."

"Father, are you the happier for it?" she slyly inquired.

"Well, Lizzy, her presence influences the girls to a better degree; they respond to her goodness. And, Lizzy, I do believe she has your wit; she presents herself with a high spirit such as yours. I feel you near in her presence; I do believe there is a likeness," he expressed with elevated excitement.

Elizabeth, watchful of his expression, contemplated his words. She was influenced by his manner of speaking. She was not disposed to make any immediate answer after having received his undisclosed described felicitations with pleasure. She wondered if her father was conscious that he chiefly expressed delight in Emily's company. After additional thought she looked at him, "Father, did you ever play that next game of backgammon with Emily?"

"To be sure, she defeated me," he stated with pleasure.

"I see; well, Father, did she win of her own account or did you allow it?"

"It is fact, Lizzy, she won on her own merit."

Curiously, she pressed on. "That would make the challenge stimulating; is that not so?"

"Oh, yes, indeed, she is a fair challenge, a most enjoyable opponent."

"What do the girls do whilst you play backgammon?"

"They sit, read, play the pianoforte, yes; and, Lizzy," his voice raised with excitement, "I must relate, Emily has taught Mary voice; she has improved her methods. She sings much better now; is that not the best of news?"

"Oh, yes, that is very good news, indeed. Does Mary still read?"

"Yes, but Emily has taught her to appreciate prose and poetry as never before. I daresay, I can see where Mary has improved on every account."

"Well, I hope Mary is grateful."

"Yes, Lizzy, I do believe both the girls enjoy her company immensely. She adds delight to any day. She affords pleasing attentions; her company is found to be most enjoyable."

"Yes, Father, I imagine so; Emily is quite the character."

"Yes, a most delightful creature. Her visits are not of ordinary occasions, no indeed; I've requested the use of the fine china and the best silver when she visits. I've challenged the cook to excellence. We look forward to Thursdays; yes, indeed we do."

"Oh, on Thursdays? Well, Father, with Mr. Bingley's move to Derbyshire, what will you do on Thursdays?" she asked, observing his expression.

His features drained of excitement. "Well now, Lizzy, I confess the thought downcast me, the girls so look forward to her visits. They are sure to be disappointed."

"Indeed, and you, Father, will you be disappointed?"

"Quite so, yes indeed, for the girls sake of course, they will sorely miss her, there is sure to be a void felt there. Longbourn has taken on unexplainable freshness. I awake feeling an enthusiastic admiration for the old place. I confess, I rather enjoy my situation; perhaps it's the girls, they are so altered, quite comforting. Yes, I do believe they will miss Emily's attention."

"I'm sure they will, Father; I'm sure they will," she said as she noticed her husband and Mr. Manley nearing them.

"Mrs. Reynolds wishes you to know dinner will be served in five and twenty minutes. Where are the girls?" Mr. Darcy inquired.

"With the children out of doors; perhaps I should tell one of the servants to fetch them."

"Visit with your father; I shall fetch them."

"Mr. Manley, after dinner might you be interested in billiards?"

"I would be delighted, Mrs. Darcy."

"Mr. Manley, I believe my daughter intends a game of partners," Mr. Bennet explained.

"I see, Mr. Darcy and I have not allowed her a win, although I confess she has improved on closer examination."

"Yes, she has improved, but has not the ability to defeat her husband as yet," Mr. Darcy added with a jovial tone as he entered the chamber with Kathryn and Mary.

"Where are the children?" Elizabeth inquired.

"I had Bessie take them above the stairs to the nursemaids."

"May we watch the billiard game?" asked Mary.

"Yes, I'm sure there is no objection," Elizabeth was quick to answer.

"I do believe we better direct ourselves to the dining hall," said Mr. Darcy, motioning for them to follow.

During dinner much was said regarding the upcoming ball at Pemberley. Kathryn and Mary, now anxious for Emily's arrival, talked of nothing else but her intentions of accompanying them to the local warehouses. In an agreeable exchange of spending rights, Mary sought the opportunity to declare her personal philosophy. "We must remember, discontentment is rooted in ungratefulness; therefore, it is of the utmost importance we select a modest gown to show gratitude for the generous opportunity our father affords us. We must not lack good sense; it would not be prudent."

Mr. Bennet looked at Elizabeth, then winked before looking at his youngest daughters. "Girls, you may acquire complete attire for the ball. Allow Emily to assist your decision; I believe she will do you credit."

Kathryn's lips separated with excitement. Her eyes became wide. "Oh, complete attire; Father, are you sure of it?" she squealed with excitement.

"Yes, my dear, I believe complete attire is in order for such an event."

"Thank you, Father, we shall be sensible in the selection," Mary ecstatically cried. "Such delight, such pleasure, how shall we abide the wait; to be sure it will be distracting, will it not?"

Elizabeth's lips parted. "Father that is quite generous of you," she declared, worried her father stretched his generosity beyond his means.

"Such an occasion calls for new attire, perhaps I should consider it also."

"Father, that would be wonderful; you will be handsome," Kathryn cried with joy of the thought. But Elizabeth struggled to conceal her concern. Awareness sprung up within her of her father's need to make the occasion exceptional. "It has been some time since you last purchased a dress coat, is it not now, Father?" Elizabeth asked.

"Yes, indeed it is, too long to be sure. It is settled; new dress attire for the ball it is," he stated with certainty. Mr. Darcy slyly looked at his wife. "Mr. Bennet, are you trying to out-swagger us all?" he inquired with a grin of approval.

"You'll hardly need worry on my account, Mr. Darcy."

"Well, I shall wear my best so I am not to feel left behind," Mr. Manley added.

Mr. Darcy looked at Elizabeth. "Dearest, are you intending the trip to town as well?"

"I had given it thought; why do you ask?"

"I desire you do so. Perhaps you should request they send to Paris for a few gowns to choose from. This is your ball; I rather think it requires a definite level of elegance."

"This is a consideration I may undertake."

The rest of dinner passed quickly, with a variety of conversations. Elizabeth looked at her father. Like her sisters, he was no less eager to indulge in a shopping venture. Elizabeth understood her father's desire to look his best, perhaps better than that of his own understanding. It was not hard for one who imagines to realize the reasoning of new attire. Happy in the thought of her father's sudden interest, she delighted in his youthfulness of spirit.

With dinner soon past, the girls continued to converse of the ball whilst Mr. Manley and Mr. Darcy decided they would accept a challenge of partnership in a round of billiards, much to Elizabeth's undeniable delight.

"Well now, Lizzy, I daresay, do not get too excited; I have not played these past two and twenty years," Mr. Bennet announced.

"That long? Oh, Father, just the same we shall enjoy the game. I'm not accustomed to a win; indeed I assure you I am not," she said with a sarcastic tone marked by a teasing smile meant for her husband's attention. The four competitors directed themselves to the billiard chamber. Kathryn and Mary followed. Mr. Darcy assisted his wife with the mace. He observed with curiosity the manner in which Mr. Bennet thoroughly examined each stick, realizing he lacked no understanding of the game or equipment. He noticed Mr. Manley's eyes fixed on Mr. Bennet's behaviour as well. Managing a shared look, they resolved that perhaps they did indeed have competition. Making sure he understood correctly, Mr. Darcy asked, "Mr. Bennet, you say you have not played some two and twenty years?"

"That is so; but a man never forgets his skills. I imagine they surely come back now, do they not?"

"Perhaps you would wish to practice to refresh yourself before the game?" Mr. Darcy offered generously.

"I think not; I believe my skills have survived these past years. I am confident they will not fail me."

Mr. Darcy looked at his wife. He smiled coyly. "Very well, Elizabeth, should you require a few refreshing shots?" he said teasingly.

"No, I shall depend on my skills as is," she replied playfully.

"Very well then, shall we play the game?" Mr. Manley inquired.

The billiard parlour became quiet of prattle. The players were eager for their turn, but more eager to witness the skills of Mr. Bennet, whose confidence left them wanting. Mr. Bennet, being second in turn, proceeded successfully as the five intently watched in amazement. He took each shot with precision, astonishing them with his "side" shot, clearing the table of balls.

As soon as he finished, he asked with a measure of wit, "Shall we play another?"

With a broad smile overspreading her features, Elizabeth looked at her husband. "I do suppose this advantages me a win?"

"You—you never had chance to shoot!" Mr. Darcy replied, his features revealing a bit of unexpected shock.

"No matter. I am half of the winning team, am I not now?" It was plain to see Elizabeth enjoyed the victory. Her smile broadened, then turned to laughter at his amazement.

"Mr. Bennet, wherever did you learn to play?" Mr. Manley inquired.

"In my youth I was taught by my father. I played daily at my uncle's estate; indeed, when I reached this level, very few would play me. I have not deceived you to be certain. Surely I had not played these two and twenty years. I suppose I had a little luck just now."

"Shall we play again in hopes of a turn?" Mr. Darcy inquired whimsically.

"Yes, indeed," Mr. Manley stated, then added, "perhaps Mr. Bennet should go second in turn to assure us at least one shot." He then laughed with delight at the astonishment of his friend. It was not often that Mr. Darcy was caught in an expression of steadfast surprise.

Mr. Manley listened with impossible avoidance as Mr. Darcy expressed his compliments to Mr. Bennet of the skills he demonstrated. At first he seemed immovable from surprise, but, once recovered, he advanced toward Mr. Bennet. Speaking now with perfect composure, he commented of his beholding awe with which he admired his skills. In completion of his admiration, he humbly bowed.

Kathryn and Mary, as well as Elizabeth, had never witnessed their father in the sport. They were equally astonished.

Elizabeth, now in a complete state of felicity, was in a hopeless state of gloating without restraint, which did not escape notice. Mr. Darcy looked in his wife's direction. Their eyes instantly met, causing her face to be overspread with a smile of contentment. He faintly smiled back, enjoying her reaction to the win, realizing she would surely not allow it to be forgotten. Her reaction exhilarated him. There was elegance in her fancy, igniting a sense of excitement. Inwardly, he delighted in her victory. The very thought of her teasing him insufferably on the subject caused pleasing anticipation at the notion of the fancied torment.

In the end, Mr. Bennet's skills remained unmatched, although he did manage to miss one shot, allowing some sense of challenge. The billiard games caused much excitement. The laughter afforded the night a complete success in Elizabeth's reasoning. Mr. Darcy was certain her success in having such a skillful partner was affirmation of constant amusement.

The remainder of the evening passed with much entertainment as Mary played the pianoforte, singing to her tune. Kathryn exhibited her needlework to Elizabeth as the gentlemen discussed a variety of subjects with the conversation of the billiard games rousing laughter every now and again. Elizabeth, remembering her father's comments regarding Mary's voice, found he was absolutely correct; she had noticeably improved.

Mr. Manley parted their company rather late. It was shortly thereafter that the remainder of the party quitted the sitting room in search of rest.

They had no sooner reached their bedchamber than Elizabeth unmercifully expressed delight in the victory. Mr. Darcy appeared somber, his face grew grave as he made himself ready for bed with no verbal reaction to her. Instead, he ignored her completely as she continued her taunt. After a time of unrelenting teasing, she became disturbed by his sobriety, and all frivolity ceased from her expression. She turned suddenly quiet.

Mr. Darcy stood at the window, peering out over the moonlit grounds. Still he said not a word but instead lingered there for a time. Now troubled that he would not speak or react to her, she quietly made herself ready for bed. He eventually joined her but lay in silence. As she attempted to snuggle closer to him, Mr. Darcy turned his back to her.

The two lay quite for what seemed forever to Elizabeth. "Good night, dearest," she said meekly, hoping for a response.

Mr. Darcy continued his silence. It was but a short time thereafter that he heard her release a pitiable sigh. Upon hearing her, he turned to lay on his back with his eyes closed. Conscious now of her awkwardness over his silence, he began to pity her. She lay silently, sorry for herself, wishing she had not been quite so insufferable.

Realizing she was on the verge of tears, he cleared his throat as if he were going to speak. Suddenly, unable to control his silence any longer, he burst into laughter. "Upon my word, Elizabeth, I confess, you are easily caught in a tease; your vanity so anxiously assured you my unjust anger true, you could not believe otherwise." He continued to laugh, then added, "You must admit, I had you in want. I suppose you may say you received your just reward."

"Mr. Darcy, you quite amaze me; I should have known," she said, relieved it was a tease.

Michaelmas

As she breakfasted the morning next, Mary asked, "When is Mr. Bingley expected?"

Mr. Darcy looked at her. "I do not expect him before the afternoon, as previous word from Bingley announced his intentions were to go directly into town."

Mr. Bennet perked up. "Indeed his journey to Derbyshire is to settle on the property he resolved to lease. Surely you know, Mary, it is the custom to settle rents on September 29, the day of Michaelmas." He turned to Mr. Darcy. "I suppose Mr. Manley refers to it as the feast of St. Michael the Archangel. Nonetheless, Mr. Bingley expects to come together with the civil magistrate."

"Yes, I know, Father, the magistrate is elected at Michaelmas, one of the four traditional quarterly rent days on which occasion all tenants settle property," Mary replied with testimonial knowledge. Mr. Bennet winked at her. "You see, my dear, you do know."

"Indeed, Father, I am quite educated with regard to the Holy Day of Obligation. Did you know it is celebrated by the Roman Catholic Church as well as the churches of the Anglican Communion?"

"Yes, Mary, I believe we are well aware of it."

"All tenants look forward to Michaelmas, do they not now, Mr. Darcy?"

"Yes, Mary, I plan to join Mr. Manley at the parsonage after breakfast to assist with the arrangements. My involvement in the festivities affords me opportunity to receive my community. It is one of several times I make my presence socially among those residing on this property."

Kathryn quickly asked, "Mr. Darcy, might Mary and I join at the parsonage to assist?"

"I should be delighted to have you do so."

The girls excitedly anticipated the difference in the celebration in comparison to what they were accustomed to at Longbourn.

"Dearest, it is my intention to accompany you, but I plan to return early to look in on the children, if that meets with your approval?"

"Yes, Elizabeth, that would please me."

Mr. Bennet gained Mr. Darcy's attention. "I should like to go to the parsonage as well. Do you think Mr. Manley will view me officious if I offer my services?"

"Not at all." This pleased Mr. Darcy inasmuch as he viewed it an opportunity to introduce his father-in-law to the tenants on the property.

Mary perked up once again. Her eyes brightened with wit. "Eating roast goose is one of the popular customs traceable at least as far back as the days of Edward IV. The feast falls in the season in which stubble geese are reputed to be in their highest perfection."

Elizabeth eyed her father. He looked back at her over top of his spectacles. Elizabeth rolled her eyes. Mary's inherent propensity to educate them in that which they already knew, had surfaced once again.

Mr. Darcy, having caught his wife's expression, looked over at Mary, who was now two shades of red. Rescuing her from embarrassment, he quickly added, "At Pemberley we serve nothing less. According to an old English proverb, 'one who eats goose on Michaelmas day will not lack money all the year.' Thank you, Mary, for bringing it to my attention; it does one good to be reminded."

Elizabeth looked somberly at her father. From the corner of her eye she viewed her husband. It was she, now, who was embarrassed. She weakly smiled at him. Elizabeth then felt the warmth of his consoling hand pat her knee. Elizabeth saw this as yet another example of his excellence. Now sorry for her slight ridicule of Mary, she wondered if she was ever to live up to his level of graciousness.

It was late morning when Elizabeth returned to the house. She went above the stairs to play a game of bilbocatch. Joseph especially liked watching Elizabeth do the cup and ball game. Elizabeth held the two, reading and singing to them until it was time to nap.

She descended the stairs feeling content in her situation, encircled in felicity to which her children provided vast joy. She felt greatly appeased in her comforts, realizing she experienced love from a man upon whom she was so wholly dependent.

She went out of doors to enjoy a brisk walk, which she always found exhilarating. High in spirit, she followed the same path she and Mr. Darcy strolled on her very first visit to Pemberley. Happy in her own sense of propriety, she freely admired the grounds, renewing her prejudiced opinion of its beauty. The grounds were remarkably handsome and the long summit of a path proved even more inviting, promising to afford a breath of fresh, abounding beauty. She eagerly eyed everything within view, concluding the sum total of the estate was beyond admiring words of description.

"Oh!" she thought aloud, spinning herself around with her arms outstretched, "I hear the church bells off in a distance." She rallied herself to a faster pace. With each trodden step her mind raced with thoughts of him. "Has he any notion how I esteem him? His kindness to my family is far more than anticipated," she said aloud.

Elizabeth stopped and closed her eyes as she drew in fresh air. "Oh," thought she aloud, "my wants are nil. How sacred is the passionate love we share! How precious is the air of moral discipline surrounding him! How shall I ever deserve such a man?"

Her thoughts suddenly sank her spirits. She continued to muse aloud as she started her walk again at a slower pace, examining her conscience. "My faults are numerous indeed; perhaps I should pray for forgiveness." As she continued her walk, she examined her heart. "I love him so very much. He is beyond expectation, but why can I not fully recognize what makes him so totally unrivaled? Surely the answer is plain and simple!" she mumbled to herself.

Admiration for him caused her to pause in a grassy area. Although alone, she found it arduous to suppress a smile while reminiscing. She stood for a moment remembering their wedding night when he poured out his heart and soul to her of his most intimate beliefs. He expressed his thoughts of God's making woman for man. His words freshly surfaced in her mind, "woman was taken not from man's head to rule over her, nor from his feet to be trampled upon, but from his side, under his arm, to be protected and closest to his heart, to be loved." How she cherished those words.

She stopped beneath a tree. Leaning against its trunk, she closed her eyes to give greater thought to the depth of his beliefs. He expressed so eloquently the sacredness of marriage. "The bond of love unites us, making us one. The purity that characterizes that love gives honour to the virtue of our union. Cannot you understand the loving heart of God doubtlessly rejoices in the institution of our alliance? We are expected to be an elevated example of His true meaning, with clear perception to go out into the world to represent all that He intends."

With pleasantries in mind, she twirled about with her arms stretched out, absorbing the glorious creation surrounding her. She longed to totally understand all that made him great. She reached her outstretched arms upward as she ceased to twirl. She started her journey once again in a trot, until she stumbled. She then stood still to voice her thoughts aloud. "Each time I am convinced I know all there is to know of you, you unsettle all such confidence. Am I to ever comprehend the complexity of your countenance?"

She looked at a nearby tree. It seemed to reach to the heavens, providing yet another reminder of his religious views. Her memory, having not failed her, forced his past spoken words to surface once more. "When sacred marriage vows are taken, the two expect to unite to make the completed whole, thus establishing the eternally significant institution of marriage as intended. It is of utmost importance that our character and companionship, our shared love, trust and devotion in the intimate circle of a family relationship, hold to that sacredness. Without you, my dearest, loveliest Elizabeth, I would be less than complete."

For a brief moment she considered the unfairness of it all. His descriptive aspirations were of strong faith, a loving partner as well as expected heirs. He declared that a family is the central unit in society, whose character is determined by marriage. She pondered, had she not the very same thoughts? Did he not reveal to me his innermost conviction of marriage stating, "Lest it is wholly and completely in the deepest felicity, I should not desire it?" She paused. She called out to the heavens as she looked to the sky, "Then why, oh why, can I not fully comprehend his complexity?"

Putting the smile back upon her features, her thoughts took a contented turn. She walked leisurely swaying back and forth, occasionally swirling around to drink in the beauty of the grounds she called home. She clearly remembered well his artlessness on their wedding night when he desired her to kneel with him for their bedstead prayer. There was such unrestrained humbleness in his character. There was no trace of awkwardness in his shared faith as he urged her to follow his illustration. She knelt aside him, sensing satisfaction in beginning the marriage with such depth of virtue.

She continued her walk feeling flustered by the honesty of his convictions. He expressed the natural loneliness he felt before their intended marriage as well as his lack of full contentment, desiring a companion who would satisfy the unfulfilled yearning in his heart. He expressed his beliefs in a partner to share his faith, respond to his nature with understanding to love, and wholeheartedly join together with him in working out a sacred plan.

She now stood before the lake. Looking down at her reflection in the water, she smiled at herself. She sat down in a grassy area, drawing her knees to her chin. Closing her eyes, she remembered him confidently expressing his recognition of her as being a divinely created companion, fashioned to provide all his hungry heart required. The satisfaction of being so important and wholly connected to him caused tears of joy to moisten her eyes.

As she got up from the ground, she looked at her reflection once again, making a little curtsey to excuse herself from it. Somewhere in her mind there was a consciousness of her own powerful feelings. She began to walk at a slow pace. All she could think of was how she loved him. In him she discovered a sense of implacable honour together with a loyalty that gave her strength. Yet she felt he was so much more, but what could that be? She felt bound to him and obligated to uphold him, viewing their union an indissoluble bond of love. She beheld their wedded vows, founded in the scriptures. She was certain they shared the kind of love that unites husband and wife in purity, characterizing those who typify the expectations of the very best relations. His character exemplified every man's notion of all that is desired and expected of a man in every sense, whether it be courage or those powers of authority necessary to get on in the world. In her own opinion, she concluded, women could only regard him as evidence of that which illustrates courage, virility, strength, masculine beauty and all that is preferred when choosing a mate. She smiled at her thoughts of the attentions he received from admiring ladies.

Having acquired affections of great value, her heart was deeply rooted in his soul. Yet his actions depicted perfection, complete in all respects, accurately and precisely adding an extreme degree of excellence according to his own standards of constancy, which she discovered were undeniably hers as well, although he seemed to live up to them with greater ease. She endeavoured to fashion her own character to that of his, which she held in the highest esteem, trusting that some day she may find such improvement, surpassing her own expectations of merit at his level of perfection.

As for his sentiments regarding perfection, she thought he would surely not claim himself flawless. She concluded that he would say no one could possibly achieve perfection one hundred percent of the time before professing his weaknesses. One flaw he could claim was his quickness to rise to a level of anger when justified. He lacked a tolerance for the suffering of those he loved. One could easily lose the grace of his good opinion when connected to the loss of respect, honesty or virtue. He could be reduced to quick temper when confronted with subjects distasteful to his principles. His opinions could be viewed forceful when he felt a certainty of correctness. He was known to be honestly forthright. There arose occasions when his frankness was viewed as arrogance, but those so wholly connected to him could be certain his openness held truth. He had little tolerance for false flattery or mixed words expressed for the sole purpose of contriving schemes. He had no wish to alter his conviction to secure the comfort of another's good opinion. There was no false dignity in his language, although his anger could be regarded as severe on occasion. She had to admit she saw him quick to anger when confronted with less than honourable deeds. She herself had long ago decided she should not wish to be on his opposing side. Nay, on such occasions, he was sure to be the winner, as he was most likely to be sure of himself before committing to a battle of wits.

She neared the house, now emotionally intoxicated in her reflection of him, the children and the whole sum of her life at Pemberley. "I love him so much; I trust him more than anyone in the world," she verbally reflected with contentment. She realized he was part of her favourite memories as well as her most important dreams. She could not imagine what life would be like without him or his love. She concluded she had indeed been blessed far beyond her deserving.

Her thoughts now went in another direction. While the others still remained at the parsonage, Elizabeth seized the opportunity to concentrate on the plans for the upcoming ball.

Mr. Darcy had encouraged her to render any changes to the house to her own delight, making ready money enough to satisfy any want of greater elegance. She was content with the chambers. She admired her husband's taste, finding nothing pretentious or ineffectual, instead she discovered refined elegance. She had no desire to make any drastic changes. She had no wish to alter its charm, but thought that perhaps some tapestry in one particular area might be advantageous. She planned to decorate Pemberley in such a fashion surely not to escape anyone's notice. Elizabeth desired the Pemberley ball to be infinitely superior. She passed the day writing lists, drawing details, but saved the delicacies for last. After additional thought, she decided she would need a special gown. As she continued to design her elegant decorating notions, she found that she had drawn a gown very pleasing to her taste. Perhaps she would purchase material to do it justice, she pondered. She continued to study her design, smiling at her own intriguing notions. After drawing further details, she resolved a gown should be specifically formed to complement the occasion—something extraordinary, something uncommon—surely a gown so elegant as to leave her husband speechless. Since Georgiana was to arrive home within the week, she anticipated sharing her design with her; to the rest it would be kept secret. Georgiana was her dearest and closest friend now that she unhappily discovered Charlotte's turn against her family, her opposing convictions matched with her willingness to agree with the ill opinions of her husband. She was certain she could entrust her plans with Georgiana.

She entered the music chamber, occupying a seat in the corner of the sofa continuing her plans. When it came to the delicacies, she decided nothing should be spared. She planned to acquire imported chocolates as well as the finest wine from France. She resolved to secure the finest musicians in Derbyshire, having already had notions of the melodies she favoured. Since her husband challenged her with the arrangement of the entire ball, she judged the splendor of her plans would be kept a guarded secret, any intrigue would only prove to crest his curiosity. In the end, she would ascertain by his expression the success of her undertaking. She plunged into her plans with dedicated fury. Each new idea seemed to stimulate another inspiration, granting her sensational notions pleasing to her taste.

The afternoon passed swiftly. She put aside her plans, not wishing to have them viewed by anyone. Immediately after having done so came the greatest relief. She had no more removed the plans from view when she heard the familiar voices of the party as they freely entered the music chamber.

"Oh, Lizzy, such a happy time we had. The children were so delightful; they played card games, spillikins, riddles and conundrums all afternoon. Mr. Manley was so kind, it is unlike our celebration at home to be sure," Mary claimed.

"Well, Mary, there is a vast difference in estates. You must remember, Mr. Darcy has the means to do more than Father. You must not judge what you do not understand. Our father is kind to the servants at Longbourn; I should not like you to judge him ill."

"Oh, no, Lizzy, to be sure, I should not judge father less than good, I would not want you to think I would do so. I only meant to say that Mr. Darcy provides for the servants well. We did have a splendid day, we did indeed."

"It is quite all right, Mary, do not be anxious," Elizabeth said with greater patience. In an attempt to change the subject, she went on, "I do believe I shall join you when you go to the warehouses in town."

"That will be delightful; we shall be a gay party," Kathryn voiced with exuberant joy. Having heard that part of the conversation as he entered the room, Mr. Darcy wasted no time addressing his wife. "I must say I am delighted with the plan. I urge you to purchase a new gown; after all, the arrangements are of your own doing; you should indulge in whatever you desire. It would not be fitting if you did not."

Elizabeth smiled; little did he know of her secret plan. "I shall do just that."

Mrs. Reynolds entered to announce, "Mr. Bingley, sir."

Charles Bingley quickly bowed upon entry. His face beamed with a broadened smile as he announced, "We may be considered neighbours from this day forward."

"Mr. Bingley we are delighted; are we not now, dearest?" Elizabeth asserted.

"Yes, Bingley, we certainly are at that. I was rather concerned; it is almost time to dine. I had rather expected you a bit earlier."

"Mr. Bingley, it is indeed an honour to see you again. Your family—I trust they are in health?" Mr. Manley inquired.

"Yes, very well indeed. I had expected to arrive earlier, but was delayed in town. The magistrate was quite busy. I must say I am wanting; I have not had a bite since breakfast. I trust you are having the expected roast goose?"

"Indeed, Bingley, I expect you'll not have a long wait," Mr. Darcy assured him.

"Mr. Bingley, the ladies and children, are they not expected to journey here tomorrow?" Mr. Bennet inquired.

"Yes, they shall, some of the servants have already arrived at Foxshire Estate to air the chambers in anticipation. Just the same, Darcy, I do plan to accept your offer to stay the night, if it is still agreeable."

"Why, yes, Bingley, of course."

Mrs. Reynolds entered to announce their presence was required in the dining hall for the planned feast. Having wasted little time, they found themselves in deep conversation over a feast of goose. Kathryn and Mary were anxious for the arrival of Mr. Bingley's party, inquiring if they might join him at Foxshire Estate the morning next. Mr. Bingley readily agreed to the plan. Mr. Bennet instantly decided to accompany them as well.

Mr. Manley and Mr. Darcy planned to sport the day following, while Elizabeth was occupied with the planning of a special dinner for the new neighbours. I know, thought she, since the intended ball is but a fortnight away, I shall rehearse my skills at the dinner party. I shall attempt to delight my guests as well as my husband with unexpected pleasantries. My attire shall have to be exceptional. Looking over at her husband, like a girl in her youth on the threshold of womanhood, she suddenly had notions to set out to gain his notice with her presentation. She was convinced—should I excite them to notice, my plans for the ball will undoubtedly prove successful. She felt satisfied with her convictions. Lost in eagerness to present her plan, her mind was elsewhere. Mr. Darcy was aware the laughter around the table escaped her notice.

"You are quiet this evening, you have scarce made conversation; are you unwell?"

"On the contrary, dearest, I am very well, thank you. My mind was agreeably engaged with the delight of seeing Jane again." Granting him a warm smile, she turned her eyes to Mr. Bingley. "I should expect you all here no later than four o'clock tomorrow for dinner; is that agreeable to you?"

"Very agreeable."

The remainder of the evening passed quietly. Tired from a busy day, Mr. Bingley retired early. Mr. Manley quitted the great hall earlier than usual. The girls were anxious to occupy their chamber to work on embroidery before Emily's arrival. After playing the pianoforte, Elizabeth announced she should like to rest early as well. The whole of the party retired with anticipation of the joyful arrival of the Bingley family the day next.

As for Elizabeth, she secretly concentrated on her design to utilize the unsuspecting as a test for her future plans for the Pemberley ball.

Unexpected Delights

ELIZABETH AWOKE EARLY to find her husband had already quitted the chamber. After making herself ready, she found him in the breakfast chamber. He was sitting with her father, deep-rooted in conversation over a cup of coffee.

"I did not hear you rise;, I must have been resting very soundly," she announced.

Mr. Darcy looked at her. "Good morning, dearest," he said. He seemed uncommonly cheerful.

"Good morning, Lizzy; I trust you slept well? Your husband and I plan to sport early, and then accompany Mr. Bingley to Foxshire. I believe the girls are still tucked up."

"I did rest well, thank you, Father," she said just as Mr. Bingley entered the breakfast chamber.

"Well, what a delightful morning it is. I shall see my dear family today; you know I have missed them excessively; I restlessly found sleep difficult."

"No doubt, you are not accustomed to being from home," Elizabeth interjected.

"You know I believe it is so; I should not like to do it often."

"Being away from a most agreeable, loving wife can prove agonizing," Mr. Darcy stated, glancing at his wife, emitting thoughts of his own happy situation.

"Yes, indeed it is; I should like to join you in sport to pass the time more quickly until their arrival."

After having breakfasted, the gentlemen departed the hall for their intended shoot, allowing Elizabeth time alone with her designs. It was not often she wished her husband's absence, but on this day she had purpose she

482 — HONOUR AND HUMILITY

did not desire to share. She related to the cook to plan the evening meal for the party of twelve, ordering special dishes to be lavishly prepared. She applied for their finest wine to be served. She shared with them her expectations as to the exquisite appearance of the table, ordering fresh flowers and greens to be brought in from the out of doors. She desired desserts to be delectable, sweet as well as advantageously displayed. She applied for the use of the fine china, linen and silver flatware. She directed the silver candelabras and cutlery be polished to perfection.

She discovered satisfaction in her intended appearance; surely Mr. Darcy would not expect her formally attired. It was not in her nature to dress elaborately in their home. Although he never said as much, she often wondered if he had wished it otherwise, realizing other ladies of her situation dressed advantageously in finery as standard attire. She anxiously arranged her apparel for the evening, planning to wear the jewels he presented to her at the coming out party for Ann.

The post had arrived. Responses and acceptances of the invitation to the Pemberley ball were arriving in small parcels each day. Most of the replies were of a positive nature. She marveled at the number of attendees that she was to expect. She received a letter from Lady Catherine expressing their delightful anticipation of the event, articulating pleasure in the extended invitation to John Gibson, who most readily accepted upon learning of it. From the Earl of Matlock she received a definite acceptance by the whole of the family, but most pleasing, perhaps, was the acceptance from the Gardiners. Many acquaintances of Mr. Darcy had responded in consent. Of course, Mr. Manley would attend without a doubt.

Kathryn and Mary, having already breakfasted, proceeded to the music chamber to accomplish additional needlework in hopes of impressing Emily. They talked much of the intended trip to the warehouses, the visit to Foxshire as well as the upcoming ball. Elizabeth played the pianoforte, later taking up a book.

The gentlemen returned in the early afternoon for nourishment before departing with Mr. Bingley to go to the newly leased Foxshire Estate. It was not long before the whole of the party, with the exception of Elizabeth, quitted Pemberley. Elizabeth immediately put her plans into action, spending the entire early part of the afternoon overseeing the table setting as well as the placement of greens and flowers. She restated the evening's plans with the servants, reiterating her expectations regarding the dinner and how it was to be served. Having completed the directions to her satisfaction, she proceeded above the stairs to prepare for the dinner, entrusting the servants to carry out her wishes.

The maidservant prepared the vat of water for her to bathe. Allowing herself ample time to leisurely soak, she had her hair washed as well, later having it arranged to her approval. As she sat at the dressing table, she peered into the looking glass. Her complexion was radiant. Elizabeth's eyes sparkled with a look of contentment, which only enhanced her relaxed, gleeful face. Mrs. Reynolds had the gown she wore at Rosings prepared fresh and made ready. Her maidservant laid everything out she intended to wear that evening. Her chambermaid placed fancy combs in her hair after preparing it with locks about her face. When the time had come, her chambermaid assisted her with her gown and jewels. She completed her preparations in time for the arrival of her husband, father and sisters, who returned little more than one hour before the expected guests. She heard their voices as she stepped from the bedchamber. She descended the stairs with poised strides, her carriage gracefully elegant. At the base of the stairs a very awestruck Mr. Darcy awaited her with unquestionable delight. His eyes were bright with pride.

"Elizabeth, dearest, you look radiant; I had not expected you to go to such lengths this evening; I must say I am more than pleased."

"Dearest, should you not be preparing yourself as well? You shall have to make haste," she declared with deliberate lingering charm to entice him.

"Indeed I shall do so directly," he retorted, directing his strides hurriedly above the stairs. He paused amid his elevation to turn to capture a further glimpse of her, which did not escape her notice. This was exactly what she had hoped for. Mr. Darcy was no sooner out of sight when Elizabeth happened upon her father and sisters. They looked at her with astonishment.

"Well now, Lizzy, you are well dressed for the occasion, I perceive. I believe I shall refresh myself as well," her father said gleefully, requiring no persuasion.

"Come, Kathryn, we shall make ready ourselves," Mary said as she grabbed Kathryn's hand, pulling her in the direction of the stairs.

Elizabeth smiled, now anxious for the next planned reaction. Thus far her expectations were met, but the real challenge looming was the dinner. Surely Emily would notice the fruits of her labour, but would Caroline or Mrs. Hurst, she wondered. And, if they were pleased, would they dare be so kind as to voice any favourably formed opinions?

Within the hour, Mr. Darcy joined his wife. Her father and sisters had not yet come below the stairs. He deliberately neared her, placing his face near the side of hers as he whispered in her ear, "My beautiful Elizabeth, thou tempts me, such a lovely creature. Indeed you must know your appearance gives me the greatest pleasure. I had not expected such extravagance; it pleases me tremendously."

She lovingly smiled at him, fixing her eyes deep within his stare as she answered, "Dearest, I am delighted you are pleased; I trust you will experience a most enjoyable evening. How did you find my sister and the rest of the party?"

"Very well, I believe Jane is eager for your company, to be sure."

"And I am eager to see Jane. Pray, tell me of Emily; did my father thrill at her sight?"

"Yes, I do believe Emily is sensible of your father's interest, although I am uncertain if he recognizes his own true feelings. Caroline and Louisa, however, have apprehended the notion. They seemed quite displeased with them both. Caroline especially—she attempted to occupy Emily from your father quite unsuccessfully. She affords them no gain. I detected deliberateness in her manner in dealing with the situation. I do believe Emily fancies provoking them with attentions she easily allows him, undermining their every attempt at separation. It was quite entertaining; you would have thought it amusing."

"Well I'm sure of it; oh, I do believe I hear Father," she whispered.

Elizabeth spun around on her heels. Mr. Bennet was approaching. "Father, you look very handsome this evening."

Although he now sported his usual dress, she thought he appeared quite dashing, but in need of a new dress coat. It had been many years since her father had purchased formal attire, and Elizabeth found pleasure in his anticipated purchase. His presentation was fresh and sharp. She went so far as to believe it advantaged him in height as well as youthfulness. He maintained a sophisticated air about him, which was most pleasing, thought she.

It was but a few moments when Kathryn and Mary entered, each wearing fine dresses, each with their hair fixed favourably about their face in ringlets. She noticed her father under the watchful eye of her younger sisters, who studied him with curiosity. Following the scrutiny of their father, they put their heads together in a whisper. Elizabeth graciously stepped back to near them. In a low voice she reminded them it was impolite to stare or to join their heads in a whisper. Surprisingly, Mary sarcastically pointed out, "Your husband stares at your every move; he is unable to remove his eyes from you; perhaps you should enlighten him on the subject as well."

"Mary, that was unnecessary; why should you say such a thing?" Elizabeth asked, surprised by her quick rebuke.

"I am so sorry, Lizzy, I am a little out of sorts at the moment."

"Whatever for?" Elizabeth asked.

"I'm not quite sure of it; may I discuss this later with you, Lizzy?"

"To be sure, I look forward to the discussion."

As the party arrived, Mr. Darcy and Elizabeth greeted Emily, Caroline and the Hursts. Elizabeth and Jane greeted one another with expected delight. Mr. Manley followed close behind, arriving just in time to join the rest of the party. Caroline's expression bore an icy stare at Elizabeth's presentation. In the beginning, her envy was without obstruction as she obviously struggled to gain composure. Emily wasted no moments in granting compliments, which were graciously received. Elizabeth indeed felt the successful start of her plan, first with her husband, now with Emily, but most assurance came from Caroline Bingley's direct response. Jane was thrilled to see her, complimenting her dress. She was in awe of the jewels about her throat, claiming them to be stunning, proclaiming her all that is graceful. At last Caroline managed to say, "Elizabeth, my dear, I see you have improved in taste. Wherever did you acquire such a bold necklace; I daresay was it handed down from your mother; is it genuine?"

Caroline, unaware of Mr. Darcy's hearing the comment, was shocked when, without hesitation, he swiftly turned to her. He interrupted. "It is quite genuine, I assure you. It was with certainty a selected gift from her husband, who thought of no other throat to do it justice. I am of the opinion it is she who enhances the beauty of the piece rather than it adorn her."

After having addressed Caroline's rude remarks, he passed off a look of decided satisfaction to his wife, then to his friend. His words were directly sober, causing Caroline to blush, realizing she was caught in her own scheme.

As Caroline's face lost its luster, turning a deep shade of red, she tried to maintain a stance of superiority in regaining her composure. Having insulted Mr. Darcy was the least of her intentions. Elizabeth's kind demeanour only proved to add to her self-inflicted injuries. Elizabeth remained graciously welcoming, affording Caroline civility far beyond her deserving, in spite of her ill-mannered attempts.

"Well, thank you, dearest, that is quite a compliment," she exclaimed. She then turned to Caroline. "I am so glad you have come this evening, Caroline; it has been some time since you last visited Pemberley. I trust you will enjoy the evening."

"Your dress has an elegance we are not accustomed to seeing from you, Elizabeth," Mrs. Hurst managed to say foolishly, expecting no one to believe it was meant to be anything other than a compliment. Her husband, thinking it so, added, "Yes, Mrs. Darcy, it is quite an exquisite gown."

Mr. Hurst then stepped closer to examine her jewels. "These jewels are extremely fine; you look very handsome this evening indeed."

Elizabeth blushed at his remarks, mainly out of the realization he earnestly had not understood his wife's comments. But it was of little concern to Elizabeth, she was confident in her appearance, and more importantly, she was knowledgeable they harbored begrudging feelings. She decided she would not take seriously any expression made by Caroline or Mrs. Hurst.

When the party entered the dining hall, Mr. Darcy studied the table with pride. He smiled with gratification at the reaction of all those entering. Mary was sure to manage a seat near Mr. Manley, engaging him in conversation whenever possible.

Emily wasted little time in her admiration of the beautiful presentation.

"As fine a table as ever I saw," Mr. Bennet boasted. "Elizabeth is quite accomplished, yes indeed it is so. I expected as much. I daresay she is deserving of a husband of Mr. Darcy's character," he continued to chant.

Mr. Darcy thoroughly enjoyed his father-in-law's explanation of his true feelings on the subject. By virtue of his shared opinion, he detected enjoyment to be had in the scorned look on Caroline's face along with the frown brought to Mrs. Hurst's expression upon hearing it.

Mr. Manley voiced his approval. "The arrangements are exceptional, not only in placement but in purpose; I believe them to be so elegantly emphasized."

Mr. Manley's words caused additional pain to those opposing. If all such compliments were not well enough, unwittingly Mr. Manley continued, "Mrs. Darcy, did you have one of the servants do the arrangements or were they by your own hand?"

"Indeed it was my own design with the aid of the servants' hard work. I thank you, Mr. Manley, for all such compliments; they are greatly received."

Jane complimented her again, delighting in the colours. She could not avoid mentioning the magnificent details to which the displays flourished admirably. Mary and Kathryn were impressed and stated so in many ways.

"Well, dearest, I confess, I am not at all surprised by the superiority of your extensive design. My only wonder is that you do it all with such ease," Mr. Darcy expressed openly.

"I find it all most agreeable, yes indeed, very delightful, Elizabeth," Mr. Bingley added as his sisters shared a sneering exchange. Mr. Bingley winked at his friend.

Elizabeth determined such excessive flattery was perhaps not for her sake alone but more fitted for sport of Caroline and Mrs. Hurst, who now struggled to regulate themselves. The presentation of the extravagant meal seemed another source of contention to Caroline and Mrs. Hurst, who now were attempting to do their best to hide their opinions, lending shallow compliments to Elizabeth in Mr. Darcy's presence.

Their sarcastic disregard for Elizabeth did not go unnoticed by Emily, who immediately agitated them further with the sincerest form of flattery she could bestow on Elizabeth. "Elizabeth, I am not at all surprised by such accomplishments. From our first meeting I was so totally convinced of your discernment that I should wish myself to your likeness. I was certain this evening would prove my suspicions correct. I daresay it has. I believe you have reached the highest level of society in your design. Judging by the distinction of this evening, the Pemberley ball is certain to be pure elegance beyond all imagination. I know of no one who has impressed me thus far to this high degree. You truly present yourself superior in character, taste and elegance. Might I be so bold as to say I should wish to claim you as a dear friend, always."

Such high praise made Emily a contender in the battle of discontentment plaguing her sisters. Her difference of opinion was sorely noticed, providing further amusement to Mr. Darcy as well as her brother Charles.

Later in the evening, whilst Mr. Manley entertained the party at the pianoforte, Elizabeth had an opportunity to talk to Mary, who now had altered her disposition. She told Elizabeth she had earlier realized her father's attraction to Emily, stating upon first thought that it gave her alarm. But now she claimed a difference of conviction. She expressed her thoughts on the subject, concluding she realized she enjoyed her attentions.

Elizabeth paused, then said, "Father has not expressed any designs toward Emily. I believe he has no understanding of his feelings at present."

Much to Elizabeth's amazement, Mary retorted, "Perhaps that was so this morning, but I think not now; you need only to watch him. You will be forced to agree. I daresay you are quite in error of the subject. I do believe Father realized it this evening when she made her entrance. I could tell, surely I could. Imagine that, Lizzy, I, whom everyone believes to be the most unromantic, perceived the very moment Father realized his affections for

Emily. And Elizabeth, my initial trepidation ceased after much thought. Indeed I now delight in the thought of Emily's daily presence, should they marry. I have not chanced to discuss the subject with Kathryn, nor do I have knowledge of her feelings."

"Really now, Mary, I rather doubt our father is contemplating matrimony."

"We shall see, Lizzy. I for one do not agree; we shall have to wait and see."

It had been a comfortable day. The evening sky was spattered with stars. Mr. Bennet and Emily stood at the threshold enjoying the night air as the rest of the party remained indoors.

The remainder of the evening passed unchallenged, with no additional sarcasm toward Elizabeth. Mr. Darcy perceived their concern of Emily and Mr. Bennet must have hastened their thoughts in another direction. Seated on the sofa aside of her husband, Elizabeth enjoyed the success of her plans.

Mr. Bennet and Emily were observed in a delightful exchange, which appeared to be on intimate terms, causing a disapproving exchange of sentiments to pass from Caroline to Louisa Hurst and vice versa. The only member of the party unmoved by any actions during the evening was Mr. Hurst, who upheld his reputation. As usual he was sprawled across the sofa, managing a moderate snort every once and again. The evening belonged to Elizabeth—everything she did, said or planned, including her appearance, was outstanding. No one present could deny the success of it, not even Caroline.

When the guests departed, the remainder of the party sat about in an exchange until Mr. Bennet requested the use of Mr. Darcy's office to speak with his two youngest daughters. The looks on the faces of Kathryn and Mary were that of defense. It was obvious they expected to be reprimanded or scolded for some ill-mannered words spoken or improper decorum on their part. Elizabeth's curiosity swelled as they quitted the room. Mr. Darcy noticed his wife's reaction. "So I imagine you will not rest until you know all."

"Surely my father may just wish to compliment the girls. I could see where they did nothing wrong, but if that be the case, he would have no reason to quit the room. Whatever do you suppose is his meaning?"

"Well now, it matters little until he makes it known, does it not?" he asked, amused by her wonderment.

Within the half-hour, Mr. Bennet and Mary returned. Elizabeth immediately inquired, "Where is Kathryn?"

"She ran above the stairs in tears, Lizzy," Mary hastily blurted out.

"Whatever for, Father?"

"Well, I thought it best to inform the girls first, since they reside with me. I decided it necessary they should hear the news from me. Lizzy, Mr. Darcy, I do believe I shall ask Emily for an interview."

"Oh, that would please me, but is Kathryn unsettled by it? Does she weep of your announcement?" Elizabeth anxiously inquired.

"She'll get over it sooner than she thinks. I believe Kathryn's youth makes it difficult for her to realize how lonely a man can truly be. I was once of the opinion I should never wish to entertain thoughts of marriage, having had more than twenty years of the institution. I believe I thought I should never be longing to revisit such a challenging experience, but much to my surprise I find I have sensitive yearnings of the opposite nature. Lizzy, Emily Bingley is pure delight; why only this very morning I realized my heart is captured by this creature of loveliness. Kathryn need not worry of her taking your mother's place; there is no likeness there to be sure, I daresay none at all. Now, Mary here is a young lady of deep reflection, she affords me understanding. I am sure once Kathryn has given it more thought she'll come 'round."

Before Elizabeth could comment, Mary turned to her, smiling smugly. "Lizzy, did not I tell you so earlier; it is all as I have said. And to think I happened upon his notion almost as soon as he did himself. No one would have suspected me to detect such romantic tendencies." Then Mary turned to Mr. Bennet, "Father, I'm sure it will pass over quickly with Kathryn. I was angry all the day until Emily arrived. I soon realized I experience inexplicable feelings of happiness in her presence."

"Father, when do you plan to seek Emily's hand?" Elizabeth inquired.

"Well now, Lizzy, that I have not decided as yet, these things take time; perhaps I shall give Kathryn time to come to an understanding. I should not wish to let it drag on though, nay, I say the sooner the better, but we'll allow your sister time to reflect."

"Well, Mr. Bennet, may I speak frankly?" Mr. Darcy asked.

"I wish you would, Mr. Darcy, I hold your opinion in the highest regard."

"When a man meets a woman who induces feelings of deep admiring affection and the felicity he experiences is so ardently expressed, I believe he should not squander a moment approaching the subject with the lady whose attentions he desires."

"I see we are of the same opinion, Mr. Darcy."

"Indeed we are, Mr. Bennet," he said, fixing his eyes on Elizabeth with pride.

"Well, when I marry it will surely be only for the deepest affections. I should not wish to marry only to be unhappy or miserable," Mary explained.

"Indeed not, Mary, I believe you possess correct understanding of the subject," Elizabeth voiced.

"Well now, I must consider the prospect that Emily may not wish to accept my offer of marriage. Perhaps the meager comforts of Longbourn are far less than she may be inclined to settle upon. But we shall see now, won't we?" Mr. Bennet lamented with pleasure.

"Well, Father, if this is your desire, I wish you every success," Elizabeth said pleasantly.

"Well, thank you, Lizzy, I do believe I shall go above the stairs just now; I am not at all tired at the moment but I should like to read. I should reflect on my thoughts if that is agreeable to you both?"

"Of course, Father, good night."

"Mary, might you go above the stairs to your sister for her comfort?" Mr. Bennet asked. Then he turned to Elizabeth and Mr. Darcy. "I bid you both good night."

"Good night, Mr. Bennet," Mr. Darcy called to him as he quitted the room.

"It appears we are alone," Mr. Darcy said with a smile.

"So it appears we are."

"It was indeed an exceptional affair. You achieved at great length a truly satisfying evening. Your elegance was most assuredly envied. I am sorry you were put upon by their lack of manners. I do suppose they had not counted on my hearing their snide remarks regarding the exquisite necklace you are wearing. Allow me to assure you, it is genuine indeed."

"I never doubted it. I confess, tonight I resolved to gain reaction of my abilities as mistress of Pemberley. I was in want to experiment prior to the ball. Caroline's and Mrs. Hurst's reactions convinced me the evening was a success; had it not been so, they would have enjoyed the evening more," she giggled.

"Yes, I suppose it would be so. What of this news of your father's; does it really please you? Are you indeed happy with the notion?"

"Oh, yes, very much so. I do hope Kathryn changes her opinion. I never had expected my father to announce such thoughts tonight, but I confess I have noticed his gaining spirit these many months, I suppose I'm still shocked a very little at least."

"Why should you be? A man can't abide forever on chanced meetings. If he is to secure his beloved, he must make his feelings known."

"Such as you did once?"

"Once? I believe I made mine known a second time, if you recollect. I shall make them known this very moment if I choose," he said, moving closer to her. "Dearest Elizabeth, with your skin wonderfully fragrant, your extraordinary beauty fascinates my desirous heart at the very thought of you. You indulge my senses to the fullest," he whispered.

"Dearest," she whispered, "it is just we two; why are we whispering?"

"The servants are directly beyond the door. My words are for you alone."

"Your appearance is strikingly handsome. I daresay it excites my romantic notions. I find you a man of distinction, excessively appealing. Perhaps your handsome appearance is further reminder to Caroline of what is lost to her."

"Perhaps, dearest. The Pemberley ball is but a fortnight off; I do suppose you have plans for its success as well?"

"Indeed I do, but I'll not tell you one thing more," she teased.

"As you wish; if you desire my assistance you need only ask."

"Yes, I am sure of it. You may depend on my asking if I should have a need."

"What of your sister Mary? She advantageously gained a seat next to Mr. Manley at the table again. Poor Mary, he is very kind but there is no interest there."

"I recognized it as well; my sister is persistent is she not now?"

"Very, but she is young. She admired you greatly this evening."

"Me? She admired me?"

"Yes, you were so intent on the gathering you had not noticed her eyes fixed on you most of the evening. Perhaps she thought her sister very beautiful as I made notice."

"Speaking of fixed eyes, as we joined together in the sitting room before our guests arrived, I scolded Mary and Kathryn for their ill-mannered whispering and staring. Mary in turn made me aware I should remind my husband it is impolite to stare."

"Stare? Whatever is her meaning?"

"She claimed your eyes were fixed on me, following me as I walked across the room."

"Ah yes, your sister is perceptive indeed, and I am guilty. Can a man refrain from the temptations of such beauty? Can he deny himself the pleasure of expression of elegance so beckoning to him? I think not, at least it would have been hopeless to try not to gaze on you this very evening, to be sure. I confess—no I boast—yes, indeed, I am deserving of blame or censure. I did fix my eyes upon my wife as I do at this very moment. Why should I not? Thou art mine, my beautiful Elizabeth! If it be criminal, if I am proven guilty, I show no reproof. I forbid myself to claim it unpardonable; therefore, madam, I suggest you shall forevermore suffer to hold me your prisoner," he whispered teasingly, causing her to blush.

Preparations

IT WAS BUT A FEW DAYS before Georgiana's carriage arrived. Elizabeth was elated to see her again. She anxiously waited for a time when she could discuss the plans for the ball.

Mr. Darcy, no less eager to see his sister, had many questions regarding her education, but first expressed his delight in her safe journey.

When Elizabeth presented her plans to Georgiana, she listened intently, then expressed her delight to be called upon for her opinion. Although she was eager to learn of the shopping trip, she revealed her purchase of a new gown in London for the occasion.

The evening prior to the shopping journey, Elizabeth visited Georgiana's room to share her completed plans. "May I come in, Georgiana?"

"Yes, indeed, please do."

"I have brought the plans. I entreat your good opinion. I have shared these with no other."

"I am honoured you grant me the privilege."

With outstretched arm, Elizabeth handed her the many drawings. She stood watching Georgiana as she examined the plans. Georgiana mused profoundly until she viewed the sketch of Elizabeth's gown. A smile overspread her face. She looked at Elizabeth. "It is remarkable. Who will make it?"

"I have not the smallest notion. I was hoping you could direct me."

"Mrs. Reynolds will know."

"Georgiana, I must know, you surely approve of the design?"

"My dear sister, I only wish I had such talent. Read nothing into my reserve, it is my general manner. This is a superior design." Georgiana's expressed approval provided Elizabeth with a sense of confidence, assuring her there was nothing wanting in her plans.

"Do sit down, Elizabeth."

When Elizabeth took a seat, Georgiana expressed her eagerness to see the finished gown, table settings and decorative arrangements.

"Georgiana, are you acquainted with Emily Bingley?"

"Very little, why do you ask?"

"My father plans to seek Emily's hand in marriage."

"Are they well suited?"

"Yes, I believe so."

"Well, then, I am happy for them."

Having no Jane present to comfort her, she discovered Georgiana a pleasing confidant, quite open to discussion.

The morning next, Mr. Bennet, Georgiana, Elizabeth and her two sisters departed Pemberley for Foxshire Estate to gather the rest of the party for the shopping journey. Upon arrival at Foxshire Hall, they were greeted affably.

Jane positioned herself in front of Elizabeth. "Lizzy, Caroline and Louisa are on their way to London to purchase new gowns for the ball. They claim nothing of superior quality could be found at the local warehouses."

"We shall see, Jane," Elizabeth answered with a smile. The absence of Mr. Bingley's sisters induced a flutter of relief.

Mr. Bingley decided he should like to join them, requiring two carriages. To Kathryn's dismay, Mr. Bennet suggested he might like to ride in the Bingley carriage.

They spent hours visiting several shops, making selective purchases. Kathryn, now fancying a gown, laid aside her ill thoughts, once again attaching herself to Emily. Both girls found gowns flattering to their form, but feared the cost beyond their father's expectations.

With dresses in hand, Mary and Kathryn quickly sought Elizabeth. Kathryn seized Elizabeth's elbow, pulling her aside. She anxiously spoke without hesitation, "Lizzy, I'm certain the gowns may be too costly for Father. He says we are to purchase complete attire. But, Lizzy, I think we ought to think the better of it. Such expenditures may put Father to ruin."

Elizabeth faced her sister. Clutching her shoulder, Elizabeth smiled. "Since it is a ball at Pemberley, I wish to purchase the gowns. Only charge to our father the other necessities; he'll not surmise the difference if you do not make it known. I may say your concern for our father's economy pleases me. You and Mary quite surprise me at times."

"Oh, Lizzy, thank you, that is quite generous of you." Mary chanted gleefully.

"Lizzy, how may I ever thank you? Such a gift, it is so very beautiful, is it not?" Kathryn said with a voice full of excitement, holding up the dress.

"Let it be our secret. Father need not know; tell no one. I shall settle it with the clerk," Elizabeth whispered.

Elizabeth felt fortunate finding a shop with the finest choice of dress goods. With Georgiana at her side, she talked to the clerk, exposing her drawn sketch. She explained that Mrs. Reynolds told her to inquire if the clerk were acquainted with a particular woman named Emma well known for her fine stitchery. To her delight, the clerk herself was the very woman. She accepted the challenge of such an impressive design. She and Georgiana assisted Elizabeth in carefully choosing the material and trimmings, discussing border designs, brocades and a slight trailing piece. Upon gaining Georgiana's approval, she confirmed her decision.

Georgiana waited while Elizabeth disappeared to the back of the shop for measurements. When all the details and expectations of the gown were completed, Elizabeth purchased accessories to complement her creation. She was pleased to learn she was to return in a week to fit and approve the finished finery.

Mr. Bennet, having found fitting attire, was in a state of euphoria, humming with distinct contentment. Elizabeth watched with interest as he wandered about the shop, taking notice of a variety of inventories.

Kathryn and Mary, having all their purchases approved, delighted in their father's compliments regarding money well spent. Elizabeth afforded her sisters a reassuring smile. Mr. Bennet gleefully wandered about the warehouse, happy to accompany Emily. Elizabeth raised her brows to Mary and Kathryn. His actions furnished a source of amusement. They, having never known their father to delight in shopping, snickered at his attentions. Surely at one time he would have fervently claimed it a task for women alone.

Georgiana discovered a few unexpected items, while Emily, who had announced earlier that she already had her gown for the ball, appeared delighted in a pair of gloves.

Jane purchased an elegant gown, fitting perfectly to her form, along with additional items Mr. Bingley encouraged her to acquire. Mr. Bingley was extremely attentive with Jane, allowing her to want for nothing. His devotion to her was constant.

Mr. Bennet, still delighted with the situation, thanked his youngest daughters for their consideration of his purse, complimenting them on their economy.

In a moment alone with Elizabeth, he lamented, "I sorrowfully give thought to the many occasions I chose to deny your mother her purchases, but to be truthful they were seldom within reason, causing friction when the requisitions arrived. Looking back on the situation, perhaps there were admittedly times when I could have been less severe with criticism. At times, I find I am quite ashamed of my actions. Now here I am with a new dress coat."

"Do not distress yourself, Father, surely you were within good reason. You need not reproach yourself for acquiring a dress coat, indeed you deserve it; say no more of this. I have not forgotten the many trips to the warehouses that were not to be."

"Just the same, Lizzy, I am sorry for having tormented her with words on the subject. I do hope you and your sisters understand my rationality."

"Father, think nothing of it; you must put that behind you now."

"Yes, I do believe you are right, my dear; I shall indeed. I just desired your opinion of it before I ask Emily for her hand in marriage. You know, Lizzy, how very much I value your opinion."

"Yes, Father, I do. Rest assured you have my blessing where Emily is concerned."

Elizabeth noted an almost apologetic tone in his explanation. She was grateful he had not realized there were no charges for the girl's frocks, fearing he would be embarrassed at her attempt to alleviate his expenses.

Elizabeth observed her sisters' immediate feelings toward Mr. Bennet's intended proposal to Emily now seemed vastly altered. Since the night last at Pemberley, Kathryn's unpleasant reaction of the upcoming proposal seemed to have palliated. She presently fixed her concentration on Kathryn's interaction with Emily, believing it as it ought to be. They were friendly confidants once again, with Emily never really having noticed any change in Kathryn's demeanour.

Elizabeth had little chance to speak with Jane in private. She wondered if she knew of their father's intentions. Mr. Bingley never missed an opportunity to be at her side, allowing nothing to be revealed on the matter.

They rode to Foxshire Estate after departing Lambton to visit a short while with the children before returning to Pemberley. Elizabeth had forgotten Mr. Hurst, who was in the sitting room taking a nap. Startling him upon entering, he abruptly stood, then bowed, "Forgive my idleness, shameful to nap on such a fine day indeed."

Jane ordered tea for her guests as they discussed the afternoon purchases. Elizabeth was astonished by Mr. Hurst's desire to join them. He spoke with easy interest. For the first time since their meeting she found him to be receptively eager to speak with her on any subject. He even went so far as to say how very much he enjoyed her entertainment at the pianoforte, believing her talent to be of superior quality. It seemed a strange occasion to be quite taken aback by his agreeable countenance. She credited his wife's absence as reason enough to grant him the freedom to be cordial in her company. Another incipient reaction was her compassion for this man to whom she had previously given little thought. She could like him as an individual, thought she. With profound conviction, she concluded he was a prisoner within the married state, a man who seldom spoke, allowing his wife the authority to direct his views.

Now Elizabeth, in an attempt to talk to Jane alone, requested to see little Charles, but, much to her dismay, Mr. Bingley chose to accompany them along with her father and sisters. Upon their return to the sitting room Elizabeth long resigned herself to believe she should not attain a free moment with Jane. The subject would have to wait. Then almost as if Jane were aware of her desperation of an exchange, she suggested she show Elizabeth a bit of material she had purchased for another project. To her satisfaction they found themselves in the privacy of yet another chamber. Upon closing the door, Jane turned quickly to say, "Lizzy, I must speak with you." Her voice grew urgent.

"What is it, Jane? You sound so severe."

"Lizzy, Caroline and Mrs. Hurst have taken leave to London to purchase fine gowns for the ball, scoffing at the local warehouses. They intend to make a grand appearance. I am concerned on your behalf."

"Whatever for, Jane?"

"Lizzy, you did not purchase a fresh gown for the ball; whatever are you thinking? Surely you will not wear the same gown you wore for our dinner; they will surely make it known among your guests, their having witnessed it at a lesser event."

Elizabeth laughed. "Jane, do not concern yourself on my account; I shall have a fresh gown at the ball. I shall explain, but it must be kept a guarded secret. I have sketched my own gown. The clerk at the warehouse is stitching it for me. You see, I expect I should have it within a week. I'm not at all concerned with any purchases connected with Caroline or Louisa Hurst. I am confident my gown will be acceptable. You shall have to remain patient, Jane, you will see.

"Truly, Lizzy?"

"Yes, Jane. My only concern is with my husband. It is my desire to overwhelm Fitzwilliam with my presentation. Surely I care nothing of the opinion of Caroline or Louisa Hurst. Besides, Jane, surely you understand we are all equal in the eyes of Caroline and Louisa, as commoners, that is," Elizabeth said with a laugh.

"Oh, Lizzy, do be serious."

"Jane—there is something I would speak to you about; there is another concern. It is a matter of which I must make you aware."

"Whatever can it be, Lizzy? Your look is quite serious."

"Our father intends to make an offer of marriage to Emily Bingley."

Jane's lips parted. A look of horror overspread her features, uniting her brows. "Good gracious, when does he intend to do this? What will Caroline and Louisa say? What will Charles say? Oh, Lizzy, pray tell me it will not cause further pain."

"Does it really matter, Jane? After all, cannot Father, a man of sound scruples, make an offer without concern of the opinions of others? Is not Emily's reaction the only one of his concern? Certainly you would not wish him to refrain on their account or ours to be sure, would you not now?"

"Well—Lizzy, are you aware Emily has money of her own? Emily's father provided for the girls. I do believe she inherited the handsomest sum of £20,000 as did Caroline and Mrs. Hurst. Surely this will cause much dissatisfaction if she accepts him."

"I was not aware of it, and I am sure Father is not. Why should that matter?"

"It should not; perhaps Charles would not mind, but Caroline and Mrs. Hurst are sure to feel put upon with the thought of their sister marrying our father. I'm sure Longbourn is not a grand enough estate. Consider their family history. Oh, Lizzy, I confess they will no doubt be offended; other struggles may arise when they learn of it. I do believe they have slight suspicions. They will surely voice their disapproval through their selfish, capricious natures. I am not privileged to know the whole of it, but one evening I overheard them scolding Emily for her attentions toward Father."

"And what was Emily's retort?"

"She defended her obligation to her own happiness."

"Well then, Jane, do you not see? If Emily were not interested she surely would have no reason to defend her right to happiness."

With fresh thoughts of concern, Jane covered her mouth with her fingers. "Poor Caroline, poor Mrs. Hurst, they will be quite put out!"

"Poor Caroline, poor Mrs. Hurst indeed! Come now, Jane, why do you concern yourself with their opinions on the subject? Emily Bingley is their elder; surely they have no influence. Say what you will, I do believe she will act honourably in her own interest; after all, is she not entitled to a bit of contentment? Should she not be the one to decide her own fate? It angers me, Jane, how her own father robbed her of happiness once; now she must concern herself with the ill opinions of others."

Jane became less anxious. "Well, since you put it that way, Lizzy, I do suppose you have made an important observation; still, it will not be to their liking."

Elizabeth patted Jane's arm. "Jane, do not worry, perhaps she will reject Father; but I rather doubt it. I have witnessed the attention she affords him; she finds a certain attraction there to be sure."

"Well, Lizzy, I shall say nothing of it except to Charles. You do not wish me to keep it from Charles, do you?" Jane's eyes widened with each word.

"No, Jane, no more than you should ever expect me to keep anything from Fitzwilliam. We are fortunate in our choice of husbands. I should never like to keep anything from Fitzwilliam."

"I agree, Lizzy, we are fortunate. I cannot believe we are situated with a nearness to Pemberley. How very much my life has altered these past months. Charles exceeds my expectations, especially having accepted our Lydia's children as his own. You know, Lizzy, there is something artful in him that allows his manner to be so endearing to others. I esteem him far beyond my initial fancy."

"Yes, Jane, your life has certainly altered."

"And what say you, Lizzy? Your Mr. Darcy has surely proven to be quite the gentleman. I had given him great thought on our wedding journey as being quite honourable, but now, after many months passed, I view he is so much more of a man than first thought. Indeed, he is without question agreeable, highly educated as well. We both have been victorious in our choosing, have we not now?"

"Certainly, Jane. Fitzwilliam continues to astonish me. I believe I know and understand the full meaning of the man. I must say he far exceeds that which he reveals publicly, for he has a most tender heart."

"Lizzy, your mutual esteem is evident. I do believe it is that which rakes the nerves of Caroline and Louisa Hurst. Among strangers, Mr. Darcy appears reserved, but there is a noticeable difference when he and Charles are in company. I do believe Caroline and Louisa had not expected to witness such felicity within your marriage, and I fear they have grown increasingly bitter against you. As time passes, it seems to become more difficult for them to accept your happy situation; there is evidence they grow more cynical. Your radiant appearance at the dinner party tended to put them on their guard for the upcoming Pemberley ball. I do believe they expect to expose you to be inferior in comparison with their presentation on that very evening. I fear it is their intention to injure you publicly."

"Jane, you have a propensity to worry for naught; do not be anxious on my account. I have no fear of Caroline or Louisa Hurst. In fact, I view their disapproval complimentary. They cannot harm me with words. Reason of it, Jane; it is I who lay to rest at night with Mr. Darcy at my side—all their resentment has no effect on our felicity. As for Mr. Darcy, indeed he is reserved in strange company. He has not that fancy some men possess in speaking with strangers; he has no pretentious desire to be noticed; he has little tolerance for frivolity of exchanged intercourse for reason of being heard."

"Yes, I believe it is so, Lizzy; I do believe you are right."

Elizabeth quickly hugged Jane. "Good then, perhaps we better join the others, lest they become suspicious; we have long been absent."

As they joined the rest of the party, Elizabeth suggested they return to Pemberley directly. Kathryn and Mary were anxious to return, but it was obvious Mr. Bennet reluctantly agreed. Georgiana remained willing to go whenever the carriage was ready to take its leave.

Mr. Hurst expressed his delight in their company, noting he looked forward to the Pemberley ball. Again Elizabeth felt warmness toward him, as though she had made a new friend. She bid him farewell, expressing she expected to see him at the ball.

Significance of Elegance

$\mathcal{W}$ITH HER DRESS NOW SECURE in safekeeping at Pemberley, Elizabeth sought the servants' understanding with regard to the significance of elegance of all preparations. With the ball nearing, the well-thought-out menu was written out for the cook. Elizabeth stressed the prominence of the evening, desiring it a success, with amenities delightfully in abundance.

Mrs. Reynolds kept the servants busy the better part of the week. The freshness of the great hall could be sensed immediately upon entry. They exhausted much time preparing the greens and flowers with Elizabeth overseeing the surety of their display as being beautifully grouped with sophistication. The ballroom was pleasantly decorated, providing ample room for the musicians. To her own credit she discovered she had an unexpected talent to express her imagination well enough to visualize the finished whole, with taste enough to carry it out well.

The tables were first covered with white damask cloth patterned in the design of Irish linen which showed the mark of the linen press.

A plentiful supply of servants made ready for the lengthy dinner. Endless service for a socially successful evening, along with the employ of what was reputed to be the best French cook and pastry cook in Derbyshire, was secured through Mrs. Reynolds. The undercooks had worked exceedingly hard for incredibly long hours in preparation.

Lavish centerpieces of extremely ornate epergnes made of glass and silver were used to display the hanging bunches of white grapes along with white fleshed peaches. All were garnished with greens of palm with fern at their base along with carefully placed larkspur, pom-pom dahlias, blue salvia, tamarisk and santolina foliage, all picked at the height of their bloom and dried in a dark attic for the grand occasion. The many silver candelabras were garnished at the base with dark greens adorned with lighter ferns sparingly used around them, alongside silver saltcellars, serving dishes and silver breadbaskets.

Elizabeth was well satisfied in her choice of the Spode "Tower" pattern, which now lined the long tables. Each setting was richly placed between the silver cutlery and fancy table decorations. Chandeliers, individual candelabras and crystal goblets brought sparkling elegance to the dining table, which exhibited high-back chairs with seating on both sides. The elaborate decorative pieces, as well as silver food platters, lent an appearance fit for royalty.

The sideboard boasted crystal candelabras with prisms and drops, with a glass bowl arranged with white roses, white anemones and white tulips with the petals curled back to show the dark centers. Atop the sideboard were displayed arrangements of confectionery of all sorts—candied fruits, sugared nuts, French imported chocolates and liqueurs.

Elizabeth planned a prodigious meal consisting of a variety of meat, fowl, fruits and vegetables; sauces and a fresh salad were to be the first serving along with sweetbreads.

The finest wine reserved was sure to please the palate of any connoisseur whose understanding and devotion to the wine's perfection would have certainly identified him as aristocracy.

To grace the feast, Elizabeth carefully planned desserts consisting of an admirable collection of jellies, dishes of creams, cakes and sweetmeats, disposed to surely make the whole of the party contented.

Mrs. Reynolds, now delighted with her master's wife, could hardly contain such feeling of pride as she looked about the chamber declaring the evening a sure success. She delighted in the thought of Pemberley engaging a grand ball once again.

After prudently giving instruction and reiterating her expectations to the servants, Elizabeth gracefully acknowledged her faith in their services, giving merit to their proficiencies. Then upon doing so, she bid them well and went above the stairs to prepare for the evening.

Elizabeth ordered the maidservant to prepare the vat of rose water for her to bathe. Once the vat was prepared, she immersed herself in the refreshing water, leisurely soaking as she gave wishful thoughts to the evening's success. Her hair washed and later arranged according to her instruction brought out a freshness of spirit. As she sat at her dressing table in her robe, she heard a knock at the bedchamber door. Pulling her robe shut tightly, she requested the visitor to enter. Georgiana appeared.

"Oh, Elizabeth, I could not help myself. I entered the dining hall. I cannot tell you how delightful it truly is. Indeed it is all so indescribably wonderful. I should like to hear my brother's thoughts on the subject."

"Thank you, Georgiana, I was sure you would tell me honestly. I had no doubt you would find favour in it. Surely you are a true test. If you approve, I am sure it will be to your brother's liking as well."

"I know my brother; tonight he will be caught in a state of absolute pride. Elizabeth, you are sure to be a sight of superior elegance. I know my brother recognizes your exceptional qualities. He has expressed as much to me on more than one occasion. I must go now; they have prepared my soak and I should like to make ready myself."

"Very well, we shall join later when we greet our many guests with all the charm and grace expected at a formal ball," Elizabeth said with a giggle, then went on to say, "I shall be happy to have such a sister near."

Alone once more, Elizabeth eyed her gown, still astonished to believe it her own creation. After her hair was designed to her satisfaction with curls slightly on the temples and her application of face cream completed, she peered into the looking glass, feeling she had achieved a state of relative excellence. Her complexion disclosed a soft, fine texture. Her fine eyes gleamed into the looking glass at her reflection, producing excited emotions, which now generated eagerness for the anticipated reaction from her beloved. She now found the wait a test of her patience. Mrs. Reynolds made ready everything she intended to wear, but she was undecided as to which of her jewels would complement her attire. She tried to read but lacked the ability to concentrate. Her apprehension of the whole of the evening would not allow her to focus on a book.

Hearing the chatter of her husband, father and the girls advancing above the stairs, she supposed they now planned to make ready for the evening.

Mr. Darcy entered the bedchamber. In viewing his wife, he made notice of her supremely soft skin. Closing his eyes, he allowed his senses to drink in her delicate fragrance. Then making himself nearer to her, he closed his eyes once more to absorb her beauty. Teasingly, he suggested he would find it impossible to think of sharing her with guests. She begged him to go at once to prepare himself, pointing out the necessity of their being prepared along with Georgiana to greet the guests.

"Very well, dearest, I shall make haste. I visited the dining hall. I must say I am astonished, such an impressive array; why the splendor of the incredible detailing and extensive design is outlandishly wonderful. The servants tell me you have done all of this yourself; they are merely following orders. I daresay you are deep in their favour; when they speak of you, they do so with great admiration. I am continually reminded that I am a most fortunate man."

"Thank you, dearest, but should you not get ready just now? While you bathe I shall complete my dress. I have ordered your manservant to make ready your bath and evening dress; I'm sure it is waiting for you. I have little more to do while I wait."

"Very well, my dear," he said, then quitted the room.

She breathed a sigh of relief when he exited. She needed the privacy of the moments next to dress. She anxiously secured her chambermaid to assist her with her gown.

Elizabeth's dress lacked neither sophistication nor elegance; there was nothing common in its delivery, and the same could be said of the form within. Mrs. Reynolds' recommendation of the lady known for her fine creations in needlework proved successful. The dress Elizabeth donned was made of the finest material available in England. In sum, it was fashioned according to her exact drawing, resulting in a gown of royal extravagance, revealing the richness of the fabric, brilliance of the design and gracefulness in treatment. The colour was superfluous light beige trimmed with slightly salmon edging with hues of gold, harmonious in colour, pouring its luxury through the richness of the fabric. The edgings, beautifully arabesque, were exceptionally extensive, having been stitched to absolute perfection. It was of unsurpassed distinction, bestowing its inherent aristocratic taste, surely not to go unnoticed.

Mrs. Reynolds ensured the chambermaid satisfied all Elizabeth's concerns. She studied Elizabeth. "May I be so bold as to say, knowing the master to some degree, I am certain your presentation will far exceed his expectations. You look lovely, my dear."

"Thank you, Mrs. Reynolds," she said as she dismissed her chambermaid.

"Mrs. Reynolds, I am so very anxious to have his reaction, silly of me is it not?"

"Not at all, Mrs. Darcy, this is sure to be a delightful evening. I shall leave you now. The master is soon to join you. I believe a private audience is perhaps desired?"

"Mrs. Reynolds, you are so attentive. I value your services as does my husband, and I should like you to know it."

"Indeed I have understood it. This is such a wonderful occasion at Pemberley. The hall will come alive with the grandest ball ever to have taken place within these walls," said she as she curtsied, then quitted the chamber.

Elizabeth had dressed with more than her usual care. Her skin was richly tanned and soft. She felt refreshed by her light, delicate fragrance, wonderfully acquired through the vat of rose water. Her intoxicating spirits were high, yet she yearned for the conquering of all that remained unpresuming in his emotions. She glanced in the looking glass again. She viewed her attire with concern, well aware it revealed her mature carriage, which accented her frame advantageously, promising to please any observer. She tugged on the front of her dress to raise the level a bit. It did not budge. Her gown revealed the fullness of her bosom spectacularly. The relative notion of conviction that her husband would find her exceedingly appealing, now caused anxiety. As she awaited his return, she understood the probability of his being delighted with her sight, yet she still continued to be apprehensive for his unknown reaction.

Abundantly satisfied with her design, she delighted in the way in which her silk frock trailed slightly in the rear. While she turned once again to face the looking glass, her husband entered the chamber. His initial reaction was intrigue. His eyes expressed the aggregate of qualities in his observation, giving pleasure to his senses, filling his mind with enthusiasm. Her beauty physically and mentally captivated him.

He stood momentarily detached, scarcely daring to remove his impassioned eyes from her. His looks permeated her with pleasing astonishment, discovering himself distracted beyond his ability to speak. Remaining transfixed by the awe of the moment, his eyes filled with suitable emotion. Overpowering his will was an intensifying affection which resulted in the prevention of an immediate response. He could scarce contain his adulation of her as he continued to gape in a mused state, suffering an extreme degree of unwavering speechlessness. He struggled to gain control of his will, to speak the absolute intensity of his violent affections, which were now long deliberating upon his lips. Thoughts of love swept through his body and spirit with tender desire. At length, every notion seemed to fail him. After standing with amazed expression a few additional moments, he instinctively endeavoured to recover himself, languidly advancing toward her with his hands behind his back. Within his breast his heart beat with overwhelming emotion as he made himself still nearer to her. He took in air, then swallowed hard as his heart leaped with fresh hope of the ability to speak. He spoke, not in terms of perfect composure, but with absolute tenderness, expressing slightly above a whisper, "I should desire you not judge me by my hesitating manner. Forgive my prolonged silence. I confess your radiant appearance surpasses charmed sophistication. I beg you consider my taciturnity, distracted meditation of your loveliness, as I find you breathtakingly incomparable. Such splendid attire is so uniquely donned. Your magnificence exceeds beauty, and I do willfully confess I believe nature has had its last words."

Elizabeth swelled with endearing pride. If there had been any doubt in her mind of his finding her pleasing, all such thoughts now dissipated into the thinness of the air by virtue of his countenance alone. Such eloquence of speech induced a peaceful influence to her nature, causing her to find refuge in his admiration.

"Why, Fitzwilliam, surely there is nothing of your respectful silence to forgive," she replied, reaching out to touch his face. "Although you had not declared it openly, your expression implied the highest degree of regard;

your enthusiasm is little hidden. I am inclined to believe my appearance the cause of your wavering. Surely you require no words to convey such tender notions. I perfectly understood your full meaning. In your silent watch I perceived admiration. In your admiration I felt the depth of your esteem. Altogether I sensed the warm commitment of your unyielding, loving devotion; no explanation is required, surely not."

He pleasantly smiled at the articulation of her spoken observation. He hesitated, then said, "I must ask you to regain your seat in front of the looking glass."

With a curious look, Elizabeth did as he requested.

Moving closer to her, he bent down to kiss her cheek while he placed before her a gold box. "These are yours now; open it, dearest."

Elizabeth opened the box. She could scarcely breathe at the sight before her. Now it was she who experienced a restriction of words. Her heart pounded within her chest at the sum of its contents. Astonished by her own discomposure, she lastingly stared at its substance in disbelief, trying to overcome her failing power to respond. She turned to him with an expression of extraordinary graciousness. Fixing her questioning eyes on him, she overcame her unbending reserve, as her desire to speak enabled her to gaspingly express, "Oh—dearest, wherever did you acquire these? They are exquisite, so generous; it is just too much, indeed a most generous gift."

"These were my mother's jewels; choose from among them tonight's wearing. I should like to place it round your beautiful, wanting throat," he intimately whispered as he viewed her through the looking glass, allowing his eyes to search her form.

Elizabeth's eyes quickly became fixed on an exquisite diamond jeweled necklace, which would surely complement her dress, thought she. So busy was she with the contents of the box, she made no notice of his setting aside another. Carefully she handed the necklace to him. "I am uncommonly at a loss for words; they are so breathtakingly brilliant. Are you pleased with my choice?"

"Indeed, if you look further you will encounter diamond earrings to match."

"Oh, Fitzwilliam, these are exquisite. But perhaps you should like to render your sister your mother's jewels, surely she would desire to own them."

"I have already selected several pieces for Georgiana. I plan to present them directly. I desire you to have these particular pieces with the understanding Deborah shall one day possess them."

He carefully placed the diamond necklace about her throat, gazing at her again. "I am delighted you chose the diamond necklace as I have another box you should open; this will complement the neckpiece rather well." Then reclaiming the rather large box he had put aside, he put it down before her. She carefully removed the lid. Her eyes widened as she placed her open hand upon her chest, taking in air. Her gaze settled on a diamond tiara glistening before her. Its sight paralyzed her. She viewed it with gratification, faintly uttering, "Dearest, your mother wore this?"

"Yes, it belonged to my grandmother. My grandmother wore it at a royal gathering, my mother at court. Tonight you are the royalty of Pemberley; enjoy its splendor. Before we descend the stairs, let us visit briefly with the children. I should wish them to view their mother as a picture of pure elegance. Then, we shall visit Georgiana. Perhaps we shall have Mr. Armstrong do a sketch. Yes, just as you are this very evening; what a delight it will be. I should like it very much, especially if it is hung next to mine in the gallery. I daresay this attire, so flattering to you, will colour a portrait quite well."

Elizabeth, no longer at a loss for words, rallied her general frankness. She united her eyes with his, unleashing all she felt. "You render much happiness in every aspect of our lives. I am never in want of affection or in need. I should wish my conduct command you rewards of happiness. I have long regretted that all I have to offer is the luxury of my honour. I shall always desire our union never be viewed a degradation to your society."

Mr. Darcy's demeanour took a sudden turn. His face drained of the gentility of moments ago, instead inducing a baffling expression. "A degradation! Such preposterous language, I'll hear no more of it. By no manner of means could you ever be thought of in that sense, and you are entirely mistaken in supposing it. I deserve no extraordinary praise; it is you to whom I owe everything. You influenced me to be the man I am presently, and ought to have been prior to our acquaintance. In considering past events, it was your study of truth which properly humbled the erroneous pride of my situation. The painful recollections of my prejudice I can never forget, no more than your reproof, which forced me to examine the selfish arrogance prevailing upon my social condition. My manners were wanting. Until then, I cared for none beyond my own relations. I mistakenly thought meanly of the rest of the world. Their significance or worth compared with my own was given little thought."

He paused, then he touched her cheek before continuing. "Although I enjoyed the admiration of my people at Pemberley and have always treated

them well, you taught me how I had overlooked the true meaning of gratifying kindness. My self-regard was at fault, not intentionally but certainly
undeserving of their good opinion of me. Even so, they continued to afford
me undeserved respect, never having been aware of the unpleasant circumstances of my corrected principles. At times I find I am still tormented by
the thoughts of my misappropriated enthusiasm regarding duty as well as
honour. I well nigh lost your affections due to my foolish pride, and I
remain much in your debt for such as you humbled me. I was saved from
my arrogant thoughts, insufficient in my pretensions to please a woman
worthy of being pleased. Your love is so much more than I deserve. Few
men receive or even deserve a second chance. The very fact that you would
have me is a tribute to your goodness. Your forgiveness is more invaluable
than anything I have to offer. Your happiness is far more important to me
than my own or anything I possess. Dearest, loveliest Elizabeth, you shall
always have my undying love and devotion; you and the children are my
whole."

Elizabeth's face warmed with the risen redness to her cheeks. His words
provided her with comprehending purpose. She felt the gravity of his honour, which now surged the intense love within her. She afforded him a smile
of embarrassment as she managed to say just above a hushed tone, "Dearest,
you have the ability to swell me with love; I wish always to strive to be your
equal."

She began to express her gratitude again, but he halted her words.

"There is nothing left to be said except perhaps continued words of gratitude to God for happiness not eluding us," he expressed tenderly.

Decidedly, she felt it best not to approach the subject any further. She
touched the jewels with continued disbelief of the splendor displayed about
her throat as she viewed them through the looking glass propitiously. She
glanced up, catching him admiring her reflection in the glass. His expression emanated the passion of his desire.

Again she coloured at his stare. He tenderly took the back of his hand and
brushed it against her cheek. "There was a time I possessed a definite confidence in my ability to completely regulate my will. The only time I have
been controlled by my desire over my will was in discovering my violent
affections for you and again tonight viewing the beautiful creature before
me. Your gravitating power exceeds my direction. Surely you are aware you
are all I desire; in you I lack nothing. I believe God willed you to me, my
precious gift."

She turned to him with aroused sensibility. Romantic impulses of effervescent spirit ignited her enthusiasm, making her a prisoner of his unguarded affections. He responded, drawing her to him, holding her desirously as he placed his head together with hers. He turned her to face the looking glass. "Look, there is my admiration, my desire, my wife, the mother of my children, my life. The beauty before me is more than I deserve; such deep felicity is rare indeed, yet it is mine to boast."

"Oh, Fitzwilliam, you flatter me. I daresay I rather enjoy it."

"Truth, not flattery, my dear. I must say again, your gown is exceedingly superior. Your choice demonstrates excellent taste. Was it your own choosing, or did your sisters assist?"

"I must confess I did not choose it, I designed it. I had it stitched. Mrs. Reynolds directed me to a woman to do it justice; I am pleased you find it appealing."

Still captivated by her, his passion by conviction of her valuable qualities was now only enhanced. He gasped, "Permit me to say, it exudes grace and sophistication. The very notion of it being your design only embellishes its magnificence. I see it boasts incredible detailing. I should dispute my awe; I should have expected as much from one as incredible as you are. It is excellent, truly elegant, nothing wanting.

His eyes glistened. "I daresay it flatters your form," he expressed in sultry language, fixing his eyes slowly over her frame. He drew her near to him in a most delicate embrace, whispering, "Your eyes are beguiling; from the moment I first made their notice I was challenged by the turn of nature's compelling emotions."

Again she blushed at his admiring words. Although she found his attentions quite desirable, his comments regarding her form affected her composure greatly. His indulgence in making his thoughts expressed orally were out of his common manner. Despite being pleasing, seldom had he expressed them with such burning passion. She now realized, through her aspirations to surprise him, she had not anticipated a reaction so permissive, proving her appearance more successful than planned—in fact, exceeding her intentions.

In an attempt to distract his attention in another direction, she voiced, "The jewels complement my attire admirably; your mother was beautiful as I witness from the portrait in the gallery. I shall cherish them. Indeed my gratitude is inexpressible. And you, look at you, so decidedly handsome in your dress coat; your appearance is splendid. I find I am quite taken by your manly beauty. So you see, dearest, you are not alone in your admiration, no indeed. Perhaps we should make ready to greet the guests; it cannot be long before their arrival."

Discovering her own passionate will increasingly difficult to direct, Elizabeth did not desire to long dwell on her admiration toward him. She was well aware how his fine appearance could disengage her to distraction upon studying him at length.

"Yes, I believe we must go if we are to view the children. I should like to present a box to Georgiana as well," he said as he walked to the secretary to secure a silver box.

They attempted to visit the children, but they were already sound asleep.

Georgiana answered the knock at her door with a receptive invitation to enter. Mr. Darcy placed the silver box before her. As suspected, she was delighted to share a portion of her mother's jewels. In her excitement she embraced him with gratitude. Elizabeth smiled with affection as Mr. Darcy placed the necklace of Georgiana's choice about her throat.

"Beautiful, Georgiana, you wear them well; our mother would have been pleased, I'm sure of it. Georgiana, look, these were mother's as well; are they not exquisite?" he asked, touching the jewels Elizabeth was wearing.

"Oh, Fitzwilliam, they do flatter her attire. You are so very good to me. I do believe our mother would have approved your choice of wife, surely she would," Georgiana expressed earnestly with her usual reserve. "Fitzwilliam, tell me at once, what thoughts have you on your wife's apparel. Is it not the most magnificent creation, what say you?"

"Yes indeed, quite magnificent; I suppose you knew she sketched and designed the whole of it."

"Yes, I confess, I have known for a time. I was most anxious for your reaction. You are certain to be pleased with the dining hall as well."

"Indeed, I saw for myself; surely tonight's affair will be much talked about. Come now, we should take our positions; the guests will arrive momentarily; shall we?" he said proudly, offering his disengaged arm to Elizabeth.

As they descended the stairs, the musicians were tuning their instruments.

"Mrs. Reynolds has already directed the musicians where to stage themselves," Georgiana remarked.

"Mrs. Darcy, the musicians are ready. The negus is made hot. It will no doubt put the colour back in the cheeks of the guests. Would you like the musicians to begin?"

"Yes, that will do nicely; thank you, Mrs. Reynolds."

Mr. Darcy presented himself aristocratically handsome. Elizabeth struggled to avoid concentration of his appearance, only to be caught in a weak moment, relinquishing her will to an uncontrollable urge to study him in depth. She discovered herself captivated by his virile presentation. She struggled with perseverance, but discovered it impossible to disengage her fixed eyes from him. At last, she acquired much needed escape through Georgiana's distraction. "Elizabeth, tonight is sure to be regarded a success."

Elizabeth looked at Georgiana. She judged her decidedly elegant in her pastel gown of lace trimmings. The jewels about her throat only enhanced her natural, refined elegance. Her graceful appearance added sweetness to her already alluring character. Elizabeth concluded she exemplified everything she had ever desired to be—conformity with formality of propriety, good taste, education and talent, together with a perfect understanding of prescribed social behaviour expected in polite society, and with the ability to carry out all such expectations with relaxed grace. She looked at her husband, then next to Georgiana. She imagined, if she had ever longed for a place in the world, this surely would have been her desire. She stood tranquil, with disciplined harmonious poise, stimulated by the certainty of love and with titillating anticipation of the duty of receiving guests. The three stood in gracious elegance prepared to welcome invited guests to the impressive array of carefully planned delights awaiting them.

Before the first guests arrived, Mr. Bennet, along with his youngest daughters descended the stairs. Elizabeth observed her father's spectacular presentation. She had little remembrance of him in such handsome form. His new dress coat was well fitted. Her sisters' pleasing appearance and poised nature impressed her as well. She viewed the elevated manner in which the three directed their performance. She could not help but conclude they now engaged in a society vastly different from the past memories of her mother's days.

The Arrival of Guests

THE FIRST TO BE ANNOUNCED was Mr. Manley. After being greeted by his hosts, he immediately expressed admiration of the elegance of the decorations. He addressed Georgiana. "Miss Darcy, how delightful to see you again; you are looking rather well. Might I impose on you now for a dance later in the evening?"

"Thank you, Mr. Manley, I am quite well. Yes, it would be my pleasure. I should enjoy a dance. I look forward to it."

The next to arrive was Lady Catherine, Ann, John Gibson and, surprisingly, Mariah Lucas. Mr. Darcy greeted his aunt with a humbling bow, Georgiana did so with a curtsey, but Elizabeth greeted Lady Catherine first with a humble curtsey, then a sincere smile, before stating, "Lady Catherine, it is an honour to have you here once again, you are always a welcomed guest."

Lady Catherine closely eyed Elizabeth's dress. "Thank you, my dear. Your gown is most beautiful indeed, such exquisite needlework; why the quality is sheer perfection. Wherever did you acquire such a gown; did you have it sent from Paris?"

Before she could answer, Georgiana leaned toward Lady Catherine. "It is Elizabeth's own design; she sketched it first, then had it especially stitched for this evening."

"I'm delighted you approve; it is indeed an honour to receive your compliments," Elizabeth said, humbly blushing. •

"Well— I must say you do quite well; it is superior work. It is beautifully designed, my dear," she said as she moved on to Georgiana.

"Why, Mariah, I had not expected you; I thought you to be at Hunsford. I am delighted you are come indeed. Surely Kathryn and Mary will no doubt be pleased to see you; they are in the ballroom. Such a beautiful gown, Mariah," Elizabeth expressed.

Before Mariah could respond, Ann replied, "Mariah visited this morning, relating to us Charlotte and Mr. Collins had decided she should attend after all. I afforded her the use of my gown. It befits her rather well, does it not? How fortunate for her we are of equal measure."

"I'm happy to attend, Elizabeth; I should like to join Kathryn and Mary now if you have no objection," Mariah blurted out in a hasty fashion.

"Yes, but first I wish to introduce Mr. Darcy's sister, Miss Darcy."

"Delighted to make your acquaintance; I do hope you enjoy the ball."

"Thank you," said Mariah as she quitted their presence hurriedly.

"Well, Ann, how do you do? You look exceptionally well. Such a lovely gown—we are delighted you are come, I am happy to see you," Elizabeth expressed.

"Has the Colonel arrived yet?" Ann inquired.

"No, I do not believe so, although I'm sure we may expect him before long."

"Very well, I'm delighted to be here, Elizabeth. Your gown is quite luxurious; you have wonderful taste. I did hear my cousin say you designed it. I am all astonishment, but I should have expected it. You remember Mr. Gibson," Ann expressed, turning in his direction.

"Yes indeed, Mr. Gibson, delighted you are come. I do hope you enjoy the evening."

"Thank you, Mrs. Darcy, I'm delighted to have received such a gracious invitation. Ann has told me much of Pemberley. I certainly understand her appreciation of this great estate. I am quite taken in by its elegance; it exceeds my expectations."

"Thank you, Mr. Gibson," Elizabeth stated as they moved on to Georgiana.

Georgiana embraced Ann, expressing her delight to see her looking so well. Although she received Mr. Gibson graciously, his overstated charm toward Georgiana did not escape Elizabeth's notice. Georgiana received him coolly, seemingly unaffected by his charisma.

Several other distinguished couples of great wealth and situation arrived from town. After having been greeted, they moved in the direction of the ballroom.

Dr. Gordon arrived with his wife. "Mr. Darcy, my gratitude for your kind invitation; we are delighted to come. I confess we thought we should not want to miss an event such as this. I must say you are looking rather well this evening; no doubt you are feeling quite well?"

"Yes, indeed, quite well, Dr. Gordon, thank you for inquiring. I do hope you both enjoy the ball; will you not join the others?"

"Yes, we shall, thank you," Dr. Gordon replied as he and his wife were greeted by Elizabeth and Georgiana, before moving in the direction of the gathering.

The party next to be announced was the Earl of Matlock, James, Charles, Frank, Fanny and Lord Fitzwilliam.

"Uncle, welcome, so glad you are come," Mr. Darcy expressed.

"Delighted you are come," Elizabeth reiterated.

"Thank you, we have so looked forward to the ball; I shall speak with you later," the Earl told them after receiving his greeting from Georgiana.

Lord Fitzwilliam, the eldest son and his wife Fanny were the next to be received. After Mr. Darcy greeted them, they moved on to Elizabeth. "I am so glad you are come, delighted to have you here. I trust you will enjoy the ball," Elizabeth expressed, directing her remarks to Fanny.

"Indeed it is wonderful to return to Pemberley. Fanny has never been here. I daresay it is as elegant as always. If I might be so bold as to add you are looking well this evening," he said as his wife just nodded, appearing to be occupied. Although her eyes examined everything in sight, she remained indifferent, saying not a word.

"We so looked forward to your attending. Fanny, I do hope you enjoy the ball; it is so very nice to see you again," Elizabeth graciously stated with a smile.

Fanny's haughty disposition caused Elizabeth to feel awkward, but she was determined to not allow it to affect the evening, surely nothing could tempt her to feel anything but gratification.

"James, we so looked forward to seeing you. You are looking rather well."

"Delighted to be here, Elizabeth," he retorted, before turning to his cousin. "Darcy, grant me your permission to flatter your wife on her appearance."

Mr. Darcy smiled with pride as he nodded his head.

"If I may be so bold to indulge in flattery, you are a vision of loveliness. My cousin is indeed a lucky man to have a wife owning such beauty and sophistication; I find I am quite envious, to be sure."

"Thank you, James, your comments are well taken. I do expect you will enjoy the ball. There are plenty of partners to be had this evening; I daresay some anxious for a dance. We shall be honoured to introduce you."

"And, Georgiana, you're elegant as always, excellent attire too, I see. Perhaps you will allow me the pleasure of a dance this evening?"

"Yes, of course, Cousin, I believe I should like that very much."

"Very well then, I shall go now to survey the ball," he said in a droll fashion.

"Frank, Charles, so glad you are come, delighted," Mr. Darcy addressed them.

"Darcy, it has been quite some time since we last visited Pemberley; why is that?" Frank asked.

"No doubt the reason being that when my father died there was little company received here at Pemberley. Now that I have wed, I find Pemberley has come alive again."

"I am glad you are come, Frank, Charles; I look forward to speaking with you later in the evening when I am excused from the duties here," Elizabeth stated.

"Welcome, Cousins, delighted you could come; so happy to see you again."

"Yes, and you are looking rather well, pretty as ever. You ladies display such superior qualities of dress; how shall the other ladies compete?" Frank said to Georgiana.

"Yes, Cousin, your elegance never fails you," Charles told Georgiana, leaning on his cane with a look of pain on his face.

Mr. Darcy immediately motioned for his manservant. "Do see that my cousin receives a comfortable chair once he enters the gathering."

"Very good, sir."

Charles and Frank made their way to the ballroom while several other of her husband's acquaintances were announced, none of whom Elizabeth knew, but was glad to meet. They were welcomed, then proceeded to the ballroom with the others.

The party next to be announced consisted of the new residents of Foxshire Estate.

"Bingley, Jane, how good to see you; do come in," Mr. Darcy stated.

"Oh, Jane, Mr. Bingley, I know you will enjoy the ball; I have anxiously awaited your arrival," Elizabeth said, embracing her sister.

"Gracious, Lizzy, your jewels, such a spectacular display! Why—you look like royalty! I can scarce believe how you glisten," Jane gasped. After catching her breath, she continued, "Incredibly elegant, such superior quality, your gown is breathtakingly beautiful. You must be contented in your achievement. To think you sketched it, then had it stitched to your own liking. I should never have believed there could be anything so beautiful;I am quite overtaken, Lizzy. It is quite wonderful, yes indeed. I should never have attempted a task of such magnitude. And your husband, Lizzy, I'm sure he noticed?" Jane asked, with Caroline near in line.

Mr. Darcy managed a wink in Mr. Bingley's direction, inducing smug grins.

At once Elizabeth felt the chill of the cold, hard stare of Caroline upon sight of the diamond tiara. As her eyes lowered to the splendor of the diamonds gracing her throat, she appeared to inhale. Her expression became rigid as she pressed her lips tight together with resentment, arching her back, making her form stiff. She narrowed her eyes until her brows all but united with scorn. Caroline could no more escape the raptures of Jane's adoration, nor ignore the unsurpassed quality of elegance in Elizabeth's attire, than deny the existence of the royal crown. She seized the opportunity to stare across Elizabeth's entire form as she caught the words Jane spoke, forcing the reality of the elegant beauty emanated by the woman about to offer her hospitality. Caroline's resentment raised to a level beyond suppression, causing a momentary loss of forbearance. Her brows came together again in disturbed agitation at the moment she witnessed Elizabeth's refined grandeur. With all the sourness of her assessment, she cast a look toward Mrs. Hurst; none of her actions eluded Mr. Darcy, however. When returning her eyes toward Elizabeth, she attempted to conceal her exasperated manner, but the colour drained from her face as she caught a glimpse of Mr. Darcy's watchful eye. With disturbance of mind still visible in her guise, she painfully tried to speak, but her language failed to shroud her jealous nature. She turned to Mrs. Hurst. "Louisa, have you taken notice of Eliza's frock. The local warehouse must have imported additional gowns. We saw nothing of that nature there, did we? Pray tell me, is it possible she designed such a gown?"

Louisa Hurst struggled to shadow her own disturbance when her eyes caught view of the sparkling diamonds. In searching Elizabeth's form, she could not escape such finery. She plunged into a shocked state, unable to part her lips to answer Caroline. Her face bore an expression of combined disbelief and mortification. Now caught in a position of disguise amid their reprehension of Elizabeth, they were consequently prevailed upon to speak complimentary language against their will.

Mr. Darcy, having heard Jane's remarks, observed the sentiments of Mr. Bingley's sisters, who stood before him. For their benefit, he addressed Jane,

"Yes indeed, Jane, I most definitely approve of my wife's beauty. Such an exquisite gown created by her, there is certain to be no likeness of it anywhere. She does my mother's jewels justice; is she not the vision of elegance? She is simply radiant, as you say."

Now having agitated them further, he decided the gaiety of the evening had its start. He was not sorry his words frustrated them to distraction.

"Yes, Mr. Darcy, my sister is a vision of loveliness, quite beautiful."

Jane's remarks had an immediate effect on Caroline and Mrs. Hurst. Their restraint was obvious, as was the redness in their cheeks—a deepened haughtiness now overspread their features.

"Enchanted, your gown is flattering," Caroline managed to say hastily as she maneuvered to escape paying too much attention to Elizabeth. She gave her a superficial grin, then quickly moved on to Georgiana. "Delighted to see you at last; it is indeed always a pleasure. You look wonderful, my dear. Your dress is simply marvelous, quite beautiful." Caroline said, addressing Georgiana. Her speech now turned sincere as she complimented Georgiana at length, redirecting her composure to what it ought to have been.

Mr. Darcy reveled in the folly. Their strained expressions bore silent contempt with insolent smiles as they repulsed at the slightly laboured conversation with Elizabeth for his sake. The forced compliments threw them into nervous exhaustion. Having exposed their ill manners, they soon realized, much to their embarrassment, their actions had not escaped the notice of Mr. Darcy, the very individual they wished to impress.

"Delighted, your gown is elegant," Mrs. Hurst icily added, her words shallow with intrepidity as she quickly turned away with a sneer, now fixing her eyes on Georgiana. "My dear Miss Darcy, you look quite splendid this evening, such an exquisite gown."

Georgiana looked at Elizabeth wondering if she would respond to such vagueness of flattery. "Thank you," was all she could manage as her face coloured.

The look on Caroline's face was proof enough for Elizabeth of her own elegant appearance. Caroline and Mrs. Hurst remained perfectly indifferent, as not to bestow half the consideration such finery deserved. But nothing escaped them. She was aware their eyes searched her form with scrutiny, surveying every minute detail of her gown, the arrangement of her hair as well as the authenticity of her jewels. Their insufferable conceit failed them as they lacked the ability to control their vexation. Elizabeth thought it was gratifying to have Caroline and Mrs. Hurst so disconnected by her appearance. She was amused by their inability to endure, finding their resentment implacable. Happy was she the moment they moved from her. She did not wish to long dwell on their mean spirits, nor did she desire them to destroy the prospects of a fine evening.

Ironically, the discontented jealousies seemed totally to escape the unsuspecting Mr. Hurst. He thought his wife sincere. He approached Elizabeth in a most agreeable manner. "Yes, beautiful, just beautiful," Mr. Hurst said sincerely, as he studied the diamonds at length. He also studied with interest Elizabeth's attractiveness before capturing looks of contempt from his wife, who awaited him. With her eyes fixed on Elizabeth's face and catching his words to her with no less resentment than surprise, Mrs. Hurst became pale. Mr. Hurst, abruptly heeding the disdain of her countenance, quickly moved to Georgiana. He expressed brief compliments before hastily moving out of the region of contempt.

Mr. Darcy quitted his attention of Caroline and the Hursts. He now fixed his eyes on Emily, who was next to be greeted. "Emily, it is always a pleasure to welcome you here; I trust you shall find the evening most agreeable."

"I believe I shall, Mr. Darcy, thank you."

"Elizabeth, I am in awe of your stunning presentation, exquisite jewels to complement such an impressive gown," Emily expressed with genuineness, providing additional displeasure to her sisters, who now stood impatiently awaiting her.

"Thank you, Emily, your kindness is greatly appreciated. Thank you indeed, delighted you've come. I am confident you will enjoy the evening."

"Is your father in the ballroom?"

"Why, yes he is; I'm sure he'll be delighted to see you again."

"And I, him," she answered.

Then she turned her attention to Georgiana, indulging in momentary conversation until she realized Caroline and Louisa restlessly awaited her, so she hurried on.

While Caroline and the Hursts waited impatiently for Emily, still more amusing folly presented its opportunity inasmuch as Mr. Bennet appeared, approaching Emily immediately upon making her notice. "Miss Bingley, might I have the honour of your hand for the next two dances?"

"Of course, Mr. Bennet, it would please me; I'm delighted you asked," Emily answered with eagerness unfavourable to her sisters. She took his disengaged arm, allowing him to lead her into the ballroom, leaving her sisters behind in their vexation.

As Mr. Darcy and Elizabeth continued to greet guests, Ann approached Georgiana. "Georgiana, do you know if Colonel Fitzwilliam has arrived as yet?"

"I do not believe so, Ann; when he arrives, shall I tell him you inquired?"

"Please do. I am most anxious to see him. I must return; I promised Mr. Gibson the reel next," Ann said, immediately quitting Georgiana's presence.

The Gardiners arrived, much to Elizabeth's elation. "Aunt Gardiner, Uncle, I am so glad you are come. I have anxiously awaited your arrival; at last you are here."

"Well, Elizabeth, are you not the most exceptionally elegant sight? Exquisite jewels, such finery, it is delightful indeed. Wherever did you find such a well-appointed gown?" Mrs. Gardiner inquired with admiration.

"I had it stitched. I am quite pleased with it, I must admit."

"Well, it suits you well. Mr. Darcy, my niece is exceptionally beautiful this evening; would you not agree?"

"Well now, Mrs. Gardiner, how can I not agree? I find her breathtakingly exquisite, but then I am a prejudiced man, my eyes are fixed in her direction indeed."

"Well, Elizabeth, you are certainly radiant; I do believe your happiness renders you additional splendor; you are lovely, my dear. We are delighted to be here. Oh, Mr. Darcy, I do have some results on that business venture with which we were dealing in London."

"Well, Mr. Gardiner, I should like to find a moment to discuss the matter if possible. We shall talk later to be sure," Mr. Darcy said, then added, "I must agree, Mr. Gardiner, my wife is radiant, and, if her heart be equal to that of her husband's, there is no doubt she is a most happy, content woman."

Having greeted the Gardiners, they noticed the Colonel. "Colonel, I thought you should never come; where have you been?" Mr. Darcy asked.

"Darcy, I had a difficult time getting away; I'm delighted finally to arrive. Is our cousin Ann here?"

"Yes, Colonel, but allow me to warn you, Mr. Gibson is here as well. We had no choice but to invite him. Ann has inquired about you more than once," Mr. Darcy said in a low voice.

"It wondered me. Well, Darcy, I have given it considerable thought. I confess I am resigned—I know such a union can never take place. I have nothing to offer, she deserves better; and, what's more, Lady Catherine would surely never approve of me. Why, I am merely the youngest son of an Earl; it would be insupportable to say the very least. I daresay it would be viewed a most unsuitable match. No, Darcy, I am quite resigned regarding the whole of it. You need not concern yourself with me."

The Colonel had a disappointed look about him as he advanced toward Elizabeth. "Elizabeth, you look exceptionally fine. Darcy, I daresay I should keep a watchful eye on your wife this evening, she looks quite splendid, and, Georgiana, you have grown into a most elegant young woman. You are lovely as always. I'm so happy to see you. Might I seek your hand for a dance a bit later?"

"But of course, Cousin, that is agreeable to be sure."

The Colonel disappeared into the chamber. The three continued to greet guests until it seemed most had arrived. The time neared when they would be free to intermingle amongst them. At the Darcys' suggestion, Georgiana entered the ballroom.

Elizabeth took this opportunity to inquire, "Dearest, this business venture you wish to discuss with my uncle, does it involve Mr. Wickham?"

"Not at all; why do you ask?" Mr. Darcy said with a surprised look.

"I believe the association of London brought Mr. Wickham to mind; I am happy to hear we have no further dealings with the man."

"None at all, I do believe we have heard the last of him."

"I daresay it is a welcomed relief."

When it appeared all those invited had come, Elizabeth and Mr. Darcy joined the others.

The Great Ball at Pemberley

*W*HEN THEY ENTERED THE BALLROOM, they approached Lord Fitzwilliam and Fanny. Edward turned. "Darcy, a magnificent ball, exceptional musicians. I am excessively happy to be here."

Then Fanny said, much to Elizabeth's surprise, "This is such an elegant affair, quite the height of society, I observe. It is evident you enjoy the company of the foremost circles. Mr. Darcy, your estate is quite impressive. I have no doubt such effects must be greatly envied. I see your propriety no doubt lends itself to such possessions. I confess I had not expected such elegance. Elizabeth, I notice you so richly dressed. I may say your gown is of royal extravagance; it no doubt profits your society most advantageously. Your jewels are richly worn as well. I had not expected such grandeur or such fine furnishings. My husband's family described the elegance of Pemberley, but I had not expected it to be this fine. I daresay it far exceeds my expectations in every sense. I had not the notion your society was so highly elevated; I am quite pleased to be acquainted here indeed, yes, most pleased."

Mr. Darcy looked at Fanny solemnly. "Indeed, Fanny, your compliments are well taken. As for this ball, it is all my wife's doing; it is her efforts alone you witness, carefully planned for the enjoyment of our guests. While it is true we do enjoy a handsome society here in Derbyshire, I doubt our friends envy our position. I find they are deeply satisfied in their own comfort. I trust they are just happy to enjoy our society, no pretenses I'm sure."

Mr. Darcy was uneasy with language suggesting he drew rivalry from friends or acquaintances. He did not desire to be envied, nor did he yearn to seek recognition for his wealth or position. His aspirations were only to be viewed an honourable gentleman, a person of superior integrity, nothing with regard to his ownership or elevation.

Elizabeth quickly added, "We thank you for your compliments. We are delighted you are come; perhaps we should venture about the room with our other guests now."

She was relieved to quit Fanny's company, finding her a most perplexing character, failing to comprehend her lack of contentment in her own status. She obviously desired more wealth than in her immediate possession. Elizabeth understood her to be captivated by means or any social advantages drawn by such people who acquainted themselves for advantageous reasons. She believed Fanny not quite accepting the pursuit of felicity in life, but more preoccupied with the demands of her purse. She could not help but wonder how Lord Fitzwilliam managed to unite with such an ill-mannered creature, whose sole purpose thrived on obsessive gain and nothing beyond means.

Within the hour, after Mr. Darcy and Elizabeth intermixed with several guests, a servant entered. "Sir, it is time for your guests to enter the dining hall."

"Very well, announce it."

To Elizabeth's satisfaction, the elegance of the dining hall captured the undivided attention of her guests. Expressions of intrigue could be heard along with gasping sounds from those delightfully scrutinizing the dressed table.

Dr. Gordon's wife, among the first to be seated, was quick to voice her opinion. "I have never been witness to such fine taste of natural elegance. It is of no surprise, judging the graceful distinction of Mrs. Darcy. I should have suspected as much."

Caroline, sitting across from Mrs. Gordon, carefully listened. Elizabeth watched her shrewdly. She made no comment; however, the scowl of Caroline's countenance revealed her ill will. Judging by her reaction, Elizabeth was certain Mrs. Gordon noticed her opposing demeanour. Marking herself with ill conduct, she inflicted no one any pain other than herself. Louisa, in an attempt to conceal Caroline's soured expression, managed to remark, "How delightful, the table appears to be well arranged. Perhaps Mr. Darcy employs exceptionally talented servants."

Much to Elizabeth's astonishment, Georgiana spoke, "Oh no, not at all, Elizabeth planned every last detail; I was witness to it. I'm sure you must agree it is splendid, I am in awe of the elegance; my mother would have been pleased, as my brother surely is."

Elizabeth watched as Louisa and Caroline sipped their wine, avoiding further discussion. Mr. Hurst appeared to wish to comment. He leaned forward, giving a pleasant smile before parting his lips slightly to speak, but, after glancing in his wife's direction, he obviously thought the better of it and sat back in his chair, taking his glass to his lips.

Mr. Manley stood to give the blessing. All eyes instantly fixed upon his natural dignity. With immense satisfaction, Mr. Darcy listened to his friend beseech so eloquent a prayer as to astonish his guests with his rectitude. Following the prayer, a sobering spiritual hush fell upon the chamber. The guests had been drawn to a state of awe in being allowed to grace the same table as Mr. Manley. After a few moments, Mr. Darcy stood, breaking the silence to toast his guests.

"To our honoured guests, I wish you all health, wealth and happiness. Be assured it is our desire that you enjoy the evening whose delicacies were so scrupulously designed and arranged by my wife; her 'savoir faire' is sure to bring you enjoyment. And in closing, I should like to express my indebtedness to God, who, in His infinite wisdom, granted me such a superior partner."

He stood above her, lifting his glass to her, his eyes piercing deep into hers. His swelling pride, now unavoidably evident to their guests, emanated his natural feelings. He appeared not to wish to conceal his felicity or adoration.

Elizabeth smiled demurely. Suddenly aware of the many eyes now in her direction, she felt her face colour as she tilted her head forward to nod acceptance of his endearing public recognition.

When Mr. Darcy took his seat again, Georgiana, seated at Elizabeth's side, leaned toward her. "My brother's pride is made public, Elizabeth; I do believe he is well pleased beyond his imagination for I have never known him to be so unrestricted. He revels in the awe of his guests. It is just as I imagined; I suspected as much. I must say when I saw for myself the dining preparations and your gown, I could only anticipate his reaction. It is indeed so, as you can well see."

"Thank you, Georgiana, your encouragement affords me the satisfaction of genuine respect. I cherish your kindness; you are so very dear."

Guests expressed jubilation of the excellence in food preparations. Delight could be easily interpreted through looks of amazement of the lavish feast. The food was prepared to perfection. Endless quantities were served hot, and the variety lacked nothing. Elizabeth had additional musicians as an integral part of the dinner, serenading the guests softly while they ate, causing further appreciating conversation.

Elizabeth's searching eyes rested upon that part of the table where her father and Emily were seated, deep in conversation. She noticed Mrs. Hurst glaring across the table at Caroline displeasingly. Elizabeth was not in a position to see Caroline's facial expression, but could only imagine the thoughts the two encountered. She was certain her father made no notice of their condemnation, as he appeared oblivious of anyone with the exception of Emily. But she did notice Mary at his side studying Caroline and Mrs. Hurst, her eyes changing betwixt the two. Mary appeared perplexed.

Suddenly she perceived Ann seated aside John Gibson; on his opposite sat Mariah to whom he paid equal attention. She detected Mariah's eyes seemed to glisten at his every word. The Colonel seated next to Ann, seemed to advantage conversation with her, while Mariah captured John Gibson's attention habitually. Inconspicuously, Elizabeth gracefully chanced a view of Lady Catherine, who maintained steady conversation with the Earl. She was well pleased with the seating arrangements, the only alteration having been the addition of Mariah.

The servants' attentiveness and their excellence in providing superior service pleased her guests. Elizabeth absorbed the many complimentary expressions of the variety before them as well as the conviction of the servants' merits. The servings were endless; the wine continued to flow, while the softness of the selected music graced the atmosphere, lending undeniable elegance. Mr. Darcy and Elizabeth exchanged favourable glances, acknowledging the pride the successful evening provided thus far. After having served several courses, the servants graced the feast with the carefully planned desserts, consisting of a fine collection of jellies, dishes of creams, cakes and sweetmeats, the variety of which drew attention in connection with the lavish style with which they were presented.

Long after the accomplished dinner, the guests continued to converse of the impressive meal as they gathered once again in the ballroom.

Elizabeth caught a glimpse of Caroline and Mrs. Hurst standing by the fireplace, now eyeing Mr. Darcy. To her knowledge, Caroline failed to secure a dance, as did her sister Louisa, whose husband Mr. Hurst lay sprawled in the corner of the sofa, having imbibed too much liqueur. Squinting her eyes with a sneer overspreading her features, Caroline wrinkled her nose as she glared at the sight of Mr. Darcy and Elizabeth together. Elizabeth was not sure what agitated Caroline more, the jewels, her general appearance or the combined sight of herself and her husband. Upon making eye contact with Caroline, Elizabeth broadened her smile, causing a displeased Caroline to place her head together with that of her sister. With their looks now angry, frustratingly jealous, their eyes appeared like daggers. While the entire party appeared to enjoy every aspect of the evening, the two Bingley sisters soured in their contempt, causing their own element of pain. Elizabeth was not influenced in the least, in fact, quite the contrary; she found them amusing, furthering their disdain by affording them a broadened smile at every given opportunity.

Elizabeth and Mr. Darcy set off to enjoy a much desired dance. As they took their place in the set, their eyes met, stimulating a fixed romantic inter-action. Standing opposite one another, they fell captivated in mutual desire while exchanging glances by way of dignified pleasure. She was awestruck by his masculine form. Although she viewed him daily, on this night she was spellbound by his attractiveness. He was advantageous in height, wearing sleek, well-fitting attire which afforded him marked distinction, inducing an intoxicating thrill she could scarce deny. She gasped for breath at his manly beauty as he advanced in her direction to grasp her hand in the dance. As they touched, her heart fluttered, melting with the encounter. They moved about the floor with grace, surrendering themselves to powerful, fanciful sensations emanating through the music. Lost in harmony, they reeled about with ease as their feet moved with precision to the melody while fixed eyes held them captive, until Elizabeth abruptly noticed the eyes now established upon them as the coupled guests stood round the dance in observance. A vast redness overspread her face while her heart pounded more abruptly within her chest. Realizing guests witnessed their intimate exchange, she struggled to recapture a sense of reserve as she continued the dance. She deliberately sought view of her neighbouring dance partners, whom she perceived shared equal amazement of their actions. Mr. Darcy, now sharing his wife's realization, remained fully composed. He forced himself to direct his attentions to the dance itself. He felt obliged to break the silence. She paused, following her husband's lead as he compassionately advanced her an assuring smile, leading her from embarrassment. The significance of his smile calmed her fluttering heart as they continued. For the remainder of the dance they exchanged simple conversation to divert attention from their distraction. At the finish, they felt their efforts were in vain. They continued to command attention from the majority of guests about the room. Upon quitting the dance floor they were encountered by guests to receive compli-ments regarding their superior performance. Such comments caused Eliza-beth to blush, fearing the guests perceived their intimacy.

Mr. Manley, who quitted the dance floor with Georgiana, now approached them. He quietly commented, "Well, you two certainly captured the attention of the room." He threw his head back and laughed.

Elizabeth, much too embarrassed to utter a word, felt more than common awkwardness. The anxiety of the situation caused her face to warm by the very thought of their noticed behaviour. Glancing over at Caroline and Mrs. Hurst, she was certain such conduct had not escaped their notice, as they appeared more vexed than ever. She imagined the look they cast in her direction was one of mortifying disgust.

Mr. Darcy, with seriousness of expression, related, "Henry, I must confess, I scarcely ever allow myself open to public display. Tell me, dear friend, was our conduct so noticeable as to offend?"

"Not at all, Fitzwilliam, your guests are quite captured by your superior dancing and elegant appearance; surely you are aware of your presentation? You, my friend, present yourself extremely well. Your stature, your attire, look at this marvelous dress coat," he said, touching Mr. Darcy's lapel. "You, my friend, are conspicuously distinguished. Ah, but the very sight of your wife, the jewels dazzling discreetly about her throat, has captured the whole of the party; they have talked of nothing else all evening. Have you not been aware? How is it possible it escaped your notice?"

"Yes, but I feared their attentions were drawn by our conduct. I'm afraid Elizabeth and I lost composure momentarily; it is I who am quite taken by the very sight of her," he expressed with relief, as Mr. Manley lightly touched his shoulder, then laughed at him.

Georgiana voiced, "Brother, are you not aware of the respect you command? Together you are captivating; your guests are in awe of the entire evening. As for the exchange of glances, they did make my notice, but then I am understanding of the exceptional felicity you share; I may only wish to do as well in the wedded state."

"Yes, Fitzwilliam, Mrs. Darcy, I agree. Perhaps a few guests who would only be convinced of your affections narrowly observed you. I find it delightful, very refreshing; you show an appetite for life. To view a marriage so wholly what it ought to be—now there is certainly nothing to hold in reproof. Delightful! Fitzwilliam, with a partner so advantageous in appearance, it is not difficult to see why you were caught in a moment of rapture."

Elizabeth, still affected, was solemn in her reply as she breathed a sigh of relief. "Mr. Manley, your friendship is invaluable, but, I must ask, are you sure of it?"

He laughed at her earnest inquiry. "Mrs. Darcy, trust my frankness, you give too much credit to it. We witnessed your notice the whole of the evening. Viewing you together dancing provided your guests admiring entertainment, nothing more."

"Thank you, Mr. Manley," Elizabeth expressed with another sigh of relief.

Upon Elizabeth's word, the servants set up a table filled with an admirable collection of light refreshments—sweetmeats, biscuits, fruits, cakes, French-imported chocolates and other pleasing delicacies, along with tea and liqueurs, which gained further delighted interest.

Jane and Mr. Bingley approached Elizabeth. "No doubt you are aware of the success of the evening?"

"Yes, we are well pleased."

Mr. Bingley, having just secured a liqueur, stood by his wife with a drink in hand. "When we have truly settled, we shall have a ball, nothing to Pemberley's I'm sure. Darcy, such extravagance, you certainly spared naught; I'm well amazed at this table of light refreshments, it is wonderful. There are servants everywhere; however did you accomplish such a grand event? I'm quite taken by the luxury of it all; the planning must have been extensive."

Mr. Darcy stood tall with his shoulders back. "Well, Bingley, I confess I had no hand in it; it is all my wife's doing. She arranged the whole of the evening; it is she who deserves the merit of it its success."

"Yes, Charles, Elizabeth sketched her attire and had it sewn. I am quite taken with it. Lizzy, I do believe your presentation far exceeds any other in the entire chamber. Together, I do believe you draw the attention of the entire population with your fine appearances; surely you know everyone speaks of it."

"I am grateful of your comments, Jane. When I planned the ball I sought success, but I had not expected the reaction to be this severe. We can scarce go but a few steps to receive complimentary admiration with regard to the whole of the evening. I confess I am not sorry in the least. I rather enjoyed making the arrangements. I found it altogether quite gratifying."

Elizabeth stood in homage as guests continued marveling at the array of refreshments. Mr. and Mrs. Gardiner approached them.

"Mr. Darcy, such a wonderful affair. I have always believed private balls are much more delightful than public ones, this one in particular. I do believe you have outdone yourselves. I claim it the finest I have ever had the pleasure to attend."

"Thank you, Mrs. Gardiner, you are aware, are you not, that it is Elizabeth's doing entirely; I had naught a hand in it," Mr. Darcy told her as he proudly turned to his wife, whom he embarrassed with his boast.

"Well, Elizabeth, I grant you the gaiety of the evening will remain unforgettably on the minds of all your guests as being the finest social event of the year."

"I am glad you see it as such, Uncle," Elizabeth expressed.

"I do believe you discovered your own capacity for particular actions in planning an admirable evening. You possess a polished sureness in your social adaptation," Mr. Darcy said to his wife.

"I agree, and I certainly have never witnessed her so radiant, except perhaps the day you wed," Mr. Gardiner added.

Elizabeth smiled. "Thank you both. We should move about now to speak with other guests; I should like to speak with you both again."

While moving about the room, Elizabeth and Mr. Darcy paused for a few moments to observe the dancing.

"I beg you will excuse me a moment, dearest; I shall return directly," Mr. Darcy said to his wife. Within an instant he disappeared.

Elizabeth remained to observe the dancing. Mariah seemed unavoidably happy in her partnership with Mr. Gibson. They appeared equally content with their dance. The Colonel had the good fortune to claim the hand of Ann. Ann looked radiant as she moved about with the Colonel, exhibiting marked felicity. They appeared to lack notice of the other guests. Elizabeth felt they, as well, were caught in that state of captivity she herself had experienced earlier. If Ann minded the attentions Mr. Gibson now afforded Mariah, it was not evident. She seemed unaffected by their gaiety. Once again, Elizabeth studied Mariah's actions as she danced about, seizing the opportunity to delight in the pleasures of it all. She seemed captivated by his presence and preoccupied with his flattery, if it was so, thought Elizabeth.

Kathryn appeared happy with the Colonel's brother Frank as her partner, while Mary managed a dance with Mr. Manley. She noted Georgiana secured a dance from her cousin James, who had no difficulty in securing partners. Throughout the evening he had danced with every available lady at least once. Elizabeth watched with enjoyment, then realized she should seek conversation with Charles, who she thought must be alone since Frank was dancing.

She immediately passed through the crowd to Charles, who was now deep in conversation with her husband as she approached them.

"Charles, may I get you anything?"

"No, your husband offered; I am quite fine, thank you. I am delighted to be here. Surely this is the very best of balls. Even Fanny is content. I believe she approves of your high society; she made note of the noblest families present. She has joined in the festivities, can you believe it?"

"Yes, she does seem to be involved at the moment," Mr. Darcy said, taking notice to her dancing with her husband.

"She revels in the majesty and variety equaling that society which she treasures. Such aristocratic notions, she surmounts endless difficulties with enthusiastic dignity in pursuit of the highest order. Cousin, she voiced her impression of your fine furnishings and noted art, establishing you incredibly prosperous. I do believe her a prisoner of privileges; she desires treasures at her disposal. I can only wonder if it is inbred in her. Such pretentiousness is precisely what one should wish to avoid. She has a natural curiosity of those who live in wealth, which is evident in her response to Pemberley as well as her questions regarding one of your guests."

"Who might that be?" Elizabeth's curiosity aroused her to inquire.

"Mr. John Gibson. Fanny quickly became aware of his family's wealth at Ann's coming-out party. She is quite impressed, even educating herself to his father being advantaged in years. Poor Edward, he is a prisoner as well in his marriage. I do feel quite sorry for him, yet it was his own doing. He should have listened to Mother, who was not happy with his choice," Charles stated, his voice filled with sadness at the thought.

"It is our understanding Mr. Gibson will inherit quite an estate, substantial in fact. I do believe at least equal to Pemberley," Elizabeth answered.

"Well then, is it no wonder she is entirely taken in. By the bye, Darcy, I must tell you, Cousin, the music is most stimulating, such fine musicians, very grand indeed. I find it a most noteworthy performance. To concentrate, listen and experience the greatness is gratifying indeed. Since my situation does not allow me a dance, I have developed what I believe is a real taste for the performance as well as the performers themselves. I am quite taken in by the whole of the evening."

"Thank you, Charles. Your compliments are well received; indeed we are most happy to have you here, but more so knowing you derive pleasure from it," Elizabeth expressed. "Here comes my sister, Mary; allow me to introduce you. Mary, this is Mr. Darcy's cousin, Charles Fitzwilliam. He is a clergyman on his father's estate. Charles, my sister Mary is quite the reader of many books; she enjoys religious writings."

"Yes, Charles, Mary is an ardent reader; I do believe she shares your passion for poetry as well," Mr. Darcy added.

Mary curtsied. "Delighted to meet you, sir. I do indeed enjoy reading; I enjoy poetry, sonnets as well as prose. Are you an enthusiastic reader?"

"Indeed I am, I do believe we share a common interest. I am a devoted reader of religious books. I enjoy poetry and prose, preferably William Shakespeare; are you acquainted with his work? What say you?" Charles enthusiastically inquired.

He appeared refreshingly interested in continuing a conversation with Mary. Elizabeth and Mr. Darcy excused themselves, quitting their company, believing they had rendered a service to them both as well as Frank. Once they reached a bit of distance, Elizabeth turned to view the success of her introduction, finding, much to her satisfaction, Mary sitting next to him, engrossed in conversation. At that moment Frank was dancing with Kathryn, looking quite pleased in his choice of partners. Little time passed since their departure from Mary and Charles. When the dance ended, Elizabeth deliberately watched to view the consequences. With the immediate dance now over, Frank returned to Charles to find him occupied with Mary, allowing him to secure Kathryn's hand for another reel.

As they wandered about the room, Elizabeth's searching eyes rested upon Lord Fitzwilliam and Fanny with John Gibson. As Elizabeth started to turn away, she observed Mr. Gibson extending his hand to Fanny, leading her to dance. Her propensity to be curious forced her to encourage her husband to go on without her, promising to rejoin him directly.

As she stood in observance, Georgiana approached her. "I noticed your attentions toward Mr. Gibson are as curious as my very own."

"Yes, Georgiana, I cannot sketch his character. He is too pleasing, too eager to be known. He seems gentlemanly enough, but there is something lacking. What is your success in watching?"

"Oh, I am conscious of Mr. Gibson; he is quite the gentleman."

"You speak as though you know him."

"Yes, I do, Elizabeth, I met him in London after Ann's party, where he recognized me and was quick to seek me out. He talked as though he was intimately acquainted with you and my brother."

"Indeed, and what were his thoughts on that subject?"

"I believe he realized I was edified on the subject, so he chose to try flattery instead, causing me to remember our conversation on the very subject. I conceived truth in all your words regarding such forced flattery. I believe I understand his attentions to my cousin Ann but I have not the understanding of his attentions to Mariah, for indeed they are deliberate. Surely you must have noticed how he is drawn to her. Perhaps he prefers a younger woman."

"Why, Georgiana, such serious reflections, is there real significance?"

"To be sure," said she without hesitation. "Elizabeth, when he discovered me unaffected by his flattery, realizing his attempts lacked success, he quitted the notion. I do believe he thought he should approach me no more for fear of offense, perhaps to my brother as well. He has a cautious, flattering manner about him. To be truthful, he brings to mind George Wickham, and in that thought I was repulsed. I have no accounts of him, but I feel there is something very definitely deceiving. Although he is of a celebrated family, I fear there is something we do not know, definitely something wanting. Perhaps I should not judge him in the same company as George Wickham. I do believe him more dignified, but his designs are as such that he strives to make gain, although I cannot see that his wants are for more than comfort. I am well aware of his inheritance. It makes little sense, him coming from the first circle, being the eldest son. I cannot quite sketch the character of such a man. He leaves me quite perplexed; what say you?"

Elizabeth was amazed at the alteration of Georgiana's language. Her accentuation of words had none of their usual sedateness. She spoke with a sureness of insight increasing her interest of the subject. Now wholly engrossed in thoughts of Ann's vulnerability, Elizabeth grew alarmed, realizing she was easy prey for a designing scoundrel, but, without surety, there was nothing to be done.

"Well, Georgiana, I am all amazement; you have taken me quite by surprise. I see you are truly on your guard; you are sure you are not mistaken?"

"Not at all," Georgiana told her with confident certainty.

"I see; well, Georgiana, are you aware your brother shares your feelings on the subject? He fears Mr. Gibson recommends himself too strongly. Um— from this conversation and my notice of the pair dancing, I daresay I entertain a notion disagreeably intriguing. With an inheritance of such a great estate before him, it presents itself rather odd do you not agree?"

"Yes indeed, Elizabeth, it does."

Mr. Darcy, noticing Elizabeth was occupied with Georgiana, seized an opportunity to escape to his office with Mr. Gardiner. The two men hastily quitted the ball, quickly closing the door behind them once they were in the confines of the office.

"Mr. Gardiner, I thought I should never find a moment of escape. What do you have to relate?"

"It is just as you thought; the man was indeed Mr. Bennet's great-great-grandfather. It appears he was a British nobleman, a Lord, a man of high ranking position—a feudal tenant holding directly of the king. As I understand, his great-grandfather sold the title under duress. Having fallen on hard times, deriving from a son's extravagance, he did so and was forced to accept a lesser estate, being Longbourn in the settlement—and a mere £2,000 per year for his family, which was considerably more than Mr. Bennet now enjoys. Interestingly enough, the title can easily be purchased, and the sum is quite reasonable—£2,000 to be exact, perhaps less. I have checked into the matter. Arrangements can be made as to the purchase."

"Very well done, Mr. Gardiner, but I am curious, why so little?"

"It appears the present owner of the title is a most indifferent character, similar to George Wickham; need I explain further?"

"Not at all, offer him £1,000; if his character be like that of George Wickham, he'll probably settle upon negotiation. I will provide you with a bank note to secure the title. This is indeed pleasing, Mr. Gardiner. I do expect you'll make me aware of your expenses as well as your fee."

"Mr. Darcy, as a businessman I'll allow you the expenses, but as for a fee, I'll not hear of it. With respect I have done this. Perhaps a visit to Pemberley and the use of your fishing tackle will be payment enough."

"Very well, Mr. Gardiner, but it is always a pleasure to have your company. I had better be getting back to my guests. I should not wish Elizabeth to be curious of my absence. Your wife is waiting as well, to be sure. Mr. Gardiner, is she ever curious of our affairs?"

"Indeed, no doubt she is, but my wife is a sensible woman. She makes it a point never to interfere with my business. I am a fortunate man as well, Mr. Darcy. I enjoy deep felicity with a woman who is kind, tender and respects my wishes."

"Thank you, I consider myself a fortunate man indeed. Surely she is curious though. I must return before we are missed; shall we?" he said, leading him from the office.

Before they could reach the ballroom, one of the servants anxiously sought Mr. Darcy.

"Mr. Darcy sir, pray excuse me, it cannot be helped. There is a lady and gentleman most anxious to see you at once regarding an urgent matter. They insist on speaking with you."

"Who is it?"

"I'm sorry, sir, he would not say. The gentleman demanded I fetch you at once."

"Mr. Gardiner, if you will be so kind to excuse me, I have business to attend."

"Very well, Mr. Darcy," Mr. Gardner answered as he parted his company. Darcy followed as the servant led the way.

"Mr. Collins, Charlotte, what do you do here?"

Charlotte, in an anxious quivering voice, hastily replied, "Mr. Darcy, is my sister Mariah here? She has been missing since daybreak; we cannot find her anywhere!"

"Why, yes she is; she arrived with my aunt. We were under the assumption you approved her coming."

"No, we did not," was all Charlotte could say with a stern voice.

"Please wait here; I shall return directly," Mr. Darcy stated as he quitted their presence to fetch Mariah and Elizabeth.

He entered the ballroom, immediately noticing Elizabeth conversing with Lady Catherine while Mariah danced with Mr. Gibson. He approached his wife and aunt, telling them of the arrival of Mr. Collins and Charlotte along with the nature of their despair. Lady Catherine suggested they not inform Mariah of their arrival for the moment, further advising she and Elizabeth return with him. When they approached, Charlotte hastily stepped forward, "Lady Catherine, we understand Mariah is here with you."

"Yes, indeed she is; am I to understand you are unaware of her doing so?"

Before Charlotte could answer, her husband interrupted. He abruptly used his arm to push his wife into the background, causing her to stumble. He swiftly directed his words to Mr. Darcy. "Be assured, my dear sir, Mrs. Collins and I hold the Bennets responsible for our present suffering. With all respect to you, Mr. Darcy, we believe their actions profit from a fault, which is a severe misfortune. Surely the Bennets persuaded her to practice deceit. Do you care to explain her presence here?"

"I do not offer any explanation," retorted Mr. Darcy.

"The circumstances of my sister-in-law surely proceeds from a faulty degree of licentious behaviour derived from the Bennets' indulgence, afforded them through their nurturing at Longbourn. I need not remind you of the indulgence of their mother, she allowed them to run absolutely wild. Its proof lies in the grave of her youngest. As for the two remaining at home, their behaviour is naturally inclined to be bad. The enormity of their guilt now lies with their father. In this, I am joined likewise, I'm sure, by Lady Catherine de Bourgh. She will surely agree, now that we have related this unfortunate affair to her." He lowered his head as if to slightly bow humbly at Lady Catherine, affording her a shrewd smile upon his elevation.

Lady Catherine took a step forward. She parted her lips, but before she could speak, Mr. Collins went on. His voice turned more cunning as he continued now to address Lady Catherine and Mr. Darcy.

"I am certain her ladyship will agree, such behaviour will reflect on your immediate family connections. Should anything have happened to Mariah, the disgrace would be at your threshold. I am confident we are of the same sentiment, to be sure."

Having stated his beliefs in overbearing terms, his chest swelled with haughtiness. He smiled with a look overspreading his face that exuded a sense of pride in his revelation. His deep satisfaction was evident, as was his certainty of Lady Catherine's opinion on the subject.

By her expression, Mr. Darcy was well aware of his aunt's unsettled state. Long ago he learned to interpret his aunt's wrath, knowing full well never to speak when her face revealed extreme annoyance coupled with suppressed anger, as was now the case.

"Mr. Darcy——" was the extent of Mr. Collins' words as Lady Catherine hastily interrupted, saying, "Let me rightly understand, Mr. Collins; do you have the presumption to aspire to speak for me using such language?"

Not being of the same understanding, Mr. Collins slowly tilted his head humbly to submit himself to Lady Catherine again. He foolishly dared to say, "Your ladyship, I have the supreme conviction that all the world regards your excellent judgment in all matters within the scope of understanding. Permit me to educate you of several individuals now in your company whom you may judge beneath your favour. I do believe we are of the same mind to realize the Bennets' situation in life. Surely you agree they are wanting in this respect," he said, assured of her agreement, with a smirk of satisfaction still overspreading his face.

Mr. Darcy stood completely upright; he inhaled, allowing swelling to his breast as he placed his hands behind his back, realizing Mr. Collins was about to encounter the wrath of his aunt. As he witnessed the redness fill her face, he awaited the extreme anger about to be unleashed. Elizabeth, unaware of what to expect, stood quiet, absorbing the confrontation with intrigue. She was well aware of the depth of anger of which Lady Catherine was capable.

"Mr. Collins, allow me to state my business. You are not entitled the privilege of speaking for me, nor are you to assume me ignorant of the many times you as well as your wife have insulted my dear niece Elizabeth. Your imprudence shall not be endured," she stated angrily, deliberately enunciating each word.

"Your ladyship, I thought——" His eyes widened. His face bore fear as he began to apologize, humbling himself to no avail as she interrupted, halting him from speaking further.

"No, Mr. Collins, that is the difficulty; you give no thought. You ought to know not to trifle with me. You are aware my frankness is universally known. I have long been aware of your sentiments toward the Bennets. I have deliberately not shared mine as of late with you for the sole purpose of understanding your celebrated insincerity coupled with your cruelty to them. Unbeknownst to you, I have been in their company often. I have formed a friendship here, but, most importantly, I'm sure you must realize—we are family. You have industriously circulated ill thoughts, spreading reports, scandalous falsehoods of blame and discredit upon the Bennets at every possible opportunity that was most advantageous to yourself. You believe you impress me with your ill language on the subject. Nay, Mr. Collins, you have erred in judgment. I believe Mariah's behaviour is that of her own will. Tell me at once, has she received correspondence from the Bennet girls while at Hunsford?" Lady Catherine's voice was filled with anger. Her eyes were piercing as her brows united in scorn of such hateful thoughts.

"Yes, she has; is that not so, Charlotte?" Mr. Collins nervously replied.

"I'm not sure."

"Elizabeth, please bring Mariah and Ann here at once," Lady Catherine said in a much calmer tone.

Elizabeth quitted them at once, returning directly with Ann and Mariah. Mr. Collins and Charlotte stood waiting their presence. Mariah's face drained of colour upon seeing them; she looked nervous, as though she could scarcely breathe.

"Come here, Child, you too, Ann," Lady Catherine told them, motioning Mariah to come near. "Ann, are you aware the Collinses knew not where Mariah was?"

"No, Mother, I did not," Ann replied softly.

Lady Catherine hesitated for a moment, then cautiously asked, "Mariah, is it not so you allowed us to believe your sister and Mr. Collins gave permission for you to attend the ball with us? Did you not indeed relate this to us?"

Lady Catherine spoke in a soft tender voice that Elizabeth thought advantageous to Mariah.

"Yes, ma'am, I only wished to attend the ball; they did not wish me in Kathryn's company. I confess, I did not speak the truth."

"And, Mariah, while at Hunsford, did you receive letters from Longbourn?"

"Why, no, Lady Catherine, I did not," Mariah answered with a puzzled sound in her voice.

"Mariah, you should think the better of indiscretions, they will only bring you grief as well as slighted displeasure. Under such circumstances you may be despised and censured by those of your connections. Promise me now you shall not do it again." Although Lady Catherine said this with sternness, she afforded Mariah the courtesy of sincerity with a sense of concern.

"I promise, Lady Catherine, I'll not do it again."

"Very well, Child. You and Ann may return to the ball while I converse further with your sister and Mr. Collins."

"Lady Catherine, we should like to take Mariah with us; we do not wish her to be here," Mr. Collins said rather emphatically.

"I sent Mariah back to the ball so we may continue our conversation, Mr. Collins. I am quite displeased in your treatment of Mrs. Darcy and your continued language with regard to her family. You pay no regard for the honour and distinction of my nephew. You willfully insist on insulting with a passion I can no longer endure. You prove not to be a sensible man; your accusations are shallow, as is your character, which I have too long overlooked. You lack the honourability becoming of a man of the cloth. Do not deceive yourself into a belief I will alter my opinion on the subject. I am extremely vexed. I demand you quit Hunsford at once—this is my final resolve."

"But your ladyship, surely you cannot mean this?" Mr. Collins replied with exasperation, obviously shocked by her declaration.

"Silence, Mr. Collins, let me be rightly understood; upon my return to Rosings, I will learn you have vacated Hunsford. Your services are no longer desired."

Then looking at Charlotte, she added, "Mrs. Collins, you have often found it necessary to share correspondence from Meryton which contained offensive language toward Elizabeth and the whole of the Bennet family, many times pointing out erroneous accusations. Your husband has continuously made known to me your agreements on such subjects regarding them;

always stating you share his opinion. If it be so, let me warn you to cease your public opinion lest you be unable to secure any position in all of England. Should so much as a whisper reach Rosings of any negative discourse regarding the Bennets, I will take immediate action to have you discharged from any position you might be so fortunate to secure."

Although Lady Catherine was seriously angered, she made her voice soft again as she turned to Elizabeth. "Elizabeth, please do me the honour of bringing Mariah to me once again."

Elizabeth nodded her head, then quit their presence at once. Mr. Darcy continued to stand upright, with his chest high, his hands still behind his back. He looked down at Mr. Collins with intimidating expression, swelling in the victory of the moment.

When Elizabeth was out of sight, Lady Catherine turned to them once more. She projected her chin forward, lowering her brows as she squinted her eyes in their direction. "Have I made myself clear? You will vacate Hunsford at once!"

"Yes, your ladyship," replied Charlotte in a surprised voice, her eyes not knowing where to look, avoiding Elizabeth's direction as she returned with Mariah. Mr. Collins bore the look of mortification, and, together, the two stood unmistakably nervous and anxious to quit Pemberley.

Lady Catherine turned to Mariah. "Mariah, you are to return at once to Hunsford with your sister, where you may leave the gown."

"Come, Mariah," Charlotte said, obviously unnerved as she hastily whisked her to the door, applying strong language, saying not a word to Elizabeth. Mr. Collins followed behind in a hurried trot with mortifying expressions throughout his gestures.

"Elizabeth, you should choose your friends more wisely," Lady Catherine stated. "Since they are come to Hunsford, she has been less than flattering on your behalf. As for your family situation, from whom do you believe I learned all I confronted you with at Longbourn? Mrs. Collins receives letters frequently from Meryton. Both Mr. Collins as well as Charlotte briskly related most of the information regarding your family to me. Now that I look back on it, I daresay they were eager to report any injurious intelligence. Charlotte, as well as Mr. Collins, granted neither you nor your family compliments or respect to be sure. When you first visited Rosings, I had little understanding of your friendship, as her criticisms flowed rather loosely from her tongue, expressing otherwise ill-favoured remarks. Even then, I wonder how you considered her your friend. Good gracious, I'm thankful my nephew brought me to my senses—to think I was looked upon as I now view them." She gasped at the thought, then added, "Come now, your guests must not be kept waiting; we better make haste."

"Lady Catherine, you relieved Mr. Collins of his position at Rosings? So severe—I can scarcely believe it!" Elizabeth uttered.

"Why should you not? I have been anxiously awaiting the proper occasion. Months ago I decided not to make my altered opinions of the Bennets known to them. In keeping silent, my eyes were excessively opened; any pain they suffer is of their own consequence."

"Oh," she gasped, then said, "Lady Catherine, I admired your affording Mariah a lack of harshness; she appeared frightened indeed, poor girl."

"I had not the heart to scold her to a higher degree, understanding her worst punishment comes in the carriage ride with Mr. and Mr. Collins. In that, she is grievously to be pitied."

Mr. Darcy could not help but put his arm around his aunt's shoulder to give her a squeeze. He said not a word. His face was serious until his exchange with Elizabeth, who was still in a surprised state. They returned to the ballroom, where the three joined Georgiana.

Elizabeth willfully looked in Charles' direction. Not to her surprise was Mary at his side, still engrossed in an exchange. Charles' hands were in motion as he conversed in descriptive terms. Elizabeth reveled in the thought he received more attention than no doubt anticipated. She then turned in Georgiana's direction.

Georgiana, observing the dance, intently watched Mr. Gibson as he reeled around the room with Fanny. Elizabeth noted her expression to be of a serious nature, soberly deep in thought as she continued to eye their every move.

As Elizabeth neared Georgiana, she asserted, "Well, Georgiana, such lively dancing, perhaps you should partake; shall I find you a partner?"

"No, thank you, Elizabeth, I am quite content to observe."

"What is your success in watching?"

"Oh, I am curious of Mr. Gibson; he now dances with Fanny."

"Georgiana, I see you examine Mr. Gibson; I presume his dancing with Fanny disturbs you to some degree. Pray excuse my being so bold, I only inquire upon reading your expression. It appears she is quite taken with him; what say you?"

"Yes, my cousin's wife is a queer sort, is she not? I understand she has the ability to be rather unfriendly, even rude at times, but I daresay the splendors of Pemberley impressed her enough to display a certain amount of civility. She has danced much with Mr. Gibson, quite insensitive toward Edward, I would guess, although it would appear my cousin is glad for the imposition, as it affords him freedom to enjoy the ball."

"I see to what you allude, Georgiana. When we visited at Rosings, as the family gathered, she would not participate in the exchange of social intercourse; she sat indifferent to the conversations, appearing rather mean-spirited. My every attempt at conversation was greeted with extreme rudeness. I finally quitted her presence upon first opportunity."

"Yes, Elizabeth, I can believe it; she quite lives up to the reputation she formed long ago. My brother is directed toward us. I do believe he looks for you," Georgiana said as she and Elizabeth stood eyeing Mr. Gibson, who was still engaged in a dance with Fanny.

Elizabeth wondered of Ann's whereabouts. Her eyes searched the chamber. Ann was with the Colonel, unmistakably happy to be in his company.

Lady Catherine watched as Fanny danced with Mr. Gibson. She neared Elizabeth and Georgiana. "I'm happy the Colonel is here to distract Ann from the neglect of Mr. Gibson. I noticed he danced with Mariah as well as Fanny a great deal this evening. But my Ann does not seem to mind. I daresay she appears to prefer the Colonel. She always delights in his presence; it is quite interesting to notice."

Upon hearing his aunt's remark, Mr. Darcy dared to approach her. "Yes, Lady Catherine, it would appear Ann most always reverts back to the Colonel, and he to her. I must say, they seem to be comfortable in each other's company."

"Yes, indeed, Fitzwilliam, you need not trifle with me. I am shocked. I expected to find you more sensible; I see to what you allude. Do you take me for a fool? I take infinite pride in my acute senses. I see your meaning; do not suppose I lack the understanding of the exchanges between them. I'm not so sure they understand their own connection."

"To be truthful, the Colonel all too well understands his true feelings. He chooses to do nothing about it, realizing he has nothing to offer Ann." Mr. Darcy dared tell her.

"I am no stranger to the particulars of your cousin; he descends from a noble line. From his father's, he gains respect—honour with family connections. The voice of every member in his respective family would chant his praises; this I know as truth. These are valuable offerings indeed. Why has he not come to me?"

Elizabeth and Georgiana's eyes swayed between Mr. Darcy and Lady Catherine, occasionally sharing a look of shock.

"The Colonel has too much pride to do so. He feels unworthy of Ann. To be truthful, I do believe he might be of the opinion you would not consider such a notion as well. He has long resigned himself to love her from afar," Mr. Darcy reported with less caution.

"Does he now, indeed? Well now, this John Gibson concerns me; he flaunts himself about. I have had reservations where he is concerned. I have not been pleased with his actions at Rosings. Many evenings he stops by to visit but parts early, always providing a convenient excuse. I have long suspected he has other interests. But I cannot understand why he should seek Ann. He has much to offer in terms of wealth, but lacks qualities deserving of a girl of Ann's nature. The Colonel may lack wealth, but he possesses a definite depth of integrity. He is what a man ought to be. I do not believe this John Gibson is suitable for my Ann. She is too delicate; she requires an understanding of her fragility. Ann's happiness is my exclusive concern; I should not desire to chance her with a less than honourable gentleman. Ann's dowry is more than desirable. She lacks nothing anyone can provide. Fitzwilliam, the three of you go talk with Ann. Send the Colonel hither; make haste."

Elizabeth, Georgiana and Mr. Darcy immediately followed her instruction, directing the Colonel toward his aunt.

As they stood making conversation with Ann, Lady Catherine captured the Colonel's attention. "Colonel, you ought to know my character has been famed for its frankness. It is not my intention to depart from that now. I wish to make my sentiments clear. I take notice you desire my Ann. I can see clearly your thoughts; can you deny this?"

The Colonel's face turned a deep shade of red. As he gasped to answer his aunt, he managed to say, "Well—Aunt, indeed I do love Ann. I have no wish to deny my feelings on the subject; however, I can assure you I have made no designs on her; you may be certain of it."

"And why is that, Colonel?" she asked in a stern voice.

"Lady Catherine, I know you wish the best for Ann. I have nothing to offer. I have not revealed my feelings; truly I tell you I adore her from afar. I have made myself content with her laughter and smiles. I know a union is out of the question; I know it is impossible. You must believe me; I have not approached Ann, to be sure. You need not fear my attachment. Darcy can verify my position," the Colonel nervously defended himself.

"Allow me to be explicit; I am entitled to know my Ann is happy. She is a delicate creature to be sure. She requires a sense of suitability in marriage; would you not agree, Colonel?" his aunt said in a strained response.

"Why, yes, of course," he answered, looking her in the eye with curiosity.

"Tell me at once, Colonel, why have you not come to me?" she asked as her voice softened with affection.

"Lady Catherine, I have nothing to offer other than my honour. Indeed, I love Ann, but she deserves more. I know your wish is to have Ann marry in the best circle."

His words angered Lady Catherine. "Have you no regard for the honour or credit of your lineage? You are of the exact circle, are you not? Have you no regard for Ann? Do you think me ignorant of the importance of felicity within marriage? Speak up, what say you?"

"Lady Catherine, I'm not quite understanding your meaning. I am at a loss for words," he said in a voice filled with nervous fear of her pending reaction.

"Very well, Colonel, allow me to speak plainly. You are a most honourable gentleman. I know you to be the best of men. I might add, I am of the knowledge you descend from the same noble line as Ann. You are respectable; more importantly, you have formed an attachment. You are in love with her, are you not? Tell me at once!"

"I do love Ann."

"Well, Colonel, what say you?"

"Are you approving a union?"

"Indeed I am. You say you have nothing to offer; I say that is not so. You offer her love, honour and deep felicity. You are aware of her delicacy. I know you will care for her as she ought to be taken care of. Tell me now, is this not so?"

"Why, yes, of course it is so," he said with a voice filled with surprise.

"Well, Colonel, whatever are you waiting for?"

"Now?" he said in shock, his eyes wide with surprise.

"Now, Colonel, go, make haste, take her for a turn, grant her an interview. Send those three back to me at once."

"Very well," he said with a voice of excitement, squeezing her hand hastily before quitting her presence. She stood with a broadened smile on her face, feeling satisfyingly smug in her dealings. Elizabeth, Mr. Darcy and Georgiana returned to Lady Catherine. When they approached her she was silent, appearing rather stern.

Mr. Darcy dared cautiously to ask, "Well, did you speak with the Colonel on the delicate subject of matrimony?"

"Indeed I did; I sent him to her at once. He is, without any doubt, applying for an interview as we speak. I have encouraged him to waste no more time."

"Lady Catherine, I am surprised, but quite delighted."

"Why should you be? Next to you, the dear Colonel is equally as honourable," she said sarcastically with a smile as she turned to wink at Elizabeth.

Georgiana and Elizabeth shared a look of surprise, making no attempt at conversation.

"Well, I can plainly see nothing escapes your notice. I daresay your intelligence is only exceeded by your love for Ann. It may interest you to know his love for her is severe."

"I believe I can see that for myself."

Elizabeth stood in astonishment; the whole of the event had taken her aback; she could scarce believe her hearing.

"Look, they are no doubt going to secure a quieter place for an interview," Georgiana remarked with joy.

"If you will excuse me, Aunt, I believe I should like to dance one last dance with my wife," Mr. Darcy explained, smiling.

"Yes, do; and, Darcy, allow for less public display on this reel."

Elizabeth and Mr. Darcy exchanged a look of shock at her comment, realizing their earlier behaviour did not escape her notice.

"Lady Catherine, are you telling me you noticed our ill-mannered behaviour while we danced earlier?"

"Certainly, although I would hardly call it ill mannered. Darcy, do not concern yourself; it was not such a public display. I managed to watch both of you intentionally, wishing the same felicity for my Ann. It was through my witness of your exchange that I realized I wanted nothing less for my daughter. Suddenly material worth was at a loss. Then viewing Ann with the Colonel, I realized he would care for her in the same tender sense. You know me well enough to know nothing escapes my notice. I will never lay myself open to be a victim of foolery. No indeed, you have to rise early in the morning to put one over on your old aunt!"

Elizabeth and Mr. Darcy smiled broadly, avoiding an exchange of looks as her words echoed about their ears. He bowed, then swiftly swept Elizabeth away to secure a last dance. They managed a laugh within an easy distance from her notice.

"Mrs. Darcy, your hand please," he teased as he reached out to guide her to the dance, smiling with satisfaction as they stopped to observe before joining the set.

Elizabeth once again observed her father with Emily, near the fireplace, engaged in earnest conversation. Elizabeth studied their moves as they engrossed themselves in each other, an exchange she was familiar with. She recognized that mesmerizing stare capturing the inability to remove one's attentions from the other. There was no trace of awkwardness in their expressions. She quickly looked away, feeling embarrassed by her notice. Having never experienced her father in rapturous emotion, she momentarily became uncomfortable watching him.

She renewed her attentions in the direction of Charles, who was sitting alone. She immediately examined the room for Mary, who was advancing in his direction with a drink. It was obvious her attentions were received well.

As a new dance was about to begin, they joined the set. She returned her eye to her father in time to see him extend his hand to Emily, leading her to dance as well. Before she realized it, they were at her side awaiting the start of the music.

He had a glow about him, thought she. Although she had always known her father to be a gentleman, she readily noticed how much more dignified he was in Emily's company. She had a definite influence over him. Emily instinctively drew the greatness in him to the surface. The thought of Emily and her father pleased her. Although he was still quick of wit, he no longer used it for unsettling purposes. There was a definite distinction over him as well as Kathryn and Mary—they seemed more settled, more accomplished and well bred—but most importantly her father appeared happy.

The music turned livelier, having a stimulating influence over their guests, causing an exhilarating eagerness to dance. The air overflowed with excitement. Guests less eager to dance now stood at length to catch a glimpse of the fervor of those indulging in the activity. Mr. Darcy stood opposite Elizabeth. He bowed to her with superior courtesy. She was once again caught in the rapture of his infinite superiority as he stood fixing his eyes on her form, swelling with impregnating pride at his partner. She thought him a bit more stately than usual, his unpretentious manner lending her acquiescence to lavish him with her subtle elegance. Her heart fluttered with each instance the dance forced them to touch, as they reeled about the floor with smoothness and grace. As they continued to dance, he suddenly became aware of the watchful eyes of a few guests. He attempted to bring the situation to her attention, but Elizabeth heard not a word at first. She remained wholly engrossed in her admiration of his manly figure, experiencing no awareness of the same until he caught her attention with a nod. Such notice diverted her alertness to the dance, avoiding repetition of their earlier display of less-shrouded emotions.

Their guests continued to watch with jubilation, delighting themselves in the amenities and amusements of the evening.

With no lack of exhilaration, Mr. Bennet and Emily danced, moving about with ease. When the music ended, Elizabeth and Darcy quitted the dance floor to take a turn out of doors. It was not long before they decided they must return to the ball to visit with their guests before the close of the evening. As duty and honour would have it, they proceeded to do what was proper, returning to the ballroom without further delay. As they directed themselves to the ballroom, Elizabeth felt the compelling notion that she would always seek to be guided by her husband to do what was expected, honourable and just in the eyes of the universe.

They rejoined Lady Catherine in time to take notice of the Colonel and Ann coming in their direction.

"Mother," Ann said, embracing her, "the Colonel said you approved; we are engaged. Is that not the most wonderful announcement? I'm happy beyond belief." Ann's voice was filled with joy as tears streamed down her cheeks, all the while a smile broadening on her face. The Colonel stood tall, obviously overtaken with inexplicable happiness.

"Well, Ann, what of John Gibson?" Lady Catherine slyly asked.

"Mother I have long felt his lack of sincerity; I cannot make him out. His character confuses me. At times he is evasive, oftentimes coy. I have never really desired more than friendship. Even in his friendship I felt uncomfortable of his flattery. I have long thought his attentions not necessary for my future happiness. I believe I may find contentment without him."

"Very well, Ann, when we arrive at Rosings we shall make plans; I shall have to secure clergy first."

"What do you mean, Mother?"

"Mr. Collins will be gone upon our arrival at Rosings; I asked that he vacate the premises at once. He insulted Elizabeth's family for the last time."

"Oh goodness gracious, I am exceedingly pleased!" Ann retorted hastily, clasping her hands together beneath her chin with a broadened smile. Putting her fingers up to her mouth quickly, she voiced, "I am so sorry, Mother, that was indeed unkind of me; but Mother, I should not have wished Mr.

Collins to perform the ceremony. I have long thought him less than expected of a man of his position. I'm sure our cousin would spare Mr. Manley. It is my wish; will you not, Cousin? Mother, please say it is so." Her speech advanced rapidly as she begged.

"Yes, yes, you know I cannot deny you such a wish. If Mr. Manley is agreeable, it will be so. Now perhaps you and the Colonel may wish to dance, the evening is near end. There are so few to be had. Later you must make announcement to the Earl."

"Oh, Mother, thank you again," a very delighted Ann said as she once again embraced her before hastily running off to enjoy a dance with the Colonel.

During the course of the evening, several of the privately invited guests, mostly family, were shown to the gallery by Mrs. Reynolds to see the newly hung family portrait, which drew much praise. The Gardiners and Lady Catherine especially appreciated the privilege to view the work of art.

Hours passed rapidly as the close of the evening drew near. Many guests parted Pemberley with fond memories. The Earl and his family were gathered to leave, only to discover Fanny's absence—much to the embarrassment of Lord Fitzwilliam. Throughout the discussion of her whereabouts, Lady Catherine looked at Elizabeth; next she turned to glanced at Mr. Darcy, while Georgiana's eyes danced between the three. All four harboured the same thought, realizing John Gibson's absence as well. No one dared to voice their suspicions. Finally, the two appeared, explaining they became overheated by the dance, deciding to step out of doors for a bit of fresh air, having no realization of the late hour.

The Earl abruptly bid farewell, as did his sons. Quite astonishing was the comment from Fanny, who delighted in saying she had a most spectacular evening, the finest she had ever experienced at any ball, even stating further she should wish to be invited back to Pemberley. Soon after the arrogant display, the Earl and his party quitted Pemberley, leaving John Gibson once again in the company of Ann.

Mr. Gibson seemed rather agitated upon learning of Ann's engagement. Lady Catherine wasted no moment in setting the record straight. She was now nonetheless more eager than the Earl to quit Pemberley, if only for the reason of their now unwanted guest.

Before departing Pemberley, Lady Catherine turned to Elizabeth. "Elizabeth, I believe tonight you aspire to fame; your elegance was surely admired as was your perfection of performance. And you, my dear nephew, the day next you shall no doubt be universally known for having had one of the country's most spectacular balls, not to mention a most handsome wife whose captivation of her guests will linger in many a memory. My lingering memory of the Pemberley ball will lie in the engagement of Ann. I could not be happier for having been invited to such a celebrated event. Do come and visit your old aunt soon."

The Rapture of Memories

Mr. Darcy and Elizabeth were amongst the earliest to rise, lending an opportunity to exchange thoughts of the evening past over breakfast.

Mr. Darcy reached for Elizabeth's hand. "Elizabeth, the excellence of the ball was executed uniquely; I believe our guests were taken aback. I understood many to confess their awe of the tasteful application of the entire affair, admiring the infinite superiority of elegance. Surely you were regarded accomplished; I believe Lady Catherine was absolutely correct in her prophecy."

"Prophecy?"

"Lady Catherine predicted the raptures of the ball to linger in many a memory. I must say my aunt quite astonishes me."

"Oh, yes, I do eye it a success. I find I'm consumed with a sense of satisfaction; it is quite gratifying indeed. In terms of congratulatory language, Dr. Gordon's wife, I believe, paid the highest respect. The very expressions of our guests spoke volumes; words in some senses were not necessary; would you not agree?"

"Quite, considering the contemptuous expressions of Bingley's sisters; surely their disdain was highly complimentary. I found it most gratifying to witness their expression upon seeing your elegant attire. The intensity of their scorn made concealment difficult," he expressed with a smile as he winked his eye.

"Yes, I believe it was so. But, think of Lady Catherine's dismissal of Mr. Collins; was that not quite shocking? I still can scarce believe it. I must tell you, to the best of my judgment, I was shocked beyond all capacity."

"Lady Catherine may have given up her harsh ways, but she rightfully lacks tolerance for injustice. Had she been of her present sentiment, they should not have lasted this long; perhaps he would have never gained the position at Rosings. Now that she has regained her own society, the need for such shallow, flattering company has dissipated. I firmly believe she was a prisoner of her own making. Once she became mean-spirited, her society failed her. The only consoling agreeable to her was found in a complimenting, condescending, apologetic clergyman whose sole benevolence was to flatter and say whatever it was he believed would delight her ears."

"I suppose they went to Lucas Lodge. I wonder what they will tell Sir William; no doubt my name will rise with unrestrained convenience."

"Dearest, do not concern yourself; why should it matter? All that you desire is yours; their opinions are nothing."

"Yes, I suppose that is true. I am still overcome by Lady Catherine's approach to the Colonel. In that I am still quite amazed."

"I confess I am at a loss for words. My aunt accepting the Colonel so readily, I should have thought it would be some time until her realization. I suppose I had not allowed her enough credit. There has never been any doubt of her love of Ann, but not her disdain of John Gibson. Luckily for the Colonel, Mr. Gibson was invited to the ball. Perhaps one could say he has Mr. Gibson to thank for the swiftness of my aunt's acceptance."

"You know, dearest, I dared not look in your direction when Lady Catherine claimed her inability to be tricked. I was equally grateful the Colonel was not present. Such composure would have been a strain, I imagine," Elizabeth expressed with certainty.

"Lady Catherine was very generous with you; were you aware of her reference of you to Mr. Collins as her 'dear niece Elizabeth'? Considering her compliments of the evening, I do believe you have attained a high level in my aunt's eye."

"Aye, I confess, I truly appreciate her acceptance. In recollection of the past, I do believe I was persuaded to her dislike, not only by her own harsh ways, but through Mr. Collins' constant necessity to boast with added condescension with respect to her. Now I have only to be heartily ashamed of my own feelings. I look back on that time with abhorrence; my sentiments have undergone so material a change since. I now delight in the reconciliation of the family, which brings great pleasure. Now, what say you about Fanny and Mr. Gibson?"

"My Cousin Edward's wife is a foolish woman indeed. She wallows in a dreadful, detestable spirit toward anyone not of her circle. You must have noticed her disapproval of you at Rosings, but here at Pemberley you represented quite the opposite, so she found you readily agreeable. I suppose once she witnessed Pemberley, she was convinced with assurance that it carried immediate conviction of wealth. As for John Gibson, I am more convinced in my suspicions. Although he accompanied Ann, I detected a certain indifference toward her in general terms, as though his attention were directed to her in appeasement; then he seemed more naturally drawn to Mariah, next moving on to Fanny. I'm not quite sure what misrepresentation he intended to impose upon these ladies. As for the latter, I know not what her conduct tends; surely she should reproach herself for such ill manners toward Edward. It makes little sense, I know. I believe he preferred the youthful character of Mariah first, the wealth of Ann second. As for Fanny, perhaps it was she who preferred him." he told her with uncertainty in his voice.

"Yes, I believe it is quite true. I felt sad toward Lord Fitzwilliam; he was embarrassed as was the Earl. Frank was occupied with Kathryn as was Charles with Mary; I believe they hardly noticed the sordid event. As for James," she chuckled, "he was oblivious to all as he danced with every available female in the room. I must say he certainly enjoys a dance. Do you suppose the Earl will discuss this with Fanny or Lord Fitzwilliam?"

"I do not know. My uncle speaks little, unless it is important or to make direction. He is a principled man; such a violation will no doubt be censured as it certainly goes against his philosophy. Edward will inherit a substantial estate upon his death, but so long as he lives, my uncle's tolerance for such undesirable behaviour is at naught. It will be viewed disrespectful, of that I am certain. I do believe he is not in the habit of accepting such disreputable conduct; his situation at present will not allow her to divide his respective house. I have no guess of the consequences."

"Oh dear, Lady Catherine was less then civil with her. The Earl being her brother and John Gibson having arrived with her as a guest brings that situation near her threshold; I'm sure that cannot be agreeable."

"I'm sure of it. And what of Jane and Bingley, has your sister mentioned anything with respect to Caroline and Mrs. Hurst?"

"Only that Caroline and Mrs. Hurst are eager to separate Emily from Father; they are quite uncomfortable regarding the association. Apparently Mr. Bingley is less than happy with their residence at Foxshire Estate. They demonstrate a total disregard of the children. They are civil, but no more, to Jane. You know Bingley values his marriage to Jane. The children are his delight. As for Emily, whom he dearly loves, Jane claims he is weary of their habitual abuse of their own sister, relating to me that once upon her quitting the music chamber, they indulge their mirth at the expense of her interests, much to his disgust. Jane said he was quite displeased."

Their attention was suddenly drawn to the sound of voices. They perceived the remainder of the family had finally decided to join them in the breakfast room.

Mr. Bennet was in high spirits, claiming he had risen earlier, but not desiring to intrude on their intimate conversation, he had been out walking.

"Father, you should have joined us; we did not hear you."

"That's quite all right, Lizzy, I preferred to take a turn. It clears the mind, a man can think better with a walk, but a walk does make one hungry."

"Well, Mr. Bennet, that can easily be attended to," Mr. Darcy told him as he rose from his chair to ring for service.

The subject of conversation circled round the evening past. Elizabeth sat listening to the varied opinions. The happiness derived as well as descriptions of her own dominance was found to be agreeable to her ears. Her sisters talked continually of the raptures of the evening, the overheard expressions of delight along with the joy they experienced with such charming partners.

Kathryn, still swelling with excitement from the ball, expressed her happiness in having had only one dance to sit out. She claimed the delightful, smooth actions of Mr. Darcy's cousin Frank were not matched by any other dancer in the room, declaring him to have been the best.

Elizabeth looked at her husband with a warm smile. She leaned to him to say in a half whisper, "I am most certain I had the superior partner, but we shall allow Kathryn her belief."

Mary sat bright-eyed as they breakfasted. She soon related her interesting conversations with Charles, claiming him to be well informed on many subjects. Then she suddenly stated with slight alarm, "Lizzy, Mr. Darcy, I hope it is of no objection to you, I do expect your cousins Charles and Frank to visit the day next. He is lending me several of his books. Frank is accompanying him; I do hope it is agreeable."

"Certainly, Mary, but I do wish you had mentioned it; I would have insisted they dine with us," Mr. Darcy expressed.

Mary's face first paled, then heightened in colour, turning a deep shade of red. Her now obvious embarrassment delayed her reply. She hung her head, then bringing it up again she looked at Mr. Darcy. "I did mention to Charles that I thought you should like them to come for an early dinner; since they are your cousins I should think that was appropriate."

"Mary, how could you?" Mr. Bennet scolded.

"That is quite all right, Mr. Bennet. Mary, accept my gratitude for having done so. Although my cousins live within an easy distance, I see little enough of them. I shall be delighted to entertain an early dinner. Elizabeth, shall you invite those at Foxshire? I'm sure it will be a pleasant evening. I shall include Mr. Manley; he is always eager for the company."

The thought of inviting all those from Foxshire Estate quickly turned Mr. Bennet's emotions to Emily, giving no further discouragement to Mary.

Elizabeth gave immediate thought to Caroline and the Hursts. Although she was always happy to see Jane and Mr. Bingley and delighted in the thought of bringing her father and Emily together again, the notion of an additional evening with them was exhausting. Perhaps she could convince Mr. Manley to assist her by diverting Caroline's attention in another direction; surely Mrs. Hurst would be more receptive when not so wholly influenced by Caroline or vice versa. This plan would surely make the evening more tolerable, thought she. She decided she would speak to her husband for his opinion on the matter.

The day altogether passed off pleasantly, with the inhabitants of Pemberley feeling quite relaxed. Mr. Darcy and Mr. Bennet set off for a few hours of fishing, promising to return early with enough fish for the evening meal. Elizabeth and the girls played with the children for several hours, taking them out of doors until they napped; then the three passed their time in the music chamber.

Mary played lively melodies on the pianoforte while Kathryn embroidered a pillow. After a time, Mary occupied herself with a book of poetry she borrowed from Mr. Darcy's library, declaring the collection to be the largest private selection she had ever seen. Elizabeth explained that Mr. Darcy's family had added to it for many generations. Since Mary's adventures to grand estates were few, Elizabeth laughed to herself at her believing it to be such a large selection.

The girls were a joy to have near—the days of high-pitched voices, tattling and spats were long past. They were calmly dignified, their manners polished as were their characters elevated. Elizabeth could not help but think them a striking contrast to the family she resided with at Longbourn when her mother was alive, always giving way to unnecessary excitement over the most inconsequential developments.

As Elizabeth sat in an armchair with her head back, she closed her eyes, reflecting on the evening last. Never in her entire life at Longbourn had she entertained thoughts of planning a ball; nay, such prospects were never to be afforded. With great satisfaction she relived parts of the evening in her mind. Having given the grandest of balls was surely beyond any aspirations she ever had. She marveled at how it all came to be—first her longing to make her husband proud, then working on her lists followed by her sketches, and all this with the support of her husband, whom she had not called upon for assistance. The knowledge of his pride contained her as she pictured him standing in his dress coat, bowing before her at the dance set. Extremely satisfied in her thoughts, she fell asleep for a short time, only to be awakened by her husband's touch upon her cheek.

"Elizabeth are you unwell?"

"Very well, dearest, I was dreaming, you were in your dress coat."

"Was I behaving myself?" he teasingly said above a whisper.

"Yes, you were a gentleman."

"I see; well now, this gentleman and your father did very well fishing. We will be dining on trout this evening. We did so well I invited Mr. Manley to dine with us; I knew you would have no objection. I even mentioned a foursome at pool; are you game?" he asked smiling, with a teasing tone.

"Mr. Manley is indeed always welcome; I need not tell you so. I believe I can do with a bit of fish. As for the pool, may I claim Father as my partner?" she said, allowing a giggle to slip.

"If you insist," he replied, laughing at her. "Did you have a pleasant afternoon?"

"Very pleasant indeed; we played with the children, then took them for a turn about the grounds. I'm sure they were fagged out. I sent an invitation to dinner for the evening next to Foxshire Estate. Dearest, would it be presumptuous of me to seek Mr. Manley's assistance in occupying Caroline? Would that be improper? He is a dear friend; I do believe he would favour me; in fact, I'm sure of it," she said in a whisper.

"It is not a common request; I should not wish Caroline to get the improper notion that Mr. Manley seeks her attention. Since he is aware of the situation, perhaps he'll consider it a challenge; allow me to inquire."

"Thank you, dearest, you are so good to me. The thought of Caroline and Mrs. Hurst together is indeed trying; but if Mr. Manley occupies her, I believe she can do little harm."

The remainder of the evening passed in a quiet fashion. Mr. Manley joined the party for dinner. Elizabeth and Mr. Darcy noticed Mary less eager to gain a seat near Mr. Manley; her thoughts were in another direction as she scarcely participated in the table conversation. Mr. Darcy, thinking perhaps she was ill, inquired only to have her say she was quite well, just meditating in thoughts.

Elizabeth rolled her eyes at her husband for not perceiving the direction of her notions. Kathryn was less talkative as well, but ostensibly practicing a bit more elegance in manners. Elizabeth observed as she followed Mr. Darcy's lead, seemingly mimicking his every move. Dinner ended with an abundance of conversation as the party made its way to the pool parlour with little anticipation of the winning team. They entered the parlour in good spirits, Elizabeth's perhaps higher than the rest of the party, as she was absolutely sure to win according to her own proclamation. Mr. Darcy gained in laughter at his wife's jubilation with each win. After three unsuccessful attempts at winning a game, Mr. Manley and Mr. Darcy concluded Mr. Bennet's team the best, to the delight of Elizabeth, who failed to get one ball in a pocket. Mr. Darcy just shook his head with laughter at her euphoria. Mr. Bennet smiled at her, then, turning toward Mr. Darcy and Mr. Manley, he rolled his eyes in an elevated position in light of her excitement over the winning of a game to which she contributed naught.

The remainder of the evening passed with an impossibility to evade Elizabeth making her wins a celebrated event. The only one in the party fortunate enough to escape her overzealous joy was Mr. Manley, who quitted the place early to return to the parsonage.

Entrapment

With two days passing, the prospect of dinner that evening presented additional obstacles to overcome.

Much to Elizabeth's relief, Mr. Manley considered Caroline a challenge, providing her with as good a grace as she could hope to receive. She was eager to see Jane and Mr. Bingley as well as allow her father his attentions toward Emily. Surely the plan would ease the tensions of the evening, especially since Mr. Darcy's cousins would be a welcomed distraction.

It rained the whole of the day; the ground was soaked, leaving roads in a muddy state. Elizabeth conceivably found some trial of her patience in the dreary weather, which totally suspended any out-of-door activity, as it rained hard into the late afternoon without intermission. The clouds united, darkening the sky as the driving rain continued, resulting in pure gloomy thoughts as torrents of rain, directed by a breeze, caused it to beat against the windowpanes with fury. Elizabeth peered out of the window, perceiving the dreary weather had an effect on the music Georgiana played on the pianoforte.

Surely the farmers would welcome the rain, thought she. She decidedly sought to find the best in the dreary situation, as would her sister Jane. Wondering how Jane would perceive the storm, she quickly concluded Jane would revel in the notion of a beautiful rainbow across the sky, but not before giving value to the farmer's delight in the watering of crops. An inner, pleasing feeling swelled within her as she laughed at her own thoughts.

With the whole of the party forced indoors, the activity circled around reading, needlework and the pianoforte, with an occasional turn about the room or visits to Mr. Darcy's library. The Bennet girls played cards before returning to their bedchamber to prepare for the gentlemen whose presence they anticipated with unguarded eagerness.

Georgiana kept her position in the music chamber, first on the piano-forte, later at her harp. Elizabeth and Mr. Darcy remained there as well, each reading a choice book.

As noon neared, an express came for Mr. Darcy, informing him of a most unexpected and serious situation. Elizabeth studied her husband as he immersed in the written word, which drained the colour from his face, leaving him in earnest meditation while reading its contents. As soon as he finished his reading, he immediately made strides toward his office, with his wife a fleeting distance behind him. He gained a seat at his desk.

Heavily breathing, she stood in front of his desk with her palms flat on its surface; she leaned forward, anxiously questioning, "May I inquire of your letter? Who is it that writes? Why does its substance deprive you of the pleasant spirit you enjoyed moments ago?"

"It is a letter from your uncle."

But before he could respond further, she quickly took a seat, nervously quizzing with urgency, "What is it? How is it possible a letter from my own uncle shocks you to distraction?"

Elizabeth's heart pounded; her eyes searched his expression. Unable to sit still, she nervously twitched, biting on her lower lip, wondering to what end such trepidation should be given by the contents of the letter.

"Perhaps you better read it," he said, placing the letter in her hand to cease her fervent curiosity. Although his look was severe, there was a certain air of control in his countenance. Elizabeth realized, whatever the contents, her husband had already contemplated its final resolve. He studied her, knowing such grief, disturbing as it was to read, must take its course. He perceived her reaction as she read the letter written in her Uncle Gardiner's hand.

Gracechurch Street
November 22ND
Pemberley Estate, Derbyshire

Mr. Fitzwilliam Darcy,

After discussing the subject at great length, Mrs. Gardiner and I have devoted much of the morning hours deciding the merits of sending you word regarding such horrendous circumstances made known to us. We mutually agreed, since there has in the past been a connection, first to you as a child, and in latter years through your relationship in marriage, perhaps these circumstances should be known to you to avoid the shock of learning the information from another. Further reason is, I was hard pressed to give my word to do so.

Mrs. Young, your sister's former governess, who was dismissed from her charge on cause of disapprobation, resides still on Edward Street in London, continuing to maintain herself by letting lodgings. She being so intimately acquainted with George Wickham, visited the day before last to inform us Mr. Wickham has but a few days of life left in him. She implored I write to inform you of his circumstances. I am not of the understanding why she thought it necessary to make us knowledgeable of his now sorry state. She hesitantly revealed his last months spent in revelry with drink in the company of courtesans, which are now wholly connected to his illness, claiming he is no longer of his own mind. His declining health has forced him into invariable confinement. She desires to know if you may be reduced to reason of burial, revealing Mr. Wickham is penniless and seemingly has been abandoned by his friends to die deranged and in filth. She begged my promise that such a letter would be written, stating it will not be long. She thought it might only be fitting if he were buried next to his father. Having given my word, I regret the necessity of the information penned. I entreat your forgiveness of what can only assure to bring indignant astonishment, thus only further increasing your abhorrence of such a man. To his inexpedient end, may we all be in prayer for his soul.

Yours very sincerely,
Mr. Gardiner

In her urgent reflection of the contents, the concerns of the letter threw her into a flutter of mortifying spirits, finding difficulty in determining the depth of pain its reading must have produced. Her concerns were not for herself but for her beloved Mr. Darcy. She could not help but feel he had endured more than any man should be obliged in life at the hand of such an evil character whose every discontented situation seemed to require his rectification, often causing pain and suffering. Yet he bore it with a grace and dignity not of her understanding.

"Elizabeth, my dear, are you all right?"

Elizabeth's mind raced. Was there ever to be an end to the demands of such a man? Was this yet another plot to involve her husband in his reckless indiscretions? The very thought of George Wickham caused her head to ache. She nodded her head as he secured paper with his quill in hand.

She delicately placed the letter on the desk, noticing her husband steadily writing a response. He was universally known for his close hand with the pen. She thought his handwriting a testimony of his excellence as his letters were always finished off handsomely, even when they bore the gravest words, as was the situation at present.

Unable to sit still any longer, Elizabeth stood. She folded her arms while fixing her eyes on her husband's actions, studying him with curiosity. He looked intense as his pen moved swiftly across the paper.

His intent was obviously to do what he believed was required of him. It was difficult to imagine his thoughts, the only surety being his integrity, his inability to ignore Mr. Wickham's predicament without dishonouring his father or his own character, which in the end would lead him to be generous.

As he finished, she inquired, "Dearest, what are your intentions?"

He looked at her with a grave expression. He slightly raised his shoulders before answering. "What else is there to be done? I shall send word to your uncle at once. If there be any truth in this report, I shall have your Uncle Gardiner arrange to have his body brought to Pemberley to be buried next to his father. For his sake alone I am grieved, shocked and glad he is not alive to endure the pain in the disgraceful finish of his only son."

He sat back in his chair. "I'm convinced your uncle received the news with difficulty in determining its vague, unsettled suspicions of uncertainty contrived by Mr. Wickham's blemished past. I am quite persuaded it pained him to write. Although I owe this man nothing, my own father held his father in the highest esteem. I cannot ignore the request. For his honour alone I find I am plagued by the pain of obligation. Certainly this one last act will be the final supplication."

Elizabeth returned to the chair. She shook her head, letting out a sigh, as she looked at him. "You are so good; I cannot imagine what you are feeling at this very moment."

Mr. Darcy sat upright at his desk once again. He looked at her with resigned relief. "I find I am reduced to bury the man whom I most wished to avoid, whose name is punishment for me to pronounce and whose penetrating ways have weighed heavy upon the hearts and lips of those I hold dear to me. Nevertheless, I shall give him proper burial, employing the services of Mr. Manley. I am thankful that he knows of the circumstances, saving me the pain of explanation. I beg your aunt's forgiveness in keeping your uncle's interference in making such arrangements as necessary, sparing me that anguish."

Mr. Darcy sat forward, bringing his hands together upon the desk. Compelled by love, Elizabeth reached forward to place her hand on his.

He afforded her a faint smile. "I implore you as my partner as well as my faithful council—have I secured your compassion? What is your opinion on the matter?"

Keeping her hand on his a moment longer, she hesitated before answering. "Dearest— I see what you are feeling; perhaps I may alleviate a bit of your suffering. Do not concern yourself on my behalf. I confess I am quite apathetic to the consequences of George Wickham. He has done wrong with no regard or value of those lives he has touched. He requires no reflection on my part. My sentiments were once extreme abhorrence, but now I find I am quite indifferent. I have no desire to think of him, not even with despise; there is nothing due to me on that score. I have made my peace long ago. Nay, not even in death will he pilfer from me so much as an ounce of despair; I have long set such feelings aside."

She sat back in her chair, taking in a deep breath. She stared at him for a moment, then continued, "I conceive it is necessary for you to do what is morally right; I know you view it as your duty."

She walked around the desk. Placing her hand on his shoulder, she leaned down to caress him, kissing him gently on the cheek. "It is your qualities I find essential to my happiness. I believe I understand your necessity to always do the honourable. I am guided by your judgment." She returned to her chair once more.

"You provide me great comfort, my dear. I shall put him to rest with the knowledge I have your support. I can do nothing less, lest I reproach myself if I had not done so. This I know is certain. Although these may be viewed as trials of the living, I find I am a fortunate man to so easily secure your compassion. To have a wife with such tolerance and comprehension is comforting indeed," he said, twirling the quill between his fingers.

Elizabeth sensed he was rather relieved by the discourse. She faintly smiled back at him. "I do believe you can be nothing less than honourable."

She sat back with more comfort, but struggled awkwardly with her thoughts. She was puzzled. How is it possible I know him so well, yet so little? She studied him at length. His powerful presence intrigued her. She believed she grasped his unwavering loyalty, but lacked understanding of the whole of the constancy which made him unvaryingly wise and magnanimous. His ability to reduce himself to do with ease that which other men would surely view impossible, bewildered her.

"You aspire to such noble magnificence in distinction of reputation that I should only wish my character to be viewed in your likeness. In confessing thus, you should certainly be aware that it is your opinion that matters most to me. With pride, I acknowledge the understanding of your character, which requires you to take on this last honourable action. Surely you realize I lack no insight of your necessity. When the deed is done, it will truly be finished."

She paused, studying him at length, sitting back in the chair as she stared at him.

"What—? What is it? Why is it you study me?"

Elizabeth paused. The words seemed to linger on her tongue. She took a deep breath, deliberating her words. "Although I am convinced I understand your position, the power of your ceaseless honour seems to elude me. How it is you are consistently apt to rise to grievous situations with such easy air of dignity and serenity of mind?"

"My dear Elizabeth, it is not a matter of rising, more a matter of falling."

She immediately stood. "Pray, excuse my ignorance. I find I am less certain of your purpose. What do you mean, falling? When have you ever fallen beneath dignity? When have you failed to be constant, to do what is proper? You always do your duty. Pray tell me, when is it that you have fallen?"

"When I fall to my knees seeking guidance through His absolute power, I am lifted to a level of direction by grace. By the rules of England I am required to obey that which is set forth as law. Through my father, I am required to do what he taught me is proper to honour the family name by way of duty, but by God I am required to do all that is good and righteous for His name's sake. I charge myself to keep always a faithful void of offences toward God as well as my fellow man, which enables me to humble myself to endure suffering and pain. In Him I find comfort. In Him I gain refreshed spirit in times of distress. It is only by the grace of God, I am what I am. I realize my imperfections. I cannot count my life dear to my own credit or any of my deeds; nor can I attribute unto myself any goodness or virtue. I do not claim majesty or any level of greatness, but ascribe any and all goodness in me to God's grace alone. There are times I struggle to do that which is required of me. In cases such as this, my faith is tested. I must seek His guidance through prayer. It is constancy in Him."

As he spoke, she slowly lowered herself into the seat. She faintly gasped. "Oh—Fitzwilliam," she said, breathing heavily. She sat forward with a reddened face and tear-filled eyes, staring at him with parted lips. "The depth of your character makes me ashamed of what mine has been. Until this very moment I have never fully understood the whole of your integrity. Your veracity causes me to blush. I have never known anyone of your nature. To think—all this time I have fancied myself of your understanding, I confess I have been quite ill-judge of it."

Mr. Darcy once again sat forward. A look of placid benevolence overspread his features. With his usual prudence and thoughtful sensibility he determined he was glad the subject had been mentioned. He shook his head slowly. "Do not reproach yourself, my dear. I beg you will not allow this to weigh heavy upon your mind."

"I comprehend clearly now. It is not your wealth that makes you among the richest of men. When we have knelt to pray together, often I have felt a powerful force of goodness about you; indeed I have frequently been in awe of it, but now I understand its meaning. At such a moment I can only give glory to God who has favoured me with the honour of such a partner."

He sat quietly. With fresh admiration, his feelings ignited with joy of her confession. He composed himself without further hesitation. Folding up his finished letter, he placed a seal upon it with a look of serenity. Then his voice cracked with emotion, "Elizabeth—I must confess I am delighted by your disclosure. I——"

"Yes, but, dearest—" interrupted Elizabeth, "there were times I felt so unworthy of you. Most recently I have felt closer to your understanding, now only to find how full of error I have been. I earnestly desire to take my place at your side, drawing myself unto Him as I ought to have done from the beginning. I would have done so had I true understanding of the glory and honour of your desire to serve Him. With such discernment I can only tell you I shall never be the same person." She paused, then looked at him as if she perfectly understood. "Fitzwilliam, you are infinitely my superior. She paused again. "What a pity Wickham had not the same understanding, a great pity indeed."

Mr. Darcy sat silently tranquil for a moment. Seized by her discovery, he leaned forward at his desk to place his face in his hands. His eyes filled as his breast swelled with the captured understanding of his wife's revelation.

"Are you quite all right, my dear?"

"Yes, dearest, I am very well indeed," he answered, removing his face from his hands. He took a deep breath, then sat back in his chair.

"You look a bit tired. This has been an eventful day, has it not?" she asked.

He struggled to compose himself, making no response regarding the inner joy he felt of her spirituality, not wishing to embarrass her further. He soberly looked at her, then nodded his head, accepting her words before directing himself back to the delicate subject of George Wickham. "Dearest, what of your father? Perhaps it is wise to educate him of Mr. Wickham after the guests have gone. I have invited your Aunt and Uncle Gardiner to visit with us. This is agreeable to you, is it not? Surely it will divert attention from the grievous deed."

"Yes, I daresay it is best to tell father," Elizabeth answered, taking in a deep sighing breath of air as the subject was now concluding.

"Well, I do believe our guests have arrived; come, let us greet them. Then I shall excuse myself briefly to send the message. I will rejoin you when the deed is done," Mr. Darcy stated as he arose from his chair, taking charge of the situation.

They quitted the office to greet their guests, who were eagerly joined by the Bennets and Georgiana in the entrance hall. The gentlemen expressed that the muddy, wet route in such cheerless weather presented the otherwise beautiful countryside a dreary, unpleasant journey, whose endurance caused Charles to suffer additional aches through dampness about the air. Upon giving up their dampened cloaks to the servant, the gentlemen appeared no less eager to the greeting, first assuring in their delight to pay respects to their cousin as they moved in the direction of the music chamber, chiefly occupied in conversation with Kathryn and Mary. Mr. Bennet followed close behind, while Mr. Darcy excused himself with intentions of tending to the chore of sending the message. Elizabeth excused herself to order hot tea to be served with a bit of food, first suggesting Charles acquire a seat by the fire.

Upon entering the sitting room, Elizabeth heard Mr. Bennet express his delight in seeing them once again; then he excused himself, stating it was his wish to continue his reading of a book once started.

As Mr. Bennet passed Elizabeth, he paused. He viewed her momentarily, "Elizabeth, you appear well rested; your general colouring adds much to your beautiful complexion. I might add you seem rather peaceful. Marriage to such a partner agrees with you, my dear. It makes me feel rather content to know you are well settled."

"Thank you, Father," said Elizabeth, linking her arm in his to walk him to the stairs. Allow me to tell you, Father, until this very day I had believed myself to be most fortunate, but today I fully understand the depth of my felicity. Dare I tell you, the values my husband affords me far exceed the worldly possessions visible to mankind. We are kindred spirits united by a force far greater than human desire."

"I can see that, my dear. You go along now, rejoin your company."

"Very well, Father." She smiled, then turned to direct herself to the music chamber.

Upon Elizabeth's entry, Frank introduced an exchange of intercourse complimenting the splendors of the ball, proclaiming it to have been the finest of his attendance. There was no wanting of discourse. The gentlemen proved to be exceedingly well bred, similar to the manners of their cousin Mr. Darcy. Kathryn and Mary needed no courage to join in; they ventured into discussion with no worry of forwardness, yet they were careful not to exert too much talk. They remained perfectly at ease in their exchanges.

Above one-half hour passed when Elizabeth was roused by the entrance of servants with cold meats, cake and a variety of what little fruit was in season, along with a selection of the finest fruit jellies on the premises. The beautiful pyramids of grapes and nectarines soon collected them round the table, thus still fully engaged in conversation.

Kathryn and Mary seemed perfectly at ease. They seemed unembarrassed by the attentiveness so strongly marked by Frank and Charles. Mary and Charles were captivated by deep discussion of the publications he wished to lend, while Frank and Kathryn's communication reflected their notions of composition.

Elizabeth watched with curiosity the actions of the happy foursome, which awakened a new awareness of their developed friendship. She had at first thought Charles was the reason for Frank's presence, as it was universally known that Charles seldom was seen in public without the guardianship of his brother; but Elizabeth concluded the visit a favoured opportunity for Frank as well. When Mr. Darcy entered, brief attention was spent in conversation inclusive of him, only enough to express delight in a more intimate visit to Pemberley. Soon after the words were spoken, the young ladies and gentlemen quickly turned their attentions toward each other, leaving him to himself.

Mr. Darcy raised his brows to Elizabeth in submission as he took his place at her side. They watched as Kathryn and Frank moved to the pianoforte with discussion of music while Charles and Mary buried their faces in a book.

Elizabeth and Mr. Darcy excused themselves to go above the stairs to dress for dinner, anticipating the arrival of the party from Foxshire Estate. Georgiana soon followed, leaving behind the Bennet girls to entertain the guests, since they had already dressed for the occasion.

As the day progressed, Elizabeth noted no less shortage in subjects among the foursome. She waited in anxious anticipation for the expected party, having dressed well for the occasion. Her husband had admired her choice in dress, affording himself the pleasure to place her necklace about her throat as she prepared herself for scrutiny by Caroline and Mrs. Hurst.

Fortunately, Mr. Manley arrived before the dreaded company of the Bingley sisters, who proved not to be far behind.

Jane and Mr. Bingley, were, as always, a welcomed sight, and Elizabeth could not have been more delighted to welcome Emily. Mr. Bennet eagerly awaited her arrival and soon whisked her away for conversation all his own.

Although Elizabeth's gown was more than adequate, it had not the magnificence of attire she wore at the ball. Still, she found herself once again under the watchful eye of Caroline and Louisa Hurst. In spite of all this, Elizabeth noticed a detectable difference in their behaviour; they were more civil, affording easier conversation. Mr. Hurst seemed to be his usual quiet self, securing a glass of port shortly after his arrival.

Elizabeth managed intimate conversation with Jane, learning Mr. Bingley was unhappy with his sisters and growing increasingly tired of Mr. Hurst slumping over the furniture in a state of drunkenness. She supposed the children now occupied his interests, and Mr. Hurst's dullness of character along with his inability to correct his wife's ill manners were wearing on Charles to a point of discontentment. Jane related that although Louisa was his sister, Charles felt it was Mr. Hurst's place to settle his wife to some degree. She further expressed the present unhappy state rendered no excuses as far as Mr. Bingley was concerned for their lowness of opinions. Jane feared Caroline and Louisa were so occupied with hard opinions that they failed to notice their brother's increased displeasure and, therefore, were in danger of a conflict in which she feared Charles would cast them out under no uncertain terms. None of this revelation came as a surprise to Elizabeth. Yet such information still seemed unsettling to Jane.

If there had been any implied doubt of the attentions Mr. Bennet possessed for Emily, their intimate exchange now furnished Caroline and Mrs. Hurst affirmation of their affection for one another. The present unfavourable expression borne by Mrs. Hurst escaped Caroline's attention, as Mr. Manley carried out his task well. Mrs. Hurst was careful to not allow her eyes to stray from the two. Emily and Mr. Bennet left her in agitated spirits upon announcing their intended turn about the gallery, which was out of view of the whole of the party. To add to her injury, upon her inquiry to accompany them, Emily quickly wished it not to be so. The two escaped to the gallery to admire the wall hangings, with Mr. Bennet's desire to specifically introduce her to his grandchildren.

Their absence caused considerable uneasiness to Mrs. Hurst. Mr. Hurst, having enjoyed several glasses of port, was slouched in the corner of the sofa. Caroline was involved with Mr. Manley, leaving Louisa to keep watch.

Upon their return, Emily's face bore the look of excited felicity, drawing the attention of the whole of the party. Mr. Bennet directed himself toward Mr. Bingley. "Mr. Bingley, your sister has granted me an interview. My proposal has been accepted; you see before you a happy man." Then turning to Emily, he stated, "I had asked your brother if I might request your hand in marriage, to which he did not refuse; I thank you, my dear, for honouring me with your acceptance."

Mr. Bingley burst with excitement. Emily declared the happiness now felt was such as she never experienced before. She spoke warmly of the man whose asking brought promising excitement of the future. She smiled with pleasure as Jane welcomed the news with delight. Jane had wished it so; such news she expected, although perhaps not on this evening. Kathryn and Mary were equally delighted with the news. Kathryn had altered her opinion of the union when realizing her own love for Emily as well as her desire for her father's happiness.

Caroline and Mrs. Hurst were overwhelmingly astonished by Mr. Darcy and Elizabeth's expression of congratulations. Mr. Darcy, believing Elizabeth's father a suitable match for Emily, viewed the intended union agreeable. But the Bingley sisters, in total opposition, believed Elizabeth would have not desired her father to quit the pattern set by her mother, believing Emily to possess those superior qualities the prior Mrs. Bennet lacked.

Georgiana welcomed the news with delight; although she had not known Mr. Bennet for very long, she took pleasure in learning of their intended nuptials. Charles and Frank quickly expressed happy sentiments to the newly engaged couple.

Mrs. Hurst's and Caroline's reactions were less than excitable. They said not a word, exchanging glances of mortification as Mr. Hurst remained at the end of the sofa, snoring loudly until his wife nudged him, startling him to an awakened state. He remained expressionless with regard to the news. His indifference was only made more obvious by his rising to fill his glass.

Mr. Manley offered his congratulations, expressing his wish to perform the ceremony.

A servant summoned them to the dining hall, which interrupted the excitement. It was viewed a welcomed diversion by Mr. Darcy, who was aware of the disappointed reflections of Caroline and Louisa.

Mr. Manley occupied Caroline as promised, with his careful manner devoid of any assurance to lead her to believe there was any real interest other than association through the social intimacy of her brother's friend. He sought a seat next to her at dinner, keeping her conversation in other directions.

Convinced as Elizabeth was of Caroline and Mrs. Hurst's dislike of her father, she could not help feeling their regret of the evening's invitation. It was obvious they had not expected such an announcement. Elizabeth soon noticed her father and Emily closely scrutinized by Mrs. Hurst, sitting an easy distance from her view, making her quite uncomfortable. Even Mr. Manley's attentions to Caroline seemed to fail. Both ladies were now in an obvious state of despair, making Mr. Bennet the object of their desperate condemnation. Caroline viewed the engagement with indiscreet anger, taking the first opportunity to boldly say, with sneering impoliteness, "Emily, just where do you intend to reside? Surely Longbourn is considered a lesser estate than you are accustomed."

Mr. Bingley's face reddened with embarrassment. Next, he appeared angrier as he clenched his lips together, attempting to control himself in mixed company.

Emily ignored the question, pretending she heard not a word. She immediately turned her attention to Mr. Bennet. "Mr. Bennet might I further trouble you to take another turn about the gallery after dinner; perhaps we may visit the grandchildren as well?"

Mr. Bennet, about to take a bit of meat to his mouth as he heard the remark, looked at Caroline and Mrs. Hurst with raised eyes. He was quick to address Emily's question, rescuing her from the abomination of her sister's snide remarks. "I should be delighted."

Altogether the remainder of the dinner passed as mildly successful, given the strained sentiments. Emily directed her attention to Mr. Bennet, while Mary and Kathryn involved themselves in the attentions of Mr. Darcy's cousins, who collectively seemed untouched by any other concerns. The remainder of the party struggled through general conversation, with relief provided by the conclusion of the meal.

They moved once more to the music chamber, where Georgiana entertained them with her exquisite performance at the pianoforte. Jane nervously made light conversation centered on Georgiana's music, while her husband conversed with Mr. Darcy and Mr. Hurst of an upcoming fox chase. Mr. Bennet and Emily had disappeared once again for a turn about the gallery in a hasty escape from Caroline and Mrs. Hurst.

Shortly after Mr. Bennet and Emily's hasty escape, Charles and Frank bid their farewells, insisting they were required to start for home. They expressed their regrets on having to quit Pemberley so soon after the meal, noting Charles' early rise the morning next to provide wedding services at his parsonage as their reason for having to end their visit so soon. Much to the girls' delight, was their request to return the week next to fetch the books and visit Pemberley again, which was met with satisfaction.

The rain had stopped shortly after the arrival of the party from Foxshire Estate. The clouds dispersed, allowing the sun to make a forced appearance whenever possible. The freshness of the evening had more appeal to those leaving, as a gentle crisp breeze seemed to erase the dampness in the atmosphere, making it more tolerable for Charles to endure. It had been viewed a favourable day by the two gentlemen, who departed in high spirits. With pleasant humour, they eagerly determined they would return before long.

Kathryn and Mary, having had a most delightful afternoon, reluctantly bid them good-bye. Mary thanked Charles for the loan of the books, promising to treat them with great respect. The two gentlemen disappeared as quickly as they came, or so it seemed to the two Bennet girls, who were most sorry to see the visitors take their leave.

Georgiana and the girls excused themselves, venturing above the stairs. Mr. Manley occupied the pianoforte in an attempt to direct attention to a more delightful atmosphere. As Mr. Manley played, he seemed to bring about a sense of calm to a much excitable evening.

Jane and Mr. Bingley expressed a wish to visit the gallery to see the portrait which had escaped their notice during the ball, taking this welcomed opportunity to quit the presence of Caroline and Louisa.

After giving the party much pleasure with several melodies, Mr. Manley announced a need to return to the parsonage. He bid them all good-bye, making a hesitant exit. As Mr. Darcy and Elizabeth saw him to the door, Mr. Manley said, "Well, my friends, once again I enjoyed a most welcomed meal. In parting, I can only wish you well to the evening's end. I have a new appreciation for the challenges before you. As for Mr. Bingley, he has my sympathy. His embarrassment is obvious; luckily for them, his tolerance sustains them. I shall remember them in prayer; surely the situation requires it."

They returned in time to hear Louisa request to play the pianoforte. As they sat listening to the tune, Mrs. Reynolds entered, requesting Mr. Darcy and Elizabeth to please follow her, to make haste, as Bessie had a mishap and was in need of their assistance. They begged to be excused by their guests who had no alternative but to surely agree to part with their company.

On their arrival near the kitchen, they found that Bessie had not been feeling very well; she had fainted, but was alert presently. Mr. Darcy exchanged a few words with her for several moments as she tried to reassure him. "Mr. Darcy, I shall be quite all right, only a bit weak; surely you should not be concerned with me. I suppose I was feeling ill, but I'm quite well now. You have guests, please, do not concern yourself with me."

"Nonsense," replied Mr. Darcy, "I cannot have you ill. Surely you need to be looked after. You need rest, I insist. Mrs. Reynolds, please have one of the servants accompany Bessie to her quarters. Have the apothecary summoned at once. I shall check with you a bit later, Mrs. Reynolds; perhaps she does only feel a little weak, but we shall take no chances."

"Bessie, may I do anything for you?" Elizabeth asked.

"Not at all, ma'am; please, I should feel better if you returned to your guests; I should not have wished Mrs. Reynolds to disturb you."

"Surely we are glad she did," Elizabeth retorted.

Mr. Darcy looked at Bessie. "We shall leave you now as you wish, but I intend to check on your behalf later. I suggest you get some rest."

Mr. Darcy and Elizabeth started to make their way back. As soon as Mr. Darcy closed the door to the servants' quarters, they suddenly became aware of angry voices approaching within an easy distance. They realized they could not enter the servants' quarters again without being noticed, nor could they venture further. The angry parties were now in the entrance hall, preventing them from proceeding in that direction. They realized the voices belonged to Caroline and Mrs. Hurst. Now caught between the service chambers and entrance hall, Mr. Darcy and Elizabeth remained motionless, expecting their guests to move on. To their discouragement, they learned that was not to be. They were now entrapped in a position to overhear a conversation not meant for their audience. As they stood quietly, they heard a third presence in the conversation, whose voice they immediately accredited as belonging to Emily. Caroline and Mrs. Hurst, now having Emily in private, were deeply rooted in vexed conversation regarding the engagement Emily so happily announced earlier. Mr. Darcy and Elizabeth listened with unintended interest.

The two Bingley sisters, intending to vent their opinions against Mr. Bennet, chose, without much thought, to approach Emily with language so angry that Mr. Darcy and Elizabeth dared not make their nearness known. The unplanned situation in which they found themselves afforded them the chance to hear Caroline's and Mrs. Hurst's unfavourable opinions toward Mr. Bennet and their own sister regarding the intended nuptials.

Believing they were far removed from the remainder of the party, Mrs. Hurst bitterly turned to Emily. "Surely you cannot be serious, Emily; this is highly scandalous, absolutely absurd. Is it not unfortunate enough Charles has regretfully connected the Bennet family to ours? Is it your wish to humiliate us further? Is it not horrid enough he has married a Bennet; now he raises two children from a disgraceful marriage of her very own sister, calling them his children, even naming the boy 'Charles.' Such nonsense, this is not to be borne, why he is damn foolish! His children indeed. Whatever can he be thinking? What can you be thinking? You are not accustomed to life in a meager manner in which they reside; there can be no foundation for such a foolish act. You will be viewed as a lonely lady of society caught in a moment of infatuation, having been flattered beyond your own reason. How is it possible you consider such a low match?" She advanced a few steps closer. "Why—he is coarse, unpolished; he is certain to be considered unacceptable amongst our relations, to be sure."

"Coarse, unpolished? You two are preposterous, simply absurd," Emily retorted.

Elizabeth and Mr. Darcy, dazed but careful not to make a sound, continued to stand quietly side by side with their backs to the wall, hidden in the shadows, astonished at what they heard, uncomfortable with hearing it.

It was Caroline's voice they detected next. "I'm sure Mr. Bennet is a very good humoured sort of man, one who obviously appeals to you at a weak moment, but I beg you to reconsider. Think of the sphere in which you were brought up. You would be quitting it, not to mention Mr. Bennet is advantaged in years. I have no understanding of this notion. Why, he has absolutely nothing to offer. The whole of his society lies in Charles and Mr. Darcy, whom I daresay humiliate themselves greatly by the institution of marriage within such a family. I still have yet to recover from the horror of their unions. I simply cannot get over it; indeed it is most insufferable."

Emily could no longer hold her tongue. She reached out to touch Caroline's arm. Her voice turned cold as she swallowed back the nausea arising in her throat. "How cruel you are. I had not thought you this heartless."

Caroline and Mrs. Hearst stared at her inexpressively. Emily could only guess their cruelty escaped them. They were unaccustomed to contradiction. Emily's emotions ran high. She now fought to govern her thoughts enough to express them openly. With a voice railed with anger, she addressed her sisters in an authoritative tone, stepping closer to seize Caroline's arm.

"I am quite astonished. Mother and Father did not raise you to act as you do. Although our father once held similar opinions, he altered them in later years, having realized the error of his ways as well as the respect it cost him. Upon his learning the strength of that attachment, which in spite of all his endeavours to end I found impossible to forget, he felt my loss of respect for him. It was the pain he bore. To his end, he regretted his actions; he told me so. Surely, even if they shared your opinions of my intended marriage, they should never display ill manners publicly; nay, that they indeed would never do. Your exhibits continue to amaze me. You both quitted that sphere you speak of by your own actions. I am heartily ashamed to call you sisters."

"Come now, Emily, you understand our society. You are merely angry of our disapproval. No doubt you can see the reason for contempt. You cannot pretend to be ignorant of his family situation. If your behaviour is to merely make us anxious, you have succeeded, now we ask you to quit this silly nonsense. Put an end to it at once," Louisa said, still disbelieving she could be seriously contemplating such a union.

Emily looked at Louisa. "No, I will not break my engagement. Mr. Bennet is one of the finest men of my acquaintance. He is witty, intelligent and is indeed a gentleman of the old persuasion, not as some men I know who indulge in drink, then lounge all day, slumped over furnishings wherever they may be." Her remarks caused Louisa to colour with embarrassment. Louisa knew all too well the description was befitting of her own husband.

Mr. Darcy gave Elizabeth's hand a comforting squeeze. It was hard to contain their emotions, being caught in a position affording them privilege to hear a most private exchange of words and sentiments with regard to themselves as well. Mr. Darcy leaned toward his wife to whisper in her ear. "Dearest, I do believe we are abominable for listening."

Elizabeth whispered back, "Yes, I agree, but we can hardly make our presence known now, nor do we have a means of escape."

Mr. Darcy leaned to her again. "Indeed you are right; I confess there is no reason to suppose I shall not feel guilty for a long time to come for my witness of it, but most for the enjoyment of hearing the whole of it."

Elizabeth faintly smiled. "Yes, and I, too."

It was Caroline's voice they recognized next. "Surely you cannot suppose him to make you happy; why are you so anxious to place yourself in his keeping? Do you care nothing of honour, decorum and prudence? Why do you willfully act against the inclinations of your family, friends and acquaintances? Such an alliance will be censured; you will risk everything, making our family situation contemptuous in the eyes of the world! Why, he does not even posses a title; what possible purpose can sway you to submit to such a whim?"

"Yes, I agree," Louisa interjected. "Mr. Hurst will one day soon inherit his fortune and title."

"A title! Oh, I see, a title means he has character; is that your meaning, Louisa? And this character will give his family distinction; is that not so?"

"Why yes, of course, I see you understand us a last, Emily," Louisa replied triumphantly.

"Oh, I understand you all too well. Such a pity you lack understanding. In your estimation, Louisa, being a gentleman does not require one to have integrity, like that of, shall we say, Mr. Hurst?"

Caroline stepped forward. "Really, Emily, your situation will be looked upon as pitiable, surely not respectable! What arguments do you use to support this frivolity, this decision of family ruin? I resent your attempts to burden us further with your poor choice of a man who no doubt has set his designs on your inheritance. There could be no other reason for his choosing to marry you, none at all. Why not wait before giving him your answer; tell him you need additional time to reflect. Tell him you answered too hastily, at a weak moment. Then let him down gently."

Such remarks angered Elizabeth though she dare not make a sound. Luckily for Caroline and Mrs. Hurst, Elizabeth's newfound understanding of the ability to deal with the trials and tribulations of life had brought about a generosity of tolerance to her nature. A few hours earlier, Elizabeth's wrath may not have been under such deliberate regulation.

Receiving their remarks with disgust, Emily fixed her eyes on them. Caroline's mouth curled, sneering, as Louisa's blistering eyes narrowed with unleashed disdain. Together, miserably angry, they stared back at her. Then Louisa's face turned ashen, and she snarled, while Caroline turned her face angrily away, but in an instant swung around as if she would speak.

Caroline, now at the height of contemptuous scorn, seemed a trifle unnerved by Emily's defense. Such looks induced Emily's desire to deprive her of speaking next. Her words had been puffed with resentment. Their ridicule of her intended marriage inflicted unguarded pain. Straightening her shoulders, she stepped closer to Caroline. She shook her head, letting out a sigh of displeasure. "Really, Caroline, you are like well-polished glass; I see right through your attempts. Do you think me unaware of the lengths you have gone to keep me from Mr. Bennet's company? Your devious disdain is offensive. Your behaviour toward Elizabeth is dreadful. Do not be so arrogant to believe Mr. Darcy is unaware of your evil deeds; he saw through your designs of his wealthy position. At first I was quite perplexed as to why you should dislike Elizabeth so, but now my understanding is quite clear."

"Come now, Emily," Caroline said halfheartedly.

Emily looked her directly in the eye. "Your attempts at recognition by Mr. Darcy went unnoticed, but she was able to secure him, making you increasingly jealous. You foolishly believed the manner of your dress as well as the sphere of that society you view yourself part of, made you worthy of him. Nay, Caroline, Elizabeth is far worthier. Her genuineness of character greatly outweighs any disadvantage she may have been born to. I am certain that you will end an old spinster. There is no man of character to tolerate you. Such scorn from one whom only dares to dream of companionship. Truthfully, I find it hard to believe Mr. Darcy was ever within your grasp. I do not believe I ever heard you talk of any beau expressing a desire to grant you an interview. Is the fact that you have never attracted a possible suitor, the reason you believe it unfair that I, for the second time, have been sought after as a partner in marriage? Is this the cause of your mean-spiritedness? Your chances of ever marrying may be doomed by your unprincipled nature. Surely these are not attributes men would view appealing. I fail to understand you. You have only to dare hope to find the beauty of commitment that is real, that is absolute or perhaps that would bring you on a sphere that rises above the realm of spirit and love. Perhaps it is the thought of my gaining simple beauty in pure love coupled with the reality of felicity that troubles you. Should you be lucky enough to secure a man, it will be for reasons of means or comfort for which you are accustomed, but real felicity in marriage is sure to be beyond your reach, as it surely escapes your reason."

Emily stopped to take in air. She stepped toward Louisa, startling her. "Louisa, why is it you allow yourself to be led by Caroline's shallow opinions? It's odd isn't it?—you married a mere country gentleman with little to recommend him for he has not yet inherited his family fortune, forcing you to bide your time under your brother's roof. Perhaps he married you for your £20,000. What say you, Louisa, is it not so?

"Really, Emily!" Louisa gasped.

"You both would be wise to hold your tongue. Resentment is a hard burden to carry. It will weigh you down while I will enjoy a life of felicity. I assure you, your misery will have no effect on me. You are a sad pair indeed. You are so far removed from the sphere in which you were raised that you have traveled a narrow path of indignity. For the first time I clearly understand you both, I daresay I do not like what I see. Mr. Bennet is not penniless, nor does he desire me for my inheritance. I may say I wouldn't care if he did! You two are further proof that wealth cannot keep shame from rich people's houses; indeed you draw dishonour to our family. I am all too sorry for our association. Did you two believe I was so much like you that I am devoid of feelings? I have simply secured unto myself a welcomed match, a good, honourable man—I had never expected to find such felicity. Perhaps if Mr. Bennet were the son of a Baron rather than a country gentleman you would have no reason for dispute. I can assure you his affections are not marked by gain; he knows not that I have inherited £20,000. I will indeed marry him in spite of you both. If you two continue in your prejudice toward him or his family, I will have no choice but to disassociate myself from your society, to which I might add, that, at this moment, I find the notion quite agreeable."

Elizabeth and Mr. Darcy heard movement near the servants' quarters. They continued to stand quietly, afraid one of the servants would open the door behind them, causing them to be seen in the shadows. They feared causing their guests embarrassment at having been caught in their close proximity hearing what was not meant for their ears. There was no means of escape without discovery. They heard footsteps, signaling Emily's exit.

Emily started to quit the room, but stopped suddenly, turning back to her sisters. "By the bye, you two are afoot on very thin ice. It is my understanding Charles will not tolerate your selfish piety directed at his wife or their family much longer. He can easily be persuaded to listen to my telling him of your interference in my affairs as well as the insults you have placed at his threshold. But have no fear, I am not born of the same meanness of spirit. I find I cannot do such without conscience, not even toward two sisters whom I once believed had better sense."

Emily turned to quit the room, but before she could take but more than a few strides, Charles entered, securing a look of mortification from Caroline and Louisa. They stood frozen in horror. Mr. Hurst stood behind him as their brother approached.

"Perhaps tomorrow I shall feel guilty for having the ill manners to deliberately listen and invade the privacy of my sisters' most intimate conversation. When I heard the angry mention of my name, Louisa, I could not help
but take it all in. What was that I heard pass over your lips? 'Is it not unfortunate enough Charles has regretfully connected the Bennet family to ours?
Is it your wish to humiliate us further? Is it not horrid enough he has married a Bennet, now he raises two children from a disgraceful marriage of her
very own sister, calling them his children. Whatever can he be thinking?' Be
assured there is no explanation due me. You have related feelings offensive to
me. There is no apology that I could accept without the thought of its
absurdity. I believe I understood your meaning well enough; perhaps you'll
be so kind as to afford me the same understanding. Make no attempt to
approach me; I am beyond anger. It will be of no benefit to you, be assured
of it!"

He stepped closer. "Tomorrow, early, vacate Foxshire Estate. Visit your
other sisters if you wish, but be assured it is my intention of messaging them
information as to what has transpired here. You are no longer welcome in
my home. The whole of my connection to you is a disgrace. I can only think
of you with abhorrence. I am resolved to wholly separate myself from your
ill society. Your ambitions toward my friend have been long noticed. Your
deep-rooted dislike of Elizabeth was unveiled long ago, yet for my sake
Darcy and Elizabeth chose to overlook your faulty principles and receive
you in spite of the inferiority of your society. Be assured Caroline, you are
the last person in the universe to which Mr. Darcy would have ever set his
designs. There is no mistake in this; do not flatter yourself otherwise. You
were merely too foolish to understand. I can assure you, you were never a
consideration in Mr. Darcy's pursuit of a partner. There is no motive to
excuse your injustice. Your inferior society lacks sense and good judgment.
Your conduct is reprehensible. Allow me to revisit Emily's words—you both
have quit the sphere to which you were born. I suggest you quietly take your
leave."

Louisa's looks drained of the horror she had felt. Now overcome with
rage, she looked angrily at her husband. "Mr. Hurst, why do you stand
there; speak up, why did you not stop him? How dare you allow him to
listen in on our most private sentiments; have you no value for your wife?"

He loudly cleared his throat. "SILENCE! I have no desire to speak to you
at present. I have long suffered the ill effects of your inferior behaviour."
With his voice still angered, he spoke with emphatic agitation. "Quite frankly,

I have not the toleration to discuss the matter publicly. I daresay there is truth in his words. Tomorrow I will direct myself toward my family home; you will join me, Louisa. Now come, both of you; I shall request the carriage be brought to the front." He turned, bowing to Mr. Bingley. In a milder manner, he addressed him, "Please accept my apologies; I do not share the sentiments of my wife. As for my own ill manners, I beg your forgiveness; they do desire corrective action to be certain."

After receiving their cloaks from Silas, Mr. Hurst bowed once again before directing the ladies toward the threshold.

"Has anyone seen Mr. Darcy or Lizzy?" Jane said, entering the entrance hall innocently. She heard not a word, and Mr. Bingley could not have been happier for it.

"No, they were called away by the servants above half an hour ago," Mr. Bingley said, composing himself, his face pale from the confrontation.

"Perhaps they returned to the sitting room," Emily said, moving in that direction. Mr. Bingley and Jane followed.

Mr. Hurst, Louisa and Caroline hastily quitted the entrance hall. Elizabeth and Mr. Darcy heard them take their leave of Pemberley Hall. It was with relief they heard Mr. Bingley, with the rest of the party, depart to those in the music chamber. With the party having now quitted the hall, they breathed a sigh of relief. He embraced her with comfort until suddenly the door behind them opened, startling them. Mrs. Reynolds quietly unrestricted the door. "Come, they have taken their leave. I safeguarded the door, realizing your entrapment; indeed you were not noticed, we guarded all the doors."

"Mrs. Reynolds, you quite astonish me. I wish I had been so certain of our solitude as you; nonetheless, I am grateful for your guard. Your perseverance to deliver us from a most horrendous situation is greatly appreciated. Surely it must be through your guidance Silas brought their cloaks from another direction. I wondered why he did so; I thought certain we were doomed for discovery at such a moment. Surely our presence would have been revealed had you not done so; is there no end to your competence?"

"Surely you know I am always at your service, sir."

"Indeed, Mrs. Reynolds, thank you," Elizabeth added.

"We must join the others. I do wonder where your father has been."

"I'm sure I do not know," Elizabeth said above a whisper.

Upon entering the sitting room, where the whole of the party gathered, they noticed Mr. Bennet had set up the backgammon board, supposing it was the reason Caroline and Mrs. Hurst were free to gain a oneness with Emily.

"Darcy, Elizabeth, do come in; I have an announcement to make," Mr. Bingley said, much to his wife's astonishment. Jane look perplexed; her eyes became wide. Her mouth partially opened, anticipating the announcement.

"My sisters and Mr. Hurst quitted Pemberley and are headed toward Fox-shire. They will quit our company in early morning. I confess I requested they take their leave. I have long suffered their ill society. I have, too, long endured their disregard of you, Jane and Elizabeth, with embarrassment. They treat Emily with disrespect at their objection of her intended marriage. I'm sorry to pain you all with such revelations, but it cannot be helped. I daresay their sentiments were no secret. Given thought to it, I decided it best to make this known to you, lest you wonder where they might be."

"Charles, you told them in the entrance hall, that was the reason you appeared so pale. Oh, Charles, I imagine the pain you suffer. Poor Caroline, poor Louisa and Mr. Hurst, they are sure to be sorry for such thoughts; perhaps they are sorry now," Jane said with sympathizing emotion.

"Jane, have no concern, be assured they are capable of looking after themselves. I feel it was indeed time for them to quit our company." Charles was secure in his thoughts of never revealing to anyone the whole of their sentiments, which brought about the hasty departure.

"Well, Emily, a backgammon game awaits us; what say you?" Mr. Bennet asked.

"Yes, I am up to the challenge; shall we?" she answered him, as they sat down to play. Emily, now eager to change the subject, directed the conversation to more pleasant thoughts.

"Elizabeth, please delight us with an air," requested Mr. Darcy.

"Very well, is there anything particular you wish to hear?"

"Indeed, the tune I first heard you play in Hertfordshire."

"Mr. Bennet, have you given notion as to when you should wish to wed?" Mr. Bingley inquired.

Emily looked at her brother, then turned to Mr. Bennet. She detected his eagerness.

"I do not wish a long engagement. I confess it is my wish Emily should not like a long wait as well."

"Indeed, I should like to be wed soon."

"How very exciting, Father; I am so very delighted in your announcement. You know I wish you both every happiness," Jane excitedly announced.

It was with great pleasure the whole of the party shared the delight of the newly engaged couple. The absence of Caroline and the Hursts only proved to lighten spirits and erase any discontent about the impending nuptials.

"Mr. Bennet, this afternoon I messaged the Gardiners, inviting them to visit Pemberley. Perhaps you would wish to wed within a fortnight; it would be an honour to have you do so at Pemberley. I am equally certain Mr. Manley would welcome such an honourable task. Perhaps you should like to think upon it. I shall await your sentiments on the subject."

"Oh, Father, such a delightful thought; it would please me greatly should you decide to do so," Elizabeth expressed.

Mr. Bennet and Emily exchanged approving glances. "Mr. Darcy, I do believe we will take you up on that offer."

"Very well, Mr. Bennet, you shall have to apply for a special licence as soon as may be."

"Yes, Mr. Darcy, you do think of everything," Mr. Bennet said as he winked at Elizabeth with a twinkle in his eye.

The matter being well settled elevated the spirits to the occasion.

Mr. Darcy moved in the direction of the pianoforte, taking a seat on the right side of his wife. For a time he listened to her play as he sipped his port. To her astonishment, he put his glass down to join her in the tune on the high notes.

"My dear husband, I did not know you could play! You quite astonish me. Am I ever to fully know you?"

"I certainly hope not," he replied with a chuckle.

"I may never again own to the certainty of knowing you to the fullest; surely you have a tendency to prove me in error. You never mentioned you could play the pianoforte."

"You never asked," he continued to tease. Then he leaned toward her. "To be truthful, I very seldom play. Indeed I do not play well." He nudged her before continuing. "Since it is my nature to surpass my own expectations in all my endeavours, I confess I prefer not to expose my inferior talents. But tonight I dare just about anything, my dearest, loveliest Elizabeth," he whispered as he made himself closer to her.

Mr. Darcy was good to his word. Before the evening ended he inquired after Bessie. He was assured she had been well cared for by the apothecary. It satisfied him greatly to care for those who cared for his family.

Within days a licence was secured. All that remained was the arrival of Mr. and Mrs. Gardiner, which transpired within the fortnight.

Their arrival was in the guise of a visit. Unnoticed by Pemberley's guests was the second carriage, carrying the body of George Wickham, which was quietly and discreetly laid to rest without pomp or ceremony, just a few spiritual words given by Mr. Manley. Having kept the sad consequences of Mr. Wickham from the whole of the party, only Mr. Darcy, Elizabeth and Mr. Bennet knew the task performed by Mr. and Mrs. Gardiner. To the rest remained the belief the Gardiners coming was an intended visit, nothing more.

As soon as they were afforded time alone, Mr. Gardiner and Mr. Darcy had a most private conversation, which began with Mr. Gardiner's report. "Well, Mr. Darcy, I have accomplished it. The title was secured for £1,000, no more."

"Very well done, Mr. Gardiner; I cannot be more pleased."

"There is more, Mr. Darcy; I have arranged through my connection in Parliament to release it upon my request, it will be done officially with a royal seal bearing his family crest for a price of £5, to which I gave approval. It will all be done officially; that is quite an accomplishment, is it not now?" Mr. Gardiner said with great satisfaction.

"Indeed, Mr. Gardiner, I could not have done any better myself."

"Mr. Bennet will receive the title through the post, officially marked, returning the title to its rightful owner upon the release of such by its present holder, who will remain nameless."

"This could not come at a better time, with his marriage tomorrow, Mr. Bennet's life will change far more than anticipated. Now allow me to settle the expense of the delivery with you."

"No, Mr. Darcy, you have done quite enough; allow me this pleasure. It will be our anonymous gift to him. I have always had a fondness for Mr. Bennet. Although my sister, God rest her soul, was not the best match, he remained loyal to the end. I daresay Miss Emily Bingley is well suited to him. I delight in his felicity. I will be well pleased to see him so happily situated. Have you noticed, Mr. Darcy, the very resemblance her character is to that of your wife?"

Mr. Darcy smiled. "Yes indeed, Mr. Gardiner, they both have that curious, delightful spirit about them. I surmise that is the attraction, considering Elizabeth is his favoured."

"Yes, well, I must agree that is the attraction." They both laughed.

"Perhaps we should join the others; having come this far I should not wish to be discovered now. I have but one regret, Mr. Gardiner, that is the concealment from my wife; it pains me to think of it. We possess a most extraordinary closeness. As much delight as is derived from the success of it, I find equal despair in keeping it concealed." Mr. Darcy's eyes turned glassy as he tenderly relayed his most intimate feelings to her uncle.

"Mr. Darcy, rest assured, I understand. I share a bond of the same likeness with my wife. Indeed it is difficult to do something so honourable, yet so secretive, keeping it from the very one with which you most wish to share."

"I believe you do indeed understand," Mr. Darcy said, making eye contact with Mr. Gardiner before turning to move in the direction of the door. As he reached for the door handle, he turned to his guest, granting a humble bow; they then quitted the office.

In joining the others, they anticipated a quiet day aspiring toward the upcoming marriage. Mary and Kathryn scampered about to finish embroidering a pillow they wished to present as a gift to Emily, both equally excited at having been asked by Emily to stand up with her at the ceremony.

Caroline Bingley and the Hursts vacated Foxshire as requested, making no attempt to rectify their relationship with Mr. Bingley or Emily, much to Mr. Bingley's satisfaction.

Through correspondence from a distant sister, who had declined Caroline's company, Mr. Bingley learned Caroline soon realized the superior society she had generally known was now lost to her. Louisa resided at the Hurst's family residence with her husband, where Caroline was not a welcomed guest, forcing her to seek other family until that time she could settle upon a property of her own. Having limited choices, as Charles did not allow her access to his London house, she resided far off with a sister who had not married well. Having wedded for love, her situation was near equal to the estate of Mr. Bennet, which she would surely describe as a meager existence according to her own calculations. Her existence there required her to help support the family of twelve, leaving little connections to that elevation of society she had grown used to. Having no other alternative at present, Caroline remained there. As far as Mr. Bingley was concerned, she had her just score.

Joyful was the day on which Mr. Bennet and Emily exchanged vows, uniting in felicity, joined by well wishes from so many. Mr. Manley, having officiated at the ceremony, joined in the celebration feast brought about by Mr. Darcy, whose orders were to display the whole of it in such a manner as to bring delight to all who did partake.

It was Mr. Bennet's intention to return to Longbourn, now having secured a life of felicity with a woman he admired greatly.

Having taken a moment to thank Mr. Darcy for his kindness, Mr. Bennet expressed his contentment in Elizabeth's situation at Pemberley, stating he should not painfully miss her so much as experienced in the past now that Emily had accepted him. He further went on to say he supposed her likeness to Elizabeth's character had much to do with the attraction. Mr. Darcy, in total agreement, concluded his choice to be a good match. He earnestly gave his best wishes for their health and happiness, expressing that if the felicity they found in marriage was half so much as he had secured for himself, they were guaranteed wedded bliss.

Honour Bound

AFTER THE MARRIAGE CELEBRATION, Mr. Bennet, Emily and the girls directed themselves toward Longbourn. It was with pride he settled into domestic life, but it was only upon their arrival at Longbourn did Emily reveal her inheritance of £20,000. When united with Mr. Bennet's income, it brought their estate to a handsome level.

Mr. and Mrs. Gardiner remained at Pemberley an additional week. While Mr. Darcy and Mr. Gardiner enjoyed their planned sport, the ladies occupied themselves with time well spent with the children. Mr. Manley joined them the entire week for dinner at the great hall, often spending much time in the company of Georgiana.

Mr. Bennet and Emily now wed for a month, dispatched a letter to Pemberley which brought about great excitement. The letter produced further delight to those residing at Foxshire Estate upon its sharing.

Longbourn
December 12TH

My Dear Lizzy,

It is with the greatest pleasure we write to thank you and Mr. Darcy, as we ought to have done sooner for your kindness in sharing in our wedded joy. We are among the happiest in the world. We have much news to share on this occasion.

My dearest Emily brings with her to the marriage a handsome inheritance, providing us opportunity to move to Netherfield. The great house, still uninhabited after the Bingley's vacating it, seemed to beckon us beyond resistance. We have settled the lease and have found an interested party to lease Longbourn. So, my dear children, after this date you may forward all communication to Netherfield. I daresay Kathryn and Mary are quite excited. They presently plan a ball with Emily to take place in about a month, or very soon after. My dear wife affords me opportunity to increase the family library as we both enjoy much of the same readings. I cannot tell you how happy I am to awake each morning with Emily at my side; I dearly look forward to each day.

Your cousin Mr. Collins and Charlotte still remain at Lucas Lodge, inasmuch as Mr. Collins has not secured a position. Upon learning of our leasing Netherfield, he expressed interest in moving to Longbourn estate before his presumed inheritance, to which I denied such a foolish notion, much to his displeasure. Presently he could not afford to maintain it. In leasing it, we are provided with a handsome income. I do believe we will find much solitude and happiness at Netherfield. Although within close vicinity to town, it is not so close as to render our neighbours opportunity to learn our every activity.

And now, my dear Lizzy, the most astounding news I must share. We were home but a fortnight when the post come, delivering a letter with an official seal addressed to your very own father. It seems I am born of title. As I understand by the document, my great-great-grandfather was a 'Lord.' He was forced to sell his title, having fallen on hard times deriving from a son's extravagance, losing a grand estate so valuable I cannot comprehend. He accepted a lesser estate, 'Longbourn,' in the settlement and a mere £2,000 a year for his family, which as you know is exactly my family inheritance. The document states I am to be given back my inherited title due to the present owner's release of it, at no cost to me. As for the rest, well it is gone.

My best regards to your honourable husband, affections to the children; we hope to see you at Christmas when we may all gather to feast on plum cakes.

Yours sincerely, Lord Bennet

"Dearest, can you believe it?" Elizabeth voiced with excitement as she finished reading the letter aloud.

Mr. Darcy sat reserved with a serious look about him attempting a response to comprehend the letter as though he knew nothing of its contents. Choosing carefully his words, he spoke, "Dearest, that is extraordinary news; imagine your father a Lord. I daresay 'Lord Bennet' sounds quite dignified. I am delighted indeed."

Elizabeth closely scrutinized her husband's manner. Her propensity for curiosity peaked. He added nothing more to the conversation, so she paused to see if he would seek to continue the exchange, which he did not. Probing further, she looked him directly in the eye. With a slight grin she viewed him for a moment more. "My father, a Lord? I know my husband had something to do with this."

"Dearest, what ever gave you such a thought?"

"I don't know, I just have this feeling."

"Well, I daresay it would be quite an honour to bring about such a happy situation, yes I do believe it would be exceedingly gratifying to have a part in it. It all sounds so official, does it not?" he answered truthfully.

"Perhaps, I suppose it is of little matter from whence it derived, but I do believe it could not have arrived at a better time. Even if what you say is so, it is the sort of honourable deed I would suspect of you. You would tell me, would you not now?"

"Well, if you wish to believe it was of my attaining, I suppose there is nothing I may do to alter your thoughts. I must say such a feat would be flattering indeed if there were truth in it. Such an honour deserves a celebration, does it not now?"

"Yes, dearest, we shall send a reply to felicitate."

Still unable to determine his having a hand in it, she decidedly put the subject to rest. Although her curiosity was left wanting, she had not the proof to press the matter further. But still she possessed natural intuitiveness regarding the whole of the situation, failing to expunge all doubt from her desire to learn the source of it.

After the passing of several quiet days at Pemberley, the post delivered two separate writings—the first being for Elizabeth, the latter addressed to Mr. Darcy.

Mr. Darcy opened his with jubilation, exclaiming delight in the invitation to the wedding of Colonel Fitzwilliam and Ann. They were to be wed at Rosings, which would require them to journey there for the happy occasion. He stated his intentions to immediately dispatch their delighted acceptance.

Elizabeth recognized the handwriting of her letter as belonging to her sister Kathryn. She gasped as she read the letter with great speed. Mr. Darcy inquired what information it contained as to cause her such shock, to which she read the following aloud to him:

Pemberley Estate, Derbyshire
Netherfield

Dec 18

My Dear Lizzy,

Be assured we are all in health at Netherfield. I write with intelligence of the purchase Father and Emily recently made. Lizzy, they have purchased a barouche box. You won't be surprised to learn we expect a turn about the countryside this very afternoon.

We had a visitor the day last; it was Charles, Mr. Darcy's cousin, who come to call upon Mary. Can you guess who accompanied him? I daresay you can; it was Frank. Now I must tell you, I hope Mary does not mind my doing so, perhaps she would prefer to tell you herself. I shall tell you anyway. He desired she grant him an interview. Lizzy, Mary is engaged to Charles and our father is quite delighted. Our father believes Mary will make a fine vicar's wife, given her study of the church writings and her interest there.

I have alarming news. Our cousin Mr. Collins has suffered a severe blow to his spirits. Mariah Lucas has been missing for days. It appears she has run off with a Sergeant Waverly much to the mortification of the Lucases and Mr. Collins. The whole of their family is in uproar, as Sergeant Waverly was often a welcomed visitor at Lucas Lodge. They afforded him the privilege to visit, never suspecting there was an attachment. It would also seem Sergeant Waverly is much of the same character as George Wickham. In view of this, Mr. Collins rarely leaves Lucas Lodge, only leaving once to attend church services this past Sunday. Mr. Collins swiftly quitted the church as not to be approached. It is said he is despondent. I have been in Mariah's company little since we moved to Netherfield, as I have no interest in the regiment encamped at Meryton. We design a ball to be held in January and plan to invite the regiment only to provide dancing partners for provincial ladies. Do not concern yourself on my account; I have no intention of fleeing with anyone; I surely delight in the confines of Netherfield. My regards to your husband along with our affections to Joseph and Deborah; we will see you all soon, as Christmas is near.

Affectionately, Kathryn

"The news concerning Mariah is unfortunate indeed; there is no pleasure to be had in it. I am sorry for it. I am fond of Mariah. I always thought her to be a dear child owning to better sense. Whatever could have possessed her to do such a thing?" Elizabeth said alarmingly.

"I'm sure I do not know. Surely I cannot venture an assumption; I have no knowledge of the minds of young ladies. I can only desire she has wed. I have compassion for the Lucases, surely they are not deserving of such grief. I too thought her a sensible girl. Their waiting must be a wretched suspense. As for your cousin, Mr. Collins, although I take no pleasure in the news, I find no sympathy for him. I'm sure his concern is not for Mariah but for his own reputation. He must realize he is now in the very standing for which he so contemptuously ridiculed others in the past. It would seem his sins revisit him in an altered manner. I am certain, in his present situation he would wish he had not passed his ill judgment upon anyone now that he suffers the same ill effects. He no doubt is mortifyingly ashamed for those of his society to know he was forced to quit Rosings, now this. Such disgrace—there is justice in it, although I cannot delight in it, indeed I cannot," he said soberly.

"Yes, I do agree; poor Mariah, I had not thought her silly as this. It is quite shocking. I too cannot delight in such misery, not even for Mr. Collins' sake."

Georgiana was shocked to hear the news of Mariah, as was Jane upon her learning of it. Jane's fondness for Mariah left her quite undone by the news. She anxiously expressed her hope of their finding her well and married.

The whole of the Bennet family assembled for the Christmas season, gathering at the church on Pemberley Estate to attend services conducted by Mr. Manley, next assembling at the great hall for a shared meal. Pemberley Hall was alive with Christmas music as its inhabitants gathered about the pianoforte with gaiety. It was to Mr. Bennet and Emily's delight to share in the festivities of the reception Mr. Darcy maintained for his staff and families about the estate. Their Christmas remained a marked occasion of time well spent with closeness of families.

Shortly after Christmas, Elizabeth, Georgiana and Mr. Darcy, along with Mr. Manley, attended the expected wedding of Ann and the Colonel, which was characterized with happiness as to exceed Ann's anticipation. Lady Catherine delighted in Ann's union to such a character in whom she had the surety of his conduct as both honourable and wholly in love with her daughter, assuring felicity of the best offering with comforting realization that the riches he brought to the union were invaluable. As expected, nothing was spared with regard to the wedding feast. A journey to Paris was planned as a favour from Lady Catherine. Ann blossomed in every respect, proving there was strength to be gained through felicity. Sensitive emotions stirred within Mr. Darcy and Elizabeth as they witnessed the happy event. Their own sense of felicity was heightened by remembrance of their wedding day, still enhanced now with their exchange of exuberant affections. He touched her hand unpretentiously as they stood witnessing the exchange of vows. It was of little wonder to Elizabeth what joyful thoughts must be passing in her husband's mind. At that very moment she was reliving those very words within her joyful heart as each spoken declaration passed the lips of Ann and the Colonel.

Elizabeth once again enjoyed the unrestricted sentiments of Lady Catherine, who continued to treat her with exceptional courtesy and regard. Georgiana delighted in the time she could spend with family, entertaining them with her musical talents. Although Mr. Manley had been requested to officiate at the ceremony, the newly appointed clergy made his presence known. Upon closer acquaintance with the clergyman, Mr. Darcy congratulated his aunt on securing a rector with exceptional character and exemplary integrity, stating his belief that such a man added much to the estate's valuable reputation. Upon hearing her nephew's remarks, Lady Catherine accepted them with pleasant satisfaction.

The day next, before their departure, Lady Catherine explained the absence of Fanny at the marriage ceremony. As it was told, Fanny's increased desire to gain further wealth induced her to run off with John Gibson, later learning he had little or nothing to offer as his family was in bankruptcy due to the poor management of business within the great estate he was to inherit. To further add pain to her injury, brought about by her ungovernable desires, was her father's intolerance of her behaviour. He first forced her to divorce Edward, insisting she follow with a marriage to John Gibson to right the wrong she had brought upon the family reputation. Upon having done so, he then turned her away from their family, further depriving her of the monthly income he once granted, forcing her and Mr. Gibson to make their own way in the world.

Lady Catherine noted Fanny's discontent with the extravagant means she enjoyed, as well as the society afforded her, was not sufficient, which caused her own demise. Fanny now suffered the loss of everything known to her through greed. She expressed her satisfaction in her once uneasy feeling regarding John Gibson. She was troubled at the thought of his earlier designs on Ann. Such revelation made sense of his once disturbing but perplexing actions. It was now that they all understood him perfectly well.

They were informed that Lord Fitzwilliam, having quietly divorced, planned to be more selective if the opportunity should ever present itself again. Lord Fitzwilliam, now released of his obligation, expressed his good fortune at not having to go through life with such a disagreeable wife, whose pleasing was unattainable. As for his father, the Earl, he found little reason to be contrite, Fanny not being of his blood, he concluded that the disgrace was all on her family. He further thought it quite fortunate that Edward would have a chance at a more amiable match.

Lord Fitzwilliam's brothers, being of the same opinion, expressed it a little more openly, stating their delight to be rid of such a scowling, mean-spirited sister-in-law along with their delight to have their brother back with them as the free spirit he once was.

Once again they made their journey back to Pemberley, with Elizabeth anxiously awaiting the sight of their home. Georgiana looked forward to returning to London. She was impatient to make plans. Mr. Manley was eager to return to his work.

Their life was prosperous as they enjoyed family among the best society. Elizabeth wanted for nothing. The attentions her husband afforded her were always welcomed with the sheerest delight. Those of their association judged their excellent reputations implacable.

Happy now in all maternal feelings was the family who resided at Fox-shire Estate, which after six months of residing there, had waited several months beyond surety to give great pleasure in announcing an upcoming event. The events that followed would later prove to enhance the affections of both Jane and Mr. Bingley beyond their imaginations. Theirs was a happy existence of mutual love and affection.

Having now enjoyed the wedded state for more than two years, Mr. Darcy and Elizabeth shared a deep, abiding love and an unselfish esteem experienced by a privileged few. They understood the secret of happiness is to be found in charitable giving and placing God foremost in their lives. Such felicity never escaped them, as they were fortunate to understand how honour and righteousness, mingled with the example they resolved in their lives, could touch even those whom they may never have chanced to meet.

With Mr. Bingley and Jane so near a vicinity to Pemberley, the easy affections in the hearts of the sisters were drawn closer through the years. They grew in wisdom as their children grew in age. The constant communication created a strong family affection amongst the children. The friendship of Mr. Darcy and Mr. Bingley remained impervious. Such abiding respect and devotion was only to be understood by those who learn sincerity of the heart. The happy four spent much time together in a society so superior that Elizabeth was ever mindful it was far beyond their past experiences. As they traveled in the first circles, Elizabeth and Jane soon became universally known for their superior characters. Their husbands were known to be honourable gentlemen with outstanding integrity.

Within the year next, Mary and Charles were wed, affording Mary the satisfaction of an existence so becoming to her design. She experienced felicity as the wife of a clergyman, sharing her husband's love of children, intending to produce a large family over the years. Mr. Bennet, determining her most deserving of her station in life, celebrated her accomplishments, which later were disclosed by the establishment of an orphanage.

Kathryn remained at Netherfield, feeling no haste to marry, as she enjoyed life at the estate, supposing the day would come when she would desire a gentleman she would chance to meet. She continued to enjoy her visits to Pemberley. She became known as a most dignified lady, well received within her circle of society.

Mariah was eventually discovered in London. Unmarried and left destitute by Sergeant Waverly, much to the family's embarrassment, she was sent off to reside with an aunt in the low country, hidden from the sight of society known to her, kept quietly to conceal the family's shame as she bore an illegitimate child. Having settled into a meager existence without so much as a visit or communication from her family, she eventually married a farmer who treated her fairly, the most she could hope for as a woman of her situation.

There was no further society to be had with Caroline and Mrs. Hurst. Mr. Bingley found his amiable character too kind to ignore the letters sent to him. In spite of their humble apologies, Mr. Bingley chose not to expose his family to them, but kept communication through the post alone, never having given in to their pleas. Caroline and Mrs. Hurst wrote of repentance regarding their misconduct with a minute sense of sincerity. Their punishment remained in the lack of society shared with those residing at Netherfield and Foxshire. They were destined to learn of the splendours there through other sources, except the disclosure of Mr. Bennet receiving the title of "Lord," which provided Mr. Bingley pleasure when penning it. Although their requests were denied, it did little to halt the attempts of the sisters, whose insincerity seeped through the guarded words of their communications. Their punishment, continuously being that of rejection, never halted their perseverance.

Failing to secure a position as vicar, forced Mr. Collins and his family to remain at Lucas Lodge beholden to Sir William Lucas. His self-appointed righteousness only proved to bring him humiliation and censure from those who had been the objects of his condescending opinions in the past. Charlotte's indifference toward her husband grew, as his insufferable ideals regarding her character and that of their son became increasingly difficult to aspire to. She viewed the unreasonable rigid conditions he placed on them falsely directed, as he himself failed to be humbled to follow those same demands he required in others. The ill fate of her sister Mariah was only harmonized by her mother's gossiping, eventually causing Charlotte to become so downhearted she turned from all good society, sinking into habitual gloom of temper. She became a sad figure, known about town to have married for comfort only to suffer misery through her choosing. Adding to and only worsening the fate of the Collinses was a third and fourth devastating blow, chiefly to the designs of Mr. Collins. The first was his expulsion from Rosings. Only unto himself could he recognize blame. Lady Catherine afforded him extensive opportunity to reverse his steadfast reproach of the Bennets to which his loose tongue proved the source of his own ill fate. Second was his failure to secure a clergy position. His condescending reputation followed him, casting a shadow over his ability to find a church, forcing his need to be sustained at Lucas Lodge. The third disgrace was brought about by Mariah's indiscretions. This humiliation was only to be augmented through his past fixed condescending opinions regarding the Bennet family and others within Hertfordshire to whom he made himself superior. His past wry public opinions caused firm reprisal from those who suffered his condemnation. As for the Bennets, they remained silent on the subject, with full knowledge of the affliction he now suffered receiving that same repulsive language and reprisal from others of Hertfordshire society whom he so foolishly censured in the past. The last misfortune, perhaps the most personally devastatingly suffered, was the loss of Longbourn Estate. Mr. Bennet and Emily, so happily settled into the raptures of marriage, birthed three sons in the years following, providing an heir to the Bennet property.

Through all the misfortunes suffered, perhaps the saddest remains in Mr. William Collins' willful lack of repentance of his ill opinions and condescending ways, which thus brought its own punishment through the loss of respect from his immediate family. His continued envy of those residing at Pemberley combined with a lack of regret of his conduct, made him universally known as contemptuous in the sight of his society.

As for Elizabeth and Mr. Darcy, they were viewed a prolific match, having birthed three additional sons and one other daughter. Word of the family having spread throughout Derbyshire, made it universally known to many that theirs was amongst the most handsome families. Further proof of this hung in the gallery, where Mrs. Reynolds often took pride in its showing when her master took his family to their house in London.

Elizabeth continued to maintain a sense of curiosity throughout her life, viewing it as part of her inbred, spirited character, but she learned to govern it well. She lastingly desired to strive to live up to her husband's nobility. She would continue to be in awe of his greatness, always believing his plateau was exceedingly high. Many times she had pondered the secret of his extensive success, but soon learned through the error of her certainty, that it was all quite simple. He was extremely disciplined in his convictions. He was unquestionably incapable of being anything less than honourable. He was a man devoid of artifice, but instead followed those principles and laws set by God first, his country second and his father third. Although he was acquainted to many, he was intimate to few. He remained rather shy in public and quite uncomfortable speaking of himself to any degree, but, instead, was constant in his approach to duty. He was dedicated to those he loved, and he loved with unwavering passion.

Fitzwilliam Darcy's prosperity afforded him greater wealth than even he had once imagined. His extremely handsome looks enhanced with age as his love for his family brightened within his reflections. The deepness of his dark eyes still flattered his captivating form. His excellent breeding and superior character remained evident.

When in public, Mr. Darcy maintained that quality of air conspicuous of his good breeding, but still in a reserved style. While at Pemberley he was more at ease, but when alone in the confines of his wife's presence he proved an exceedingly sensitive husband, passionate lover and a bit of a tease.

Uncommon was any improvement needed within the wedded bliss of Fitzwilliam Darcy and Elizabeth, whose relationship was one of perfection. As their union was from the beginning far superior than most could boast, never having quitted that realm of ecstasy they shared, instead striving in its growth, they found their reciprocal admiration never ending. And to their merit, theirs was a relationship so filled with truth and honour it was often noted, mostly by those who had an intimate friendship with them, that God had surely done his best work in allowing them to become a match.

They were well known and admired in Derbyshire, as well as in London, as enjoying superior society, but more so for their benevolence unto others, often designing charitable committees to care for the poor. Pemberley Estate was known far and wide as having not only well-maintained grounds and some of the finest woods and lakes, but more so for the superior clergy and the wanting by so many who sought to be under its employ as part of its everyday existence.

As Mr. Darcy grew more prosperous, it was said his treatment of those who served at the great estate of Pemberley were not only greeted with respect but handsomely rewarded. Pemberley's employees were often viewed with envy for having secured a position on one of the foremost estates in all of England. His estate seldom suffered a void, usually only by death. His reputation as a desirable landlord clung to him to the end of his time. Perhaps this was due to the fact that he never forgot the lessons learned earlier in his life, first from his parents, later from his dearest beloved Elizabeth, whom he looked upon as a standard of perfection in women, bearing no comparison to anyone he had ever known.

Mr. Darcy was recognized throughout Derbyshire as the master of Pemberley, owning to vast wealth, a beautiful wife and handsome children. His reputation as a gentleman was not to be exceeded by his excellent character; his pride and morals became deeply rooted in the teaching of the church. He was known to be a man of perfect good breeding, owning knowledge of etiquette of court. Together with his dearest Elizabeth, he was valued for continual, unselfish charity. Tales of the lavish balls at Pemberley Hall became universally known throughout the surrounding countryside. Those receiving invitations considered it an honour, having been so fortunate to be invited into their society. Mr. Darcy's reputation remained steadfast, tending more toward spiritual teachings with age, but, when alone with Elizabeth, he remained true to his teasing fashion, deriving pleasure in his ability to invariably catch her off her guard. Elizabeth never failed to provide him with anticipated excitement with her everlasting folly in claiming victory of her celebrated win in the billiard parlour.

Elizabeth, never tiring of the freshness of the out-of-doors, retained her healthy presentation. Her reverence for the beauty of Pemberley Estate never wavered. She acclaimed every opportunity to further her education through extensive reading, proposing her a complementary challenge of wit for her husband. Fully understanding the source of his strength, she as well asserted that same integrity necessary of a godly life, giving a wholeness to their marriage far beyond her expectations. Although she remained in the highest of spirits, she relinquished much of her frankness and her challenging nature. She did maintain a level of curiosity, however, continually affording her an unrelenting sentiment to which she lastingly sustained the notion that somehow her most honourable husband had indeed had a hand in her father gaining the title of "Lord Bennet."